## Ambitions

AUDREY HOWARD was born in Liverpool but has lived most of her life in St Annes on Sea. After nearly twenty years working on and off as a civil servant, she did not begin to consider herself an author until she entered a competition which resulted in the publication of her first novel, *The Skylark's Song*. She has since written three further novels set in Liverpool, *The Morning Tide*, *Ambitions*, and *Between Friends*, and *The Juniper Bush*, set in nineteenth-century Cumbria, which won the 1988 Boots Romantic Novel of the Year Award.

# AUDREY HOWARD

# *Ambitions*

## Fontana
*An Imprint of* HarperCollins*Publishers*

Fontana
An Imprint of HarperCollins*Publishers*,
77–85 Fulham Palace Road,
Hammersmith, London W6 8JB

Published by Fontana 1987
7 9 8 6

First published in Great Britain by
Century Hutchinson Ltd 1986

ISBN 0 00 617408 6

Set in Ehrhardt

Printed in Great Britain by
HarperCollinsManufacturing Glasgow

For Gerry
with my love

# CHAPTER 1

The room was hushed. The only sound was that made by the pregnant woman as she moved heavily between the table and the child who stood docilely before the fire. The woman's face was unutterably sad. She stirred the pile of clothing upon the table, then picked out a bodice, inspected it and held it against the girl. It seemed to suit so she dropped it upon a separate mound and repeated the procedure, this time with a skirt.

The child's face was impassive, but her eyes held a shadow as though some anticipation of the future, unknown and mysterious, had her fast.

The room was barely warm. The sulky fire had difficulty in maintaining even the feeble flame which lit it. The fireplace was small with bars across its front to hold the coals in place, and on either side was an oven, its blackleaded surface as polished and gleaming as wet coal. Several pans stood upon its top and an appetizing smell leaked from one, whilst on the bed of embers a kettle whispered steam.

The woman sighed and the child looked gravely into her face. She bent and kissed the girl's cheek then, in a sudden surge of motherhood, drew her into her arms and held her fiercely.

'Oh darlin', darlin', sure an' what will we do without you? I can't bear to think. It's such a way up there an' you just a baby, that's all, a baby.'

She rocked the child in her arms, and her tears flowed across her cheeks and fell on to the dark, curly head pressed to her breast. The child, stoically dry-eyed, remained quite still, but the mother's sorrow brought to life what seemed to be a multitude of scattered children who sat or stood about the room. They moved to form a protective, anxious circle about the woman and the child, and the youngest, barely out of infancy, began to cry in sympathy.

A man rose from a chair, tossing a small ginger cat which he had held on his lap to the floor. He gently disengaged the woman's arms from around the girl, led her weeping to the chair from which he had just risen, and sat her down, shushing her tenderly, stroking her abundant hair and murmuring in the brogue of his forebears.

'There, macushla, there. Hush now, for 'twill only upset the child. 'Tis a good place, yer know that. She'll come to no harm. Don't I know Mr Hemingway's a decent man an' keeps a good home.' He searched about in his mind for some further comfort to give the grieving woman, but his own eyes were damp and his heart was as anguished as hers. 'Sure an' she'll be home in four weeks an' no doubt as fat as butter with all the good food. Now don't yer be frettin', Mammy. Would I let me own daughter go to a place that wasn't fit? Would I now, would I?'

As he spoke, Sean O'Malley knew the words he uttered were a vain attempt to alleviate his own fears as much as to comfort those of his wife, for he had no knowledge of the life in the great man's house. Though he himself worked for Charles Hemingway, it was in his shipyard, and the routine of his master's home was unknown to him. It was hard, sending the child into another world and him not there to protect her. To be sure the family of the man would live grand, for wasn't himself one of the wealthiest men in Liverpool, but for those who laboured in his kitchens as his daughter was to do – at the cleaning and the scrubbing and the score of menial tasks which a house of that size and grandeur would require – what of them? Better there than in factory or mill or, worse, in the hell of a mine. But did they eat enough and were they warm in winter? Were they overworked and would she be safe?

Sean looked down at the bent head of his wife and felt the hopelessness wash over him. What was the use? He had no choice. He turned and looked about him at the room which was their home. He had painted every surface of it himself with whitewash worked for at the dockyard after he had done his shift, and his wife had scrubbed it until the stone floor could have been eaten off, but despite that what was it? A cellar. A basement in a tall and tottering house which numbered its occupants in the hundreds, most of whom lived in filth and squalor.

The men were all unskilled and without regular trade, working at whatever came their way and glad of it, most of them. Dockers, factory hands, labourers, street pedlars and the worst poor, like himself: the Irish immigrants who were willing to take the most menial jobs. The soup kitchens fed them; there had been times, though Sean's pride took a beating over it, when his own children would have starved but for that daily bowl of 'broth' with its slab of grey bread to soak up the unsavoury thinness. On good days they had tea, oatmeal and potatoes, and on very good days a bit of mutton or bacon with it. But those times were scarce.

The room in which he and his family lived was no better than the sod cottage in County Clare beside the River Shannon from which he had come, and the view from the window decidedly inferior. He looked towards it now. The bottom half was below street level. He stared at the filthy, rutted courtyard and saw for a lovely moment the lilting green of the land of his fathers, and heard the rushing gurgle of the stream as it passed by his door down to the river.

But you could not eat the lush green grass, though once in desperation he and Bridie had tried, nor clothe the children who came year after year, in a pretty landscape.

A small hand crept into his, and Sean looked down into the deep green eyes of his daughter. They were framed in a thick spiked fan of black lashes, tilting upwards at the corner, wide-spaced and luminous, the pupils dark as sable. The face in which they were set was as pale and thin as paper.

'Will I be tryin' the skirt, then, Daddy?'

The composure of the child contrasted strangely with the distress of her parents, and her words brought the weeping woman to her feet. She wiped her eyes and blew her nose savagely. Sean was glad to see a glimmer of her old spirit. Strong had been Bridie O'Malley, but weaker now with the blows which fell on her, and this, the loss of her first born, was the worst.

'Yes, darlin', an' let's be lookin' to see if there's a pair of drawers to suit. Yer'll need two pairs, one to wear an' one fer the washin', an' a bonnet.' Bridie's face was determined now, as though she must put on a show for the child if nothing else. Garments were tossed hither and thither in a frenzy of activity.

'See now, will yer look at this, the very thing.'

From the accumulation of discarded clothing, most of them barely more than rags which she had bought for threepence at St John's Market that afternoon, Bridie triumphantly produced a bonnet fashionable a decade ago. It was of Italian straw, much frayed, and trimmed with the sorriest assortment of silk and velvet flowers under its brim and on top of the small, flat crown.

The child, in drawers of flannelette and a mended but scrupulously clean chemise, a size too large to allow for growing, stood whilst her mother reverently placed the old bonnet upon her rough tumble of curls, tying the fretted velvet ribbons beneath her chin. The small face peeped out from under the brim and the girl looked from one to the other, her gaze coming to rest at last upon her father. He winked and a smile tugged the corners of his mouth. In a moment the room was in an uproar as they all began to laugh.

Suddenly, at a word from Bridie, Mary Kate and Seamus were away like two skinny rabbits to the standpipe at the entrance to the alley, turned on for only an hour each day, fetching buckets of water. There were chores for each of them: washing, drying clothes about the fire, heating the flat iron upon the stand above the coals, stitching a hem, taking a tuck or two at a waist or sleeve, polishing boots with spit, elbow grease and a bit of rag from the pile ... even the youngest children of the family were busy at some task within their scope, to make them feel important.

They stopped at five and ate their meal, squashed together on the rows of wooden boxes which served as seats at each side of the table. The meal was a treat for the occasion. The pan of stew with scrag ends of mutton and a few carrots was filled up to its brim with potatoes, and was followed by a bowl of moistened oatmeal in which Bridie had mashed some fat

10

blackberries gathered by the children in the hedgerows beyond Everton Brow. They thought themselves as well fed as the Lord Mayor of Liverpool himself. They were each given a cup of weak tea, without milk or sugar of course, for the 13s 6d earned by Sean each week must be carefully manipulated to feed, clothe and house ten persons.

The meal finished, the dishes washed and put away, the baby drowsing against his mother's swollen stomach in the hour before bedtime, apprehension settled once again upon Sean and Bridie and their eldest daughter, though Rose's anxiety was threaded with other emotions. Curiosity was there, and also a certain determination to make the most of the opportunity which had been presented to her. The prospect of the unexplored sat more heavily on the parents' minds. They had gone through it all before only a year since, when they had stepped from the gangplank of the packet ship which had brought them from Dublin, with the thousands of others who suffered as they did. The men, defeated by the potato failures of 1845 and 1846, and by the consequent famine in Ireland, lured by work which could be found in the industrial mainland, had come to be 'navvies' on the building of the railroads. Many had travelled from remote villages and had belonged to small communities whose inhabitants had for generations never been further than five miles from where they were born and, until they got to Dublin, had never in their lives seen more than three or four dozen people in one place at a time, and most of them relations.

In the busy dockland, they had felt themselves to be placed upon another planet.

They wore moleskin trousers, hob-nailed boots, double-canvas shirts, gaudy neckerchiefs and, placed upon the back of each dark head, was a small bowler hat with a curly brim. Each man held a knotted bundle. Some had their womenfolk with them and even children, but most were alone for fares could not often be found.

Suddenly they had all fallen silent and watched with respectful awe the progress of a splendid company who strolled along the wharf towards an awaiting carriage.

Rose O'Malley, soon to change again the pattern of her young life, remembered that strange day on the quayside. She recalled the group of handsome people who had averted their eyes from the tatterdemalion assembly as though they were so many grubby packages which had been left inconsiderately in their path, and had moved hurriedly by. There had been a tall man, seven feet at least, all in black and with a stern countenance; and a woman dressed like a queen, Rose imagined, though she had never seen one. There were young men, limp, languid and high-nosed; young girls the same . . . and a child.

She was like nothing Rose had ever seen.

So fair, silvery and bright she might have been a star in the heavens. *She* had not turned her eyes away, but had gazed directly into Rose's own with a look penetrating and imperious, as though her curiosity would know more but she was too grand to enquire. Rose's head lifted proudly and she had returned stare for stare, ready to be as haughtily stiff-necked. But suddenly, inexplicably, the fairy child smiled at Rose, and Rose, enchanted, smiled back.

Tomorrow, she, Rose O'Malley, was to become part of the household which belonged to the family of that child.

Now, as darkness fell, Sean and Bridie lifted down the pile of straw palliasses and spread them about the room. A length of cloth was draped between the shelves which held the family's crockery and pans and the corner of the room where Bridie and Sean slept, to give husband and wife some measure of privacy. Boys top-to-toe in one bed and girls similarly arranged in another, the O'Malley family settled down to its last night with its numbers complete.

Rose regarded the square of window. The light from the stars which pricked the autumn sky reflected on the scrap of snowy net which Bridie had put up. She heard from some far-flung corner of the house the familiar shrieks of the woman whose husband stumbled from the pub, and in bilious temper beat her every Saturday night, before subjecting her to his ardour. A baby howled, a dog whined piteously, and something clattered in the yard as though unseen hands had fumbled through the rubbish which lay there. Mammy and Daddy murmured for a moment and then were quiet.

Rose's eyes were bright, like stars in the darkness which finally fell about the room as the last flicker of the fire died. She hugged herself and a small pin of excitement pricked her then, as the ginger tabby tapped her face with its paw. Rose took it into her bed between herself and their Mary Kate, and dreams rested heavily on her lids until they closed and she slept.

In the early morning Bridie did her best. It was the bonnet that broke her resolve.

'There, alannah, that's it.' She gave the bow a final tweak, straightening the bonnet until it was precisely lined up with the centre parting in Rose's hair. She smoothed the material of the bodice down the child's back and shifted the skirt a fraction. It fell to the girl's ankle bone, showing, unfortunately, the bare white skinny legs which did not completely fill the top of the shining boots. She looked in distinct possibility of stepping out of the footwear at her first movement.

Bridie studied her daughter. The set of her shoulders and the way she held her head bespoke of brave determination, and yet, within the clear depths of her eyes, the mother could see her child's dread.

Bridie's mouth quivered, but her voice was firm.

'Yer look like an angel all dressed up on its way ter Heaven, so yer do, and not even the missis of the house will be so grand. A fashion plate so ya are. Now then' – she turned to the close circle of admiring children who crowded about the table – 'did yer ever see anything so grand? Did yer? Now, did yer? Mary? Patrick?

They all agreed unanimously that they had not, and Bridie added to the clamour by calling down the blessing of the Holy Virgin Mother in recognition of her child's appearance.

Next it was Sean's turn.

'Will yer look at her, Daddy. As lovely as the shamrock, wouldn't yer say? Tell her, Daddy. Tell her how lovely she is.'

13

'Oh, she is that, Mammy. Lovely. Yer look grand, darlin' . . . grand.'

Sean's voice cracked and he turned away, making a great show of looking for his cap and muffler and stumbling over the cat.

'It's the bonnet, Rose, the bonnet. It just seems to finish the outfit off.'

Bridie's voice shook and she put her hand to her mouth. 'It makes yer look like . . . like . . .'

She had made up her mind in the night that she would not cry again, but it was too much for her. She and Sean were rare amongst their peers in that they did not share their neighbours' apathy towards the well-being of their children. The couple loved every one of them devotedly, and both were prepared to sacrifice anything for them. The true family spirit bloomed, brought with them from their homeland, and nurtured in the good Catholic household they had built there.

With a sharp cry, Bridie sank to her knees before her child as though she knelt in church. Rose was swept dementedly into her arms, and the flood gates opened. The bonnet was knocked unceremoniously to the back of Rose's head, and she was clutched in frantic arms, her face smothered in the hollow of her mother's chin. Bridie's shoulders shook, and her voice came out from the region somewhere at the back of Rose's neck where her face was pressed.

'Sean. Please, Sean, don't let her go. It's too much ter expect her ter do the work of a grown woman. She's only a child. I'll not sleep in me bed at night worryin' about her. Look at her, feel her . . . so thin, and . . . Oh, Sean darlin', as soon as the babe comes I'll get another job . . . nights somewhere . . . Rose could see to the little 'uns whilst I . . . Could we not manage another year until she's . . . Oh Sean . . . Rose . . . she's . . .'

The others began to cry. The baby, frightened by his mother's grief, wailed and clung to his sister Teresa, only three years older than himself. And Mary Kate, whose turn

14

it would be next year, put her head down upon the kitchen table and sobbed in fright.

'Bridie, woman. Will yer control yerself, or will I land yer one. Holy Mother of God, yer'd think the child was away to the other side of the world on a slaver instead of ter a grand job in a mansion in Toxteth Park, an' sure, won't she be back in a month. Yer know she must go. Don't make it any harder for the child. And how could yer work the way ya are. Look at yer.'

All the children looked, eyeing their mother's familiar swollen belly with the understanding of a large family.

'Seven months gone nearly, an' we can't manage unless . . . The child must work. She'll be well fed an' looked after an' . . . an' her wages will help ter . . .'

In an agony of frustration, Sean's voice thundered through the room, echoing hollowly off the old walls, and the very sound of it brought the babble to an abrupt halt, even that of the hiccoughing baby. He never raised his voice nor his hand, their Daddy. Never. Whenever he spoke, it came from him in a soft musical lilt which seemed to penetrate the most noisy argument. The very strangeness of it surprised them into silence and, though Bridie still wept, she rose obediently to her feet. Quietly she kissed her eldest daughter, and spoke a soft word of farewell. Turning, she took her youngest into her arms, clinging to the infant as though daring anyone to take this one from her. She did not watch as Rose kissed her brothers and sisters in turn, nor did she look round to see her go up the area steps with her father.

'Goodbye, Mammy.'

'Goodbye, darlin', an' may the blessed Mother watch over yer. I'll say a prayer . . . don't forget yours an' . . . be a good girl.'

At the last, Sean thought Rose would break. She turned back to look at her mother, who stared fixedly at the empty grate, blinked, made a small sound in her throat, and then continued up the worn steps.

Sean held Rose's hand, her bundle firmly under his arm

as they began the long walk from Naylor's Yard, along Naylor Street. They passed through a warren of narrow, filthy passages, divided into vile smelling lanes and dark back alleys. Some were scarcely three feet wide and thronged with a farrago of persons, all bent on some frantic errand. It was not until the man and girl came to the fine thoroughfare of Castle Street that they glimpsed the pale bluebell sky which edged the roof of the Town Hall. It was the most ancient highway in the town, so named because it was the only road to the castle from the north. The site of the castle, demolished in the last century, was now occupied by St George's Church. Beyond was North John Street and, as Sean and Rose passed the post office in Canning Place, the only delivery of that day, a Sunday, was just starting. The postmen wore scarlet cut-away tailcoats with blue lapels and cuffs and, beneath, blue cloth waistcoats. To top this finery each sported a tall beaver hat. Rose stared in wonder. She had never seen a postman before. Not many in Naylor's Yard required their services.

It was just a quarter past seven.

An assortment of street musicians were already setting up in preparation for the day's business. Rose pulled on Sean's hand and they stopped for a moment to watch. Her heart, dashed to pieces it seemed by the parting with her mother, lifted a little as she glimpsed the gleaming black eye of the scarlet-jacketed monkey perched on an organ grinder's shoulder. It chattered, grinning, and lifted its tiny pillbox hat in a comic parody of a gentleman greeting a lady, then ran down its master's arm and relieved itself on top of the organ. Even Sean had to smile, but then moved away. They were to be at Silverdale by nine, and there were several miles to be walked. Rose followed reluctantly.

They went on, into St James' Street and into Mill Street, at the end of which were the quarries from which came much of the sandstone that had gone into many of the fine new buildings then being erected. They came to New Park windmill and, though the sails moved round in the capful of wind which came off the river, their whirling was in vain for no corn was ground on the Sabbath. The man and child turned left into Wellington Street, then right into Aigburth Road, and it was here that the fine houses of the lesser gentry began.

Soon, the road narrowed to a pleasant country lane, hedged in quickthorn. The trees were every shade from pale cinnamon to rich tobacco, from faded gold to chocolate brown, from magenta to rusty pink; and the leaves which covered the ground, dried out and crunchy from lack of moisture, rustled delightfully beneath their feet.

A stile on their right led to a field waving with grasses and meadow rue. Campion grew in a drift of rosy pink. Lady's smock, white and lacy like a Madonna's veil, dazzled the eye, and the man and child stopped involuntarily, their breaths caught in their throats with the delight of it.

'Oh, Daddy, will yer be lookin' at that,' Rose gasped. But Sean needed no telling, and they leaned against the steps, the man's hands on the child's shoulders. ''Tis lady's smock, child. We used to call it cuckoo flower in the old country, for it was the cuckoo's call which seemed to fetch it out. And see, there in the ditch,' — Rose followed Sean's pointing finger — 'that's great willowherb. See the lovely purple flowers. And the red ones, them's poppies. Yer can get a fusion from them to ease pain, did yer know that? 'Tis a wondrous thing but not to be taken carelessly.'

On the other side of the lane, the field contained a herd of grazing soft-eyed cows, the udders beneath them limp and empty for they had just come from the milking shed. They raised their heads and, staring curiously at the two humans, they began, in the way of their kind, to wander towards them.

'Oh quick, Daddy, they're coming.' Rose began to edge away, her town-dweller's mind filled with trepidation as the placid creatures heaved their horned heads against the hedge. Sean laughed and took her hand.

'They won't hurt yer, darlin'. They're just nosey like Mrs Geraghty, wantin' ter miss nothin'. Come up, come up,' he said to the nearest. 'Come up, Buttercup.'

Rose was fascinated. 'How d'yer know it's called Buttercup, Daddy?' Her face was lit by the magical moment, and she held Sean's hand and stared into the liquid brown eyes of 'Buttercup'.

'Sure an' isn't there always a Buttercup in a herd?' Sean laughed. But then, as though blown out by ghostly breath, the candle of joy left Sean's eyes and his face became expressionless. Rose saw it happen. Her hand tightened about her father's fingers and, without another word, they continued along the lane.

Away in the distance, beyond the enclosed grounds of Silverdale, a gleam off the River Mersey rippled like a moving sheet of pewter as the sun touched the water. For a moment, Sean had been returned to the lovely countryside of his birth, and he was overwhelmed with a feeling of homesickness so great it took all his strength not to break down in front of the child. The lane meandered on for another mile or so but they did not stop again. And there was St Anne's Church and, opposite, the gates of Silverdale. They stood open as if Rose were expected.

Sean stopped, putting his big, work-scarred hands upon the child's shoulders.

'Before yer go, there's something . . .'

Rose looked up into her father's face and saw there his love for her, and his searing sadness.

'What is it, Daddy?'

He put his hand in his pocket and brought out a little packet, holding it out to her.

''Tis nothin' much, darlin'. I made it for yer out of bits of . . . Yer've never had a lot . . . so I thought . . . Take it, child.'

Rose unwrapped the bit of cloth and between her fingers threaded a slim, beautifully made rosary. The beads were only glass, but tiny, and each one matched and was the exact size of its neighbour. The chain in between had been worked with infinite patience from slivers of silvery wire as fine as the strands of her own hair, and the whole was as light as the down which flies from the dandelion in summer.

Her mind had only a moment to wonder how her father had found the time and the materials for such a dainty thing when she was swept into his arms and cradled against his chest.

'Don't speak, macushla, but 'tis so yer can say yer rosary when ye're alone. Without Mammy it might be . . .' Bridie's was the only rosary the family owned, and it was she who led them each day in the telling of the beads.

'Come now. Let's be off, or Mr Hemingway will be after sending out a search-party for yer.'

Rose held the beads in her hand, the feel of them a link between the world she was leaving and the one she walked towards.

'Will I come ter the kitchen door with yer, darlin'?' the father asked softly.

For the last time Rose O'Malley allowed herself the indulgence of being a child, with a child's natural entitlement to a parent's protection.

'Please, Daddy.'

It was another half mile through the wood and parkland of the estate to the house – a mile to be put on his journey – but his child's eyes, terrified now by the enormity of what lay before her, begged his understanding. The wrought iron gates, massive, as though they guarded a prison, made her timid and she held Sean's hand so tightly her small imprints were left, white and clear in his flesh, when he prised her loose.

They went by a lodge and tall, gracious trees grouped themselves like inquisitive prisoners come to see the newest inmate, along the driveway. The gravel was swept so neatly they were almost afraid to step on it. They crossed a small wooden bridge which spanned a clear stream that was edged about with water violets and bladder wort, and the rushes made a song as they tiptoed across.

He delivered her to the kitchen door of the vast and gracious house of his Master, and watched as Rose vanished with a last despairing glance over her shoulder into the bustling alien environment that was to be her world.

No one spoke to him. At that last moment the little girl clung and, when she had gone, he stood for several minutes staring desolately at the closed kitchen door. Then he turned, straightened his shoulders and began the long walk home, leaving his child to her fate.

She was just ten years old.

# CHAPTER 2

It was Robert Hemingway who began it all. The youngest son of a prosperous wine-merchant, he married in 1776 and, for want of an occupation, he bought shares in a trading ship. He launched his first merchantman three years later, laying the foundation of what was to become one of the greatest shipping lines to do business out of Liverpool.

But it was his only son, Thomas, who had the vision and the drive to compete in a commercial atmosphere of a thriving port, making the name of Hemingway one of the most respected, and the family one of the wealthiest in the north-west.

In the year 1540 there were but twelve vessels sailing from the village of 'Lyverpoole'. By the 1800s the ships numbered some fifteen thousand, a good number of which were owned by Thomas. From the crowded docks went salt, coal, glass, iron bars and hoops, manufactured goods and pottery. In return, spilling on to the teeming quayside, came from all corners of the world, sugar, tobacco, rum, raw cotton, silk, sandalwood, green ginger, spikenard, redwood . . . and slaves.

Despite Thomas' impatience with public indignation over slavery, by the early nineteenth century the Hemingway fortune was assured. He became a major influence in the borough, respected and admired for his business acumen and when, as the century progressed, the vast tracts of land he had purchased in West Derby were sold for huge profit to the railway companies, his name was spoken of with envy.

In 1830, at the age of twenty-nine, Charles, grandson of Robert, took control of the shipping line and inherited not only responsibility for the Hemingway name, and the enormous wealth, but also the elegant mansion in Toxteth Park that Robert had built in the style of Robert Adams.

It was a beautiful house of perfect symmetry, softened by curving stairways and arches. Outside, acres of wood and parkland were surrounded on three sides by the chequered fields of farms, orchards and small woods, and on the fourth by the great River Mersey. Here, ornamental gardens hewn from what had once been farmland, flanked by dim tunnels of yew, descended from the house in terraces down a gentle hillside almost to the water's edge.

Charles Hemingway sat at the head of the table and watched as his wife and four daughters glided, like so many swans on a lake, into the morning room. The hem on his wife's full skirt touched the floor, and she appeared to be without feet as she skimmed the velvet of the carpet. His daughters, the eldest fourteen, and already begging to put up her hair and let down the hem of her dress; the youngest nearly eleven, revealed neat, white-stockinged ankles and black kid slippers, though their gowns were a demure replica of that worn by their mama.

They took their places about the breakfast table: his wife at its foot; his daughters opposite; his two sons, who were already seated, bowing their smooth heads above clasped hands, as did the servants who stood at the back of the room, whilst Charles murmured Grace. A way of life was made up of such small matters, and it pleased and soothed Charles's mind to keep up such traditions.

The room faced south and, though the sun did not shine, the light which fell through the tall window was clear and bright, polishing the glowing mahogany of the long, oval table to a mirror in which the faces of those about it were reflected.

Charles and his two sons, Thomas, sixteen and Robert, a year younger, were soberly dressed in dark, well-fitted frock coats and tight trousers, all alike. They wore waistcoats of grey silk, and their necks were swathed in cravats of the same colour and material. They wore their hair rather long, curled and liberally applied with pomatum. Charles affected mutton chop whiskers, but no moustache. A great deal of time was spent in making up one's mind about appearance and the smallest gaffe was observed and ruthlessly acted upon.

Sarah Hemingway wore a morning gown of sprigged blue

22

muslin, and a small lace cap. Her daughters were charmingly youthful in day dresses of soft pink grenadine, the style copying that of their mama to the last stitch. Well-fitting bodices, except in the case of Mama of course, were smoothed across flat chests and straight backs, and the slightly full skirts revealed a fraction of white lace petticoats. Their hair, brushed and brushed until it gleamed, was long and smooth, that of the three eldest being forced into long ringleted curls, induced there by papers each night. It fell below tiny waists, held from their faces with broad bands of velvet in the same soft pink as their dresses.

Six young heads rose simultaneously as Charles Hemingway spoke. 'I heard yesterday that Andrew Jenkinson's *Susan Jay* has done the trip from the Far East to London in just over one hundred days, Thomas. Is that not remarkable? She is a fine clipper ship and one day we shall have one just like her, or even superior.'

The young boy to whom the remark was addressed cleared his throat, and a rather desperate expression took the place of politeness on his face.

'Yes, Papa,' he ventured, and his eyes slid away from those of his father, as though hoping the older man's attention would go with them.

'They still have it over us, you know, the American ship-builders. But only, I hasten to add, in the matter of the clippers. The day will come when our yards will equal, no, surpass, theirs. Do you not think so, Robert?'

'Yes, Papa,' Robert said hesitantly.

'And what do you mean by that, Robert? Have you no opinion on the comparison between American and British shipbuilding? I admit the Americans are well ahead of us at the moment, but mark my words, British clippers will come into their own.'

There was a deep, implacable sigh from the other end of the table, but Charles chose to ignore it. On his right, the child beside him hung on his every word, her face rapt, her eyes fixed upon him with intense and earnest admiration.

'The *Mary Munro* will be a fine ship, though only a fore and aft schooner. Yes, a fine ship. Tell me, Robert,' he turned swiftly to his younger son, who jumped and went quite limp, 'can you tell me the difference between a topsail schooner and a fore and aft?' He smiled and waited.

There was silence, and the boy's eyes became glazed.

'Come, sir. You are the son of a ship builder, and one day will have the directing of one of the largest shipping lines in the country. Do you mean to tell me that you are ignorant of one of the most simple technicalities? Topsail, and fore and aft. Which is which?'

The child who sat beside him held her breath, watching avidly as her brother searched for words.

'Why, Papa, I believe . . .'

'Yes, Robert. What do you believe?'

'A topsail schooner is . . .'

'Yes?'

She could hold it in no longer.

'I know, Papa. I know! A fore and aft schooner has only two masts, and the sails run in the same direction as a line from the bow to the stern, and . . .'

'That will do, Alexandrina. I would be obliged, Charles, if we might dispense with this talk of clippers and schooners at the breakfast table. It is hardly suitable to discuss business in the presence of our daughters.'

Charles turned immediately and courteously to his wife.

'Of course, my dear. I apologize. This is neither the time nor the place. It was just that the news of the *Susan Jay* was of such interest. I thought the boys would be . . .'

The two boys threw thankful, furtive looks at their mother's severe face and exchanged glances. Though the subject was for the moment dropped, they knew their father would renew it when they reached his office where they were to spend the day with him. They were both on half-term holiday from school, but Papa had insisted that they accompany him, saying that if they were to take his place one day they should at least know where that place was.

'And what will my daughters do today, my dear?' he asked, as the silence stretched out emptily.

The question again raised six heads and the polite, smiling expressions returned. Charles Hemingway expected little of his daughters except that they behave as well-brought-up young ladies, and they had little option to do ought else, for they were watched every moment of the day. The question was asked merely on behalf of good manners. His grey eyes moved from his wife to the straight-backed figures of the four young ladies who sat on his right. His eyes lingered a moment longer on the one who sat nearest him, and his eyes softened.

He and Sarah Beaumont had been married in 1831, and in the following six years she had borne him six children. She had, as was her duty, submitted to the odious business of conceiving and the painful task of giving birth, and had accepted, with little enthusiasm, her husband's conjugal embrace. She was fervently thankful that she had produced two sons and might therefore, she thought, reasonably be allowed to discontinue the distasteful practice. But Charles Hemingway thought otherwise. She was his first wife and, despite her apathy, he still found her rounded figure of interest. When the need arose, he would call on her in the luxurious bedroom in which she slept alone, and take her with enormous pleasure; the act giving his wife a weapon through which she ruled him, if not at his place of business, at least in their home.

She wanted no more children. Her slim, white body had thickened, although this was not, it must be added, due entirely to childbearing: her main pleasure was to recline upon her chaise longue and sip thick and creamy chocolate, whilst her maid brushed her curtain of long, pale hair. This was her greatest claim to beauty, being luxuriant with a springing curl at the end. Her husband gloried in it, wrapping it about himself – quite indecently in her opinion – in the privacy of their room, and secretly pleased with the growing plumpness of her figure. He seemed to find no fault in her indifference to his attentions, for he believed that to be the mark of a lady.

Sarah's eyes, a pale myopic blue, somewhat vague and deceptively ingenuous, looked up from the sliver of toast she

25

was buttering and regarded her husband. She was an intelligent woman and, after seventeen years of marriage, not the slightest bit in awe of her husband. She knew him well, and how to handle him. She was cunning in that she let him think he had his own way. Providing she was allowed to continue her pleasant life – entertaining, calling upon and receiving visitors; conferring with Mrs Johnson, the housekeeper who ran the big house, and with Nanny Wilson who ran the nursery – she let him believe he was the master. Her day drifted smoothly by from breakfast with her husband and children, the only meal she shared with them, to dinner with her husband and whichever guest or guests they might happen to entertain. She did little in between but visit, and gossip, and see her dressmaker and milliner, and Charles Hemingway expected no more of her.

'They are to go with Miss Robertson and Nanny,' she replied, 'to the Royal Institution in Colquitt Street, Charles. I believe Miss Robertson wishes them also to see the fine collection of paintings in the Gallery of Art. It is as well for them to have an appreciation of things artistic, do you not agree? It gives a young lady a certain poise to be able to converse on such topics.'

Charles nodded his head and addressed himself once more to his breakfast. Silence fell once more, and the eight figures around the table resumed eating. Empty plates were removed efficiently and others, upon which hot kidneys, bacon, kedgeree or eggs were heaped, were put in their place. When he had finished, Charles glanced idly about the table, his mind already in the carriage which stood at the front door of the house, waiting to take himself and his sons to town. His eyes met those of his youngest child, and again his face softened. She smiled warmly, as though she had waited only for his glance, and he could not resist smiling back.

She was his favourite, this slip of a thing whose bright spirit Sarah was doing her best to stifle, as she had done with the others. She was his treasure, precious beyond belief, though wild horses could not have dragged the admission from him. He was fond of his other children, particularly the girls, though he was disposed to a certain disappointment in his sons. He was strict and fair, but they lit no fires of love in him as this one did. This child was not the same as his other children. Patternless, unpredictable, showing a quality which the rest lacked, she seemed to question all that went on about her with her bright inquisitive mind, which he only regretted had not been given to either of his sons.

Alexandrina Victoria Hemingway. Named for the young queen who came to the throne three days before she was born, his daughter was called by all except her mama by the simple abbreviation – contrived by her sister, a year older and unable to get her baby tongue around the difficult christian name – of Lacy.

Lacy. Lacy Hemingway.

And that was what she was. No name could have suited her more admirably. She resembled exactly a scrap of exquisitely worked lace. She was dainty and fragile as gossamer with her silver-streaked, tawny hair, silken and curly just like her mama's; her clear grey eyes; and the fine ivory and rose of her skin. She reminded her fond papa of the mock orange that grew so profusely in Sarah's winter garden. The cup-shaped blossom, oval and flushed with pink in its centre, was no more delicately lovely than this child of his.

But there the simile ended. Though she was slender as a willow, a fluff of swansdown to be blown through the summer air by any chance breeze, her fragile looks were deceptive. She had a brave, strong spirit, and a natural confidence which quickly overtook and dominated her three older sisters. His daughter's bright expectant eye was upon him still.

'And will you enjoy the excursion, Lacy?' he asked fondly.

There was a brief silence, and five pairs of eyes turned towards their sister as they waited for her answer; and five hearts beat faster. Would she really say what she had threatened? The tension began to be felt by the rest of the occupants of the room, and the servants exchanged uneasy glances. Even her mother's face, so calm and unruffled now that the talk of ships was out of the way, took on a faint look of alarm.

27

'Lacy?' Her papa's voice was questioning.

She took a deep breath.

'Yes, thank you, Papa,' she said clearly, 'and on Wednesday I should like to go with you and Thomas and Robert to see the launching of Great Grandmama's ship, if you please.'

The maids melted into the corners of the room as though seeking shelter from the coming squall, and Chapman froze behind his master's chair. It seemed to go on forever, the silence which followed, and apart from the movement of five heads as they looked from their papa to their sister, everyone was still.

Sarah Hemingway came to with a gasp, a great floundering heaving moan, and her pale skin flooded with colour from her high forehead to the frilled neck of her gown. Even her hands became red, and she had time to wonder in the midst of her horror if that dreadful part of a woman's life, that which was never spoken of except in hushed whispers amongst matrons, was upon her.

'Alexandrina!' she wailed, and in a moment began to slip from her chair in a faint. She had never really fainted in her life, but she found the pretence of one convenient at times; and now was one of them.

Charles' mouth hung open in disbelief. He ignored his wife's flapping arms and graceful glide to the floor, and it was left to an expedient maid to gather her mistress into a sitting position.

He stared dumbfounded into his daughter's face. It was brilliant with hope. Her eyes never moved from his, and she scarcely seemed to breathe as she waited for him to speak. He could feel his own denial begin to well up, and yet, at the back of his mind, a small but logical part of him said, why not? Where was the harm?

But no, the very idea was preposterous. To take a gently reared young girl amongst the rough workmen who would be crowding the slipway, and to introduce her into the company of his own all-male world was unthinkable. He would be censured not only by his business associates but by their wives, for it was they who made the rules. But as he looked into her ardently expectant face he felt his resolve slip away. She was so like him. In her he could see the way he had been at her age.

Sarah Hemingway watched them, her hand to her heart, ready to shriek and slip away should Charles agree; ready to take her stand as a mother should, for what woman can see her husband reproached, and her daughter whispered about by society, and do nothing?

Lacy saw the look of uncertainty on her father's face and knew he wavered. She rose from the table and on light, slippered feet moved gracefully towards him. No running or acting in any way which might displease Papa. He must believe that she was able to conduct herself as a lady should. She stood demurely before him, her hands clasped, and looked at him with eyes enormous with longing.

'Oh, please, Papa. May I not go? I will be no trouble, and will be so good and . . .'

'Charles.' Sarah's voice sounded warningly.

His face soft with indecision he said, 'Lacy, my dear. It would not be proper for a . . .'

'But, Papa, I will be so good no one will even notice that I am there.'

'I'm sorry, Lacy. It is out of the question,' he said sadly.

At the other end of the table Sarah relaxed against the back of her chair, and her breath sighed from her lungs in relief.

'But why, Papa. Why?' Lacy's voice was tense, her small frame rigid with the effort to hold herself still, and act as a well-brought-up young lady was supposed to.

'Alexandrina. I will not have you questioning your Papa in this fashion. He has said you may not go, and that is an end to it. Now please leave the room at once, and go to the nursery. I shall be up directly.'

She might have addressed the flowers upon the table for all the notice that was taken of her. Jane, frightened by the tension, began to cry silently, her tears running in tiny ladylike rivulets down her pale cheeks.

Sarah opened her mouth to speak again, furiously angry now, but nothing came out. The maid, seeing the flush mount to her mistress's cheeks once more, began vigorously to fan her with a folded napkin.

'Lacy, you know why. The yard is no place for a . . .'

'Papa, I will stay by your side. I shall not move even an inch.'

Charles looked into the lovely, determined face and doubted it.

'But, my dear, it would be unfair to take you and not your sisters,' he said, trying another argument.

Lacy turned passionately towards the three correct young ladies at the table. Their backs were poker-straight, their hands folded primly in their laps; only their faces moving in consternation. Go to the yard, their expressions said, amongst those rough men, and the noise, and the dirt, and the smell!

'You do not want to go, do you? Do you, Amy? You should not like it. Should you, Margaret? Or you, Jane?' Her head turned fervently from one to the other, and her composure slipped. 'You would hate it, would you not?' She veered back to her father and put her small hand on his. He looked at it, and into her eyes in which her soul shone, and he was lost.

'Well,' he began, but he got no further. His wife rose to her feet and waved away the maid with a gesture of mad imperiousness. Though Sarah was mild and amiable in most matters, this was, perhaps, because she had never in all her life been put to the test.

'Charles, I must protest most strongly. You are allowing the child to speak to you as though it was the most natural thing in the world to ask to go to the launching. It is the height of impropriety to permit the child this foolishness. Heaven knows what language she may hear, and those uncouth men will no doubt be about the most . . . the most indecent . . .' Words failed her.

'Sarah, if I may be allowed to . . .'

'I am amazed that you should even contemplate the possibility!'

'Sarah, if you would . . .'

'No, Charles. No! I absolutely forbid it. We will speak of it no more.'

Perhaps it was this, for no one had spoken to Charles Hemingway in such a manner since his days in the nursery, which firmed his resolution. To be told in front of not only his family, but his servants, that he was forbidden to take his own daughter to his own shipyard, to see the launching of his own ship, steeled his resolve.

He rose to his feet, and husband and wife faced one another.

'Thank you, Sarah. Your objections have been noted but, despite this, I intend to take the child. I can see no possible reason why she should not attend, none at all. She will be constantly under my protection and will come to no harm.'

Sarah's eyes flashed and her bosom heaved. For a moment, the thought passed through Charles Hemingway's inflamed mind that, if his wife brought some of the fire she now showed to their marriage bed, what they did there might be a great deal more interesting; then he was horrified that such an indecent idea should slip in, as it were, when he wasn't looking.

The notion made him hesitate. Had she chosen the right words, the correct attitude, his wife might have had her way even then, and many lives would have taken a different route, but she stared in venomous silence, unaware of the still flickering doubt in his mind.

But Charles could not now go back on his word and still retain his position as head of the household; as the father whose word was law; the master who had the respect of his servants.

He said firmly, 'The child will go. This is my last word.'

# CHAPTER 3

Rose was at the brussels sprouts when she came in. The hands which were stripping the outer leaves from what seemed a hundredweight of the things, hesitated, as she stared in wonder at the vision which never ceased to bemuse her. In the past seven months Rose had seen her a hundred times, dressed on each occasion, or so it seemed, in a different outfit. The sight of her, vivid as the sunshine which fell through the kitchen door at noon, reminded her of that day when they had first become acquainted on the quayside. Her hands, floating in the water which contained the discarded leaves of the vegetables, became still. She held her breath, as though the expulsion of it might blow away the delicate sprite who was making her way through the activity created by a dozen or more people preparing a meal.

There was much brisk stirring, chopping, whisking, pounding, kneading; a tumultuous frenzy which might have led the ignorant to believe that a banquet at least was being got up. It was, in fact, a simple luncheon for the mistress and her four daughters. Cook was leaning over the range, the wooden spoon with which she had just stirred a sauce to her lips. She tasted the mixture speculatively, her rubicund face set in lines of deep concentration, then she turned to the kitchen maid and, with an air of one who makes a momentous decision upon which the lives of thousands might depend, said,

'A half teaspoon more of salt, if you please, Nora, and not a speck more.'

Rose stood on tiptoe, her pale face a scant inch from the glass partition which divided the scullery from the kitchen. The bowl in which the sprouts were heaped rested upon a high bench, perfectly suited to an adult, but to reach it Rose was forced to perch upon a wooden box. She leaned forward until her tiptilted Irish nose was pressed to the window. The box almost overturned, but Rose righted it deftly, balancing precariously, but unwilling to miss a word spoken or a gesture made by the elegant little girl.

The disturbance in the morning room had been described, every word, even embellished a trifle by those who had been there, and the kitchen had seethed with excitement since breakfast time. The very notion of the Master and Mistress almost at fisticuffs! Or so Polly would have it, and hadn't she been the one to help her mistress from her faint, so she should know. And here was the cause of it all, as calm as the River Mersey on a still day, smiling about her as though she were the Queen herself, taking a turn about the royal kitchens.

Lacy Hemingway was dressed in an outdoor costume of misty blue, glossy and rich, trimmed with buttons and cross bands of velvet in a deeper shade. The short jacket fitted snugly into her waist and high up her slender neck, like those worn by the soldiers of the Queen's Guard, and upon her incredible silver hair was a tiny pill-box hat, tilted above her forehead, and secured beneath her chin with a narrow velvet ribbon. The full, gathered skirt reached the top of her black-buttoned kid boots and, as the skirt swung, it revealed a fraction of her lace petticoat and the frilled edging of her drawers.

The kitchen was filled with a delicious smell of a meal being cooked, and by the trays of Cook's biscuits which had just been taken from the oven. On the table lay a variety of cooling gingerbreads, shortcakes, almond squares and a multitude of shapes, upon which a maid, trained up by Cook, and now in a position of some responsibility, iced pretty figures of children, animals and flowers. It all spoke of Cook's genius with a 'bit of flour and an egg or two', as she modestly put it.

The child in blue moved towards the table, considered the assortment set out thoughtfully for a moment, then selected half a dozen, putting a gingerbread man to her lips, biting off his head casually, and stuffing the rest in the pocket of her

33

skirt. Rose watched intently, and her mouth watered as she saw the crumbling sweetmeat disappear between soft, pink lips. A small tongue came out and delicately licked a crumb which clung there. The girl was laughing, saying something to Cook, as another biscuit, this time an iced oval on which a brown chocolate dog scampered, made its way into her mouth. In that instant, as crumbs were brushed carelessly from the fine blue jacket to the floor for the mice to enjoy, Rose felt the first stir of resentment. (Blessed Mother, wouldn't their Terence love the very sight of the beautiful thing, never mind the taste?)

The words the girl spoke drifted across the top of the partition, which did not reach the high ceiling but served only to keep those not actively engaged in the cooking separate from those who were.

Rose listened intently.

'. . . and I am to go with them, Cook.'

Well, and we all know that, thought Rose dryly. Haven't we heard nothing else but Miss Lacy this and Miss Lacy that for the past hour, and what the Master said to the Mistress, and her to him, and a storm in a teacup if you asked her. She gave the sprouts a stir and cocked her head in order to hear better.

'It is most unusual for a lady to go to a launching, you know, Cook. I am probably the first to do so.' The small girl spoke airily then, pretended sophistication gone, she became again a child.

'Oh, Cook, is it not wonderful?' Her eyes glittered like bright slivers of crystal caught in sunshine. 'To watch as the *Mary Munro* slips away to the river to rest upon the water. To be there in the dockyard when . . .'

A footman in another cubicle began to turn the handle of the wheel which sharpened the knives and the rest of the words the girl spoke were drowned, though Rose could see the excitement flowering in the expressive face, the bright eyes, the hands which flew about in description of some momentous feeling, and in the very way she stood and moved from foot to foot. Rose wished the footman would hurry up and finish, but for five minutes the knives ground against the wheel, and when they were done, the girl's words could be heard again, the conversation had taken another turn.

'. . . and when Jepson told me there were new puppies in the stable I gave Miss Robertson the slip, saying I must go to the . . .' The girl stopped abruptly, her eyes widening, her hand going to her mouth as she realized what she had been about to say, and where. One did not mention the closet . . . Oh, dear me.

Lacy Hemingway was a strange mixture of rebel and conformist, too young and unformed as yet to be either. She gave the appearance of longing to be about all the wondrous activities allowed to the male; to escape the confines of her upbringing and reach the freedom so far denied her, yet taking the time to stop and put on her bonnet, as convention demanded of a lady who stepped out of doors.

'. . . just imagine, there are seven of them, and Bess scarocly two years old herself. Is it not a marvel to be a mother at two years of age? I could not wait another moment . . .' She looked around, and her eyes sparkled, and Rose saw that the servants were drawn to her as though she had cast a spell about them.

'Amy, Jane and Margaret would not be persuaded to come, though I begged of them not miss Bess's pups.' She pulled a face, and Rose felt herself begin to smile as foolishly as the rest. 'They were afraid they might soil their boots, but I could not resist.'

'If you ask me, they done right. It's me what 'as the bluddy cleanin' of 'em,' the boot boy muttered behind Rose.

'Ssh!' Rose hissed.

'You won't tell Miss Robertson, will you, Cook, should she come looking for me?' The smile was conspiratorial.

Cook said fondly that she would not.

'I thought to take Bess some of your biscuits as a reward for her endeavours. You know how she loves your biscuits.' Cook preened as though Bess's fondness for her baking was commendation indeed.

Rose clamped her soft mouth into a thin line of disapproval. Biscuits for the dog, now, was it? And here was herself longing for a taste, and almost in tears at the thought of her baby brother having just one of the lovely things. The Mammy'd have a fit if she knew.

'. . . and I had better take an apple for Holly. If I went to the stable without one, that horse would never forgive me.'

And then a strange thing happened.

In the grip of a compulsion she was never able to explain, even years later when everything was changed, Rose wiped her wet hands upon her apron and leapt across the back of the startled Jack, running the length of the scullery into the kitchen. She was aware at the edge of her consciousness of faces, mouths hanging slack, and of figures brought to a standstill.

From a tumbling pile which stood on a side table waiting for her own hands to peel, Rose selected a smooth, green baking apple. It fitted her hand as though it were meant for it, and a voice said that was how it should be. Moving between the open-mouthed, motionless figures of the servants, Rose crossed the kitchen and arrived beside the table on which the biscuits were cooling.

Cook had her back to Rose, but Lacy saw her coming, and her expression altered. Cook turned and, before her own face had time to change from warm and doting interest to cold horror, Rose's hand shot out. Upon its small, red palm lay the apple.

Alexandrina Victoria Hemingway looked at the hand. It was attached to a thin arm, pink and raw to the elbow, where miraculously it became as white and smooth as porcelain. Her eyes followed the arm to the thin shoulder, the delicate neck, the stubborn chin in which a tiny dimple hollowed; to the defiant yet vulnerable eyes of the scullery maid. The servant's hair was completely enclosed within an enormous billowing cap of an indeterminate mushroom colour, and her dress, floor length and of the same neutral shade, was covered from neck to knee by a sacking apron. Upon her feet were a pair of hob-nailed boots from which her legs emerged, like a pair of white candles. She was without a doubt the most completely unattractive girl Lacy had ever seen.

Silvery grey eyes with pupils as black as night looked into green and, for a moment, everything melted away into some distant place as the two children recognized each other. So it is you, mind seemed to say to mind; and both remembered that day almost two years since. Then, grand Miss Hemingway had become just Lacy, smiling at Rose as though kindred spirits had met; and now it was the same.

The incongruity of it did not seem to matter. If they had stood side by side looking into a mirror, dressed as they were, neither would have laughed. They had been brought together – a poor Irish girl from the stews of Liverpool, and the daughter of one of its wealthiest men – by a chance in a million. It was fate, and they both knew that their futures would take them on the same route.

They knew it unquestioningly.

Cook was blessed with no such foresight. She was infuriated. Why, not even a parlour maid, dressed decently and accustomed to moving about the house, would presume to approach one so high above her.

Then in a voice as soft as Irish mist and as hard to cut through, so thick was her brogue, Rose gently put the apple into the hand of the child and said politely,

''Tis fer the 'orse, if yer please, miss.'

Lacy, captivated by the strangeness of the incident, and startled by the empathy which seemed to exist between herself and the girl, smiled and took the apple.

Rose O'Malley smiled back.

'Why, thank you . . . er . . .?'

'Rose, miss.'

'Thank you, Rose. It's a lovely apple, just the kind Holly likes.' Lacy was enchanted. Always moved by anything which was out of the ordinary, the maid's unparalleled rashness in approaching her, her obvious scorn of the consequences, spoke of the recklessness which awoke something in Lacy which she could not yet identify. It was like the feeling of a moment ago when they had looked into one another's eyes. There was an invisible link between them, invisible that is to all who were about them; but they knew it.

By this time, Cook had regained her senses. This was her territory and, though Lacy was the Master's daughter in it, even she must be directed as Cook thought fit. As long as Miss Lacy did not overstep the mark of what Cook considered seemly, for even here lines were drawn, she might come and go as she pleased. And she did, and was most welcome. But now look at this! She had never seen such outlandish behaviour. No, not in all the years she had been in service. A chit of a scullery maid in conversation, if you please, with the daughter of the house; and in the middle of her kitchen, with every servant lolling about as if they hadn't a thing to do but stand and stare.

'*Rose.*'

Her voice shattered the pleasing moment and the interested looks with which the two children eyed one another. Rose jumped and turned, startled, to look at Cook. She put her hands to her cap and pulled it firmly down to her eyebrows. The small, peaked face was almost drowned.

Backing away from the situation, hoping by doing so to divert Cook's anger, Lacy began to babble.

'I must go now, Cook, or Miss Robertson will have me before I have even seen the pups.'

Her eyes flashed a message to Rose, as if to tell her to run back quickly to whatever hole she came from, but, as she put the apple in her pocket and edged towards the kitchen door, the sharply defiant face was still turned in her direction.

'Thank you, Cook. I'm sure Bess will . . .' She smiled again, and shut the door on the tensely silent kitchen.

That night, Rose lay on the straw-stuffed mattress on the narrow iron bedstead which she shared with Nelly. Nelly was her superior, though herself only a scullery maid, by virtue of the fact that she had worked at Silverdale two months longer than Rose. The girl moaned in her sleep and turned, dragging the coarse blanket which covered them from Rose's shoulder. Rose pulled it back, for she was no longer the slavey who would run here and go there at everyone's beck and call; not after today's happenings.

Her ears still throbbed where they had been boxed by

Cook's heavy hand, and her eyes dripped silent tears into the ticking of the pillow, but she had not cried then. Not a tear. She had taken the blows which had almost knocked her from her feet with dry eyes, and tightly clenched lips and hands, but no one had seen her cry.

Rose knew she had made a blunder. Cook ruled her; Cook owned her to all intents and purposes and Cook's approval, or otherwise, could make or break Rose. But even as Cook had set about her, scarcely before the door had shut behind Miss Lacy, Rose knew something else about Cook. She was old, stiff on her legs and slow; and she was afraid. If Miss Lacy should mention today's happening, and all the other days when Cook had covered for her on her escapades, the matter of Cook's age, her increasing inability to do what she had done so well for over thirty years – to render discipline amongst her own kitchen staff, might be brought to attention. The woman's eyes had been sad, as though to tell Rose that really she was sorry to be so severe. It was the way of the world.

Rose had understood. She knew that if she was to amount to anything she must keep on the right side of those above her. If she had to eat humble pie every day of her working life, an' lick Cook's boots an' all, begorra, she would. Whatever it took, she'd do it, and she'd get there. She would.

Where 'there' was in the mind of a ten-year-old child was not yet clear; but she'd know when she arrived.

Rose smiled in the dark. What a tale she'd have to tell Mammy and Daddy tomorrow. The young mistress would not forget her in a hurry, that was for sure.

Sean O'Malley eased his aching body into the sagging comfort of the dilapidated chair which stood before the fireplace. He closed his eyes, rested his dark head against its back and felt the tiredness pulse along his limbs, making them heavy and reluctant to move.

The room was dim and peaceful, and he savoured it, for it was not often so – not with eight children, one of them a baby a few months old. The piece of net at the window, white as a snowflake and as insubstantial, stirred in the draught which forced its way through cracks stuffed with sacking and paper, and the fire blew out a cloud of smoke which drifted to the ceiling. Sean opened his eyes and watched it, and his mind considered the never-ending problem of keeping the place clean. The times he had painted it, and still it came back: the dirt and the green stained patches. Bridie scrubbed ceaselessly untill her hands became cracked and sore with chilblains, but it did no good. When the weather was wet and the sewers could no longer cope, the water seeped through the floor, evil smelling and dangerous.

The quiet was sublime. Sean's head slipped sideways and his body melted into the relaxed stillness of a child. The fire snapped cheerfully and, now that they had a firm hold, the coals no longer belched smoke, but blossomed a bright orange. The ginger tabby turned a time or two upon the bit of rug before settling into a ball, her tail curled neatly about her.

It was Saturday night, the end of a long week, and Sean slept the almost unconscious sleep of the exhausted. He had worked for fourteen unceasing hours that day, for it was to be the launching on Wednesday. Glad of it, he was, for it meant his pay packet would have another shilling or two in it. With the new baby, and Bridie as yet unable to work, they needed it. Rose's few bob helped and, when the baby was weaned and could be put in the care of Mary Kate, Bridie could get back to the washtub. The worst would be over. Please God.

The sound of feet clattering on the area steps broke the peace and had him starting from his chair as though the army of Wellington himself had just marched in. And so it seemed, as the door burst open and in a matter of seconds the cellar was filled with noise. Children were everywhere, all speaking at once, and not one appearing to listen to another.

The woman, who was the last to enter, put her shawl and the baby within it on the table where the infant lay in perfect equanimity, as though already at four months it knew its place in the order of things. Talking with as much garrulity as the younger members of the party, she moved towards the fireplace. It was not until then that she noticed Sean. Her good-natured face softened and she turned fiercely, shushing the irrepressible crowd about her, but it was too late.

"Tis no good you hushin' them now, woman. Could anyone sleep with that lot jabberin' like drunken Irishmen at a wake?' It was said with a smile, and Bridie returned it, as she bent to kiss her husband lovingly.

'Aah, darlin', I'm sorry. We didn't mean ter wake yer. I wasn't expectin' yer home yet awhile with them workin' late on the owd ship. We've bin away ter market an' wait til yer see what we got.' Her face was like that of a child who has been brought a present and is about to unwrap it, and Sean smiled. She was always the same. No matter what happened, she would spring up and be about the getting on with life, determined to make the most of it. She had that rare quality, a truly happy spirit, and he didn't know what he would do without her.

'Look,' she was saying gleefully, 'a whole bag of scrag ends fer tuppence Tuppence!' she exulted, 'an' carrots an' onions thrown in ter be shut of 'em. Seamus carried them all home fer 'is mammy, there's a good lad.' She brushed the hair from the brow of the young boy. 'Who should we bump inter but Mrs Geraghty, an' wouldn't yer know she kept me talkin' about her Mick an' herself, in the family way again, an' 'im without a job. It'll be the work'ouse next, yer mark my words,' she went on cheerfully, though a kinder heart never beat. 'So I told 'er ter tell Mick there was jobs ter be had at 'emingways with the launchin', well, before I knew it it was half past, an' the kids were all at me to come away . . .'

Bridie O'Malley kept up the breathless flow of words which was her normal method of conversation. She needed no answer and got none; she gave of her opinions and herself without stint. On and on her conversation swirled, eddying about the room as she reached for the teapot, placing within it a small teaspoon of tea from the old tin box which served as a caddy. The box was a measure of the ups and downs in the financial life of the O'Malley family. If there was tea in it they were, by their standards, in good times.

The kettle on the fire was lifted and hot water was poured

into the waiting pot. Without once pausing for breath, Bridie pressed nine thick mugs of thin tea into waiting hands, and nine mouths sipped the brew appreciatively. Even the baby was given a drink for, without even bothering to sit down, Bridie opened her bodice and put the child to her breast. Somehow, between mouthfuls of tea and a soothing word to the suckling child, she managed to continue her ceaseless monologue, regaling Sean with the evening's events, and constantly harping back to poor Mrs Geraghty, for whom she felt inordinately sorry.

In all the flurry of loving activity Sean remained contentedly silent. In twelve years of marriage, though he loved her dearly and she him, she had gradually taken from him the merry wit and lively tongue which had been his as a youth. From the moment she opened her eyes in the morning until they closed in sheer exhaustion as she lay against Sean's chest at night, she kept up a continual discourse with whoever happened to be within earshot.

There was always someone. In June 1837 her first child was born. Rose, they named her, for Sean said she looked like the rosebuds which grew round the windows of their tiny cottage. When Sean was away digging peat, or potatoes, or any other job he could find, however menial, Bridie would talk to the baby. As each year passed, her audience of listeners grew, and she was never short of an ear in which to pour her blithe chatter. The losses of children, one at birth and the other two of the 'fever', had grieved her heart but had not taken away her spirit, for she had her Sean, her mainstay.

The tea drunk, the baby fed and sleeping at her breast, Bridie turned once more to Sean.

'Why don't yer get ter bed, my lovely,' she admonished him, gazing solicitously into his tired face. 'Yer look all in. Drink yer tea an' then be off. I've put yer clean shirt on the line over the fireplace t' air a bit. See, 'tis lovely an' warm. Slip into it an' take the hot water from the kettle an' 'ave a nice wash. Now will I do yer feet fer yer? See, stay there an' I'll fetch the bowl. It'll make yer feel better. Patrick can bring some more water from the pipe.'

Any activity to do with water and cleanliness must automatically, in Bridie's view, improve the situation. To be clean and warm, whatever else ailed you, was surely half way to being cured.

'I'll boil up some more water fer the children an' don't you worry about the mess' – the place was like a new pin – 'I'll see ter it. Mary Kate will help, won't you, alannah? An' when yer've 'ad a rest Joseph'll bring yer a bit o' supper.'

Sean had taken Terence, himself only eighteen months old, onto his knee, and he and the toddler stared in amiable silence into the heart of the fire. He rested his cheek upon the boy's soft hair and let the moment settle into him, comfortable as a well-worn jacket.

'I think we'll be away ter our beds early the night, with our Rose comin' tomorrow, an' we'll be wantin' ter go to early mass. Father asked after yer last week, Sean, so if ye're not too tired p'raps yer'll come.'

'I do feel a bit tired.'

Even though Bridie's voice rose and fell in a perpetual peal of words, filling the room with its Irish lilt, when Sean spoke everyone heard him and paid attention. All eyes turned immediately to look anxiously at him, but he flapped his arms at them, and in a moment their worried faces relaxed, and they laughed with him. The room, bare of all but the sheer necessities of life, was warm and lovely, and full of love.

It had taken two years to achieve what little they had.

Within a week of being spilled like so many empty crates upon the quayside Sean had found a job: a weekly wage and a full-time job as a yard hand at Hemingway's. Bridie went to mass each day to thank the Holy Mother for her goodness.

Leaving her babies, the youngest only a year old, with Rose – just eight years of age, and a sensible and trustworthy child – Bridie went to work cleaning: early mornings and evenings at the Northern Dispensary in Vauxhall Road; and, in the day, six hours at a tub in a laundry in Banastre Street. Her arms became red and inflamed to the elbows. But the farthings mounted up; they ate decently, and they had a basement room

43

with a few sticks of furniture and its own entrance all to themselves. At last they were getting on their feet.

Sean and Bridie, unable to love one another in the night, for it would not be decent within earshot of the children; forced to lie side by side without touching, for fear it would give life to their need, now found the necessity to sleep with space between them was no longer required. They were both so exhausted when they fell onto their mattress that the longing died away, and for a long time Bridie's 'monthlies' came as regularly as the moon which controlled them.

They had lived in Naylor Street, just off Scotland Road where most of their own countrymen had settled, for six months when, on finding themselves alone one Sunday afternoon, the children having gone to stare at the horses and carriages on St James' Walk, Sean and Bridie spent a most satisfactory hour upon their bed, and would have spent another, when the sound of the children on the area steps had them reaching for their far-flung clothing. They had only time to pat themselves into place, smoothing one another's tousled hair, when the children were upon them. But that evening, Bridie and Sean, flushed and sated, could not get enough of loving looks and fond touches.

The joy did not last long. Four weeks later Bridie knew she was pregnant, and in her despair threw the chamber pot at Sean, and wept as he took her lovingly into his arms. He knew it was not at him that she railed, but at the fates which would, just as they were getting a grip on their future, fling them back into the dark pit of poverty. They were poor now, the Blessed Virgin knew, but there were degrees, even of poverty; and worse would come if Bridie could not work.

She was ashamed as she knelt before the altar. 'It's not that I mind another, Holy Mother,' she whispered to the serene face above her, 'I'd 'ave another dozen, yer know that, but Sean can't manage without me, yer see, an' it would mean our Rose takin' my place at the washtub, an' 'er so young. Forgive me, Mother, but take this burden from me.'

But the Holy Mother disregarded Bridie's plea and in January 1848 her twelfth child was born; three months after

44

her first, Rose, went to be scullery maid at the big house – spared the washtub.

Now their Rose had been seven months at her grand job. The few shillings she fetched home brought a jug of milk for the little ones, and a bit of good meat now and then, and put a pair of boots on their Joseph, who grew like a sapling. Soon Bridie would be back at the washtub, and another crisis got through. And the best of it was, Rose could come home every fourth Sunday. Only for a few hours, to be sure. Less in the winter months, for her Daddy liked her to be back before dark. But they were lucky, for many girls went into service far from their homes and were virtually exiled for life.

They might not have seen her for four years instead of four weeks, the fuss that was made. Kisses and hugs, and cries of wonder at how the new one had grown; and anxiety that Rose might have lost weight, and was working too hard, and that the walk was more than she could manage; and take off your shawl macushla; and how was Mrs Geraghty, and the latest was another boy and Mick, Glory be to God, had a job . . . It was like the bird house at the Zoological Gardens. The younger children exclaimed over the basket of leftovers, mainly bits of cakes and biscuits which Cook had unaccountably allowed Rose to carry home; and Mary Kate must tell her of her skill at the cooking, now that Mammy had weaned the baby and was to be away to another job, leaving her in sole charge.

The quiet voice of Sean silenced them all, and father and daughter faced one another.

'Well, my Rose.' His eyes searched hers. Though he loved all his children, this girl had a part of his heart that had once been gay, and cheerful, and bright with confidence. She had been the first to leave the shelter of his protection, and he still felt the pain of it.

'How is it then?

'Fine, Daddy.'

'They're not workin' yer too hard?'

Rose thought of her day. Up at five and often not falling into her bed until eleven, after the last pan had been scrubbed and polished and put away, and scarcely a minute to herself; but she smiled impishly and going on tiptoe, kissed her father's cheek.

'No, Daddy.'

Green eyes looked into green then, satisfied, Sean put his arms about her, resting his cheek against the brown silk of her hair, soft and tumbled, for she had loosened it on the road from Toxteth. Watched by the rest, no one speaking, Sean put Rose from him, gave her one last enquiring look, then turned to Bridie.

'Well, Mammy. Time to eat.'

It was a signal for pandemonium to break loose again and, for the next hour, as they tucked into the Irish stew and the sweetmeats Cook had sent them, it continued unabated. But it was Rose who held the floor as she, Bridie, Mary Kate and Teresa cleared away and washed the crockery, and also what appeared to be every movable object in the room. One expected to see Bridie going carefully over each child, and even her husband in his chair before the fire, with the wrung-out dish cloth.

The rest were silent as Rose spoke.

'. . . an' yer'll never guess where Miss Lacy's goin' next Wednesday, Daddy, never in a hundred years. Go on, 'ave a guess.'

Ten pairs of eyes stared at Sean, whilst minds were busy with the teasing question of where the never-seen but always-fascinating Miss Lacy was away to. China, perhaps, or London, or on a railway train to Manchester.

Sean smiled into his daughter's expectant face.

'I give up. Where?'

'Go on, Daddy. Guess. Yer'll be there too.'

Sean looked from Rose to Bridie, and then at the circle of dazzled children, whose minds marvelled at the very idea of their Daddy going to some place where the exquisite Miss Lacy was to be.

'Rose, darlin', sure an' I'm flummoxed at the . . .' Then the expression on his face began to change as revelation dawned on him. Amazement, wonder and the beginnings of a smile crinkled his brown face, and his mouth opened wide in a great shout of laughter.

'She's going to . . ?'

Bridie looked, mystified, from one face to the other. 'What . . . what, our Rose? What's she goin' to?'

Rose turned to the enraptured audience whose mundane lives gained a little colour every fourth week, through the 'doings' of the great Hemingway family, as seen by their scullery maid.

'Miss Lacy is ter go ter the launchin' with her Papa.'

There was a further protracted silence as those about Rose digested this, to them, inconsequential bit of news.

It was Mary Kate who spoke for them.

'But what's so special about that, our Rose?'

Rose stared in horror at the ignorance of her sister.

'Ladies do not go ter . . . ter these sorter dos,' she said primly. 'Not without a chaperone, an' anyway it's only fer gentlemen, an' 'er mama 'ad a blue fit an' stamped out o' the mornin' room, an' she's never spoke ter the Master since.'

'What's a mornin' room, our Rose?' questioned Patrick interestedly, seven years old, and quite bemused by the whole thing. His mind had separated the only words which, to him, seemed worthy of mention. Rose gave him a look in which was written amazement that someone should not know what a morning room was, then explained that the family took their breakfast there.

'Where do they eat their dinner, then?'

'In the dinin' room, of course.'

The boy was silent as he considered the marvel of eating one meal in one room, and a different meal in another. He could barely imagine having two rooms to do anything in, let alone just for the eating. Bridie was enthralled, as were they all, though they could scarcely comprehend half of what went on at Silverdale. There appeared to be so many rules to be followed. Why was it not right for a girl to go about with her daddy and her brothers there to protect her?

Rose's face was gravely solemn, as though the consideration of Miss Lacy's coming out into the world of commerce was of critical importance to them all; her own involvement in it after seven months at Silverdale giving her, in her own mind, a worldliness not yet shared by her sisters.

'Well, Mr Chapman says she's not supposed ter go about without a lady with 'er. Miss Lacy, or any of 'em fer that matter, an' Mistress says Miss Robertson or Nanny Wilson aren't ter take 'er. In fact . . .' Her voice lowered conspiratorially, and even Sean found himself leaning forward in order not to miss what she said. '. . . in fact, Mr Chapman says that if Master takes 'er, Mistress 'as threatened she'll not share 'is . . .'

'That's enough, Rose.'

Rose stopped abruptly as her father became stern. She knew she had gone too far in repeating the gossip at the big house, and her Daddy didn't like it. Not that sort of talk, and certainly not in front of her brothers and sisters.

'Yes, Daddy.'

The nights were beginning to draw out but Sean was anxious that his daughter be safe at the house before dark. She was not quite eleven years old, and as pretty as heart's ease, and who knew what ruffians hovered about the rough district through which she must walk to reach safety.

She said her goodbyes, and again it was as though she went to the far side of the world, and would not be seen for years. Each must have a kiss, and Bridie clutched her to her plump bosom, beseeching her to be a good girl and not to forget her prayers; she'd light a candle for her next Sunday, and was there any chance of her going to mass. She was to try and eat a bit more, and to thank Cook for the sweeties; and on and on and on, until Sean took Rose from her mother's arms and led her towards the door.

Now that she was to be away, Rose's pose of sophistication fell from her, and she turned at the foot of the area steps to look back at the sad faces who watched her go.

'Be a good girl, lovely, an' we'll see yer in four weeks.'

'Yes, Mammy.'

'Goodbye, our Rose.' A chorus from the children.

At the top of the steps father and daughter clasped hands,

and began to walk through the yard to Naylor Street and Vauxhall Road. Sean would see her to the gates of Silverdale and, once inside the estate, she would be safe.

When they reached them, he looked down into her pale face, a blur in the falling dusk.

'I'll be all right from 'ere, Daddy.'

'Good girl. God bless, darlin'. Yer've got yer rosary?'

'Yes, Daddy. 'Tis in me pocket always.'

A kiss, a small sign of the cross on the child's forehead, and she began to run up the gravelled drive towards the house. She turned to wave a half dozen times, and he stood and watched her until she was out of sight. Then began the long walk back to his home.

# CHAPTER 4

It was a grey day with a hint of rain in the cool air, but the noise and sheer energy and vitality of the scene filled the child with an intoxication she had not imagined could exist. She dared not speak for the wonder of it. She marvelled at these creatures who shouted and sang and whistled; who hammered and sawed, and carried huge bundles on their brawny shoulders; and the incredible thing was, they did it every day. This world of theirs had been here yesterday, and would be again tomorrow, and they seemed unconcerned by the miracle of it.

Men with huge hammers struck blows which made her ears ring. They wore caps and aprons of sacking, and touched their eyebrow with stiff fingers, in salute to their master and his children as they went by. Each time his daughter looked up, her eyes were brilliant with excitement, and they smiled as she passed.

A thicket of ships' spars hung above her head until she could barely see the washed grey of the sky. An anchor, bigger it seemed than Papa's carriage, stood against the dock's edge, and a man in half-hose and breeches, an oil lamp hanging from his belt, a bottle protruding from his pocket, leaned unconcernedly against it. He sprang to attention as Charles Hemingway's eyes fell upon him.

Figureheads at the prow of each ship reared at her at regular intervals along the wharf. A wooden binnacle boy, with an injunction to 'mind your helm' inscribed upon his hat, caught her eye, and she speculated as to what it could possibly mean. There were women with buckets upon their heads; dogs, children, casks, horses; steam, smoke; chains and rope; and, everywhere, tools which lay about as though owned by no one.

There were oak for hulls, stout and sturdy enough to

withstand the demonic rage of the Horn; pine for masts; poplar for elegant ornamental carvings; deal and mahogany brought from New Brunswick, all lying in tidily stacked piles about the dock. The redolent aroma of timber mixed with salt and tar – with every smell of a great sea port – filled the enchanted child's nostrils, and her young head with dreams.

What would it be like to be poised on the deck of the ship which was, even now, making its way to the mouth of the river? To look to the top of its mainmast, to command a view of the swaying sail and lines; the ropes, the cable and chain which supported mast and spar? To lean into the wind at the prow and feel the spray sharp against your face? To know the dip of the vessel as it leaned into the jaws of a squall, sails full and cracking with the power of the tempest which drove it? She wanted to know.

How would it be if the waves rose like the sides of a mountain tipped with snow, and the high wind tugged at her hair until it flew about her head like the wings of a great sea bird? How would it be to sail the polished turquoise of the southern oceans to the shores of the lands of cotton and tea, of sugar and nutmeg? Or to feel the hot sun brush your cheek, and to hear the strange tongue of the peoples who lived there? What did the words spoken by a woman from China sound like, and what would she wear?

Would she ever know; would she?

The yard was a feast for Lacy's eyes. Frigate and brigantine. Four-masted barque and schooner. Small, full-bodied merchantmen running up the Mersey on the flood; racing to catch the tide to enter Garston Dock. Nearer to shore, the dumb vessel of the Mersey lighter, carrying freight from ship to dock. It unloaded wheat from Canada and Argentina, fruit and wine from the Mediterranean, Indian tea, and silk and rice.

Lacy Hemingway was entranced. For a moment, Papa and her brothers moved ahead of her. Papa was bending politely towards an acquaintance who had claimed his attention, and his eye had momentarily left her. Her keen gaze whipped from one delight to the next, and she was so absorbed she failed entirely to see the thick, snaking whip of rope attached to a barrel of rum just unloading. It lay in her path and, as she walked, her head turned to the river and the shining water at its mouth, the hands which were releasing the barrel from its burden gave the rope a twitch. It rose six inches above the ground directly in her path, and she was suddenly upon it, her full skirt caught in its length.

A shout, an oath quickly stifled and, as she felt herself go, strong hands were about her waist lifting her from the danger. It took only a fraction of a second. She barely knew what had happened before she was set gently upon her feet again. Papa was still courteously engaged with the persistently questioning gentleman, and Thomas and Robert, fretting on the state of their dirtied boots, were too concerned with themselves to take heed of their sister's plight.

Lacy looked up, startled, into the smiling face above her, and her hand rested briefly on the man's sleeve as she steadied herself. Green eyes, thickly lashed, shone into hers. A full mouth, gentle and humorous, lifted at the deeply grooved corners to disclose big, square teeth. A weathered, freckled skin; dark, slightly greying hair; black eyebrows; and in the strong chin, a hollow which might have been put there by the tip of a child's finger. A strange face, not handsome, but with a Celtic charm which brought a smile to her own lips. A memory tantalized her, for though she had never seen the man before, she felt she had seen the face within the last few days. Those eyes, that flashing smile, surely she knew it . . .

Suddenly becoming aware of where she was and at what had just taken place, the manners instilled into her by Nanny Wilson returned and, without thought, she curtsied as if to a close friend of her mama. Her mittened hands went to the skirt of her blue woollen dress, which dipped gracefully. Her neat bonneted head bent politely. The man stood bewitched. She smiled.

'Thank you, sir. I would have fallen had you not been there to catch me.' She turned her head and looked about her curiously. 'What can it have been, do you think, to appear so quickly from nowhere. I am sure there was nothing in my path.'

''Twas the rope, Miss Lacy.' The man grinned, doffing his cap with a flourish. 'The dockie was unloading the barrel, and the owd rope kind o' sneaked up on yer, sudden like.'

'The owd rope . . .' Lucy, gratified beyond measure, as she always was at the manifestation of something unusual in her day, could only repeat the man's strange remark as she stared up into his face. Where had she seen him before? He knew her name, too. He had called her Miss Lacy. He would know who she was, she being here with Papa, but only the family and close friends called her Lacy; and one or two of the servants . . .

*Servants*. Like a taper which had just put a flame to a lamp it came to her and she beamed, transported for a second to the bustle of the kitchen at home, and the remembrance of that funny creature with the droll hat. The green eyes, the sharp cleft chin, the laughing mouth. They were all here in this man's face. Her own lit up, and she held out her hand.

'Why, you are Rose's papa, are you not? I spoke to her only last week. She works in the kitchen at home.'

Sean took the small hand which Lacy held out to him and, not quite knowing what to do with it, shook it gently.

'That's right, Miss. Scullery maid she is.'

'And have you just come to see the launching as well, Mr . . . er . . .?'

'The name's O'Malley, Miss.' Sean almost laughed out loud at the very idea. Come to see the launching! As though he were one of the fine gentlemen who flocked beside her father, with nothing better to do with their time than stand and stare at a ship going on its way. He bent his head, and his eyes twinkled humorously.

'Bless yer, I work here. 'Twas me that helped in the buildin' of the vessel, and a foin ship she is an' all. I'm a yard 'and, yer see.'

Lacy was fascinated. To actually be talking to a man who had had a hand in the construction of the *Mary Munro* must

53

surely be one of the most exciting moments of her life. But, what on earth did a yard hand do? She must ask him at once.

'Why, that sounds most interesting,' she said seriously. 'And which part of the ship are you concerned with?'

'Well, Miss Lacy' – It seemed the most natural thing in the world to call her that, for didn't he feel he knew her well, with Rose forever having the child's name on her lips – 'yer might say I'm a jack of all trades.'

'A jack of all trades?' Lacy repeated his words raptly, her eyes on his face, unaware of the growing circle of silent, mesmerized spectators who surrounded them.

'And what is that, Mr O'Malley?'

'Why, 'tis meaning I can turn me hand to . . .'

'Alexandrina!'

The implacable voice of Charles Hemingway cut like a sword through the delightful exchange, and Sean O'Malley straightened instantly, his hand going deferentially to his forehead. He stepped back from the enchanting slip of womanhood who had spoken to him with the respectful cordiality she would show one of her own class, and he had time in that moment to consider that all Rose had said about her was true. There was something about her that drew you to her, and yet she spoke with none of the condescension with which those of her standing addressed his.

'Alexandrina.'

The voice could not be ignored.

Lacy turned reluctantly and looked up at her Papa, ready to tell him of her encounter. But the instant her clear sparkling eyes met his, she was aware that somehow she had displeased him. His expression was as usual: polite, rather stern; but the flesh about his mouth was white and his eyes, the same colour as her own, were bleached to a pale silver. He had called her by her full name, a thing he never did unless he was vexed.

In a moment she was by his side. This lovely day must not be spoiled, not for a second. She took his hand placatingly and smiled up at him, the words of what had happened tumbling from her lips. He must have thought her caught up in conversation with a total stranger, and that is why he looked so cross. An introduction must be effected immediately. When he knew that Mr O'Malley had saved her from a fall, or perhaps even a ducking, he would smile again and shake Mr O'Malley's hand, and thank him, and all would be well.

'Oh, Papa. This gentleman saved me from falling. He is . . .'

'Thank you, Alexandrina. That is enough. It was most resourceful of . . .'

'But, Papa, Mr O'Malley caught me when I . . .'

'Yes, Alexandrina, but that will be all.'

Charles Hemingway nodded coolly to Sean O'Malley, who touched his forehead again. Then, with Lacy's hand clasped firmly in his, he steered her away through the crowd. Thomas and Robert followed closely upon her heels, their faces bleak, for they knew they would share the blame for this shameful happening.

Charles was simply appalled. He should not have brought her. Barely inside the dock gate, his back turned for a moment, and she was in conversation with one of his own workmen. Sarah was right. He should have left her at home where she belonged, in the schoolroom with her sisters and, by God, that is just what he would do from this day on. He held his head high, though in his heart lay the demoralizing knowledge that Sarah had been right, and he wrong.

But for the next half hour the beautifully dressed little girl charmed the gentlemen who had come to see his ship launched, curtseying with the grace of a debutante and the assuredness of a grown woman. She kept her eyes demurely lowered, the thick fan of her eyelashes shadowing her pink, rounded cheek. She smiled modestly when addressed, but answered each question quietly, and spoke only when spoken to. She was the epitome of decorum, moving not an inch from his side, as though to compensate for her previous behaviour. Her gentle reserve and ladylike constraint turned Charles's scowl to a look of approval, and his expression relaxed. She could not help the incident with the yard hand, he told himself. She would have fallen had the man not been there. She was not accustomed to the dock, to the hazards which lay about waiting for unwary feet. The fault was his in not watching her.

'Mr Hemingway, sir.'

A voice spoke behind him and a deferential hand touched his arm. He turned. It was Joseph Marshall, the designer who had created the beautiful ship which lay passively on its bed of keel blocks, waiting for its journey from womb to world.

'Good morning, Mr Hemingway. A good day for a launch, sir. The water is calm and there's not too much wind.'

'No indeed, Mr Marshall. Is all ready?'

'It is, sir. I was wondering . . . Perhaps you and your family might care to be aboard when she goes. I myself am to ride on her deck. I am anxious to see how she takes to her element.'

Lacy stood beside her father, her small cloaked figure as still as the ship behind her; but her face was glowing, flying poppies in her cheeks, and her eyes shone with radiant hope.

'Would you like that, my dear?'

'Oh, Papa,' she breathed, and her hand crept into his.

They stood on the deck, the planks smelling of that lovely fragrance which only new timber has; and the tang of the tar-soaked hemp which had been forced between each one to seal it, to caulk it, filled her nostrils. The wind was stronger up here, and she could look directly away to the far side of the river. Her bonnet fell to the back of her neck, her hair became loosened from its ribbon and lifted about her head as she stood, like a tiny figurehead in the bow. Silence fell for a moment, for those of the sea are of a superstitious nature, and it was held to be bad luck for a woman to be aboard a ship as she was launched.

There was much shouting of directions to the men who stood far below, where the ship's frame curved under its keel. Lucy ran to the side, decorum gone, looking down at the yard men as they prepared themselves for this moment; the moment they had worked towards for nearly a year. A brown face looked up at her, green eyes laughing and merry, and Rose's papa winked at her. He held a huge wooden hammer, and flexed his muscled arms in preparation for that first blow. The excitement was intense.

To start a vessel down the ways a pair of men must smash the blocks of wood that support the keel. As the blocks are knocked away, the weight of the hull is thrown onto the cradles, piles of beams built up along the hull's underbelly. An interface between two layers of the cradle beams is greased and, as the weight settles onto the cradles, the top layer begins to slip letting the ship move down the incline and into the water.

Sean O'Malley looked up at Lacy, and waited for the order to strike. What a tale he would have to tell Bridie and the little ones tonight.

There was a signal. From which direction it came Lacy was never to know. Her eyes blazed with intoxication. Her face, like a cameo set in the frame of her tumbled mass of hair, smiled down at Sean. It was the last thing he would ever see.

He swung his mallet.

With a clattering of falling keel blocks the vessel began to move.

Sean looked up again at the child's enchanted face. His eyes gazed into hers joyfully, as they shared that last moment. His foot almost missed the patch of grease which lay in the shadow of the slowly moving vessel, but it was meant for him. Suddenly he could feel his body begin its slow gliding descent to death, but he could do nothing to stop it. His eyes were still on the child when the keel neatly sliced away his legs where they met the trunk of his body, carrying the mangled stumps with it.

With a tremendous splash the new vessel entered the water, stern first.

Lacy Hemingway watched the vivid scarlet blood pump in a vast tide across the jumble of wood and clutter left behind by the ship. She could no longer see his face, only the poor defiled remnant of what had been, only moments before, a vital laughing man. The horror was so great she was like a moulded clay effigy of herself. Colourless, motionless, speechless, she stood by the ship's rail, seeing, but not seeing, the frantic scramble of men who ran to Sean. Though they were mercifully hidden from her sight, his eyes still blazed at her; not with excitement, but in agony.

The men who stood with her father on the far side of the deck shouted and cheered and threw their hats in the air, and all about them was the joyous hullaballoo which is incurred by the initiation of any new ship. Horns blew and men whistled, unaware of the tragedy which had taken place in the space of two or three minutes.

Charles Hemingway turned to the still, cloaked figure of his daughter, surprised by her quietness. He walked towards her across the deck, which had come alive as the ship took its first breath and, looking down at her, was vastly embarrassed when she began to scream in a high, thin voice.

# CHAPTER 5

The house was quiet. There was no sound in any of the
spacious and elegant rooms, save that made by dozens of
clocks which ticked away the minutes. From the deep pro-
fondo resonance of the grandfather clock in the hall, to the
delicate carillon of the ormolu on the mantelshelf in the
drawing room. Clocks under domed glass whispered almost
without sound, muffled by their polished covers. Calendar
clocks warned not only of the slipping by of the hour, but of
the day, the month and the year. There were bob clocks,
cuckoo clocks and pendulum clocks. They tinkled and
trumpeted and, on the hour, exploded into an orgasm of
chiming like the sound of an orchestra as it tunes up before a
performance.

The clocks chimed, and as they did so, a wraith in a white
cap and apron slipped from the rear of the house and began to
repair the fires which burned in each room, although no one
sat before them. Suddenly the silence was broken again by the
clatter of tongs on a coal scuttle. The girl winced visibly, then
retreated thankfully to the familiar comfort of the kitchen.

Here was normality of a kind, though the atmosphere was
charged with a certain morbid excitement. It was not often
that its occupants were treated to a break in the tedious
routine of their lives, and although they were for the most part
kindhearted, they could not help but feel that strange,
vicarious thrill which comes when tragedy in which one is not
personally involved strikes another.

At Cook's command, the kitchen maid refilled the kettle in
readiness for another cup of tea, for the woman had gone, in
her own words, 'all peculiar', when she had been told the
news. She and Mrs Johnson sat, one on either side of the
fireplace in the servants' hall, sipping the revitalizing brew. By
virtue of their seniority and age, they felt they were entitled to

cosset themselves after the dreadful shock they had suffered. Their heads nodded together and, as they explained to one another, it was not the passing of the poor man which upset them so, for they had not known him, but the manner in which he had gone. Horrid fascination filled them as they dwelled on the sight which had been witnessed by their little mistress, and her so young, and Madam had been right to protest at her going where no child, especially a female, should be allowed. Had this not proved it?

The maids, exclaiming as the dreadful details were revealed, waited in groups of two or three, keeping an eye on the house door at the top of the steps for Mr Chapman to return, or anything else which might feed their lively curiosity. Only Jack Talbot, the boot boy and the one who teased Rose O'Malley unmercifully just to see the flash of her green Irish eyes, seemed disinterested. He sat upon his upturned box in the corner of the tiny room he had often shared with Rose, and was mystified by his own sadness. Her eyes wouldn't be flashing again, not for a long time, he thought, poor little sod; and his own drab, hardworking day would be the poorer for it.

Upstairs in the warm luxury and resplendent comfort of her bedroom, attended by the family doctor, Sarah Hemingway lay for the first time in a real faint. Her screams had surpassed even those uttered by her daughter earlier but, just for a moment, before the genuine swoon overcame her, she had felt a surge of triumph. Then the child's voice, so strange and high, jerked Sarah from her brief spell of self satisfaction and, before she could stop her ears, her daughter's words slipped greasily into her head.

'. . . and his legs were cut right off, Mama, and were carried away by the ship, and in a moment the blood poured from him like the stream at Pyke fell. He just lay there, Mama. Just half a man, just half . . .'

Sarah, appalled, sickened, speechless for a moment, found her voice.

'Stop it, stop it, *stop it!*' she screamed. 'How could you speak so? How could you . . .?' Her senses reeled and tilted and, in a moment, the hand-painted Chinese wallpaper which covered the walls of her bedroom fell in on her, mercifully, silencing the strange, rhythmic chant of her daughter's voice.

Charles Hemingway stood between his fainting wife and mindless child and wished with all his heart he had listened to Sarah when she had deplored his decision to take Lacy to the shipyard. It had been pride, he knew it now. Pride in his own judgement, in the bright intelligence and beauty of his daughter, and in her rapt attention to himself. His sons cared not a jot for his world; only for the privilege it brought them. They had gone to see the ship because they were made to, and had shown scant interest in all he attempted to instil into their empty minds. Only Lacy cared. Only Lacy hung on his every word, listening intently, making him feel that, to her, he was second only to God. The infallibility with which he had believed himself endowed had proved as treacherous as quicksand. His unshakeable confidence, well founded he had thought, and proven by his success in life, was slipping away as surely as Sarah's senses.

It was at that moment, although she did not as yet know it, that he gave his children, even his sons, entirely into his wife's hands. Never once in the remainder of their lives together was he to go against her wishes. He was beside himself with horror at what the child had witnessed and was never to forgive that part of him which had defied what he now perceived as Sarah's good judgement. He had tortured himself with the belief that, but for him, the tragedy might never have happened. Why, the man himself might still be alive, he thought, for had not Lacy told them that he had looked up at her as the ship moved down the slipway?

He, Charles Hemingway, had been wrong, wrong. Did not the look, the bone-white look of his daughter confirm it? After that first piercing scream she had lapsed into shock, staring at him with deep pewter-grey eyes, as though in some way she felt him to blame. As still as a small animal caught in the eye of a storm, she sat huddled in the corner of the carriage, refusing his agonized attempts at comfort. She had alighted from the coach, dignified as a duchess, pitiful in her frail hold on her childish reserves of strength. It was as though, deep in shock as she was, she kept herself in hand for some task which lay ahead of her, although Charles was at a loss to know what it could be. He felt himself to be in a nightmare, his self control completely gone. Sarah's maid scampered about the room searching frantically for the sal volatile which always lay close to hand, she said, in the event of one of her mistress's faints. But it was unaccountably missing, and the fact seemed to unnerve her more than the account of the tragedy. The girl seemed terrified, sobbing as she tore drawers from the tallboy, scattering their contents on the thick carpet.

At last Charles pulled himself together. The maid's distress seemed to calm him, and he rang the bell beside his wife's bed.

Lacy and Sarah Hemingway lay in a drugged sleep when Charles summoned Sean O'Malley's daughter to his study, and told her that her daddy was gone forever.

When the command came, Rose was wondering what all the fuss was about. Intent upon the scraping of half a ton of new season's potatoes, and quite fascinated by the ease with which the peel fell, she was surprised by Mr Chapman – his face grave but strangely wondering, for could not he have done the job himself, he thought – who told her that the master wished to see her.

Rose almost fell off her box, and a potato slipped from her limp fingers with a small plop into the water which contained those already peeled. Her mouth opened and closed, and her eyes hazed in fear, for the one thing Rose dreaded most of all was to lose her job and, she wondered, whatever else could the master want to see her for? She did not stop to consider that Cook and Mrs Johnson conducted the hiring and firing of servants within their responsibility, but stepped down immediately, wiped her hands upon her apron, straightened her lopsided cap and followed humbly the rigid back of Mr Chapman – up the stairs and into that part of the house which she had never once seen in her seven months in service. She was not aware of the compassionate glances of the other servants, and she did not observe the strange silence as she went.

The study was pleasantly warm, for the maid had only just replenished a leaping fire. The room was large and square, and completely masculine. There were guns in cases and fishing rods upon the walls, and on the round table set companionably before the fire were a box of cigars, several newspapers and a book or two. Three or four red leather easy chairs stood about the room, and against the far wall beside the window which overlooked the drive was an enormous leather-topped desk. Charles Hemingway sat behind it.

For a wonderful moment, before the pain entered Rose's spirit and quenched it, she felt an enormous thankful relief that she had not lost her job after all. Then the lights went out, and Rose O'Malley stood in the darkness alone.

Charles looked at the girl curiously. Her face had the same expression as his daughter's. The maid, still dressed in the shapeless garments, the boots, the sacking apron and the oversized cap which appeared to be the uniform of a scullery maid, stared at him as though he were speaking in a foreign language. He had never, to the best of his knowledge, seen a scullery maid before, at least not at close quarters, and he wondered idly if they were all as puny and undersized as this one. God, but her eyes were strange. Like deep, dark green pools of water covered by a film which he could only compare to a fog. They stared and stared, and he wondered irritably why he had thought it necessary to tell the girl himself, instead of leaving the task to Chapman or Mrs Johnson, which would have been perfectly reasonable. Something to do with the chap dying beneath his own child's gaze, he supposed.

'Jepson will take you to your home,' he said, not unkindly. 'It would not do for you to have to walk . . . er . . .?' What the devil was the girl's name? He could not remember, nor the name of the man who had died. Irish, he knew, but the name had gone. 'You will be allowed to remain until after the funeral,' he continued.

Her eyes looked at him unblinkingly. He began to wonder

if she was perhaps a little simple, and did not understand what he had said.

'You do know what I am saying about your . . .?'

'Yes.'

He breathed a sigh of relief and stood up.

'Very well . . . er, I'm sorry this had to happen. It was most . . .' What the devil was he doing talking to this child as though she was . . . well, *someone*?

'You may go now. There will be a small sum for your mother and I, of course, will pay all expenses. It is the least . . .

Abruptly, Rose turned and left the room before he could finish speaking.

Waiting until Nanny's back was turned, Lacy had poured the sleeping draught into the bowl of flowers which stood on the table beside her bed, then closed her eyes and pretended to sleep. The doctor had come in and stood at Nanny's side, and watched her as she breathed deeply. They had both gone away satisfied: the doctor murmuring of shock, of the restorative powers of sleep and of a good night's rest working wonders, and to keep an eye on her; and Nanny, all injured satisfaction, for had not she and the Mistress been proved right, assuring the doctor that she would look in from time to time, and would send a maid to sit with the child.

Now Lacy stood, a small white shadow in the dimness at the top of the gently curving staircase. Parallel stairways ran down each side of the wide hall, the one on the left finishing in front of the door to Papa's study, through which the girl had just been led. Lacy stared intently, her breath light, her ears listening to catch any sound which might break the utter silence which filled the house.

The hall was square. In its centre stood a lovely round rosewood table, on which a copper bowl of hothouse roses was arranged; a bright splash of pink and scarlet in the gloom. Their scent filled the hallway and the child was reminded suddenly of Grandmama Lucinda's funeral two years ago. Grandmama had loved roses and had grown them in her winter garden all year round.

Around the walls of the hallway stood fragile chairs up-holstered in green velvet. The grandfather clock, standing sentinel between the arches which split the rear of the hall, ticked gravely. Wall sconces held unlit candles and, through the long Georgian window at the back of the hall, daylight fell on the handsomely framed portraits of Robert and Mary Hemingway, serious and charming in the clothes of the pre-vious century.

With a soft click, the door to the study opened and the girl re-appeared, outlined for a moment against the light which came from the room. Then the door closed. Lacy watched her as she stood with her back to the staircase, her hand still on the doorknob, her face pressed to the door. It was as if she had lost the power of movement; as though, having got this far from the horror of the previous minutes, she had not the vaguest notion of how and what to do next. She made not a sound.

On flying feet, her nightdress billowing about her like a huge bell-like flower, Lacy ran down the stairs. She stopped as she reached the bottom step then tiptoed silently across the last few feet, until she stood directly behind the stiff, silent figure of the maid. She waited for a moment holding her breath, then reached out a gentle hand and touched Rose's arm. Now that she was here, Lacy did not know what to do next. They had exchanged no more than a few words, but Lacy had known as she lay in pretended sleep that Rose had need of someone at this moment. Lacy was not quite eleven years old, but her heart was filled with pity, and her impulse was to give without stint to her father's scullery maid.

'Rose,' she whispered, 'Rose, it's me.'

The hand which clung to the doorknob fell, awkwardly, to Rose's side. She turned, her body rigid. Her eyes were blind with shock. The hand which had just fallen plucked limply at her apron, then lifted, and she steadied herself on Lacy's arm.

'Me Daddy . . .' Her voice faltered. 'Me Daddy's . . .'

'I know, I know.'

'Master's just said me Daddy's . . .'

'Ssh, I know. I know . . .'

65

Rose's eyes became alive then. The blankness went and the agony came, and she began to shake. She faced Lacy and looked into her sad, frightened, pitying eyes. Then, with a tiny cry, she fell into Lacy's open arms. The same age, of the same slight and slender build, the two little girls clung together; wet cheek to wet cheek, shaking silently in a storm of grief neither was old enough to bear. For five minutes they wept, a strange sight should someone have come upon them. But Charles was before his fire, whisky glass in hand, and the rest of the household either slept, went about their daily business, or hovered, waiting for the next episode in the day's drama.

Lacy was the first to regain her composure. Keeping her childish arm protectively about Rose's shoulder, she began to lead her, stumbling and shaking, across the hall and towards the drawing room door. Rose was crying openly now, great gasping sobs which echoed about the hallway.

'Come,' Lacy whispered, looking over her shoulder to her father's study door. 'Come with me, just for a moment, until you are able . . .' She dragged her nightdress sleeve across her wet face, wiping her dripping nose upon it in a most un-ladylike manner. They moved into the drawing room and Rose's cries became wilder. She was but a child. The one who had been her strength, her rock of protection, was suddenly gone, and she was not only filled with grief at the loss of him, but with fear. Who would look after them all now?

The two little girls staggered through the drawing room and beyond the glass doors which led to the winter garden. In normal circumstances Rose would have been enchanted. The glass-walled room had been built in the early days of the marriage of Lacy's grandmother, Lucinda, to Thomas Hemingway. It had white gingerbread moulding and rose to a high, domed window of glass and fretted woodwork. The floor was of parquet. Clustered here and there in pleasant groups were white wrought iron and wicker tables, and chairs covered in gay cushions. There were plants everywhere: on shelves and tables; on the floor in huge terracotta pots; on fluted pedestals, and in hanging baskets. There were fragile ferns and exotic flowers from other countries; magnolias, camellias and every tender bloom which would not survive an English winter outside this protective environment.

Drawing aside a curtain of dense green ivy, which hung from pots on a shelf about three feet from the floor, Lacy revealed a space beneath in which a pile of sacking had been left by the gardener. The place was Lacy's own: a private, warm, tranquil and secret spot, where she could hide from Nanny or Mama or Miss Robertson; take a book and read; smell the hundreds of plants which grew there; or just while away the hours with dreams.

The two children sank down upon the coarse sacking and, in the fashion of young animals, curled together for comfort. Rose was quieter now, as her grief deepened, but she was taking hold of herself, becoming aware of the girl who wept with her. This girl had seen her terrible grief, but it had not mattered. They seemed to share something which drew them together, and there was no need of explanations. They understood each other.

'Rose.'

Rose turned her head and looked into the steady grey eyes of her young mistress. What she saw there gave her courage, and she wondered why it should be so. Lacy Hemingway had known neither grief nor want in her life. Their backgrounds could not have been more different, but Rose knew that of them all, even her own family, Lacy was and would be the only one amongst them to know exactly how she, Rose, felt. She did not know as yet that Lacy had seen Sean die. Later, when she was told, she would wonder whether it was that which linked them together in such a strange way.

Her eyes were filled with a sorrow which told Lacy that her heart was, in this moment, broken. But she was steady now. There was worse to come and Rose quailed at the thought of Bridie and the children – she who was but a child herself. They would be rudderless without Sean. She looked about her in-curiously. Although she did not recall how she came to be in this hidey-hole being comforted by the master's daughter, these moments had given her the support she needed, and a shield to protect herself from what she knew must be done.

'Thank you,' she said softly.

'Oh, Rose. Will you be able to . . .?'

'Yes, I'm meself now. I must get ter the Mammy. Yer Papa said Jepson'd take me ter the . . . funeral . . . Then I'll be back.'

'I shall watch for you, Rose. Oh, Rose. *Rose.*'

Lacy, too young to have the words with which to ease Rose's sorrow, but with a heart filled with childish compassion, hugged Rose to her. Rose clung to her for a moment, then broke free gently.

They parted silently at the foot of the stairs, the relationship which was to be theirs cemented that day into a friendship unbroken even by death.

When Rose climbed into the carriage which was to take her to Naylor's Yard, in her hand clinked the two guineas Charles Hemingway thought to be the value of Sean O'Malley.

The coffin lay on the table, the lid resting beside it, waiting to be closed for the last time on the sleeping face of Sean O'Malley. Sleeping. That was how Rose thought of him, as she stood in the neat row of children ranging from herself at its head down to Terence, eighteen months old and only just able to stand by himself. She pushed hastily from her mind the thought of the emptiness at the lower end of the coffin – was it packed with something to stop Daddy from sliding down? – and concentrated with all her youthful optimism on willing her daddy to come back to them, for she did not think she could manage her mammy and the eight children all by herself.

The room was thick with people in their good black shawls and jackets. They stood two deep about the walls and sat upon the boxes next to Bridie, who nursed the baby. But the chair, the one in which Sean had rested, was left empty. No one could bring themselves to sit where the man of the house, may the blessed Mother and all the angels rest his soul, had so recently reclined. Sean had been well liked by those of his compatriots who lived beside him, for though he could not give financial aid, being as poor as they, he had always had a good-natured word or smile for his neighbours, and his advice had been much sought after. They had all come from Naylor's Yard and the street off which it lay, and many who could not cram into the small room stood patiently in the courtyard waiting to join the cortège. They were all as Irish as Sean himself, congregating together now in death as they did in life, staying close to their own kind, giving them comfort and support.

The soft murmur of the five decades of the rosary hummed about the kitchen like a well beloved and comfortable lullaby, sighing musically from two dozen throats. Beads clicked through fingers, work-worn and scarred, old and twisted. The men and women owned nothing of monetary value, but each had their beads. Rose fondled the beads which Sean had put into her hands on the day she began work at Silverdale, and her soft lips formed the words automatically.

Each decade represented some part of the life of the Mother of God and the almost inaudible words were whispered by young and old alike. The first bead was the 'Our Father', followed by ten 'Hail Marys'; the chain between, the 'Gloria'.

'Hail Holy Queen . . .'
'Eternal Rest . . .'
'De Profundis . . .'

It was well known, as intimate, as dear and understood as the homes they had left behind in Ireland and they clasped the words and the beauty of them to themselves as the one stable element left to them in this heathen place and the impoverished lives they led.

In the midst of the mystical solemnity which pervaded Bridie's kitchen, the cheerful Irish voice from the top of the area steps sounded almost blasphemous. Heads which had been bowed in devotion rose sharply in surprise. They had been deep in that state into which utter belief and repetitive prayer had taken them and they felt a sense of outrage as the solemn reverence of this last farewell was interrupted. Feet clattered down the stairs and, in a whirlwind of cold spring air, excited Irish vitality and a huge sense of his own importance, Mick Geraghty put his head round the door and informed the comatose Bridie, 'Faith, 'tis the 'earse, Missis, an' wait 'til yer see the glory of it. 'Tis like a bloody ship, the size of it. Bejasus, Sean would be proud ter go ter 'is Maker in it. Shine! Yer could see yer face ter shave in it, so yer could! 'Tis a miracle ter behold an' 'orses black as coal an' better than any ter be seen at Aintree.'

The wondrous splendour of it had Mick in a spell so intense that the need for respect on this sad occasion quite forsook him. The vehicle could not get between the narrow entrance to the alley which led to the close, so Sean was carried shoulder high by several neighbours together with the man who had been his partner in the smashing of the blocks of wood which had released the *Mary Munro* from her cradle. No blame fell on him, but he had felt a compulsion to assist in this last ritual.

Rose and Joseph walked behind, Bridie between them. They linked their arms through hers, guiding her faltering steps and supporting her sagging frame. She cradled her baby to her passionately, but seemed to be unaware of what was happening, allowing her children to lead her up the steps and across the rough and filthy yard to the alley. Her face was like the wax on a candle, and a sheen of sweat filmed it, though the day was cool.

Rose stared numbly at the plain unvarnished wood of her father's coffin, resting lopsidedly upon the shoulders of the men who bore it. It was not right, her mind said, that Daddy should be carried by mere aquaintances, by strangers. His own should take him to his last resting place, not the likes of a ne'er do well such as Mick Geraghty, who she knew her father had despised for a drunkard, a wife beater and an idler. But Joseph was only eight years old and Patrick, Seamus, Declan and Terence even younger, and the uncles and cousins and brothers and nephews, of whom there were dozens, were all in Ireland.

The hearse was as magnificent as Mick Geraghty had described it, its shining splendour rising between the scabbed walls of the tenements on each side. Four black horses stood before it, plumes nodding, heads moving nervously with the amount of attention they were receiving from the gathering crowd. There were no flowers. The walk to the church was not long but, as the cortège proceeded on its way, the procession grew. Open-mouthed spectators threw on shawls or caps and joined on at its end, unwilling to miss the spectacle.

Father O'Shea, the parish priest of St Xaviour's, met the hearse at the tiny arched gateway. Rose, standing patiently in the tiny area of calm she had begun to build around herself in Lacy's embrace, held Bridie's arm. She could feel her Mother sway, and saw Joseph put out his hand to ensure the baby was safely held. Behind, in a tightly knit and silent group, as indivisible now in grief as they had been in happiness they had shared with their father, were her brothers and sisters. Mary Kate held the hands of Terence and Declan who, although they could not comprehend the horror of what had happened, sensed the misery, and clung to her like limpets. Patrick and Seamus, seven and three years old respectively, stood together behind the others. Not one cried. United they had laughed and in the same manner they shed no tears. The strength of Sean was bred in them and though they might despair they did not, children though they were, display it here.

The priest led the bewildered group to the altar, and Sean's coffin was placed before it. They sat, Rose held Bridie's hand, and Mary Kate took the baby upon her knee. The Requiem Mass passed them all by in a blur of colour and sound, and drifting whispers of fragrant incense. They watched calmly as Father O'Shea donned the beautifully embroidered purple cope, took the thurible and, intoning softly, swung it to and fro, incense misting in a pattern of feathers as he faced the foot of the coffin. He moved around the plain wooden box until he reached its head, bowed in veneration to the Cross held there by an acolyte, then returned down the coffin's other side to its foot.

Words were spoken and Rose heard her father's name, but she remained in the merciful state of calm which had been granted her. She was conscious of movement, of the weight of her mother against her shoulder. Then, suddenly, sunlight

71

dazzled her as she and her family, and the mourners who had crowded the church, were led by the priest to the graveside. She felt the gaze of Father O'Shea upon her, and he smiled kindly, indicating the soil which lay heaped about the open mouth of the grave. It was black and damp, and smelled as lovely as that in which her Daddy had planted the 'taties' they ate in Ireland.

Bending, holding Bridie's hand and guiding her gently down, Rose clutched a handful of soil and threw it onto the coffin, which she did not remember having seen lowered into its place. Bridie did the same and, as the small sound of it hitting the wood rang conclusively in Rose's ear, Bridie began to weep as though the full realization of what she was about had finally shattered her awful calm.

She fell to her knees.

'Sean, Sean, *Sean*!' she screamed. She wept loudly, harshly, angrily, cursing the fate which had taken from her the one complete, unchangeable joy of her life.

'Sean, Sean, Sean.' Over and over again her voice pierced the sacred quiet of the moment, as Sean O'Malley's widow struggled to leap into the grave which contained the mutilated remains of her husband.


'What will yer do, Mammy?' Rose's voice was anxious.

'About what, darlin'?'

Rose clutched her black cloak, the one lent her by Cook on the day she was driven from Silverdale to Naylor Street, pulling it more closely about her. It was cold in the cellar, for no one had thought to light a fire, and she herself must be off soon if she were to reach Silverdale before dark. No pan of stew bubbled on the stove, and no kettle whispered steam in preparation for the familiar, comforting mug of tea. Rose shivered. It was not just the cold that made her tremble, but the sense of purposelessness: the emptiness; the feeling that all of them, Bridie and the children, waited to be told what they should do now. Without Sean's quiet but steadfast presence, they appeared to be lost.

Rose, with as yet no inkling of the true state of her mother's mind, nor of where it would eventually lead them, thought only of the desperate necessity to plan for the immediate future, to drag them all through the next few weeks. And, to do this, she must get the Mammy to herself again. The children only needed a firm voice; the appearance of a return to normality, and they would rally; but it needed Mammy to take up the lead.

'Mammy.' Her childish voice trembled as she tried again.

'Yes, acushla?'

'Will yer listen, Mammy?'

'I am, acushla.'

Bridie sat upon one of the boxes at the side of the table, her shoulders hunched uncomfortably as she leaned her elbows on its once scrubbed and spotless surface. It had not felt even the wipe of a cloth since the day the man had come to take her, unbelieving, to the mortuary. She stared unblinkingly at Sean's chair standing in splendid isolation beside the unlit fire. The chair was still unused, although Sean had now been dead a week.

Bridie answered when spoken to, but Rose knew she had made no sense of her question. She was still in that twilight world to which Sean's death had flung her and resembled nothing more than a waxen dummy propped at the table in a grotesque tableau. Only when the baby was put to her breast did she seem to be herself for a few moments. It was as though the small puckered mouth clinging to her nipple – an act which had been repeated so many times in her life, and which was as familiar to her as once had been the washing of her own face – brought her to an island of blessed peace, and her eyes never left the face of her baby as the child suckled. But her milk was drying up.

The flesh had been stripped from Bridie O'Malley in the past week. Her face was hollowed at cheek and temple, and her eyes, once bright and lively, were pale, faded and lifeless. Her lovely burnished hair, as dark and glossy as the black stallion in Charles Hemingway's stable, and falling to her waist in a living mantle, was lank and greasy, dragged back by Rose into a tidy knot at the nape of her neck. Already lice

73

moved in it and in the heads of her children; for it took only a glance away, a moment's relaxation from vigilance, for the teeming life of the neighbourhood to infest the unwary.

At twenty-eight, Bridie looked a filthy and dilapidated fifty.

Rose fidgeted from one foot to the other. She felt exasperation wash over her, and for a second she was tempted to give her mother a good slap. A 'fourpenny one' might bring her to her senses; make her pull herself together, so to speak, for it was evident words were doing no good. Instantly she felt ashamed. Her Mammy was sick with grief and couldn't be expected to be as she once was, not just yet. But she, Rose, couldn't just go off and leave them like this.

Six frightened pairs of eyes stared at her, apprehension plain on each face at the thought of being left alone with the empty woman at the table, with no Rose to direct them, and the Daddy gone forever.

Rose smiled at Mary Kate, the eldest, and, instantly relieved, Mary Kate smiled back and waited. Their Rose had smiled and it would be *all right*. Rose's eyes moved from Mary Kate, going from one child to the next. They stood docilely about the room; all except Terence, who, too young to understand what had happened to Sean, waited impatiently by the basement door for his Daddy to return.

Rose turned back to Bridie and attempted another smile. She cleared her throat, trying to rid it of the dreadful dryness which attacked it, but she was at a loss for what to say. Something must be arranged before she began the long walk back to Silverdale.

Alone. Alone for the first time. A shaft of desolation stabbed Rose, but she pushed it firmly away. She could not allow herself the consolation of grief now. She had no time.

'Mammy, will yer listen to me?' Rose said.

'I am, darlin'.'

Bridie's eyes gazed blankly into Rose's.

'No ye're not. Yer say ya are but ye're not. I've ter be away soon, Mammy, an' we must get things . . . done.' Her voice was desperate. 'The money Mr Hemingway sent will last yer a few weeks, but 'tis a job yer'll be needin' now, an' Mary Kate,

74

too. Joseph can see ter Kathleen. I can fetch yer me money next time I'm home, but we've got ter make up . . . what Daddy earned.' Her face contorted and her eyes misted in anguish, but she went on. 'The rent's paid an' . . . Oh, Mammy, please listen . . .'

Bridie's eyes had slid away to stare without interest at the wall somewhere above Rose's left shoulder. The irritation Rose had felt returned more strongly, and with it came fear. Holy Mother! Bridie seemed to care not a jot about money, or a job, or the well-being of her own children. It was as though the spine of her had gone with Sean, and she sat like a crumpled doll at her own table. Waiting, waiting. But for what? Rose turned distractedly to Mary Kate looking for support, some reassurance that she was not alone in this nightmare. But her sister, only nine years old herself, was as frightened as she. But there was no-one else. Someone must hold them together until Bridie was better. Like a clock which had ticked loudly, cheerfully all day long, she had seemed the very centre of their world, but Sean had been the mainspring and with him gone the timepiece sat, silent and useless, waiting to be wound up. With herself up to the house there was only Mary Kate to do it.

'Mary Kate,' she said firmly.

Mary Kate stepped forward bravely.

'Yes, Rose.' Her voice quivered.

'Can yer . . . can yer manage fer a week or two? See ter the money? Just 'til Mammy's . . . I wouldn't ask yer, acushla, with yer so young . . .' Rose was ten years old, but the irony was quite lost on her. 'Give 'er a week or two, she'll be right as rain. But 'til then, if yer could just . . . see ter things. I've got ter go. 'Tis the only money . . . Will yer be all right?'

Mary Kate nodded. She held the baby in her arms, fiercely, protectively, trying to be brave like their Rose. Though she was just nine years old, she had expected soon to have been put to a good job, perhaps in service, as Rose had last year. But then, Daddy had been there to look out for Rose. He it was who had found the work Rose did. He had taken her there on her first day, and watched over her. Now she, Mary

Kate, must find her own job or her brothers and sisters, younger than her and unable to work, would starve. But where to start looking? Oh, if only Mammy would be herself again!

She looked at Rose and clamped her mouth into a straight, tight line to stop herself from bursting into loud, childish tears.

'There's enough ter keep yer 'til I come 'ome again. Yer'll 'ave ter leave Kathleen with Joseph while yer look fer work.' Rose nodded in the direction of her brother, but his face was turned from her now as he skulked in the corner. She could not see his expression, but something in the slump of his shoulder and the set of his head sent a shiver of disquiet through her. He had always been the one to stand a little apart from the others – his head in the clouds, as Sean used to say – dreaming his boy's dreams. It was not that he had shrugged off the worries the others shared so closely, but it seemed he had not found them as absorbing. He had never shirked his work: the fetching of water or the jobs set him by Sean; but he had done them with only half his mind, the other half off somewhere in some place only he knew about.

'Joseph.' Rose's voice was sharp.

He turned slowly and looked at her, and she was alarmed by the terror and confusion which flared in his eyes.

'Yes,' he said sullenly.

'Yer'll see ter the others while Mary Kate looks fer work?'

'Yes.'

'An yer ter . . . try ter cheer Mammy up, there's a good boy.'

Without speaking again, he returned to his contemplation of the wall.

''Tis only 'til Mammy's better,' Rose pleaded, 'then we'll decide what's ter be done. Ye're eight years old, Joseph. Nine next, an' a man yer'll be. The 'ead of the family, 'tis true, an' a foin job yer'll be gettin'. We'll manage, darlin', we will.'

She waited for an answer, but none came.

'Mammy's not 'erself yet, so yer'll 'ave ter look after 'er. She's grievin' fer Daddy.' The children's faces, wise beyond their years, turned compassionately towards their mother; all except Jospeh, and Terence who still lingered at the door.

'But she'll be well soon.' Hope tried to overcome despair, as Rose looked into Bridie's empty face, and she felt the tears well into her eyes. But she must not let them see her cry. They must have the small security of one person in their lives who was still the same; who looked to their welfare as Mammy and Daddy had once done.

Rose sat down opposite Bridie and undid the clasp of Cook's cape, placing it neatly on the box beside her. Cook would have her hide if it was spoiled. Taking her mother's hands in hers, she gave them a little jerk, as though to get her attention.

'Mammy, will yer listen?'

'Yes, darlin'.'

'Mammy. I'm off now, but Mary Kate's got the money an' will do the buyin' 'til . . . fer a while.'

'Yes, darlin'.'

It began to penetrate the child's mind then that Bridie was not going to be 'well' for a long, long time. Rose turned away, and with the dreadful burden of knowing that in one week she had lost not only her father but her mother too, she lifted Cook's cloak from the box, and slipped it about her shoulders. It seemed to drag her down with its weight, and she felt she could scarcely walk to the door, let alone the miles which had to be journeyed to Silverdale.

The fungus on the ceiling had spread in a circle of lacy green, and a patch or two crept insidiously down the wall. A dozen minute, black specks slid from a thin crack, moving slowly, forming and reforming in a hideous dance, then vanished. The enemies of the poor: filth and vermin, and their attendant follower, disease, were beginning already, with no one to give battle, to encroach upon the home of Sean's family.

Wordlessly Rose crossed the space between the table and the door. She felt she should be saying more, giving instructions to the children who looked from her to their mother. In a few days, when she had pulled herself together,

Mammy would be able to see to things. To get a job in the laundry, perhaps, and something for Mary Kate. Joseph was a good lad and would mind the others, and they would be fed and housed for a week or two by Charles Hemingway's munificence. The money wouldn't last forever, but it would tide them over.

Sighing, the feeling of trepidation growing within her, Rose turned and, opening her arms, hugged and kissed each one of them; beseeching them, as her mother had once done, to be good and mind the baby, to be careful with the money, not to forget their prayers, and to have a good wash every day.

With an ache in her heart almost too great to be borne, the child began the walk back to the big house.

# CHAPTER 6

It had been two months, and still the nightmare came to claim her each time her eyes closed in sleep.

The ship was like a monster, huge and black and shiny with the tar which leaked from its sides. It had a mouth in which teeth the size and whiteness of a sail tore at her limbs as she scrambled from its path. It tried to catch her, snapping and snarling, and her petticoats flew about her legs as she kicked at it. And then, then . . . Oh, please . . . Dear God . . . Then her legs disappeared, and there was the blood, the blood, oh, the blood . . . It was bright, so vividly scarlet it hurt her eyes to look at it. It washed over her and filled her mouth, and she choked as she screamed.

Lacy's face, once creamy and pink with the healthy colour of the young and well-fed, became transparent. Her eyes grew enormous and haunted: deep, grey holes in the fine parchment of her skin.

She slept in the nursery again now, afraid to lie down without someone beside her who would awaken her the moment she began to twitch and moan. In the little bed, the one that had been empty for years, since the day she had been considered old enough to leave the night nursery for a bedroom of her own, she lay beside Nanny Wilson. The old woman, who had brought up a dozen children with stiff reserve, opened up her heart and comforted the terrified child as she had never done before.

Lacy's clinging arms, her despairing, tear-steaked face and, above all, her sheer desperate need cracked the self-protective shield Agatha Wilson had placed against her heart when she had taken up her profession and cared for, and lost, her first child. But Lacy was to be her last charge, and she clung to the girl's dependence as a sign of her own importance, and did nothing to ease the child back into the world of normality. Sarah Hemingway washed her hands of the whole affair.

Lacy had scarcely quit the nursery or schoolroom since the day Rose left Silverdale in Cook's black cloak to go to her father's funeral. It was as if the courage and compassion she had given the little maid when it was needed had been used up in their few moments together. With Rose's departure had come remembrance, and it would not leave her.

Her screams had brought Nanny running, and the doctor, who had not yet left the house. In Nanny's arms, and then in those of her Papa, who had come tearing like a mad thing when he heard her, she quietened, and after the administration of another dose of sleeping draught, eventually, she slept.

Sarah was jubilant in her triumph, and Charles was filled with remorse. He could not do enough for his wife, to make up to her for the distress he had caused her by his disregard of what he now knew to be her supremacy in matters of propriety.

Lacy was scarcely recognizable to her father as the vital, adventurous, eager girl who had begged his attention for stories of the sea and his ships; who had craved freedom and the knowledge which was usually only allowed a boy; and who had tried to lead her sisters, and anyone who had the courage to join her, into escaping the chains which society placed upon her. Her bright, brave spirit was quenched and she hurtled from one moment of hysterical terror to the next, with little respite. The doctors gave her draughts to let her sleep, but she existed for days afterwards in a half-dazed torpor which frightened him more than the fits of hysteria. She was no longer his lovely shining girl.

The sight which had met his eyes when he looked over the side of the ship had been enough to bring his own breakfast heaving into his throat, and Robert, in whom he would have hoped for a little more manliness, had wept and sunk to the deck of the *Mary Munro* like a girl in a faint.

The ship's launching had been quite spoiled, and those who worked upon her, and many who would sail in her, would call her haunted, for she had been sent to sea on a tide of blood.

'Perhaps you will listen to me now, my dear, when it concerns the upbringing of our children,' Sarah had said complacently. 'I do not wish to be one of those horrid persons who persist in saying "I told you so", but you must see now that such places and occasions are not for ladies, and certainly not for impressionable young girls.'

Charles agreed most heartily.

'The child will stay in the nursery, where she should have been in the first place, until she has recovered. That is, of course, should she ever do so . . .' Charles choked in horrified contrition. '. . . I am sure that with time and care and the careful elimination of all that might excite her brain, Alexandrina will become as her sisters are. Nanny will stay with her at all times, and I will make certain that she does not leave the grounds.'

Sarah gloried in her vengeance: on Charles, and on her daughter. She said, 'It might also be reflected upon, Charles, that the unfortunate man's . . .' A slight look of disgust twisted her lips as though she spoke of something not quite nice. '. . . that the man's daughter, the scullery maid . . . It might be advisable if she was dismissed. Should Alexandrina see her, be reminded . . .'

Charles turned swiftly from the long narrow window of his wife's bedroom, through which he had been watching the pale orange ball of the sun slide gently into the trees beyond the lake. The light from it stood about him like a nimbus hiding the expression of his face, but the strength of his consternation was clear in his voice.

'I cannot do that, Sarah. Do not ask it of me. The man died in my yard and, for all I know, might have other children dependent upon the girl's wage. If I were to send her away it would seem a double injustice.'

'Injustice? Do you consider you were to blame for the man's death?'

'Of course not. It was an accident. The will of God. Call it what you like, but I feel it would be heartless to . . .'

'As you like, my dear, but if Lacy should . . .'

'But she does not know the girl.'

'That is true at the moment, but should someone point her out . . .'

'Oh, surely not.'

'I am only indicating, Charles, that to have a constant reminder in the kitchen of this dreadful day, namely the man's own daughter, might have an adverse effect upon the child's progress towards recovery.' Sarah sighed and glanced from beneath lowered lashes at her husband, gratified by her new-found power over him. 'But that is up to you, my dear,' she murmured.

Yet, penitent, guilt-ridden and saddened as Charles Hemingway was, he could not bring himself to charge Chapman with the dismissal of Sean O'Malley's daughter, and as far as he knew she continued to work in his kitchen.

He did not enquire, and Sarah, secure in her new position, and charmed by the final taming of her youngest daughter's spirit, forgot.

The days passed into weeks, memories faded and distress eased, and as summer reached its peak, the incident lived on only in the minds of the two young girls who shared the same roof, but who had not seen one another since the day it had happened.

The schoolroom was quiet as the four demure, pretty daughters of Charles Hemingway sat about the long table in its centre, and listened to Miss Robertson as she read a piece of poetry which was considered suitable for the ears of such sheltered creatures.

They were dressed alike in dresses of creamy tarlatan, although each had a broad velvet sash in a different colour about her tiny waist. Necklines were modestly high, sleeves short and puffed, and their soft, full skirts reached a point mid-way between knee and ankle. They wore white stockings and cream kid slippers to match their dresses. The colour of each girl's sash was repeated in the ribbon they wore in their long, curling hair.

It was July and the French windows of the room, which was on the ground floor, stood open to allow in bright sunshine. The warm rays as they moved along the wall reached Lacy's shoulder and, as at the touch of an old friend she had not seen for a long time, she turned her attentive gaze from Miss Robertson and looked through the window to the garden beyond, brought for a moment from the quiet shell into which she had retreated. The schoolroom faded into shadow, and from somewhere far off a bright, excited voice called to her.

'What on earth are you doing, Lacy Hemingway?' it said, 'sitting like a pretty doll in the schoolroom, when you could be out here in the sunshine. The lark singing her silly head off high above Elms Wood has more sense than you. Come on, come and play in the meadow, or roll down the bank to the river's edge. Take off your shoes and stockings, and feel the sand between your toes . . .'

The voice was her own. Her own voice, which she had locked carefully away with her daring heart, where it was safe and could do her no harm. It was invading her silent spirit, pleading with her. But if she listened to it, allowed it to direct her, would not, would not . . . *he* return . . ?

Miss Robertson was speaking of Keats and his 'season of mists and mellow fruitfulness', but the full glory of the summer day seemed determined to intrude, and Lacy's memory tricked her again.

She was sitting astride Holly, defying Nanny and Mama and the groom, the mare wading belly-deep in a field of oxslips and speedwell and, above, the periwinkle blue of the sky went on forever, merging completely with the heat-misted heights of the Pennine Chain. As she looked about her at the moving ripple of colour, she heard Bess barking in demented excitement as she fell on the scent of the dog fox who had sauntered that way the night before and, with a quick pressure on her knee, she guided the little mare towards the dog. They laughed at one another, she and Bess, as though to say they would follow the trail wherever it led and . . ?

'Lacy, Lacy! Pay attention, my dear, if you please. I have just asked you a question.'

Lacy turned back from the daydream, looking round at the faces of her sisters as they waited for her to speak. For the space of thirty heartbeats she had felt the wonder and joyousness that had once been hers, together with the certainty that life was good, and the memory of it bewitched her. She blinked, disorientated, seeing Jane's eyes smiling, encouraging, her young face filled with gentle affection.

In Jane's heart there was nothing but kindness, and a desire to be a friend to her younger sister. Just recently, Lacy had become the kind of person Jane longed for in a companion. Submissive and amiable, and willing to listen to Jane's confidences and dreams. Her two elder sisters paired together, two of a kind, the eldest daughters and therefore senior and superior to the others. It had seemed to Jane that Lacy and she must naturally form a sisterly friendship of a similar kind, which would fill the small hollow of loneliness she felt. But, truth to tell, Lacy had always frightened her somewhat. She was so venturesome. Trying to lead Jane and the others into what she called 'escapes'. Jane did not want to escape. She was content to read or paint; to go for pleasant walks and pick flowers, which she pressed in a book. Lacy had wanted none of that.

But now she was different. Since the day Papa had taken her to see the launching of Great Grandma's ship, and some dreadful thing had happened, she had been different. Jane did not know what it could have been that turned Lacy from the exciting – yes, Jane admitted she had been exciting – hoyden she had once been, into the quiet mouse she now was, and she had no wish to be told. Things alarming were not welcome in Jane's world. She had heard Lacy scream in the night and, until the quick arms of Nanny reached her and quietened her, Jane hid her ears under the pillow waiting for the fear she heard to go away.

Now she touched Lacy's hand, and said softly, 'We were speaking of the line "Where are the songs of spring . . ?" Lacy, and Miss Robertson asked . . .'

'I am so sorry, Miss Robertson, I was . . .' Lacy smiled hesitantly.

Miss Robertson, who was not very old herself, smiled back.

'I know, dear, the day is lovely and very inviting. Shall we go and see what Mr Keats speaks of, instead of reading about it?'

The four girls rose obediently, putting their books into neat piles and arranging pens and pencils in symmetrical rows beside them. They waited politely as Miss Robertson moved ahead of them towards the open French window, saying as she went, 'I do not think it necessary to take our mantles, but perhaps you will fetch the parasols, Amy? It is very warm and the sun is strong. It might be as well if we kept beneath the trees where the shade will protect us.'

'I shall just go for Nanny, Miss Robertson.'

Miss Robertson turned, astonished, as Lacy spoke. She looked at the young girl, just eleven years old, and wondered for the hundredth time when the dreadful event which had turned the high-spirited but always lovable girl into the quenched ghost she now was, would fade from her mind. She seemed able to go nowhere without her Nanny, and an excursion which would once have filled her with joy appeared to fill her with the greatest anxiety. Miss Robertson knew of the man's death. But, surely, the child had not been witness to it?

Lacy did not speak of it, or of anything, that was the pity of it. Hiding her dismay, Miss Robertson said, 'Just as you like, my dear. But I think the walk might be too much for Nanny. It is rather steep. Come, hold my hand, and Jane shall hold your other, and we shall go together. Look out for sweet cecily when we get to the meadow. Remember how I told you it smells of aniseed when it is bruised. It is white and fern-like, and will make a good pressing for your book, Jane.'

Without being aware of it Lacy was led like an infant upon its first steps: down the grassy slope from the terrace, across the smooth perfection of the lawn, and onto the gravel path which led to the ha-ha and the meadow beyond.

They made a charming picture. Their full skirts swung

decorously as they walked. Parasols, pretty and fragile as a butterfly's wing, were held above bright heads, high and proud on straight backs, and Sarah Hemingway watched smugly from her bedroom window.

Her world was just as she wanted it.

It was October before Lacy finally recovered, and it was a stranger who cured her. No one knew how he got into the house, for to do so he had to pass a score of people in the kitchen; escape the attention of maids repairing fires in drawing, morning and dining rooms; of footmen standing stiffly in the hall; and of chamber maids in the upper halls, looking to the contents of the linen cupboard on which Mrs Johnson lavished her attention before the onset of winter.

Charles was in his study, where he had retired after lunch, mending the boredom a morning at church and the vicar's interminable sermon had placed upon his spirit, with a stiff glass of whisky and the Sunday newspapers. It was the moment of the week he relished most. The duties placed upon him by his standing in the community had been discharged – he had read the lesson this morning, a task he detested – and the rest of the afternoon until it was time to dress for dinner was his own; a pleasure not afforded him at any other time of the week.

The soft pitter patter of feet past his door went unnoticed, for the whisky, the warmth of the room, and his own peace of mind had carried him into a light doze.

Lacy was alone in her room.

Though she still slept each night in the nursery, trusting in Nanny to wake her should the need arise, she was becoming accustomed to spending an hour or two of the day by herself. As time went on, and summer slid away into autumn mists, she had begun to grow constrained by the constant presence of her sisters, and had been made restless by the feminine pursuits they followed. The sewing, which had seemed so peaceful and so completely safe, had begun to irritate her, and the sampler she worked was starting to take on the untidy, rumpled look it once had, months ago.

The book she read aloud to the others as they embroidered, the one which she had loved so for its undemanding simplicity, became stupid and silly. And, week after week, the sight of Nanny nodding approvingly in the corner, and of Mama 'popping' in, as she put it, to smile complacently upon her eminently suitable daughters, made her fidget.

There was one thought, however, which was never allowed to slip into her mind; one picture, one memory at least, that she had become adept at keeping from herself. Although it sometimes hovered on the edges of her consciousness, Lacy was too mortally afraid even to acknowledge it might still be there.

A sound made her raise her head from the easel at which she worked. Beyond her window, rain lashed the tall cedar trees into a frenzy, and clouds tore across the sky. They were pulled into long, trailing streaks of silver grey, their undersides a deep, mystic charcoal. It was with this colour that she was currently absorbed, as she tried to put it onto the stiff, white paper. The painting was a delicate, ethereal water colour. She did not paint exactly what she saw, in the manner of a perfect copy, but only hinted at it. Her work was like the impression one gets when one looks at an object for a fraction of a second, then looks away: a hazed outline of a tree, for example, with a wisp and a smear of cloud, all seen through a mist, like the wash of rain as it ran down her bedroom window.

The sound came again, and it was one she did not immediately recognize. It seemed to come from beyond her closed bedrom door and, for a moment, she was afraid. But the fire crackled in the grate, its glow on every surface of the room, and lovely objects gleamed and shimmered as it touched bowls of flowers and silver-mounted photographs with gold. Everything was as it should be. Warm, pleasant, familiar. There was nothing to be afraid of. Nothing at all.

Taking a deep breath, Lacy crossed the room and opened the door. The hall was dim, for the day was overcast and, as yet, no lamps had been lit. She did not see him at once. His burnished copper coat blended with the panelled door at which he was sniffing but, at the sound of her door opening, he turned and, seeing her there, ran towards her joyfully.

It was one of Bess's pups.

Lacy let out the breath she had been holding and sank to her knees. The dog was all over her, placing his paws, muddy still from the day outside, upon the pale green saxony of her dress; sniffing, licking and lurching. After an ecstasy of delightful greeting, he lolloped beyond her into her bedroom, cavorting like a clown at a circus, then rushed back to where she still sat in the doorway, and lay down, his heavy chest across her knees, his tail swishing wildly in complete abandon.

Lacy was overwhelmed with happiness. Words deserted her. She held the dog's head between her hands, looked into the velvet depths of his eyes, and saw there simple joy and trust, and a willingness to be friends.

'What is your name, you great silly thing, and how on earth did you get up here? Mama would have a fit if she knew. Quickly, come inside before you are seen, and let me think.' She pointed to the rug before the fire.

The dog sauntered amiably across the pale cream and pink of the soft carpet and flopped down in front of the fire, putting his fine head upon his paws, and going into that contemplative coma all animals assume when confronted by the lovely warmth of a fire. Lacy looked up and down the hallway, then quickly shut the door. She stood for a moment or two, a smile upon her face, shaking her head. She began to laugh, and the dog twitched a long soft ear, and turned a smile of idiotic joy upon her.

'Oh, you beautiful, *beautiful* dog!'

Words failed her again and, going to the fireplace, she sank down on the rug, and placed her hand upon the silky back. Bess was a Cocker spaniel but, even to the untrained eye, it was obvious that her partner in the making of this handsome dog had been a setter. The lovely domed head, the warm red of his coat, the feathers just beginning to come, and the long, plumey tail told of his parentage.

Lacy lay upon the floor and put her head down, until her silver veil of hair fell across the dog. He sniffed at it, and gazed at her adoringly. Her arm wound round his neck, and he sighed contentedly as she whispered in his ear, 'I shall call you Copper, and you will belong to no one but me.'

Mama did have a fit, several in fact, and swore that she would not have a moment's peace with that great, wild creature loose in the house. But it did no good.

With the dog beside her, standing obediently to heel as though he knew his future depended upon it, Lacy glittered her way back to life again as she implored her Papa to be allowed to keep Copper with her. Charles had not seen her so animated since that May day almost six months ago and, for a moment, his joy faltered. She was at it again, seducing him to go against his wife's wishes, as she had then.

But it was such a little thing, he reasoned. To have the company of a dog was all she asked, and many young ladies of good family kept a small dog in their sleeve. This was hardly a lap dog, to be sure; but look at her, just look at her. Lacy's face was flushed with longing, and her enchantment stoked the fires of his love and pride.

She bargained with him, promising to be everything that Mama and Nanny asked of her, if only he would let her keep the dog. She would be diligent in her lessons, and heed Miss Robertson, and be kind to her sisters, and not a bit of bother to anyone. She would sew on her sampler, and sing, and learn the quadrille, and never, never 'escape' again. It was the first Charles had heard of her 'escapes', and he smiled inwardly. She would never be as the others were, this delightful child of his, and he praised God who had restored her to him.

And Copper was certainly a good looking animal; one that did the child proud. Lacy did not pause for breath, as she saw her father's hand go to the dog's head. She promised to keep Copper in her room, or in the stable, and on a leash when she was about the house, and would see that Seth, the Coachman's boy, groomed him every day.

'Oh, Papa,' Lacy said, 'if you should allow it, I think I might sleep in my own bedroom from now on. With Copper beside me I shall not be afraid again.'

He could not withstand her.

# CHAPTER 7

'Don't yer worry, Missis. They'll be well looked after. Three good meals a day they'll 'ave an' decent beds ter sleep in, an' the master o't mill'll give 'em some warm duds ter wear an' all. Why, yer won't know 'em in a few weeks time.'

The man speaking smiled derisively to himself. *If* yer ever see 'em again it'll be a bloody miracle, he was thinking. But it did no good to let what went on in your head show in your face.

'Fat an' bonny they'll be,' he continued, smiling, 'an' carnin' a few bob ter send 'ome. They'll only be one night in't work . . . on Brownlow 'ill, an' termorrer they'll be away ter fine new jobs. They could 'ave bin sent ter the Female Orphan Asylum in Myrtle Street if they'd bin orphans. But they're not, are they, not with a mammy livin'. Don't yer fret now, they'll be right as ninepence, yer'll see.'

The man from the workhouse was cheerful. Insensitive after so many years at the job, he was blind to the desolation on the faces of parents forced to relinquish a loved child to poor relief. Paupers they were, all of them, and unable to feed the children who came year after year. So they sent them, those who survived, to the parish, which in its turn found them work. The overseer of the Poor Law collected them, or sent this man to do it, and, with the unconcern of a farmer driving a flock of sheep or a herd of cows to market, they were distributed amongst the men willing to hire them.

Those gathered in would be sent within a few days, in cartloads of a hundred at a time, to the mills and factories of Lancashire. It was almost a certainty that their parents would never see them again. The overseer was glad to be rid of them, for their departure not only reduced the Poor Rates, but also frequently provided him with a nice little re-muneration from the factory owner.

Four years old he started them. It was a good age, for they were still small enough to crawl about the whirling machinery in the cotton mills, collecting the waste which accumulated there. They were, or so the observer confided, housed in comfortable dormitories. He did not upset delicate sensibilities by divulging that each one, whatever their age, would work for fourteen hours a day; or that, at the end of each shift, the unfortunate child would stumble to a 'bed' just vacated, one falling in as one staggered out; or that the 'beds' were two blankets – one under, one over – on a bare floor. He did not distress with tales of exhaustion and semi-starvation. He did not describe the fate of those who fell asleep at the machines they minded; or talk of the beatings, the kicking, and the buckets of cold water poured about dazed heads to ensure they stayed awake. The overseer did not worry his superiors with such details; nor enumerate those who fell, mercifully, into the machines they worked, the wheels and gears ripping them into oblivion.

The two little girls clutched at one another, their thin faces looking back in anguish at the woman who stood at the top of the area steps. Their feet were bare, plastered with the filth in which they trod, and their puny legs – those of the youngster, bowed and rickety – were barely covered by the threadbare dresses they wore. Little shawls as thin as vapour were tied around their shoulders: folded pathetically across thin chests, under their armpits, and knotted at their back, as though their mother had done her best to give them warmth. Their dark hair was dusty and lifeless, but for the vermin which romped there. Only their eyes, green and washed with tears, were alive.

'Mammy, please, Mammy . . .' The elder held out her hand to the woman. 'Mammy, let us stay. Please. I'll get somethin' tomorrer, really I will. At the laundry, or . . . Oh, please, Mammy. Yer know the woman said when I were bigger . . . I'll grow. Please don't send us away.'

'Come on now, lass. No 'angin' about. I've a few more ter pick up yet, an' we can't stand 'ere jawin' all day.' The man's genial chat bore no relation to his job. He took the arm of the

92

older girl in a rough grip, and began to move her sharply towards the alley which led from Naylor's Yard into Naylor Street. It was packed with people standing or sitting apathetically against the walls of the houses, watching with little interest a scene which was as common a sight as the cats who fought over the refuse which lay in littered heaps in the four corners.

Around the courtyard, men leaned against the wall, a black tide-mark at shoulder level testifying to where their backs had rested. They were all unskilled men, relying on casual work to keep them and their families fed. Despite their poverty, many smoked a pipe, and several would be seen later on making their way to the 'Stout House' on the corner. Their wives and children might starve but there were those amongst them who thought a man was not a man without a pint now and again Despair made them unfeeling, and many of the children who lounged in the pale sunshine would soon follow the two girls who struggled in the grip of the workhouse man. Every soul in the yard had the stunted physique, pale face and curved legs of malnutrition.

The two children began to tug away from the man, the elder screaming in her fear. The younger seemed dazed, uncomprehending of what was happening, but still she instinctively pulled with her sister, in the direction of her mother and her home.

'Give over now.' The man's face became churlish, and he aimed a cuff at the head of the girl whose stick-like arm he held. 'I can't be 'angin' about 'ere all day. Stop yer clap, or I'll land yer one.'

'Mammy, Mammy, *Mammy*!'

The despairing cries rang out above the noises of the streets, and for a moment activity was stilled and heads turned to look. Picking up the tiny figure of the younger girl, and tucking her under his arm, the man pulled the other along behind him until they vanished down a narrow alleyway. The girls' voices died away.

The woman standing at the top of the steps remained, unmoving, long after general interest in the scene had gone.

Her eyes stared mutely at the spot where her daughters had disappeared. She lifted a trembling hand to push back the cascade of bedraggled hair which fell about her face, and her lips moved soundlessly, but she seemed untouched by emotion. Her fingers touched her cheekbone and, as she turned her head dispiritedly, a livid bruise the size of a fist glowed against her skin. It was the colour of a greengage, fading to yellow at the edges.

She continued to stand, as still as the iron post to which she clung. She shivered in the cool October air, but still she made no attempt to re-enter the house. Her hands clenched for a moment, as though she were in the throes of some deep and terrible despair, but nothing showed in her blank face.

A man came from the doorway of the cellar at the bottom of the steps. His hair was the colour of a carrot, as bright and curly and full of life as a field of marigolds, but from there downwards he might have been made from granite. His face was lumpy, pitted with old smallpox scars, and as grained and grey as a boulder. Although he was not tall, his body was massive; the breadth of his shoulders that of a shire horse. His arms were far longer than those of a normal man; and his hands, hanging almost level with his knees, were the size of the hooves on the same shire. But it was his eyes which forced the rest of his grotesque appearance into shadow.

They were black: small, black, deep-set, and completely expressionless. No light shone in them; no hint of warmth or humour, only a plunging nothingness. There was an air of malevolent cruelty in the very way he stood and, as he walked slowly up the steps, and his head appeared for those in the close to see, a curious silence descended, like fog in sunshine.

'Come away in, woman. What d'yer think ye're doin' gawpin' at nowt. Get down an' make us a bite, an' shut them kids up, or they'll be next.'

He turned and surveyed the mass of quiet onlookers, his eyes touching first one and then another and, as they did so, the recipient of his gaze turned away; even Mick Geraghty, who was renowned for his pugnacious Irish temper. The man continued to stare about, as though daring anyone to as much as blink an eyelid and, when a dog growled savagely, more in fear than in anger, he turned and spat at it, showing his broken teeth. It cowered away behind the privy and whined. The man laughed, at what no one knew or cared to ask, then turned and followed the woman down the entry steps, banging the door behind him.

No one tangled with Lancer McGhee.

Rose O'Malley turned from Whitechapel into Byrom Street, pausing for a moment to watch a man who entertained a small crowd with a dancing bear. The man, dark-haired and shabbily dressed, who appeared to have had little contact with soap and water for many a month, smiled falsely as he prodded the beast with a pointed stick, in an effort to entice it into more enthusiastic activity. The bear, its eyes glazed in anguished resignation, stood obligingly upon its hind legs, a foot taller than its tormentor, waving its paws pathetically in an attempt to please, and shuffled in a caricature of a dance. The evilly smiling man yanked on a thick chain around its neck, which had worn away the animal's fur down to raw skin, and it redoubled its struggle to entertain.

A few yards on, a gypsy played a mouth organ. The woman with him, earrings clinking lethargically, banged a tambourine equally apathetically against her hip, and did some steps in the dust. An organ-grinder fought to gather some of their custom as he energetically turned the handle on his instrument, his bearded face split into what he thought to be a merry grin. After a bar or two, some barefooted children began to waltz in pairs around him.

Two young boys, their clothes little more than rags, their bare feet as black as the bear's pelt, and as tough, plied their brooms at the crossing. Mud, horse manure and refuse collected almost as swiftly as the boys swept it away, for many horses – some carrying riders, others drawing smart carriages from muddy lanes on the outskirts of the town and beyond – passed along Whitechapel and into Dale Street. The children, no more than six or seven years old, were as thin as matchsticks. Their eyes were enormous, black and sunken in their little, worn-out faces. As each carriage or rider passed by they ran into the roadway on their pathetic, rickety legs, sweeping as though their lives depended upon it, as indeed they did; clearing away the offending ordure, and returning after each attack to press tiredly together against the corner of the building.

Rose looked eagerly at the taller, who was about the same age as Joseph. Piercing him with her direct gaze, she walked across the busy street until they were face to face. She searched his undernourished body and listless eyes for some sign of familiarity, but there was none. The face she examined was not the one she looked for.

Men in bowler hats stood against railings and in shop doorways, pipes in mouths, hands stuffed in the pockets of their baggy trousers. The day was fine and mild, a faint memory of the summer remaining in the pale, cloud-streaked sky, and in the sunlight which patched the cobbles at intervals.

People jostled Rose from both directions. It was Sunday, and those amongst the respectable working class who had the energy and inclination were off on an outing. Entire families moved along Grafton Street into the countryside which circled the town. Some crossed the footpath to the Pottery Beach, or to the 'Cast Iron Shore', as those of Liverpool called it. The riverside was pleasant beyond the Herculaneum Basin, with meadows filled with grazing cows, and many lovely walks. On a sunny day, some brave soul might be drawn down to the water's edge in a bathing machine for a ducking, but most walked on beyond the Pottery Beach to the sands of Dingle Point and Knott's Hole. At low tide, it was possible to go as far as Jericho Shore. The air was fresh and unpolluted. It was the ideal spot for a picnic, with a never-ending pageant of sailing ships spread out upon the river to stare at.

Large numbers dawdled along Hill Street to St James' Walk at the top of Duke Street. It was a popular site of excursions for those of all classes, where one might view the other with keen interest, the gentry safely ensconced in their carriages. The promenade was very fine with a long, gravelled terrace from which the far off hills of Flintshire might be seen, across the silvered surface of the estuary, with the lighthouse at its mouth.

For those with money in their pockets it was possible to have one's photographic portrait taken at St James' Mount. The establishment which was positioned there boasted it was the most complete of its kind, being entirely independent of direct sunlight, and commanding the most favourable site and views in all of Liverpool. There was a garden in which to walk, kept in order by public monies, and a rockery, and the grove and shubbery behind it was most popular with courting couples of the working class.

A whole afternoon's excursion would be, of course, entirely free.

Rose continued along Byron Street to Scotland Road. Young boys, barefoot and mucky, pretending to play the popular Lancashire game of 'purring' – in which two contestants in clogs kicked one another until one was too badly beaten to continue – stopped their pantomime and ran after her, whistling, for it was not often one saw a young person dressed as she was, and in shoes as well. A howling toff she was, to them. But Rose, streetwise and unafraid, turned on them, giving as good as she got, and they ran off laughing. Girls, more constrained, sat on doorsteps and voiced their opinions of her to one another in lilting Irish. The 'bejabers' and 'begorras' fell thick and fast.

Turning into Naylor Street, she walked along it until she reached the courtyard which was her destination, but, as she drew near to the steps which led down to the cellar which was her home, she hesitated. Much as she longed for her mammy's arms, and the greetings of her brothers and sisters, she was reluctant to go down.

She was afraid.

Afraid of what she might find this time. Would they be there, or would she find it deserted as it had been on one of the Sundays when she had come home? No one had been able to tell her, or had cared to be bothered where her family might be and, though she had stayed almost until nightfall, giving the place as good a cleaning as once Bridie might have done, not one of them had returned.

She had gone back to Silverdale, sick with worry, and was for the next four weeks, and to Cook's consternation, 'fit for nothing'. In her mind she imagined the lot of them, Bridie included, in the river.

Bridie had been there the following month, mumbling and fractious, aggrieved by the interrogation her daughter put her through; saying fretfully that she couldn't remember where she had been, asking why she should be expected to recall every moment of her time whilst Rose was away, confirming that she had forgotten Rose was coming. She must have done, she said, or she'd have been there else; and, yes, the children had gone with her, she thought. Bridie said that she didn't know where Mary Kate was at, nor Joseph neither. And so it went on.

Rose, despite the flesh which had begun to build up on her as she fed on the good meals which were put in front of her at Silverdale, was thinner now than she had been when she first started there almost a year ago.

She tried to peer through the net which still hung at the window, but it was stiff with dirt, and she could see nothing. It was very quiet. Were they there, or had the Mammy forgotten it was her Sunday again, and left on some mysterious business of her own? Would the children have gone with her, or would they be in their beds, lying reeking and listless in the dirt and confusion which always filled the place now? Would Bridie have come by a job and, more to the point, if so, would she have kept it? In the past few months, she had obtained several but, somehow, those who employed her never kept her for more than a week or two. Some fault was found, and never of her own making, Bridie swore. Her work at the tub, at scrubbing floors, even at the cleaning away of refuse, was taken from her and given to those with more enthusiasm.

Bridie's cheerful obsession with the disposal of dirt had died with her husband. Her once spotless home was filthy. Rose could sweep the lice in handfuls from the floor, and the walls, once as white as Cook's apron, now grew a pattern of black mould from ceiling to skirting board.

Squaring her shoulders, Rose slipped quietly down the steps.

The horror was upon her before she had time to brace herself.

Three little boys, the eldest just four years old, sat about the room, naked but for the scraps of rags which barely covered their thin frames. They gave the appearance of shrunken dolls, without movement or life, their faces contoured into expressions of detached resignation. Their heads veered incuriously as she entered and Seamus, his eyes the exact shape and colour of those of his dead father, smiled as he recognized her, before he turned again towards the entertainment on the bed which he and his brothers watched. Rose followed the direction of his dulled eyes and could not, for a merciful moment, comprehend what the struggling heap of arms and legs and other parts of the human body were about, or even how many were involved. There were horrid noises, and she thought wonderingly that Mick Geraghty's pig had wandered in and somehow become entangled in . . .

Rose began to moan deep in her throat, and her head moved in desperate denial. A heavy drumming filled her mind, and she thought she would be sick. She stood in a tiny circle of beastliness and she could not move, even to look away.

Bridie's eyes, which stared somewhere over the shoulder of the man who heaved on top of her, turned slowly, jerkily, towards the paralysed figure in the doorway. Little by little, proper consciousness returned, and she regarded Rose with the growing anguish and shame of a woman caught in an act of such gross indecency it cannot be named. Gone for the moment was the uncaring drab, whose loss and snd sorrow had rendered her incapable of protecting her own children these past months, and in her eyes shone the agonized spirit of Sean O'Malley's Bridie. It was as if the six months just gone had never been, and she, the beloved and loving wife of Sean, faithful always and true to her one love, had been discovered by him with another in his own bed. Mortification invaded her, flaming in her, strong and hopeless. It seemed to communicate itself to the beast who rode her and, bewildered, he stopped his dreadful performance, staring indignantly down into her face. It was as if her absorption in something other than himself had quite spoiled his pleasure.

Instantly, with the unthinking reaction of a mother protecting her child, Bridie's mind, the one she once had, took over from the thing she had become. Turning to smile at the face above her, she began to move her hips in eager, obscene pantomime, trying furiously to keep the man's attention on herself. In the far reaches of her soul, the place in which she had quivered since Sean had gone, was the essence of the woman she still was; of the wife and mother she had been, and beside it was Sean's face, begging her to protect this child of his. Here in this room was the bestiality of what was being done to her and what had been done to the sweet young flesh of the one she had let go. The instinct which is given to a mother had worked in her then and she had sent them both away. Both her daughters. Probably to a life of drudgery, even to their deaths, for who had not heard of the life children led in factories, mines and mills. Sean had fought to keep his children from them, but surely the life there was better than what they would have endured here, with *him*. Holy Mother, it must not happen to this one as well. Not her sweet little Rose . . .

But it was too late.

The man's head turned angrily to see what had taken Bridie's concentration from himself. His face was suffused with lust, his eyes hot and wild, and Bridie began to moan as they fell on the pretty, slender figure of her daughter. The man humped himself to a kneeling position, the lower part of his half-naked body horribly revealed, and as he did so, it was very evident to everyone who cared, or dared, to look, why he was named 'Lancer' McGhee. His 'lance' stood out before him, thick, swollen and huge, and Rose began to whimper in terror.

Lancer McGhee stared, surprised. Then, slowly, his

mouth widening in a wolfish grin, he stood up. Bridie's white body lay splayed upon the bed, the bites and bruises he had inflicted in previous encounters exhibited there in varying shades of colours, from paling yellow to vivid purple.

The little boys watched impassively. They had seen it all before.

'Mammy, Mammy.' Rose's terrified voice became high and shrill, as Lancer McGhee took a step towards her.

It was his trousers which saved her.

In his eagerness to reach her, and the sweetness he remembered from the other one, he quite forgot that they were round his ankles. With a crash like the fall of a bull in the ring, he hurtled to the floor at her feet. Even then he might have had her, for his hand reached for her skirt, but Bridie began to scream. Her voice was filled with such unspeakable torment that even Lancer turned to look in surprise.

'Run!' she screeched. 'Fer God's sake *run*.'

Rose stood like a rock upon the shore, unable to move.

'Run, Rose. Fer the love of Christ will yer run!'

Bridie's voice reached Rose at last and, as Lancer turned venomously, his hand searching for her, she leaped backwards and, like a hare cornered by dogs, flung herself at the open doorway. As she fell up the area steps and into the pale sunshine which filtered into the courtyard, she could still hear her mother's voice. But Bridie was imploring now: disgustingly, shamefully imploring, as she strove to defend her child.

'Lancer! Lancer, darlin'. Leave 'er. See, come back to bed. See, look what I got fer yer. Look, look what's waitin' 'ere fer yer.' Her voice was cracked and desperate and, for some reason known only to himself, the hulk of a man turned from his pursuit of the girl. Bridie had spread her bent legs, flinging her arms wide as though she were crucified. Her grotesque gesture caught the man's lustful obsession. He fell upon her and, watched by her children, he abused her until she fell senseless, and her blood flowed into the foul mattress.

Lancer had gone to the 'boozer', his lust fed for the moment, his clothes flung carelessly about him, when Rose crept back. The silence as she stood in the doorway went on and on, and nothing came to interrupt it. Not even a moan from Bridie's poor, battered body.

The dog which had cringed from Lancer McGhee fell with savage intensity upon some unfortunate rat, and its triumphant voice echoed off the scabby walls. A child grizzled monotonously and, from over the rooftops, like a benediction, filtered the carillon call of the bells of St Xaviour's. Still there was utter silence within the room.

Rose moved a step. Like a doll, one of those delightful mechanical mannequins which walk stiffly at the turn of a key, she lifted her feet, one after the other, until she reached her mother. Bridie lay, her left arm still outflung, her hand gripping the snarled blanket ferociously. Her other arm covered her face in desolate shame. Her body was red, blotched, rubbed raw in places, and her blood stained the bed beneath her. Rose looked down at her. Her mind was sick, dazed with revulsion and horror, and, deep down, beneath the unendurable, shaking mass of her devastation, was hatred. What she had witnessed had sent her hurtling into a brief, crushing shock; into fear so great it had paralysed her. She had seen in the man's eye what he wanted, and she knew as she looked at the pitiful wreck upon the bed, that it was this that had saved her.

Love and compassion flooded her, and her hatred for the man was drowned for a moment, as she knelt. She gathered the woman who had once been her mother into her arms, and, crooning, soothing her with soft words, she rocked her until Bridie wept her desolation. As her mother had once comforted her when she was younger, the eleven-year-old child brought the woman back and learned, little by little, of the terror which had come to her family.

"'E's gone, Mammy. Ssh, ssh, 'e's gone. I watched 'im go. Ssh, ssh.'

In singsong voice, like a child reciting a well-learned piece with which to entertain guests, and still naked as the day she was born, Bridie told Rose of Lancer McGhee.

'I couldn't stand it 'ere on me own, Rose, with yer Daddy gone. So I went ter the Stout 'ouse an' I met a chap or two, an' they came back, 'cos I was lonely. Lonely, acushla. Sean was gone, yer see, an' I needed . . .' Some remembrance of propriety, obscenely incongruous in view of what Rose had just seen, stopped her for a moment. 'Nice chaps, Rose, nice chaps . . .' Her voice was vague. '. . . an' they give me a penny or two. Faith, it didn't seem wrong. I bought the baby . . . the baby . . .'

Tears dripped disconsolately and, for the first time, Rose became aware that Kathleen, as sweet and bonny as a plump kitten six months ago, was nowhere in sight. She stared over her mother's head, searching each corner of the room, as though the dimpled legs might kick the air, or a fist lift to grab at some imaginary toy. But there was no movement, except the stirring of the three small boys with old men's faces. Her eyes met those of Declan, who explained in the voice of one who speaks of nothing more important than the absence of an acquaintance.

'Kathleen's gone, our Rose. The man took 'er when she went ter sleep.'

Went to sleep? Holy Queen! Dear Mother of God, what had happened? In just four weeks the world of her childhood, her family, had shattered. Mary Kate was missing, and Teresa, where was she? A man had taken Kathleen when 'she went ter sleep'. What man? Taken her where? Rose's heart was like a huge stone, and she felt it move, crushing her inside until she could scarcely breathe. Dear Virgin Mother, don't let this be happening, she pleaded. But Bridie went on, and it was happening.

'. . . the man at the abattoir said I'd not ter be late again. Mary Kate was out lookin' fer a job an', with Joseph gone, Patrick went ter be a climbin' boy, an' the baby wouldn't stop cryin' so Seamus gave 'er some of the stuff Mrs Fitzpatrick let me 'ave . . . ter keep 'er quiet like, d'yer see, whilst I was away ter the work, fer the poor wee lad couldn't manage 'er on 'is own. 'E's only four, our Rose. 'E couldn't be blamed. It was good stuff Rose. Cordial. Jus' a drop o' treacle wi' opium in it, only a teaspoon, our Rose. It kept 'er quiet fer the boys, but Seamus, 'e gave 'er too much, Rose an' . . . Oh, Rose, darlin', the baby died. She's with 'er Daddy in . . .'

It was like the Bridie of the old days, her voice rattling on non-stop; but the contrast was tragic. Then, she had run on merrily, speaking of all life's humour and sadness, seeing it as a backdrop to her own contentment, and her tongue had not been able to move quickly enough to tell of her fine experiences. The people she described, as poverty stricken as herself, had taken on a measure of drollery, brought about by her own. Her family had loved her, their ears attuned to the melodious flow of her words which went on from morning until night.

This was different. This was a proliferation of stinking matter, which broke through as if an abscess had been lanced, and the badness within allowed to break free. Bridie faltered, clinging to Rose as if she might collapse under the weight of what she was about to say. Her voice fell to a frightened whisper.

'. . . an' then I met . . .'e was there in the pub . . . Lancer . . . Lancer McGhee.' She shuddered as she said his name and her eyes glazed at remembered horrors. ' . . . 'e made me . . . 'e came 'ere, Rose, an' forced me . . . I didn't like 'im, Rose,' she said pitifully. '. . . 'e hurt me an' then 'e . . . Oh, Rose. Oh, Rose . . .!' A memory so appalling it could barely be acknowledged, let alone spoken of, came to her, and she began to wail, her voice on the edge of hysteria.

'. . . 'e got our Mary Kate, my little girl, my little Mary Kate, an' her only . . . Oh God, Rose!'

Bridie shook her head from side to side, and her tears flew about like raindrops. Rose held her and held her, and they wept together while the small boys watched. Then she quietened.

'I 'ad ter send 'er away. She's gone ter the poor 'ouse, Rose, where 'imself can't get at 'er. She'll get a foin job, the man said, an' I sent our Teresa as well.' For the first time Bridie looked without shame into her daughter's face.

'I ad ter send 'em away, our Rose, both of 'em. Yer see, I

104

was afraid what 'e'd do. Ter Teresa as well, though she's barely five. I can stand what 'e does ter me, Rose. I 'ave ter, but I can't allow the daughters of . . . I can't let Sean's daughters 'ave done ter 'em what 'e does ter me.'

Rose bent her head to her mother and held her against her own thin chest. The tale was harrowing, and the telling like a nightmare, but Bridie seemed to take comfort now it was told. They rocked together for a minute or two, then the mother, conscious for the first time of her nakedness, reached hastily for her clothes and, while her children watched woodenly, drew them about her. She seemed to have regained a little dignity now, as if her sacrifice and the steps she had taken to protect her daughters, had lifted her self esteem. She stood. Rose looked up at her and realized desolately that, if her father had returned miraculously from the grave, he would have passed his beloved wife by without a flicker of recognition.

Rose left within ten minutes, her mother's terror that Lancer McGhee might return communicating itself to her.

'Yer musn't come again, alannah, not . . .'

'Oh, Mammy, please. I must see yer . . .'

'I know, ssh now, ssh. Let me 'ave me say, darlin'.'

Rose's eyes were agonized, and she shivered in Bridie's arms. Their roles had reverted again, with the mother soothing the child.

'Yer can't be comin' while 'e's about. I'd never 'ave a minute's peace. Not that I get one . . .' Her face contorted, and Rose clung to her.

'Mammy, what will we do?'

'Sure, an' we'll see each other, we will, praise be to God.'

She took Rose's face between her hands. Her own face, once as bonny as a bright, new apple, was ravaged.

'I'll get word ter yer, when 'e's away. 'E goes ter the purrin' on a Sunday afternoon, on ter the cock fights in Jasmine Street. When I know 'e's goin' I'll send word. Somehow, I'll get word ter yer.'

They kissed lovingly. Rose hugged the unnaturally silent boys, blessing them in a murmur of incoherent pleadings to the Mother of God to look after what was left of her family. Then she began the long walk back to Toxteth.

She did not know when, or if, she would ever see any of them again.

# CHAPTER 8

Lacy stopped on the gentle slope of the hill, and turned to look down at the landscape spread out before her. The path on which she stood had become overgrown during the summer, and the remains of the wild flowers which grew along the verge had crept towards its centre. Coltsfoot and cowberry crowded the hem of her skirt, and yellow vetch stood out in the green of the waving grasses which ran down the slope. A narrow, placid stream which curled like the lash of a whip, leaves floating gently upon its surface, ran quietly a hundred yards below. Trees grew thickly to its banks, their glory dying in the autumn winds. Beyond lay squares of lush green fields, their hedges neat and symmetrical, and in each, like specks of white fluff, and seeming from this distance scarcely bigger than the chickens which pecked in the stable yard, were scattered sheep.

The village was sheltered in a fold on the wide, shallow valley. The roofs of the cottages were red and pink and brown and grey: some slated and tight against the weather, others still thatched; but all in good repair, for Charles Hemingway looked after his tenants.

There were more trees beyond the stream, thick as the grass in the fields and, where the horizon met the sky, tiny wandering clouds, palely white against the blue, made a backdrop for the row of great chestnuts which stood there.

Lacy sighed with deep pleasure, her eyes absorbing the loveliness. She turned as her sisters caught up with her. She was always ahead of them now, running as fast as her six petticoats would allow, thankful only that Mama had not yet insisted upon the dreadful contraption of horsehair and whalebone which was beginning to be fashionable. The crinoline was very much in vogue with those who had style, replacing the mass of petticoats previously worn. It was very

107

graceful when one walked, but to sit down, enter or leave a carriage, or even give Papa a kiss, required the greatest tact and skill, and much time in manoeuvring the cumbersome thing. At least petticoats were flexible, and might be removed when one was out alone, and hidden behind some convenient bush to await one's return.

But not today.

This time, Lacy sighed in exasperation. Amy, Margaret and Jane followed her up the path, walking one behind the other, their heads bent, their eyes on the ground, anxious that they might step in something horrid. It was so . . . so wild up here, they thought; so far from the security of the house, and who knew what nasty thing might have been deposited here. After all, there were sheep. They glided as though they were on wheels, and Lacy longed to give each of them a push, sending them rolling down the hill, and back to the uniformity of the ornamental gardens in which they preferred to walk. It had been her turn to choose the direction they would take today and, naturally, as they knew she would, she had chosen to walk – well, they walked, *she* darted hither and thither like a gad-fly – up behind the house and over the gentle hill of the parkland. The path was smooth enough to have been danced upon, for nowhere did Papa allow neglect, and an army of labourers kept the estate in an impeccable condition. But it was so much more genteel in the gardens.

They were all warmly wrapped. The sky was winter blue, but the sun shone without warmth. Amy was in deep blue, the colour of a harebell. Her costume was made of the finest Valencia, and over it she wore a warm plaid woollen cloak and shoulder cape. Her tiny bonnet perched on the back of her head, allowing the arrangement of her ringlets to be seen. Margaret was dressed similarly, but she was in forest green and carried a tiny fur muff. Around her neck was a collar to match. Jane, decorous, gentle and disappointed to tears at the reappearance of the old Lacy, was dainty as a flower in rose-coloured merino, her mantle being several shades deeper. A handful of wild flowers were held tenderly in her small hands, and her eyes darted from side to side, as she looked about her

108

for suitable specimens to press between the pages of her book.

The four young girls stood along the path and looked with varying degrees of interest at the gentle valley, which lay like a chessboard of many colours before them. Although it was November, it was almost mild, the autumn wind which had stripped the trees taking itself off temporarily to the wilds of the north. The three oldest girls moved impatiently, eager to return to the environment they found more satisfying, but Lacy looked about her with keen interest.

From away down at the bottom of the slope, a demented barking lifted three magpies from a bush, their black and white plumage flashing against the pale circle of the sun. The noise scattered the sheep in the meadow into an idiotic gallop, and in their midst a fast moving blur of red whipped the game to further intoxicating heights.

'Dear Lord, it's Copper!'

Without thought, and certainly with no concern for the words with which she had just shocked her sisters, Lacy gathered up her petticoats, and with the agility of a mountain goat and the speed of a diving eagle she was away, her sturdy boots skimming the soft grasses as she ran down the hill towards the enchanted dog.

'Copper!' she shrieked, decorum forgotten. Indeed, even if it had been remembered it would have been ignored, for the sheer joy of running had her in its grip. She hurtled to the bottom of the slope, crashing into the trees, her breath coming in frenzied gasps, her eyes like stars in her crimson face. Her pale lilac bonnet fell to the back of her neck, the pretty velvet violets which crowned it bouncing joyfully. Her hair flew about her head in a swathe of flying silver, the bows and clips which kept it in place springing into the undergrowth as she crashed through it. Her shawl, its fringes waving like seaweed under water, snagged on a tree, and she let it go, aware only that Farmer Pilkington would not only be incensed by the worrying of his sheep, he would be within his rights to shoot the animal which chased them. Though the land was her father's, Farmer Pilkington was its tenant, and the sheep which Copper chased in delirious circles were his.

The sheep heaved together, then parted, running in twos and threes until they came to a hedge, which one tried to force its way through. The noise of their terrified baa-ing and the dog's barking rang as true as a bell through the clear air.

'Copper, Copper!' her voice rose as she plunged onwards. The stream was at her feet before she knew it, and one black boot actually sank, her foot within it, to the stony bed, before she came to an abrupt halt.

Oh Lord, the dratted dog! He was over there, and she was here, and the river between, and she could hardly wade it in her lovely new promenade costume. If she did that, not only would Mama have Copper banished from the house, and Farmer Pilkington have him shot, but she would be confined to her room for the rest of her life.

'Copper,' she wailed despairingly.

'I'll get 'im. 'Old me boots.'

From nowhere, the phantom appeared, or so it seemed to Lacy. Boots – thin, much mended, but so clean and polished they were like a mirror – were thrust into her limp hands. A pair of stockings was draped unceremoniously across her arm, and there was a splash as someone dumped into the stream. Holding the boots, the stockings, her face split into a grin of huge enjoyment, Lacy began to shout her encouragement. She wished it were she who had the sense to strip off her things to ford the stream. The water would be cold, but what fun it would be . . . Then, the girl who waded the stream with her back turned was suddenly as familiar as Lacy's own face in the mirror. It was Rose.

Rose.

Suspended in memory, Lacy stood as still as the trunk of the huge oak tree from behind which Rose had come. Though Lacy could not see the girl's face, it was drawn in her mind and would be forever. Green eyes, starred with black, sooty lashes; eyebrows winging dark in a white face; hair like midnight, swirling about thin shoulders; and legs as white and slender as the cleaners which she had seen Jepson draw through the stem of his pipe.

The water sprang up in a shimmer of spray about Rose's knees, and she turned to laugh in dismay as her skirt slipped from her clutching fingers, trailing in the water like the sail of an upturned yacht.

'Bejasus 'tis cold,' she gasped, and Lacy's face relaxed from the rigid stiffness which had set there as memory returned to her. She laughed back, and the ghost of Sean O'Malley was laid forever.

She had never seen anyone quite like Rose in her life.

'Oh, do be careful, Rose. The water is moving so . . . mind that branch . . . Oh Lord, your skirt, it will be quite saturated. That dog, that damn . . . dratted dog. I shall thrash him for his pains, believe me.' Both knew she would do no such thing.

Rose reached the far bank of the stream, stumbling and slithering on the smooth, mossy stones beneath the water. She flung out an arm and caught a clump of chickweed which grew there and pulled herself up. In a moment she was away, running like a whippet on feet as red as a signal light and cold as frost, her skirts bunched up about her knees. Her legs twinkled in the sunshine, pumping vigorously in the soft grass.

'Copper, Copper, Co-o-o-o-pe-e-r! Here, boy. Here, Copper!'

At last the senseless dog heard her, and in a frenzy of extravagant affection ran towards his new friend, eager to include her in his game, his ears flopping up and down, and his tail sweeping the air with ecstasy. He leapt into her arms in the firm conviction that he was still only eight weeks old and the size of a kitten, and with a shrill cry, Rose and he vanished into the flowing greenness in a tumble of legs and tails and flying skirts. For several minutes her merriment rang out, the laughter of a child whose joy is complete, then like a gypsy urchin, her hair full of grass, her bare feet covered in black soil, the girl rose from the flattened pasture where she and the dog had floundered.

Grabbing Copper's collar, Rose turned and, seeing Lacy, a

tiny elegant figure on the river bank, waved and pointed, shouting gleefully.

'I've got 'im, the daft creature.'

The sheep in the field, with the mindlessness of their kind, the memory of their former terror gone, began to crop the grass and Rose, her face flushed now, her eyes as merry as once her Daddy's had been, dragged the buoyant animal behind her. Bewildered, he pulled back, but as Lacy's voice came to him, he started to run towards its beloved sound, and the hapless girl who held him had no choice but to go with him. Down the bank, across the stream, her skirt dragging like a trawling net, they careered, dog and child, up the slippery bank, and before Lacy could steady herself, they were upon her. Both of them.

Down they went again, the dog overjoyed that a third member had joined the romp. He jumped, and barked, and licked any area of bare flesh he could: hands, ears, soft childish necks, and, particularly, he relished Rose's bare feet and legs. Mud splashed, and water, as he ran in and out of the stream, and each time the shrieking girls sat up, he felt it was his duty to show his love by tugging them down again, and giving each face a good going over. Lacy's pretty outfit looked exactly as though the whole of Bess's litter had raced across it, and her bonnet, falling from her head, was seized rapturously by the dog, and thrown into the air with a playful toss.

The laughter, the silly, senseless, childish giggling which is the right of all young girls, the carefree moments that are for them alone, had the two children in a spell of a timeless instant. And then, as the excited dog lay down suddenly in the way of a puppy, for he was no more, putting his head upon his paws, they sat up at last.

They looked at each other warmly, their eyes still filled with joyful laughter, their faces glowing, and then, as suddenly as the dog, they were quiet. Their eyes still smiled, their lips curved gently, but the hilarity faded as they remembered the last time they had met.

Lacy put out her muddy hand impulsively and took Rose's.

112

She held it as she searched Rose's face earnestly. Although the horror had gone with time, as it does – with the companionship of the dog, and now with Rose laughing beside her – her heart still became saddened as she remembered that day.

'Rose, dear Rose. It has been so long. Nearly seven months, and in all that time we have not spoken. It is my fault, I should have come, but you see . . .' A cloud passed across her shining eyes, dimming them for a moment '. . . but you see, I was . . .' She did not know in what way to explain how she had been for how was she to tell Rose that the memory of Sean O'Malley's death had haunted her to the edge of madness, and that the nighmare would never quite leave her. But it seemed Rose understood, and the words were not needed.

'Don't, Miss Lacy. Don't. I know, yer see. I know 'ow me Daddy died an' I'm sorry yer saw it. Faith, it must 'ave been . . . but there, 'tis done now.'

She patted the hand in hers consolingly, feeling at peace for the first time since that day. She and Lacy seemed to step to the same rhythm, perhaps through the sharing of their grief, and it was evident that neither felt the need to speak further of it.

The leaves stirred in the breeze and both girls shivered. Rose's red toes were turning blue and Lacy, becoming suddenly practical, soon had her in her darned stockings and old boots, searching about until they had retrieved their shawls. They found a patch of sunlight in a protected grove of fallen trees, the huge mossy trunks forming a pleasant break from the wind. The grass was dry and the carpet of leaves crackled as they sat down. The dog lay between them, in heaven as two hands fondled his head, and stroked the gleaming bronze of his coat.

'Tell me about yourself, Rose. What has happened since we last met? Is everything well at home? Your mother? Is she recovered?'

A ghastly picture flashed in dreadful detail before Rose's eyes, and she caught her breath. Bridie and Lancer McGhee, white, heaving flanks. Black, crawling body hair. Three wizened faces, impassive and still. Eyes, blue and filled with agony as Mammy . . . Recovered? What did it mean, that word? What image did it bring to mind? It spoke of being as you once were. Being whole again. Well. In good health. Her heart slipped sickeningly, and she felt bile flood her throat.

Bending her head, Rose pretended an intense interest in Copper's silky ears, gaining a moment before speaking, for how could she tell this funny little sheltered thing of what her family did. She asked so compassionately, probably imagining Rose's mammy sitting in resigned composure in her chair, a bit of sewing in her hands, the children at her feet, the cat before the crackling fire. There would be a bubbling pan of stew upon the hob and the kettle waiting for the inevitable cup of tea, and Bridie would be in her warm black, good shoes upon her feet, and the boys with boots, and Mary Kate would be about the table with forks and plates, and Teresa cutting the bread and Kathleen . . . the baby . . .

It was the lovely picture of what might have been that did it. It was out before she could press it back to where it festered. Inside her, deep inside where no one went, where no one saw or even knew existed, the great aching pain of it – more than could be withstood by a grown woman, let alone a child – flowed through her mind, and from her sore and bruised and bewildered heart, poured in great gasping breaths from between her lips.

Mercifully, much of it meant nothing to Lacy. She could not comprehend the beastly pictures Rose painted with stumbling, weeping words. The very phrases used were unknown to her, and the idea of Rose's mama and a man with no clothes on, of three starving children, Mary Kate raped – what did that mean? – of the death of the baby through some comfort given to her to make her sleep, of workhouses and factories, of Joseph gone and Patrick a climbing boy – whatever that was – passed her like the vision of a jig-saw puzzle from which many pieces are missing. She knew vaguely what the outline represented, but it was hard to imagine the whole with so many gaps.

'. . . I should've gone today, it's me Sunday off. But Mammy said I wasn't ter come, in case 'e was there. 'E'd ave me, Miss Lacy, like 'e 'ad Mary Kate. That's why I'm 'ere. I didn't know where else ter go. Them in the kitchen don't know about Mammy an' Lancer McGhee, an' I couldn't tell 'em. It would shame 'er if they knew, but I can tell yer. Yer saw me Daddy. Yer know what a lovely man 'e was.'

The eyes of Sean smiled in both their minds, and the clean goodness of him cut through the heart of his child, as she pictured her mother in the arms of Lancer.

'I don't know what ter do, Miss Lacy. I daren't go 'ome. Ter be sure the man'd . . . Well what 'e does ter me Mammy, 'e'd do ter me, an' I'd kill meself if 'e did.' She shuddered violently and, appalled, Lacy tried to imagine what it was the man did that was so awful. She patted Rose's hand, staring intently into her face, trying to understand what it was that made her in such terror. She could envisage the weight on Rose's mind concerning her brothers and their poor starving bodies, and she had flinched at talk of rats and lice and dirt piled up all about, but surely there was someone who could stop this man inflicting pain upon Rose's mother. A policeman should be brought, and the man sent to gaol. It must not be allowed. Papa would see to the matter at once, she knew, when he was told. The problem of food for Rose's brothers was simple. Was there not food enough in the kitchen to feed three hundred children, let alone three? She would ask Papa for some money to give to Rose for her mother until she found suitable employment.

She was so glad she had met Rose today, for now all the difficulties of which Rose spoke would be swept away. Poor Rose. What she must have suffered during these last months with no one to help her. But everything would be put right now. She herself would see to it. How ashamed she felt, wallowing – there was no other word for it – in her own misery, when poor Rose had so much more to trouble her. But, she vowed, this would happen no longer.

Rose was still speaking, weeping brokenheartedly.

'. . . if I could just find 'em, Miss Lacy. Teresa's only five.

She can't work in a mill at 'er age. Me Daddy'd turn in 'is grave if 'e knew. Holy Mother of God, five years old an' workin' in a mill! Still, I suppose it's better than bein' . . .' Here she used the word Lacy did not understand again. '. . . by Lancer McGhee. Yer should've seen it, Miss Lacy. Like a donkey's, it was. At least a foot long an' . . .'

It struck Rose then what she was saying to the unworldly child who stared in bewilderment at her, and the full comprehension of what she had done in despair swept over her. To speak such words, gross and offensive, to this girl who had been guarded all her life from even the most simple fact of life beyond her father's estate, was surely a sin before God. She, Rose, had had it forced upon her by circumstances beyond anyone's control but, in kinder times, both Bridie and Sean would have killed to protect her from it, she knew. Now, without thought she had . . . Dear Mother, forgive me, forgive me, and don't let her understand, she cried inwardly. For if she does, and tells her papa, I shall be out of the house at the end of his boot.

Appalled, her hand went to her mouth, her eyes grew wide, and became a dark, dark green, like a lake in a storm.

'Oh, Miss Lacy,' she whispered. 'I'm that sorry. I shouldn't 'ave. I'm sorry. It came out before . . .'

'Hush, Rose. Now hush. It can all be sorted out in a matter of hours.' Rose breathed a sigh of relief. The words she had spoken in her despair had meant nothing to Lacy. But Lacy went on coolly, 'Now we shall go home and I shall see Papa at once.' She began to scramble to her feet, the dog leaping with her, eager for another game. 'Fortunately it is Sunday and he will be in his study . . .'

'No, no! Oh no, Miss Lacy, yer mustn't.' Horror gripped Rose again. 'Faith, don't yer see, if yer tell 'im 'e'll sack me.' She began to gabble incoherently, holding Lacy's arm, but Lacy interrupted coldly.

'Don't be silly, Rose.' She was shocked, and not a little affronted. 'Why should he do that? My Papa is good, and kind, and very generous. He will see that your family does not starve, and I am convinced that if we were to go to the . . . the

116

poor house, he would soon discover the whereabouts of your sisters. No, leave this to me, Rose. Something shall be done for you, and before the day is out.'

Rose lost control.

All that had happened snapped her hold on her own tongue. Fear made her as she was. All she had to hang on to was her job, such as it was, and the corner she occupied in the big house, and the few shillings she had tucked away there to give to Mammy. She had that, and hope, and it was all slipping away from her now, swept along by this girl's good intentions. Without stopping to think, to understand that Lacy acted only in an effort to ease her burden, Rose sprang to protect what she had.

She stood up, her face a blaze of fury. Dear God, she would go to her Papa, an' all, the silly little madam. Full of herself and her own importance, she'd be away up to the house and tell her Papa, and yes, 'before the day was out', so would Rose. Out of the house, out of a job, and forced to return to the seductions of bloody Lancer McGhee. Gone now was the terrified demented child, and in her place was a young creature filled with celtic fury.

'Don't be so daft. Faith, 'tis touched ya are, yer eejit. Can't yer see what's plain as the nose on yer face? D'yer think yer papa is goin' ter be bothered with the likes o' me? 'E did what 'e thought was 'is duty when 'e paid fer the funeral an' give Mammy a couple o' guineas, but that's it as far as 'e's concerned, an' if 'e thought 'is darlin' child was down 'ere talking, aye an' listening ter 'is scullery maid, 'e'd 'ave the law on me.'

Lacy stood like one of the pillars which marched across the front of the Custom House in Canning Place. Her face was white as bleached calico, and her eyes stared in consternation. But something glimmered there, not quite ready to surface. Copper stood quietly, his tail down, his eyes pleading, for he knew that these two lively friends of his, one of whom he loved devotedly, had created a tension between them which he did not understand.

'D'yer think yer daddy will get in 'is foin carriage an' race down ter Naylor Street, an' go in our 'ouse?' Rose laughed hysterically at the very idea. 'D'yer think 'e's goin' ter get a policeman ter lock up Lancer McGhee fer what 'e does ter my Mammy? 'Tis not against the law, yer know. Yer daddy does it to yer mammy all the time.'

Lacy began to breathe unevenly, and her face went from white to bright crimson. She had not the faintest notion what her papa did to her mama all the time, and the mention of the law and the pastime connected with it was an enigma to her, but she was very sorely provoked. It was unthinkable that her papa would shrug off his responsibility to a girl who worked so hard for him, and who was in such trouble.

'. . . an' me little brothers, what about them? Is 'e goin' ter bring 'em up 'ere, is' 'e? An' will 'e take the trouble ter go up ter Brownlow Hill an' ask the overseer where they sent Mary Kate an' Teresa, if yer please?' Her voice sank to a whisper. 'There's thousands of us, Miss Lacy, thousands, all starvin' and' dirty, an' crawlin' with fleas, an' lice, an' . . . an' . . . Please, please, Miss Lacy!' Her anger was ripped apart by fear, and the awful dread of what Lacy, in her misguided desire to help, might do.

She was pleading now.

'Yer Papa is a . . . good man. Kind ter yer an' 'is family an' decent ter us, 'is servants, but there's nowt 'e can do fer the likes o' me, fer me Mammy an' all the others like 'er. Leave well alone, please. If yer've any . . . feelings, not just fer me, but fer the rest of me family, don't do it. The few bob I earn can be got ter me Mammy somehow, an' will put a bite in the little uns' mouths. If I lose me job . . .'

But Lacy had found her tongue now, and she interrupted savagely. 'How dare you say my Papa would not care to help. How dare you!' She stamped her foot. 'He is a wonderful man who would do anything, *anything* to assist those less fortunate than himself. If I should ask him he would . . . call a carriage, and . . . he . . . and be down to . . . well, he would . . . he would send . . .'

Like Rose, she felt the fury slip away to be replaced by an uneasy feeling of uncertainty. In her mind's eye she tried to picture her papa in surroundings described to her so graphically by Rose. Rats running over his foot, and lice falling into his . . . Lacy felt her skin prickle, and she scratched her shining head vigorously. Papa would not be afraid to tackle Lancer, would he? The constable would go with him and tear him from Rose's Mama, and Papa . . . Papa would . . . What would Papa do? Give her some money to buy food, her mind said confidently. But what if Lancer should come back and take the money from Rose's Mama? He would return as soon as Papa had left and they would be no better off, those little boys, than they had been. The awfulness, the dread and indisputable finality of what Rose had said about the thousands who were as Rose's family, and whose lot could not be changed by anyone, no matter how well meaning, began to waver her conviction, and an unease as strong as her previous certainty sat about her. Suppose, just suppose, Papa said . . .

Lacy looked at Rose, her eyes bewildered, lost in the maze of her own tangled thoughts. She had been so positive only moments before that Papa would take up his sword, like the knights of old, and charge full tilt at the horrors of which Rose spoke. He would right all wrongs and undo all injustices. He was her Papa, and she loved him, and always she had trusted him. But, somehow, the truth of what Rose had said was so vivid, so absolutely clear, it blurred her own sureness.

Rose spoke softly, taking Lacy's hand again – the one which had clasped hers in friendship.

'Believe me, Miss Lacy, please. Yer daddy is a good an' great man, but 'e can do nothing' fer me an' mine. He could if he wanted to, her cool, disillusioned mind said, but he wouldn't want to and it was no good going on to this one. She believed in her daddy, and there was nothing to be gained by repeating what she herself had just said. The important thing was to keep Lacy from telling him, because Rose knew, as sure as Ireland was a little bit of heaven, that if he knew of what had been said this day, or even that they had spoken, he would put a stop to their relationship, insubstantial as it yet was, in the only way he could.

By giving herself the old heave-ho.

119

'Don't say 'owt ter 'im, Miss Lacy, please. We'll work somethin' out. Ter be sure, me sisters will be right as rain in the owd mill. 'Aven't I 'eard they eat meat every day an' sleep as warm as could be of a night? They'll be fit as a butcher's dog, begorra, yer'll see.'

She could see the doubts growing, the expressions chasing one another across the other's face, and she knew that Lacy wanted to be convinced. Quick to take the advantage, learning even now that that was the one way to achieve her own ends, she smiled brightly.

'Let's give it a day or two, shall we? Bejabers, before yer can say "Mick Geraghty's pig" everythin'll be turned round an' as lovely as the day. Now let's not be botherin' yer papa. 'Tis our secret.' She was serious now, her small white face as wise as though she had lived through a lifetime of such experiences. Her eyes, still dewed with tears, the lashes spiked and wet, looked imploringly into Lacy's.

'Promise me, please, not ter say anythin'. Not yet. If things . . . if it needs . . . but fer now, promise yer'll say nowt.'

Lacy sighed, pressing the hand in hers, longing to be up to something to take the tragic shadow from Rose's face. In her mind, as in those of most who are young, was a belief that black was black, and white white, and that there was always an antidote to all the world's ills. For the time being her innocence protected her. She was not to know the truth just yet.

'Very well, Rose. I promise. But I want to see you often. If I came to the kitchen and signalled, would you be able to slip away? I should like to speak to you again.' It was said almost shyly.

Rose smiled and relaxed. She felt her heartache ease a little. It would be grand to have someone to talk to, to confide in. But not, she thought hastily, of what was happening at Naylor Street. She must keep that to herself, or Lacy might . . . She watched Lacy's expression light up and sparkle with excitement. Her words interrupted Rose's thoughts.

'I know, we will use Copper. When you are free you must write me a note and slip it under his collar. We will fix a little

120

clip or something and when he comes up after lessons, I shall find it and . . . What is it Rose? Do you not think it a splendid idea?' She looked quite put out to have her SPLENDID IDEA frowned upon.

Rose sighed. A different world the child lived in, to be sure, so how could she be blamed for her daft schemes.

'What is it, Rose?'

'I can't write, Miss Lacy.'

'Can't write?'

The notion was so astonishing, and so unexpected, that Lacy was lost for words. Imagine not being able to write and, therefore, to read. Why, it must be like being in prison, and never seeing the trees, or the lovely sky. And not to know what the history books said of the past, or . . .

'I can draw.'

'Draw?'

'Sure, an' can't anyone draw a bit of a thing on a scrap of paper?'

Intrigued, aglow with excitement as the novelty laid a hold on her, Lacy sat down again, resting her slim buttocks on the crusted trunk of the fallen tree. The dog moved to her and put his head upon her knee, and his tail thumped the log. He was happy now that the anger had gone, and he licked her hand, then turned to Rose as though he knew something was brewing which concerned himself.

'Oh, Rose, do you mean you will . . .'

'Yes, I'll draw a little tree fer 'ere.' She swept her hand in a vague circle to indicate the spot in which they sat. 'Or a . . .'

'A little house for the back of the stable, you know, where it joins the wall of the paddock . . .'

'. . . or a lake if it's ter be down by the . . .'

'. . . a horse if you should decide the paddock, and I will answer the same, and we could put strokes, one for each hour, so that we shall know what time . . .'

'It won't be every day, Miss Lacy. Faith, Cook'd skin me . . .'

'I know, but you must have a few minutes now and then . . .'

"Ow about a bird fer down at the beach . . .?'

'Oh yes!'

Their excitement grew. Once again, they were children without a care in the world, as they expanded upon this new and delightful game they would play. Ideas poured from between their soft, pink lips, and grey eyes laughed into green, whilst the dog rolled on his back in ecstasy.

They parted, Lacy racing behind the bronze flame of her dog, up the slope and onto the path. The others had gone, of course, Amy and Margaret and Jane, as she knew they would, and her heart beat in rapid thumps. Mamma would be told of her unladylike behaviour, and Papa would talk to her sadly of the need to be more decorous, but as long as her sisters had not seen her meeting with Rose she did not care. Life was such fun now . . .

She stopped abruptly, the glow left her face, and it became quite sober, settling into a mould of maturity which would one day be hers. The dog looked back, waiting for her. She called to him and he came. She knelt down and looked into his intelligent eyes.

'We will do something, Copper, whatever Rose says. We cannot let her family starve. It would not do. We shall think of something, shall we not?'

Copper licked her face, his devotion shining. Then away they went again, two lively young animals, full of joy and hope, and the wonderful certainty that all would be well.

# CHAPTER 9

Slate steps were built into the dry stone wall which divided Charles Hemingway's estate from the meadow belonging to Jericho Farm. But the two boys jumped with the suppleness of youth from the top of the wall into the knee-high rippling counterpane of grass. It moved in the breeze, the colours of thrift, cowbane and wild thyme making a patchwork of pink, green and lilac. The passage of the boys, as they waded through the sea of wild flowers and newly greening pasturage, bruised the plants, and the sweet aroma of spring filled the air.

The boys were followed closely by a handsome dog.

They were dressed in almost identical clothes of a style fashionable eight or nine years before. Their light tunic jackets, trimmed with military-style rows of buttons, had deep, gently pleated skirts, and the trousers they wore were wide about their ankles. Each had a neckerchief tucked under the collar of his jacket. A cap, pulled down low about eyebrows and ears, covered each small head. Their clothing was stained and torn, and their square-toed shoes, dusty and cracked, were fastened with string. They both had extremely dirty hands and faces.

They did not speak as they ran. After a last glance back at the wall over which they had just clambered, they looked directly ahead. Legs blurred with the speed of their movements, faces glowing through the filth, breath gasped from laboured lungs as they sped on.

The dog was ahead now, turning his head every few seconds or so, as though to check that no mishap had befallen his companions. He ran low to the ground, his coat feathers picking up burrs, seeds and scraps of grass. Field after field was crossed. Some had a stile, some did not, but the children and dog leaped nimbly over each obstacle. Cows lifted placid heads, then turned and backed in alarm. A man behind a plough stared in astonishment. The horses he was guiding, feeling the lead go, moved to one side. The furrow he made lost its symmetry and he cursed.

The boys came to a closely planted orchard, and as they raced between the slim trunks of apple trees, the blue sky vanished behind a dense canopy of white blossom. The last stile was climbed. They were in Aigburth Road leading to the town. At last they stopped.

Sinking down upon the grass verge which edged the lane, they gasped and floundered like two landed fish. The dog lay between them, his tongue hanging from the corner of his mouth. His flanks rippled, but his breath was scarcely disturbed by his exertions. A bed of coltsfoot, dandelion and clover made a softness on which to lie, and a tiny ditch, hardly wider than a man's hand, was screened by fool's watercress, green and delicate. A skylark sang its heart out somewhere high above them.

One boy spoke. 'I've never run so fast in all me life.'

'I know, but was it not a wonderful experience? I did not realize how lovely it is just to let go and never stop. I feel I could go on forever, once we have regained our breath.'

There was silence again. The first boy to speak looked speculatively at the other, running his eye over his clothing, from his large peaked cap to his down-at-heel shoes. He chewed a piece of grass, his eyes shaded by the peak of the check cap he also wore.

'Listen,' he said. 'I think it'd be a good idea if . . .'

His companion sat up, turning to look eagerly, only too anxious to be told what to do.

'What?'

'I think it'd be a good idea if you said nowt.'

'Nowt?'

'Mmmm. Let me do all the talkin'.'

'But why?'

''Ave yer ever 'eard yerself speak?'

'I'm not sure I know quite what you mean.'

'Oh, come on. Listen ter me, will yer, then yerself. Yer know the difference. Faith, a deaf man could tell . . .'

'Oh, I see. Perhaps I could attempt to . . .'

'It's not just the way yer speak, it's the words. There's not a spalpeen in Naylor's Yard would say "attempt", fer a start.'

'Oh.' The second boy showed a keen interest. 'Why ever not? It is quite an ordinary word.'

The first boy was becoming irritated. 'Just do as ye're told, will yer? If anyone speaks to us, let me do the talkin'.' A serious, very serious expression crossed his pale face. 'This isn't a pleasure trip, yer know. It could be dangerous. If . . . if 'e's there, we'll 'ave ter be away like the wind. Me Mammy says 'e won't be, but yer never know, so don't treat it like it's a bit o' fun. An' no names.'

'But could we not call each other . . . Arthur and . . . er . . .'

'Begorra, will yer stop yer blather. No names, I said.'

'Yes, Ro . . . Yes, I'm sorry.'

'Are yer ready then?'

A slight shiver shook the frame of the second boy, but he stood up and lifted his head bravely.

'Yes, I'm ready.'

The piece of paper for Rose had been handed in at the kitchen door, by a carter who had plainly shown his vexation at having to come nearly a mile out of his way to deliver it. He had not been told, he said, of the long drive from gate to kitchen, and the man at the lodge had stated flatly that it was not his job to deliver personal messages to the staff.

By now, Rose's worth was well recognized. Her passion for cleanliness was a byword in the kitchen, and her genius for removing dirt in any shape or form, or for shining up some dull surface to mirror-like perfection, had found favour with those above her. So, a word in Cook's ear was sufficient to ensure that the carter was mollified by a vast tankard of ale and a couple of freshly baked pork pies, and that the note reached Rose's hand.

Rose knew it was from Bridie. All day it lay, seeming to Rose to be still warm from Bridie's hand, in her apron pocket above her heart. It was not until she was alone, in the tiny candle-lit cubicle she called her own, that she was able to read it. Nelly had fallen by the wayside, or more specifically, flat on her back – knocked sideways by the impish smile of a casual labourer brought in to help with the harvest at the home farm last September – and had been shown the door when her condition became apparent.

Rose opened the first letter she had ever received. A stick man had been drawn, like those done by children, although anyone less like a stick than Lancer McGhee Rose had yet to see. An arrow pointed from him to what was clearly meant to be an animal with four legs, and above it all was a cross.

Rose marvelled at Bridie's ingenuity, and her heart warmed. Surely it meant her Mammy had regained the spirit which had beguiled them all a year ago. Her mind must be sharp, for not many would have had the ability to 'write' a note such as this. It told Rose what her mother wanted her to know without one word being written or read. The stick man who was Lancer McGhee was going to be away from home. He was going somewhere connected with animals, and the cross was the Cross of our Lord. Sunday. It must be Sunday.

It came to her then, and she smiled, and the candles lit stars in her eyes. Lancer McGhee was going on Sunday to the bull baiting, and Mammy was telling her it was safe for her to come home.

Home.

Not since last November had she seen her family, and now it was May, and in all that time she had had no word. Dead they could all be, and she would not know of it. So many times she had been tempted to walk the miles to Naylor Street, and had been ashamed by her own fear. She had wept for her mother and the family they once had been, but fear, terror of the man who brutalized her mother, had kept her from going to them. The money she earned was put by each month, every shilling of it, and she took it now from beneath the mattress, and listened to it clink, and smiled, for on Sunday she would put it in her mammy's hand.

'Let me come with you.'

'Yer what?'

'Let me come with you, Rosie.'

126

'Yer must be out of yer 'ead.'

'I'm not, Rose. Really I am not.' It was said seriously, and Rose had to smile.

'Miss Lacy,' she said patiently, shaking her head as though the ideas the child had were beyond belief. Rose always thought of Lacy as 'the child', and always would, although they had discovered to their mutual delight that they had been born on the very same day. To share a birthday made it seem as if they were almost twins, said Lacy, and Rose had to agree.

Now, she disagreed most strenuously.

'Miss Lacy, I'm away ter see the Mammy, not ter Bootle on a picnic. It's not the sorta place someone like yer can go. Why, it's . . . Well, I've told yer what . . .'

How could she make Miss Lacy understand?

Her standing there with lamps in her eyes, and her face all pink with excitement. She must make her see the rotting houses, mouldering piles of human excrement, walls which ran with slimy water; the rats and vermin which scampered about like kittens in the stables, and just as unheeded, bold as you please. And the people. The poor, devastated, poverty stricken thousands who crowded into close, and alleyway, and foetid room, and who fought to stay alive on less than was thrown away from this child's plate each day. And the stench. Miss Lacy would gag, and retch, and slip away senseless when it hit her. But more to the point, should the master find out, he would not only dismiss Rose, but send her no doubt on the first available convict ship to the other side of the world.

How to describe the indescribable. How to tell a child what the other side of the moon was like. For one must see a wonder, or a blemish, to understand and tell of its freakishness.

'It's not what yer used to,' was all Rose could manage. 'An' yer not goin',' she said.

But she should have known better. There was only one who could withstand Lacy Hemingway when she put her mind to it, and she lay placidly sipping chocolate in the

127

delightful conviction that Alexandrina was a changed person to the one who had wished so indecently to visit the shipyard a year earlier.

Lacy did nothing to disillusion her. She had taken to carrying her easel and paints outdoors, where she spent many hours sketching and painting – a most ladylike pastime, and one which served to persuade her mama that her youngest daughter was finally becoming what she had always envisaged. But Lacy's paintings were not just the pretty pictures her mama thought them. They were good with a delicacy which reminded the beholder of the fragile paintings etched on the vases and bowls which come from the East. A drift of blossom, a smudge of hyacinth in the shadow of the spinney, the outline, barely discernible, of a bird lifting on the wing. But, and to Lacy this was the most important thing, although she lost herself for hours in her work and loved it, it also gave her a legitimate excuse to be absent from the house, and alone, for hours on end.

Copper was always with her, and even Sarah Hemingway was forced to admit that the animal watched over his young mistress with the ferocity of a lion. His devotion to her was as tangible as the ground beneath her feet, and he was never more than an inch or two from the hem of her gown. He was a young dog, just over a year old now, but his instant obedience to a word or the click of her fingers was a credit to Lacy's patience in his training. Should some insolent fellow so much as look at her with an expression which the dog did not care for, he would be dispatched from her presence as fast as the animal could remove him.

He watched each face now, as the impending visit was discussed.

'We can take Copper. Old Lancer will be quite terrified,' Lacy said beguilingly. Rose was quite titillated by the idea, and it was perhaps this which swung her from a determined *No*, to an indecisive *perhaps*, and then to reluctant agreement. The picture of Lancer with Copper's teeth in his . . . Well, it would be worth it for that alone. And Lacy was right. No one would get within an inch of either of them with the dog to defend them.

'Please, Rose. Let me come. I can pretend to be sketching up in the wood, and listen. Oh, listen, Rose. I have a splendid idea.'

Lacy's eyes sparkled, and Rose felt herself drawn as she always was to the sheer exciting vitality which shone about her.

'Let us dress up as boys.'

She grinned wickedly as Rose gasped. Then, the plan fitting together in her mind like the petals of a flower, she began to explain.

That night, had any of the servants been on the top floor near the attics, or even lying sleepless in their beds, they might have thought the spirits of those gone before had come to haunt the great Hemingway house. Lights flickered, as the flames of candles moved in draughts from invisible cracks, and they might have seen a blur of white as a small form slipped around a corner. The pit-a-pat of feet, stealthy and hesitant, the squeak of an unoiled hinge as the lid of a chest was lifted, and soft laughter would have moved hair on scalps and prickled the skin. But none heard, for those who work from dawn to dusk, and many hours beyond, do not spend the night hours awake.

The following Sunday, after luncheon had been served, eaten, and the remains cleared away; when Papa had retired to his study, and Mama to her boudoir; when Amy, Margaret and Jane had announced that they were not in the least interested in a walk to Elm Wood; when Cook was dozing in a comatose state of exhaustion after her morning endeavours; and when Mrs Johnson had finally settled to the monthly housekeeping accounts in her room, the two 'boys' slipped from the summer house into the stand of trees to the side of the house, and climbed that first stile on the start of their journey.

It was all Rose could do to keep Lacy on the move when they reached the town. Of course she had seen organ grinders, and street musicians, hawkers, knife sharpeners, men with bears, monkeys and performing dogs. But only from a distance, and always from the safety of the carriage. Her steps slowed as she stared in fascination at the performers.

A blind penny whistler played a piercingly sweet tune and,

scarcely before she had time to consider it, she had reached into her pocket for a coin to throw into the cup which lay at his feet. She turned in surprise as Rose's hand clamped on her wrist, and her hissing voice told her to, 'keep yer 'and in yer pocket. D'yer want us fallen on?'

The hurdy-gurdy man had a dozen barefoot children about his instrument and Lacy's eyes were drawn to the half-inch-thick callus of skin upon their soles, built up from years of walking without shoes on setts and cobbles. They danced in little shuffling groups, their tattered garments swinging in a merry rhythm that was pitifully inappropriate.

When they reached Scotland Road, Lacy's hand crept into Rose's. The stares of those who lolled in open doorways and leaned against the dirty walls began to frighten her. Rose shook her hand free, whispering fiercely, 'Boys don't 'old 'ands round 'ere, Arthur.'

Copper walked quietly by Lacy's side, his flank brushing her leg. His ears moved constantly in the way that an animal has when it is uneasy, listening to the strange sounds which he had never heard before. The ring of steel-rimmed wheels on cobbles; the shouts, rough and angry; the screams of children; the sounds of harmonicas, bellringers and fiddlers; the noise of women arguing, and his instincts told him there was danger here. He nudged his head against the small hand which hung just by his nose, and was reassured when it grasped his collar. He would protect it, and his beloved friend, to the death. His beautiful coat gleamed in the sunshine, for it had been brushed that morning, as it was every day, by the brisk hand of Seth Arkwright's lad. And it was this, more than the sight of the two ragged boys, which drew the eyes of the inhabitants of Scotland Road. Boys, even those with shoes, were a common sight. But a glossy, well-groomed setter was not.

The dog's glance was captured by movements in the shadows of a house, and he longed to be away, chasing the sneaking, four-footed, long-tailed creatures who he knew to be his enemy. But he remained by Lacy's side.

They turned the corner into Naylor Street. Lacy felt her stomach begin to lurch. Her face was the colour of Cook's

130

pastry before it was put into the oven. She had felt a strong desire to vomit for the past ten minutes, as the stench became worse the deeper they got into the squalid district. Her feet had cringed from contact with the loathsome mess – she could think of no other word, for she knew none – which clung to them. The smell was so appalling it filled her head, her throat, her mouth, and her lungs. She could taste it, feel it clinging to her skin, creeping down beneath her collar, and up the arms of her coat sleeves.

She began to scratch vigorously. Clamping her lips tightly together, both to contain her feelings and her nausea, she continued to step with Rose. At the entrance to the courtyard in which her family lived, Rose stopped.

The close was empty, save for a starving cat and three children who attempted to catch it by the tail. Evidently the women of the hovels which lay about were indulging in a Sunday afternoon siesta, whilst their menfolk took themselves off to the bull-baiting which had attracted Lancer McGhee.

'Just a minute,' Rose whispered. 'Yer wait 'ere wi' Copper.'

Tiptoeing, as though Lancer might hear and come roaring back from wherever he might be, Rose skirted the dripping walls of the houses until she came to the area steps. She bent down, and Lacy saw her peep hesitantly through a window, the top of which could just be seen. As she did so, there was the sound of a door opening, and Rose stood up abruptly, backing away, ready to run. Copper's fur bristled, and he growled deep in his chest, but he stood like a rock at Lacy's side.

'Rose, Rose . . . Is it you, darlin'?'

A dark head, smoothed roughly into some appearance of neatness, rose above the step. A face, clean, smiling, apprehensive, peeped like a dormouse. In a moment, Rose was down the steps, and she and the dark head vanished.

Lacy stood indecisively where Rose had put her. Her hand trembled on Copper's head, and they leaned together for comfort. She glanced about as though feeling eyes upon

131

her, and jumped when Copper growled again and made a threatening lurch towards something which scurried against the wall.

Oh Rose, dear Rose, where are you? Her heart hammered. Please don't leave me out here alone. I am so afraid. It is so dreadful . . . The smell . . . I shall be sick in a . . . What is that . . ! Oh, Rose, Please, please . . .

'Lacy, Lacy. Quickly!'

A white hand waved from the shadow of the area steps, and Rose's anxious face flashed for a second between the bars. Holding the dog's collar, her feet slipping in some unmentionable horror which oozed from the small building in the centre of the courtyard, Lacy ran to the steps and stumbled down, clutching at Rose's steadying arm. In a moment she, Rose and Copper were all inside. Her heart pounded. The fun had long gone, sent scurrying away by the aura of fear, the anxious glances, the fidgety way in which Rose looked constantly over her shoulder, and by the surroundings in which Lacy now found herself.

Never in her wildest imaginings – like most young Christian girls of good family she had been told of the 'poor', and how one must do all in one's power to 'help' – had the pictures which crowded her lively mind been horrific enough, squalid enough, revolting enough to bring to life what she had seen today.

Bridie had evidently gone to some trouble to prepare for her daughter's return. A tiny fire crackled in the grate, and the kettle sat in its centre. The place had been swept and tidied, and the straw mattresses were stacked in a corner. But only a cursory wipe with a damp cloth had been passed over the table, the oven top, and Bridie herself. Although her face was sufficiently clean, dirt rested in the folds of her neck, along the rims of her eyes, and in and around her ears. As she reached out loving arms again to Rose, and her wrists were exposed, the line where cleanliness ended and filth began showed clearly. Fetching water was a chore which had evidently been given up long since, and the reason for it showed in the line of Bridie's figure.

She was in the last weeks of pregnancy.

Lacy stood beside the door which Rose had closed behind her, and watched as Rose and the filthy, fat old woman murmured, and hugged, and looked, and murmured again, and felt she was in a nightmare. Her eyes rested unbelievingly on the old table from which, in a moment of drunken rage, Lancer had knocked one leg. It teetered crookedly now upon one of the boxes which served as seats. The once white walls were green and black and grey, a mossy fungus growing on every inch of the surface. The floor was wet in places where water had seeped through, and the window at her back was so dimmed with dirt it might have been boarded up.

Rose turned absently to Lacy and indicated that she should sit down. Sean's chair was still there, basically unaltered since Sean had sat in it, for it had been battered even then. Edging around the table, the dog attached to her as though his nose was glued to her trouser leg, Lacy sat down by the fire. The woman acted as though she did not exist. A mug of tea was thrust into her hand, and she took it hesitantly, wishing she had brought a handkerchief with which to wipe around its brim. She sipped it gingerly, and gagged again on its bitter, sour smelling taste.

The woman, Rose's mother Lacy supposed, was speaking.

'. . . an' so we 'ad to be wed, acushla. 'E did the right thing by me,' she said propitiatingly, as though all that she had suffered at Lancer's hands was wiped out by this blessing he had bestowed upon her. 'An' 'e works hard.' Which was true, and the only virtue which could be attributed to him. '. . . so we don't starve . . .'

Rose looked as though she had been struck by a bullet and mortally wounded. Her face was like death itself. The shadow of the peaked cap she wore could not hide her expression of stupefaction, nor the raw despair which clouded her eyes.

Although she had as yet made no plan, she had been certain in her mind that in some way she would rescue her mother and the three little boys. One day soon she would fetch her from the hell in which she lived. She did not know when it would be, for it would take money to do it, and all

133

Rose had now was what she earned. But she was determined to go up in the world, and when she did, she would bring her mammy and the boys from here, and put them in a decent place. Until then, Bridie would find work and someone to see to her sons. Between them, Mammy and her, they would work and save and . . .

With a few words her mother had taken the bright innocent dream, the hope from her. She could have wept with the pain of it.

'. . . an' so we 'ad to be wed . . .' she had said.

The words went round and round inside Rose's head, and she felt dizzy and sick. The woman who had been loved with all his goodness by Sean O'Malley was tied forever to that foul beast, and Rose would never get her away. Never. Not her, nor the little boys, the sons of . . .

Rose turned swiftly, her crushed spirit surging to frantic life as some dreadful intimation of worse to come flooded over her. Her head swivelled from side to side, searching every corner of the squalid room and fear, terror washed over her in sickening waves. Terence? Seamus? Declan? Where were they? Oh, Sweet Mary. Where were they?

What had happened to her little brothers?

The last time she had come they had sat, tiny motionless creatures, in the rotting palliasse which was their bed, pale replicas of the impish rascals they had once been. Now they had gone. A terrible dread rose in her, and nausea threatened deep in her throat. Dear Mother, her eyes pleaded, tell me it's not . . . don't let him have . . .

'The boys, Mammy. The boys . .!' Her voice cracked.

Bridie McGhee's blue eyes became vacant. Her face was still as death. And when she spoke, the words came from lips which were as stiff and colourless as those of a corpse.

Rose began to cry even before Bridie had uttered the first sentence. She knew, without being told, that her little brothers had gone the same way as the rest of the family. As Bridie's words of horror whispered about the quiet room, she stared at something only she could see – some awful memory which numbed her senses. It was the only way she could bear it.

134

'Patrick went ter be a climbin' boy, Rose. 'E's eight years old now.'

'I know, Mammy. I know that. Yer told me the last time.' Tears ran unchecked from Rose's eyes.

'When we saw 'im in the street, Lancer asked the man 'oo 'ad 'im did 'e want any more, an' the man said ... Yer should 'ave seen me Patrick's poor little legs, Rosie, an' 'im all black from top ter toe, with only 'is lovely green eyes just like 'is Daddy shinin' in the soot. 'E began ter cry, an' said, "Mammy, don't let the man take Seamus." Then 'e ran away, an' I ran after 'im, an' Lancer an' the man couldn't catch us. We went inter the church, an' 'e showed me ...'

Her voice faltered, and her eyes widened with remembered pain. Then she reverted to her former trance-like state and continued. "E told me the man said 'is skin was too soft, an' it kept bleedin', Rosie, so 'e rubbed brine into Patrick's legs ter 'arden them, an' made 'im stand afore a hot fire, an' hit 'im with a cane. Patrick cried and cried, Rosie ...'

Her voice trailed away, Rosie's sobs stuttered in her throat, choking her.

'... When I got 'ome, I 'ad ter leave Patrick, Rosie. The man was there, an' Lancer, an' the man said they liked them small to go up the chimneys. There's not much room, yer see. So he took Seamus an' Declan ...'

Rosie's screams filled the room.

'No, no!'

Lacy jumped up dropping her mug, and Copper began to bark dementedly, terrified to savagery by the afternoon's outing and the creeping tension which filled the room. He backed against Lacy's legs, fiercely protective, his eyes wild and rolling.

Rose's screams continued.

Lacy was ready to flee. She scarcely knew what it was Rose and her mother talked about, but it was all becoming too much for her. With all her heart, she longed for the safety of the nursery.

'No, Mammy, no! Not Seamus, not Declan ...'

135

'Yes, child. Lancer got . . . a good price for them . . .'

'Don't, Mammy. Please don't. Yer didn't let 'im . . . And Terence? Not 'im as well? 'E's only two. Please, Mammy . . .'

Rose was incoherent in her grief. She began to hit out, striking her mother about the head and shoulders. Lacy flinched and moved as though to stop her. The dog barked, and with a terrified moan the girl sat down again, cowering to the back of the chair, her hands covering her white face.

Bridie sat, her words still flowing like the babble of water over the stones in a brook. Her daughter's blows had fallen upon her unheeded.

'. . . but there was nothing else for it,' she continued. 'I couldn't do the work, yer see, child. Not like this, an' Lancer likes me 'ere all the time. Fer when 'e wants me. All the time, even now, an' I prayed to the Holy Virgin to let 'im 'urt me, so that I wouldn't 'ave this one, but it's done no good. An' then there's Joseph. I've not 'eard a word from . . .'

'Terence, Mammy! Where's Terence?' Rose sobbed. She begged to be told that Terence was out in the yard, or with Mrs Geraghty, or anywhere, but that he would be coming in soon, with his bright eyes smiling in welcome, and his toddler's legs scrambling in his eagerness to get to her.

Bridie had stopped, the gush of her words suddenly corked. She looked about her with the air of one who gives her attention to the contents of a room in which she had never been before, then said abruptly. 'The fever came. A lot went that week. Mrs Geraghty's Liam, and Con Rafferty . . .'

The silence was appalling.

It lasted for several minutes. Even the dog was quiet now, as though he sensed he was in the presence of sudden death. Lacy shivered and thought longingly of her papa. Her words had been brave when she had begged Rose to bring her. What an adventure it would be. How exciting to see the way in which other people lived; those without the advantage she had. They existed in a state of poverty, she had been told, but in her naïvety she had not known what poverty really was. She had known the dictionary definition of the word, but she had not had the slightest notion of what it actually meant. She had known, for Rose had told her, that they starved. But the word was meaningless to one who ate more food in one meal than they did in a week. And dirt! Dirt to Lacy had been mud on one's shoes, or paint on one's fingers, or at worst, the manure which momentarily lay about the stable yard. Even the obnoxious aroma of cow dung which patterned the meadow beyond Elm Wood was as sweet smelling as lavender, compared to what she had known today. Brutality she had not even considered, for she had not known it to exist.

She hoped Rose would not be too long. She really did not think she could manage another moment, and besides, she wanted the water closet. But where . . ?

Lacy stood up awkwardly, putting the mug which she had retrieved from the floor where she had dropped it, upon the table.

'Rose,' she whispered.

Rose and Bridie turned wet and swollen faces towards her, their eyes dulled and lifeless. They seemed surprised to find her there, as though the tragic events Bridie had confided had driven out all but their own shared sorrow. Bridie looked at her indifferently, but in Rose's face there grew an awareness of who she was and what had brought them here, and the horror faded a little. She had brought this sheltered child into this, and she was responsible for getting her out of it. She had come with excitement and hope in her heart, convinced that she and Mammy would be planning their bright future together.

But that was all gone now. She had nothing. Her Mammy was lost to her, committed to the evil man she had married, and set upon another path than that which Rose would take. Rose had her job, her life to lead, and she must lead it alone. This was not her place now. This was *his* place. And in the midst of it sat Miss Alexandrina Victoria Hemingway, frightened out of her wits, and longing to be gone.

Lacy tried to smile.

'Rose, do you not think it is time to go home?' Her voice trembled. 'Mama will be wondering where I am.'

She turned to Bridie, and with the impeccable manners bred in her from infancy, she continued as though she were making her farewells to Sophie Osborne or Dorothy Bradley, who were Mama's dearest friends.

'Mama will be anxious should I not return soon Mrs . . . Mrs . . . er.' Bridie's name eluded her. Her fear and shock had taken her spirit and flashing mind, leaving her with only the conditioned reflexes of her class. Even the gift she had in her pocket for 'Rose's poor mama' was forgotten. She bobbed a curtsey, her hands feeling for her skirt, and was bewildered when she found none.

'Thank you, ma'am. It has been delightful, but I fear we must take our leave,' she parroted, the lines she had learned as a young child coming automatically to her lips. Mesmerized, speechless, Bridie watched her as she began to edge towards the door, the dog close to her heels.

Rose stood up and wiped her nose on her sleeve. She had retreated again under the spell of temporary shock, and her goodbyes, her soft kiss on her mother's cheek, were perfunctory. Like a doll, she performed the little ceremony she had gone through a dozen times or more in the last eighteen months, and Bridie was the same. For the moment, the strong family thread of loving care was frayed, and neither wanted to make a gesture or speak a word which might snap it.

'I'll send a note, child, when . . .'

'Yes, Mammy.'

'I'll say a prayer.'

The two small 'boys' melted up the area steps, silent as mist, the dog between them, and began to move across the courtyard towards the slip of alley which led to the street.

They did not speak, or touch, or even look at one another until the dog's warning growl brought them to a nervous stop. They were in a state of such dread that the sound of a leaf falling to the ground would have made them swoon.

But it was not a leaf at which Copper growled.

138

There were footsteps. Boots with iron tips on the cobbles, faltering and unsteady; and a thick, blurred voice cursed obscenely. There was a crash and a harsh cry; a dog yowled, and again the voice swore.

Rose clutched Lacy's arm in a grip so tight she gasped with pain. She turned as though to remonstrate, but before she knew what had happened she found herself being dragged backwards towards the small stinking erection which had excited her curiosity when she had first entered the yard. In a moment, she and Rose and the dog were flung this way and that in a heap of matter to which she could put no name, but whose smell and consistency made her faint.

She began to vomit.

'Quiet,' hissed Rose, holding Lacy's head down close to the slimy ground. Her terror was so great that she vomited the contents of her stomach without the slightest sound. Copper quivered by her side, his instinct telling him that this was no time for a show of bravery.

The squat, mumbling bulk of the man stumbled from the alley. It was evident from the state of his clothes that he had fallen in something nasty. His face, as hard and dangerous as a maddened beast, was smeared and filthy, and his tiny eyes pricked brutishly in his face. He reached the top of the area steps, and as the two little girls who cowered behind the privy peered, terrified, around its crumbling corner, he undid the front of his trousers, extracted his penis, and urinated in a long, thick, yellow stream down the area steps. Putting himself in order, he followed his own mess down to the basement door and fell inside, crashing it behind him.

'Come on,' breathed Rose, and rising up, began to run.

Together they went, the dog beside them. They never faltered as they sprinted, their feet gathering momentum as they fled. Their faces like chalk, eyes burning and enormous, as though they had seen the devil himself, they ran until their breath rasped in their throats and the pain of it seared them.

But they did not stop.

Heads turned in consternation as they passed, and mouths

hung open, but not until they reached Aigburth Road and the stile into the field did they slacken their pace.

During the whole silent, heart-pounding run, Rose cried broken-heartedly for the family she had finally lost.

# CHAPTER 10

They grew together.

Their brave hearts, their vital spirits, maturing characters and strong minds – so amazingly alike – bound them closer than sisters. Whilst the experiences, sorrows and terrors they alone shared fortified the two children, creating an even more fundamental and lasting bond.

They lived beneath the same roof, forming a friendship made more precious by its secrecy and, as the years passed, grew increasingly dependent upon one another, although they were at first innocently unaware of it. When they slipped away to the tiny beach that edged Charles Hemingway's estate, or crept silently amongst the tall trees in the spinney to while away a sweet half-hour in the dappled sunlight, they did not realize that each encounter placed another brick in the building of a relationship which was to stand until death. They were children, relishing the game of hide and seek; the clandestine meetings and the release from the confines of their enclosed world, be it for only moments at a time. The fractured hours they spent together were noticed by no one for who in their right mind, whether servant or family, would consider the possibility of an association between a scullery maid and the daughter of the man who employed her.

It was pity that had started it.

Although Lacy was a wilful, high-spirited girl, she had a warm and loving heart. Her first feeling for Rose had been one of compassion, but from that had grown sympathy and admiration, and she had felt compelled in some way to seek out the girl whose life impinged so strangely on her own. The courage of Rose, her fortitude and sheer blind determination to carry on, to beat what life had thrown at her, filled Lacy with awe. It made her think for the first time of her own character. Would *she* have the courage, should it be needed,

141

to take up the burdens of loss, loneliness and desperate anxiety that Rose knew and carried alone? She began more forcefully to question the rules and clichés which were trotted out a dozen times a day by those who had guardianship over her. And she began to appreciate that in some strange way she and Rose could draw upon one another; learn from each other, so that what each knew and understood could be shared.

What had begun as a delightful game, soothing Rose's wounded heart, and giving her something to which she might cling in the months following the visit to her mother, at the same time released the tension which gripped Lacy when she was forced to bend her will to that of her mama. Their friendship became vitally important to each. Without it, they might both have lost their composure and given way to the repressed emotions which grew in them.

The defeat Rose had felt when Bridie told her that she and Lancer were married had turned once more to determination, and she still had one compulsion: to rescue Bridie from Lancer McGhee. Had it not been for Lacy, she would have thrown caution to the winds and her own good sense to the chimney pots of Silverdale, and gone running the miles to Naylor Street in an effort to wrest her mother from the life she was forced to endure.

The little notes came occasionally. One when Lancer's son was born, another which told Rose that Bridie was pregnant again. Despair gripped her at this, for how was she, Rose, to support not only Bridie but two babies on what she earned? She re-doubled her efforts to please in Cook's kitchen, gaining another promotion from kitchen to parlour maid when she was fourteen, and clung tenaciously to her goal.

Lacy, growing from sweet and childish loveliness into the stunning beauty which was to be hers, was encouraging, loving and concerned, but cautious and strong in her determination to keep Rose from such folly.

Several times the paper with the simple drawings scrawled upon them informed Rose that Lancer was away from home, and she went to Naylor Street – without Lacy this time, for no amount of pleading would persuade Rose to take her again. She would spend an anxious hour with her mother and her growing brood of red-headed babies, on pins and needles in case Lancer should return. She saw, surprisingly, that Bridie was reasonably well fed, for in his bull headed way Lancer was vain of his good looking offspring, and saw that they ate decently. Although they had his bright copper hair, their eyes were as blue as once Bridie's had been, and their features were just as pleasing, with none of Lancer's granite countenance. Her maternalism returning, Bridie ensured they were all well cared for as had been her first family. They were strong and sturdy like their father, especially the boys, but his daughters were quaint little creatures with Bridie's volubility when they were allowed, and none of his temper. They seemed to have taken the best of both their parents

Bridie guarded them all with her white body, which still had the power to divert her husband when the drink was on him and his temper was cruel. She muddled along from day to day, living in a state of filthy squalor which appalled Rose on the few occasions she saw her. She sported many a black eye, and once a broken wrist which never mended properly, leaving her hand at an awkward angle from her arm. But she and her children, six in five years, survived and thrived, and Rose accepted sorrowfully in her heart at last that her brave dream was just that.

A dream.

'I know now I'll never get her away, Lacy. I suppose I've known for a long time, but I just couldn't face it.' Rose's expression became reflective as she gazed inwards at some lovely image.

'I always thought that when I had enough money I'd get her a cottage, perhaps round here.' Her hand indicated the countryside beyond the stream where she and Copper had once had a wetting. 'She could have found a bit of work and the boys, my own brothers I mean, not *his* . . .' She tossed her head scornfully, her eyes flashing at the idea of Lancer McGhee's progeny being related in any way to herself.

'She could have had a few hens, like we did in Ireland, even a pig. A bit of a garden with a vegetable patch, but it won't happen now. Six kids. Imagine, six kids to that devil. And more to come, no doubt. Oh, Lacy! What would me Daddy say if he could see what's happened to us all.' Her face was unutterably sad. 'All of us gone but meself.' Although Rose had unconsciously aped Lacy's way of speaking, and no longer slurred her words and mouthed the brogue of Ireland, now and again, when she was upset, a word or two of dialect slipped in.

''Tis sad, to be sure.' She shook her head in remembered pain, and her thick black hair moved like a velvet cape about her shoulders. Her back rested against the same tree trunk where she and Lacy had sat over five years ago. The dog was between them, and but for the change in the two girls from children to young womanhood, it might have been the same scene.

Shoulder to shoulder they sat, looking across to the full foliage of the trees on the far bank of the stream, and to the sheep-studded meadow beyond.

Lacy said nothing. She knew her presence, her sympathetic ear, her concern and affection were all that Rose needed at these times. Rose felt the necessity to speak like this at intervals, as though to ease what Lacy privately thought was guilt, although God knew she had no need of it.

Guilt that she could not complete what Sean would have wanted.

It was poignantly sad, Lacy thought, for how could a scullery, kitchen or parlour maid, no matter how hard she worked, bring about such a miracle? But, nevertheless, Lacy recognized what was in Rose's mind: that her inability – despite her determination – to succeed, scalded Rose's heart with remorse. If only Lacy could have helped. But she had no money, and could not even acknowledge her friendship for the girl, without causing further devastation by losing Rose her job.

Sometimes it was Lacy's turn. They fled to many places on her papa's estate, hiding in favourite sheltered corners

144

where no one came, talking endlessly of what they wished for in life.

'I feel so utterly useless, Rose. So stupidly, hopelessly useless. Where is the satisfaction in learning to dance the quadrille, to sing some foolish song about "sunshine and cloud, love, still there must be", or to play "The Lost Chord" for the amusement of Mama's silly friends? We are "wife material", that is all. Nothing but machines trained up to amuse and bear children and agree the sentiments and ideas of our menfolk to the last echo.

'The others love it so, Rose. Especially Amy. And of course Mama turns to me, and smiles and says pointedly, "Look what these accomplishments have brought to dear Amy", and all I can see is her boring fiancé, Edward Lucas. I feel like saying that if playing "The Lost Chord" has the effect of putting oneself into the arms of such an oaf, then I shall desist immediately. I asked Papa again yesterday if I might accompany him to his office. "Just to see it", I said innocently. But he saw right through me. He always does.'

She sighed gustily.

'He seems to have it fixed in his mind that every time I go anywhere it must be with Mama, or Miss Robertson, or Nanny. Am I never to have the company of a gentleman, Rose? Sometimes, after dinner, when we have guests and the gentlemen remain at table with their port and cigars, I slip from the drawing room and listen at the dining room door, and the conversation is fascinating. The ladies are discussing children, servants and fashion, or Her Majesty's latest addition. But the men . . . Oh, Rose! They talk of ships and railways and trade and soldiering, and so many things I do not understand but long to. Did you know there was a dispute between Russia and Turkey? Well, neither did I. But I mean to find out. Oh, if only . . .'

If only. If only. If only . . .

In the seclusion of the winter garden if the weather was inclement, or in a dozen secret places when it was dry, they would pour out their hearts to one another.

'If Mammy would only do a bit of a clean now and then, the

145

place wouldn't be too bad, Lacy.' Rose had dropped the 'miss', which should have preceded 'Lacy', long ago. 'But, no. She sits about, happy as a pig in muck, it seems. And her so fanatical once . . .'

'If I have to listen one more time to Mrs Bradley extol the virtues of her last grandchild, or hear again of the wonder of Amy's forthcoming nuptials to Edward, I shall run away to sea in one of Papa's ships . . .'

'. . . she makes me want to fetch her a good clout . . .'

'. . . Mama nearly had the vapours because the poor fool left his hat in the hall. Imagine, Rose, if you can, after all you have suffered and I have shared, being offended by the impropriety of not bringing one's hat into the drawing room . . !'

They used each other, in their affection, as valves which release steam when pressure is building up too dangerously, threatening to explode the machine it drives. Both were burnt up with a driving ambition to be other than they were; to be about something which was beyond them in their present world.

But both were totally ignorant of what that was, or how to attain it.

They stood about the lawn in their tight-fitting trousers, the young men, and as a concession to the temperature, their host permitted them to remove their jackets, which they slung carelessly over a shoulder. Their freshly laundered shirts shone white in the sunshine. It was very warm, and now and then one would surreptitiously wipe his sweaty brow or sticky palm with a pristine handkerchief.

Several jaunting cars and small traps had been lined up along the gravel drive, ready to be off when the last laden picnic basket was aboard. The hampers were filled with every delicacy which was considered necessary to tempt the appetite including pâté, lobster, pheasant, game pie, jellies, cake, biscuits, fruit and ices, bottles of hock and claret, and madeira for the ladies.

The servants stood in a row beside the grass verge, respectfully silent, a dark frieze against the variegated green of the shrubbery. There were two small phaetons waiting in the stable yard, should any lady feel the walk too much for her – it was quite a hundred yards or so to the summer house which stood at the edge of the vast lawn – and, piled neatly in the dog cart pulled by a docile grey pony, were rugs and Persian carpets to be spread upon the smooth grass, pillows and cushions, parasols and umbrellas, perchance the weather should turn inclement, and a great number of small folding chairs.

One might have been forgiven for thinking that an expedition was to be mounted across the vast wastes of the Sahara Desert.

James Osborne leaned gracefully against a cedar tree, one of those planted eighty years ago by Robert Hemingway, the present owner's grandfather. It towered above him, shading him from the heat of the noon sun, and he wished irritably that he had withstood his mother's persuasions to come. It was too damnably hot to be dressed up like a tailor's dummy, when he might have been cooling himself in the tumbling waters of the spring which erupted on the top of the hill behind his father's house. And all for the sixteenth birthday party of some child who would simper and blush, and to whom he must pay some attention, for she was the daughter of his mother's oldest friend.

It would be solitary up on the gentle hill, surrounded by trees, dappled and still in the windless day; with the green slope winding up to the scatter of boulders which lay at its summit, hiding the ice cold stream and his own naked body from all eyes save those of the swift and lark which flew there. He sighed deeply, and shifted his booted foot to rest upon the tree trunk at his back.

His tall figure, although slender still with a young and athletic man's suppleness, had an arresting, vigorous physique. He looked splendid in his well-made whipcord breeches. He had ridden over that morning from Highcross, his parents' home, and the occasion being considered informal, it was recognized that he was not required to change. His shirt was open at the neck and he had loosened his cravat, revealing a firm brown throat. His sun-darkened face was strong, almost aggressive, in its masculine beauty. His hair was a deep chestnut brown, short, curly and unfashionable in its unruliness, for he scorned the scented pomatum with which most gentlemen of his acquaintance smeared their locks. His eyes were thickly lashed and a rich melting brown, especially when they observed a pretty woman, the pupils big and black. They were usually merry and unconcerned, for James enjoyed the life he led. But today he was prepared to be bored, and his demeanour showed it.

He was the second son of Richard and Sophie Osborne, and although he was wealthy in his own right, due to an inheritance from his maternal grandmother, he had no expectations of his father's vast business estate. His elder brother, Matthew, would have it all.

Indifferent to his lack in this direction, at the age of eighteen he had entered the Military Academy as a cadet, had purchased a commission, and through eight years of soldiering had seen some active service in South Africa, and had served in Ireland. It had all been enormously enjoyable, but since Waterloo Europe had been at peace, and the British Army fought mostly in her colonies. James had been too young for the wars in Afghanistan, or the Sikh wars of the 'forties against the Lion of the Punjab. Still he had, as he nonchalantly put it, seen a skirmish or two.

He was shortly to rejoin his regiment, and was secretly longing to be away, for the tedium of this parochial life had him yawning.

There would be a war soon, of that he was convinced. The Russians were making threatening overtures towards Turkey, eager to carve up the tottering Ottoman Empire. Her claim was that she wished to protect the interests of the fifteen million or so Greek Orthodox citizens of the Turkish Empire. There were squabbles over certain Christian shrines and religious sites in the Holy Land, and early in the year, the Tsar had dispatched his envoy to Constantinople, where he was joined by the Russian Admiral commanding the Black Sea fleet. Russia threatened war on Turkey, and Britain was desperate to keep the port of Constantinople from their hands. The situation looked alarming, and already France and Britain were gathering troops to send to the Dardanelles.

Captain Osborne was convinced it would not be long before he saw some *real* action, and he could scarcely wait. He stifled another yawn and sneaked a third look at his watch.

The sunshine washed the back of the house and the beautifully ordered garden with gold-edged brilliance. The lawn on which a dozen children, some of them his own nieces and nephews, played a sedate game of 'tig' watched by several starched nannies, was a vivid green. It had been watered early that morning by the gardening boys in order to give it time to dry out for today's events. Fuchsia frothed its scarlet bells, frail clappers hanging delicately from within against the dark green of the yew hedge. Wisteria climbed like a curtain against the house wall, a dense violet blue, its fragrance brought out by the heat of the sun. Below were lupins, vividly pink, and roses and massed stocks, and in hanging baskets at each side of the open French windows, verbena breathed out its lovely scent.

It was into this setting that she came.

The older men, waiting patiently for wives who were supervising the assembly of the young unmarried girls come to honour Alexandrina Victoria Hemingway on her birthday, stood in groups beneath the shade of the trees. Here and there comfortable chairs had been arranged for the relief of the young married women, who no longer mixed with their unmarried friends, but sat with their own kind, excluded from the excitement of demure flirtation. Even chaperoned as they were, an unmarried girl might still find the thrill of a bold glance upon her, and should her mama look away for an instant, the glance might be returned. Married ladies, however, were forever denied this small pleasure, and must make do with babies, husbands and nannies.

'Whatever do they do with themselves, do you suppose, to take such an interminable time in there? One would imagine they were making their own gowns, the time it takes.'

James turned, smiling, and looked into the world weary

face of Thomas Hemingway. Thomas lounged indolently beside him, resting a hand upon the trunk of the tree, as though the very act of standing was too tedious for words. His eyes were glazed, whether with the heat or boredom James could not tell, but he looked with as little interest as James towards the French window through which the young ladies would come.

'I don't know why I allow Mama to drag me into these family affairs, I really don't. Especially after the night I have just spent in Juniper Street. You know the place, James, the one where . . .'

'Yes, I seem to remember being there a time or two.'

James grinned amiably as he spoke, his good white teeth flashing in his brown face. So that was it. Master Thomas was not only bored and hot, but hung over. He had heard rumours that the young man had a fancy for lively horses and livelier ladies, and was to be found on most evenings at some gaming table. What a life. Thank God he did not have to live it. There was some advantage to being a younger son. One might not inherit the family estate, but one could pick the kind of life one preferred. Although he had been as wild as Thomas at his age, and was still able to enjoy the boisterous parties which his fellow officers engaged in, he found at the age of twenty six that he was beginning to lose his taste for the foolish pranks which others considered such good fun.

Thomas was speaking again, his eyes barely focused on the French window.

'I swear, if I have to sit beside those frumpish sticks the Bradley daughters, I shall die of ennui. Now promise me, James, if you should see me cornered, you will have the goodness to rescue me. I beg of you, if you value our friendship . . .'

James, five years older than Thomas, and not aware that in the past they had been such chums, was about to concur – for what did it matter who he sat with? Each young lady would be as boring as the rest. Young unmarried girls always were – when Thomas straightened hurriedly, his papa's eyes upon him.

'Here come the ladies, James. Stiff upper lip, old chap.'

The two young men leapt politely to attention.

They were like a cloud of butterflies, drifting and insubstantial in the benevolent sunshine. The wings of their wide skirts of creamy white, palest lemon, flush of pink and tender blue swung and dipped to reveal the tips of their satin slippered feet. They skimmed gracefully in their tulle and muslin and tarlatan over the shaved green smoothness of the lawn, arranging themselves in nosegays of colour before parting to move separately, or in pairs, towards the gentlemen.

She was the last to step from the doorway. She had the light, almost wary tread of a fawn. Not cautious, more with an air of one who suspects that a delightful danger lies ahead but is prepared nevertheless to enjoy it. Most of the others were graceful, although some, like the Bradley girls, moved with the awkwardness of sticks pinned together at the joints. But she had an added fluency which drew the eye to the elegance of her straight back, the proud tilt of her head, and the sweet girlish curve of her shoulders. Her small breasts, thrust forward by her upright carriage, showed clearly beneath the bodice of her gown. The others were demure, their eyes for the most part ingenuously cast down, even amongst those they knew. But she looked about her with keen interest, her glance filled with bright expectancy and warmth. She showed none of the restraint inculcated into young girls of good family, and where the others peeped from beneath lowered lashes as was proper, she stared directly into his eyes. In the years to come, he was always to remember his first thought and smile, for he was to be proved right time and time again.

'I imagine her Mama has trouble with this one.'

Her beauty took his breath away.

He had known her almost from the day she was born. Although he was ten years older, he had noticed her vaguely as she grew. She had been elfin, dainty and ethereally pretty, the daughter of his mama's dearest friend, but he had not seen her since the day he had become a soldier. She had been eight years old then, a little silvery thing with the penetrating gaze of a curious kitten, and he had been amused by her

151

continuous flow of eager questions regarding his forthcoming departure for the army and the wonderful – her word – career he was to have.

Now he saw her for the first time, as a man sees a woman.

She wore cream muslin striped with cream silk. The skirt of her gown was full with a tight waist, around which was fastened a narrow, golden, velvet ribbon. Balloon sleeves flowed gracefully from her shoulders, ending at her fragile elbows in a binding of the same colour as her sash. The neckline was modest, high and boat-shaped, from which her white neck rose, slim and delicate as a flower stalk.

Her hair was like nothing he had ever seen. A mixture of silver and gold and pale streaked amber, as though sunshine had become trapped in it, and so thick and curly it hung to her waist like a living curtain of silk. A narrow golden ribbon held it from her face, leaving tiny ringlets in a bunch over each ear. She wore a wide-brimmed cream straw hat with a flat crown, which tipped over her forehead, the golden velvet of its ribbons framing her face and tying in a bow beneath her chin.

Her eyes were the colour and transparency of crystal, like moonlight on water; the pupils deep and black. They pierced him with their steadfast gaze, and he could not look away.

Her skin was the cream which tops the milk; the curve of her cheekbone flushed to palest rose; and her mouth was full, with lips soft and parted. They looked almost bruised, bee-stung, and if he had not known her for the innocent, un-touched girl she was, he would have sworn she had just spent the past half hour being thoroughly kissed.

They looked at each other across the stretch of garden, and she began to walk towards him, smiling with pleasure. It started then for him.

Sophie Osborne and Sarah Hemingway watched them, then turned to nod complacently at one another.

The several nannies who shepherded their flock from spot to spot about the wide lawn were engrossed in their work. Nanny Wilson, bereft of infant these past ten years and eager to share in another, was so enthralled in the details of the latest

152

Osborne grandchild that she did not see Lacy go. Sarah Hemingway, too old for picnics, she declared with an arch smile at the gallant Captain Osborne, had returned with Sophie to the comfort of her salon, secure in the knowledge that her troublesome youngest daughter was in good hands. And Charles, overcome by the heat and the several glasses of hock he had imbibed, had dropped off in his chair, his hat comically askew upon his nodding head.

James saw her slip away to the edge of the trees at the back of the summer house. She turned, looking to see if anyone had noticed her, then vanished into the green tunnel beneath the motionless canopy of leaves.

They had been seated together at the picnic. James had been startled, and faintly alarmed, when she had asked him in forthright fashion for his opinion on the possibility of war between England and the Allies and Russia.

'It seems to me,' she said calmly, 'that Russia considers most of the Turkish Empire to be her own, and the news that Prince Menshikov has issued an ultimatum to the Sultan regarding the Turkish troops is most worrying. Do you not think so, James? Will we fight? Will our troops go?'

James, who longed only to compliment her on her attractions, to flirt in the way one does with a pretty woman, had barely time to recover from that bombshell and attempt to answer coherently, when she launched another, asking about his soldiering, questioning him on his garrison duties in Ireland and the discontent there. She was most concerned, she said, regarding the morality of shooting natives in South Africa, when they were only doing what any Englishman would do in the same circumstances in defending what was theirs. Did he not agree?

Just as he was beginning to think himself saddled with a blue stocking, she proceeded to delight him with a wickedly humorous description of last Sunday's visit to church, where, made soporific by the warm sunshine which fell upon him through the window, Parson Adams had leaned comfortably back in his pulpit, and fallen into a light doze in the middle of his sermon. The consternation which had befallen the congregation in the small church was drawn with such vividness that James felt himself to be there, and his laughter turned all heads towards them.

He was fascinated by her clever tongue, inexperienced and lacking sophistication as she was; by her quicksilver mind, and by the fount of knowledge she had stored in her young head. She seemed to be cognisant of not only the current affairs of her own country but also of most of what was happening abroad. It appeared that recently her papa had allowed her *The Times* when he had done with it. His library was at her disposal, she said, and she was going to read every book in there before she was twenty.

'I started as soon as I was able to read,' she said impishly, her grey eyes shining into his. He felt himself lean forward unconsciously drawn towards her by a force he could not control.

'I used to slip downstairs after I had been put to bed, and take the first book I could reach from the shelf nearest to the door. I waded through *The Decline and Fall of the Roman Empire* before I was seven years old, desperately trying to grasp its meaning, and convinced because I could not that I must be half-witted. Aah, but when I reached the Waverly novels, then I was rewarded for my devotion. What a joy . . .'

He watched her, bewitched to the point where he felt himself to be a green schoolboy again. He tried to recapture the tatters of his earlier longing to be back with his regiment – heart whole, carefree – the feeling of being his own man. But could not. She had a freshness, a delightful directness and simplicity which captured his attention as no woman had before, although he had known many. She seemed to care neither for etiquette nor the rules of polite society, and during the meal he was bewildered to see her turn her head away and smilingly wink at one of the serving maids.

The maid winked back.

Intrigued he tried to capture the eye of the young girl who took his empty plate from him, but she turned away as though in defiance. He felt so lighthearted he might have been

154

sixteen again, and he smiled to himself. The day became more interesting by the minute.

Lacy encouraged him to talk of himself, to tell her of the countries and peoples with whom he had been concerned. She was so obviously enthralled with his words that he found himself recounting incidents, feelings and emotions he had told no one of before. Her eyes were serious, full of compassion, as he spoke of the deaths of his comrades in minor skirmishes in Africa, and of the cholera and malaria which decimated the ranks of the ordinary soldier. His feelings for the men he commanded, which he had revealed to no one except the men themselves, shone in his eyes as he spoke to her of the harsh discipline they suffered, and of the meagre wage they received for death or mutilation in the service of their country. She reached out and touched his hand gently, as he told her of their courage and fortitude in lands far from the green and gentle place where they were born.

They were interrupted by Thomas, who came to share the rug on which they sat. As James turned politely, silently cursing the young man for breaking the spell, Lacy slipped away.

'What do you say to an evening in Juniper Street, James?' Thomas asked. 'This is your last, is it not? I can promise you some good sport, my dear fellow, although I fear I have not the, er . . . My dear Papa has decided I must manage on my allowance, and will not advance me another guinea. It is devilish tricky to enjoy oneself on the pittance he allows me, and I shall be deuced glad when I reach twenty one and can draw on the money Grandfather Thomas left me. Imagine having to wait until one is twenty one before . . . Hey, where are you going! Did I say something, my dear chap . . .? There is no need to dash . . .'

But James, with a mumbled apology, was gone, and Thomas was forced to return to the company of his brother Robert, who was flirting decorously under the watchful eye of the family Nanny with Alice Taylor, seventeen and palely pretty.

The dim, chequered tunnel through the narrow strip of woodland beckoned to James, and he stepped lightly across the soft bed of grass and wood anemones, skirting a thicket which stood guard. It was delightfully cool. The greenwood swallowed him up. As he drew further into it, the subdued murmur of the party faded, and all James could hear was the chatter of a finch in a holly bush, the friendly drone of a browsing bee as it busied itself in a tangle of celandines, and his own light breathing.

Where the devil had she gone?

He came to a tiny clearing, where the trees stood back to allow in the benign warmth and light of the sun. It illuminated the variegated shades of the leaves from pale, pale lime, to willow green and apple, and the dark colour of holly. Dogwood grew in profusion and, trailing like the delicate lace of a shawl, fern hung from oak and beech and maple.

But that was not all.

Draped on the branch of a chestnut tree, like a huge bell about to be rung, was the crinoline, horse hair and whalebone, with which the fashionable lady of the day must dress if she was to be considered at all stylish. Beneath the branch on which it hung, flung this way and that, as though the wearer had discarded them in some hurry, lay two small slippers and a pair of cream stockings.

James stared in astonishment, his face a study of mixed emotions. Consternation opened his mouth to foolish proportions, indicating that he had never seen the like before, although he had helped many a pretty lady in the removal of certain such articles of clothing.

He moved slowly across the clearing and picked up a satin slipper, stained green from the juicy grass. It was still warm. He began to smile, the corners of his mouth twitching in a most personable way. His teeth gleamed, and his eyes grew a deep, deep, brown as the laughter began to rumble in his chest.

But he must make no sound. Not for the world would he raise the alarm and warn the girl, whatever she was up to. No, he must see this for himself.

What a girl!

What a woman!

Well, not just yet, perhaps. But soon, soon. And when she was, he would be there. He had not realized when he had seen her – was it only two hours ago? – that she was something special. But this escapade proved that her courage, her sense of adventure, and of rebellion against the silken chains which bound her, put her on a different plane to that of her contemporaries. How many of the young misses back there would have the nerve to . . . do what? What was she doing? What was Miss Lacy Hemingway up to, running about without her crinoline, and her shoes and stockings discarded like so much surplus weight? His thoughts became confused and darting. Surely, it could not be a man . . .

James Osborne felt the joy drain from him.

He was badly affected by the vision of the lovely girl who had held him spellbound for two hours in the arms of another man. Putting the little slipper back where he had found it, he began to walk on through the spinney in the direction of the river, and the tiny private beach which ran along Charles Hemingway's estate. James could barely force one foot in front of another. He had only just found her. Surely she was not to be snatched away before he had even had time to realize the extent of the emotions she aroused in him. She was so young, only sixteen. It was not conceivable that already she was versed in the charms of loving.

He would not believe it.

A sound broke his angry reasoning, and with it went the terrible speculation which for several moments had filled him with such panic. It was as though something precious, taken from him just as he had found it, had been restored by the joyous sound which rose above the tree tops, startling several wood pigeons, who took to the wing in fear.

Laughter. Two girls laughing.

James could hear Lacy's ringing tones, recognizing them instantly, for she showed her amusement with none of the polite ladylike smiles of her fellows, but opened her mouth and revealed her teeth and threw back her head, and made, at

157

least to her mama's ears, a great deal of noise. The second girl's laughter he did not know. But he was not on friendly terms with any of the young ladies in that afternoon's group, except for his own sisters, and this was none of them, of that he was certain.

He came at last to the edge of the trees, stepping lightly on the rough grass which led to the narrow strip of beach. It was low tide, and the sparkling water, touched by the sun to silver grey, had left a flat, rippled stretch of dark golden sand, wet and gleaming. Small pools had collected, shallow and warm, and it was in one of these that they splashed. They held their bunched skirts about their thighs to prevent them becoming wet, for Lacy's, without the width of her crinoline, was at least six inches too long. Their legs were luminously white in the spray-filled sunshine.

'Ssh! Oh, ssh,' Lacy was imploring the young girl with her, whom, astonishingly, James recognized as the maid at whom Lacy had winked during the picnic. The maid was wiping her eyes on the corner of her frilled apron in a paroxysm of mirth.

'Oh hush, Rosie, please! If we do not stop someone will hear us.'

More shrieks, and James looked around, for she was right. They were not far from the genteel place where the others were collected, and if they kept it up, these two helplessly laughing young girls, Charles Hemingway would be sure to come and investigate the sounds which pierced the air. And, no doubt, the rest of the company would be with him.

'Please, Rosie, be quiet. Now, stop it. Do not make me laugh any more, I beg of you. I know it is our birthday, but . . . Oh, Lord, I'm going to have hysterics! I shall wet my drawers if you . . .'

James felt laughter, and some other exquisitely painful emotion, squeeze his heart. He had never thought that he would know the day when he would meet, in his own class, a girl who was not only beautiful and clever, but who also had a sense of humour to match his own. His Mama had often reprimanded him for his riotous sense of fun, his ability to laugh at the ridiculous, and he had despaired of finding someone who shared his characteristic. Lacy did not know he listened, of course. She thought herself alone with the servant. But she spoke those 'unmentionable' words with all the casual ease of one who has that slight touch of humorous crudity which is the essence of a successful sexual relationship between a man and a woman. It was a small thing, and not one which would be considered by most when choosing a mate, for men of his acquaintance required a perfect lady to take to wife.

But not James Osborne.

He stepped from the cover of the trees and began to laugh. He watched in delight as the two girls froze into stillness, their backs towards him. It was as though they were afraid to turn to see who intruded into their simple pleasure, and for a moment he was startled by the rigid fear which showed plainly in both still figures. Neither moved as he walked across the firm sand towards them.

'Lacy,' he said softly.

At last she knew who it was, and as she turned, her relief was so evident, that again he was bewildered. What harm was there in laughing with a young maid servant? Particularly if they shared a birthday, which seemed apparent from the words they had uttered before they saw him. But she was so obviously afraid, he almost held out his arms to her as one would to comfort a child.

Instantly, both girls stepped from the pool of water, letting their skirts fall hurriedly. But their alarm, receding now, seemed not to care much for modesty. Four bare, white feet peeped from beneath full skirts.

Lacy was quite incoherent in her relief.

'Oh James. You devil. We thought, we nearly . . . If it had been . . .' She turned to her companion. 'You frightened us both to death, did he not, Rose?' She took her maid's hand most affectionately, even protectively, and again James was surprised.

'You see, Rose and I . . . Well, we are both sixteen today, you see. Rose is . . . a parlour maid, and when we realized we were born on the same . . .' She became confused and turned again to Rose, who as yet had not spoken.

'. . . we thought it would be nice for Rose, well I did . . . That is, I have brought her some birthday cake, as she is . . .' Her voice trailed away, and James was increasingly aware that some desperate anxiety was making her inarticulate, a trait he had not noticed before.

Then for the first time, James looked at Rose O'Malley and she at him, and again, as it had when he looked at Lacy, his breath left his body. She was not beautiful in the accepted sense, as Lacy was, but her face was as arresting, her figure as fine, and he could not seem to drag his eyes away.

She was the opposite to Lacy in every way.

Her hair was a rich, dark, curling brown, almost black, falling about her shoulders in a tangle. The droplets of sea water caught there, glittering like tiny diamonds. Her face was heart-shaped, broad of brow, pointed of chin, and her skin as white as paper. Her huge, tilted emerald green eyes looked as though some sooty finger had outlined them, and her mouth was as red as a ripe raspberry. She was as tall as Lacy, but, like her mother before her, full-breasted, with a handspan waist above hips which, with maturity, would become wide and curving.

She looked at him, spirited as her young mistress, eyes flashing, defiant chin lifted, and James' first coherent thought was that she had no need of Lacy's protective hand. A cloud shifted across her face, and her eyelids lowered. The expression in them was unreadable, which was just as well, for Rose O'Malley loved James Osborne from that moment.

James returned his gaze to Lacy, and as he did so, Rose looked up again. She was wiser than Lacy in the ways of men. She mixed with the male servants, and listened to the talk, and knew, although she had no personal experience of it, of the minds of men in love. She recognized something in James's expression as he looked at Lacy. Something joyous, yet reverent. His gaze was warm and gentle, at the same time ablaze and urgent. His feelings shone luminously from his smiling face, and his mouth moved and lifted, mobile in its urge to be about something of which even he, at that moment, was scarcely aware. But Rose knew, and her heart lurched with pain. It was plain to see that James Osborne loved Lacy Hemingway.

And yet, in that fraction of a second when he had looked into Rose's eyes, she had seen something in his own that had spoken of his interest. Before he turned back to Lacy, she had felt the intensity of his regard, and had known that he was, in that moment, passionately aware of her. For a split second, he had recognized her, had experienced the same shock as herself.

But it was Lacy who claimed him.

James Osborne spoke to Charles Hemingway that night.

'I realize that she is young, sir, and for that reason I am taking the liberty of asking you if I might wait a year before speaking to her. She is not aware of my interest, and I do not wish to startle her, but I would like you to know of my hopes. I wish to be completely honest and honourable. Lacy is very special. I will be away at first light. As you must be aware, there will be trouble in the Balkans. I do not know when I shall return, but I would like to know that . . .'

He smiled with the joy of his first love, and his mouth, which was strangely vulnerable in a face so strong, trembled.

'. . . I appreciate that this is very sudden, but Lacy has become dear to me. I have the greatest respect for her. I pray you do not think me precipitate.'

'Not at all, my boy. Our families have been friends for years, and your father and I have always hoped that perhaps one of you would . . . Well, now you are the only Osborne still unmarried, so . . .' Charles grasped James' hand and wrung it fervently. '. . . Have you spoken to your father?'

'Not yet, sir. If I may, I should like to ask you if you would allow this to be our . . . Well, I should not like Lacy to hear from any other lips but mine how things are. If a word were to be dropped, however unintentionally . . .'

'Of course, dear boy. Of course. But I trust you will remember she is only a . . . Well, James, nothing that might upset her susceptibilities, you understand.'

James smiled inwardly. He doubted whether Lacy's

161

susceptibilities were so easily upset, but he agreed, his face serious, and Lacy Hemingway's future was disposed of.

Like a beloved possession, she was handed over by her father, with no thought beyond pleasure that she had found a good home.

# CHAPTER 11

Amy was to be married to Edward Lucas in September. She and her sisters had gone that day to their mama's dressmaker and milliner in Bold Street, to choose the headdresses the bridesmaids would wear.

The Misses Yeoland had Parisian flowers and feathers, wreaths and bouquets, and were renowned for their ingenuity in turning a scrap of lace and a length of satin ribbon into the most charming headdress. Mama, Amy, Margaret and Jane were enraptured as the elder Miss Yeoland drew pretty designs, and made clever suggestions as to the kind of flowers which would be most suitable.

'All in white, you say, Mrs Hemingway?'

Sarah nodded, and six heads bent once more over the samples of lace, ribbon and pale feathers which lay upon the round, chenille-covered table in the salon. The room was elegant with soft carpets, beautifully draped curtains at the long windows, fresh flowers, and gilt-framed mirrors everywhere – in order that clients might more easily see how charming they had become, under the ministrations of the Misses Yeoland.

The two sisters catered only to the enormously wealthy.

'Perhaps I might suggest fresh flowers, Madame. I know you to have a magnificent winter garden at Silverdale . . .'

Sarah preened.

'. . . so if I might be allowed to view what you have growing there, I could make further suggestions and design a most becoming and original headdress for each of your daughters. Fresh flowers would be most unusual, particularly at that time of year.'

Sarah was enchanted. To be the harbinger of a new fashion would be quite a feather in her cap, and she was pleased by the flattering remark about her winter garden – for which in reality she could take no credit, for it was Lucinda Fraser Hemingway, her husband's mama, who had designed and had carried out the work on it. A thought struck her.

'But will they not become jaded, Miss Yeoland? A fresh flower does not remain so for long.'

Miss Yeoland, as elegantly dressed as her client, but plain and neat, for it would not do to compete, had the whole matter worked out in her clever head. That was how she and her younger sister prospered. To be one jump ahead, not only of her clients, but also of her competitors, was the secret. Politeness, calmness and courtesy all counted, of course, but they were not enough. One must always be able to meet with any event or emergency, however small or large, as the occasion arose. And this was just such an occasion. Not only would her headdresses be seen by all society at the wedding of the daughter of one of Liverpool's most prominent families, but also she would be allowed into their home. And if she played her cards correctly, she might be asked to take tea, and where might that not lead?

'Dear Mrs Hemingway,' she coo-ed, 'do not give it another thought. Do you think that such an important occasion as this will find us wanting? Having found exactly the right blossom for each of your daughters, I will instruct your gardener, and early on the morning of the . . .' she simpered archly, '. . . *special* day, he can bring them to us and we will guarantee, my sister and I, that all four will be ready, fresh as a daisy, ha ha, at the wedding hour. I myself will deliver them, and affix them to the young ladies' hair.'

Miss Yeoland the elder warmed to her theme, whilst Miss Yeoland the younger, who had no head for business, but who was the finest needlewoman in town, looked on admiringly.

'May I advocate a different shade of flower for each bridemaid. White, of course, for the bride. Perhaps camellias.' She smiled silkily at Amy, who preened and smirked. 'But the palest of . . . hmmm, let me see . . . Miss Margaret has such fine blue eyes, and Miss Jane's hair . . .'

Lacy thought she would scream.

What a nauseating woman Miss Yeoland was, with her

flattery, and compliments, and silly, simpering manner! Surely Mama and the girls could not be taken in by her smooth blandishments, her fawning references to Margaret's lovely blue eyes and Jane's mousy hair. It was as plain as the plain nose on Amy's plain face that the woman's honeyed words were meant only to obtain more orders. No one could honestly believe all that *blarney*, as Rose would call it. And what would be the fulsome compliment paid to herself, she wondered, when it came to her turn to be picked over for some colour to match her eyes, or her hair, or the pimple she was determined to get on her chin. She never had pimples, or any sort of blemish, but she was going to produce one for Amy's wedding. Just to spite them all.

She rested her head against the window frame, and stared dispiritedly into the busy street below, watching the carriages which moved in both directions along its length. It was a fine, wide street, the most fashionable in town, renowned for its elegant shops, and the gay and gallant socialites who promenaded its thoroughfare. Only fifty years ago it had been a grassy area called 'Brooksfield', but when it was built up and the fine shops appeared it had been re-named Bold Street, in honour of Peter Bold, the seventeenth century mayor.

Beautifully dressed ladies alighted from their carriages, helped by footmen, and the roadway became quite blocked as those who stopped to shop held up those who passed along to Church Street. Confusion was caused as two carriage horses coming from opposite directions took exception to one another, and the faint shouts of a carter trying to go about his business could be heard as he was frustrated from doing so.

A police constable in a dark blue coat and red waistcoat moved through the mêlée, issuing orders, doffing his tall black hat politely to impatient ladies in carriages, and sorting out the consternation in moments. He was posted there for that particular purpose, for it would not do to have the gentry hindered.

The sun broke through the clouds, shining brightly on the polished metal buttons of his swallow-tail coat and on his white duck trousers. It brought into bloom a positive sea of parasols, as the ladies protected themselves from its damaging rays. It danced on polished windows and touched to fiery chestnut the fine coats of the horses which pulled Lacy's mama's carriage. They stood in front of the window of the downstairs salon, and Arkwright the coachman tenderly stroked each soft nose, patting the animals to patience.

The padded window seat was comfortable. Resting her back against the matching cushions, Lacy let her mind drift away on the tide of utter boredom which occasions such as these afforded her. She was seventeen now and still, as she put it herself, in prison. 'A life sentence', she often said to Rose, but always allowed herself the luxury of believing that one day she would truly 'escape'.

But she did not know how.

She still attempted to cajole Papa into allowing her to go with him to his office; or to the warehouse where his cargo of cotton was stored; to the place of his cotton broker in Sweeting Lane; to the Exchange; to America on a packet ship; to London to see the Queen; anywhere, *anywhere* which would take her from the mind-numbing, stifling life that she and her sisters led.

She knew she had reached the age when young men would be trotted out for consideration in the marriage stakes, and her heart beat with dread at the thought. But, strangely, this had not yet happened. In fact, whenever some young hopeful, even the most suitable, began to show more than a friendly interest in her – and there were not a few – Papa seemed somehow to steer the bewildered fellow in the opposite direction. Not that she minded. Far from it. Once she was married, she would lose forever any chance she might have of doing anything but bearing children, and visiting the same everlasting soirées and garden parties that she went to now. She would be trapped into the life all the ladies of her acquaintance accepted as normal. She would have callers, and return them, and rear her children, and oversee the housekeeping, and be *bored out of her mind*.

To be bored was the worst affliction that could befall Lacy

Hemingway, and as she constantly suffered it, she complained of it to all who would listen, but it did her no good.

However, at least whilst she remained unmarried there was still hope And at the balls she attended she might accept dances all night, each one with a different man; and laugh; and if she could elude Mama's eagle eye, flirt a little, which was fun.

Both Margaret and Jane had suitors. Margaret's engagement to John Bradley, the son of a business associate of Papa, was to be announced after Amy's marriage. Jane would be next, which left herself, only a year younger and still, as Nanny put it, slightly alarmed, 'on the shelf'. She was surprised really, for at her age the Papas of most girls had someone in mind for their daughters. Do not look a gift horse in the mouth, she often told herself. Cherish the little freedom you have, and stop wondering why you have it.

A tall officer in a bright scarlet jacket crossed the road in front of the carriage, bowing gallantly to some ladies, who nodded smilingly. His shako, gleaming with gold lace, was set at a jaunty angle on his smoothly brushed hair, and a scabbard hung from his belt, tapping his leg as he walked. Lacy leaned forward eagerly, for it was an unusual sight. All the young officers were fighting in the Crimea. As she watched him stride along the pavement, her heart filled with pity, for the young soldier had only one arm. His empty sleeve was pinned up neatly, and she wondered in which battle he had been wounded. Names she had read in papers and in James' letters sprang to her mind.

Odessa. Varna. Silistria. Giurgevo.

Leaning back from the small-paned window, Lacy thought of James.

Every month since he had left a year ago she had received a letter from him. She was surprised at first, but pleased, for he gave her a clear picture of the situation in the Balkans, and treated her as a person of intelligence, who could understand his reports, and not as some silly nincompoop with nothing in her head but whatever female nincompoops had in their head. She began to look forward to the long, detailed, interesting and often humorous accounts of events of the war and James's part in it.

She was not to know that he carefully omitted many things which he considered might distress her. One could not speak to a young lady, no matter how enlightened, of exposure and exhaustion, and of soldiers starving due to lack of supplies, which could not be brought to them because the road was a river of mud. They had no adequate clothing, nor shelter, his men. Scantily clothed, irregularly fed, existing when on duty in the mud and water of the trenches, sleeping when they returned to their improvised shelters in wet clothes on wet floors. The number of available 'bayonets' – the name by which the men who were not sick or wounded were counted – fell appallingly each week. And James could not, of course, describe to Lacy the horror of the battles, the wounded, the blood and the carnage.

Lacy answered all his letters although she felt that she had little to say that would be of interest to him. There were balls and theatre parties, and during the summer months, picnics and garden parties. That was all. So dull. So deadly dull to a man who was living through one of the most exciting periods in British history.

How could she realize that when he opened the bright, chatty, funny letters she sent him, it was the one lovely moment for which he waited in a world of misery and pain and the harrowing ordeal of watching the men he commanded dying like flies – not from enemy action, but from cholera, dysentery, malaria and festering wounds.

He kept them, her letters, every one, in an oilskin pouch in a pocket above his heart, and read and re-read them, holding them to his cheek when unobserved, absorbing the faint smell of her perfume which clung to them. She was a sweet memory now of one perfect day, and he brought out that memory whenever he was alone, turning it over and over in his mind, remembering not her beauty but that moment of laughter when she had threatened to 'wet her drawers'. He would smile and marvel why, when men clung to remembrances of soft arms and lips, of flower filled gardens and moon-drenched nights, he should delight in this one ridiculously poignant incident. He wondered at the comfort and pleasure it gave him.

'Lacy.'

An irritable voice brought the girl in the bow window back from her reverie, and she sighed. Oh Lord, it is my turn now, she thought. Will it be zinnias, or antirrhinums, or perhaps a dahlia behind each ear? Possibly a swathe of virginia creeper to hang over my face, then no one will see the pimple or my expression of . . .

'Lacy!'

'Yes, Mama,' she murmured in resignation.

'Come here and sit among your sisters. Miss Yeoland can hardly be expected to consider your headdress when you are hanging like a hoyden from the window.' Sarah was always inclined towards exaggeration. 'We have some lovely ideas here, and a colour and a flower must be chosen for you. Now, sit beside Jane and pay attention.'

Lacy obediently sat in the chair indicated, catching Jane's eye which, unexpectedly, gave her a tiny, unobserved wink. Startled, Lacy smiled, and then almost laughed out loud, as Jane straightened her face into grave and attentive sobriety. Jane was the only one of her sisters for whom Lacy felt any attachment, for although she was quiet and plain, she did her best to understand her ebullient younger sister, and was sympathetic to her desire to be free. It was completely beyond Jane's imagination, but she did try, and her sense of humour, well hidden and often missed by those about her, drew Lacy to her when Rose was busy.

Lacy sometimes talked to Jane, lying full-length on her bed whilst Jane pressed the flowers she had gathered on their walks, knowing she was completely to be trusted and would tell no one what she had revealed to her. She knew that Jane held her in great affection, and she returned her sister's feelings to some extent, but she could no more get to grips with Jane's passivity than her sister could comprehend her own vitality and restlessness.

'Do sit up straight, Lacy, and pay attention. This is most

169

important. The most important day in the life of any woman, and it must be perfect for Amy. We must all look our best, for everyone will be there, and our behaviour and appearances must be without fault.'

When Mama said *our* she did not, of course, refer to Sarah Hemingway, for her own behaviour was always perfect. Her remark was not aimed at Lacy's three sisters either. Only at Lacy herself. Lacy's face was impassive as her mama continued.

'Do you understand, Lacy?'

'Yes, Mama.'

'Now, if we have your attention, would you be good enough to state a preference for a flower.'

'I do not mind, Mama. Perhaps you will choose for me.' She heard Jane stifle a giggle, but did not look at her. She kept her own face quite expressionless. Sarah smiled, pleased. The child was showing sense at last.

'Well, it must be suitable for a headdress of course, and something which will compliment your colouring.'

Sarah looked at Lacy dispassionately, considering in her mind which bloom would look best on her daughter's pale, silvery hair. She had to admit reluctantly, for she had had no fondness for the girl since the O'Malley incident, that she would look perfect in a headdress of cabbage leaves. She needed nothing to enhance her, for she was loveliness itself. She wondered idly why none of her other daughters, or her sons for that matter, had inherited her own and Charles's good looks, for she had been considered a beauty in her day. It was as if the attractions to be shared out amongst her six children had all been bestowed upon one, leaving the others colourless and dull.

She shrugged her shoulders. It did not matter really, for they were all either settled or soon to be with suitable partners picked out for them. Even this one. Although, as yet, she was not aware of it. Turning away from the future, Sarah gave her full attention to the delightful pastime of getting one's first daughter married.

Lacy stared at her bent head, then round the circle of bent

heads, all engrossed in the choosing of one wreath of flowers to be worn to one event, and felt despair grip her.

Why was she so different?

Why could she not be as her sisters were? Placid, content, pleased with the idea of having a husband and children. It would be so easy. Life would be made so uncomplicated if she could just accept that her future was to be exactly like that of her mama, but she could not. She just could not. Was it because of Sean, of Rose, of Bridie and Lancer? Had the things she had seen, heard and experienced six years ago made her as she was? No, they had not, she told herself sadly. She had always been the same. Ever since she could remember, she had rebelled against Nanny, Mama, Miss Robertson, struggling to be herself and not a miniature of her mother. Her sisters were happy with so little, whilst she longed for something which forever eluded her, and that was the most frightening thing. She did not know what it was she wanted, so how was she to get it? Her Mama said that a girl's wedding day was the most important day of her life, so it must be deduced that from then on life went rapidly downhill, having reached and passed its peak.

Dear God.

For the next hour, the compelling challenge of what flower would suit which eyes and look best on whose head was grappled with, and after interminable arrangements to receive Miss Yeoland at Silverdale, Sarah stood up gracefully, preparing to take her leave. Reaching for her parasol, straightening her light mantle, smoothing her wide crinoline, she graciously allowed the Misses Yeoland to accompany her and her daughters down the wide carpeted staircase to the lower salon, through the doorway, and to the carriage.

As Arkwright urged the chestnuts on their way, she was heard to say, did not Mr Ireland have some rich and elegant furs in his window, and that she must remember to send her sable to be cleaned. She bowed to an acquaintance and put up her parasol, for the sun was quite strong, and one did not wish one's skin to become as dark as that of a gypsy.

'Put up your parasol, Lacy,' she admonished her youngest

daughter, 'and bow to Mrs Nicholson. Perhaps we might prevail upon Papa to give us lunch at the York Hotel, if Mr Hamer can provide us with a private room.'

In a moment, Lacy's drooping spirits soared.

Lunch with Papa, that was treat enough. But first they must call at his office to see if he were free, and that was better than . . . She could not find an example wonderful enough to set against the joy of going to Papa's office. Even for a few moments, it was intoxication. From the wide window it was possible to look out over George's Dock, south to Canning, north to Prince's, and beyond to the mouth of the river. All the great sailing ships would be tied up, the wharves swarming with workers about their duties, docks in turmoil. The noise, the wonderful noise and smells, which were dearer to her than the sights, sounds and smells in Papa's garden, would fill her with the most complete sense of satisfaction she had ever known.

The carriage stopped at the doorway which led upstairs to Papa's offices, and she could scarcely wait to get there. She ran, actually *ran* ahead of Mama, who 'tched, tched' irritably as Lacy sped up the stairs. Half a dozen clerks at their high desks were mesmerized, raising their heads as one as she flashed past them, brilliant as a firework just lit. Mr Winterbottom, Papa's head clerk, was in his own office, his gleaming bald head bent over some papers. He stood up as she entered, confused by her sudden, lively appearance.

'Miss Alexandrina. Why, how pleasant to . . . Oh no, miss, please. You must not go in, your papa has someone with him . . .'

But it was too late.

It had always been too late, even a year ago when James Osborne had looked at her, wanted her, and had asked her papa to keep her for him.

She flung wide the door to Charles Hemingway's office, and looked directly into the bluest eyes she had ever seen. They were an unimaginable shade of blue – like hyacinths, a summer sky, cornflowers clustered in the paddock, but brilliant as if set in diamonds. Yet none of these things were

172

the colour of this man's eyes, and nothing had prepared her for the thrill of quivering excitement which gripped her now, beginning just below her heart, trailing deliciously through the whole of her body, and right down to her knees, which began to tremble strangely.

She clutched her parasol, gripping it with white knuckled fingers, else they would have fluttered ridiculously about as she had seen Amy's do at the approach of Ned Lucas. So *that* was why, she had time to think, and marvelled at her own ignorance as she sank into the senseless sea of first love.

She could not tear her gaze away from him, nor he from her.

Charles and Sarah Hemingway were for once of the same opinion regarding their wayward child, for that was how they still thought of her, despite her being seventeen, and already spoken for by James Osborne. But it was this belief in her parents' hearts which saved her. Their combined annoyance at her mannerless behaviour blinded them for a brief span to the flash of unchildlike ardour which lit her eyes, and to the electric excitement which flashed between her and the man in Charles Hemingway's office.

Charles sprang from his chair, as did the young man when Lacy entered, followed by her Mama and sisters, and momentarily all was confusion as five crinolines fought for space and five parasols fluttered. Over it all, blue eyes held grey, and spoke, and were answered, and spoke again.

'Lacy! Sarah! What on earth? Can you not see that I am engaged? Did not Winterbottom tell you . . .'

Sarah and her daughters crowded upon one another's heels open-mouthed, and behind them, unable to enter for there was no space left, Winterbottom fussed, apologized and perspired beneath his frock coat.

'She was in before . . . Miss Alexandrina ran past me, sir. I tried to tell her, but . . .'

'Yes, yes. Well, never mind. Never mind.'

Charles waved away the hapless clerk, and ran his hand across his thinning hair. He looked in exasperation at his wife, as though to ask why the child was not kept in check, unable even now to see that it was his own fondness that had allowed her to become as she was. Sarah stared back, lifting her bonnet haughtily, her expression replying that it was only to be expected, the girl having been given her head from infancy. It was an old, much chewed bone of contention between them, and Sarah never let it lie.

They did not see their daughter and Luke Marlowe stare at one another across the yawning abyss of their separate social classes, nor feel the tension which stretched between them. Then the man, older, more experienced and looking to the future, deliberately glanced away, breaking the spell. He turned courteously to Sarah and her other daughters.

Charles had no option but to present him, saying reluctantly, for the man, although presentable, intelligent and destined one day for the command of a ship, was still only one of his own employees:

'My dear, may I present Mr Lucas Marlowe. Mr Marlowe, my wife and daughters. Amy, Margaret, Jane and Alexandrina.'

'Lacy.'

'What?' Bewildered, Charles stared at her.

'Lacy, Papa.'

Charles sighed deeply and Sarah's face became a deep puce.

'My daughter likes to be called Lacy, Mr Marlowe.'

Luke Marlowe bowed gracefully over each hand, his head bent respectfully until he reached Lacy. Charles and Sarah had turned away, the proprieties done with, as he kissed the air above her hand. Taking advantage of their detachment, he looked directly into her eyes and smiled.

She felt as though she had been struck. Her skin prickled, and yet at the same time glowed, as though she stood before a furnace. In the centre of her, just below the waistband of her gown, something stirred painfully. Her lips parted moistly, and it was all she could do to stop herself from reaching for him, although she had not the faintest idea why.

Mama was speaking to Papa. Lacy heard her from the fantasy world into which the smiling eyes of Luke Marlowe

174

had flung her, and some voice – not her own surely, for she would not have dared Mama's wrath – completed the sentence Mama had just spoken.

'We were hoping you might take us to luncheon, Charles, if you can spare the time . . .' Sarah Hemingway said.

'. . . and perhaps Mr Marlowe might accompany us, Papa,' her daughter finished.

Lacy's voice echoed about the room as though it were empty. The silence which followed was complete and horrible. For an instant, Luke Marlowe's eyes changed from warm, vivid blue to deep, rage-filled purple for, with those words, Lacy Hemingway had placed him in an impossible position.

Lucas Marlowe was orphaned at an early age, and although he did not remember how he came to be there, he was brought to the 'Bluecoats School' when he was seven years of age. The school's educational qualifications were excellent, and it had been the stepping stone which had helped many a Liverpool man to success and fortune in life.

The institution was established in 1709 with just 50 pupils. It was at first a charity school and had cost thirty five pounds to build, the land on which it was erected being a gift from the Corporation of Liverpool. The number of scholars was increased each year and in 1820, when Luke was admitted, there were three hundred and twenty boys and one hundred girls. Many handsome donations and legacies were bestowed upon the charity. There were dormitories and schoolrooms, a large chapel and hall, and a capacious playground.

The boys were taught reading, writing and cyphering. There were classes in navigation for those who were intent upon the sea, and in music and art for any who showed talent. The girls learned reading, writing, needlework, knitting and housewifery. At a proper age the lads were sent to sea or some suitable trade, and the girls were put into service.

When he was twelve, Luke Marlowe was signed on a ship of the 'Hemingway Shipping Line'. He was bright, conscientious and ruthlessly ambitious. He had learned to be tough at the charity school. One fought or went under, and he had set his sights higher than someone else's boots. He would do anything to get on, to earn praise, to be liked and respected. He worked harder than any other man on the ship, including its captain, and at the age of twenty-four he had his Master's Certificate.

He was first mate on the packet ship *Sarah Beaumont*, launched in the early days of Charles' marriage to Sarah. But more than anything in the world, Luke Marlowe wanted command of one of Charles Hemingway's new clipper ships, which were being built in America to carry tea from China to Liverpool. Tea lost its flavour on the long journey down through the China sea, across the Indian ocean, around the Cape of Good Hope and up the Atlantic, and the Yankee clipper ships – fast, sleek and beautiful – had begun to steal the trade from British shipping. Charles aimed to exploit this profitable source of revenue and his first clipper, *Breeze*, was to be launched within weeks.

Luke Marlowe had coveted Charles Hemingway's ship, and now he coveted his daughter. Although he had known many lovely women, her vivid beauty had hit him before he had time to prepare himself. In those first dazzling moments he had acted as any normal, warm blooded young male would react. He had stared. He knew he had. His mouth had fallen open in an almost uncouth gasp. But Luke Marlowe was no ordinary man. He had recovered at once and no one had noticed, except the girl herself, and she did not matter.

Luke Marlow had a goal.

It was almost in his hand, and although he had been instantly and violently attracted to Lacy Hemingway, his second thought, after the one in which he had known she was to be his, was how he could turn this meeting to his own advantage. He must not antagonize Charles Hemingway. Not now. Not after fifteen years of working, plotting, scheming, biting his tongue, and stepping back from the condescension shown him by those he served. He had scrubbed decks, coiled ropes, and climbed spars and rigging to reef and unfurl sails in gales the like of which had terrified his boy's soul. His young hands had bled from splicing ropes, mending canvas. He had been taught to steer the ship at the age of sixteen, and had thought he could never attain a happier moment.

It was a rough life, filled with hard, dangerous work. He ate salt pork, beef and maggoty biscuits. He had known black terror, as men had been swept overboard in ferocious seas, but he had loved it with a passion most men reserve for only one woman. He had paid for what was almost in his grasp, and no one and nothing, not even this feeling which swept over him for Charles Hemingway's daughter, was going to stop him from having it. He must make it very plain to his employer that he knew his place, and that it was not at his table.

Not yet.

He felt a thrill of excitement run through his veins. By God, this was going to be the most exhilarating chase of his lifetime, and what a prize. What a prize!

He turned politely to Charles and Sarah Hemingway. They were comical in their consternation. With quiet amusement, he saw the expression of displeasure upon each face. They were appalled at the notion of sitting down to dine with a common seaman. And angry. The look of tight rage on Charles Hemingway's face boded ill for Miss Lacy Hemingway, but at the moment Luke Marlowe cared naught for that. He was concerned only with Luke Marlowe.

His time for her would come.

'I do beg your pardon, sir,' he said. 'It is most kind of your daughter to ask that I might be included in your family party, but I regret I have committed myself to a previous luncheon engagement, and there is an exhibition of art at the gallery in Colquitt Street I particularly wish to see. It is the last day, you understand. Please forgive me, ma'am.'

Always the opportunist, he congratulated himself that with these words he had not only politely refused an invitation which was unwelcome to his employer, but had at the same time indicated that he was a gentleman of culture. And the message had been given to the girl!

He bowed to Sarah most politely, watching her face, seeing

relief, even approval, for in it was recognition that this young man knew where his best interests lay. He was not of their social background and had not, as some would, given the chance, taken advantage of a silly girl's improper proposal.

Luke bowed again, this time to Charles, and saw in the man's expression admiration and something else. Something which told him that Charles Hemingway was pleased with him. Respected him for what he had just done. He had saved Charles the embarrassment of either accepting him, and taking the unprecedented step of lunching with one of his own employees, or of rudely turning him away. And he had done it gracefully.

'Now, if you will excuse me, sir, I must be about my duties.' Luke bowed again to Sarah, who nodded pleasantly. 'My compliments, ma'am.' Another bow. 'Your servant, ladies.'

Not by a flicker of an eyelash did he show to Lacy any other than the polite regard he offered her sisters. He turned at the door. His handsome face glowed with good health and the deep brown which many tropical suns had put there. His eyes shone with the brilliance of sapphires as he smiled politely, and even Sarah felt her heart flutter with the force of his charm. He really was quite fetching, she thought, and with such beautiful manners. He opened the door and bending his dark head, for he was tall, he went through, closing it quietly behind him.

Sarah turned to Charles, who sat down abruptly. Her breath exploded from her mouth.

'Well, Charles, I really must *insist* that Alexandrina be thoroughly admonished for her unsuitable behaviour. I have never seen such a display of . . . to actually invite not only a complete stranger to lunch with us, but a man who works for you! It is reprehensible, and I . . .'

She whirled to face her daughter, and her face took on the familiar look of distaste with which she began all her interminable diatribes on good manners, breeding and the proper conduct of young ladies. It was as though the sheer vulgarity of it could scarcely be believed and, moreover, that the chastising of that vulgarity filled her with repugnance. Her voice droned on and on, and it was quite ten minutes before Charles could drag her back to the reason for her call. If it were not that it would deprive them all of a pleasurable hour, she told him, she would have returned at once to Silverdale to deposit the chit in her room, where she would remain for the rest of the day. But she could see no reason why her sisters should suffer for her ill breeding.

In a vacuum of silence, her gaze fixed politely upon her mother's moving lips, Lacy existed in the heart-stopping, pulse-pounding intoxication left by the warm touch of Luke Marlowe's fingers, and the shock of his extraordinary eyes. The last few words he had spoken rang in her head, and she knew as clearly as though he had said it to her face what he meant her to know. A message had been given. The Gallery of Art in Colquitt Street. That was where they were to meet.

In her pale graceful gown and her fashionable bonnet, the very picture of well-bred innocence, she stood and watched her mama's lips move, hearing nothing but the strong, soft voice of the man she had just met, her mind busy with the manoeuvre which would get her beside Luke Marlowe.

And in the shortest possible time.

# CHAPTER 12

It was fourteen months since James Osborne had left Liverpool to rejoin his regiment before sailing for Gallipoli, and in that time there had been many changes in the lives of Lacy Hemingway and Rose O'Malley – all smoothing the path which was to lead Lacy inevitably to Luke Marlowe.

Perhaps the most momentous change was the promotion of Rose from parlour maid to Lacy's own personal maid. The two people most astonished by it were those most concerned, Rose and Lacy themselves. Rose had been employed at Silverdale for seven years, and in that time she had gained a reputation for hard work, honesty and a keen desire to learn from those above her; and had the sense to know which of these could do her the most good. She was even-tempered to those who mattered, clean to the point of obsession, quick, clever and bright. Cook thought the world of her and even though, as housemaid and then parlour maid, Rose no longer came under Cook's influence but that of Mrs Johnson, there was an understanding between the old woman and the young girl, dating back to the day when Cook had lent her good black cape to the child who went to the funeral of her father.

Cook admired spunk and Rose had it and besides, did you ever see a girl for work like Rose. Clean! She nearly took the pattern off the plates when she washed them. The best little worker she had ever known, was Rose, and she had seen a few come and go. She was always willing and, for all her troubles, cheerful. Quiet, keeping herself to herself, a good girl, but always with a smile. Cook was sorry to see Rose leave first the scullery then the kitchen, but she deserved to get on, did Rose.

Rose's neat, scrupulously clean appearance about the house excited the notice of neither Sarah, who had never clapped eyes on the girl until she appeared one day to repair the drawing room fire, nor Charles, who had last seen her as a skinny ten-year-old in a shocked state of grief for her dead father. The modest, attractive young parlour maid with downcast eyes and a respectful manner, who bobbed a curtsey at the door of his dining room, was so vastly changed from the child she had been. Charles would not have believed it was she, had he been told.

'Good morning, Rose,' he would say, the name ringing no bells in his memory.

So when the question of a personal maid for his daughter was brought up, he and Sarah agreed equably with Mrs Johnson, when she suggested Rose. The events which followed Sean O'Malley's death in May 1848 were not mentioned, if indeed they were remembered by Mrs Johnson, and the connection between their daughter and the maid Rose was not even thought of by Charles and Sarah Hemingway.

Now the secrecy was done away with and, for the first time, the two young girls went about openly. Lacy was given slightly more freedom than would be normally allowed a girl of good family, but it must be admitted that James's commitment to Lacy played a large part in Sarah's gradual relaxing in her guardianship of her youngest daughter's life. Lacy's future was arranged and the girl would soon be off her hands. When the war in the Crimea was over and James returned, Lacy and he would be married and, in a sense, only the scantiest interest need now be shown the girl. The long and harrowing consideration of a suitable husband for one's daughter might be, in Lacy's case, thankfully disposed of, and the concentration needed could be transferred to Margaret and Jane. Margaret would be betrothed to John Bradley in October, and the young man who was paying court to Jane could then, with Charles's permission, take his turn.

Matters had worked out most opportunely in Sarah's opinion, and so she relinquished her vigilance a little. Not too much. It would not do to allow the girl to run about willy-nilly, but this interest she showed in painting and the arts fitted in very nicely with Sarah's plans. It kept her occupied out of harm's way, and mischief, until James came to claim her.

Later Sarah was to be blamed for what happened.

Was it not a mother's duty to see to the strict chaperonage of her unmarried daughters, they said. But how were she and Charles to remember *all* of their servants, she was heard to remark plaintively, or to know that Rose was *the* Rose, the daughter of *that* man, and obviously the one to blame.

But by then it was too late.

They were allowed to go out alone.

Lacy's new maid proved to be a serious, thoughtful and conscientious young woman with none of the headlong enthusiasms of her young mistress. She had a good head on her shoulders and was unlikely to be led into any unseemly behaviour. Did her job not depend upon it? As the months passed, Mrs Johnson's confidence in her proved justified.

They went to the Royal Institution, then to the zoological gardens at the top of Brunswick Street, so that Lacy might sketch the wild animals which were caged there. Arkwright and one of the footmen were always in attendance.

Because of her talent for sketching and painting in water colour, Lacy was allowed to become a member of the Royal Institution, a society which furthered the careers of Liverpool artists. Mama had been convinced that well-known families of their class were involved, and was quite charmed to see her daughter's work on display and praised by close friends. It was impressed upon Lacy that she painted as a hobby only. There was no possibility of a career in that direction. Privately, Sarah suggested to Charles that he might wish to consult James on the advisability of allowing his future wife to show her work in public but, after receiving a note from the captain to say that he had no objection, and could see only good in keeping Lacy occupied whilst he was absent, Sarah was doubly pleased and magnanimously gave her consent.

The annual exhibition of painting took place in the gallery in Post Office Place, and artists from all over the country displayed their works there. There were four small rooms and one large salon all lit from the top, and well suited for the purpose to which they were devoted. The exhibition opened in August and continued until December – yet another circumstance which favoured Luke Marlowe's intended seduction of Lacy Hemingway.

Lacy's 'little pictures', as Papa fondly called them, a most ladylike occupation, he thought, kept her happy and busy until the return of James. She was absent from the house rather more than he would have liked, but diplomatic questioning of Arkwright, who was as trustworthy as the Bank of England, only confirmed the innocence of her whereabouts, and his mind and Sarah's were at peace as the summer began its slow glide towards autumn.

It was thirty-four days before they met again.

The packet ship carrying Luke Marlowe to New York took thirty-three days for the round trip, and the day after he docked in Liverpool, he and Lacy Hemingway stood face to face in the Permanent Gallery of Art in Colquitt Street. Beneath the statue of William Roscoe, one of the gallery's founders, Luke lifted her hand and brought it gently to his lips, and saw her eyes fill with stars, and her face blaze with worshipping love. He looked into those eyes and was, for a brief selfless tick of time, turned from the one thing in life he had wanted since he had been able to discern the difference between a schooner and a brigantine and, should she have said a word, he would have thrown it all aside in an instant and done whatever she commanded.

Just at that moment, their first alone together, she had him in the palm of her hand. She might have done with him as she wished, and he would have submitted gladly, for he knew he loved her as he had never loved another human being in his life. She took the breath from his body, and he wanted to hold her to him forever.

He stepped back, although his eyes never left hers. His hat was in his gloved hand and he stood tall, his head proudly set. Did he not have the love of Alexandrina Victoria Hemingway? His fine body was taut with checked vigour and high-charged emotion, but he moved with the supple grace of an animal. He was young, alert, sensuous, and yet he moved instinctively in a way which showed restraint; a fear that he might alarm.

As yet they had not exchanged a word.

At last he spoke.

'Will you walk with me?' It was said diffidently, almost humbly, and Luke Marlowe had not been humble since he reached manhood. It was a token of his regard for her. He wanted, longed to treat her with all the deferential respect a suitor would show a young girl of good family, and although he knew he never would or could be considered as such, for that moment he felt compelled to it.

'Will you not take my arm and walk with me?' His voice was soft and deep, and completely irresistible. He held out his arm. Lacy put her hand in the curve of it, and he drew her to his side, enfolding the softness of her fingers against his broad chest. She felt the strength and warmth and complete masculinity of him. She felt his heart beat against her hand, and thought she would swoon with the sheer joy of it. Besides Papa, she had never touched, nor been touched by, a man.

They stepped out of the doorway of the art gallery into the small garden which lay to the rear. Luke seemed to know exactly where they were going. The building had once been a house, someone's home, and the area at the back was still attended by an old man who had worked for the previous owner.

It was a cool, overcast day and not one for summer finery. Lacy wore an apple green day dress in soft Vienna wool, very fine and clinging. The huge skirt was held out by six flounced petticoats, every one edged in the finest Honiton lace. Even in the depths of the hypnotized state in which she had prepared herself for this moment, her mind had told her coolly to wear, not a crinoline, which was unwieldly and awkward, but soft, manageable petticoats. Her dress was patterned with uncut velvet and had a wide belt of the same material. White lace undersleeves fell about her slender wrists, and her glowing face was framed by a small green bonnet, whose brim frothed with a delicate spray of lily of the valley.

The sky lay like a pale blanket above the rooftops, soft as lambs' fleece and the same colour. The ornamental, stylized garden of the last century was set with symmetrical rows of herbaceous plants, box hedges, neat paths and wooden benches, all canopied with ancient oak trees.

It was empty.

Taking Lacy's hand in his, Luke led her to a bench hidden almost from view in the furthest corner of the garden. Honeysuckle laden with fragrant blossom grew up the high brick wall in great swathes, and the smell was overwhelming. Lacy, shy as a fawn now, looked down at her clasped hands, which trembled with the depth of her feelings.

Again, Luke was seized by a passionate longing to protect, to treat with reverence the lovely young girl who sat beside him. She seemed to draw out everything that was best in him: everything that was warm, tender and idealistic in his deeply hidden, self-seeking heart. He ached to treat her as she should be treated: to speak the first soft and tentative words that a man speaks to the woman he loves; to make the slow, hesitant steps through courtship, the gallant and courtly beginnings; to follow the gentle movement of wooing through months of delightful approach, response, acceptance, betrothal and, when she was ready and her father willing, marriage.

That was how it should be, but it did no good to dream of what might be. The reality of his own humble origins left him with no illusions as to what he was, nor how he would appear to her family. No day dreaming would ever make him acceptable as a son-in-law to Charles Hemingway and though, in his new-found love, he wanted for the first time in his life to do the 'right thing' by a woman, he could not. He would have her – there was no doubt of that in his mind – and he would be Charles Hemingway's son-in-law, but not in the way he would have liked. Not in the way it should be.

Luke shook his head regretfully, cleared his throat, smiled winningly and began the way it would be.

As he reached for her hand, beginning to withdraw it from her glove with the practised ease of the born seducer, Lacy felt her heart pounding in her chest, and for a brief second she felt fear. But he whispered her name so tenderly, and his eyes were so soft and loving, she felt herself to be as safe as she was with Papa. But when she was with Papa her breath did not become trapped in her throat as it was now, lying somewhere between her lungs and her lips. Her cheeks burned bright flames of crimson in her pale face. She let him kiss her bare fingers, felt his lips burn her flesh, and beneath the skirt of her gown she quivered, as she had on the day she first met him. It was the loveliest of feelings, but at the same time painful, and she felt an urgent desire to put her hand, or have Luke put his hand . . .

She did not know what it was she wanted, or what to do about it. The touch of his warm lips, the hard masculine feel of his arm and chest, so new, unfamiliar, exciting, frightening, was driving her almost to the edge where restraint ended and submission began. She knew now that if he were to take his lips from her fingers, and put them to her mouth, she would be beyond help.

In her ignorance she had no idea what it was she would be driven to, only that she wanted more than anything in the world to have him do it. Her heart knocked frantically. Her mouth was dry, and if he had asked her to speak, she would have been unable to do so. Oh Lord, if she could just stop her fingers from fumbling and flustering beneath his touch. If her knees would stop quivering, and her thighs. If her stomach would only stop its cartwheels . . . Oh Lord, she thought she was going to cry.

Rose O'Malley stood in the shadow of the doorway, lurking uncomfortably, feeling foolish and ill at ease, not sure whether her role was that of chaperone, lookout or spy.

She did not like it whatever it was, and she did not like Luke Marlowe either. Two minutes in his company, for Lacy insisted upon introducing them, was all it had taken. Her instinct, unclouded by passion, distrusted the easy confidence of the man. It spoke of experience in the ways of a man with a woman; of an inability to allow himself to be thwarted; of determination to have his own way. He was set on a course in which Lacy was to play a part, Rose could see that; and he seemed completely assured of finishing it.

Her senses warned her that though he looked like a

gentleman, acted like one, he was not. No man of good family would bring a young unmarried girl of his own class to a private place such as this, would treat her as wantonly as he was treating Lacy. Kissing her hands and wrists, hiding away in corners. Just look at him. All over her like a rash, he was, and her lapping it up like a kitten at the cream, a face on her red as a poppy.

She had been like one possessed of the devil since the day she had come home from her papa's office, and her mama after her like a mad woman. Her eyes had been brilliant, looking away into some world where, for the first time, Rose was forbidden, and though her mama and papa had been incensed by her conduct over some chap in her papa's office, and had kept her to the confines of the estate for several weeks as punishment, Lacy had not seemed to care.

Now Rose knew why.

The man had been at sea. Lacy had been content to sit and wait, taking her easel to the beach or the wood or to the top of the hill behind the house, whilst he did his trip to New York and back. On this very day – no doubt worked out by the little madam to the very minute, for did she not know the sailing departures and arrivals of every one of her papa's ships? – she had asked her mama most humbly if she might go to the gallery to see the new exhibition of artists' work just come from London. Almost five weeks she had been confined, and in all that time she had been mim as a mouse, her poor Mama taken in by it all, thinking her repentant.

It was not until they were safely in the carriage, passing the busy approaches to St James' Market, that Lacy had told her about Luke Marlowe. Despite Rose's pleading, threatening, and then her blunt refusal to have anything whatsoever to do with the meeting, here she was like a fly on the wall, fluttering about, not knowing whether to alight or wing away to a place where she need not watch her beloved friend's madness. That was what it was. Madness. Anyone with half an eye could see the man was up to no good, else why did he not call on her at home? Look at her. Just look at her! All eyes, glowing cheeks and . . .

Wait a minute! Just wait a minute, Rose O'Malley, a voice within her said. Who are you to judge? Surprised, as though a fourth person had entered the garden and sidled up to her, speaking her name, Rose turned away from the spectacle Lacy was making of herself and listened.

Would you not be there yourself, the voice said, drawn like a flower to the sun, if James Osborne were to give you the time of day? One smile, or the beckoning of a finger would have you exactly where Lacy is now, and bewitched by it. Blushing and yearning, face aflame, eyes burning with a longing her innocence does not understand.

But Rose understood. She had seen it long ago in her mother's eyes and on her father's moist lips. As a child reared in close proximity to two loving human beings, sleeping beside them, listening in the night when they thought her asleep to their coupling, she knew what Lacy wanted even if Lacy did not. And in her honesty did she not admit that, given the same chance, the slightest encouragement, she would run to James Osborne and . . . Rose's heart shifted heavily, her eyes became soft and unfocused. The cool walled garden, Lacy Hemingway, Luke Marlowe and the details of the day vanished. She was surrounded by sunshine and bright flowers, laughing children, white dresses and sailor suits, by pretty girls and young men and, in the centre, like a king holding court, was James Osborne. His dark glossy hair had turned to russet in the sunlight and, as he bit into an apple he had taken from a dish offered by Mr Chapman, his strong white teeth had closed about it, and his lips had moved in sensuous pleasure. She had been unable to look away. He had laughed and shaken his head, and his hair fell about, curly and thick and, for an unbelievable moment, she had felt her hand stray, still clutching the napkin with which she held a silver dish of pâté, to smooth it back from his bronzed forehead.

His deep brown eyes, warm with the emotion Lacy had awakened in him, looked up at her. She was a servant, a parlour maid and, as such, only a hand which held out a dish or a spoon. The sun was behind her and he did not see her face, but if he had it would have made no difference, for he was unable to keep his eyes from Lacy Hemingway. It was there in his, what he felt. Lacy did not see it or recognize what she saw, but Rose did. In that moment, Rose O'Malley hated the girl who had given her nothing but trust and affection, and jealousy ran through her, hot and scalding. It took but a second for the emotion to form, and the same for it to die, for her own honesty told her that even if James Osborne did not look at Lacy as though she were the answer to all his masculine yearnings, he still would not see Rose. Not in that way. She was not of his world and never would be. Many a master had tumbled a maid, and would again. Did not Master Thomas try it out on her, at every chance he had. But *that* was not what she was after in this life. Not Rose O'Malley. Only fools allowed liberties to be taken, and she was no fool. Yet, if James . . .

He had been gone so long.

Fifteen months of writing, writing, and in all his letters ran the steady stream of his love for Lacy. Not in words. Not recognizable as love to those who read them – Lacy, her Papa – for she gave them trustingly to anyone who cared to read them. But Rose, who loved him, saw it. Sometimes, when she had pressed carelessly into her hand the notepaper which he had held, she wished Lacy had not taught her to read all those years ago. Then, the pain she felt as she read his words could not have struck her. She knew, though she said nothing to Lacy, what was in his mind.

Then, when they were both overcome with wonder at the sudden leniency of Lacy's papa and the freedom he allowed her, Rose's mind was tantalized by the idea that some bargain had been struck between Charles Hemingway and James Osborne. Lacy was guarded like a precious jewel by Arkwright wherever she went, but it seemed strange that somehow each suitor who showed the smallest degree of interest in her was never good enough, no matter how eligible.

Not that Lacy noticed.

Unawakened, unashamedly relieved as each young man was whisked away, she never stopped to ask herself why.

The couple in the corner of the walled garden stood up.

Half a head taller than Lacy, Luke Marlowe looked down into her face and, for the last time, his heart contracted in unaccustomed pain. The trust and adoration he saw there almost unmanned him. For an incredible moment he wanted to go down on his knees and begin the gentle wooing he knew was her right. Later, much later, there would be ardour, passion, but now . . .

If only.

He felt anger, and sorrow and envy of those who had the right to court her openly, and cursed the gods who had put him on earth so far beneath her. His eyes smiled, crinkling attractively at the corners, and his lips moved to show his white teeth, but his heart hardened, and he felt a return of the resolve which had always been his.

The moment was gone.

'Lacy.' He murmured her name and watched her pupils widen. He had only to speak and she was ready for him.

'Luke.' It was barely a whisper.

'Tomorrow?' The question was asked, but he knew she would come. She would always come. Whenever he smiled at her, his eyes brilliant in that way he had, she would come running.

Their passion for one another was to grow until one of them lost control, but at this their first moment alone together, they were equals.

Rose shivered, and turned away as they walked slowly towards her.

# CHAPTER 13

The wedding was lovely. It took place in the tiny church of St Anne which stood on Aigburth Road, and occupied a small portion of ground on the estate of Silverdale. In it the family had worshipped each Sunday since Lacy's great grandparents had built their home there.

The day was mild. It was an Indian summer, Walker said, as he supervised the raking of the gravel in the drive, but it boded no good for winter. Well, it stood to reason. Nature had her ways, and if summer lingered on when it should have long gone, it was bound to upset the balance and produce a hard winter. But then, Walker was a real Job's comforter, and what did it matter if winter should be as cold as charity as long as it was nice today. Mantles would not be needed, that was certain, but parasols would, and they were produced and gone over urgently to ensure their perfection.

The bridesmaids, the bride's mother with her two sons, the bride and her father were drawn in three open carriages along the newly raked, curving driveway, across the wooden bridge which spanned the stream running through the wooded parkland, and on down to the main gateway. Here, scores of estate workers were gathered in their Sunday best – mostly black, for then they did for funerals as well. A woman or two, particularly the young, had pinned a scrap of artificial flowers to her bonnet, or a splash of coloured ribbon. They lined the bit of lane from the gateway of the estate to the lych-gate of the church, bobbing and smiling and doffing caps, straining to get a good look at the bride. But most agreed, shame as it was, that Miss Lacy outdazzled her as usual. She always had, so that was no surprise.

The Misses Yeoland had outdone themselves in their creation of four exquisite flowered garlands. After careful consideration of all that Sarah's winter garden had to offer the

191

elder Miss Yeoland chose simple rosebuds for them all, even Amy, although orange blossom was just beginning to be fashionable. White for the bride, of course, with white satin ribbon entwined with pale green velvet. Palest pink, so delicate as to be almost without colour, for Lacy; golden yellow, to bring some brightness to Jane's mouse brown hair; and tenderest apricot for Margaret. It seemed that apricot 'went' with blue, blue eyes. Miss Yeoland had found satin ribbon to match perfectly the shades of the rosebuds and, to give credit where it was due, she had sat up most of the night with her sister, preparing the coronets for the flowers. When Walker had brought these, cut less than half an hour earlier, at seven o'clock on the morning of the wedding, she had them finished, delivered and arranged on the four shining heads an hour before the wedding party was due to leave for the church. She had designed and conceived a small posy for each girl to carry to match the headdress she wore.

Sarah was so gratified she almost wept.

And so Charles and Sarah Hemingway's first girl passed from daughter to wife, exchanging one unequal status for another. She was completely ignorant of what lay in store for her that night, but then so was poor Ned Lucas, although he at least knew the rudiments of what was expected of him. However, each must have done their duty for, nine months later, Amy gave birth to their first child, a boy.

All society came to the wedding, and many of the household servants to the church ceremony. Rose was elegant in a soft, blue afternoon dress of rich silk, the finest gown she had ever owned and, were it not for the worry which hung over her head, this day would have been the happiest her hard life had ever allowed her. But, as it was, she felt as though she and Lacy stood in the lee of a high cliff, on top of which a huge boulder teetered.

Tomorrow, Luke Marlowe sailed for Philadelphia. Tonight, when the wedding feast was done, when the bride and groom had set off on their wedding journey, and the house guests and family were safe in their beds – stunned senseless, no doubt, with exhaustion – Lacy meant to slip down to the summer house to meet him. As she had done for the past week.

St Anne's was a protestant church, plain and somehow lacking in all the comforting symbols which Rose's faith provided, but it was a church nevertheless, and if the Hemingways' God was present in it, it followed that His Son and the Holy Mother would be about somewhere. Rose prayed passionately to the Blessed Virgin to keep Lacy Hemingway as pure as *Herself* and safe from the attentions of *him* who lurked, she knew, somewhere on the fringes of the estate.

Nanny Wilson stood beside her and cried to see the first of her 'babies' go, and as she did, Rose wondered bleakly where it would all end.

The wedding march rang out triumphantly and the trembling groom was borne away by his composed, innocent bride, from the dimness of the church into the lovely sunshine outside. Servants clapped respectfully, eyes shining, faces beaming. Sarah cried a little, for was it not the thing to do? And Thomas eyed appreciatively the lovely curves of his sister's maid.

As they were helped into their carriages for the short drive back to the house, a man far away raised his head to stare at the causeway heights above Balaclava. The sun shone benignly, cooler now that summer was passing, on the valley which would later be recorded in history as the 'Valley of the Shadow of Death'.

The British army had left Varna on 5 September for the Crimea and on this day, 26 September 1854, James Osborne's mind flew across oceans and continents to the girl who was never far from his thoughts, and he smiled.

He imagined her in a white, virginal bridesmaid's dress and he felt he knew the joyous exhilaration she would show, for Lacy Hemingway did nothing without enthusiasm. The excitement of her sister's wedding and her own participation in it would be intoxicating to her. He remembered her forceful vitality, the spirited drive with which she applied her whole nature to whatever interested her. Never one to be half-hearted about anything, she poured herself and her energy into everything she did. He would never, even when he grew old, forget that moment when she had stamped in a pool of seawater, her skirts bunched to her thighs, as she pleaded with her maid to stop making her laugh.

The child had enchanted him then and he knew she always would. But months had passed since James had last seen Lacy. Over a year, and she was no longer the child he thought her. To him she was still sixteen, a girl verging on womanhood, untouched and innocent, still consumed with youthful activities, frozen in time until he returned. Her mind still grew, as her letters showed him, but her emotions were as yet unawakened, waiting for him to return and give them life.

That night, as he lay in his cot, the lamp extinguished, the sighs and sleeping moans of thousands of men and horses about him, he smiled in the dark, and his hand folded about her last letter. In it she told him of the fitting they were to attend the next day. Letters took so long to reach him: the garlands she spoke of, then still unmade, had been worn today.

'We are going,' she wrote, 'for wreaths to wear in our hair. Can you imagine us, dressed in our white, with flowers in our hair, and poor Mama chivvying us from pillar to post, exhorting us to *behave*! . .' He could, and his teeth gleamed in the dark in a grin of pure pleasure. 'You know how I seem to have a gift for quite spoiling her day by my impropriety. But I promise to be good on Amy's wedding day, James . . .'

There would be a battle soon, but that night James Osborne slept peacefully, Lacy's letter beneath his pillow. The one written on the day before she had met Luke Marlowe.


Rose watched cheerlessly as the slender figure in white slipped for the third time that week, like a sliver of moonlight, from the door of the winter garden, through the trees which lay beyond the lawn, to disappear between the stand of woodland into the night.

'She has not even the sense to put a dark cloak about her,'

she said bitterly to the dog who strained in her grasp, crying deep in his throat to be allowed to go with his mistress.

'Lost her mind, she has, the great daft thing. If her papa should catch her, or if someone sees her and tells him, I shall lose my job, for a start. That does not even occur to her, and if it did she would only say, "You shall come with me and Luke, Rosie, when we leave. Do not worry." Worry! I'm off me head, Copper, an' that's the truth, so it is. An' it's no good you cryin' like that, me lad. She doesn't want the likes o' you with her, not where she's goin'.' The more distressed Rose became so did the brogue deepen. 'Faith, will yer be stoppin' that noise.'

Reluctantly, the dog allowed her to lead him through the silent house and back to her own bedroom. He lay at the foot of her bed, his head upon his paws, and watched as she took off her lovely blue silk, slipping her white flannelette nightgown over her head, brushing the long dark cloak of her hair. A dozen times she went to the window to stare anxiously beyond the garden, straining her eyes for Lacy's return. She had promised, 'only half an hour, Rose'. But her face was already lit up with that almost holy look it took on when she spoke of him, and her spirit had gone on ahead of her, and Rose knew Lacy was not really aware of her. She lived now in the acute and enchanted dream world to which Luke Marlowe had introduced her.

The dog watched Rose quietly, not dozing as he usually did, and when he pricked his ears and turned his head towards the door, her heart lurched thankfully. She had kept to her half hour, well almost, thank God. Rose did not know how she was to survive this nerve wracking existence on which Lacy seemed to thrive, but at least the divil was to be away tomorrow.

With this comforting but meagre hope in her heart, Rose moved with Copper towards the door. His tail flagged gently, and he stood ready to greet a friend as her hand reached to the door knob. Rose was smiling with relief when the handle turned and the door opened slowly inwards, and there, dressed in a quilted dressing gown, clinging to the door post, was Thomas Hemingway. He was smiling foolishly, obviously drunk, and for a moment Rose almost laughed out loud. It seemed that more than one person was bent on seduction this night, and if she had not been in such a cold sweat she might have been delighted with the joke.

Thomas was a poor thing in her opinion, as easily handled as a child, and had it not been for the urgency of removing him at once, she would have charmed and teased him from his goal, turning him from her door and back to his own with the ease a trainer leads a docile animal. There was no real badness in him, and only the spirits he had drunk had given him the courage to approach her, but she had not the time to jolly him along. Supposing Lacy were to turn the corner of the landing all unsuspecting. Even a drunken oaf such as this would have to be blind not to see.

For a moment she felt hysterical laughter well in her throat, as she considered the irony that her own virginity should have to be sacrificed in order to protect Lacy, who might at this moment be chucking away her own on a bastard who wasn't worth a bottle top.

Thomas was staring lasciviously, his eyes greedy, at the curved silhouette of her body beneath her nightgown. Oh, sweet Mary! It looked as though the only way to get rid of this daft sod was to go with him to his room. If she could just get her hands on the divil who was the cause of all this . . .

But Thomas was not that drunk.

As the dog leaned against his leg in companionable fashion, ready for a pat and a friendly word, the strangeness of seeing him there, and not in Lacy's room where he always slept, seemed to penetrate the man's blurred mind, and the fatuous expression slipped away to be replaced by bewilderment. It was so much taken for granted that Lacy and Copper were inseperable, bar when she was at table or away to the art gallery, the animal looked quite lost without her, like a carriage separated from the horse which pulls it. Rose watched his eyes darken in that way all Hemingways had. It came over them when some emotion claimed them, whether it be joy or anger, surprise or dismay, and her heart dropped like a stone.

He was going to be awkward.

'What is Copper doing with you?' Thomas asked truculently, as though it were some crime. In his mind was an odd feeling of uncertainty. He did not know why he felt as he did. The dog could be with Rose for any number of reasons, but something, perhaps Rose's own reaction, made him uneasy. And Copper seemed content to be with her. He was not whining or pawing the door to Lacy's room, which he always did when she inadvertently shut him out.

Rose stood like a thief who has been caught with her fingers in the till. Like a mouse in a thicket as an owl swoops, she was completely still. The light from the lamp beside her bed cast a golden glow around her, outlining her body beneath the thin stuff of her nightgown. Thomas's eyes narrowed. Her face was in shadow, but her enormous eyes glittered in the pale oval of her face. Dear sweet Mother, she thought, I'm going to have to do it. Nothing else will distract him from seeking an explanation to the mystery of Lacy's whereabouts, and Copper's presence in my room.

Thomas was like his mother in many ways and, once he had an idea in his head, be it something important or completely senseless, he would cling to it like a terrier to a stoat. The only way to take his silly mind from it, was to place before him some diversion which would have him in such a thrall that Lacy could walk the hallway with Luke Marlowe himself, and he would not heed them.

'Why is Copper here, Rose?' he said again. 'Is there something wrong with Lacy? She does not usually leave . . .'

As the words were spoken, Rose realized jubilantly that Thomas had given her the answer she herself had been too disconcerted to arrive at. She was tempted to cross herself and give thanks to the Holy Queen, who must surely have put the idea in his head so that he might transmit it to her. She nearly laughed out loud, this time with relief. He did not know how close he had come to having his lusty dreams fulfilled, the fool. The sudden trance into which his appearance had thrown her vanished and she said, calm as you please now, but with the Irish brogue on her thick enough to cut,

197

'Sure, an' hasn't she just been sick over the poor creature, Master Thomas. Can yer not smell the nastiness of him?'

Instantly, Thomas wrinkled his nose distastefully. God, he *could* smell it! If there was anything he detested, it was the stink of puke. Even his own. He moved back hastily and Rose supressed a smile. Poor old Copper. Clean as a whistle and groomed to perfection, but branded as a smelly animal in order to save not only Rose's honour – her mouth twitched, she couldn't help it – but his mistress' reputation. If Thomas had known Rose better, as Lacy did, he would have realized at once that she was lying. Her lilting childhood tongue gave her away.

'I 'ad to bring the divil in here ter give 'im a good wash. Begorra, he was like . . . well, 't wouldn't be nice ter be tellin' yer what he was like, sir. Now, mind him, he's still . . . Aah, come here yer spalpeen. Don't be gettin' too close to Master Thomas or yer'll be makin' him as ill as Miss Lacy.' She lowered her voice conspiratorially. 'Too much madeira an' her not used ter it, yer see, but don't be tellin' your mama, I beg yer. She only 'ad a glass or two, but it went to 'er 'ead.'

Rose glanced at the door leading to the dressing room, which lay between her own and Lacy's bedroom, and put her finger to her lips.

'She's asleep now, the poor wee thing, so we won't be makin' a noise. Now is there somethin' I can be gettin' for yer, Master Thomas? A cup of chocolate to make yer sleep?'

Her face was as guileless as a child's and Thomas's ardour vanished without a trace. Whether it was the smelly dog, his sister sleeping off a hangover, or the virginal quality of Rose's nightgown, which looked remarkably like the white habit of a nun, he was not certain. But, thanking her rapidly, apologizing for disturbing her, forgetting in his confusion why he had come in the first place, he turned about and closed the door behind him.

Rose ran to the wardrobe, tore open the door, and began to pray.

He kissed her as he had never done before that night, for he

198

knew he must bind her to him whilst he was away. She was mad for him now, and he felt his own control begin to slip away. Those first few days he had gone slowly: a touch of his hand upon her cheek, a finger caressing the skin of her arm just inside her elbow. His kisses had been gentle, hesitant, a mere brushing of his lips against hers. His arms had held her to him with the tenderness and delicacy of a lover cradling the dearest treasure he had, and she had trembled against him.

He had not dared to be seen with her in public, for if her father had heard one word, the merest whisper, that her trips to the art gallery or the library were anything other than the innocent outings they appeared; if an acquaintance should ask Charles the identity of the young man in Lacy's company, Luke Marlowe would lose not only this girl whom he loved as he had loved no other person, but also the dream he had worked towards since he was twelve years old.

He begged her to be patient when she would have him come to the house, saying it was not yet time; that her Papa must be brought round to the acceptance of himself as a suitor slowly, for she must realize that he was far beneath her in the matter of class. He said it reverently although his eyes gleamed strangely as he spoke. She had denied this hotly, saying he was her equal in everything, *everything*, and that Papa would welcome him. But it was she who had suggested the beach house as a place for them to meet.

'Only until it is time, Luke, and then I shall be proud to have you . . .'

Each night, when the house was silent and asleep, they met in the summer house, and he kissed and held her circumspectly, and spoke of the future, and filled her head with new dreams.

She was bewitched.

She still wore the diaphanous white dress in which she had accompanied her sister to the altar. Although all the proprieties had been observed during the wedding meal, and not a word or gesture had been spoken or made that might be considered unseemly, the atmosphere in the house, and amongst those who had peopled it, was charged and mysteriously different that day. Those who were already married, and many gentlemen who were not, knew what it was.

Lacy felt it.

She was puzzled by it and by her own restlessness. Hours later, as she stood in Luke's arms, he sensed it in her and, as he felt her lips go soft, sweet and open beneath his, caution and for the moment his whole future, were thrown carelessly to the winds.

Before Thomas Hemingway had discarded his fine quilted dressing gown in his own room, Rose was down the stairs and through the winter garden, her long black cape, the one she wore for country walks with Lacy, held closely about her. The dog strained under her strong young hand.

The sound reached her ears before she was within twenty-five yards of the summer house. She recognized it immediately, although she had not heard it for over seven years. It was the one Mammy had made deep in her throat when Daddy loved her.

He would have taken her.

The white dress, like a wedding gown in its simple purity, had slipped like silk from her shoulders to fall about her feet. Her small, naked breasts were in his greedy fingers, and her moaning, sighing, yearning voice had quietened the small animals in the undergrowth. He was reaching to her waist for the ribbons of her drawers, tearing feverishly at the lace in his blind need, when Rose came upon them. She let go of the dog's collar. Copper made no sound, and Luke Marlowe's cry of pain had a dog fox two hundred yards away frozen to a statue, not even his whiskers moving.

In his madness, his urgent sexual desires denied outlet, the teeth-marks in his leg on fire, red and burning, Luke Marlowe turned on Rose O'Malley and struck her violently across her white face. Lacy, support gone, fell to the floor of the summer house in a swoon, her discarded clothing beneath her. Copper stood over her, his teeth bared in a snarl of hatred. Rose looked with loathing at the man who in the next moment would have violated Lacy, then returned his blow with all the force she could muster.

He looked at her venomously.

'I'll not forget this,' he whispered.

'Nor I.'

When he had gone, she lifted the bemused weeping girl from the floor, and wrapping them both in the voluminous cape, led by the enraged dog, took her back to her room, and put her to bed.

# CHAPTER 14

Her face was cold, her expression frozen in bitter rage.

'You had no right, no right! I shall ask Papa to dismiss you.'

'Very well, ask him and I shall tell him of your . . .'

'You would not. How *dare* you speak to me like that! You are a maid in this house, no more, and as such . . .'

'Oh, I am, am I? Just a maid? Well, let me tell yer, missy, if that is so I shall 'and in me notice right now, for 'tis underpaid an' overworked I am.'

'Underpaid! Underpaid! You go too far, Rose, as you did last night. To interfere in what was none of your business . . .'

'None of me business is it! So that's the way of it. Yer, set ter fall inter the divil's hands, like an apple from a tree in September, an' yer say 'tis none of me business. An' who would 'ave the mendin' of yer when that . . . man had done with yer? Tell me that! Not yer mama, nor Miss Robertson or Nanny, ter be sure, for wouldn't yer be off to Scotland to yer cousins' an' meself out on me ear.'

Lacy's face was white now, as her anger at Rose's words provoked her to whip like madness.

'Stop it. Stop it! You seem to think me a flirting housemaid caught in a cupboard with the boot boy. Someone having "a bit of fun".' Her eyes blazed with passion. 'Do you consider me wanton, Rose? A loose woman who will allow the first man who comes begging to . . .'

She was lost for words, for she did not know how to describe the act which had so nearly taken place. Although she knew of the mechanics, for Rose had gently granted her an explanation when she was thirteen and her periods had come, how was she to speak to Rose, or to anyone, of what had so nearly happened? But Rose was boiling in a fury as violent as her own, as her speech betrayed.

'Don't speak to me of what yer were about. Sure an' didn't

I see it meself. D'yer think I would've allowed yer ter go up ter the owd summer 'ouse if I 'ad thought he would . . . 'e's no gentleman, that's fer sure. But, faith, I though 'e might respect the daughter of 'is own master. 'E was treatin' yer no better than a cheap . . .'

'Don't, Rose. Do not say it, or it might never be forgotten. And let me add that you did not *allow me* , as you so quaintly put it, to do anything. I do not need your permission to mix with friends of my own choosing. I went of my own free will . . .'

'Aye, ter meet a blackguard an' a seducer . . .'

'He is not! He is kind, sweet and gentle, and, Rose, I love him, love him beyond . . .'

'Love, love. Yer don't know the meanin' of the word an' neither does 'e. If I'd not come when I did, can't yer see, 'e'd have taken yer like some cheap . . .'

'And can you not see, Rose O'Malley,' Lacy hissed, 'that is what I wanted. If you had not come when you did I would have been his . . . his . . .'

The silence which fell was terrible in its intensity. Rose went rigid with shock. The passionate face before her was as white as the bed sheet, and the girl to whom it belonged shook like a flower beaten by a violent storm. The house was completely silent, for it seemed that none of the guests who had come to see the wedding, nor the family, were as yet risen from their beds. Only the servants were up.

The housemaid had gone from Lacy's bedroom. The fire burned beautifully in the freshly cleaned grate, but the hot water she had brought went cold as Lacy and Rose fought their bitter battle.

'You thought me unwilling?' Lacy lifted her head scornfully.

'Yes.' Rose whispered the word. 'No . . . I don't know. I thought . . . you did not know what you were about, I . . .' Lacy had not been struggling in Luke Marlowe's arms. But it had not once occurred to Rose, through all the long night she had sat with Copper beside the exhausted girl in the bed, that she had been as eager as he; that she had known what he was about, and longed for it just as impatiently.

'You must think me a slut or a simpleton, Rose,' Lacy said

bitterly. 'I love Luke Marlowe, and he loves me, and we are to be married. Do you think I could love a man who would use me for his own ends? Do you? We have known one another only a few weeks, but it came upon us in that first moment of meeting. Who is to set the time when one falls in love, Rose? Must it be a month after one has been introduced, six months, a year? Or can love be born at the first encounter of two pairs of eyes?'

Yes, yes, yes! said Rose's heart, and she understood. She remembered a mouth, a smiling mouth, the strong and obstinate face in which it was set, a thick mass of unruly hair, and James Osborne's eyes as they looked, startled, into her own on that day at the beach. Oh yes, I understand, for given the opportunity, I would have done the same. My body would be as eager as yours to love, be loved. But as her mind conjured images that set her breasts tingling and her body tightening just below her navel, the word 'married' plunged her, unpleasantly, back into the present.

'Married?'

'Yes.'

'Married!'

'Oh Rose, for God's sake take that look off your face. Of course we are to be married. Do you think I would allow . . .?'

'Does your papa know?' she interrupted rudely.

'You know he does not.'

'And, when he does, do you think he will permit it?'

'Why not?' Lacy was perfectly confident. 'Luke is a presentable and charming man. His manners are perfect, and he has had a good education. He has worked hard and has prospects. He is to have command of *Breeze* as soon as she is commissioned, and as her captain will have a place in Papa's employ . . .'

'Exactly.'

'I beg your pardon.'

'*In your papa's employ.*'

'I fail to see . . .'

Rose shook her head in exasperation. Her anger was draining away, and a great sadness had come to fill the empty

204

space it left behind. She could not condemn what Lacy did last night, but if she could stop it happening again, she would. That much she was determined upon, although it now seemed that the problem was bigger than she had thought. However, the man would be away for long periods, particularly if he gained command of the clipper. A hundred days it took to reach the Far East, and the same back, and in that time anything could happen. Whilst he was gone, the distance put between himself and Lacy, the thousands of hours to be got through, could work wonders on an impressionable young girl who thought herself in love. Without the stimulus of his presence she would forget. The war in the Crimea might soon be over, and James returned, and surely, with him to . . . to . . .

Dear God! Dear Holy Mother, Rose cried inwardly, I love him so much. I want him to love me and I know he never will. He is the only one who can save Lacy from this madness, with the love he has for her, but I want it. I want it. I want him. Yet all I can do, all I *must* do, is try to keep her safe.

For him.

The pain gripped her unbearably. She turned away to stare blindly through the window at the mellow autumn day which was just beginning. Let her do it, she thought. Let her get involved with this adventurer, then maybe James will . . .

But she could not, and she knew it. As she knew that, even if Lacy married Luke Marlowe, James Osborne was hardly likely to turn to her for comfort. And besides, Lacy talked of marriage now as blithely as though her partner was to be one of the Bradley boys, or William Taylor, sons of Charles Hemingway's dearest friends and socially eligible. Rose turned back to the girl who sat on the bed, crumpled like the roses in the garland she had worn only the day before.

'You know your papa will not allow it.'

'Why not?'

'Dear Jesus and all His angels. Give over the blarney. You know as well as meself he wouldn't have it. The fellow's a seaman, a common seaman brought up in a charity school and, as such, beyond the reach of Charles Hemingway's daughter. Come on Lacy, be honest with yourself. You always have been that. Don't blind yourself with love.' Rose's lip curled and Lacy saw it.

She leaped to her feet, the dog with her. She began to walk towards Rose, and Copper, bewildered, walked with her. The anger in the room frightened him and he whined uneasily.

Lacy stopped a foot away from Rose, who stood quietly by the window. For the first time in their long friendship they stood against each other. Always in the past they had been in agreement about things which were important. They had been firm in their championship of one another. Unwavering mutual support, comfort and dependence had made them close, like two sides of the same coin. But now they were divided, and Rose knew that one must make way for the other. And she knew it must be herself. She had no choice, for she loved Lacy Hemingway second only to James Osborne.

'You sneer at me and my love, Rose. Why, Why? Luke has done nothing to harm me. Why should you dislike him so?' Lacy's voice was confused. 'Oh, I realize we were precipitate last night . . .' A lovely flush deepened her skin to rose and her eyes glowed softly at the remembrance. '. . . but I'm not ashamed. Rose, you know me as no one does. You are my friend. My one true friend, and I feel that between friends there should be no secrets. I love him, and I want him. As a woman wants a man I want him. I know it is not considered correct to speak so, but that is your fault, Rose. Yes it is,' she said, as Rose, startled, would have protested.

'You brought me years ago from the straitjacket my sisters and friends wear. I know more about life than any of them, thanks to you. I should imagine none of them but myself knew what Amy and Ned were about last night, and that is because you told me of it. So although I am protected like some jewel, I am, in a way, free. For in knowledge is emancipation. And in my freedom I have found the man I love, and I will marry him. There is no more to be said. If Papa disagrees I shall run away, but you must come with me, Rose. Wherever Luke and I go, you will go too. Please Rose, do not turn from me. Please!'

What could Rose do?

She had known, admitted to herself once her anger had fled, that she must range herself with Lacy against whatever came. They would never be married. She knew it. Not that it would be Charles Hemingway who would stop them. Not him, for Lacy would defy him and have her way. It would be the other one. Would he allow his fine career to be jeopardized, by going against the will of the one man who could give him what he wanted? Not he. When he came to his senses, and realized what his relationship with Lacy would do to him, he would be off like a fox caught raiding the hen coop.

Lacy took both of Rose's hands in hers, and smiled that brilliant smile which no one could withstand.

'Do not be cross, Rose. All will be well, wait and see. Luke and I love each other, and all will be well.'

He returned each trip.

All through the dying months of autumn and the long frozen days and nights of winter he came. But they were never alone again, for Rose would not have it. Wherever they went she was with them, and Luke Marlowe hated her as he had hated no one in his life before. Not the second mate who had made his life a misery when he first went to sea, and who beat him savagely for the most minor infringement. Not the captain who had taken a fancy to his young boy's body and who, when thwarted, had tried to have him dismissed. Not the many men who had wanted what he had, and who had tried to take it from him. None of them had filled him with the loathing which he had for Rose O'Malley.

The enmity she aroused in him was born of the knowledge that she was aware of what he really was, and of what he wanted. He knew exactly what she thought of him, it was in her slanting green eyes whenever she looked at him. She despised him for an adventurer, a schemer, who would use her mistress as a stepping stone to success. And from that night, the night when for ten minutes he had let his reeling senses get away from him, and she had found Lacy almost naked in his arms, she had let him see her contempt.

To do him justice, he had not meant to seduce Lacy.

She seemed to him to contain all that he had ever wanted in a woman, and she had offered it to him eagerly, in her pure white dress. He had been startled by her passionate response to the first of his more sensuous kisses and, as she clung to him, her slim body leeched to his from breast to knee, he had been overwhelmed. In a way, although he had been ferocious in his foiled rage, he was relieved that Rose had come. He was not ready to put into being the scheme he had planned.

Not yet.

He wanted the ship first.

Rose thought he did not love Lacy Hemingway, but he did. As much as his eager, self-seeking nature would allow, he loved her, and he would, should events turn out as he planned, treat her as she deserved. He vowed to be a good husband when the time came, and to do his best to make her happy. He also vowed that after he and Lacy were safely married, he would get rid of Rose O'Malley. She had far too much influence over his beloved. She was forever stating her mind on subjects which should have been forbidden her and her interference, stubborn and strong, seemed to him to prevail far too deeply upon his courtship of Lacy.

His courtship! It was all he could do to keep Lacy from confronting her papa. Ever since he had come back to Liverpool from Philadelphia in November, she had been eager for him to approach Charles.

'Please Luke. Go and see him. Tell him we love one another and we wish to be married. He respects you. I know he does. He must admire what you have done, or he would not consider letting you have *Breeze*.' She laughed, and looked around to see if Rose watched. Seeing that her attention was momentarily elsewhere, she leaned forward and kissed him softly. 'That ship is dearer to him than . . . I am. He would not let just anyone have her, you know that.'

And he would not let just anyone have his daughter either.

Luke was not fool enough to believe that Charles Hemingway would be pleased to accept a seaman from one of his own ships as a son-in-law. It stuck in his craw. Was he not as hard working and ambitious as Charles himself? And did he not mean to get ahead and, perhaps one day, own his own ship? Even so, he was fully aware that in the eyes of Lacy's family he was less than nothing. No matter that for thirteen years he had worked himself up from cabin boy, to the command, almost in his grasp, of a clipper ship. No matter that to all intents and purposes he was a gentleman – for his manner of speaking had been copied from their own, as had his impeccable behaviour.

It would not make the slightest difference to Charles.

No doubt some young jackass had already been picked out for her and, when the time came, she would be told who he was and when the marriage would take place. She was seventeen. That was the age when young girls of good family were groomed for what was to come: an advantageous marriage.

Sons were bred to continue the line; daughters were bartered and married young, whilst they were still malleable, moving like children from the guidance of father to husband. They were expected to submit happily to this change of guardianship, although he doubted whether Lacy ever would. She was too high spirited. However, as yet, he had been able to bend her to his will. He always meant to.

Luke liked vitality in a woman; it made for excitement. But she must also be aware that his word was law. She would in time, but that was in the future and, meanwhile, he must keep her from taking her love to her papa and demanding that it be acknowledged by her family. Her honesty irritated him at times. Out in the open, she said, for she was proud of him, and wanted to be seen in public on his arm. Not furtively hiding in summer houses and behind rocks in the park, she said, lugging her protective easel about with her; not scurrying about the rear garden of the art gallery, ready to dart behind a mulberry bush if Rose should indicate that someone approached.

He quietened her each time, promising that he had a plan, and extracting her undertaking that she would keep their secret a little while longer. And he waited impatiently for his ship. For it would be the talisman which would tell him that all he longed for was his.

Lacy and *Breeze*.

They were inextricably linked, the woman and the ship he loved, the futures of both bonded together forever. Without one he could not have the other, he told himself. So he put her off, holding her in his arms, soothing her with kisses, gentle and loving. And she waited obediently.

The Fediukine Valley was quiet on the morning of 25 October 1854. The mist had lifted with the dawn, and only tiny eddies remained, like wisps of smoke trickling from a camp fire. The sky was clear, heralding a fine day although no one was ever to remember whether it was or not.

The Russian army, twenty five thousand foot, thirty four squadrons of horse, and seventy eight guns, began their advance towards Balaclava.

Lord Lucan was heard to exhort the men of the 93rd Highland Regiment who stood with him, 'Remember there is no retreat. You must die where you stand.' And Captain James Osborne, who watched the fighting from 500 yards up the valley, saw that they did stand firm, turning aside the Russian cavalry. The 'thin red line' they were to be called afterwards, for a great many legends grew from this day.

But even the 'thin red line' could not hold the Russians on their own.

Despite Lord Lucan's order to charge to their aid, the 'Heavy Brigade' continued to dress their lines immaculately, giving a parade ground display to please the heart of the most demanding commander whilst men fell to their deaths, bewildered, waiting on those who did not come. James ground his teeth in frustrated rage, but just as he felt he must surely be away himself to get them on their charge, they went. In a flurry of flashing sabre blades, the Scots Greys, the Inniskilling Dragoons and the Dragoon Guards crashed into the Russian ranks, which then began to waver. British artillery fell upon the enemy's rear and within eight minutes the Russians were fleeing over the Causeway Heights.

The cheering was ecstatic from those who watched: the 673 men of the Light Brigade, commanded by Lord Cardigan. The 'Heavies' had won an amazing victory, and the impatient cavalry, James Osborne amongst them, waited for their commander to give the order to charge the retreating Russian army.

It did not come.

James put his hand on the neck of his restive grey, looking along the lines to where Lord Cardigan sat his own horse. He heard a junior officer ask diffidently, 'My Lord, are we not to charge?'

'No, we are not. We are to wait here,' he was told.

'But, my Lord. It is our duty to follow up this advantage.'

'We will remain here.'

'Allow me to charge them with the 17th, sir,' the young man beseeched.

'No.'

And so began that historic day of unprecented confusion and military bungling, of matchless heroism and sacrifice.

A young officer was given the order to relay to Lord Lucan to begin the charge. The officer was renowned only for his superb horsemanship, and nothing else, and the message he took was not clear. Guns, he told them, the guns must be attacked. He stared in consternation when asked which guns, for there were many.

With no choice but to obey, unsure of the direction they should take, the 673 young men charged down the valley into the mouth of the guns they thought they were to attack and, everywhere, they toppled from horses which were dis-embowelled beneath them. Limbs flew in haphazard fashion from bodies, and heads rolled about like footballs. Animals and men screamed in agony, and when they finally reached the guns, the Russian cavalry awaited them.

The Light Brigade, outnumbered, wheeled and retreated. Of those 673 brave young men, only 226 came back, and of those a mere 173 could still ride the horses on which they had charged, bewildered, into battle.

James Osborne was one.

Through the indescribable hell of stench and smoke and awful noise he stumbled, but before the day was out, the wounds he had received, untreated and filthy, were beginning to fester.

He arrived at Scutari on a stretcher, rambling deliriously of laughter and drawers. The men who carried him were heard to remark that the officer, half off his head as he was, still had thought for his loins.

On the same day, a ship arrived from England, and from it stepped a woman called Florence Nightingale. It was she who brought the means to save James Osborne.

The news of James came in the first week in November. The battle was blazoned across all the newspapers, glorified by its very confusion and ineptitude into one of the most celebrated cavalry charges in British history.

Rose thought she had given herself away, when Charles Hemingway came to his daughter, and told her gently that James had been wounded and lay seriously ill in hospital at Scutari. The next words he spoke seemed to come from some vast, echoing chamber, distorted and incomprehensible to her, and she felt the sweat stand out ice-cold on her body, and her stomach heave, and she knew she was about to fall. Her hands went blindly to the back of Lacy's chair and gripped it – the only stable thing in her tottering world.

'. . . and so you must write at once, my dear, and I implore you, make the letter as fond as you are able.'

Lacy, saddened by the news and anxious for James, who had become dear to her through his letters, looked startled. Charles talked on, and Rose's frozen fingers and flour-white face went unnoticed for the moment.

'. . . any small token of your, of *our* esteem that might help him to fight off the effects of his wounds, can only be beneficial, Lacy. If he knows we are all thinking of him, praying for him and worried about his condition, it will help to revive his spirits. I am a great believer in the power of the mind over the body, and if he knows . . .'

In that moment, Charles's attention was caught by the

rigidity of his daughter's maid and the beads of moisture which beaded the ghastly pallor of her face. Her eyes were haunted, great pools of dark green horror. They appeared to look at some scene of indescribable agony, and a touch of ice slid down his spine. A memory, some feeling of having enacted this moment in a distant dream, of seeing such pain in the eyes of . . . who? Where . . .? He shook his head and blinked.

'Whatever is the matter with you, girl?' he said irritably. 'Have you lost your senses?'

Turning to Rose who stood, the brush still in her hand, just behind her chair, Lacy looked in wonder at her blanched face and shock-filled eyes, and cried out, leaping to her feet to take Rose's hands in concern. But for a brief span of time Rose was oblivious to everything but the deathly fear in her heart.

James hurt.

Images in her mind of bleeding flesh, torn and gaping. He was wounded, seriously ill, dying, perhaps already dead. That strong, laughing face, pale and ill, or closed and silent, eyes empty or glazed in pain, and she here, not knowing, with no one to comfort her, for no one was aware that she loved him.

'Rose. Rose, dear. What is it?'

Someone was holding her, shaking her gently, pulling her back from her nightmarish imaginings. She shuddered violently.

'Rose, what is the matter? Are you ill? Sit down. Here, see . . .'

Suddenly she was aware of what was being said, of where she was, and of those who stood about her. Charles Hemingway stared in astonishment, and Lacy had her arm about her, holding her; anxious, but as puzzled as her father.

'What is it, Rose? What happened? Do you not feel well? Sit down, and I will fetch a glass of water.'

'No. No, Miss Lacy. Please, I'm sorry. I don't know what came over me. Faith, I think 'twas the thought of all the brave young men. To be sure . . . It must have been. No, no, begorra, what must yer think of me! I'm that sorry, sir. Please go on. The brush, if yer please, Miss Lacy.'

She smiled a tremulous smile in Lacy's direction, and bobbed a respectful curtsey to Charles Hemingway, though her stomach churned so she felt she might empty its contents all over his good black suit. Her mind writhed from thought to thought. Dear Mother of God, help me to get through the next few minutes . . . James, stay *alive*! Oh, dear Lord, let me reach my room without arousing further suspicion. Let me be alone . . . Sweet Mother, no one must know.

No one.

She began to brush Lacy's hair with long, steady strokes, and listened to Charles speak of the glory of the charge of the Light Brigade, and the heroism of the men who had taken part in it.

Holy Mother, keep him safe . . .

'So you see, my dear, we must do our best to help one of the heroes who fought so bravely in the battle.'

'Of course, Papa.'

'James is a dear friend, not only of the family but of . . . Well, I think it would be appropriate if you were to write at once, and tell him how much we look forward to his homecoming.

Homecoming. James. He will be home . . .

'Will he come home, do you think, Papa? Or will he be nursed by Miss Nightingale at Scutari? The newspapers say she is performing miracles with those who are in her care. How lucky that she is there to look after James.'

'That is so, child, and I suppose his homecoming depends on the extent of his wounds. We must pray that he will recover. Now, you will write at once, will you not, Lacy?'

Blessed Mother of God, in Your mercy look down upon James Osborne and keep him safe. Heal his wounds and give him the strength to stand the pain. Hold him in Your loving care. Let no more harm befall him and in Your wisdom protect him from all adversity. Hail Mary, full of Grace . . .

'Rose, Rose!' Lacy's voice was sharp. 'That is enough, Rose. You will have my hair out by the roots. Now, let me get dressed, and then I shall write to poor James. What do you suppose are his injuries? Last week I heard that Emily

Longman's poor brother, the one who went to school with Thomas, has lost both legs at the Battle of Alma. Is that not dreadful? He is only twenty two, and will be forced to sit in a wheelchair for the remainder of his life. Oh Rose, poor James, I do hope he will survive. I thought him so charming at my birthday party. I wonder if he has someone who loves him? Do you suppose he has, Rose?'

Lacy gazed into the mirror, her young face soft in its sadness.

'I hope he has, Rose. Someone who loves him, as I love Luke, and will not care a fiddle for his wounds as long as he returns to her. Not even if he has lost both legs like poor Tim Longman.'

Rose moaned, and again Lacy looked at her in consternation. Then in a storm of passionate, sorrowing remembrance, she held her in her arms, soothing her, comforting her.

'Rose. Oh Rosie, I am so sorry. Please forgive me. How could I be so thoughtless! I did not think. To be so insensitive . . . Talking about Tim Longman and his . . . Oh, Rose, I beg of you, do not cry.'

She wept herself, her heart aching for the grief of her friend, and for what she thought she suffered for her dead father.

'I am sorry, Rose. I am so sorry,' she whispered against Rose's dark hair, and Rose cried out her longing and fear for the man who loved the girl who held her in her arms.

# CHAPTER 15

'I cannot go, Luke. Not without telling Papa.'

Luke's handsome, aggressive face closed up in that particular way she was beginning to know so well, and Lacy felt a minute flicker of doubt. Doubt, apprehension, dread. It was really none of those things, and yet it was a mixture of all three, that in just a moment his expression could change from a look of tender pleading love to a stubborn, implacable obstinacy. He was this way more frequently now, as he tried to persuade her to do what she quite honestly could see no reason for doing.

If they had spoken to Papa and he had said no in that adamant way he had – when you knew there was not the slightest purpose in arguing, and that if you continued to do so he would be angry – well, she could have understood Luke's beseeching, and she would have agreed immediately. But Papa knew nothing of the love she had for Luke, nor of their wish to be married. So, surely, it was hardly fair to just run away without a word.

She knew it would not be easy to approach Papa. Her own intelligence and upbringing told her that Luke was not . . . It seemed an unkind thing to say, but that he was not of her own class. But surely that would not matter to someone like Papa, who so admired a man who could start with nothing and become in fifteen years the captain of his own ship. Well, not exactly his own. The *Breeze* belonged to Papa, but Luke was to command her, to be wholly responsible for her, her crew and her cargo, and he was just twenty-seven. Not many men could have done so well with so little. She admired him for it, and she knew Papa did too.

To be married to Luke was all she asked: to marry him with her father's blessing; to have her family stand with her whilst she pledged her vows to the man she loved. It was a simple thing, and she could not understand why Luke would not even hear of her speaking to Papa. If he refused, and there was a possibility that he would, Luke knew she would still go with him wherever he went. To the ends of the earth, if necessary. And on the *Breeze*, for the clipper would sail very soon.

They would be married.

She had promised him.

But he would not listen.

He had this plan, he said, to take her with him when *Breeze* sailed, and they would be married at the first port of call.

'I'm afraid he will prevent our marriage,' he pleaded passionately. 'He will talk you out of it. He will put forward a thousand reasons why you should not marry me, and you will listen to him.'

She had been shocked and angry. 'Luke, how could you say such a thing. You know how much I love you. More than anyone in the world. Oh, my darling, believe me. I will be with you whatever happens.'

'He will lock you up and prevent your coming to me. I shall have to sail without you, and when I return you will be promised to some fine gentleman . . .'

'Luke, Luke!' She pressed her fingers to his mouth and leaned against him, diverting him from his frenzied attempts to force her to his will in the only way she knew.

*Breeze*.

She was his now.

Long and lean with knifelike bows, she would go at a good 'clip', the term from which the word clipper came, and her sails, 'cloud-cleaners', would compel her to sing her way across the water with a life of her own. The lovely sleek hull, fast and beautiful, had been designed and built to compete with the steam ships which, though ugly and dirty, were reliable for they were independent of wind. Luke scorned them. *Breeze* had over twenty sails, was bigger, and would eat up the journey to Canton in eighty four days. Less, if he could coax it from her.

Steam was fine in its way, he knew, but those in the world

217

of shipping had quickly come to the conclusion that sail was the more economical way of carrying cargo. True, steamships held the promise of more regular sailings and arrivals, but coal consumption was high. Their boilers needed to be regularly de-salted, the ships themselves were small and profits too. Except on short voyages, they were useless. But *Breeze*, his *Breeze*, she would fly like a gull across oceans to bring back tea, carried in ornamental Chinese chests; and porcelain; silks, paintings, fans, silver dishes, ornate ivory; objets d'art and furnishings of polished wood and lacquerware; and, if he could wean Lacy from this stubborn determination she had to tell her papa, his ship would bring her back as Mrs Luke Marlowe.

Luke was not afraid of Charles Hemingway. He was afraid of no one. He was only afraid of losing *Breeze*. He wanted Lacy Hemingway as he had never wanted any woman before, but if he was forced to make a choice, he knew where it lay. Women were easy to come by, but there would never be another *Breeze*. She was his chance to be someone; to get somewhere. With her helm beneath his hands he could conquer the sea, become its most famous master.

Then, when he had enough money, he would have his own ship. The *Lacy Marlowe* he would call her, or better yet, the *Alexandrina Victoria*, or perhaps *Alexandrina Marlowe*. His eyes glowed at the thought. He knew that if he could keep Lacy from telling her papa it would all come true, for he could have them both by the time *Breeze* came home to Liverpool, and there would be nothing Charles Hemingway could do about it. Lacy would be Mrs Luke Marlowe. The *Breeze* would have won the annual Tea Race and be laden with cargo, bringing vast profits to the pocket of his new father-in-law.

Fait accompli.

But if Lacy told her Papa before *Breeze* sailed, he would lose them both. A new captain would be found. Lacy would be packed off to some distant relative far away, guarded like the crown jewels, and he would be back where he had been fifteen years ago as a raw lad embarking on his first ship. It would be worse than that, for then he had had the expectation

218

before him that one day he would fulfil his dream. Now he would have nothing, for Charles in his outrage would hound him from the seaport of Liverpool, and with the might of his wealth and position behind him, would see that Luke Marlowe never set sail on a vessel going from there again. Not even as a deck hand.

For months, Luke walked a tightrope of uncertainty, afraid each time he left her that Lacy, in her innocence – or was it naïvety? – would confide in her Papa.

In February 1855, the lovely *Breeze* left her launch in New York and began her journey across the Atlantic to her new home in Liverpool. At her helm was the man who had designed and built her, and beside him stood Luke Marlowe, her new captain. As she ploughed gently into the rollers, which caressed her hull as though to welcome her, Luke lifted his head. His bronzed face held a look of reverent love never seen before by anyone, even Lacy Hemingway, and on his cheeks tears of joy dried in the fresh wind.

He had never been so happy in his life.


'Can we not be alone for a moment without her forever staring at us? I want to tell you about *Breeze*, and what your father said to me. I am to do one more trip on the *Sarah Beaumont*, to New York this time, whilst some further fitting out is done on *Breeze* and then, next trip, in April I am to take her to Canton. CANTON, Lacy! Oh, my love, if you could have stood beside me on that deck and felt . . . But you will, you will. She is so beautiful. The sails seem almost to lift her from the water, and she glides, she really just . . .'

'Luke, Luke! I shall be jealous if you go on so.'

He kissed her upturned face, lingering at each eyelid before moving his mouth to hers. Taking her bottom lip between his, he sucked it gently, teasing her tongue with his own. He felt her sink towards him, the bones of her scarcely able to hold her upright, and in that second he knew that in the way the ship was now his, so must he have this girl. Before another hour had gone by he must put his mark on her and claim her as he had claimed the *Breeze*. No one would know, not yet – only himself and Lacy. But that would be enough. She was already his: captured as the ship had been captured. She must be made aware of it in the only way a woman knows.

'Where can we go, where?' he breathed, sliding his lips beneath the curve of her jaw. His hands moved from her shoulders, slipping down to cup her breasts. Through the thick, warm wool of her dress he felt her nipples peak in the palms of his hands.

'There is nowhere, Luke. We cannot leave the . . .' Her voice was husky, sensual in its longing, and she trembled with the need to be in his arms. 'We . . . Arkwright is waiting in the carriage outside the gallery and Rose, she would not allow . . . You know how she is.'

'Damn Rose and damn Arkwright.'

'Ssh, Luke. She will hear you and . . .'

'I don't care if she does hear. Oh, my darling, I only want to be alone with you for half an hour, ten minutes. In all these months we have never been alone. Not once since . . . not since the night . . .'

Lacy's eyes, which had stared mesmerized into his face, fell shyly to the knot of his cravat, then rose again to gaze with hot longing into his, and he knew that if he could find a way to spirit her out of the garden without the coachman or Rose being aware that she had gone, he might spend a most pleasant half hour with her. That was all it would take to turn her from the virtuous, innocent child she now was into a passionate woman. Her lack of experience showed in the way she allowed him to do as he pleased with her, and but for his plan, that which was almost come to fruition, she would have been in his bed as soon as he could have got her there.

Success made him careless. The heady events of the last few days put a certainty in him that he could do no wrong. Even if he made her pregnant, it would not matter now, for in six weeks he would sail on the *Breeze*. And she would be with him.

His senses raced, and a pulse began to beat furiously in his temple. His rooms were close by in Rodney Street. If they could find some way out of this damned garden without that bitch seeing them go, he would have Lacy back here before she had noticed their disappearance. And if she should discover that they had gone, what did it matter? She could do nothing. Was she likely to run into Colquitt Street crying to Arkwright that Miss Lacy had gone and her lover with her? Hardly. To admit that she knew her mistress was meeting a man, and that she, Rose, was keeping lookout whilst she did so, would scarcely be acceptable in the eyes of her employer. No, Rose would know where her future lay. It would be in some factory or the poor house if Charles Hemingway knew of her involvement in this. Luke meant it to be there anyway, when he and Lacy sailed on the *Breeze*. He had no intention of taking Rose with them. His mind looked forward to that moment when he would beat down the river and look back at Miss Rose O'Malley standing beside her trunk on the dock.

But, first things first.

'Come,' he whispered smilingly, taking Lacy's hands.

Delighted with the adventure, and in her artlessness thinking how exciting life had become since she had met Luke, Lacy tiptoed like a child eluding the watchful eye of a disapproving parent and, hand in hand, they began to search the high wall of the garden.

It was cold. A hoar frost had covered the winter grass and lay like a coat of fine spun sugar on the trunks and branches of the big oak trees. It was crisp beneath their feet as they made their way between the shrubs in the beds against the wall, and Lacy's heart raced with joy. Her clear grey eyes had turned a dark, dark silver, like gunmetal with the moon upon it, and her cheeks were flushed to crimson in the cold. Her bonnet fell to the back of her neck, knocked there by the low branch of a tree, and she had to put her hand to her mouth to hold in the laughter. But she did not need to worry, for the intense cold had sent Rose inside to sit on a little seat by the closed door. It was 'taters' out in the garden, she said to herself, and she had not her love to keep her from the cold as Lacy did.

Relaxing, the long spell of uninterrupted meetings without discovery or incident lulling her into a false sense of security, Rose dreamed of Captain James Osborne, recovered now

221

from his wounds, and returned to his regiment at Balaclava. She dozed a little, for the gallery was warm, and smiled as she did so.

They found the small gate in two minutes. The honeysuckle, the scent of which had almost overwhelmed them in September, had spread brown, bare arms about its frame, but it was not locked.

It took but minutes to reach Luke's neat set of rooms, and less to take the clothes from Lacy's eager body. She could not wait and neither could he. He did not speak of *Breeze*, nor of what Charles Hemingway had said to him, nor of anything. Not even of love. It was all done in ten minutes. In fifteen they were both dressed, scarcely looking each other in the face.

Lacy tried to speak, to beg to be reassured that what they had just done though they were not yet married, was pure and honourable, made so by their love for one another. She longed to be told that she was still the beloved, the rare and precious treasure of this man, but he was in too much of a hurry to get her back to the garden before their absence was discovered. He kissed her hurriedly, tucking her hair absentmindedly beneath her bonnet, searching her clothing with a keen eye to see that she was as she had come in. Her heart felt frozen in bewilderment that this was all it was. Was the lovely tingling warmth, the aching joy, the softness, the gentleness, the happiness to end as it had just done in that swift act of . . . Of what? She had scarcely got to grips with the wonder of Luke's body, and her own welling love for it, when it had all been over.

'Come on, my love. We must be quick. Rose will be looking out of that door like a hen after its chick, and we must have it back before she notices its disapperance, or she will cackle fit to wake the whole farmyard.'

Lacy was trembling. Her breasts ached and her body, that part which had no name, was so painful she could barely walk. She hurried beside her lover back to the garden from which she had set out delightedly only half an hour ago, and wondered why her heart felt as though it had died within her

222

breast. Her face was set in the lines of a child who is confused by some unexpected, and rather frightening turn of events.

Lacy sat with Rose before her bedroom fire, and looked into its flaming depths. The curtains were drawn against the night, and the room, so spacious and elegant, was warm and secure against the things which lurked outside. The owls were hunting in the woods beyond the garden, and the noise they made could be heard clearly on the night air. There was a silver moon to light their way, but it did not intrude into the golden, glowing room. Sounds, other sounds, infiltrated the sense of the two girls; sounds that told them they were safe, and protected by the man who ruled them both. The logs crackled in the fireplace, carried that morning by Jonas from the stack behind the stable, and brought to keep them warm in a cold world. A clock ticked upon the mantelshelf. It was made of mother of pearl; the frame which held it of gold. The chair in which Rose sat creaked gently as she rocked it; her dark head, her cap thrown carelessly to the dresser, rested upon soft velvet. Everywhere was rich comfort, even the dog lying between them was accustomed to sleeping upon the thick pile of Turkish rugs.

Rose watched Lacy as she stared, hypnotized by something inside her head, into the heap of burning logs. One spat, as the sap within it dripped into a flame. Copper leaped to his feet, dismayed, then with a hurt look at Lacy, as though it were somehow her fault, resumed his dreaming contemplation of the day's events. Rose laughed, and bent to stroke his head saying, 'Did it startle you then, poor old thing?' and looked again at Lacy. But there was no response.

Rose sighed. Lacy was busy, no doubt, with thoughts of that varmint, who held her in the palm of his hand like she belonged to him. And much good it will do her. Or is doing her, by the look of her face tonight. So white and strained, and tired too. There were deep, lilac circles beneath her eyes, that had not been there this morning. And would you look at the way she sat. Like she had the troubles of all the world upon her back. He did not appear to be making her very

223

happy with his sweet talk and languishing looks. Thanks be to Jesus, he was away to America tomorrow, and they would have a few weeks of peace.

She thought she could not stand much longer the furtive sidling from one corner to another, in order to escape possible encounters with acquaintances of the Hemingway family. It was only by the Grace of God that they had been lucky so far. Some day, someone would see them together. When the warmer nights came, and he and Lacy could meet again in the summer house, it could only be a matter of time before Lacy's long absences were discovered. Or would they have arranged something else by then? Like marriage, perhaps? Not very likely, she'd be bound. Not unless the devil could benefit by it, and he wouldn't, if Charles Hemingway had anything to do with it.

Rose sighed again, looking compassionately into the pensive face opposite. It appeared that Lacy did not want to talk of whatever it was that troubled her. So, putting her head back on the velvet headrest, she closed her eyes, and waited for the call to brush Lacy's hair, as she did every night.

Lacy was scarcely aware of Rose, or of even where she herself was in that last hour she was to spend in her father's house. She could not understand why she felt so wretched on this lovely day; the day on which she truly belonged to Luke in a way a woman belongs to the man she loves. He had made her his wife in all but name, and that would come soon. So why did her heart rest in her breast like a lump of dough from which the yeast has been forgotten? Today should be the happiest, no, one of the happiest days of her life, and she refused to believe there would be no other. So why then, did she not sing, and sparkle, and dance about in her newfound status?

Because of the underhanded, stealthy way in which the encouter took place, a tiny voice inside her replied. It should not have happened as it did. Not in a back room, a place hidden and clandestine, and performed as though one had a train to catch. It might have been a footman grappling with a parlour maid in the cupboard beneath the stairs; the function squeezed in between the cleaning of the silver and the polishing of the master's boots.

Oh Luke, she wept tearlessly, why was it not as I expected it to be? Why did you not hold me, and kiss me more, and say you loved me when it was over? Why did it seem so . . . so . . ? SORDID, her honest mind said, and she flinched. That is the word for which you seek, and that was what it was; and it was so because you have allowed it to become so.

Luke is wrong. She knew it now. Wrong to hide our love from everyone as he is doing. His reasons are valid in his own mind, and I respect them. He is afraid that whilst he is away Papa will pair me off, but that is all the more reason to speak to Papa. To . . . put in a claim. To show the world that Lacy Hemingway is the beloved of Luke Marlowe. Oh Luke, Luke, she cried silently. Can you not see that? Tomorrow you sail away, and I shall be lonely for six weeks, when I might be employed making arrangements for our wedding. Think, just think: if we were to be married quickly I might sail with you. Oh, I know Mama would wring her hands, and say that people will talk, but who is to care. Not I, for I would be your wife. We would leave together on the *Breeze*. It would be our wedding journey. If only I had persuaded you to speak to Papa we might have saved this . . . the time we spent in your rooms . . . until we were alone and married, and had the right, the honest right to do as we did, and all the time in the world in which to do it. If only . . .

With a gasp that brought the dog to his feet, Lacy jumped from her chair, standing in a dither of uncertainty that changed rapidly to excitement, and then to bright conviction. She began to move across the room towards the door.

'Of course, of course,' she was murmuring. 'Why did I not think of it? That is why . . . It was because . . . But if I tell Papa . . .' Unaware of the gaping Rose, or of the bewildered dog, her face alight with rapture, Lacy opened the door and was gone, banging it behind her.

'What in the name of all the angels was that about!' Rose gasped and looked into Copper's velvet eyes. But he was as mystified as she, and his expression said so.

\*

225

'Papa, may I have a word with you?'

Startled, Charles turned towards the white-clad figure in the doorway, putting the glass of bedtime whisky he was drinking upon his desk with such force some splashed upon its polished top. He took his cigar from between his lips and blew out some smoke, then coughed, for the sight of his daughter in her nightgown had quite shaken him, and he had swallowed a mouthful.

'Lacy, have you no wrapper with which to cover yourself?' he said severely. For the first time Lacy was made aware that, in her eagerness to put into action the lovely plan which had sprung, fully formulated, into her mind, she had quite forgotten the trappings which modesty demanded.

'Oh, Papa. I am so sorry. I will this instant return . . .'

She turned towards the door, intent on going back to her room for her robe. But Charles stopped her with a wave of his hand, smiling, for her nightgown was so completely voluminous that not one inch of her flesh was visible, bar her hands and feet. Not a curve was revealed, and she might have been a child of ten, standing there with her hair falling down her back.

'Never mind, my dear. I am sure no one will see. Your Mama and the servants are all in their beds. It is hardly worth returning now.'

His eyes fell on her fondly, and his thoughts were warm and self congratulatory. He had imagined years ago that he might have some difficulties with this child of his. Self-willed she had been, and eager to do the things only men were allowed. But now look at her! She had become a lovely young woman, well behaved, and though still inclined to be a trifle immodest, that was obviously because of her innocence.

What a day it would be when the Osbornes and Hemingways gathered to see the joining of the best of their respective offspring. Admittedly, James was a second son, and would inherit no part of Richard Osborne's estate but, nevertheless, he was a wealthy and eligible young man. They were well suited, he and Lacy, and when this damned skirmish in the Crimea was over, it would give him the greatest pleasure to see them married. Perhaps it might have been expedient to drop a hint to the child. But there, when James was home and began to pay court, she would, no doubt, be as thrilled as any young girl. She was, after all, not yet eighteen.

'Papa?' Lacy's voice questioned the long silence, and he brought himself back, smiling a trifle fatuously upon his favourite child.

'Yes, my dear. What is it that brings you here at this time of night? You should be asleep by now.'

'Yes, Papa, but I have something to tell you . . . to discuss, and I felt it could not wait until morning.'

'Well, my dear, what is it?' His voice was indulgent.

At the last moment her conviction almost deserted her. In her bedroom, with Rose and Copper and all the sweet, familiar things of her life about her – all the warmth and luxury provided by her papa, and given to her with love – it had seemed so easy to decide that Papa had only to know and he would instantly understand, and give her this one last thing she asked of him. But now, looking into his kind grey eyes, those which had scarcely ever been more than sternly reproving, her confidence began to slip away.

'Yes, Lacy, what is it?'

Without another thought, impatient only to have the words out, and brave the explosion which she knew would come first; longing to be about the arrangements which would have to be put in hand immediately, she said abruptly,

'I love Luke Marlowe, Papa. And he loves me.'

She thought he had been taken ill. What was it that attacked older men who have some terrible shock, sending them out of their minds, like poor Mr Whipple from Aigburth Farm? He had toppled head-first into his own pig pen, and if the pigs had not set up such a terrible squealing and grunting, he would not have been found until he had failed to return home for his dinner.

A seizure, that was it. A seizure.

'Papa,' she said tentatively, and stood up as though she would run from his dreadful face. His countenance took on the look of a red cider apple when it was over ripe, and will burst if pressure is brought to bear upon it. Purple veins stood up in his cheeks and at his temples, pulsing with blood; and his eyes protruded from their sockets, the pale greyness of them turning instantly as black as a dark night. Only the whites remained pale: a pale, suffused pink.

As suddenly as it had come, the dreadful face vanished. But as it did so, Lacy was left with the feeling that she stood before a stranger. A person she had never met before, and one who looked at her so icily she felt herself begin to tremble in the warm room, as though a window had been opened on the freezing February night.

'Sit down,' the stranger said. And she sat.

'Tell me about it.'

'Well I . . . Well, Papa . . . Do you not remember the day when we came to . . . the day on which . . .' Her voice trembled and became a little shrill.

'Yes.'

Lacy's heart skipped a beat, and fear dribbled a finger across the back of her neck. The staccato voice with which Papa spoke filled her with unease, and she wished the interview over and done with. She was, as yet, not sorry that she had come, for it must be said if she and Luke were to be together. But she did wish Papa . . .

'Go on.' She jumped, and her heart did a cartwheel.

'Well you see, Papa, we fell . . . We fell in love and . . .'

'Fell in love?'

'Yes, Papa. You see . . .'

'You have met this man since that day?'

'Yes, Papa. You see . . .'

'Where?'

'I beg your pardon, Papa.'

'Where have you met this man?'

'Well, you see . . .'

'Where have you met this man? Tell me!'

'We met in the . . .'

'Yes, yes?'

'. . . in the art gallery.'

228

Charles Hemingway appeared to relax a trifle, and so did Lacy.

For a moment only.

'Who was with you on these occasions?'

'Oh Rose, of course, Papa. You see . . .'

'She will be dismissed immediately.'

The shock hit her as though Charles Hemingway had leaned across the desk and struck her full in the face.

'Dismissed? Rose? Oh no, Papa. For what reason? It was not Rose who . . .'

'That will do. Tell me what . . . occurred at these meetings.'

'Occurred, Papa?' Lacy blinked, her mind still on the turmoil of Rose being dismissed. Why, oh why? Rose had done nothing. Why should . . ?

'If you do not tell me exactly what took place, what was said, *everything*, not only shall I dismiss the girl, but I shall see she works nowhere in this town again. Now, begin.'

'Please, Papa. Please listen to me. We wish to be married, Luke and I. He is an honourable man.'

For a split second the scene in Luke Marlowe's rooms flashed into Lacy's mind. The milk whiteness of his body where the sun had not touched it; the hot, aching blue of his eyes as he had shuddered in some mysterious emotion upon her; and his cry – was it HER name he had called out? She had not been sure, and as the memory burned within her, she could no longer look her father in the face. An honourable man? An honourable man? The phrase beat like a pulse in her body and she felt her skin slick with perspiration. Her father saw it, and was desolate, and his anger grew with his desolation.

'Did you visit any other . . . place besides the gallery?'

'Papa, I beg you . . .'

'Answer me!'

'It was only in the garden . . .'

'Which garden?'

'At the gallery.'

'Were you alone?'

'Rose was . . .'

'Were you alone?' His voice was like flint, grey and implacable.

'Yes.' She hung her head and wept.

'Did he . . . touch you?'

'Oh, Papa.'

'Did he touch you?'

'Yes.'

'In what way?'

'Please, Papa, please. We wish to be married.' She mumbled it hopelessly into the frill on the bodice of her nightgown.

'In what way did he touch you?'

'He . . . kissed me.'

Not in his worst fears, those which had crawled into his mind during the past ten minutes, had Charles Hemingway imagined that his lovely untouched daughter might have given more than a kiss. She was a child, as inexperienced of such things as on the day she had come into the world. There was the question of a quiet and convenient location in which to . . . to perform any other act. And the man. No man would dare, would have the temerity, the sheer effrontery to interfere with the daughter of the man upon whom his whole life depended. He had only that day been given the most precious thing – apart from the girl who stood before him – that one man can give another.

His ship.

Luke Marlowe was to take his, Charles Hemingway's, ship, and command her. There was not a seaman in the whole of Liverpool who would not change places with him. It was not likely that such a man would play fast and loose with his career by playing fast and loose with the daughter of the man who was to give it to him. A kiss. Charles's mind took him mercifully no further than this for, if he had known, he would have killed Luke Marlowe. The man was finished, of course. Finished forever. For a kiss, he was finished. Things could be hushed up, for no one would know. She would go away until James . . . And the maid . . .

Charles Hemingway stood up, towering like a gigantic tree above the trembling, weeping, distraught girl who had thought in her brave honesty to make things 'honourable'. Her papa, her beloved papa had exhorted her always to 'tell the truth, for no harm can come from it, Lacy'. She had, and her world was falling about her like the leaves which whipped to the ground in an autumn storm.

'Get up.'

She got up. She stood before him, her lovely brightness dimmed as he had seen it only once before. But his anger, his disappointment, his hurt pride in her gave him no grounds for pity.

'Go to your room and stay there . . .' She began to turn, stunned, in the direction of the door.

'. . . and send the maid to me.'

In a moment, the passionate, loyal heart of her had her fighting again. Fighting in defence of the girl at whose door this would be laid and on whom no blame could be put.

'Please, Papa. Do not blame Rose. It was not her fault. She tried to stop me. Take her from me, if you must. Put her back in the kitchen, but do not take her job. She helps her mother and her brothers and sisters, and if you . . .'

'Have her pack her bag and be in my study within the half hour. That is my last word. I shall be upstairs to lock your door as soon as she is out of the house.'

He turned his back on her, and not until he heard the click of the door as she shut it behind her, did he collapse into the chair.

They were gone, with the dog, when he went to look for Rose. He never saw his daughter again. The woman Lacy Hemingway became was not his daughter.

# CHAPTER 16

They took nothing but the clothes they stood up in, the dog, and the emerald necklace and ear bobs to match which had been left to Lacy by Grandmama Lucinda. They were all she had of any value, and even she was ignorant of their true worth. That would come later.

Lacy did not weep or explain to Rose, as they set out to walk the long, cold miles to Rodney Street. And when Rose questioned the taking of Copper, Lacy hissed, whitefaced, 'He is coming. Do you think I would leave him here with HIM? He would be dead by this time tomorrow.' Appalled, Rose dressed herself as instructed, in her warmest, most durable clothes, and crept behind Lacy through the winter garden for the last time.

The dark mass of wood was on their right and the wall climbed into the meadow of Jericho Farm before she spoke. The bright, white moon lit their way. It was as easy to see the path, along which they had flown dressed as boys nearly seven years ago, as it had been then in broad daylight. The stubble of the winter grass cracked beneath their booted feet, the frost making it as crisp as sugar sticks. Birds nesting for the night in the denuded trees fidgeted, as the subdued murmur of the girls' voices faded away. The dog, uneasy at being out at night, and scenting all manner of dangers absent during the day, padded warily beside them, ready to spring to their defence.

They were slipping by Mr Whipple's farmhouse when Lacy spoke again.

'He threatened to dismiss you, so we could not stay.'

'What the divil are ye blatherin' about?' Rose stood stock still, the moonlight turning her white face to translucent pearl. Her eyes were like great holes of midnight beneath the brim of her best bonnet, which she had not been able to bring herself to leave behind. Lacy walked on, saying matter-of-factly,

'If we do not hurry and get to Luke's before Papa does we will be caught. You will without doubt be imprisoned on a charge of kidnapping, and I shall be flung into exile with Aunt Marie in Greenock and never be seen again. Do hurry up, Rose.'

Rose hurried up, dancing along sideways beneath the bare apple trees in Mr Whipple's orchard, until they reached the lane which led to Aigburth Road. The freezing night air kept them on the move, but they were not cold, for their good warm clothes and their young warm blood fought the chill. Their breath rose in rhythmic gasps about their heads.

'Lacy, will you tell me what all this is about, please? What has your Papa done? Where are we going? Will you stop and tell me, or I swear I'll turn round and go back, so I will. What in bejabers am I doin' out here, when I could be home in me warm bed? Has your Papa . . ? Is this something to do with *that* . . . with Luke Marlowe, is it?'

'Yes.' Lacy's face was set in the direction they were going, and her eyes were like pale glass in the shimmering white of her flesh. Although it was dark, the moonlight put an expression there which Rose had never seen before, and she shivered.

'What's happened?' she asked softly.

'I told him of Luke.'

Rose's breath rasped in her throat.

'You told him of . . ?'

'Yes.'

'But why? Surely you have been for the past five months doing your best to keep it from him.'

'That was Luke's idea.'

They were in Aigburth Road now. The hedgerows rose on either side, stiff with frost. A pale blue mist hung a foot from the rutted surface of the road, and the movement of their skirts sent it hurrying away as they walked through it. They had left behind their crinolines, knowing they would have the need to climb stiles and cover the ground quickly.

233

There was not a light to be seen anywhere. As the two girls passed each silent farm and cottage, dogs barked, and weary heads were lifted from pillows for a second or two, as those who had been disturbed wondered what had awakened them. The two quiet figures passed by without a glance.

'Tell me, Lacy.'

Lacy sighed and pulled her fur-lined mantle more closely about her. The first madness had gone now, leaving her drained and silent, but she knew it was only fair to tell Rose. She had followed Lacy without a murmur, beyond that concerning Copper. Blindly, she had left her home – it was as much that to Rose now as it was to Lacy – and her job, the one which provided a small measure of security for Bridie and her children. She had come unhesitatingly with Lacy, who had offered no explanation. She had asked for none in that desperate half hour of escape, but now she was owed one.

'Luke and I are to be married, Rose.'

Rose kept her face averted, staring at the silvered ruts beneath her feet, her breath even in her throat. But her heart pounded furiously in her chest, and she felt the chill of fear move in her. Dear, sweet Jesus, they were to put their trust in that . . . Dear Mother! Before she could collect her scattered wits into some form of coherent thought, the girl beside her continued.

'I must be honest with you, Rose, for I want you to understand why I took this action. You see, I always thought . . . hoped that if Papa knew about us, about Luke . . . Well, you know how highly Papa thinks of him, Rose.' She turned fervently and took Rose's arm whilst they continued to half walk, half run along the cold lengthy, tunnel of Aigburth Road. 'If he had known, or so I believed, there would be no need for the secrecy we had maintained. I could see no necessity for it, Rose. But for some reason, Luke did. I think he was afraid to lose me,' she said uncertainly.

Rose shivered. Of course he was, you foolish girl; that and his fine position with Charles Hemingway. He wanted both, and some weasel in his brain was working twenty four hours a day to devise the plan which would give them to him. What would it have been then? Rose knew, even as the thoughts flickered in her mind, and she marvelled that an intelligent girl with the benefit of such a fine education could not see what was as plain as the nose on your face.

He had the ship.

He was to sail on her in the spring. Away to China, or some such place. No one could reach him once he took to the seas and if, by chance, Miss Lacy Hemingway should be abroad . . . Well then! Just a few more weeks of keeping Lacy's trap shut, and he would be home and dry. A marriage ceremony in some foreign port, and Charles Hemingway's son-in-law would have it all. And there'd be no part in it for Rose O'Malley, a voice said. Didn't she and himself hate each other like the hen hates the fox?

'But you see, Rose . . . Oh, Rose! I don't know how to tell you this. You are so fine and honest, and ever since we have become friends we have kept nothing from one another, but . . . well, this afternoon . . . Luke and I, we . . .'

Rose felt it come. Fear. Even before the words were spoken, she knew what they would be. In the midst of her terror, a face appeared suddenly: a face smiling and warm with humour, eyes dark and glowing with awakening love; not for herself, but for the girl who spoke.

James, her heart said sadly, and she felt the tears start.

'You see, knowing we were to be married soon, we did not . . . I did not think it wrong to . . .' Lacy manfully took the blame upon herself for her own seduction in Luke Marlowe's bedroom. 'It seemed . . . Do you know what I am trying to say, Rose?'

'Yes.'

'We found a gate in the wall, and Luke said . . . and I agreed, of course, that we might go . . . to Rodney Street where he has rooms, and we . . .'

'Don't be tellin' me the details. I know what happens between a man and a woman.'

There was silence; dead and horrid.

Then, 'You do not understand, Rose. We love each other so much. It is difficult to restrain . . .'

235

And Rose understood. Of course she did, and laid no blame upon the girl who stammered excuses, for she loved a man too. She took Lacy's hand which still lay on her arm, and squeezed it gently.

'Don't tell me any more, acushla. You are a good girl. Why, your heart's as big as the moon, and you can see nought but good in the . . .'

She was about to say the word 'bastard', but stopped herself in time. She despised him, and the thought that she might, just might if Lacy was allowed her way, spend the rest of her days in his household, filled her with dread. But if it took every ounce of her Irish cunning, she'd be with Lacy on that blasted ship. She'd not leave her alone to the mercies of that divil.

'What did your Papa say?' Rose continued. 'No, that's a silly question. 'Tis obvious what he said, or why else would we be traipsing along this owd road in the dead o' night. But you can't blame him, Lacy. He does love you, you know, and I suppose he feels you could aim higher than . . .'

Again, Rose stopped herself from heaping derision on Luke Marlowe's head. The girl loved him, and it did no good to blacken him. She wouldn't believe it even if Rose did. Say nothing, and wait and see which way the cat jumped, she thought. If she was any judge of character, this cat would not only jump a mile, but be kicked on his backside from here to the China he hoped to sail for.

'He was going to dismiss you, Rose. He said, or implied, that you were at fault in allowing me to meet Luke. He seemed to imagine that you should have reported it to him. As though you would. Of course, he knows nothing of our friendship, so I suppose there is some excuse. I would have been prepared for . . . Well, even a beating. But to dismiss you out of hand, *knowing* that you help to support your family, and *especially* after your Papa was killed in his own shipyard! It was not to be borne, Rose. Nor the knowledge that he would lock me up away from Luke.'

Rose walked silently beside her, clothed in the breath which wreathed about them. She does not yet realize what

236

this night has brought, she pondered silently. Does she really believe that Luke Marlowe will stand beside her against the man who holds his future in his hand?

'Where are we going?' she said quietly, expecting the answer when it came.

'To Luke's,' Lacy said simply.

He was asleep when the hammering on his door began. It took almost five minutes to get him from his bed and his appearance – dishevelled, with eyes still full of dreaming sleep that had been clamouring with great sailing ships and chests of treasure – made Lacy laugh with delight, like a child who surprises an adult with some prank.

But Luke did not laugh, nor Rose; although, as yet, Rose was the only one who realized what Lacy had done to Luke with her bold escape.

'Great God, Lacy! What in damnation . . ?'

'Hush, Luke. Do hush, and let us in. We are almost frozen to the marrow. I swear my feet are like ice inside . . .'

'What the hell is going on? Why are you . . ?'

'Let us in Luke, and I will explain.'

Luke Marlowe, his face drooping in comical disbelief, his nightshirt clutched just below his stomach as though he feared a concerted attack upon his private parts, stepped back obediently from the doorway, stumbling over the dog who had whipped in behind him. He turned to see what had thrown him, and again his consternation was almost laughable.

'Wha . . . what . . ?' he said again, then cursed, his face creasing in temper, his bare foot lifting as though to aim a kick at the half-frozen feathers which hung from Copper's belly. He seemed as if he did not know which way to turn, for the room, so peaceful only a moment ago, appeared suddenly to be filled with dogs and women, laughing women who found nothing surprising in the situation. Indeed, Lacy seemed to be overjoyed about something.

His stomach, that barometer of all emotions, particularly fear, began to churn. And although he did not as yet know what she had to tell him, he was fully aware that it would be something so terrible he would not be able to bear it. Oh God! Oh, dear God. What had she done? What had she done? She could not possibly have gone to . . . Not even she, with her stupid ideas of . . . she could not have . . . Surely . . . Please, dear sweet Jesus, the silly little bitch had not . . . Sleep and its residual disorientation left him in the time it took for him to close the door and turn to face her.

Then with shattering certainty he knew.

Luke Marlowe's face became as white as the nightgown he wore, and Rose edged closer to Lacy who was at the fire, stirring the flickering embers, still prattling in that artless fashion she had when she was afraid.

'. . . and the moon was so bright, Luke, it lit our steps. We had not the slightest difficulty in making our way here. I was much afraid some footpad might set upon us, but we met none, did we Rose? There was just one moment when we were coming along St James' Road, when we saw two police constables, but we were able to dive into a basement. Of course Copper did not want to come, naughty boy.' She looked at Copper archly who, at the sound of his name, pricked up his ears and strolled over to her outstretched hand. He still kept a wary eye upon the man who he sensed did not care for him, but as long as his mistress was not threatened Copper was prepared to suffer him. 'It was really quite a pleasant walk, was it not, Rose, though I should not recommend it as a nightly . . .'

'What has happened, Lacy?'

Luke's voice was like steel and his expression the same.

'What brings you to my rooms so late at night?' Although he spoke steadily, he seemed at the same time to be pleading to be told that all was as it should be, and that she and Rose had decided upon a midnight stroll. Just for the fun of it.

'What have you done?'

'Done, Luke? What do you mean by done?' Lacy's voice was high.

'You know what I mean. What has happened?' he repeated. Suddenly he was so terrified it took his restraint from him, and he shouted, 'What have you told your father, for nothing else would have brought you here in the middle of the night. Your father is involved, is he not? Tell me what has happened, or by God I will hit you.'

She understood now. Perhaps understanding had been with her since the moment she had lain upon the tumbled bed which could be seen through the open doorway, and Luke Marlowe had taken her as swiftly as he might some sixpenny harlot. She had sensed his urgency then, and though her mind had told her it was necessary for they must be back before Rose or Arkwright discovered they had gone, it had distressed her. A woman loved by a man is not thrown so carelessly upon a bed, without even the comfort of a warm look.

Still she would not admit it.

'Luke! Please, Luke. Do not be angry. I felt, after what we had done, I must tell Papa . . . I was convinced that he would allow us to be married. Of course I did not say what had happened here.' She laughed hysterically and Rose could have wept for her. 'I wanted us to be married as Amy was, Luke, with my Papa to give me away . . . with my family . . . I was so sure, you see, that Papa would understand. He admires you, Luke. He has given you the *Breeze*, so he must . . .'

The effect upon Luke Marlowe was appalling.

'You stupid, mindless bitch!' Lacy stepped back blinking, confused by the words Luke spoke so venomously.

Luke stepped towards her, and Copper rose from her feet where he had flopped. The fire, which had caught and was blazing cheerfully in the dark room, brushed his coat warmly with gold.

'You stupid cow. You damned half-witted –!' Here he used a word so obscene Rose recoiled. 'What have you done to me?' His voice was shrill, high and hopeless. 'My ship, my lovely ship.' His voice cracked, and Rose saw the glisten of tears in his dark, hollowed eyes. The blue was gone now and only black remained. 'I have waited for her for fifteen years. For fifteen long years she has beckoned to me, and I have followed. Do you know what I have done to get her?'

Hypnotized by his anguish, Lacy shook her head dutifully.

'Do you? Do you? Have you any idea?' He looked quite mad as he went on. 'She was everything I ever wanted, and you have taken her from me.' He might have been talking of a woman, so tender, passionate and agonized was his tone.

'Ever since I was a boy I have loved the sea. I used to come to the quayside and watch the sailing ships, and wait and wait until I was old enough to go with them, wherever they went. Half of my life has gone into the possessing of one, and now you have taken it from me with your girlish fancy to be 'honest' with your Papa. Honest, dear God. *Honest*! Only a few more weeks and she would have been mine.'

He took another desperate, threatening step forward. Copper growled, and Rose pressed protectively closer to Lacy.

'And what did your papa say, Miss Hemingway, when you told him you fancied the idea of marriage with the new master of his clipper ship?'

Luke's voice broke and he began to weep.

'Did he give his permission? Did he? Did he give his blessing? Are we to be married then, and is the *Breeze* to be our wedding present? You little . . !' He began to call her every indescribable word he could lay his tongue to whilst she stood like a figure made of porcelain: white, glazed, silent and still.

Copper had had enough.

The evil which spewed from the man before him; evil aimed at his mistress and the other one for whom Copper felt a protective affection, was too much for him to stand without reply. His coat rippled as he began to move menancingly towards Luke. It was doubtful whether he would have attacked, for as yet his instinct was only to give warning. He stopped, drawing up his upper lip in a snarl. His ears were laid back and one paw was raised ready to spring, but Luke Marlowe was beyond fear. He wallowed in a desolation so deep that he was not aware of anything, except the need to destroy the person who had put him there.

He leaned down swiftly, and picked up the poker with

which Lacy had been sifting the glowing embers of the fire. He lifted it dangerously, and the dog sprang.

Lacy stood like a statue.

'Copper, Copper. Down, boy. *Down*! Come here, Copper. Here boy!' Rose's voice shrieked above the sounds of terror and rage which whirled about the room. The dog had the man down, and though the poker was laid about his fine head, striking him with a force which might have felled a horse, he did not let go. He growled savagely and his jaws snapped as his teeth fought for extra purchase at Luke's throat.

'Copper! For God's sake, Lacy. Call him off! He won't stop for me. Jesus, he'll kill him, an' it'll be the prison hulks for us if he does. Lacy, for the love of Heaven, call him off.'

'Why?' Her voice was devoid of feeling; like the hiss and slither of a snake.

'Lacy, please. *Please*! Oh, dear Blessed Mother, if you'll not do it for him, do it for me. As you love me, call the dog off.'

'Copper.'

He came reluctantly to the hand which clicked its fingers and the man lay on the floor, a dribble of blood about his chin. His nightgown was bunched about his thighs, shifted there in his struggles to avoid the dog's snapping jaws. His penis lay in a soft, crumpled mound in the brush of his pubic hair, and Rose's last thought as she dragged the half comatose girl and the snarling dog towards the door, was that, when it came down to it, all this great bloody fuss was all over nothing more than that silly little thing.

'Where are we going, Rose?'

Lacy had said nothing in all the miles they had walked, stumbling along beside Rose in a state of numbed despair. His words still sliced at her, cutting at her raw and bleeding flesh, not allowing it to begin the healing process, nor even to form a scab of protection, and though she asked the question, she did not care about, nor even listen for, the answer.

Rose gave her none.

The night was lightening to dawn and bird song began. The twitters and chirrups turned the dog's head. A touch of coral striped the horizon in the east. Lights appeared here and there in windows, making squares of yellow in the blue. The moon had long gone; only the stars remained, fading as daylight came to take their place.

The two drooping figures moved tiredly, and the dog crept nervously behind them, fear and anger still lurking in his mind.

There was a light in the kitchen, and when the door opened, it streamed out like a pathway to Heaven, gold and yellow and warm, and with it came the lovely smell of bacon frying. The dog was in over the doorstep like a red shadow, glad to be home from this night's doings.

Sally screamed when she saw them, and dropped the teapot she had been just about to fill with boiling water for the first, mouth-watering brew of the day. Annie came, and Kitty and Polly, scullery maids, housemaids, the first ones up in the big house. Kitty began to cry.

'There's nothing ter cry about, yer daft lump,' Rose said tartly, as she half carried Lacy over the threshold, and put her in a chair by the fire. 'Now stop yer bletherin' an' go an' fetch the master.'

Kitty shrieked and threw her apron over her head. The very idea of waking the god who ruled her, at this unearthly hour, froze the blood in her veins.

'Stop it, d'yer hear. Go an' get him at once. Tell him Rose sent for him.'

Kitty shrieked louder, cowering in the chimney corner, refusing adamantly to be the one to take the message, for he'd kill her as soon as look at her. And what right had Rose to be ordering not only her but the master about the place?

'Annie, will yer go? Someone must fetch 'im ter Miss Lacy. Tell 'im she's back. 'E'll know what yer mean. Say Rose wants ter see 'im before she goes. Have yer got it? Miss Lacy's back and Rose wants ter see 'im before she goes.'

It took only ten minutes.

The intrepid Annie, of sterner stuff than Kitty, came back to say, with a face on her like a puzzled child trying to get to grips with its first primer, 'Master says 'e ain't got no daughter called Miss Lacy, Rose. What do 'e mean, d'yer think? That's what 'e says, as plain as plain. I 'aven't got no daughter called by that name, 'e says, an' tell the person what sent the message that if she wasn't gone from 'is 'ouse in fifteen minutes, 'e was a' callin' the police. Oh Rose, what can 'e be thinkin' of?'

Annie was beside herself, her plain country face bewildered with the worry of it all. She began to weep with Kitty as Rose took Lacy's hand, and heard her say tenderly,

'Come on, my lovely. We're off again, an' the Blessed Mother's the only one who knows where we'll fetch up. Come on, sweetheart. Hang on to Rose.'

The tired dog slipped through the closing door behind them.

# CHAPTER 17

The dog's bark was as hoarse as if he had the quinsy by the time they arrived at Bridie's door, and Rose was perfectly sure that if it had not been for his presence, they would never have got there unmolested, even in broad daylight. The stinking alleys and dim courtyards through which they had passed teemed with villains, whose eyes gleamed in surprised anticipation as they stared greedily at the two elegantly dressed young ladies who passed them by.

Eyes glazed, faces white with shock, feet bleeding inside their boots, they fell down the steps of Bridie's area basement, and scarcely heard her cry of terror as she opened the door. Lancer McGhee had gone to work.

'Rose, Rose darlin'. Come up wid yer. Come up, girl. Sure, I can't lift yer on me own. Rose acushla, will yer be gettin' on yer feet?'

The hands which held her were rough, chapped and red with chilblains, but fairly clean, as was the anxious face which bent over her, but the hair, the midnight black hair of her Mammy was streaked with grey and limp with neglect. The voice was the same, though. It was thick with love, and the lilting brogue of County Clare, and went on and on in the way it had seven years ago. Blue eyes, faded now and dull with acceptance of what life had done to her, glowed again with the joy of seeing her girl, and tears wet her cheeks.

They had met from time to time. Never here, for Bridie was always afraid of what Lancer might do to Rose, but the carter who brought most of the wage Rose earned each week delivered to Rose the occasional 'note' and, leaving her family to fend for itself, Bridie would spend half an hour on Rose's Sundays off in the company of her eldest child. They usually sat whispering in the back pew of the church, the only place Lancer was guaranteed not to go, quiet and warm and peaceful, and spoke of Sean and Mary Kate and Patrick and the rest, and both were comforted.

'Come away in, mavourneen,' Bridie quivered, 'fer aren't the neighbours gettin' the real eyeful. Himself's away, so 'tis safe yer are for a wee while.' She squinted at the half-dead girl who drooped beside her daughter, and her face was a picture of perplexity. Never had the likes of this been seen in these parts, and never would again, she'd be bound.

'Get away wid yer, divils, or I'll set the dog on yer,' she threatened two young boys, who put out acquisitive hands to Lacy's muff which had fallen to the ground. One might have supposed the animal to be hers by the manner in which she flung his services about, but Copper, a bundle of agitation and nervous fear, already had the matter in hand. He had never in his life spent such a night as the one just gone, and he was almost at the end of this tether, but his snapping teeth met inches from the filthy questing fingers, and they drew back hastily. He stirred Lacy's nerveless fingers with his nose, and was relieved when the door was closed and he could ease his exhausted body to the filth of the floor. He still did not relax, though, but kept his eyes peering carefully about, moving his ears to catch the first hint of danger.

Rose was the first to come to her senses.

She looked about the room which she had not seen for six years, and wondered that it appeared to be exactly as it was then. The black mould still decorated the walls and ceiling, no worse nor better, as though there was a limit to be reached and the fungus had reached it. The same scrap of net clung to the dirt-encrusted window. The same tiny fire crackled bravely in the greasy fireplace between the ovens, and still it gave out scarcely any heat. The boxes, three to a side, stood along the table, so lopsided one wondered why the plates and mugs did not slide off to the floor. Sean's chair rested in its usual place, just as it had always done, but now it was filthy as the fire back. Rose sat in it, fearing for her lovely, blue silk dress, but too tired to care.

It was all precisely the same but for the six small figures who stood or sat about in silent astonishment. They had never

245

seen their half-sister, nor she them, and they stared at one another with blank faces. Four boys and two girls, and all with varying shades of the bright orange hair of the man who was married to Bridie. On two of the boys it stood up, spiky as a field of bright corn; on a third it curled about his head like the feathers on a hen's chest. The girls were similarly crowned, though on the eldest, a girl of about six, it tumbled down her back in a cascade of rippling apricot, and on the baby, it bounced in fat copper curls. He clung to his mother's skirts, dragged with her wherever she went, but Bridie seemed not to notice.

We are strangers, Rose thought. It was as though Bridie minded a clutch of children belonging to a neighbour, and yet they stared at her as though she were the intruder.

They were handsome children, with none of the hard cragginess of the man who had fathered them. The girls were small and delicately made, unlike both their parents. Their eyes were the pale blue of a robin's egg, although those of the youngest boy, the baby, were of the bright summer sky blue which had once been his mother's.

The children edged closer to Rose, mouths slack, eyes staring from mucky faces, clutching an assortment of rags and tatters about them. Although they were filthy, they evidently ate better than their siblings. It seemed that whatever else Lancer did he provided a decent meal or two for his children. The eldest boy had a 'mouse' the size of a saucer about the pale blue of his eyes, and there were five perfect fingerprints of purple upon the tender flesh of the baby's arm. Apart from these relatively minor disabilities, Lancer's children appeared to be remarkably well treated.

Bridie was pregnant again.

So this is how my few bob is spent, Rose thought dispiritedly, as she looked round the circle of faces. But as Bridie pushed a mug of tea into her hand, then reached a fond hand to the curls of the baby, her bitterness drained away, and she knew she would have it no different. The money, earned with so much effort; saved so assiduously, had helped to ease the burden on Bridie's back. Lancer McGhee's children they might be, but Bridie was their mother, and hers too.

Bridie spoke almost shyly. 'These are your brothers and sisters, Rose.' It was clear that she was proud of her brood. 'This is Joseph, nearly six now, he is; and Patrick,' she pushed forward a bright-eyed imp, who grinned, 'and Teresa and Seamus . . .'

Rose's heart began to thunder in her breast, and she felt the mug she held tilt in her frozen hand. Her mother's face wavered, and the six small children, bright heads gleaming in the dim room, became one, then split apart again as their names came serenely from Bridie's lips.

'. . . Kathleen an' sure this is me baby, Declan.' Bridie took the infant who clung to her skirt upon her lap, as she sat comfortably on the box. She kissed his dirty cheek soundly, cuddling the child around the bump beneath her apron. The baby put his thumb in his mouth, and stared in speechless wonder at Rose.

'They're fine children, aren't they, darlin', an' Lancer's that proud of them.' Bridie shrugged her shoulders and smiled a smile of resignation. 'Now an' again when the drink's in 'im 'e clouts us one but 'e's good ter us, Rose. We eat good. Of course . . .'

She lowered her voice and looked around in the manner of one who suspects eavesdroppers. Her glance fell on Lacy, who lay like one dead on the palliasse in the corner, the dog beside her, but sensing no threat she went on.

'. . . the money yer send is a gift from 'Eaven, to be sure. I never let 'im know about it. Not once. We 'ad an arrangement, me an' the owd carter. Well, no one takes any notice round 'ere an' faith isn't 'e a nice enough bloke, Rose, an' I thought, well, why not, 'e's no worse than Lancer. Eeh Rose, my Rose. 'Tis grand ter see yer, grand . . .'

Her voice babbled on delightedly, whilst Rose struggled from the paralysing numbness which her mother's words had forced upon her. Deep in her mind, her senses dallied with the notion of the carter, the man who came to the kitchen door and ogled the maids, the man who was clean and tidy and not very old, having a fancy for the dirty trollop who sat before her. She loved her mother, but she had no illusions as to what she had become. The carter!

247

She could scarcely keep up with Bridie as she rattled on about Mrs Geraghty, 'still up to 'er eyes in bad luck, poor soul . . .'

*Mrs Geraghty* had bad luck?

'. . . and Father O'Hara, who was over only yesterday . . .'

*Here?*

'. . . and the piece of mutton Lancer brought 'ome yesterday, pinched from a warehouse, an' what a bit of luck, fer it is bubblin' on the stove jus' now, and with a few taters . . . See, our Joseph, 'and me me purse an' run ter the shop fer a few . . .'

Rose hurt all over, and only the most rigid self control kept her from standing up and screaming her pain to the rooftops.

Joseph. Joseph. Her tall, slender, serious young brother. Green-eyed and dark-haired, and frightened into flight by the responsibility placed upon him by Sean's death. Fifteen he would be, wherever he was. And what about Patrick? Patrick whose 'legs were bleedin', Rose, and raw with the fire an' 'is skin so black . . .' Then there was Teresa, grave-eyed and trembling, but brave, so brave, clinging to Mary Kate who had promised to 'see to things' until Mammy was better. Lancer had 'gone for' Teresa, so she had been sent to the workhouse to avoid the fate of Mary Kate, who had been 'got at' by the man whose children were all named for Rose's brothers and sisters. Three little boys shunted off as though they mattered to no one, and sweet Kathleen given an overdose of opium, to keep her quiet whilst her overburdened mother tried to work.

Where were they, all those children who had been banished one by one to make room for this lot who now took not only their place, but their names.

Rose stood up abruptly, wanting to run, wanting to escape from the woman who it seemed had invaded the loving, lovable, impudent creature who had once been Bridie O'Malley. She looked down at the greasy hair; the face ingrained with years of dirt; the thick, childbearing body; the red, work-calloused hands – though how they became so was not evident in this hovel – clasped about the carrot-topped baby; and wanted to weep for what had gone.

Sean. Oh, Daddy. Daddy. Taking one step away, then another towards the door, she hunched herself, ready to run, but a quiet voice stopped her.

'Rose.' It was Bridie.

'Rose, I couldn't do any other, Rose. I've got them back, Rose. Nearly all of them. Don't, don't blame me fer what . . .'

Rose turned and walked back slowly to the woman sitting on the box beside the table. She knelt at her feet, pressed her face beside the quiet baby, and held her mother to her. The love and pity she had always felt flooded back. She did not blame her. There was no one to blame but the fate which had seen fit to tear her family to shreds.

They slept for a while, the two exhausted girls, but Bridie was afraid. If Lancer should return unexpectedly, what then? She did not know why they were here. Rose had done no more than tell her that there was trouble, then sleep had overcome her, and she had only time to fall upon the mattress beside Lacy before it took her.

Copper dozed fitfully, lifting his domed head occasionally as a sudden voice outside disturbed him. He remembered this place, and though he allowed the children to pat his head and touch the gloss of his silky coat, he was not happy.

It was mid-day. The succulent aroma of boiled mutton teased the nostrils of the sleeping girls and, almost at the same time, they awoke and sat up.

Lacy felt the thin palliasse beneath her with a hand which trembled, and heard the splash as something dripped down the wall beside her. Her ankle itched and so did her head, and she scratched it thoroughly, disturbing the pins which held up the carelessly arranged mass of her hair. Last night she had been too excited, too frightened, too enraged to do more than push a comb or two into it, and stuff the lot beneath her bonnet. She had had only one thought in her head, and that was to get Rose from the house, and herself to Luke's before her papa locked her in her bedroom.

Six pairs of eyes stared in awe at the fairy creature who lay in their Mammy's bed, and, for a second, before remembrance

249

caught her, Lacy smiled and held out her hand to the youngest. He was about twelve months old. His eyes were blue and pert, and his hair was the colour of the oranges which came from Papa's ships. He took Lacy's fingers fearfully and smiled, and then it came back to her, all of it, and she thought she was going to be sick. Her stomach clenched as Luke's words rang in her head, and she felt some part of her, that which had been bright, free and confident, shrivel up like a leaf in a fire. Her face, which had been pale with fatigue, became paler, and her grey eyes grew bleak.

Her Papa had spoken at great length of truth and honesty, and of the respect a man could earn if he was one whose word could be relied on. She had believed him. She had been naïve enough to think her papa was sincere in his utterances, and that he lived by the creed he preached. But he did not. She had thought that if she went to him with the truth, he would respect her for it, and for acting as she had been taught. But he had whipped the rug of honesty from beneath her feet with breath-taking speed, and worst of all, he would have persecuted Rose for her blameless part in the affair.

And Luke.

Lacy bent her head upon her chest with shame, and would have wept for him, but for the baby who still held her hand. Luke had called her names she had never heard before, had not understood. But she had understood the expression upon his face and knew that, though he had loved her, and he *had* she was sure, she had turned it to hate when, in her ignorance, she had taken his ship. He had loved the ship more than he had loved her, and her confidence and trust in her Papa had taken it from him. Her head was in a turmoil about the reason for it, but she knew that, when she could pull herself together, she would understand.

She was conscious of being drained of emotion, and of a feeling of inertia which took the life from everything she had loved, leaving a world of drabness and indifference.

Rose stood up and pulled Lacy with her. They shook out the full skirts of their crushed dresses, smoothing them with the instinctive gestures of young ladies of fashion. Rose's hands went to her hair, and in a moment it was twisted to a thick chignon at the back of her head. She did the same for Lacy, who had never, until last night, touched her own hair except to push it impatiently back from her face when it got in her way. Then, when they were both respectably tidy, though far from clean, they sat down at the wretched table and ate the stew which Bridie put before them.

'Copper,' Lacy murmured, and though it shocked Bridie to the core, a plateful was put upon the floor for the dog, who slurped it down almost before the hand which put it there returned to the table.

When they had finished, when the baby had fed at Bridie's pendulous breast, and the table was cleared, and the dishes washed in the pan of hot water insisted upon by Rose; when they had been put away in a semblance of the order which had once reigned here, Rose began to speak.

'Lacy and I have left Silverdale for good, Mammy,' she said quietly. Bridie gasped in horror as the meaning of Rose's words struck her. In that moment, she thought of no one but herself and her young children. What about the money which put milk in the children's bellies. Taters they got in plenty, and oatmeal, and sometimes, as today when Lancer sneaked out a bit of meat from a ship just come from Argentina, they had stew, but she would sorely miss the shillings their Rose had sent. She liked a sip of gin now and then, for it drove away misery as nothing else could. The little store of pennies she had hidden in a crack behind a brick in the corner would soon be gone if she had to rely on Lancer's wage alone. When he drank it away in an evening, as he often did, where would she get money if she had nothing from Rose?

She looked at her daughter and her face, thunderstruck, became fearful as another dreadful thought came to replace the first. They had left the big house, Rose had said, why she didn't know or really care, but surely to God they didn't believe . . . Holy Mother, they weren't thinking they could stay here? Not in the same room as Lancer McGhee.

A long agonized wail issued from her mouth.

Bridie had her home, such as it was; a bit of food to keep

body and soul together; her children to lavish her love upon; and, like a jewel to take out of its hiding place and gloat over, her pride in her first born. One of them was safe. One of them had clawed her way from her obscene life and found herself a clean and decent place. It was this more than anything which had kept Bridie brave. Rose had a fine job. She dressed like a lady, spoke like a lady; and was safe. Safe from fear, dirt and poverty; and safe from *him*.

'No! Oh, no!' she cried. 'No, Rose. No, no, no.'

'We have nowhere else to go, Mammy,' Rose said calmly.

'No, Rose. I said no. You've no idea what . . . Faith, 'tis a beast he is, a . . . monster.'

''Tis here or the workhouse, Mammy.'

'Better that, Rose. Better that. Please child . . .'

''Twill only be for a day or two, Mammy. Just until we find a place of our own.'

'But why? What's happened, Rose? What's she done to . . .?'

Bridie turned to stare at Lacy, who looked back politely, but made no effort to include herself in the conversation.

'Surely her Daddy's not chucked her out. Or is it you?' She glared suspiciously at Rose. 'You've not offended . . .?'

'No, Mammy.' Rose was patient. ''Tis nothing to do with me, but I couldn't let her come on her own. She had to leave, and I had to come with her. She couldn't manage on her own. You know that.' They both looked again at Lacy, and a look of understanding came to Bridie's face. 'Twas true, the poor creature would never manage without her Rosie.

'We've got money, Mammy. We can pay our way.'

Bridie turned about frantically, her eyes swivelling in her head towards the door.

'Hush, for God's sake, our Rose. Don't be lettin' anyone . . . If he should know you had money . . .'

Rose took Bridie's trembling hands in hers and patted them reassuringly.

'We'll be fine, Mammy, fine. We'll be out of the house all day looking for a place, and work . . .'

'Work?' Bridie looked unbelievingly at Lacy. 'Her?'

'Yes, work. Both of us. We'll find something, and then we'll be off.' Rose's voice was strong and brave. 'And don't you be worrying about . . . himself. We have Copper, and he's more than a match for Lancer McGhee, you'll see. We'll be safe, Mammy, you'll see.'

And strangely they were, but only with Copper's help, for without the animal to defend them he would have been about them unhesitatingly on their first night. When he had done staring in astonishment at the pretty creatures who sat in his kitchen, and Bridie had tried in her petrified browbeaten way to placate him, he began to smile delightedly, for he didn't mind at all. Bridie went on her knees and wept, but he pushed her away roughly. He didn't need her. He'd have the fair one first, he thought excitedly, the one with the huge terrified eyes and the skinny bosom. What matter to him if she was Hemingway's kid, as Bridie kept saying dementedly. She'd be choice, and then, his small porcine eyes circling the room, it'd be the turn of the hellion who blazed at him by her side. He liked a bit of flesh and spirit and she had both. And after that, both of them together in the one bed, and him with them.

His 'lance' grew huge in his eagerness, and his mouth, lipless and drooling, shaped into a smile. But he had got no further than the end of the broken table, when the sharp teeth of the dog sank silently into the fleshy part of his leg, drawing blood.

He had not even seen it. Cursing obscenely he floundered back on his heels, falling against the crouched, weeping figure of his wife. The children cowered in a small, tight mass in the corner, almost hidden by the palliasses heaped there, but even the baby made no sound. To draw attention to oneself when Lancer was on the rampage was inadvisable. He took off his belt slowly and began to circle the maddened, snarling dog, like a wrestler searching for a hold on his opponent. He swung the belt, ready to lay it about the streak of red frenzy, which was as eager to be at it again as he. The dog's eyes were as fiery as his coat, and his teeth seemed to grow longer and more pointed. Lancer took but a step, lifting the belt above his

253

head, when he felt the dog's teeth graze the front of his drooping trousers, just where the organ for which he was named bulged still.

For ten minutes they circled silently, but no matter what he did, Lancer could not get past the dog, and truth to tell, he was becoming alarmed. There is no more discouraging sight than a ferociously enraged dog who cares not a jot for its own safety. Only an idiot would tackle it and Lancer, thick of neck and head, was no idiot. Not when sober.

Backing away, face engorged with the red blood of his rage and frustration, he put his belt back on and sat down in Sean's chair. Immediately, Copper slipped silently to Lacy's side and leaned against her, shivering.

The man spoke thickly, and the quietness with which he delivered his threat made it doubly dangerous.

'Bugger the dog. I'll not fight it, but listen ter this, both of yer. Ther'll come a day when 'e's not 'ere, see if there's not. I'll get shut of 'im one way or t'other, never fear. That beast's days are numbered, an' so are yours, the two of yer. Stay in my 'ouse if yer dare, but watch out fer Lancer.'

Turning to Bridie, he said just as quietly. 'I'll 'ave me dinner now, an' then yer get the palliasse down fer it's your turn, bitch.'

When he had done with his heaped plate of stew, and performed a gross act of indecency upon the silent body of his wife, watched by her children and the comatose daughter of Charles Hemingway, he hoisted his pants about his waist, reached for the curly brimmed bowler he wore, tipped it in the direction of Rose and Lacy, and winked horribly.

'See what yer missed,' he said pleasantly, and grinned. 'Never mind, ther's allus tomorrow.'

It was to be like that for the next week. In that time he tried again and again, but they were on their guard; and so was Copper. Copper hated him with every bone in his body, every sinew and muscle, and the short squat man had only to turn his head a fraction in the direction of his mistress for the dog to growl. Copper watched him, stalking him, keeping his nose a foot from the man's leg, balanced to spring at Lancer's throat should he make a false move. And Lancer McGhee detested Copper as much as Copper hated Lancer McGhee. He was, if he was truthful, frightened of him.

Only Lacy could keep Copper under control, with her sharp commands or clicking fingers. He slept during the day when Lancer was gone, keeping guard all night beside the mattress on which the two young girls lay. He crawled with fleas – they all did; now wherever he went with Rose and Lacy his appearance caused no comment; they all blended in with their surroundings.

'It's the only way, Lacy,' Rose had said when Lacy protested. 'If we keep ourselves nice, we'll stand out like sore thumbs. We can be clean underneath but, you've got to see, we must look as they look, or our lives won't be worth living. Rub some dirt on your hands and face, and stuff your hair into this cap.'

After that first day there was no need to rub dirt on themselves. It just came by itself and, after a little while, it seemed easier not to bother anyway. Lacy would weep. She wept a lot these days, and Rose despaired as they trailed from place to place looking for work, for she made no effort to please prospective employers, and they were turned from job after job because of her inability to answer sensibly such questions as to how many hours she could scrub, or stand at the wash tub. She became so thin that her drawers would not stay up, and had to be tied with string over her shoulders. Her lovely mass of hair grew tangled and dirty, but Rose would not allow her to wash it. Its glorious shining would have drawn all eyes in an instant.

Rose dragged Lacy at her heels, her silent figure clumsy and comical in an overly short brown woollen dress and drab grey shawl, a cap pulled down to her eyebrows, and black boots which the hem of her skirt only just reached. They looked for work, going from door to door, factory to factory, shop to shop. The wash house was fully employed at the moment, they were told, but to try again in a few weeks. Servants were not required in the homes which festered in this area. Rose did not try the public houses. She was not desperate enough yet.

Whilst Bridie and her brood were out, Rose had worked a brick loose beneath the corner where the palliasses were stored, and in the small cavity she hid the small pouch of jewellery. It would put her and Lacy on their feet one day, but she was afraid to use it yet, waiting to see if a hue and cry ensued from its removal from Charles Hemingway's house. The emeralds were Lacy's, left to her by her grandmama, but in this society women owned nothing, not even what was inherited; men were unpredictable creatures when crossed, and Rose took no chances. Charles would know where they were and, should he come looking for them, it would be advisable to have all she had brought intact. A tiny silver pin set with a seed pearl had been reluctantly parted with at 'Ikey's', the local pawnbroker. It was a poor thing, and scarcely worth its weight in sand, or so Ikey said, but it bought the cheap clothing they wore, and provided a shilling or two, given piecemeal to Bridie.

The days passed, and now that the dog seemed to have Lancer in his place and danger to the girls was averted, Bridie began to enjoy the return of her daughter. She came to the conclusion that the girl with her was a colourless sort of creature. She rarely answered a question Bridie put to her, and was not prepared to listen like Rose. Still an' all, 'twas lovely ter 'ave the ear of another woman again, and she admitted to herself that the old place had taken on a look it had not had since . . .

She didn't want to think of that. But it was nice to see the oven shining against the wall, and she had quite forgotten how the brass handles gleamed when they were given a touch with a cloth. And would yer look at the floor! Sure, an' wasn't it as lovely as the glass in the windows of St Xaviour's. Clean, the two of 'em seemed to be demented with cleanliness, though, Bridie privately thought, they weren't too fussy about themselves. She'd never noticed the lice in her own children's hair. Well, it being such an unusual colour, so pale like, they didn't show so much; but Rose's dark hair was alive with the divils. They were like a troop of circus performers doing acrobats in the thick of it, and Rosie not seeming to care at all, thought Bridie as she placidly scratched her own heaving locks.

They had been with her a month, and she had become so used to seeing them about the place, that she was quite taken aback when Rose told her they would be off in a day or two.

They had a job to start on Monday, and had found a room in Blackstock Street, she said, but before they went, could Bridie find someone to do a little job for them?

Swallowing her disappointment, but mollified by the realization that Blackstock Street was only round the corner, so she could call on her daughter whenever Lancer was from home, she agreed cheerfully.

'Of course, darlin'. Sure an' yer know I will. What is it?'

'It's Lacy,' Rose said bleakly. 'She's pregnant and wants to be taken care of.'

# CHAPTER 18

Jane Hemingway was one of those rare creatures who are, despite their own unworldliness, completely in touch with the lives of those about them. She firmly believed in the goodness of God, but her own diffidence prevented her from forcing her ideas of Christianity upon others. She had a genuinely kind heart, was unselfish and willing to take to herself the troubles of all those who came to her with them. She went about it quietly, unobtrusively, and her own mama and papa would have been surprised to know of the many estate and farm workers who had cause to bless their daughter as she passed by in her carriage. She did what others call 'good works', but she did her good works at home. She was not pious.

The message came when she, her sister, two brothers and her mama and papa were lunching. April had just slipped quietly upon them. Daffodils and yellow iris crowded beneath the newly greening trees and along the hedgerows. Harebells spread handfuls of pale blue dust, and wood anemones peeped shyly from behind the fallen trunks of oak and beech. Celandine, dog violet and primrose grew madly at the edge of the thicket, and above them magpies and blackbirds began the anxious task of preparing homes for the arrival of their young.

It was so beautiful that day that one could only stand and wonder, and give thanks.

They were about to start on a splendid saddle of lamb in the dining room at Silverdale, and Jane was about to put a spoonful of mint sauce upon her meat, when the whispered consultation at the door of the room began. She saw Chapman take a note from William the footman, and hold it distastefully between finger and thumb. He looked towards her father, an expression of indecision upon his bland countenance, then, as though taking the bull by the horns, he placed the piece of crumpled, grubby paper upon a silver salver, and presented it ceremoniously to his master.

'Excuse me, sir, but this, er, note has just been delivered at the . . . kitchen door. I have been told it is most urgent.'

'The kitchen door?' Charles said.

'Yes sir.'

'Who on earth would deliver a note to me at the kitchen door?'

'I'm sure I cannot say, sir.'

Chapman retired gratefully to the sideboard.

Charles picked up the note with some reluctance and began to read, wiping his fingers upon his napkin as he did so.

The people around the table remained frozen in the positions in which they had been when the disturbance began, only their eyes moving as they looked curiously from one to the other. Margaret was sitting decorously, waiting as she always did for Mama's nod before starting. Thomas gripped the fork with which he had been nervously fiddling, and Robert, not sure whether to drink the glass of wine which was half way to his lips, or to put it down again, was heard to emit an anguished sigh.

Sarah, about to help herself to a tiny potato – only one, for she was putting on weight in the most extraordinary manner – looked questioningly at her husband. Jane replaced the sauce spoon in the dish with care, and leaned forward anxiously.

They all waited.

Charles Hemingway's face was as white as the damask napkin with which he still scrubbed at his fingers. An indeterminate sound issued from his lips. He stood up frantically, as though he were about to dash off somewhere, then thinking better of it, sat down again, crashing into his chair with a noise which made everyone in the room jump nervously.

Sarah found her voice. 'What is it, Charles? You look as though you have seen a ghost. Is it . . . tell me, it is not . . . Amy?' Amy expected her first child in June and news was always looked for, but then Edward would never send a dirty piece of paper to be handed in at the kitchen door. The look on Charles's face spoke of something quite extraordinary, and Sarah was alarmed.

'Charles?' she said beseechingly.

Jane stood suddenly, as though in her heart she knew from whom the note had come, and all faces turned towards her, even that of her Papa. She was frightened by the piteous look of loss upon it and began to walk towards him.

'Papa.' She put out her hand. 'Papa, you have gone so white. Is it bad news?' Her kind heart was appalled by the pain which misted his grey eyes.

'It is . . . Lacy.' Sweat stood out on Charles's blanched face, and the hand holding the dirty scrap of paper trembled.

'This is a note from . . . Rose, her maid, to say . . .'

Sarah emitted a piercing shriek and a maid dropped a serving dish with a horrid clatter, but not one pair of eyes turned to look. For a moment, Sarah was rendered speechless. But only for a moment. If there was anyone whom Sarah Hemingway loathed more in this world than Rose O'Malley, she had yet to meet her, for though it was Lacy who had struck them all to senseless shame by her behaviour, in Sarah's mind it was the girl Rose who had started it all, who had been the instigator. Her face turned a fiery red, and she gripped the fork she held as though she would dearly love to sink it into the flesh of the girl who had brought nothing but trouble to the house, leading her own daughter to dishonour the name of Hemingway.

Her voice trembled as she spoke. 'Whatever is in that note is of not the slightest importance to anyone here, Charles, and I would be greatly obliged if you would destroy it at once. When . . . Alexandrina left this house to continue her . . . association with . . .' Rage gripped her anew, and she could scarcely go on. She held the edge of the table with white-knuckled fingers.

'Destroy it please, at once, or I shall not be responsible for my actions. I do not now wish to be told what it contains nor does any member of my family. I am adamant . . .'

'She is ill.'

'That is of no concern of ours. Let her . . . new friends nurse her.'

Thomas and Robert sat stiffly to attention, eyes front, as though the present uproar was nothing to do with either of

260

them. They had held their youngest sister in great affection, but not great enough to chance Papa's outrage or Mama's wrath.

'Mama, please . . .'

Jane turned to her mother and began to walk towards the end of the table where her mother sat.

'. . . Mama, we cannot just ignore it. If she is ill she will need . . .'

'The note says she is dying.' Charles's voice was puzzled.

The quiet words brought Jane's impassioned plea to a halt, and she turned back to Charles, her face as white as his own.

'Dying?' she whispered. 'But she is only seventeen. How can she be dying?'

'It is no longer our concern.' The words rang out harshly as Sarah spoke.

She stood up, a majestic figure in her pale grey moiré gown. The weight she was putting on showed in her face, and her flesh wobbled as emotion shook her.

'I am going to my room but, before I go, I have this to say. It is my last word. The person to whom this letter refers is no longer a member of my family, and as such does not deserve the help one would ordinarily extend to a relative. She used us all as though we meant nothing to her, but she treated most harshly of all her papa, who dealt with her as kindly as any parent could. More, she lied and cheated, and consorted with persons who were not fit to sit at the same table as decent people. She chose to leave without a word, and she must now reap the harvest she has sown. I shall ignore this note, and so will you. I have stood by whilst . . . she was allowed free rein in all she desired. My wishes were disregarded, so I feel the blame for this lies not with me. If I find that anyone, *anyone* in this house, be it servant or family, gives aid to her, I will see that they regret it.'

The silence which followed was thick and terrible.

Turning, her face aflame with temper, and the memory of a dozen rebuffs and years of resentment, Sarah Hemingway swept from the room, opening the door herself, for the servants were paralysed. But she had gone barely a yard from

261

the doorway towards the foot of the stairs, when her daughter ran after her, her slippers hissing on the polished floor, her skirts held up almost to her knees. The self-distrust which had served her all her life left Jane Hemingway at that moment never to return. She forgot her misgivings, the unease which attacked her whenever she was confronted with the opposition of another, and her voice rose to a strength and resonance never before heard.

'I'm sorry Mama, but I must disobey you.'

The tension spread, like a gentle wave upon a flat beach throughout the house. Even those beyond the servants' passage at the back of the house in the kitchen fell dumb. The door between had been left ajar, so that those there might quickly get first-hand news of the extraordinary note delivered by the carter. They heard Jane's words, and were awash with amazement and admiration. Miss Jane was pleasant and kind, but so timid and shy she would barely raise her eyes to even the most humble of them, and listen to her now.

Sarah stood as still as the newel post to which her hand had just reached out. Her heart beat within her chest, and she thought she would swoon. She scarcely had time to register and wonder at this timid creature's defiance when Jane spoke again. Her voice shook with fright, but she was calm inside.

'It does not matter to me what Lacy might have done, Mama, and I am not convinced even now that her crime was so terrible. What concerns me is that my sister is ill, perhaps . . . dying, and I cannot turn my back on her. I do not wish to upset you, and should you feel it your duty to . . . to . . .' Her voice broke, but she went on. 'If you wish me to leave as Lacy did, I shall do so.'

Sarah turned, appalled, her hand held out pleadingly to her daughter. The notion that, in less than two months, she might go again through the annihilating experience of having all society whisper about her, silenced her tongue. As Jane ran back to the dining room, Sarah turned to the stairs, and began the long stumbling climb to her room and the consolation which lay there. She was defeated, and by the daughter she had thought least likely ever to give her trouble.

Charles had risen from his chair and was moving in the

direction of the doorway as Jane entered again. His eyes did not look at her. He had himself in hand now, and the memory of the injury to his pride and his absolute authority, inflicted upon him by his youngest child, returned to him as shock receded. She had rejected him, then, and gone to her lover. Defied him.

He would never forgive her.

Dying she might be, though he doubted it – the Irish had ever been excitable – but Sarah was right. Lacy had brought it upon herself, and she must recover or die in the company of those she had chosen. The despair inspired in him by the desperate words scrawled across the scrap of dirty paper had worn off, and he could reason clearly now. She had turned away from his love and the trust he had put in her. She had turned from the bright future he had planned. She had shamed the family who loved her; and held in contempt the society which had bred her.

He could do no more for her.

But strangely, when the time came, he was not there to forbid his third daughter the right to give comfort to her sister. Jonas the groom took her, and Arkwright's boy, Seth. They were both big men, and Seth had a pistol slipped to him by Chapman from the gun case in Charles Hemingway's study. It would be needed in the area where they were bound. None knew better than Chapman, for he had been born in Forth Row, only a stone's throw from Naylor Street. The carriage would need watching whilst Miss Jane went wherever she needed to go, and Seth would see to her. A good lad to have at your back, was Seth, and well able to defend her.

Blankets, clean sheets, soap, antiseptic and a bottle of Nanny's all-purpose medicine were packed, for the nature of Lacy's illness was not known, and it did no harm to be prepared for anything. A basket of Cook's lightest, most easily digested and nourishing broths and custard, milk and eggs; together with the tearful good wishes, whispered to her as she went by, of all the servants, were taken in the carriage with Jane Hemingway as she set off for Liverpool.

Within fifteen minutes she had gone. From his study

window, Charles watched her, his face as empty as the pale sky which curved above the chimneys. The horses, lashed to a mad gallop by Jonas, pulled the carriage at a cracking pace which never faltered, along the length of Aigburth Road, Park Road and into St James' Road, until they reached the Custom House, and the traffic congestion which slowed them to a crawl. The carriage took the right-hand turn into Tithebarn Street like a snail dragging not one but two shells upon its back. Jane could scarcely sit still, and but for Seth's incredulous insistence that she remain in the carriage, she might have got out and attempted to walk. When Vauxhall Street appeared on their left, the traffic had thinned and they were at it again, the speed of the carriage and the passage of its wheels over the setts threatening to break all Cook's lovely fresh eggs, each one of which she had wrapped with a tear for the girl who they said was dying.

It was the needle which was responsible, of course. It did the trick right enough, where the potion had failed. Lacy had screamed in agony as she clung to Rose; then she had bled a lot and cried a little, and though it hurt to walk, she had managed it back to Naylor's Yard.

The pain began during the night and by morning Lacy complained of the heat, and she didn't feel like eating her oatmeal, thank you Rose, it made her sick, and the fire was far too high and the room stifling, and she would be obliged if Mrs McGhee would open the door a crack.

Bridie stared, bewildered, for though it was April the day was cold and the fire barely a glimmer. But Lancer was intrigued, hardly able to eat his breakfast for the flash of long, white legs, and a sliver of smooth shoulder which Rose tried desperately to keep from his gloating eyes. Lacy grumbled as the skimpy bedclothes were persistently replaced about her fevered body, becoming peevish as Rose insisted.

'The pain in my stomach is quite bad, Rose. Do you think your mama might have something to take it away?' Even yet, after nearly eight weeks in Bridie's home, Lacy was still at times completely unable to believe that, given a particle of good will, a simple thing like a cure for tummy ache, always immediately available in the nursery at Silverdale, could not be produced. A dose of this or that for toothache, headache or that nasty twinge which came each month, was such an ordinary thing, even here. Surely Mrs McGhee would not be a mother if she did not keep them in her cupboard for the relief of her children's aches and pains.

'I feel rather unwell, Rose. Just a spoonful, if she has it, and I will be on my feet directly.'

But the dose, of course, was not forthcoming, and she was not on her feet directly. Her body became a bright, glowing pink, and she began to shiver and cry out with the pain.

Copper huddled, bewildered, at her side, getting in Rose's way as she fought the agony-wracked girl in an effort to keep her warmly wrapped. He nosed her flushed cheek and licked it tentatively, but she turned from him fretfully and Rose shoo-ed him away. His heart ached, for he had never been rebuffed in his life, nor spoken to so sharply. But he kept his post at the foot of the mattress for, although the man was out at the moment, it did not do to let down one's guard.

The fire was built up to gigantic proportions. Bridie had protested at first, demanding to know where the divil Rose thought the money was coming from to keep such a thing alive, but Rose, her eyes never leaving the fever-tossed girl on the bed, pushed the last of the money from the sale of the pearl pin into her hand, and satisfied, Bridie sent their Joseph for another bucket of coal. She and her children sat round the blaze, and enjoyed the sensation of being half roasted before the biggest, most cheerful fire they had any of them ever seen.

'Will I stick a few taters in it, Mammy?' Joseph asked light heartedly. ''Tis a shame ter be wastin' it.'

'Good idea, darlin'. Sure an' they'll be a treat for our dinner.'

But even Bridie, hapless and luckless as she was, felt compassion stir in her as the day went on. Lacy began to smell, a sour stench which was more powerful than the usual aroma which pervaded the room. Almost senseless, tossing, moaning, sweat-drenched, she fought with Rose to throw off her covers, and Rose, her eyes wild, turned at last to her mother for help.

'Mammy, will yer be holdin' her a minute. Keep her covered. I'm so tired. Just give me half an hour in Daddy's chair.'

Bridie took over and nursed the child, for she seemed no more than that, as the infection worked its way through her already slender body. Eight weeks on the poor diet Bridie's lot were accustomed to had taken the flesh from her, and she had little reserve as she grieved for what she had lost.

Her teeth chattered as rigors set in. 'Hot, hot,' she muttered. But her flesh was cold and clammy to the touch now, and Bridie held her more firmly against her own warm flesh.

'There darlin', there. Go ter sleep an' Bridie'll hold yer an' when yer wake up yer'll be better.' Shushing and rocking and stroking back the wet hair from the sunken face, Bridie put her cheek against the jerking head and began to croon a sweet Irish lullaby. There were no words, but the softness of the melody and the tenderness of the arms which held her, soothed Lacy to restless sleep for an hour.

But it did not last.

Lancer came in on a wave of cold air and began to shout his disapproval of the warmth of the room, bellowing 'where in 'ell, was his dinner, and if someone didn't shut that moanin' cow's trap, he'd do it 'imself', for his arrival had broken Lacy's light doze, and the pain came to seize her, and she cried out.

She was cold now, she said, so cold. She shivered violently as Rose bent solicitously to wrap her in the old woollen shawl Bridie used for slipping to the market, and wished she had the fur-lined cloak which reposed at 'Ikey's', but when Rose touched Lacy's shoulder she almost cried out, for the flesh was burning hot. In an upsurge like that of a salmon leaping the water, Lacy sat up and was violently sick. It seemed she would never stop, and the stench in the room became even more appalling.

Lancer made himself scarce when he had eaten. In his tiny

brain there lurked no desire now to 'get at' anybody in that dreadful room. He was glad to be out of it and away to the pub on the corner. The thin 'un was a goner, right enough, which would leave the other one, and with a bit of thought the dog could be dealt with. He'd always fancied Bridie's kid the most, anyway. A bit of meat on 'er, like 'er ma. Give it a few days, an' when she was on 'er own he'd see to 'er. Old Wilkins 'd give 'im a few bob for the dog an' all. Sell it fer mutton or summat on the market.

Lancer raised his glass and onto his face slithered an expression which might have been a smile. The landlord moved to the other end of the bar.

All through that night and the next day Lacy slipped in and out of consciousness. She burned up with fever which boiled dry the moisture in her body, and Rose and Bridie could get no fluids between her lips. She rambled now in delirium, calling for her Papa in a high-pitched childish treble and muttering over and over again of shining water. The pad Rose had placed between her thighs to absorb the blood became thick with a revolting greenish-yellow pus, and the smell was almost more than even Bridie could stand.

Rose sent a note to Charles Hemingway on the third day, to tell him his daughter was dying, and to come at once.

It was almost seven years since the last horse-drawn vehicle had stood at the entrance to the alley which led to the courtyard and the cellar where Bridie McGhee lived, and then it had been a hearse sent to take away her first husband. This one excited the same intense interest. The horses were matched greys, and the carriage a rich and glossy dark green. The fellow who sat upon the driving seat was all wrapped up in a box coat with a multiple collar, for the weather continued cold, but no one who crowded respectfully around the equipage failed to notice the handle of the pistol which peeped slyly from the man's sleeve.

Jane Hemingway, to give her her due, spent only three minutes retching miserably into a bowl, overcome to faintness by the stench. She had thought it obnoxious and scarcely bearable in the courtyard in which Bridie's house stood, but when the door was opened to her and she went inside the cellar, she reeled and lost consciousness. In later years, when she worked in a sickroom in which the smell was oppressive, those about her were amazed by her apparent disregard for what they considered intolerable; but they were not to know of this day, and of Jane's introduction to what she called 'the sickroom aroma'.

The tightly wrapped bundle on the stained palliasse was not her sister, of that she was at first certain, and she was about to rise from her knees and say so, still willing of course to help the poor soul, when the creature opened its cracked lips and white and perfect teeth shone for a second as a tiny sound emerged. Some familiar curve to the hollow cheek, the colour and length of the eyelashes which shadowed it, and the arch of the fine eyebrows, brought back suddenly a vivid memory of a laughing face in which the same white teeth had flashed. Those eyelashes had fanned sparkling eyes, full of teasing humour, and how many times had Jane seen the dip and frown of the silky brows in consternation and dismay as Mama held forth on some minor infringement.

'Lacy,' she whispered, 'Oh Lacy, my dear. What has happened to you? How did you come to this?' She turned to Rose who looked scarcely better than Lacy. She stood, swaying slightly; her fine, firm flesh whittled away to skin and bone. Dirty, her hair this way and that, hanging about her face like the witch from Macbeth; her eyes glazed, for she had barely an hour's sleep in forty-eight; she waited numbly to be told what she should do next. She had come to the end of her strength.

'What happened to her, Rose? How did she become so ill?'

'Where is her papa, Miss Jane? I thought he would come to take her home.'

'He . . . could not come.' Jane spoke hesitantly. 'But tell me how Miss Lacy came to be . . .'

'He . . . couldn't come?'

Jane lifted her head. 'No.'

'But she must be taken from here to be nursed. Taken to . . .'

'Rose, stop it. You are tired, but I have come to help. Now, what is wrong? What did the doctor . . ?'

Rose began to laugh.

Bridie, overcome to the point of gawping stupidity by the presence of the fine lady in her kitchen, and of the enormous young man who stood guarding her door, smiled with her daughter, though what at she did not know. Laughter shrieked about the room, and Cooper stood up uncertainly. On and on it went. Rose's face, as colourless and dirty as the rag at the window, was creased in a parody of merriment that was pitiful to see, and Jane, sensing the taut springs which held Rose on the edge of sanity, let her laugh; watched her laugher until it turned to impassioned weeping.

She led her to her father's chair and put her in it, and in the next ten minutes heard things more shocking and unbelievable than her sheltered life could imagine. Rose had to explain so much to her in her stumbling, weeping sorrow, for Jane did not know how a child was conceived, let alone 'got rid of'. But when she knew everything, Jane Hemingway took over, and trusting to her own instinct and the good sense she had not known she possessed, she began the job of saving her sister's life.

It took thirty-six hours to bring down the temperature which had almost consumed her. Jane's simple but logical belief that if what Rose had done – keeping Lacy warm and wrapped about, in an attempt to sweat out the badness – had failed, they had nothing to lose if they did the opposite.

The doctor refused to come.

Not even the daughter of one of the town's most influential men could persuade him to enter a district in which every known disease which lives side by side with hunger and dirt abounded.

Jonas was sent whipping back to Silverdale and returned within the hour with Annie, for Rose was exhausted and useless, and a block of pure ice from the ice house at the back of the stables. The room was kept pleasantly warm, but Lacy was sponged with iced water hour after hour, turn and turn about. As her temperature dropped and she began to respond, they spooned drinks between her parched lips; then Cook's broth, and egg beaten up in milk, to which a tot of sherry had been added.

It was like a holiday for Bridie and the children. True, they were a bit packed together, but sure, weren't they used to that. They all put on weight from the good food which arrived by the cartload, or so it seemed to Bridie, and the spectacle was a treat to one and all.

Nora came to take Annie's place, and Seth and Jonas were replaced by Sam and Harry the grooms, and in all that time, whilst his daughter was fighting for her life, Charles Hemingway said not a word – nor made any protest at the disorganization in the life of his servants.

Lancer was incensed when he could not get into his own home, and was ready to show his iron fists to the contemptuous hulk at his door, but six years of soft living had slowed him down. He was over forty now, and he had had a bit to drink he told himself in excuse, as he bristled up to Seth; but not enough, it seemed, to give him the courage to carry off what he had begun. He found a floor to sleep on at Mick Geraghty's, and stayed there a week before they all went away and he could return to his own bed. He gave Bridie a good hiding for her part in it, just to let her see he was boss of his own place, and put a 'purler' about the eye of his eldest when he told his father of the wondrous things they had eaten. He felt better then, but the one thing that really did annoy him was that he never had 'a go' with Rose.

She went with the others.

When Lacy Hemingway came back from the dreadful nightmare-filled world in which she had struggled for a week, she began to hate her father as once she had loved him; and to love the sister she had once ignored.

# CHAPTER 19

James Osborne sat upon the grey's back, stirrups hanging idle, one long leg draped about the pommel of his saddle, and allowed the animal to amble along the overgrown path which led down to the beach. Long shadows sliced it, turning the fern and rough grass to alternate shades of green. Pine trees grew straight as arrows on either side, their crusted bark still warm from yesterday's sun, and through the thickly clustered trunks he could see the dazzling brilliance of vivid pink and orange where rhododendrons grew in profusion. The grass was lushly green in there, for the trees were so dense the sun scarcely reached their roots. Wild flowers grew, for it was always damp.

The narrow archway ahead formed by the trees cast a black shadow. The ground was overgrown with ivy and purple orchids, and moss grew everywhere, even where the horse walked. No one had come by here in a long, long time.

A flush of apricot outlined the dark oaks behind the horse and rider, and the glint of the sun as it crept above the horizon polished the flatness of the water of the great River Mersey ahead to pale gold. The sky was a luminous blue, neither night nor day, and a sprinkling of fading stars winked and went out.

A fine pearly mist, heralding heat later, curled about the trunks of the trees. A late water vole splashed frantically in a tiny stream which ran parallel to the path, ending in the waters of the river. The sound carried across the silent wood as the small animal made its way along the bank towards its burrow. It would not do to be about when the sun had finally risen.

The horse wickered, and the man leaned forward and pulled his ear, speaking softly some words of friendship.

It was Midsummer's Day, and three years had gone by since he was last here.

The grey walked on, pushing through the half-grown bushes and shrubs. A blackbird began to whistle in a thicket, but was silent suddenly as the sound of the horse reached it.

'Walk on, Jason. Walk on,' the man said softly as though the animal had become alarmed by the bird's song, but the peace which drenched the spinney was as comfortable to the stallion as it was to the man, and he twitched an ear impatiently.

They broke from the cover of the trees and were there. The beach was the same. Not a footprint bar those of a rabbit or two, showed on the even surface of the sand. Even the pools were as they had been, sparkling crisply in the early morning sun.

James slipped from the animal's back and told him to stand. Walking to the water's edge, he stood looking out to the stretch of water known as Devil's Bank, wondering idly why it was named so. But he was not of the sea, nor the world of ships, and he could not hazard a guess. He turned his head and, as if it were yesterday, he heard her voice.

'Do stop it, Rose, or I shall wet my drawers.'

She would be nineteen today, the girl who had dropped off the edge of his world into nothingness. The woman, for she was that now, he still loved. If Charles Hemingway saw him here today he would think him brain-addled, particularly if he knew the reason why.

But perhaps he would not. James, sensitive on the subject of Lacy Hemingway, had seen the change in her papa since the day she had gone away. He had shrunk into the clothes which had once fitted him like the sleek coat of an otter, and his head was bent perpetually forward as though he listened for something. Her name had never been mentioned. Not since the day he had come home and made for Silverdale, like a retriever to a fallen bird. Charles's letter, the one written in August last year, in answer to his own frantic request for news of her when she herself had failed to write, had been in his pocket. It was brief, stating that Lacy had 'left my house of her own accord to find her way in the world. It appears she has no wish to be my daughter, nor your wife and, therefore, my dear fellow, I beg of you to forget her'.

No more. No explanation, and no further communications to his own letters of appeal.

It was not until April of this year, with the ratification of the Treaty of Paris and the formal end of the war in the Crimea, that James, home at last, was able to confront Charles Hemingway and discover the truth.

It was so simple he wondered why he had not thought of it, but he had not. Not once in all the months of agonizing had it occurred to him that the lovely, laughing, innocent girl had loved another man. It was ironic really, for it had been his first thought three years ago, when he had found her clothes here in the wood. Perhaps it was the sweet and untouched girlishness she had displayed then that made him think she was the same, and would always remain so, until he came to change her into a woman. But now, someone else had done it for him.

He felt quite empty. For two months he had come to the place. He did not know why. It neither hurt him, nor filled him with pleasure. Perhaps the peace of it, where she had once brought laughter, calmed him, but this was the last time he would come. He could not spend his life looking back to a girl who had filled him with delight in one special way, and whom he had not seen since. His life waited for him. He was twenty-nine years old. He must look for someone else to fill his life and his heart. But where? Where would she be? Could there exist another such as Lacy Hemingway? Could there?

James unfolded his long length from the sun-warmed sand, where he had squatted in a manner learned round the fires in the freezing Balkan nights. He flexed the shoulder of his left arm, which remained stiff from his wound, rubbing it absentmindedly. His brown eyes were unfocused as he looked across the water which, as the blue of the sky deepened, had changed from gold to pale, silvered hyacinth. He sighed, then shook his head regretfully.

It did no good to sigh over another man's wife; not unless the feelings were returned, and a pretty flirtation might happily lead to something more substantial than a stolen kiss. He had done that many times, for he was popular with pretty

273

women. His strong but strangely vulnerable mouth aroused some feeling in them which they found hard to resist, and his male tenderness towards them, his slightly impudent but always respectful charm, had turned many a warm heart over in its rounded breast.

His own had always, until now, remained intact.

But James Osborne, soldier and gentleman, was also a realist. Eleven years in the army, three of them spent on the battlefields of Gallipoli; of Scutari where he had fought his hardest in hospital; of Varna, Alma, Inkerman, Balaclava, and the confusion which had led to the Valley of the Shadow of Death, had given to him a fatalism which had enabled him to survive scenes of death and agony, giving him the strength to know when to let go of those he called friend.

And so he let go of the memory of Lacy Hemingway.

On Strand Street overlooking Canning Dock, in a tiny office no bigger than the linen cupboard on the second floor of the house in which she had once lived, Lacy Hemingway sat down slowly in the swivel chair before the desk. Her hands trembled, and to still them she placed them carefully in her lap, folding them about each other in the way she had taught herself, so that those with whom she dealt would not know of her nervousness.

The light from a window shaped like those to be seen in the cabin in the stern of a ship fell across the desk and onto her face, illuminating her fine skin to pearl, and lighting her serene grey eyes with the luminous quality of a candle. Her hair was brushed back from her forehead and gathered into a pretty chenille hair net at the back of her head. Although the style might have been thought severe for one so young, Lacy was wise enough to know what pleased the men with whom she came in contact, and she allowed several stray silvery curls to escape and drift about her ears and neck.

Her gown was of pale grey silk, very plain, with a high neck and long sleeves, but the bodice was tight-fitting, drawing the eye to her small peaked breasts and her narrow waist; and the skirt was full and graceful. Lace showed at her neck and wrists and she smelled delightfully of some light, pleasant perfume.

The only colour about her was in her warm, rose-pink lips.

It was her birthday. She was nineteen years old, and today was the first day of her new life. The old one, the first part and the second part, were all done now; and she was ready.

Midsummer Day. It was barely six thirty, but the sun shone already from a cloudless sky, gliding over the rooftops on to the quayside. Thick black shadows lay half way across the road, and Lacy could see the familiar outline of the Custom House set out like a child's block drawing, its roof reaching almost to the water's edge. As the sun rose higher, the shadow would draw back like the tide receding from the beach, and the hot sunshine would bathe the seamen and dockworkers in its benevolence, making them sweat and curse and wish for the autumn. Then, in the way of men, they would struggle in the wind-lashed rain and long for the warmth of the sun.

There were few carriages to be seen, for those who were carried to their place of daily employment in a horse-drawn vehicle were not about as yet. A hackney or two plied for trade between the docks and the streets of the town, but it was early, and those who were about came here by foot. It cost a shilling from George's Pierhead to the Angel Hotel in Dale Street, and the money was not easily found by most.

Ships were tied up, thick as the trees in a great forest and, though the day was windless, rigging moved gently as the tide inched up the pilings. Someone was whistling a tune and, further up the wharf, a voice took up the words of the song:

*'I kissed her twice upon the lips,*
*I wished I'd done it thrice.*
*I whispered, oh it's naughty,*
*She said, it is so nice.'*

Lacy smiled. She and Rose used to sing that song. She and Rose, and the dozens of other girls who had stood beside them in the pickle-filling department of 'Price and Roberts' in Mervyn Street. Hour after hour the air would be filled with the high-pitched sound of young women's voices, as they sought to keep at bay the dragging boredom of their work; to forget the almost crippling ache of backs that bent over benches too high, or too low, depending on the height of the worker; and of feet, ankles and legs which had to bear their weight for fourteen hours each day. Not many places would have allowed the singing, thinking it was likely to cut down productivity, but Mr Price and Mr Roberts were Welsh, and singing came as naturally to them as breathing. A bit of a sing-song did no harm in their opinion; they even taught the girls to pipe 'Men of Harlech'.

But that was the lighter side of a job which turned the arms of its workers to a bright, sulphurous yellow, caused by immersion in the juice of the vegetables they pickled, and made tender eyes red raw and inflamed, irritated day after day by the prickling sting of vinegar.

They were lucky to get it, they were told, and had it not been for an unfortunate accident in the vat room where the vegetables were blanched, causing two girls to be put off that very morning, Lacy and Rose would have been turned away as they had been a dozen times already that day. They had passed through the room where the accident had occurred on their way to the pickling department, scared out of their wits by the sobbing, trembling girls who stood about in the cooling water which lay in a huge lake beside an overturned vat. But Mr Price passed on, and they were glad to follow.

They worked in those first weeks in a large, low room at the back of the premises, through whose tiny windows no light could enter. Gas lights, a recent innovation, illuminated the room, and Rose marvelled in that first hour at their brilliance. But the fumes which built up sent many a girl reeling to the bucket which served as a latrine, in the corner behind the huge barrel of onions. There were many odours; one killed another, and soon they noticed none.

The gallery, as it was ironically called, where they worked, was crowded with women standing in front of counters on which were heaped enormous piles of pickles, primrose-coloured cauliflower sprouts, white onions and gherkins.

Every girl had her own 'pickle-stick', and no girl was allowed to use one which belonged to another, for each had its eccentricities, and its owner came to know them and could work with no other. A large bottle, carelessly washed in a bucket of cold water, was packed carefully by hand; the arrangement of onions, cauliflower pieces and gherkins being not too tight, nor too loose. A bright red chili was placed at either side of the jar for show and, when it was done, the 'pickle-stick' was used to move the contents about until it was to the packer's, and the overseer's satisfaction. All must be done correctly, but quickly, for each girl was expected to fill one hundred jars a day. If one was too fussy the quota was not reached; if careless, a fine was levied.

Just as they were becoming accustomed to the back-breaking monotony, the smells, and the irritation to eyes and arms of the pickling room, Lacy and Rose were moved to the labelling department. For some reason, Mr Price and Mr Roberts appeared to believe that the two girls must not be parted. Perhaps because Rose did all the talking in her broad Irish brogue, giving the impression that without her Lacy would be unable to communicate. Or perhaps it was Lacy's fragile delicacy, completely deceptive for she was fully re-covered from her illness, which seemed to need the constant support of her friend; but they were always shuffled about together. They were good workers, mind, as Mr Price told Mr Roberts: they did their hundred bottles, and more, each day neatly and artistically; the little thin one as good as the other, but he fancied she looked a bit peaked at times; so white and silvery, a sit-down would do her no harm.

Lacy was always to have this effect on men.

They were given a stool each, a bucket of water, and a pile of clean labels. It was better than pickling, Rose said, for they were away from the vinegar and, as Mr Price had mentioned, it was nice to be off your feet. But, oh, their backs when they got home at night! They could barely straighten up at first, for they were bending over all day long to the bucket on the floor, dipping in the bottle before affixing the label.

They earned nine shillings each a week, considered

themselves well paid and lucky to be working and, as Lacy said often and thankfully, they had each other. The first job, the one they had found before the 'trouble', was no longer available when Lacy was recovered. It had taken weeks of moving from factory to factory, manufacturing watches, soap, refining sugar and brewing beer before they were successful.

Jane, tearful and worried, had been gently refused when she had offered help in the way of food: the only way she could, for she had no money.

'I am able to support myself now, Jane. You have made me well again and strong with all of Cook's good food, and I thank you and her for giving me my life, but I am constrained to do with it as I must. I cannot accept anything now that comes from my father.'

'But, Lacy dear. He only did what he thought right, as you do.'

Lacy's face was coolly polite and her voice distant as she considered the statement.

'That is correct, Jane, but you did not turn from me, nor desert me when I was thought to be dying, and that is what he did. No matter what mistakes we make, are we not to be forgiven and helped when we are near to death? I would have come to him had he called, despite his attitude to Rose. But he left me to die, Jane. All my life he has hedged me about with words of Christian mercy and truth, but even to me, his own flesh and blood, he now denies it. I cannot find it in my heart to forgive him.'

'Please, Lacy. Let me tell him how you are.'

'Does he ask?'

'Well, no, but . . .'

'Then I will thank you not to bother.'

'Well, will you allow me to call and bring . . .'

'No, dear Jane. No. Call whenever you wish, but I can take nothing further from the table of . . .'

'Lacy, *I* am bringing it, not . . .'

'It comes from him. Whilst I was ill I was not in a position to refuse, but now I will fend for myself.'

Lacy's voice was implacable and she turned her head from

Jane, but Jane, having so recently gained the love and respect of her sister, would not be turned away and continued to come to the room Rose and Lacy had rented in Blackstock Street, bringing baskets of good food. It was all returned politely, though Rose's mouth watered at the sight and smell of the slices of thick roast beef, fresh baked bread, Cook's delicious pork pies, scones, and home-cured bacon and ham, and she said she could see no sense in it. Rose was as practical as her upbringing had made her. She quarrelled with Lacy for her foolishness, telling her it was a waste of good food and that she needed it after her illness, but Lacy was firm.

One thing she did allow Jane to do for her; but only then because there was no other way.

After she and Rose had moved into Blackstock Street and had been working at 'Price and Roberts' for several weeks, she began to worry about her 'nest egg' as she called it, troubled with the notion that whilst she and Rose were out, their rooms might be gone through by other persons who resided in the sleazy lodging house. They had a sturdy lock put on the door, and Copper was always there to defend it, but it put the dog in danger and, on reflection, she was half persuaded that the lock itself might invite those attentions she wished to avoid.

Taking a chance, she and Rose concocted some tale of a troublesome illness of a day's duration with which to beguile Mr Price and Mr Roberts, always conscious of how many girls were waiting to step into the shoes of an absent employee, and when Rose had gone to the pickling factory on her own, Lacy and Jane, as previously arranged, changed clothes. Jane locked herself with Copper in the room which belonged to Lacy and Rose. Then, dressed in Jane's charming outfit, and feeling strange to be so elegant and clean after four months in the tatters of a drab, Lacy Hemingway went to town in Charles Hemingway's coach, driven by a mystified Jonas.

If she could have done it any other way, she would have, but she knew the jeweller would be highly suspicious of someone looking as she had become and offering emeralds of the quality she possessed for sale. But he would be impressed by a fine carriage and handsome horses, would recognize them and her as belonging to Charles Hemingway, and would not dare to cheat her.

She got a good price for Lucinda Fraser's fine emeralds, and when she swept into the Royal Union Bank in Castle Street to discuss with its manager the most advantageous way in which to invest her money, thrown carelessly to his desk, her heart beat fast with the excitement of it.

It was the beginning.

The bank manager, though taken aback by the unprecedented event, and inclined to send a message to Charles Hemingway to tell him to come at once to give sanction to his daughter's intentions, was impressed by her astuteness.

She seemed to read his mind. 'If you should feel the necessity to contact my father, do so by all means, but I think you will find that he will not be concerned nor particularly interested, Mr Moore. Furthermore, may I point out that you are not the only banking establishment in Liverpool, and I shall be investing many such sums in the future. Now, if you feel you can spare the time to do business with me, I should like to tell you what I intend for the money you see before you.'

The girl exuded tension and authority and, despite what he considered her effrontery, Mr Moore found himself sparing the time.

He sat back in his chair and caressed his side whiskers thoughtfully. It was a gesture which his wife would have recognized, for it indicated that Mr Moore's interest was aroused. She had seen it many times in the first years of their marriage, and it always preceded what Mr Moore was pleased to call his 'conjugals'. Of late, to her relief, these looks had become rare, but Mrs Moore was aware only of her husband in the environs of his home, and she was not to know that he was apt to affect the same pose at the business table, though for different reasons. There was one element that was common, however. Greed.

Mr Moore's curiosity was aroused. The young woman who sat so confidently at his desk was a rarity indeed. As the initial shock and outrage at being accosted in his own office by such an impudent young person began to wear off, an instinct, a built-in awareness which thrived in the world of commerce and was essential if one were to be successful, told him that here was an ambition; a sense of purpose that was destined, if properly supervised, to take its owner to heights beyond his own imaginings.

There was an air about her: not just of determination; although that manifested itself in the square set of her chin and the firmness of her lips; but a resolve so obstinate, bright and positive, that he found it difficult to restrain himself from showing the same enthusiasm she did. He felt himself magnetized as she outlined her plans; and fought a desire to lean in a most unprofessional way with his elbows upon the desk-top and gaze, bemused, into her burning eyes. She seemed intent on imbuing him with her own high expectations and, like an adult who is affected by a child's vigour, he wanted to smile and say indulgently, 'What is it? What is all the excitement about?'

But this was no child.

Lacy Hemingway was a woman who had lived and breathed ships, the sea and the stimulating world of her father since she had been old enough to understand the charts he pored over. She had followed his finger along the routes his ships took, and wrestled with his adult conversation until she understood his language. Talk of exports, imports, revenues, tariffs, agents, trade winds, clippers, tides, letters of credit and bills of lading, was as exhilarating as it was bewildering. She had unlocked the mysteries of the accounts in the leading newspapers of men like Mr Cunard and Mr McIver, who had built the greatest shipping line to sail from Liverpool, making their dreams into reality. Her father had inherited what he had, building and expanding and keeping pace with them. But these men, and others like them, had looked into the future with far-sighted vision, and from almost nothing, snapping up opportunities with the sharpness of a trout taking a fly, had become legends in their own time.

They had formed a great company which sailed its vessels

not only across the Atlantic but into the Mediterranean, and away to the other side of the world. They carried the mail of two great nations and, with the accompanying grant afforded them by the British government to do so, their steamships raced backwards and forwards at tremendous speeds, covering the return trip to Halifax and New York in twenty days.

Many new companies did not survive. Uneconomical in operation and without the protection of a large mail subsidy, paddle steamships were wasteful as means of transport and, like the ships they built, the men who built them went under.

Lacy Hemingway did not intend to do so and Mr Moore, who had seen many such come and go, and who had had financial dealings with some of them, knew he was looking at that rare individuality which creates success. He did not know how he knew, but he knew he had a winner. As a breeder of fine horses will run his eye across the fine strength of several foals, and pick the one which will one day be first past the post, he sensed the potential of the girl whose candid eyes stared into his.

'Do you wish to hear further what I have to say, Mr Moore, or must I go to – ?' She mentioned Mr Moore's rival in Bold Street, and he sat back abruptly.

'I have never done business with a lady before, Miss Hemingway . . .'

Lacy leaned forward and reached for the money which lay on the desk before them, but Mr Moore had not yet finished.

'. . . so you must forgive me if I seem a little . . . hesitant.'

Lacy relaxed, leaned back in her chair and smiled. For a moment Mr Moore was transfixed. By God, he thought, what chance does any poor fellow have when in contest with that. No matter what talent he might have, business acumen be damned, she had a head start on them all. She has only to arch a graceful eyebrow, lift her chin and smile that brilliant smile, and any deal she cares to be involved with will be hers.

He was to be proved wrong, but that was yet to come.

He pulled himself together, clearing his throat and fiddling with his cravat, which suddenly appeared to have become curiously tight.

'What had you in mind, Miss Hemingway?'

It did not take long in the telling. It seemed a certain Mr Finchett, a major shareholder in a shipping line well-known to Mr Moore, was in some financial difficulty, and had been forced to realize his assets. 'I have it on the soundest advice, Mr Moore, from a reliable source,' Lacy said. 'I wish to buy those shares.'

'But it is the practice of the company that no shares should be sold to others except those in the partnership. Mr Finchett will offer them there first.'

'I believe that to be so, Mr Moore, but I am prepared to pay a little extra. And, as an added incentive to Mr Finchett, perhaps if he were to be asked at which establishment he spends every Wednesday evening, and with whom, he might be persuaded . . .'

Mr Moore gasped, turned as red as a police constable's vest, then as white as his trousers, and fell back in his chair.

'My dear Miss Hemingway . . . My dear young lady, I cannot believe . . .!'

'You cannot believe that Mr Finchett is capable of such . . . endeavours, or that I know of them? Or perhaps it is the shock of hearing me speak of them to a gentleman, or indeed to anyone. Or is it that you are speculating on the origin of my information?' Lacy smiled sweetly.

'If we are to do business, Mr Moore, and I believe we are, you must become used to my manner, and to the way in which I deal with you. I do not intend to do business as a lady. There are certain things I want from life and I have learned from . . . experience that one does not get these things by "playing the game". I have no chivalry, Mr Moore, and no compunction in attaining my goal by any means at my disposal. Now, I want those shares, I know they are for sale, though the company to whom they should be offered, does not. Do not ask me how I know, for I will not tell you. If I can put a little pressure on Mr Finchett I will do so. Men are fools sometimes, Mr Moore. They place themselves, through their own lust – yes, lust, Mr Moore – in a position where they are vulnerable. They are concerned with morals and the approval of their fellows, you see, and I am concerned with neither.'

Mr Moore sat speechless and stunned.

'I have one stipulation.' Lacy lifted her neatly bonneted head imperiously. 'You must buy those shares for me. No one is to know they are mine. Do you understand?'

Mr Moore piped that he did.

'I shall have further instructions for you on the investment of monies in the future. I have my eye on some stock which is for sale in . . .'

For a further ten minutes she and Mr Moore exchanged views on the advisability of this investment or that and, when she seemed satisfied, asking him for the last time if he fully understood what she required of him, Lacy Hemingway stood up, bowed in his direction and swept from his office like a queen.

It was hard to continue their life at the pickle factory as though nothing had happened. But something held her back. It was as though an instinct born in all animals, but atrophied by civilization in humans, kept her under cover until the moment her senses told her she might come into the open. Danger lay in exposure, safety in hiding. Although sealed notes from Mr Moore, delivered to her own box at the Post Office in the east wing of the Custom House, told her the shares were bought and thriving, and her account at the bank growing, she was not yet ready to begin.

Rose was patient with her now. They lived on their tiny wages, for Rose had had training in making one penny do the work of two. When they were not working they kept their little room scrupulously clean, putting the stamp of their own personalities into the bare attic with one or two knick-knacks they had picked up cheaply at St John's Market, and covering the walls with Lacy's sketches.

The room was at the very top of a tall house and, as such, escaped much of the noise and smells that attacked others on lower levels. Watched by the patient dog, who spent most of his days shut up in the room, Lacy would stand on a box and gaze from the window set high in the roof. On a fine day she could see across the river to Egremont and New Brighton and, if she craned her neck far enough, even to Birkenhead. With lumps of charcoal and a bit of paper supplied by Mr Price, who had taken quite a fancy to 'the little slip of a thing', and who had even found himself calling her 'Cariad' a time or two, she did sketches of roof tops, clouds, seagulls, chimneys and the swaying masts of the ships, whose rigging could just be seen.

Every Sunday, fair weather or foul, they took Copper for the only exercise he had, apart from the necessary five minutes night and morning. It was always towards the river, of course, and the docks to the north: Princes, Waterloo, Victoria, Trafalgar and Clarence. Great names with which to conjure.

From St Nicholas' churchyard, across the quays and beyond the sheds and warehouses until they reached the marine parade, the smell of the sea always in their nostrils, they would walk quickly: two poorly dressed but decently clean working girls; a strange sight with the dog beside them. But when they came to the sands which lay from Kirkdale to Bootle, they would take off their boots and run and run. The dog was a puppy again, roses whipped into their thin cheeks, and everything was forgotten in their pleasure.

They never went south for in that direction lay Silverdale. It was a resting time for Lacy, and Rose understood.

In the space of a few hours, the two men she had loved most and had trusted with her heart and innocent confidence, had taken both from her, had thrown them in her face, and had revealed them as worthless. It had almost killed her. She needed the time to repair her spirit: not the courageous spirit which had taken her to the top of the tallest trees, or had had her riding as fast and jumping as high as her brothers; but the hidden and undefined core of her which had been bruised and almost destroyed. She needed time to gather about her again the bright sureness she once had. These past months had brought the realization that though she had been rejected and thrust out to fend for herself in a world of which she had scant knowledge; though she was trained in no employment, she had survived, triumphed. And it brought her peace.

The work at the pickle factory was hard and rough; the women with whom she worked, the same. But she had gained their respect by her refusal to give in when she could have dropped from sheer exhaustion. They had known at once, of course, that she was not of their class and, in the manner of those who sense something different and therefore to be scoffed at, they had jibed at her 'posh' accent and her 'pernickety ways'. But her sharp and funny answers to their baiting made them laugh grudgingly, and her willingness to tackle anything they themselves could do earned her, at last, their friendship. She began to take pride in what Charles and Luke had turned from.

She could go forward now.

She and Rose stayed with 'Price and Roberts' until April, almost a year. Then, on a day of pale yellow sunshine, and creamy clouds which moved gently across the river like the flocks of ewes and their lambs in Farmer Whipple's field, they wrapped themselves in their shawls and began the walk to Bold Street.

There was a smell of primroses and the fresh tang of the sea on the breeze as it whipped about their slim figures. Lacy let the shawl slip to her shoulders and her lovely hair, clean and shining like polished platinum, flew about her, and men stared, for she was beautiful again now.

The salon was full when they walked boldly in, and all the ladies were afflicted with 'stickjaw', staring in amazement. The younger Miss Yeoland, about to place a scrap of foolishness upon the head of the wife of one of the town's councillors and a most prominent gentleman, nearly fainted, the wits frightened from her by the sight. The elder Miss Yeoland, summoned by an excited seamstress, could not believe that beneath the rough grey dress, the patched shawl, the heavy black boots which revealed her ankles, lay Miss Alexandrina Victoria Hemingway, whom she had last seen being fitted with a beautiful coronet of pale pink rosebuds to wear to her sister's wedding.

She whisked the pair of them out of sight in the twinkling of an eye, for she had lost none of her ability to assess and shape a situation to her own advantage, and there was none to be gained by seeming to do business with a pair of urchins from the Scotland Road.

When Rose and Lacy emerged two hours later they were both suitably gowned in simple dresses of cinnamon silk and jade moiré respectively, with bonnets to match, for the Misses Yeoland also had ready-made outfits – an innovation thought up by the elder sister, and popular with those who could not afford the exorbitant price of garments made specially.

'Walk slowly, Miss Hemingway, if you please,' Miss Yeoland hissed, 'or your boots will show.' Boots and slippers were commodities the Misses Yeoland did not stock. The girls now appeared so elegant and completely fitted to their environment that not a head turned as they left the salon. The remainder of the gowns, mantles, bonnets and underwear Rose and Lacy had ordered were delivered later to their new apartment in Duke Street where, it was said, King George IV, then Prince of Wales; and King William IV, then Duke of Clarence, had once stayed. It was named after the great Duke of Cumberland. The apartment was small but very respectable, and they had bought one or two pieces of furniture to put in it. They spent very little, for their money was to be used on more important things.

Clothes must be good and elegant, for they were to be part of the plan, but on what they slept or sat did not matter, providing their address was good.

An office was found as close to the docks as possible, furnished simply but tastefully and, on this day, their nineteenth birthdays, they were ready.

The sign on the door read simply 'Hemingway and O'Malley. Shipping'.

Lacy walked towards the bow window and looked out upon the river at the beautiful clipper ships, the sturdy merchantmen, the frigates and the barques. The water rippled gold in the sun, turning slowly with the sky to a lovely blue.

She sighed, but there was no sadness in that sigh; only the sheer pleasure of satisfaction.

There was a rustle of taffeta outside the door. She turned expectantly, her eyes gleaming in anticipation. It opened and Rose was there, smiling, confident. She wore strawberry pink and silver grey. She looked lovely and elegant, her thick hair neatly netted beneath her bonnet.

She looked at Lacy and winked, and Sean's brilliant green eyes shone from her impish face.

'Ready?' she asked.

Looking to the small mirror above the fireplace, Lacy put on her bonnet of pearl grey silk, a charming frou-frou of nonsense wreathed in white lace and rosebuds, then turned again to Rose.

'I am now.'

They both took a deep breath, and began to laugh as they walked towards the door.

# CHAPTER 20

The two-masted frigate rounded Black Rock Lighthouse at the entrance to the river and, moving slowly, for there was hardly a breeze, hovered like a butterfly on water towards the 'Northwest' floating light which was stationed in the mouth of the River Mersey. The marker displayed three bright lights after dark, but now, in full daylight, it showed its position by a large, black ball.

The sails of the sturdy ship billowed gracefully, like the skirts of a lady's gown as she curtseys, and the sun, just rising above the hills of Toxteth in the south east, flooded them with lovely early morning light, pale and translucent.

The ship, the *Annie McGregor*, fifteen days out of Savannah and 525 tons burthen, was not particularly beautiful but she was strong and, providing the wind was right, could even manage the journey in thirteen days. At this time of the year, however, when the winds were light and calm, it was all she could do to make fifteen and, had it not been for the skill of her master, the thirty-five-year-old son of a shipwright from New York, she would still be somewhere off the Irish coast.

The second of the navigational aids came up to starboard: the Formby light at the entrance to the Formby Channel, this one showing a red ball; and then the third at the Crosby channel, stationed to direct mariners through the labyrinth of channels and banks which impeded the free navigation of the port.

Orders were bellowed and obeyed as the ship approached Waterloo Dock where most of the great American ships were moored, and the complicated procedure of docking was prepared for. Barefoot sailors in loose white trousers, shirts and neckerchiefs, ran hither and thither, all seemingly intent upon some important business known only to himself; but from the apparent chaos came order. Sails were furled neatly, lines thrown and caught and carefully, tidily and with the utmost precision the *Annie McGregor* came to her moorings.

Dockers stood in groups of two or three, leaning upon the handles of hefty sets of wheels which they used to trundle cargo from ship to warehouse, waiting on the contents of the hold of the *Annie McGregor*. Most had a pipe, and smoke wreathed about their heads in a thick, blue mist. The smell of tobacco mingled with the pungency of the sea, of tar, and of coffee beans which were being unloaded from the ship in the next berth.

The men were patient, glad to idle for a moment in the pleasant morning sunshine. The next few hours would be hard, as they raced to get the cargo to the tall warehouse where it would be stored.

Strong, horse-drawn carts stood to the rear of the wharf, lined up like contestants in a race; the first ready to be down to the ship to receive its load.

At first, those who stood about believed they were dreaming, and rubbed their eyes as though to remove the last vestige of sleep. Others put hands to bewildered heads, and swore they would resist the temptation to down 'just one more'.

A curious silence fell, and in it could clearly be heard the dainty click of high-heeled slippers on the stone setts of the quayside. They might have been hewn from stone, those rough, easy-going, hard-drinking, cheerfully swearing workmen, for every activity came to a complete halt as Lacy Hemingway and Rose O'Malley, out on their first day of business, walked serenely amongst them.

The only objects which moved, beside Lacy, Rose and an inquisitive dog which sheered away, dismayed by the sudden silence, were the eyes in the men's heads. These rotated slowly from left to right, watching mesmerized the passage of the two young women. Breath was held and pipes halfway to open mouths remained there, dangling limply. One fell to the ground with a small, splintered crash which made its owner jump.

Perhaps it was this sound which awoke them from their

trance. A sibilant hissing began as speech returned. They whispered at first, like children left alone in the schoolroom, but the sounds became bolder as consternation, even indignation, took hold.

What were two women, ladies, for it was obvious that was what they were, doing down here? Surely they knew it wasn't right for such as they to be sauntering about like they were on St James' Promenade taking the air.

Thunderstruck now, and braver by the minute, but still convinced some mistake had been made, they began to move about and scratch their heads and smile, for the two women were exceedingly pretty, and it was not often, if ever, one saw such as these about here. Drabs, ladies of the street when darkness fell and trade was good; but never ladies.

Lacy held her head gracefully, her tiny white lace parasol casting a light shadow over her face. Her back was straight, her breasts lifted tantalizingly, and breaths which had been held in lungs erupted and quickened, as eager eyes devoured both her and Rose. Rose looked neither to right nor left, but walked beside Lacy as if she did this every day of her life and the rude stares of the men meant nothing to her, but her heart pounded in her breast, and she became afraid the staring men would mark its beat.

A man, a foreman by his dress, cleared his throat, removed his cap respectfully, and stepped in front of the two women.

'Excuse me, miss.' His face was as red as the handkerchief about his neck.

Lacy and Rose stopped politely. It did not do to antagonize, for their future goodwill might depend on a man such as this. A foreman had the respect of all those under him, as well as the ordering of their employment.

'Yes?' Lacy smiled pleasantly, and the man reeled under the impact of her beauty. Her eyes seemed to contain dancing sparklets of light in their silvery depths, and the warm sunshine had put a pale rose in each cheek. Her poppy lips parted on even, white teeth and, as they moved, a small dimple caught his eye.

He was transported and utterly speechless.

Lacy's smile deepened, and so did the dimple. A tiny breath of wind lifted a stray tendril of pale, silken hair and blew it across her lips. She raised her gloved hand to remove it and the man could not look away from where it clung.

Lacy took pity on him.

'I am sorry,' she said, 'I had not realized you were in charge. Forgive me. I should perhaps have spoken to you first, but with so many of you . . .'

She looked round, her brilliant smile encompassing the gaping crowd, and they all grinned delightedly shuffling their feet and ducking their heads.

Rose almost laughed out loud. They were like children, thrilled to the core to be noticed by a grown-up, she thought. One smile, a bit of flattery an' sure, they'd lie down and let her wipe her feet all over them. It wasn't fair really. They hadn't a chance, for no one could go against Lacy's charm or her beauty. A moment ago, this simpering monkey had been ready to question her right to be in this hallowed men's world, but now, with a flash of her eyes and a bit o' blarney, she had him directing her eagerly to the ship she sought.

It was going to be easier than they had imagined.

The men began to crowd about, longing to be of assistance, trying to catch Lacy's eye: deferentially, of course, for it was evident that she was no tart to be winked at. Though still perplexed at her reasons for being there, they told each other she must be related to the captain of the ship she asked for. Strange really, for he was an American and she was not, but there, the ways of the gentry were not theirs to question.

They sent her on her way, tickled pink by the few minutes of pleasure she had brought them.

Captain Paul Ellis had retired to his cabin immediately his ship was safely docked, leaving the task of supervising the unloading of his cargo in the capable hands of his first mate. The journey had been a fair one with no difficulties, but within two days they would be loaded up with a new cargo and on their way back to Savannah, and he wished to make the most of his stay in port.

There was a pretty minx who could be mighty accommo-
dating when showered with the sort of gee-gaws women love
but, if he was not quick off the mark, she might be snapped up
by some other admirer. There were several 'pretty minxes' to
be had at the house in Juniper Street, but the one he favoured
had a knack of turning a man's limbs to jelly and was well
worth the money spent on her. He had had an easy voyage
but, still, he liked to relax at the end of it, and it was nearly two
weeks since his strong sexual appetite had been fed.

He was putting the brush about his smooth, brown hair
when there was a knock at his cabin door. He eyed himself
appreciatively in the small mirror above his bunk bed, and
smoothed his waistcoat across his broad chest, pulling the two
points at the front down towards his flat stomach. Thirty-five
he might be, but he was damned fit. He thought he would
have no problem in persuading the 'minx' to his side, even if
she was otherwise engaged.

The knock sounded again, and he told whoever hammered
on his door to 'enter'.

The door opened inwards and a face appeared, the eyes in
it wide with utter disbelief, a stunned expression pasted across
it like the mask of a clown.

'What is it, man?' Captain Ellis bellowed, his gaze still on
his own reflection. Matters of business were done with as far
as he was concerned. His mind was long gone to Juniper
Street, where he fondly hoped his body would soon follow.

'Well, Jacobs? Speak up, man. Speak up.'

Jacobs spoke up. 'There's a lady to see you, Captain.'

The first mate, younger than his captain and clearly almost
beyond speech with shock, stuttered through the full beard he
wore, and for a moment Paul Ellis thought the man was
drunk.

He turned slowly, his expression comically astonished.

'A lady?'

'Yes, sir.' Jacobs was still in the state of breathless disbelief
into which the sight of Lacy and Rose had just tipped him. It
would be a while before he recovered.

'Two, sir,' he said incredulously.

'Two.'

'Yes, sir.'

Paul Ellis conjured with thoughts of discarded mistresses, outraged mamas; even of his own wife and mother-in-law, left behind in Savannah.

Still bewildered, but beginning to be intrigued, he whispered to Jacobs as though the 'two ladies' stood only an arm's length away.

'Who the hell are they, Jacobs? Do I . . . do we know them?'

'I couldn't say, sir.'

'I mean, have they been . . . here,' indicating his cabin, 'before?'

'These are ladies, sir. Real ladies.'

'I know, so you said, but what the hell are they doing . . .?'

'They are waiting on deck, sir. Shall I show them down?'

Captain Ellis scratched his head, nonplussed, then deciding some action must be taken, nodded his agreement and put on his frock coat.

Rose had to smile again. The effect that two women, one beautiful and herself as pretty as most she supposed, had on these men was most amusing. True, if she and Lacy had been as ugly as 'owd boots' they would have made a certain impression in this world of men, but the sight of Lacy, dainty as a daisy and beautiful as orange blossom in her strangely exotic way, brought the lot of them to a pop-eyed slack-jawed standstill.

But Paul Ellis, twenty years at sea, and about the same since he first charmed the pretty seventeen-year-old daughter of his father's foreman into dropping her drawers behind the timber pile in the shipyard, was well versed in taking hold of a situation and bringing it round to his own advantage. He recovered sufficiently to bow over their hands, to show them to a chair each, and to ask politely what he could do for them. He had not the faintest idea why they were here, and when Lacy began it was all he could do to hold on to his recently regained composure.

'My name is Lacy Hemingway, sir. I believe you are Captain Paul Ellis from Savannah!'

'That is true, ma'am!'

'How do you do, Captain Ellis. May I introduce my friend, Miss Rose O'Malley.'

'Miss O'Malley.' He bowed in Rose's direction. By God, she was as lovely as the other, though in a different way. More . . . more earthy, but very splendid. Light and dark. Day and night. What a pair of 'bookends' they would make. He had never seen two women who showed each other off to such advantage.

His light blue eyes, from which the sun seemed to have bleached the colour, drifted from one to the other quizzically. Who on earth were they? Surely not a couple of 'madams' drumming up business? Of course not. As Jacobs said, they were ladies, real ladies. At least the fair one was. With the instinct of a man born to a certain station in life; of a gentleman accustomed to the company of what one knew to be a lady, he was not too sure about the dark beauty. She was dressed with all the tasteful simplicity of her companion, but there was a style, a bearing, a tone of voice; perhaps the imperious lift to her head, which Miss Hemingway had and Miss O'Malley lacked. It spoke of generations of wealth and breeding, of being superior to the ordinary mortal. It was to be seen in the young Southern belles back home who drove about Savannah and Charleston in their fine carriages, cosseted by their negro slaves, protected and sheltered from life as though they were hothouse blooms – which, in fact, was what they were. This one had it but at the same time there was a look of strength, of resolution about her. Miss Hemingway was lovely, exquisite really, with an air of fragility about her; of delicacy; but in a way she reminded him of a rapier blade. Fine, silvered, but made of a steel which would last for ever.

He waited for her to continue speaking.

Lacy smiled sweetly, and her eyes sparkled as though she had some lovely secret which she was about to share with him.

'Is it not a lovely day, Captain Ellis?' she said, 'so warm already, though still early. It makes one thirsty, does it not?'

Paul Ellis jumped to his feet like a puppet brought sharply to life by the puppetmaster's hands.

'I beg your pardon, Miss Hemingway. Do forgive me. I had

quite forgot my manners. May I offer you some refreshment?' What the devil did ladies drink at this time of day? What time of day was it, for Christ's sake? Not yet seven o'clock was his guess.

Once again he was thrown into the state of confusion which had gripped him when Lacy and Rose were announced, and he looked about dazedly.

Rose smiled secretly. The events of this first morning were affording her an enormous amount of amusement. Faith, if this was life in business, it was not going to be dull. Another point to Lacy. Just when the poor man was gathering his wits into some semblance of order, she knocked his legs from under him with words which only a lady would speak. Poor devil. He doesn't know whether he's on his ear or his elbow.

'Some tea would be most acceptable, Captain Ellis.'

Tea. Did they have such a thing on board, he wondered. But he ordered it by bellowing down the passage outside the door of his cabin, and when a smart young boy appeared with a tray he silently blessed the efficiency of Jacobs, and then became flustered at the notion that he now must act as host in the serving of the beverage.

'Shall I pour, Captain?' Lacy was womanliness itself. Relieved, he breathed in her perfume as she handed him a cup of tea, the first he had ever drunk in his own cabin.

When a sip or two had been taken she began.

'You have a cargo of raw cotton, have you not, Captain?'

Her eyes looked innocently into his. Her lips curved in a smile, showing her pretty teeth. She began to remove her gloves, pulling delicately at each finger slowly, slowly, and for an awful moment Paul Ellis felt a stirring in his lap, and thanked God hc sat behind his desk. As her small white wrist, her small hand and slim white fingers slid from the glove, he thought he had never seen anything more sensuous in his life. The white flesh lay like pearl against the grey of her dress, and before he could recover his senses she began on the other. She might have been a certain artiste who was the sensation of a theatre he knew of in San Francisco, and who filled the place nightly with the erotic performance when she

296

removed every stitch of her clothing, barring a narrow ribbon and a froth of lace. By God, and all this one did was to take off her gloves! He imagined the commotion she would cause in the same pose and high-heeled shoes of the performer, and was so mesmerized he sat like a half-witted boy, unhearing, uncaring, his cup of ghastly tea almost in his lap.

'Captain?' Lacy murmured.

'I'm sorry, I . . .'

'I believe you have a cargo of raw cotton in your hold?'

'I beg your pardon, I am not sure . . .'

Lacy glanced at Rose, and the performance they had rehearsed together so many times began.

Rose leaned forward and placed her cup and saucer upon the captain's table. She took a scrap of lace from her sleeve, allowing it to drift through the air as she placed it daintily to her lips. The action freed a delicate perfume, and Captain Ellis's attention was immediately riveted upon her midnight beauty, her tip-tilted green eyes, and the full red lips to which the handkerchief was placed. Rose touched the corner of her mouth, her tongue appeared for a moment, pink and moist, wetting her top lip and she smiled a little as though at a loss as to how to begin.

Captain Ellis clung to his chair as if the slightest movement might send him floating to the ceiling of his cabin. He scarcely seemed to breathe in his enthralled contemplation of Miss O'Malley's moving lips.

'Miss Hemingway and I . . .'

'Yes?'

'We are in somewhat of a dilemma, sir, and we were hopeful that you might . . .'

'Of course. Anything, anything.'

'We had heard you were carrying a cargo of raw cotton, and it seemed you were the answer to our prayers. You see . . .'

'Miss O'Malley, if there is something I can do to help,' he breathed, 'I would be most . . .' He was about to say grateful and, indeed, that is how it seemed to him. His gratitude to

297

these two exquisite creatures would be overwhelming, if they would only allow him to help them. With what he did not know, nor care at the moment.

'Just let me know how I may assist you . . .'

'It would be of mutual benefit to us both, of course, Captain Ellis!'

His head snapped to the right as Lacy spoke. She almost heard the bone in his neck crick, so quickly did his head move.

'Mutual?' he croaked.

Lacy smiled brilliantly, but her thoughts were contemptuous. The poor fool has not the slightest notion why we are here. Her eyes met Rose's and she saw mirrored in them the workings of her own mind. Smile a little, simper, wet your lips, show a sliver of flesh and all coherent thought leaves a man. Are they all alike, or is it that the very idea of a woman transacting business has nothing to do with the flesh and is so extraordinary, even ludicrous, they cannot conceive of it? Although we speak of his cargo of cotton, all he can see are two women smiling at him, and the words we say might be of the deliciousness of the tea or the comfort of his cabin, for all the notice he takes of them.

She almost ruined it then, for her scorn curled her lip, and the smile in her eyes froze to the look of ice on the grey waters of a pond. He sensed the change in her and looked bewildered for a moment. His own smile, so eager and earnest, became uncertain. Rose saw it and, with a tinkling laugh, she who had never 'tinkled' in her life, turned his head again. When he looked back at Lacy, her attentive concern for his worthwhile advice again made him feel he was the greatest fellow who had ever worn breeches. He was not to know that Lacy's contempt for the male species was complete.

It took at least an hour before he really began to understand what they were about. Halfway through he bellowed for Jacobs and a bottle of whiskey, tired unto death of the insipid tea he drank, and finding a sudden need to bolster up his wilting body and reeling mind. Like Mr Moore, the notion of becoming allied with a woman in a way other than those usually associated with the female sex was so novel as to be laughable. How on earth was one expected to make a profit in partnership with a brain which was only fashioned to cope with the ways in which to please a man bodily, to bear his children and run his home? Women were made for no other purpose and those who demanded other than this were odd and not to be considered. The sister of a friend of his had had the misfortune to be born with, or had taken up in later life the idea that women were equal to men, and had shamed her family by stating a desire to go to university. He remembered the names she had been called, the least offensive being 'blue stocking'. His friend had scarcely been able to hold up his head for the scandal of it. There had been some small justification for the girl's actions, for she had been exceedingly plain with barely a chance of gaining a husband, but then she should have done what other women in her position have always done: remained a spinster and taken up 'good works'. But these two would not have that problem; not at all. So why . . . ?

Paul Ellis took a big step that morning, when he finally agreed to do what Lacy and Rose asked him. But it was many months, and several upward swings in his bank balance, before he felt easy in his mind about the rightness of dealing in such a way with a woman. Perhaps he never did, for it was rarely out of his mind when he was with them, that either one would have been more sensibly employed in his bed.

The sensation inspired in his loins by Lacy's removal of her gloves died an instant death when he finally understood what he was being asked, and for a second or two he felt nothing; absolutely nothing. Raw cotton. An agent. New Orleans. Consignments of cutlery from Sheffield. Cotton . . . Manchester . . . New Orleans . . .? He felt he had wandered on to a stage set in which every actor knew their part but him. The plot was a nonsense to him, and his face showed it.

Lacy's voice was quiet and her expression serious as she spoke. Rose sat silently, causing no distraction now that the softening up process was done with, although she still felt a great desire to laugh. He sat like one poleaxed and she was

299

reminded of a bull she had once seen in a street show. It had been struck between the eyes by the fist of the biggest man she had ever seen; a man with thighs and forearms thicker than her own waist, performing his act as a 'strong man'. The beast had sunk slowly to the ground with exactly the surprised expression which was now on the face of Paul Ellis. She could see his scattered thoughts beginning to gather, ready to make sense on his lips, but it took a while; and the denunciation would be first.

He came from his enthralment with the speed of a man falling from a mainmast; and he hit the deck with the same appalling thump. Lacy allowed him to rant and rave for five minutes. He strode up and down the small cabin, constantly coming face to face with obstacles which he kicked irritably aside. Rose thought he would dearly love to kick herself and Lacy, as he almost tripped over their quietly seated figures. He did not quite swear, but it was at this juncture that he called for something stronger than tea.

'Captain Ellis, I see you are surprised.' Lacy's voice was calm.

'Surprised.' Rose thought he would throw a fit, or bang his head against the bulwark at the crass stupidity of all women. It was beyond belief, his expression seemed to say.

'Surprised, madam. I am appalled. Appalled and angry, too. You are . . . both of you are . . . very attractive, and it is obvious you are ladies, and why your families have allowed you to run about in this . . . rude way, I cannot imagine. I have never heard of anything so ridiculous in my life.' He thought of the sister of his friend, the 'blue stocking', and was for a moment diverted; then, in full spate, was off again.

'Does not your father have a tighter rein on you than this? He must be mad! What can he be thinking of to let you come aboard a ship full of rough . . . It is lucky for you, madam, I run a well-disciplined ship, or you and Miss O'Malley might have been subjected to . . . Well, as you are a lady of breeding I will not go into further detail, but I can assure you . . .'

'Captain Ellis, please, I beg you, do not concern yourself with our safety. Miss O'Malley and I are well able to look after ourselves.'

A picture of Lancer McGhee flashed into her mind, and she

300

knew as she spoke, with a curious sense of objectivity, that there would never again be an occasion on which concern for her safety need be considered. She would never be afraid of a man again. It was a strange sensation, but it gave her the calmness to let this bombast blow himself out. What could he or any man do to her now, after Naylor Street? Her voice was firm as she continued.

'And as for your fears for my father's sanity, Captain, let me assure you that he has nothing to do with our visit. Miss O'Malley and I have recently gone into business ourselves, and we . . .'

'Business for yourselves! You cannot mean . . .'

'Yes, we intend to buy and import raw cotton. Later we shall consider other cargoes but, for the moment, we are looking for an agent to act for us in . . .'

'You will find no agents aboard this vessel, madam, and if I may say so . . .'

'I am sure you will say whatever you please, Captain, with or without my permission.'

Ignoring the interruption, Paul Ellis continued ferociously, '. . . and you are impertinent into the bargain. How old are you? Tell me that. No more than seventeen or eighteen, I'll be bound. You should be at home with your governess, missy, or with your mama, looking for a husband.'

The humour of the situation seemed to smite him now, and he laughed suddenly, '. . . and I am sure you will have no trouble on that score.' Gallantry took over as his rage slipped away, for he thought he had the better of them now, and did not wish to appear too harsh and reduce them to tears. He had put them thoroughly in their place, so to speak, so he was prepared to be a little kinder.

'Why, I would oblige myself, if I were not already in a state of wedded bliss. Come, Miss Hemingway, enough of this nonsense. Let me show you to your carriage.'

He was smiling condescendingly, the picture of the perfect gentleman showing the little woman the error of her ways. 'I have no notion who put the idea for this charade into your pretty head, but believe me, my dear, I should go home to Papa and . . .'

301

'Your cooperation would not go unrewarded, Captain Ellis.'

Paul Ellis began to smile. His mouth curled at each corner and his charm, that which he used to capture the 'pretty minxes' with whom he dallied when he was out of range of his wife's eye, was brought in to full play. Now there was an interesting offer. What an evening that might turn out to be. One at a time, or perhaps . . . ?

'I am talking about money, Captain. Nothing else.' The lovely silver sparkle was gone, leaving only frosted grey in Lacy Hemingway's eyes.

'Money,' Paul Ellis said blankly.

'If you were to become my representative in America, and my shipper, you would receive a percentage of the profit.'

'Miss Hemingway,' the man's voice became almost shrill as his temper took over again. 'The idea of doing business with a woman is so distasteful to me I could . . . I could . . .'

'Yes, Captain?'

Lacy smiled at Paul Ellis and stood up, bringing to an end his tramping slog up and down his own cabin. She put her hand on his arm, and shook her head as though at the antics of a foolish child. Before he knew what he was about, Paul Ellis felt the anger, the outrage and sheer, appalled amazement at this girl's effrontery drain away. The stupidity of his own prejudice, which, if he allowed it to continue, might stand in the way of his making money, became suddenly clear to him. It was as if he had become unexpectedly aware of the quiet composure of the girl who stood before him, of her certainty, her absolute confidence in herself. For the first time in his life he looked for, and found, keen intelligence shining in a woman's eye. The absurdity of what had gone before stilled him to wonderment. As he stared at her, lost for words at last, she sat down again, motioning him to his chair with a graceful gesture, and he sat obediently.

'Let me explain to you, Captain,' she went on. 'I have . . . contacts in the cotton trade, and anything you bring will readily be snapped up. I cannot be in two places at the same time, Captain Ellis. I cannot buy in New Orleans and sell in

Liverpool, so you see the necessity of employing someone who can be at one end whilst I am at the other. You can appoint an agent in the cotton belt to negotiate the purchase of cotton at concessionary rates, and ship consignments via the railroad direct to the ship, your ship, in New Orleans. You see the advantage, do you not?' she said crisply.

'The profits would be considerable. You buying and shipping, and myself disposing of the raw cotton and providing you with a cargo to take back to America. You need supply nothing but your ship and your time, and will be well repaid for both. The benefits could be . . . generous.'

Before he had time to answer, Rose spoke.

'You have been in business for twenty years, have you not, Captain Ellis?' It was like being in a boxing ring with two opponents. He stared at her, bewildered, and again she felt sorry for him. Poor divil. Between Lacy and herself, the boyo had no chance.

'Where in hell do you get your information? You must be a couple of . . .'

'And you are married?'

'I said so.'

Rose smiled enchantingly, and her eyes became as slanted as those of a cat having its ears pulled. She did not stop smiling as she said, 'and you have a fancy, shall we say, for ladies, pretty ladies who would not be invited into your wife's drawing room.'

Paul Ellis' bellow drove a flock of derisively laughing gulls from their confident perch on his yardarm. They scattered to the safety of the roof of the Goré Piazza, where a dozen men were already sorting the bales of cotton from his hold.

'. . . but that is no concern of ours, Captain Ellis. I can see that that is what you are about to say. Nor should we care that you spend your free time in a house in Juniper Street where, we have been informed, you owe a certain sum of money. A gentleman can be embarrassed by such a situation, I am sure. But then, who knows that better than you?

Rose dimpled and Lacy smiled into her hand, for Rose dimpling was a sight to be seen. It was her turn again.

'Your private life is your own affair, Captain,' she said, 'but we have been given to understand that you are . . . Well, shall we say that you would not be averse to a little extra in the account you have in a certain Liverpool bank.'

Paul Ellis sank back into his chair defeated.

Lacy smiled and, stunned as he was, the man had time to wonder what it would be like if this beautiful young woman were to smile an invitation to join her, not in a business venture, but in a romantic one. She sipped her tea with the faultless manners of a lady. Her composure was complete, but in the depths of her clear eyes, there was surely more than a gleam of anticipation of a business deal well handled. Godammit, no woman could be so lovely, so desirable, and have nothing in her head but the click of coin on coin, and a desire to put one over on those who did business at the Cotton Exchange.

'We are robbing no one, Captain Ellis. You will have a handsome profit for your trouble. The cargo will be sold legitimately to a buyer at a fair price, and I . . .'

'Yes, Miss Hemingway, and you?'

'I . . . shall be in business, Captain Ellis.'

'In business, Miss Hemingway?'

'Surely you understand the word?'

'Of course I do, Miss Hemingway, but I must admit I have not yet met a . . . lady who desired to be . . .'

'In the world of men, Captain.'

'Well, I should hardly have thought you had been brought up to enter it, Miss Hemingway.'

'That is true, but . . .'

Lacy put down her cup and saucer and folded her slim fingers about one another. This man must not know of the storm which swept through her. If she let her control slip for a second she would be lost. Lost and on her knees, begging this . . . lecher for a chance. It all depended upon him. Someone must be her agent in the cotton states of America, and men would have nothing to do with a woman in business for herself. This one was perfect! He needed money to pay his debts; he had a fine reliable ship; he knew the trade. It would

304

take so long to find another such as he. Time was wasting, wasting.

'. . . but that has nothing to do with the business in hand, sir. I wish to employ you. Do you wish to work for me?' Her serene gaze fell upon him, and she looked as though it were a matter of supreme indifference to her whether he did or not.

There was silence. Paul Ellis picked at his lip, and his expression of indecision vied with the masculine strength of him. He looked like some matron who could not make up her mind on the blue check gingham or the pink stripe muslin.

Lacy cleared her throat delicately and stood up. He rose to his feet automatically. She began to draw on her gloves, and again he watched as her soft white skin was slowly hidden from his view. She arched her back, and his eye was drawn to the cream shadow beneath her jawline, and the tendril of silken hair which lay upon her collar. He imagined one of those tiny curls around his finger, his hands at the back of her neck, just where the heavy chignon lay above the lace of her gown.

God, she was a beauty, and he thought, surprised, what a brain. As keen as that of any man he knew. What woman of his acquaintance could have thought up the intricacies of the scheme with which he had just been presented. It was simple and beneficial to them both and the implied blackmail was intended, of course, to ensure his loyalty. He had not the slightest notion where she got her information but by God he admired her for it.

'We will take up no more of your time, Captain,' Lacy was saying charmingly, as though she was making her farewells in the drawing room of her mama's friend, and was aware that she had stayed overlong.

'It seems you have not the . . . stomach,' she arched her eyebrows and her teeth gleamed like a kitten in play, but her eyes were not kittenish.

'It seems you have not the stomach for this game, sir.'

'Sit down, Miss Hemingway. Let us talk business.'

The men who waited upon the dock watched in silent homage the departure of the two young ladies, and the foreman had his day made complete when the silver one stopped to thank him for his kindness. He clapped his cap to his breast as though she were the Queen herself.

The men could make nothing of him for at least an hour after she had gone.

'. . . Papa will have the final decision, of course, but I must say I was rather pleased with the outcome. I thought I handled the whole thing rather well.'

'Oh, Thomas, I am filled with admiration. It is most rewarding to see the way you have taken to the business world. I am sure Papa is relieved to have you take so much worry from his shoulders. Shall you go to South America to settle with . . .'

'Oh, no.' Thomas looked slightly crestfallen, and turned to assure his admiring sister that it was not necessary for the man who had created the sale to travel to the far side of the ocean to put it into action. 'The agent will see to that, Jane. I must stay here and keep my eye on things at this end.'

He puffed his chest, and Jane almost laughed. It was as Lacy said. Men could be manipulated like toys on the nursery shelf. A bit of flattery and the words you wanted to hear poured from their lips, like water in a brook.

'And have you any other, er . . . deals? That is the word, is it not, Thomas? Is there another transaction which will perhaps be left for you to take care of? Oh do tell me, Thomas. I am so intrigued. What of the . . . the . . . *Annie McGregor*? Do you remember you were speaking of the captain who is your friend, and who accompanies you to . . .'

'Yes, well, that is, he is gone now, Jane. But he is a capital fellow. I find him most amusing when we . . . er, play cards at the . . . friend's house where we meet.'

Thomas drew on his cigar and the smoke billowed about his head, drifting across the darkened garden in the direction of the summer house. The night was warm and windless, and he and Jane were walking after dinner. Mama would not abide

306

cigars in the house, and one could hardly join Papa in the smoking room, not without an invitation. Thomas, even at the age of twenty four, was still a child to his mama and papa and, probably because he was treated as such, acted the child, taking the greatest delight in showing off his prowess to his admiring sister. Jane took such an interest in his affairs these days. He supposed it was because her own life was so boring, but it did a chap good to confide in someone.

'I forgot to tell you, did I not, of the cargo of wool which Papa says I might deal with? From Australia, I believe. It is due to arrive on . . . Pardon? The name of the ship? Why, I cannot remember. Yes, I can find out. It really is a wonder to me, Jane, that you take such an interest. I find it most cordial to speak to you of my work.'

'That is kind of you, Thomas, but really I am tremendously intrigued in all that you do. Now, tell me. How on earth do you dispose of a whole shipload of wool? Where are the persons situated who would buy from you? And do tell me more of that quite fascinating friend of yours, the American who sounds rather naughty . . .'

Jane felt quite sorry for him.

# CHAPTER 21

The room was of handsome proportions, a perfect square. Three tall, slender windows were set in one wall, each with a door which opened on to a tiny, wrought iron balcony, from which one might look out onto the quiet and respectable crescent which was Upper Duke Street. Across the way was a row of terraced houses identical to this one. Built in the Regency period, they were solid and reliable, but graceful in their simplicity. A small park divided the crescent: a strip of grass with flowered borders, shaded by a few trees under which benches were set. In the summer, one might find a nursemaid or two with smart perambulators in the park, for a few families still lived in the area. But most of the houses were split up into apartments, one to a floor, and occupied by prosperous, unmarried businessmen.

The area was pleasant and quietly elegant, although not quite as genteel as once it had been . Many of the houses had been built by merchants in the previous century, men who had made their money in shipping, primarily in the Guinea trade. As their fortunes had grown, they had moved their families eastwards and southwards to Everton, Aigburth and Toxteth. Their homes were bought by those of the lower middle class, who were also stepping up the ladder of success and, as they too moved on, the lovely houses became slightly more run-down with each change of owner; like elderly ladies who, though ageing, still have some claim to beauty.

Now, having been bought by a speculator and split up into 'rooms', the houses were painted and refurbished and let to their present occupants – those who wished to live close to their place of business, but in the gentility to which they were used. Windows were bright and polished. Housemaids buffed brass door knockers to gleaming perfection, and scrubbed steps to brilliant whiteness. Window boxes were gay and colourful in the spring, and the whole area had a sparkle of success about it. It was close to the centre of town, almost within walking distance of the busy commercial section, and the dockyards. One might hire a hansom cab at the corner of Upper Duke Street and be driven to Clarence Dock in Regent Road for 2s, the journey taking no more than fifteen minutes.

A slender young woman leaned against the window frame of the sitting room, on the first floor of the middle house in the row of the terrace. She gazed pensively at the white world beyond the window, but the snow was coming down so thickly and night falling so fast, she could see no further than the black-painted fretwork of the tiny balcony. The snow flakes flew about in all directions, like feathers in a farmyard battle, before landing silently on the rapidly growing drifts which were piling up in the streets.

'You will have to stay the night, Jane,' she said. 'The carriage will never get out of the yard, let alone manage the lanes to Toxteth. There is not a soul to be seen in the street. I can barely make out the benches in the gardens, the snow has become so thick.' Her eyes sparkled suddenly, and she turned from the window eagerly.

'Why do we not go down and make a snowman like we used to? Do you remember, Jane? Or play snowballs. It is beautiful out there. So clean and unmarked and, if we wrapped up well, we should not feel the cold. Copper would love it. Would you not sweetheart? Come on, say you will. Oh, Rose, say you will!' Laughter filled the room, and the dog wagged his tail in a friendly way, but no one moved.

'Lacy Hemingway, you sound just like the little girl who used to plead with me to get up to such naughtiness, you frightened the wits out of me. Will you never change?'

'Stick-in-the-mud! You are then, and you are now.'

'I know, and I do not care. Nothing will move me from this lovely fire. What about you, Rose? Do you wish to build a snowman with Lacy?'

'Bejabers, 'tis daft she is. She must go alone if she goes.'

More laughter, and the woman by the window returned her attention, entranced, to the whirling whiteness of the snowflakes, watching as they slid down the panes of glass. There was silence for several moments then she said:

'You really should not have stayed, you know, Jane. The skies have been promising this all day. Why did you not go straight home, foolish girl?' She undid the braided loops which held the thick, green velvet curtains, and drew them across the window, before turning to the second woman, who sat in an armchair by the side of the great, roaring fire. She smiled affectionately, and moved to touch the woman's shoulder.

'You know there will be a commotion at ho . . . at Silverdale when you fail to arrive. Poor Mama. She will have you abducted and on a slave ship to the east, at worst, and at best, head-first in a snowdrift in Aigburth Road. Great search parties will be sent out, and the whole house will be in an uproar, with Mama wringing her hands and berating poor P . . .' She stopped suddenly. The laughter died in her throat, and those with her saw the light leave her fine eyes, as she realized what she had been about to say.

'Perhaps Jonas could manage it alone,' she said dully and turned away, walking across the soft green and honey-coloured carpet, the hem of her velvet housegown making a swishing sound as she moved. It was of a deep, midnight blue, which turned the whiteness of her skin to alabaster. High in the neck, and tight of sleeve and waist, had it not been for the wealth of tumbled hair which curled down her back, it would have made her look as pure and virginal as a nun in a habit. She picked up the heavy brass poker and gave the leaping fire a thrust, sending sparks up the wide chimney, then bent to the dog and fondled his ears.

'What do you think, Jane? Shall we send Jonas on foot? It really is getting deeper by the minute.' Her voice had returned to normal. 'He would probably get through on his own.'

'Oh, let the poor beggar stay.' The third woman laughed, as she looked up from the ledger she was studying. 'He is having

310

the time of his life in the kitchen with young Maggie. Why should he be sent out into the snow, whilst we all stay here warm and snug. Let him enjoy himself. Those at the big house will have to . . .'

Rose O'Malley stopped speaking abruptly, and looked into the surprised eyes of Jane Hemingway. They were wide and uncertain and Rose was suddenly aware that – no matter how kindly Jane was, nor how she had changed during the past eighteen months – it seemed she could never become accustomed to sitting down beside, dining with, and being spoken freely to by a woman who had once been a scullery maid in her father's house. During the past eighteen months, she and Jane, linked as they were by their love for Lacy, had gradually formed a relationship which had grown stronger as the months passed. But she felt it to be uneasy at times. There was not the instant rapport which existed between herself and Lacy. She respected Lacy's sister and admired her courage, for had it not been for her defiance of her father last year, Lacy would now be dead and buried. Now, her implied criticism, and seeming careless disregard for the anxiety of Jane's family when she failed to come home, must have upset Jane, or so Rose thought, and she hastened to apologize.

'Look, Jane. I am sorry. I did not intend to appear heartless. I would not say a word against them up there, for all they did to . . . To be sure, are they not your family, and have you not a fondness . . .'

Jane began to laugh.

'Oh, Rose, Rose. Am I so hard to understand, or is it that I have changed so much that you do not know the new me? I was not shocked that you seemed to belittle Mama and Papa. I know what they are, and I pity them for it. Does that sound pious and "holier than thou"? I do not mean it to be so, it is just that their attitude towards others deprives them of so much. It is they who are the losers, and I have seen . . .' She became aware of the stiffness of her sister who still knelt by the dog, twining his ears around her fingers, and she changed the subject hastily, and began to giggle like a child who tells a joke.

'No, it was not that, but the notion of what Jonas and Maggie might get up to in the kitchen that made me blink. You must make allowances for my upbringing, Rose, and forgive me if things you say so freely and simply seem to alarm me. My, er, education did not include relationships which occur between men and women, and I am somewhat surprised . . .' she raised her eyebrows whimsically, '. . . by their activities.'

Rose and Lacy grinned delightedly at one another as Jane went on, serious now.

'Dear Rose. You and I are friends now, I hope. Do not think I hold you in any less affection because of the place you once held in my father's household.'

Lacy rose to her feet gracefully, throwing back the heavy fall of her hair. 'Now then, Jane, stop your blarney as dear Rose would say, and let me have your opinion on what we should place against that empty wall. I trust Jonas will be allowed to stay tonight, and you may share my bed, so do let us get down to more important matters. Now, I saw a lovely silk upholstered rosewood sofa at "Pinneys" the other day, and I think it would look just right over there. I shall have nothing else in the room but what you see. I want none of the clutter Mama had.'

She screwed up her face in a grin of glee.

'Do you remember how as children we tiptoed about the drawing room, trying to avoid a dozen small tables all crowded with knick-knacks? Constantly on guard in case one should send flying a mass of ornaments, sandalwood, lacquer vases, ostrich eggs and God knows what else. She had an elephant's foot, do you remember? The thing used to lie in wait for me. It was the most hideous thing, and I became quite nauseous every time I fell on it, imagining the poor beast limping about on three feet.'

'. . . and what about me! I had the dusting of the damn thing *and* all those ornaments. Holy Mother, it used to take us hours just doing the photographs.'

The laughter was loud and joyful. The memories no longer had the power to hurt. The healing strength of Lacy's first successes, of independence and the self confidence it brought, had laid a soothing hand upon her, and she could talk for the first time of many things that had happened to her during the past two years and before. Many of them, but not all. The names of the two men who had formed her by the taking of her love, and the savage way in which they had finally discarded it, were never spoken. Not even to Rose. She had not inquired after, nor been told what had become of Luke Marlowe. She was only aware that another man had his ship.

She and Rose, and Jane, who had become a frequent visitor to their suite of rooms in Upper Duke Street, had spent many careful hours choosing the few pieces of furniture which graced the pleasant room they now sat in. A beautifully carved chiffonier stood against one wall, a small mahogany turnover table against another. The colours of green and honey were repeated in the curtains, carpet and velvet of the low fireside chairs. The walls were washed in the palest of greens, and over half of their surface were Lacy's framed sketches and water colours. Several small cut-crystal ornaments, arranged symmetrically by Maggie their young housemaid, and re-arranged each day by Lacy, clustered on the mantelpiece, beneath which burned an applewood fire. It was built to the fiery heights of a blast furnace, for Maggie liked to keep her young ladies 'cosy', and the flickering flames danced a mad whirligig on the ceiling.

Before the fire was a beautiful rug of pure white sheepskin, a 'housewarming' present from Jane, and upon it lay Copper, his russet coat returned to glory by the grooming now given him by Maggie. She felt herself to be quite the lady when she took his elegant and handsome self for a turn about the tiny strip of park, and took great pride in his superb appearance. He was fondly tolerant of her, and he grew sleek on the titbits she fed him. He allowed her to fuss over him, waiting patiently the return of Lacy and Rose, as he had done in Blackstock Street. Then his short constitutional had been taken in the back street, padding at the heels of his beloved mistress. A change in his station, for better or worse, he accepted with equanimity, providing she was with him.

313

They had eaten a simple meal cooked by Maggie, who was from a farm near Thirsk, on the edge of the North Yorkshire moors, and who was willing to look after their rooms, their cleaning, their washing and their ironing. She was proficient – how, they never knew, for she came straight from the farm – in the special skill required in using a 'goffering iron'. The frills with which undersleeves, collars and particularly under-garments were adorned had need of particular care, and, when shown a 'crimping board' for the first time, which was a type of fluted rolling pin, Maggie took to the task with style, turning out both her young ladies each day as fresh as two daisies just picked. Not only was she willing to do all this whilst they were about their business, but she could, she said modestly, turn her hand to a bit of plain cooking.

'Well, I 'ad to Missis,' she beamed, her broad Yorkshire dialect so thick it was difficult to translate. 'Me Mam 'ad a dozen on us, an' I were eldest, tha knows, so I were allus 'andy like. She were a gudd 'ousekeeper, me Mam, an' she learnt me all I knows, so don't you fret none. I'll see to un, an't t'dog an' all.'

Maggie did see to them, cheerful and uncomplaining, and 'right set up' to be in such a lovely place with a bedroom all to herself.

It took a few weeks to wean her from her inclination to call all of them 'missis', but her pleasure in her employment made her eager to learn, and soon she was calling them by their correct titles, and even managed to sketch a curtsey. She thought the world of Miss Rose and Miss Lacy and, on the occasion of the baker's boy enquiring, rather too rudely for Maggie's liking, into the absence of a man in the household – his face a bit sly in her opinion – she hit him about the head with his own bread-basket, scattering buns and loaves twenty yards down the street.

She had gone now, disappearing into her kitchen to see to the clearing up of the pots, which had accumulated in the preparing and baking of a delicious shepherd's pie, and an apple tart from her Mam's recipe, served with cheese as was customary in her part of Yorkshire. No doubt she was also 'seeing to' the recumbent form of Jonas who lolled by her fire, enjoying the sight of her generous hips, which was all she would allow, and praying the snow would not let up until spring.

'. . . an' mind yon chimbley, when yer chuck another log on, Miss Rose, or it'll 'ave yer up ter yer eyes in soot' – pronounced suit! – 'as soon as look at yer. Reckon it needs the sweep,' was her parting shot, as she joyously banged the kitchen door behind her.

They were quiet for several minutes after she had gone. The contrast between the two sisters was sharp, even in the soft glow of lamplight, which is acknowledged to flatter the plainest. Plain Jane. It might have been made for her. She sat on the little chair, her arms about her knees, which were drawn up almost to her chin. Her eyes gazed contentedly into the heart of the blazing apple logs. She was dressed in grey, and on her it looked just that. Grey. Put the same pale shade on Lacy, and it would become silver, or smoky pearl or oyster, gleaming in folds of light and dark, rippling about her slender figure like the moon reflected in water. On Jane it hung, exciting as sacking and as shapeless, taking the colour from her already pale face, and dimming her soft brown hair to mouse.

But the happiness and goodness of her shone in her light blue eyes, and her face was kind. People turned instinctively to her smile, as though they felt that here was someone who would ease the heavy load which bore them down; and she always did. They were warmed by her, and by her instant readiness to listen to their woes. Her days were filled by these poor souls; and her thoughts and prayers at night. She was utterly and perfectly happy. Lacy was often ashamed when she saw the affection her sister had, not only for herself, but for all those who turned to her in need. She remembered the times when they were children, and she had turned impatiently from the tentative overtures of friendship her sister made, for she had been eager to be away to more exciting pursuits than those beloved of Jane.

'I was a selfish little beast,' she said softly to Jane when the

315

memories came, but Jane would smile amiably, and remind her that it was Lacy who, in a roundabout way, had freed her from the way of life into which she was being forced.

'Your courage gave me courage. I would give all I have to be able to change the circumstances which brought it about but, nevertheless, that is what freed me. If things had been different, I should have liked to ... to help Miss Nightingale in her efforts to bring respectability to nursing. But things are not, so I help those I can. I was not meant for marriage, Lacy. Men ... alarm me somewhat. What happened to you, and therefore to me, released me. Poor Henry,' she would say, referring to the young man she had refused, then smile.

She moved about her papa's estate and even, as her confidence grew, gave her time and devotion to the many charitable institutions which abounded in the town. She helped to find employment in good homes for some of the hundreds of children who were abandoned to the work-house, or to the streets; and who were destined for the mines, the factories of Lancashire, the clattering mills of Yorkshire; for prostitution, the chimneys, or death. There were so many, it broke her heart. She had even tried, using her influence and the Hemingway name, to discover what had become of Mary Kate and Teresa O'Malley, but, out of the thousands who had gone, it was impossible to trace two young girls.

Rose lounged comfortably in the fireside chair. She, like Lacy, had removed her afternoon gown, and wore a peignoir of garnet Valencia, trimmed at the wrist and about her full breasts with rich, cream-coloured lace. Her legs were crossed at the ankles, and on the toe of one foot swung a velvet slipper. Its partner lay on the floor. She held a ledger in her hands, and her face was set in a frown of concentration, as she studied a column of figures written there. Squirming round, she took a pencil from the small wine table beside her, and began to tot up the figures, jotting a note or two on the margin.

On the floor now, flat on her stomach, her feet bare, Lacy scrutinized the tables of figures on papers which lay scattered about as she discarded them. She muttered as she turned a page, and scratched her head energetically. The curtain of her hair fell about her face, and she sat up irritably and, still staring and mumbling to herself, began to plait it until it lay across her shoulder, thick as a man's wrist. The dog nudged her elbow, and she reached out and fondled his head absently. He quivered, rolling his eyes ecstatically.

'This looks good, Rose,' she said eventually, and Rose looked up inquiringly. 'Foundation, capital structure and control of the line. Number of shares, two thousand seven hundred to begin with, rising to three hundred thousand when total capital is attained. What do you think?'

She looked up at Rose, and Rose considered thoughtfully.

'How many shareholders?' she asked.

Lacy studied the sheet again.

'Thirty-three, so far.'

'What does Mr Moore think?'

'He thinks it is well worth buying into.'

'How many shares are being offered?'

'A thousand each.'

'Can we manage without liquidity problems?'

'Oh yes. Well, just about.' Lacy pulled a face.

'Then I should buy.'

Jane looked from one to the other, and wondered what it was they talked about. She was waiting for a suitable moment to bring up a subject which was dear to her heart, but she dare not interrupt whilst Lacy and Rose spoke of such important matters. It would make Lacy cross, and she wanted her sister to be in a soft, receptive mood for what she had to say. It seemed as though the snow had been sent by fate, keeping her here and giving her this opportunity. Lacy and Rose were always so busy, they had little time for anything which did not concern their business, but surely soon they would be done with their papers, and turn to other more general topics of conversation.

Jane continued her dreaming contemplation of the sweet-smelling fire. She knew she should not have been persuaded to stay and dine with Lacy and Rose, but the temptation to share a little in the wonderful freedom they had found had overcome her, as it always did, and she revelled in her own boldness in joining them.

Mama and Papa seemed enormously unconcerned about her these days. She supposed it to be her 'old maid' status which lulled them into a state of complacency. They no doubt considered it eminently suitable to have their daughter, as she had no husband, being seen to do 'good works'. She was well protected at all times by the brawny Jonas and, if she did go to places which were, in Sarah's opinion, not quite nice, at least what she did was respectable. She was almost twenty-one, and obviously destined to be unwed and childless. Mama was taken up with her two married daughters and her small grandchildren, of whom she now had three, and Amy was pregnant for the second time. Both Thomas, who had wed Emily Bradley in January of that year; and Margaret, whose fears of losing John, Emily's brother, had proved groundless, had dutifully produced a child each, nine months from the day they married. So what did one poor old spinster matter, when set against such momentous events? Particularly if she was thought a bit odd, as Jane was.

Jane's carriage was backed into the mews at the rear of the house, and the horses were comfortably installed in the empty stables, which were no longer generally used as such, now that the house had been converted into rooms. Jonas, sitting comfortably before the kitchen fire with a glass of porter in his hand, was no doubt at this very moment eyeing appreciatively the buxom attractions of Maggie.

Jane smiled, still astonished by her own matter-of-fact acceptance – and knowledge, she reminded herself – of the ways of the world, and of those whose lives had once been a mystery to her. That she could smile at the notion of Jonas admiring Maggie's figure, and not be shocked or frightened by the images conjured up, was a joy to her. Her own joy was a joy to her; her simple pleasure of smiling at the completely chaste, she was sure, state of affairs in the kitchen. Oh, stop it, she told herself. It is time you went to bed, sitting here smiling at nothing.

'What are you smiling at, Jane?'

She turned to Lacy, blushed, then began to laugh.

'Nothing. And that is what is so delightful. I find I no longer need to be so serious about life. Is that not a pleasure, dear Lacy?'

Lacy nodded, and stretched, lifting the heavy silken plait.

'The world is quite a wonderful place, Jane, if you have the courage to get out into it. I am only pleased that you have . . .'

'Lacy!'

Lacy turned, surprised by the sharpness of Jane's tone as she interrupted her.

'Yes?' she said.

'I wanted to speak to you about . . .' Jane hesitated.

'Yes, what is it?'

'It's about . . . Papa.'

Without another word, Lacy rose to her feet, the dog at her heels.

'I think it better you share Rose's bed tonight,' she said crisply. She began to stride across the carpet, and would have left the room, but Jane sprang up and barred her way.

Rose straightened slowly in her chair and watched as the sisters stood, almost face to face. Lacy's expression was one of cold rage, Jane's propitiatory.

'Please, Lacy. Listen to me. He is . . .'

'I do not wish to know how he is, Jane.'

'But do you not see how unkind it is to be so . . .'

'I do not care to be kind.'

'But, Lacy, it is so unlike you to bear a grudge. You were always the first to make up when you and Amy quarrelled as children.'

'This is not some childish quarrel, Jane. Now, if you will get out of my way, I will go to my room.'

'No. No, you will not. Not until you have heard what I am about to say.' Astounded by her own bravery Jane floundered on, even clasping Lacy's hand between her own in her determination to have her say.

'He has heard of your venture, Lacy. He could finish you, if he wished. You know he could, but he has done nothing.'

Lacy was still now, and silent, her ice-cold eyes staring at the wall beyond Jane's shoulder.

'He is not well, Lacy, but he is not senile. I think he regrets what has happened, and misses you dreadfully, but he can do nothing about it. Mama . . .' Jane hesitated, then went on, following a somewhat different tack. 'He does not speak of your enterprise to me, but Robert does.' She laughed mirthlessly at the memory of the appalled expression on Robert's face, as he told her of the rumours which were beginning to circulate about 'Hemingway's girl'.

'I can scarce believe it, Jane,' he had said. 'I had thought her in America or somewhere, with that fellow she ran off with, but she is here, in Liverpool, and there is talk that she is actually in business for herself, Jane.' His voice was incredulous. 'And it is said,' he was almost in tears, 'it is said she does not hesitate to use the most unethical methods to make a profit.'

Jane placed a conciliatory arm about Lacy's shoulders, and drew her back to the fire.

'Sit down, my dear,' she said.

Lacy's face was carved as if in marble, but she allowed herself to be placed, unresisting, in the chair which Jane had so suddenly vacated. It was as though Jane's words had brought her to the sudden realization that she was not safe from him even now. He could 'finish her if he wished', 'finish her if he wished', 'finish her if he wished'! The words clamoured in her head, and she could have wept. She knew that, despite her growing strength, she was as vulnerable as she had always been. She had only been allowed her small measure of success through her father's generosity.

Jane was speaking again, and she listened bleakly.

'Why do you not go to see him, Lacy? No, do not leave, I beg of you,' as Lacy half rose in her chair. 'Let me speak and then, if you wish, we will say no more.' Taking Lacy's silently averted face for acquiescence, she continued to talk quietly, persuasively.

'He is getting old, Lacy, and I am sure he is lonely for you. He never loved us as he loved you. We were not like you. You were brave and bright, and loved ships and the sea as he did. Do you remember how he would take you on his knee, and show you the maps of the world? I used to envy you, for I should have loved to be drawn upon his lap, but he hardly noticed I was there. He was not unkind, just distant. Even Thomas and Robert, his heirs, his sons, were not as dear to him as you. I think it possible that that is why he acted as he did, when you left. He could not bear the thought that you loved another man. He punished him ferociously, you know, taking his command, and putting it about Liverpool that he was not to be trusted. He went to America, and it was thought you had gone with him. They say the man cried and begged Papa . . .'

'Stop it, for pity's sake. Stop it! I will not listen . . .'

Lacy lashed out with her hand, nearly overbalancing her sister, who knelt before her. But Jane caught her hands and held them.

'Please, a moment longer. Papa could not bear to know you loved a man so much you would stand against him in defence of that man. And then, when you were ill, it was too late. He had made his stand, and he could not back down, but he was glad that I came. I know he was. He could have stopped me. Even now, he could stop me, but he does not. His is proud, Lacy, just as you are. Can you not understand? You are so alike, and yet he is . . . I know he is glad I helped you when you were ill.'

Lacy bent her head, and a sound emerged from between her lips. It might have been a murmur of pain or a protest. It was impossible to tell. Jane went on.

'Do you not remember how good and kind he was to us all? You especially were allowed so much. Amy, Margaret and I were quite content to stay within the confines of our up-bringing, but you, he understood you needed more, and you were permitted to wander about the estate, and ride your pony, and many other things which made Mama cross. But he took your part.'

Lacy lifted her head. A strange light shone in her eyes, and she seemed to look beyond the heart of the blazing fire to some memory which held her in a thrall. Her face was soft as she spoke.

'I remember when he took us on our first train journey,' she said, almost like a child. 'We went to Manchester and back, and it took all day, and Robert was sick.' She smiled, and Jane was quietly exultant. 'Robert was always sick wherever we went, was he not? Even when we went to London to see the Great Exhibition. Can you recall it, how fine it was? And the civil engineering section? Papa could not be drawn away. There was a model of Liverpool Docks with more than a thousand rigged ships. Papa questioned the boys, and Robert almost cried. Poor Robert. And Her Majesty came so close we might have touched her gown. I thought Robert would be sick all over her, but Papa . . .'

As she spoke her father's name again she stopped abruptly, then turned to Jane, and Rose saw the two shining paths on her white face where the tears had run. Her voice broke, but it was clear and strong.

'. . . but Papa gave up all rights to my love when he was prepared to let me die, Jane. For the sake of his pride, he was prepared to let me die. If you had not come, would he? What do you think, Jane, would he? I was his daughter, but Bridie McGhee did more for me than my own father. She had nothing. But what she had, she gave. She gave me shelter, and she gave me the comfort of her arms when I was in pain. I was to bear a *child*, Jane. My own child, and I was forced to kill it.'

Jane made a small horrified sound in the back of her throat, and her hand went to her mouth.

'I had an abortion. That is what they call it, when they kill an unborn child. Did you know that, Jane? It is done all the time in the world where Rose comes from but, if Papa had been the Christian he professes to be, I could have had my child in my arms now.'

Her voice sank to a demented whisper.

'A year old. My baby would be one year old, but Papa made me kill it. He turned me away when Rose took me back, Jane. Did you know that? Luke had discarded me and, when Rose took me home to my Papa, he told her he had no daughter called Lacy.'

Rose gasped and stood up, moving to Lacy's side. She knelt at her knee, putting a hand comfortingly to hers, and Lacy turned in her direction.

'You did not think I had understood, did you Rose? I was out of my mind, mad with grief and what Luke had said to me. But when Annie came back and told you Papa said . . . he had no daughter called Lacy, it was as if he had stabbed me in the wound Luke had left.'

Jane sobbed helplessly now, rocking in desolate despair. But Lacy had not yet finished.

'He told Annie to inform Rose he had no daughter called Lacy, and that if she and the person with her were not gone within fifteen minutes he would summon the police. No. Do not touch me, Jane . . .' as Jane tried to pull her into her own trembling arms, 'Rose, hold my hand. Rose understands, you see. I have listened to those words over and over again in my head. I had to kill my baby because my father disowned me. What else was I to do? I could not rear a child on my own. I had no support, no husband, no security, no home. My baby would have needed all these things, and I did not have them to give. I had to work, Jane, so I was forced to kill my child. My father forced me to it, and you ask me to forgive him.'

She stood up and looked contemptuously at the anguished woman on the floor.

'I will remember his words until the day I draw my last breath, Jane, and I tell you this. He will never finish me. Never. One day, all he has will be mine, I swear it. I do not know, nor care, what I will have to do to get it, but one day it will all be mine.'

Rose watched quietly as Lacy left the room, Copper at her side, then turned to comfort the weeping woman by the fire.

# CHAPTER 22

'Joanna and I could hardly believe our eyes, dear James. There she was, bold as you please, entering the Exchange Buildings, as if she had a perfect right to be there. I should not have minded so much, but beside her was Hugh Lucas, holding her arm to help her up, as though she were a lady, which she of course is not, or she would not be there . . .'

James Osborne turned the page of his mama's letter irritably, and wondered who the devil she was talking about, for in the next breath she rambled on about the wonders of her newest grandchild's first words. Either she had the pages out of order, which she frequently did, or she had left one page inside her writing case – another habit of hers – making a nonsense of many a tale she told him. Still, Mama's letters were often a nonsense, and the omission of a page could not be said to spoil the context of her news. She was always writing endless discourses on the state of her grandchildren's health, and she had sixteen now, for all of her own offspring were married, except for James; and all had children of their own, but for poor Matthew, her eldest son. However, she was certain the fault did not lie with him, but with the timid creature he had married. He was thirty-eight years of age, and the prospect that he would remain childless was a constant worry to Sophie Osborne. He was heir to a considerable estate after all and with James, her only other son, at thirty still reluctant it seemed to go to the altar, she and Richard despaired of having a direct male heir to continue the line. The girls were like gypsies, having babies one after the other. But it was not the same. And so she told James, in letter after letter, begging him to give up his commission and come home from India.

'After all, Matthew has the full load of the business upon his shoulders now that your Papa is retired, and it would afford him the greatest pleasure to have you beside him,' she wrote.

James stretched out his long legs and lifted his head, encouraging the tiny breeze which had just sprung up to lay its coolness upon his face. Shadows lengthened, black and solid, as the sun fell rapidly from the sky. The whole world was turned for a moment to a pure, dusty gold. Then the Indian night, deep and swift, was upon him.

Whittaker appeared from nowhere, shaking the veranda with his heavy tread, and exciting a flock of carrion crows, who nested in a desiccated banyan tree, to nervous exclamation with his deafening barrack room bark.

'Your whisky, sir, an' shall I be lightin' the lamp?' He bellowed as though they were in the thick of a skirmish.

James sighed, reaching for the drink and sipping it absently. He supposed he must finish Mama's letter, providing he could unravel the pages. He was never certain which was the more fatiguing: reading letters from his Mama or writing to her. His accounts of life in the barracks of Lucknow must certainly be as tedious to her, as the reading of her version of the social life in Liverpool was to him.

He glanced in the direction of the ramrod figure of his batman.

'You were saying, Whittaker?'

'The lamp, sir.'

'Oh yes, and bring me another whisky.'

'Sir,' shouted Whittaker in his best parade ground voice, and his boots rattled the structure of the whole bungalow.

The lamp was lit and, in the gleam, shared suddenly by a horde of mosquitos, James found the missing page of his Mama's letter, and read the words which were to change his life.

'. . . so sorry for poor Charles and Sarah in all this. As if it were not enough that Lacy had the exceeding tactlessness not to marry the man after all that has . . .'

Her name had been read, and the words which followed had gone marching by like a column of ants, before it hit him. The blow landed just beneath his heart and, for a painful moment, he thought it had stopped. It had come at him with the speed of a bullet and, like a bullet, he did not see it speed towards him. He had time only to feel a momentary foolish annoyance with himself as, like a trembling girl, his senses reeled, and he thought he would faint. The blood rushed from his head, and seemed to circle anxiously about his heart, which jerked in his chest. His hands shook, and he watched dazedly as the words on the page ran together.

Lacy.

It did say Lacy, did it not?

He dashed his hand across his eyes which, mysteriously, seemed to have become sightless, trying desperately to read on. Dear God in Heaven, after all these years. What was she doing in Liverpool? Had she married? Damn Mama, why could she not write a coherent letter, instead of babbling on of little Jonathan's croup, and Matthew's problem with his chest . . ? Lacy . . .

The name of the girl, the lovely young girl who had filled his wretched, agonized dreams in the hospital at Scutari, ran through his head, and he felt the full force of the shock hit him at last. He had put her from him a year ago with the gentleness of a man laying a beloved comrade to rest. He had thought her gone forever: not only from his own mind and heart, where she had rested, waiting, all these years; but also from the lives of all the people who had known her.

His hand shook and the paper on which Sophie Osborne's bold handwriting marched, wavered like seaweed beneath water, and his eyes became so misted he could scarcely read the rest of the page. Blast the light! Why did it not shine more brightly? He moved forward, placing the pages of the letter nearer to the flame, but the breeze swayed the pale, yellow glow inside the glass globe, and he cursed it, although minutes before he had welcomed its coolness upon his cheek.

Whittaker appeared at his elbow, and placed a tray upon the wicker table in front of him. Before the man had time to turn and march away, James picked up the glass which rested on it, and gulped down the liquid in one smooth motion, saying abruptly:

'Another.'

Whittaker crashed his feet to attention, his face surprised. Captain Osborne was not only an easy going, likeable officer, he was always unfailingly civil to the men beneath him and never had more than two whiskies before dining.

'Sir?' he roared.

'For God's sake man, do you have to bellow like that?'

Speechless with bewildered resentment, Whittaker picked up his officer's glass and turned sharply, beginning the route march back to the kitchen with his customary noisy flourish.

'. . . and must you crash those enormous boots of yours with such vigour, Whittaker? Can you not see I am trying to read a letter?'

Mortified, Whittaker tiptoed from the veranda, the look on his face that of the misunderstood, put-upon, poor old soldier, who will never in a hundred years understand the eccentricities of those above him. Officers, it said. Yer never knew when yer bluddy 'ad 'em. One minnit nice as yer please, next shoutin' yer bleedin' 'ead off. Still, 'is officer wasn't usually like that. Allus in command, o' course, an' respected for it, but he weren't one fer shoutin' at a bloke fer bluddy nuffink.

His thoughts ran round and round in his cockney head as he rinsed James Osborne's glass, polished it efficiently, and refilled it from the whisky decanter. 'E'd give 'im a good stiff 'un this time. Looked as though 'e needed it. 'E'd like ter get a look at that there letter what came today, fer tanner to a farthin' it were bad news. Else why should 'is officer fly off the 'andle like that?

His boots soft as feathers on the veranda, Whittaker floated like a white-jacketed ghost across the wooden floor, placed the tumbler of whisky upon its tray before Captain Osborne, waited a moment for further orders and, when none came, drifted off again. He might have become invisible for all the notice James took. The whisky stood untasted before him as he read again the re-assembled letter.

'. . . not to marry the man after all that has transpired. It really is in the most appalling taste. Even though the fellow was only an employee of poor Charles, at least it would have made the whole affair somewhat more respectable. But now, to have the effrontery to go into business for herself. Can you imagine it, James. A woman competing against men in the world of shipping. She has set up in offices in Strand Street, overlooking Canning Dock and, I believe, though I have not seen it, moves about the dockyard with only her maid to accompany her. But I think the most bitter pill poor Charles has to swallow is that she appears to be making a success of it. She has made some profitable transactions, I believe, of which, dear James, I understand nothing. She moves about in men's company and enters their places of business. Your sister and I were in our carriage in Old Hall Street last Thursday . . .' Here followed lines of unintelligible gossip. James skipped paragraphs and read on ' . . . and it has quite taken the heart from dear Sarah. She will not have the girl's name mentioned in her presence. Now for more cheerful news. Do you recall that . . ?'

James lifted his head and stared blindly across the compound. Lamps had been lit in the bungalows which enclosed the enormous square. Upon verandas identical to his own, men smoked pipes, and women beside them languidly fluttered fans, in an effort to create even the smallest breeze. It was tranquil after the dash and stamp of the day, and they were glad of the peace, and of the lessening of the awful heat. Soon, the ladies and children would go up into the hills to escape the months of killing heat on the plains but, for the moment, the serenity and comparative coolness of the evening soothed them to silence.

The letter in James's hand fluttered to the floor. Thoughts flew like swifts about his head, darting and quick, hard to grasp, refusing to alight and be studied. A baby grizzled in the darkness, and the fluted Indian voice of an ayah comforted its fretfulness. In the native quarters a dog howled forlornly, but no one quietened its misery and, in a moment, another took up the call, then another, until James was reminded of a pack of wolves he had come across in the wild country beyond the frontier. Suddenly, for no apparent reason, they stopped.

It was an evening exactly like any other. For nearly a year now, he had re-enacted the same scene with the hundreds of others who lived within the cantonment of Lucknow, and the mystic beauty of India, the calm, unhurried way of life of her people, had laid a palliative upon his disappointed heart. He could not say that Lacy Hemingway had broken it, but the day he had spent in her company had been the beginning of what he had hoped was to be a relationship that would be important to them both. She had intrigued his male sensibilities; she had stirred his senses; she had captured his imagination with her bright, spirited opinions on everything from Shakespeare to clipper ships; and she had made him laugh. Perhaps more than anything about her, even her astonishing loveliness, he remembered how she had made him laugh.

She had been young, only sixteen, and still a child in her emotions. But his mind had plunged on into the future, picturing evenings spent in the company of a woman whose sharp mind would stimulate his own; a woman with wit and charm, and the intelligence to keep James Osborne from the boredom with which all women afflicted him, once the excitement of their bodies had paled. And the nights! He was a lusty man, and he would teach her to be a lusty woman. In the dark and tumbled warmth of his bed, he would make her the bedmate who would keep him forever beside her. He had not dreamed that he would find all this in one woman, but he had been convinced it was all there in Lacy Hemingway. He had known in that first hour that he could love this girl; that he wanted to love her, for she seemed to epitomize all that men dream of. Since that day he had not foresworn all other females, for he was a man who delighted in the pleasures given to him by pretty women; but her letters had fostered a deep feeling of loving friendship, which had seemed to him a solid base on which to build a good marriage; and they had held him together with their glinting promise during the horrors he had lived amongst in the Crimean war.

But he had lost her.

In his complacency, and his certainty that Charles Hemingway would hold her safe for him until she was old

329

enough to marry, he had turned his back, and another man had taken what he had thought to be his. A child, he had thought her, held safe against the encroachment of other men, innocent and ignorant of their ways. He should have been aware that any defence can be stormed if the tactics used are well disguised. He did not know how it had come about, and he had not cared at the time. What he thought to be his had been taken, and he must accept it. With the benefit of maturity, that born on a battlefield where one must submit to the loss of a friend if madness is not to set in, he had yielded his loss painfully, and had moved on.

Now, hope had flared. He stared into the deep, purple blackness of the night sky, his hand reached out for the tumbler of whisky before him and, as he sipped it, he began to marshal his thoughts with the precision taught him by the Army. His head cleared and in the gloom a strange elated gleam shone in his deep brown eyes. A gleam like the tiny stub of the candle which had illuminated the pitchy dark of his tent during the worst fighting of the war. It had barely lifted the shadows but it had driven away the obscurity which had threatened to swallow himself and so many of his comrades. A pinpoint of clarity in a mad world. Hope. It shone in James's eye and a smile, lurking at the edges of his mouth, quivered as though longing to burst into a whoop of laughter.

She was free. Lacy Hemingway was free!

He could make no sense from his mother's letter of Lacy's entry into the business world, and was inclined to smile at the very idea. A woman in the Exchange Building! It was inconceivable, and there was not a man there who would allow it. A transaction, a successful transaction, and to do with shipping? Surely Mama had her facts muddled. He would not be surprised to find that Lacy had merely been seen talking to young Lucas, and that the rumours had started from this small incident.

Then he frowned and sat up, thumping the floor of the veranda with his feet in much the same way as Whittaker's, who was seen to peer nervously around the frame of the door. But James did not notice. So what *had* Lacy been doing for the past year? Her father had intimated when last he saw him that she was to marry some fellow of whom the family disapproved. Now, Mama stated that she had not. How had she lived then? Who had supported her and where had she lived?

He fumbled with the pages of the letter which he had retrieved from the floor, and began to read it again. Yes, here it was, Lacy had '. . . taken offices in Strand Street . . .' His shoulders slumped in bewilderment. In Strand Street? That was certainly where many shipping men did business, but Lacy . . . Lacy in shipping? It was preposterous. But as the foolishness of the idea began to make him laugh, a vivid picture clicked into his mind. It was of a young girl. Her eyes were clear and discerning. The expression on her face was full of strong determination and wayward confidence, and she showed her capacity to think for herself, and to assess what went on around her, by the sharpness of the answers she gave to his probing questions. She had had an ability to pronounce her view with a shrewd intelligence that had astounded him. He saw her laugh and shake her head. He saw her brow cloud as she argued some point with him, and he saw there the answer to his doubts.

She was as capable of starting and surviving in a business as he was himself. More so, for all her life she had hung about her Papa soaking up knowledge like a sponge. It was all there in her bright head, just waiting to be used. Oh yes, she could do it. Lacy Hemingway could do it.

Suddenly, he sprang up and his sluggish blood, slowed to languor by months of heat and the drugging charms of the great Indian continent, raced through his veins.

He was going home! By God, he was going home to sort out this muddle before that deuced girl in England saw another birthday. Twenty years old she would be next month and overripe for marriage. He had waited too long before, and he had thought her lost to him later, but now he had another chance, and he was grasping it with both hands. He was grasping it and, should it prove to be a fistful of nettles he held, well then, so be it, he would be stung; but at least he would know he was alive.

Business, Strand Street, Exchange Building, transactions . . . He would get to the bottom of the damned thing, show her the error of her sweet ways, and have Miss Hemingway up the aisle and into his bed before the end of the year.

His body tingled with the enormous vitality which surged through it and his breath flew from his lungs on a vortex of excited laughter. It was time he gave it up, this playing at soldiers. He was thirty years old and ready for domesticity. Domesticity? Could any word be more mis-matched when applied to Lacy Hemingway? Nowhere had he seen a girl less domesticated and he would insist that she remain so. Children, of course, but he and she would spend the rest of the days in one long, merry romp. He would please Mama and help old Matthew and . . . Oh Lord . . .

His spirits flew like the mosquitos which circled the lamp in demented circles and he stood for a moment, calming himself to coherent thought, then excitement gripped him again.

'Whittaker,' he roared, and all around the compound, heads turned lazily. 'Whittaker, lay out my uniform, and see to my boots. Oh, and draw me a bath. I shall be dining out. You may take the evening off, Whittaker. In fact, I wish you to stand the men in the mess a drink apiece.'

He walked jauntily towards the open French window which led to his bedroom, grinning as foolishly as a drunken dog.

'The mess will see such a celebration tonight . . .'

'Sir.' Whittaker, confused to immobility by his officer's about-face, and by his sudden vitality in this land, where no one moved faster than oxen unless driven, stood to attention.

'Do not stand there like a tailor's dummy, man,' Captain Osborne shouted cheerfully. 'Get about it quickly. I must see the CO immediately.' He grinned in the pale light cast by the lamp, and his white teeth flashed in the darkness of his face. 'I should not be at all surprised if you did not find yourself looking for another officer by this time tomorrow, Corporal, and I hope you find one as lenient with you as I.'

'Yes sir.' Whittaker stood wooden-faced until James Osborne disappeared inside the bungalow, whistling cheerfully. Only then did he relax.

'Now what the bluddy 'ell was all that about, eeh?' he asked the night in general.

As Captain James Osborne was putting in his request for an immediate resignation of his commission, and for his commanding officer's permission to leave at once for England, a group of British army officers some miles to the northwest met their deaths at the hands of the Indian soldiers they commanded. Even as they died, their astonishment was imprinted upon their faces, for none had suspected that the apparently minor unrest within the ranks would not be put to rights in a day or two. But it took a little longer than that.

The mutiny of the Bengal Army began on 10 May 1857 at Meerut, northwest of Lucknow and, as James sipped his whisky and received the premature congratulations of his superior officer – for in high spirits he had foolishly confided his hopes of marriage – the Indian soldiers, who had been placed in irons for refusing to accept the greased cartridges supplied to them for the new breach-loading Enfield Rifle, were being rescued by their comrades. Hindus and Muslims were united in the horror they felt at the pollution of their caste, for it was known that the grease upon the new cartridge, which had to be bitten before it was inserted into the rifle, was made of a mixture of beef and pork.

It was anathema to both.

The rabble of excited mutineers, leaderless as yet, but fired by the holiness of their mission, of which they were vague, made their way to Delhi – a distance of forty miles. The Indian garrison joined them and by the next nightfall, they had secured the city and fort, proclaiming an aged Mughal emperor as their leader.

There, at a stroke, was an army, a cause and a leader; and an end, hardly before it had begun, to James Osborne's dream.

As he sat in the mess that last night and drank to the health of all his brother officers and they to him, he was unaware of the events which were taking place some miles away. He could see only two clear and candid eyes shining in the sunlight and in his excited anticipation he let down the barrier

333

of reserve which had always stood between himself and those with whom he served. They were amazed to discover that not only did he have an 'intended' in dear old England but he proposed as soon as he was able to hurry home and make her his own.

'By God, James, are you not the dark horse? Why did you not tell us, my dear chap? Here we all were thinking you smitten with the delectable Miss McLellan and you had some mysterious beauty hidden away in . . . Lancashire, is it not. You devil, you.'

The dark horse, swept away upon a wave of hopeful ex-ultation by the news in his mama's letter, allowed himself to be thumped upon the back and his hand wrung until it ached. Nevertheless he enjoyed the amiable cordiality and, indeed, began to believe in his hopes himself. It seemed such a small thing, the journey home and the proposal which would make Lacy his wife.

'And when is the great day to be, James?'
'Well, I suppose as soon . . .'
'Why did you not tell us of this before, you sly fellow?'
'Well, I had not thought . . .'
'Is she as pretty as Miss Gwendoline McLellan, James?'
'She is as beautiful as . . .'

By one thirty in the morning of 11 May, 1857, Captain James Osborne was, in his own mind, firmly and irrevocably engaged to Miss Alexandrina Victoria Hemingway.

They were beginning to play those strange and foolish games beloved of officers in their mess. Even sober they could scarce be managed but, lying shrieking with laughter in a welter of arms and legs, no one cared.

It was the messenger with news of the mutiny for Captain Osborne who brought the men back to reality faster than a cold shower.

The dramatic capture of Delhi turned mutiny into full-scale revolt and, without reinforcements from home, the British fought through the summer of 1857 with their backs to the wall.

News of the atrocities which followed the capture of Cawnpore by the mutinous sepoys overwhelmed the British people. Tales of burnings, rape and murder, and of the horrors committed against British women and their children flamed in newspapers, and cries for vengeance and reprisals were loud.

In November came the relief of the British residency and the capture of Lucknow by a new commander-in-chief and, by March 1858, a campaign had cleared the countryside. It took until June before the revolt was over: 20 June, to be exact; and on 21 June, Lacy Hemingway's twenty-first birthday, and five years to the day since he had seen her, James Osborne began the long trip home which had been postponed for thirteen months by the misunderstanding arising from a soldier's bullet. He was not the same man who had grinned cheerfully on that day of decision in May. He had seen things which were to leave a scar upon him to the end of his days.

James Osborne had been at the well in Cawnpore when it was emptied by weeping soldiers of its gruesome contents.

# CHAPTER 23

It went so well at first. They did not expect to make any profit for many months, for time had to be spent in building up stocks of merchandise to send across the seas, and in constructing the myriad of interlocking arrangements which must be put into motion before the machinery of a business can begin to grind. The machine is switched on and gathers momentum and begins to work as it should and with a regular oiling and the constant supervision of a conscientious overlooker will run on for ever.

But first it must be put together.

The first cog was put into place when Captain Paul Ellis agreed to import their cotton, and to find them an agent in Savannah. On his return to America, he had made it his business to search out and re-acquaint himself with a man with whom, before he was married, he had caroused. They were of the same class and age, and had gone to school together. The difference was that, though they were both gentlemen, Paul had chosen to work for his living, and his friend had not. The small allowance he had from his father scarcely kept him in cravats.

He had the impossible name of Sheridan – Sherry to his friends – Bonfleur. His father was descended from some minor French aristocrat, who had come to Georgia in the previous century and, having a small fortune in jewels stolen from his mama, bought a plantation.

Sheridan had been brought up 'in cotton'. He had never actually been trained to it, for he was interested only in spending money, not in making it. But, somewhere between adolescence and manhood, enough knowledge and experience had rubbed off on him to enable him to recognize a bit of decent cotton when he saw it. He had many contacts amongst those of his friends who raised cotton, and the finding of cargoes was simple for him.

Sherry's family had long disowned their profligate son.

Forced to try and exist on his allowance and what he could borrow, he was delighted to augment these pitiful amounts with the commission and salary he would earn as an agent for Miss Hemingway. He had found the work surprisingly to his taste, for it meant he mixed only with those who were his equals, and the business he did with them earned him invitations to dine in the homes of many of his friends.

He travelled about the Southern States of America, buying raw cotton at low prices, and using the railroad system to transport it to New Orleans, where Paul's ship would pick it up for delivery to Liverpool. He found he also had an aptitude for selling. His 'old Southern charm', courteous and hard to resist, swept lady buyers off their feet, particularly as he worked further North, where women were more emancipated than his own. The fustians, dimity and cotton checks Lacy shipped to him were sold as smoothly and quickly as silk slipping through a ring.

Sherry's own prestige was enormously enhanced, and his father was so delighted at his son's employment and success, that he immediately increased his allowance, saying a businessman needed to be well set up.

It was Mr Moore who supplied Lacy's agents for other parts of the world. She now had an agent in Alabama, and the cotton would soon flow in a steady stream across the Atlantic, but there were other markets in the world besides America: the West Indies, the Mediterranean ports, Africa, Australia, the Baltic, Brazil; and, to do business with them, she must have agents there to buy the cargoes she needed, to arrange shipment, insurance, financial transactions; to send back reports on market conditions; and to receive the goods she would send them. The world was a vast warehouse to Lacy; she thought only in terms of cargoes: fruit and wine from Spain, Italy and France; tea, rice and cotton from India; timber and wheat from Canada; wool from Australia and South Africa; tea, porcelain, silks and fans from China.

Lacy Hemingway wanted them all.

'Perhaps Mr Moore knows of someone,' Rose suggested as they discussed the subject of agents one night at dinner.

'Well, I suppose it is worth trying, but he is a banker, Rose. Though he is invaluable to us, he really knows no more than you or I about shipping.'

Maggie had left them cheese and fruit. She had gone to her kitchen, wondering in her simple way if all ladies of quality discussed the things of which Miss Lacy and Miss Rose endlessly spoke. They never talked of gowns, or pictures, or of the latest play which was being performed at the Theatre Royal, but of ships and cargoes and freight and agents, whatever they might happen to be. She could make nothing of it, but then, she could make nothing of her mistresses, anyway. In business they were, just like gentlemen and, though it was incomprehensible to her why, or how it came about, good luck to them, she said. She was a Yorkshire lass and, as such, she admired nothing more than a bit of independence. She left them to it, singing cheerfully as she swept up for the sixth or seventh time that day, the 'muck' which invaded her kitchen.

Lacy mentioned the matter of agents to the banker on the occasion of their next meeting and was quite astounded by his answer. It seemed he had been awaiting a propitious moment to put forward an idea, which had begun in his wife's head at the last family gathering.

Mrs Moore came from a large family, and had innumerable nieces and nephews, and it was of the latter Mr Moore spoke. He did not mention Mrs Moore, for it would not do for one's clients to think he discussed their business with his wife.

'I hope you will not think me presumptuous, Miss Hemingway, nor that I am attempting to further the careers of members of my family. But I have two nephews who are not only bright, willing and conscientious, but also desirous of taking up employment in some other part of the world. They are keen to get away from Liverpool, being young men of an adventurous nature, but . . . er, financial difficulties have so far constrained them to remain in employment here. They are well educated, Miss Hemingway, and most personable, and I myself have trained them in financial matters. Ernest has always stated a longing to go to the Leeward Islands. From a base there, he could cover many of the islands which make up the West Indies. His brother, Alfred, might perhaps be sent to the Mediterranean port of . . .'

'Wait, Mr Moore. Oh, please wait! You quite take my breath away with your efficiency. Now, let us begin at the beginning. These two young men are how old?'

'Twenty-three and four, respectively.'

'And you can vouch for their honesty?'

'*Miss Hemingway!*' Mr Moore was mortally offended. 'They are my own wife's nephews, and I would not for one moment have suggested them, had I not the utmost confidence in their integrity. If you wish, I will put up a bond to ensure . . .'

'No, please, Mr Moore. I apologize most sincerely. I should have known that any member of your family would be above reproach.'

Mollified, Mr Moore relaxed.

Within two months, Ernest and Alfred Burrows were installed in their respective offices across the ocean and tobacco, rum, spices, fruit and wines began to move, like filings to a magnet, to the shores of England and a certain warehouse in Liverpool.

The foreman who had once been stunned to silent deference by her own and Rose's appearance on the wharf, when she had first visited Captain Ellis, came to mind when the matter of a man to take charge of the warehouse was discussed. Casual labour was used to unload cargoes, and tuck the freight carefully away in the warehouse ready for sale, but mistakes could be made; careless handling of fragile packages and pilfering must be stopped, and it seemed to Lacy that if one man had the managing of it, together with the trust of his employers and those who worked under him, such a man would be assiduous in the care of her goods whilst she was absent.

When next *Annie McGregor* was in port she made it her business to keep her eye out for him, and was gratified when she spied him. Smiling, she beckoned to him, and Rose had to bend her head to hide the laughter which bubbled up in her throat at his look of consternation.

It was almost Christmas, and a sharp hoar frost glistened

about the roof tops, not yet melted by the early morning winter sun. It sparkled on the rigging of the ships, and hung like children's sugar sticks from the main mast. Paul Ellis watched the scene from his deckhouse and smiled like Rose, but more feelingly, for he knew exactly what the poor chap was going through. He had fancied a time or two he might entice Miss O'Malley – he was not particular which, for both were beauties – into a warmer relationship, for they had the power to stir a man to madness. But, somehow, both seemed to treat the whole idea with amusement. It took the ardour from a man with devastating speed, when a woman laughed at a fellow's advances. He wondered what she had to say to the workman who shuffled uneasily towards her.

'Good morning.' Lacy smiled and nodded her head, and the man, red and sweating despite the cold, touched his forehead, but he could not speak. His eyes were glazed in admiration. Lacy had seldom looked more lovely.

She was dressed in a dark red velvet mantle, which fell in graceful folds almost to the hem of her gown, which was of the same rich shade. The tips of her black leather boots peeped from beneath the stiff black lace which edged the hem of her dress, and her hands were tucked in a tiny velvet muff. The mantle had a high collar, and her face was set like a delicate flower in its folds. The blue of the sky reflected a touch of pale aquamarine in her eyes, and the cold had placed a carnation of pink in each cheek.

'I wonder if you could spare a moment?' she asked graciously.

The man looked behind him, unsure whether the words were meant for him. His colleagues stood about, as still as great cart horses waiting patiently between the shafts, and just as tamed.

'Perhaps we could talk as we walk along,' she said confidingly. 'It is very cold, it it not?'

The man fell into step beside her and Rose, casting a triumphant glance at his workmates but still unable to speak. His brain was clouded with the wonder of walking beside, not one, but two pretty women. What they wanted of him he could not begin to imagine, nor for that matter did he care. Lacy's smile fell upon him like a ray of warm sunshine appearing from behind grey clouds. Her sweet perfume made his head swim and her voice reminded him of a strand of music he had once heard coming from the flute of an Irishman as he stood forlornly upon the quayside and watched the ship which had brought him from his home sail away on the tide. Sad it had been but so hauntingly sweet it had lifted the hairs on the back of his neck. She did the same to him now. It seemed to him his feet scarce touched the ground as he walked and so closely did he watch her lips that he almost fell over a length of rope, and would have done so, had she not put out a hand to steady him. He blinked, in a daze, and suddenly the words she was speaking began to sift through the stuffing which filled his head.

'. . . so, you see, we shall need someone who is trustworthy to take charge. Do you think you could do that Mr . . . Mr . . . ?'

The man realized that some word from him was looked for, his face lost its expression of vacuous bewilderment, and he was himself again.

He had a genial face, weathered by sun and wind and rain, but there was a pugnacious curve to his jawline and his nose was slightly askew, as though once it had felt the weight of a fist against it. He was in his late thirties, big-shouldered and strong, and she could see the shrewdness in his pale blue eyes. He opened his mouth to speak but realized he had forgotten the question.

'May we know your name,' Lacy smiled encouragingly.

At last he had it.

'Michael O'Shaughnessy. That's meself, missus.'

'Well, Mr O'Shaughnessy, do you think the job would interest you?'

'The job, missus?'

'Yes, the one I am offering you.' Lacy's patient voice became a little uncertain. Was the man in his right mind, she thought. Perhaps she was mistaken about the look of solid reliability she had noticed the first time she had seen him, and

341

that sharp way in which he had presented himself to help them. She was used to making quick assessments of those she dealt with in business, and was usually correct in her instincts, but she could make a mistake. Perhaps this was one. But, suddenly the big fellow grinned, and the resourceful guile of his race shone in his eyes.

'A job, missus? I have one just now.'

'I know that, Mr O'Shaughnessy, but I am offering you another. A better job, and one where you would have more responsibility.'

Michael O'Shaughnessy took off his cap and scratched his head. 'Well now,' he said, the personification of a man who, against his better judgement, is being tempted to accept something he is not sure he wants. 'I 'ave this bit of a job, yer see. Well paid, sure it is, an' . . .'

'I would pay you more, Mr O'Shaughnessy.'

A past master at the art of doing a deal, and of knowing his own worth, Michael O'Shaughnessy hesitated theatrically.

'What's it all about then, this foin job? I wouldn't want ter be leavin' the docks. Sure, an' all me life I've worked near ships.'

'Mr O'Shaughnessy, will you come with me so I can show you what I want you to do?'

The two fashionable ladies walked the length of the quayside, past Princes' Dock, until they came to the Gorée Piazza. It was only a stone's throw from Strand Street, where Lacy and Rose had their offices. The man walked sternly behind now, as though already he knew what was expected of him.

The warehouse was a humming, running, whistling, bustling bedlam of men who pushed, shoved, carried, wheeled and sometimes threw the cargoes of tea, peppers, nutmegs, coffee, sugar, rice, sago, silk, cotton, chinaware and every imaginable commodity from the farthest corners of the globe. Wherever ships could go, they went, bringing back the merchandise of countries from every hemisphere and, as the three figures entered the huge building, which was split up and let to many merchants, it seemed that that merchandise was all stacked up and stored here at the same time.

None of the trio blinked an eyelash, for they had seen it all before.

Lacy walked purposefully towards a door and, talking a key from her reticule, unlocked it. She led the way into an enormous cavern of a place. The roof was high and raftered, and almost reaching it, along one wall, was a row of high windows, dim and dusty, but letting in some light. The room was stacked neatly with crates on one wall. On a second stood bales of raw cotton. It was almost warm, and very still in comparison with the room next door.

The man stared about him curiously, then turned to Lacy. His awe had gone now, for he realized that this elegant lady had not spoken to him as a woman to a man, but as an employer to an employee. But respect was in his expression, and a keen interest.

Lacy was quite composed.

'This is my warehouse, Mr O'Shaughnessy. Mine and Miss O'Malley's. We rent this part of it, but we need someone to take charge of it. A manager, a foreman, call it what you will, but someone in whose care it will be safe. Do you understand?'

The silence was almost eerie as the big Irishman stared, mesmerized by the idea that this slip of a girl was talking to him as though she was a man, a man conducting business, and in a manner which spoke of her complete certainty that there was nothing unusual in it. He turned to look at the other one, who had taken no part as yet, and was disconcerted by her green cat's eyes stare. She seemed as indifferent as the first to his amazement.

'Mr O'Shaughnessy. I am looking for someone to watch over my warehouse. That person will be in complete charge of all that it holds, and of the men who work in it. It is a responsible job, and one that demands a high degree of honesty, efficiency, conscientiousness, and the ability to knock heads when necessary. Miss O'Malley here will see to

343

all the paperwork, and you will deal with her at all times, but the organization of the warehouse and the men who are employed will be entirely yours. You will be paid twenty-five shillings a week.'

Michael O'Shaughnessy gasped, then held out his huge fist.

'I'll shake on that, missus, and my handshake is my bond.'

It had been relatively easy to find manufacturers who would supply her with the merchandise she needed to fill, not only the holds of Paul Ellis's ship, but also the space she would take on other vessels. She and Rose travelled to Manchester to purchase fustians, dimity, cotton checks, sheeting and linen; to Sheffield for plate and cutlery; and into Yorkshire for woollen goods. In St Helens they chose the most delicate glass and chinaware, elegant enough to grace the home of the most exacting lady wherever she might reside. And though her own and Rose's appearance caused shock and consternation amongst the manufacturers from whom they bought, the sight of the money Lacy withdrew from her reticule silenced the most outraged male voice.

It was rare that merchants paid for goods with cash – more usually buying on credit and the promise of profits on cargoes – and the two young women were treated with astonished respect, at least to their faces. Odd they might be, downright peculiar even, but a hardheaded Northern businessman will not turn away brass, even when it is proffered by a woman. They did not consider her a lady, though Lacy had been born one, for no lady acted as she did. They grudgingly admitted to one another that she seemed to know what she was about; but still, it was coming to summat when a lass trod in a man's world.

With hitches here and there, wrinkles which could be and were ironed out, the small firm of 'Hemingway and O'Malley' began to move quietly forward. Merchandise bought and stored in the warehouse, and watched over by Michael O'Shaughnessy, was found buyers by Sheridan Bonfleur in the Southern States of America; by Ernest Burrows in the West Indies; and by his brother, Alfred, in Italy and Spain.

Cables arrived informing Miss Hemingway that her cargoes of raw cotton from New Orleans; of sugar, rum and tobacco from the Leeward Islands; and of mixed citrus fruits from the Mediterranean, were on their way.

The question of organizing a timetable was put in order, so that the *Annie McGregor*, and the other ships on which Lacy and Rose rented space, were in the right place at the right time to pick up a cargo and deliver it; and that the freight to be carried from Liverpool was ready and waiting to take its turn on the outward journey.

Yes, she was ready now.

She had agents in three countries. She had her office, in which she and Rose manipulated the delicate balance of imports and exports. She had a warehouse, in which both were stored, and a man she trusted was in charge. And she had Mr Moore, who held her finances in his capable hands. Her newly found company was to be operated in a way that was enormously sound. Paul Ellis was prepared to freight as much as his ship could carry, and what it could not would be taken on other ships. Her warehouse, full already of merchandise ready to be sent to its destination, was ready too to receive the cargoes from abroad.

It was done.

'Hemingway and O'Malley, Shippping' was truly born, and its lifeblood began to flow in its veins.

The first cotton broker they called upon – picked from the list of names which had poured carelessly from Thomas's lips in his chats with Jane – had been downright rude, had scarcely allowed Lacy and Rose across the threshold of his office, and had done so only because his curiosity got the better of him, before he ordered them from the building.

'Get on with yer,' he bellowed to their retreating backs. 'What do I want dealin' with the likes of you? I can buy my cotton from any importer I choose, an' I want nowt to do wi' women. Do business wi' a woman! Yer must be mad.'

The second had threatened them with the police; and the third, on hearing her name, had been eager to send for her papa, for he was convinced she was ill.

Another had treated her to a homily on the delights of motherhood.

'Go home to your papa, Miss Hemingway, and do not meddle in the affairs of gentlemen,' he said. 'A sweet little thing like you must have a dozen admirers. How old are you, my dear?'

The sweet little thing told him, gritting her teeth.

'My dear, you must look sharp, or you will be left on the shelf. Why, my daughter, who is a year younger, is already a wife and mother. Think of that, Miss Hemingway. Now get you home, my dear, and give my regards to your papa, and tell him I shall be interested in purchasing *his* raw cotton. But only from him,' he said archly. 'I really do not know what your papa is thinking of, allowing you to . . .'

'My Papa has nothing to do with this, Mr Parkinson. I am on business of my own,' Lacy interrupted quite rudely.

'On your own, Miss Hemingway. I am afraid I do not understand. I thought you to be here on your father's behalf.'

'No, Mr Parkinson, on my own.'

'Do you mean to say you are offering me this cotton without the consent of your father?'

'I do not need his consent. The cotton is mine.'

Rose watched Lacy's face anxiously. Her mouth had fined to a firm line, and her skin seemed to have drawn tight across her cheekbones. Her eyes glinted like the flash of sun on steel, and her expression of resolute and bitter determination, which was becoming familiar to Rose, gave her the look of a fox who is about to dare the hen house. I must tell her, thought Rose, for if she allows it to become a part of her, she will get nowhere. Mr Parkinson did not like it, nor the involuntary show of irritation with which Lacy was treating his words.

Lacy was dressed in a rose-coloured gown of moiré, which put a blush of creamy pink into her skin. Her bonnet had rows of delicate rose buds beneath its brim, framing her face, and again she had allowed soft curls to escape from her neat chignon. The day was mild, for it was spring now, so she was without a mantle. Mr Parkinson had been at first, though confused, enchanted by the sight of the two pretty women.

But now his temper was wearing thin.

'Miss Hemingway, I cannot believe . . .'

'Are you inferring that I am a liar, Mr Parkinson?'

Rose's foot, an inch or two from Lacy's, came down with all the force she could muster upon Lacy's toes and, as Lacy turned furiously, words quivering and about to fall on Mr Parkinson's head, Rose dropped her reticule with a soft word of apology. She bent to pick it up, saying, 'Oh, I do beg your pardon, I had not meant to interrupt. Please do go on, Mr Parkinson. Miss Hemingway and I are always delighted to have any advice which a gentleman can give us. Are we not Lacy?'

The tightness left Lacy's face, and her mouth formed a shape which might have been there in readiness for a kiss. She relaxed her stiff shoulders and sat up, peaking her breasts and smiling apologetically, and for the next ten minutes she charmed Mr Parkinson to such an extent that he invited them both to take luncheon with him. He would not buy their cotton. But he promised, in an avuncular fashion, as though he thought them ashamed of their venture into business, to keep their little secret. He spent the rest of the day smiling and shaking his head at the foolishness of women.

In the privacy of their rooms that night, Rose told Lacy, 'You must not get yer dander up when they treat you like a half-witted child. If you let them see it, sure they'll have you out of the place so quick you won't know what's happened. I know it's hard, acushla, but listen to me, will you?' Her voice was pleading and anxious, and Lacy laughed despite her rage.

'The old goat would have snapped it up if it had come from another man,' she said. 'To turn down good cotton like that, he could see how fine it was from the sample, just because it is offered by a woman . . . I don't know, Rose,' she shook her head in exasperation. 'Can you understand the workings of their minds, for I am sure I cannot. To be presented with a business deal in which he stands to make a profit, and he says

347

no. Not only that, but tells me to run home to Papa and find myself a husband.'

She walked up and down the drawing room, kicking the leg of the chiffonier before resuming her passionate pacing. She wore only her peignoir, and her hair swung about her face. She tossed it back fretfully. Feverishly impatient, she allowed the frustration of the day's events to explode, and Rose listened to her calmly.

'That idiot at "Greens" would not even allow us to enter the holy sanctum of his employer's office. He looked as though the very idea of a woman placing her silly foot upon the hallowed carpet, where no female had ever trod, might desecrate its blessed state. And what about that *lunatic*, Mason!' She mimicked the broad Lancashire accent of Mr Mason, who originated from Bolton. '"Eeh lass, I can't do business wi' a woman. It wouldn't be right". You would have thought I asked him to remove his clothes and make love to me. He probably would have done that, right there in the office for that would have been considered "right".' She sighed bitterly.

Rose put down the pen with which she had been marking a ledger.

'Nevertheless, darlin', you must put a curb on your tongue and on that face of yours as well. You looked as though you might land a fourpenny one on the end of Mr Parkinson's nose this morning. And he knew it. He was madder than Mick Geraghty on a Saturday night. Smile, Lacy. Smile and simper, and do all the daft things men expect, and when you have them eating out of your hand, as you know they will, then ask, pretty as you please, if they will buy this bit of owd cotton you happen to have for sale. Later, when we have a foothold, you can tell 'em all to go to hell, but now you have to eat humble pie. You do see it, don't you?'

Lacy smiled until her jaws ached. She simpered and fluttered her lashes, and acted like the silliest, most vacuous young maiden she could remember from her days at Silverdale.

But it did no good.

Her fruit rotted on the quayside. Her sugar became infested with mice, and the rum was sold at 2d a barrel to any pub which would buy it. Her warehouse was as still and silent as the bales of raw cotton which lined its walls.

When it was full, they bought no more, for they had nowhere to store it. The months passed by, and the machinery of 'Hemingway and O'Malley, Shipping' began to run slowly down.

# CHAPTER 24

The man stood in St Nicholas' churchyard, by the flight of steps which led to the promenade. He was looking northwards, and his eyes fixed upon the forest of masts from which pennants of all colours gently fluttered. He seemed to measure the distance between the river and the spot where he stood. Although his face was blank, his mind was busy with the idea that in the span of a man's life human encroachment upon a small stream could have been so marked. Beneath the churchyard wall, a century ago, angry waves had boiled, the raging current sweeping along unimpeded from the sea. This wall, he mused, was once the outward limit of ancient Liverpool to the west, and all her docks and quays and streets beyond this line were artificial.

He began to make his way beyond the wall, walking along the marine parade which lay beside the river. Though it was late October, the day was fine and so clear he could see the Cheshire Woods to the south and, northwards, the sparkle of the Irish Channel in the bright sunlight. Bootle Bay, and Crosby on the Lancashire coast, were also visible. And, across the water, the Rock Perch Lighthouse and Fort; New Brighton, Seacombe, Birkenhead; and, cleaving the waters back and forth, the ferries which moved between Liverpool and the opposite shore.

When he reached Waterloo Dock, he stopped to admire the superb lines of an American clipper, seeing in the beauty of the vessel a denial of the horrors he had witnessed the year before. The miles of rigging sang in a tuneful hum as the breeze plucked at it, like fingers on the strings of a harp. Her sleek hull pleased something in him, and he wondered idly if perhaps he should have taken to the life of a seaman, instead of that of a soldier. It all appeared so clean and sharp, with none of the indignity, horror and degradation wrought at Cawnpore, Inkerman and Balaclava.

He came to the last dock: Clarence, named in honour of his late Majesty, William IV; and was quite fascinated, this time, by the steam ships which were tied up there. They were coming, he supposed, to the end of the days of sail. It was a pity, for the beauty of the first ship he had stopped to admire would disappear forever. He sighed quite desolately, and his thin face became slack with some remembered sadness.

Turning, he began to walk back in the direction from which he had just come. His tall figure moved with a slight stiffness, as though he favoured a leg, and he was painfully thin. His face, which had once been burned almost black by the sun, had a strange pallor, neither pale nor sallow, but somewhere in between. The sun was on his back now, throwing his shadow before him. He watched it waver along the quayside, jumping over the coils of rope and heaped up boxes and crates which lay in his path.

The two women coming towards him did not see him, or if they did, they failed to recognize him, for the sun was in their eyes. But he knew them at once. He stopped, incurring the wrath of a labourer who, head down, intent upon his job, almost ran into the back of him with the sacks of rice he carted.

'Sorry guv,' the dockie muttered, though the fault was not his, but James Osborne did not hear him. His whole sum and substance was concentrated upon the elegantly slender figure of the woman who walked towards him.

He told himself it would happen one day. He had known that he would look up, and there she would be. Like a chimera she would appear before him, as she had done in the past, but this time the phantom was a reality. Flesh and blood instead of make-believe. He had asked himself what he would do when it happened. He had never known the answer, and he did not know it now. He stood, the sun benign upon his back, touching the shoulder which had felt the sabre of a Russian cavalry officer. The still raw wound in his knee, received in the attack on Lucknow six months ago, began to ache as he held the leg stiffly, his whole body rigid with tension.

They were laughing.

The dark one tilted her parasol so that the shade of it

351

protected her eyes, and she saw him first. He was surprised for an instant at the sudden pallor of her face. She came to a halt, carved it seemed, like Lot's wife to a pillar of salt, and Lacy slowed, turning in surprise, then stopped and began to walk back towards her.

'Rose,' he heard her say. 'Rose, what is it?'

He never knew what ailed Rose, for he had eyes for no one but Lacy. He watched her as she touched the arm of her companion then, turning again, looked in his direction, as though to see what had caused the stillness which had the girl beside her in its grip. She lifted her hand to her eyes to shade them, and stared boldly.

He watched the expression on her face change from anxiety to puzzled curiosity, and then to partial recognition. It was as though her senses knew who he was, but her mind had not yet absorbed the knowledge. He saw her eyes narrow, and the reflection of the sun placed a radiance there, like those of a cat caught in the lamplight. She took a hesitant step forward, then another, and suddenly she began to smile. She lifted her chin, her face split into a wide delighted grin, and she started to walk towards him. Faster and faster she moved, until she was running. Her lace parasol flew away as joyously as a child's kite, tumbling over and over in the air, landing on the deck of a ship at the feet of a surprised seaman, who picked it up and put it across his shoulder, grinning broadly.

Her grey kid slippers barely touched the ground.

'James!' she cried, 'Oh, Jamie. Is it really you?'

She called him for the first time by the diminutive she and she alone was always to call him, his arms lifted involutarily, and she ran into them.

Rose watched them, and her heart moved, and crashed against her ribs. She felt the pain of it as it broke.

They put James into the hackney carriage with the solicitous attention given only to elderly gentlemen with gout, or to ladies in an interesting condition, taking his stick from him as he hauled himself inside. He was embarrassed and faintly annoyed, for he would have liked to have appeared strong and virile to the beautiful woman who had once been the child Lacy Hemingway. But she seemed not to notice his stiff leg, except to say with practical ease that he might find it more comfortable if he sat beside Rose, whilst she took the seat opposite.

The composure with which she treated his sudden reappearance dismayed him for a while, and he wondered why, until it came to him that he had looked for the flustered ferment usually found in young women, particularly when in the company of a man who has been wounded in the service of his country. Since he had been home, his mama, his sisters, and all the young ladies who had been paraded almost daily for his inspection, had fussed and petted him, sentimentally imbuing him with the glamour of a hero. They had imagined him, he supposed, riding into battles, rattling his sabre and gaining his wound in the most exciting and noble manner. They had no conception of the horror and bloody carnage he had seen.

He had not enlightened them, for their sensibilities were such that to squash even an insect beneath their booted feet set them screaming and fainting. How they imagined a man could go to war and win it without bloodshed was a mystery to him, but he was indifferent now to what went on around him, and he played the returned hero, as demanded. He had begun to accompany his brother Matthew to the office in Water Street, preparing for the day when he would be fit to work, but he admitted to himself that he found the employment at his desk tedious, and the routine stifling.

He watched quietly the animated face of the woman who sat opposite, content to listen to her bright observations on the changes he would find in the borough of Liverpool since he had been away. She inquired politely of his mother and father, and of his brother and sisters and their innumerable offspring, expressing amazement at the growth of the family. Her face was expressionless as he spoke, and it was evident that only her upbringing and good manners had prompted the questions.

James was quite bewitched by the charming rooms in which

Lacy now lived and, as the dumpling of a maid took his hat and coat, curtseying so low he might have been the Prince Consort, his old merry expression came back to his face for a moment, and Maggie was quite bowled over. Except for Jonas, he was the first male person to have entered Miss Lacy and Miss Rose's place, and she was beguiled by the question of which of her young ladies he was after. But, by the look in his eyes when they came to rest upon Miss Lacy, there was not much doubt.

'This is Captain Osborne, Maggie. An old friend of ours. He will dine with us tonight. You will, won't you, James? Of course you will.' Lacy turned again to Maggie, who dimpled, blushed, and bobbed another curtsey just to be on the safe side, before slipping from the room.

'I shall go and see what we have and what Maggie is putting together for our meal. I won't be away for more than a moment.' She turned as she reached the door, her hand upon the door knob, and surveyed him as though he were some lost soul returned unexpectedly and delightfully from the 'other side'. She smiled so warmly, he almost reached out for her.

'Oh, Jamie, it is good to have you home. We had quite thought you gone forever from our lives, had we not, Rose?'

Rose nodded numbly. Neither Lacy nor the bedazzled James appeared to notice or wonder at her lack of speech. She had barely opened her mouth since the first polite, 'Welcome home, Captain Osborne', with which she had greeted James's formal bow, but Lacy had put that down to Rose's reserve in the presence of a man who had once been a guest at Silverdale, and whom Rose had waited upon. She would come round when she had grown used to James, Lacy thought, for he was the easiest person in the world to befriend. Had she not discovered that for herself? She pointed to the chesterfield, deep and comfortable, which stood before the fireplace in which a small, cheerful fire crackled.

'Please, James. Sit down by the fire, and Rose will entertain you for a moment. Come Copper, I know you are only at my heels because you hope to cajole a biscuit out of me. You're a divil, so you are . . .'

Her voice faded away into the back reaches of the apartment, and a door banged somewhere. Then there was silence.

James turned courteously to Rose, indicating that she must sit before he could. She walked stiffly towards the small, velvet fireside chair and, with rigid back and head held high, lowered herself into it. Her face was turned away from him. All he could see was the curve of her cheekbone, the long silky flutter of her black lashes, and the luxuriant fall of her dark hair where it touched her ear. Her skin was the colour of clotted cream, and he wondered if she was unwell. She was certainly quiet, and in that respect she had changed, for he recalled the brilliance of her smile, and the high peal of her laughter as she skylarked with Lacy on their sixteenth birthdays. She had been vibrant, and as lovely, in her way, as Lacy. Emerald eyes: flushed, rounded cheeks; and a wide, curving, joyful mouth.

Why did he remember her so vividly? he thought, bewildered suddenly. She was none of these things now, sitting as prim as a spinster at the vicar's tea party. He scarcely knew her, had seen her only once. But it seemed as though she resented his presence and, by the set of her head and shoulders, could barely bring herself to address him. But something must be said. They could hardly sit like two strangers, unintroduced and caught by chance in the home of a mutual friend.

'You have known Lacy for how long, er, . . . Miss . . .' Damn, what was the woman's name? He had quite forgotten in the enchantment of the last hour. Oh yes, he had it now, '. . . O'Malley?'

Rose turned as though against her better judgement, and James was mystified by the look of hostility in her eyes. The woman really did dislike him. Her face was set in a mould of chill politeness, and he could see it was all she could do to answer him. What the devil had he done to earn her animosity, he wondered, and in such a short time? He almost laughed, it was so ridiculous, and was tempted to ask her outright what offence he had committed, then thought better of it. One could hardly take up with a virtual stranger the appearance of cordial dislike which showed in her face.

'I was a scullery maid at Silverdale from the age of ten, Captain Osborne.'

Nonplussed, for what polite rejoinder could one make to continue their conversation after that thunderclap, James turned his head and began to study the lovely but simple room. It was restful, the colours muted and calming to his sorely tried spirit. The pieces of furniture could almost be counted on one hand, but they were good, and they had been polished to an iridescent glow. Velvet, soft to the touch in warm shades; soft green walls, unadorned but for dozens of water colours and sketches; bowls of flowers.

He felt the peace of it enter him gently, and he sighed. The pictures on the wall drew him and, hauling himself to his feet, he limped across the room to study the one above the fireplace. It was of seagulls on the wing, their colouring blurred as they turned in the sky. A chimney pot or two, blackened with soot, were outlined sharply against torn, drifting clouds of pearl. There was scarcely any colour: a suggestion of yellow to indicate the eye of a gull; a patch of washed blue beyond the clouds. It was the most haunting and imaginative painting he had ever seen.

'Who has done this?' he asked abruptly, good manners forgotten.

'Lacy.'

He turned towards Rose, his face comical in its amazement.

'Lacy?'

'Yes.'

'I did not know she could paint. This is incredible. And these .. ?' he indicated the others which were hung on the plain walls, '. . . she has done them all?'

'Yes.'

There was a hushed silence, as he moved from one picture to the next. A rabbit, its scut white as snow, disappearing beneath the tangle of a blackberry bush; bluebells, a mere hint of their form against a backdrop of fallen tree trunks; flowers, birds; all seasons and times of the day, and all exquisite in their simplicity.

'They are . . .' He could not find the words, but continued to stare, considering if it was perhaps his own feelings for Lacy which imagined talent where there was none. But he knew instinctively that this was not so. They were the work of a supremely able artist.

'Has anyone seen these?'

'I beg your pardon?'

'Has anyone in the world of art appraised them?'

'I do not think Lacy would like to . . .'

'But she must. They are worthwhile, Miss O'Malley.'

He turned quickly from the last painting, and this time he caught her looking directly at him, and again was disconcerted by the expression he saw in her face. The hostility was gone, but what took its place bewildered him even more. He could not name it, though he felt he should, for it was a familiar one to him. She had a look of absorbed concentration, as though she gazed into some lovely world which she would enter if only she could. A look of yearning for a prize just beyond her reach. Her clear eyes had warmed to a soft, subdued green, and her lips were parted as though they were about to speak. There was a sad and gentle droop to her dark head, and to her shoulders, and her hands were clasped tightly in her lap. She seemed oppressed, so weary and defeated that he took a step towards her, thinking again that she was either unwell, or suffering some great sorrow.

'Miss O'Malley,' he said softly.

Instantly the look was gone, replaced by the cool formality with which she had treated him since the moment they had met at the quayside. So swiftly did one expression disappear and the second take its place, he was bemused; feeling foolish, and convinced that his imagination, probably inflamed by the happenings of the day, was working overtime.

'Yes, Captain Osborne?' Rose asked politely, but he shook his head and sat down heavily, for his leg troubled him.

357

The meal they ate was simple: a clear soup, a little boiled salmon, followed by succulent lamb with brussels sprouts. Maggie brought in a bowl of fruit and a tray of cheeses and, triumphantly, with the air of a mother who bestows a treat upon a favourite child, she placed in front of James a bottle of fine, pale, brandy.

James smiled at the plump little maid who subsided in a series of bobbing curtseys, blushes and coquettish giggles.

'What's this!' he said, 'A simple meal? Plain cooking indeed! Why even the Queen and Prince Albert could eat no better fare. And then, like a conjurer at a party, you produce a bottle of brandy. You are a marvel, Maggie.'

'Oh, not me, sir. 'Twere Miss Lacy's idea. She sent young Joshua, the caretaker's lad with a message to Mr Coffler at the wine merchants to fetch a bottle of 'is best, an' this is it, sir.'

They sat about the dying fire, not speaking at first and sipping brandy, though Rose declined, saying she had no head for spirits and would take a glass of Madeira.

'Quite right, Rose. Mama always told me young ladies should drink no more than a small glass of Madeira, but I must admit I quite care for the taste of this brandy, and if I were a man I should smoke a cigar. And why don't you, James? Our feminine bower could do with a whiff of masculinity about it.' She laughed as he proffered his cigar case, and told her she should never say anything she did not mean, but when, provoked, she took him up on his dare and would have lit a cigar, he drew back, saying he could think of nothing less feminine than a woman smoking a cigar. His own was drawing before he asked his question.

They might have been only parted the day before so easy was their relationship. Even the silences were filled with sweetness, and the change came suddenly.

'Tell me about your company, Lacy,' he said.

The lovely serene face, laughing at his words of a moment ago, closed up, and her eyes frosted.

'There is nothing to tell, dear James. It moves along.'

'Moves along. What does that mean?'

'We make . . . progress, do we not, Rose? But . . . slowly.'

'You do not sound very positive. The Miss Hemingway I knew so many years ago was filled with . . .'

'That was years ago, Jamie. I was but a child.'

'But you are doing well? They say you snap up all the bargains to be had from Manchester to St Helens, from Rochdale to Sheffield, and from every corner of the two counties.'

'Do they? And what else do they say, these informants of yours?'

'Why, that you are a business woman from the top of your head to the . . .'

'Fiddlesticks.'

He blinked and turned to look at Rose, who appeared to be concerned only with the feeding of an apple log onto the flickering fire. Rose, brought up to fend for herself, had never quite got to grips with the helpless ways of the gentry, who rang a bell to summon a servant to 'throw a bit of a stick on a fire.'

The brandy had put a bright pink spot in each of Lacy's cheeks, and her eyes blazed. Her hair had become loosened, and a wisp of curl fell about her face. James thought he had never seen her look so enchanting. She tossed her head angrily, and he wanted to smile for, as yet, he did not know of the seriousness with which Lacy treated her business life. Even he, tolerant, and decades ahead of his male contemporaries in his belief that some women, although not all, were capable of quite outstanding deeds – for had he not been acquainted with Miss Florence Nightingale? – was still not aware of her single-mindedness.

His humorous, heavy lidded eyes, brown and watchful, measured her anger, and his elation grew with her temper. He did not know what it was she raged against, but her spirit delighted him. His well-defined, sensual mouth curved in a slow grin.

'Come now, Lacy, do not fiddlesticks me. You have done what you have always wanted, so why the tantrum?'

It did the trick, as he had hoped.

'Tantrum. Tantrum!' Lacy stood up and looked about her,

as if for something with which to clout him. 'Is that not typical? What did I tell you, Rose? No matter who it is, they are all the same.'

For a second, James caught Rose's eye, and was surprised to see the laughter there. Why, he thought, she knows what I am about and is amused by it. She is not such a cool customer after all. They were drawn together in a moment of intimacy, and her sudden lively warmth fascinated him. Then Lacy snatched his attention, and Rose was forgotten again.

'You do not know how hard Rose and I have worked, James, or you would not speak in such a derogatory manner. For over two years we have put our time and money, thought, organization and planning into building a business that one day will be as great as any in Liverpool. Oh, we do well enough from the interest on our initial investment, and from the profits on the merchandise we send abroad. But with that profit I have bought raw cotton, sugar, tobacco and other commodities which I had hoped to sell here, but no one will buy from us. It is a circle, James, which must not be broken, and mine has a gap in it. I *must* sell my cotton and other merchandise here to buy piece goods, and whatever else I will sell abroad, but not one damn broker will entertain us. We have even been to Manchester to try and sell direct, have we not, Rose? But we are shrugged off like delinquent children who have strayed from Nanny's care.'

Her voice shook with passion.

'We have it here, James,' she clenched her fist against her temple, '. . . and here,' this time her heart. 'But they will not allow us to do it. Nor even to try. Of what are you afraid, you men? We mean to take nothing from you. We do not wish to step into your shoes, just to be allowed to take our place beside you. Space on ships is mine, for I can pay for it, but they will not buy my goods. I have a warehouse full to the rafters with good quality raw cotton but no one will have it. All the goods I have bought which will not keep have perished on the dock, and the men, agents I have placed abroad, dare not buy any more for fear I cannot sell it. Dear God, James, why do men such as those I would sell to take this attitude? They have this damned prejudice, that will not allow them to believe a woman is capable of providing men with anything . . . unless it is in their bed.'

Rose gasped, but James sat quietly and said nothing. He wanted her to go on, to dredge the bitterness and frustrated hurt from within her, to bring it out into the open. Her pride in what she had so far achieved was being eroded by the great wall of male bigotry erected against her. The dogmatic view with which most men appraised all of womanhood would, one day, he knew, come to an end. It must. But not yet. Not for many years yet. Lacy would have to fight with the wiles, the deviousness, the underhand feminine ways that a she cat will use to obtain what she wants.

But first, he must know what it was that held her back. The jaundiced partisanship which existed in the world of commerce must be made to crack. To expose a crack big enough to allow her to put the toe of her dainty slipper in it. He was persuaded that that was all Miss Lacy Hemingway would need: a toe hold!

'Tell me about it, Lacy,' he said, 'and stop holding all men in contempt. Some believe, strangely enough, that women are able to be more than . . . a bedfellow, you know.'

Rose choked again on her glass of Madeira, and her face was a flame of indignation. For a moment, she was again the good Catholic girl who had been brought up to believe in right and wrong, and was it not exceedingly improper to speak to a lady of such things? Then she looked at Lacy, and Lacy looked at her, and with twitching lips their innate, shared sense of humour worked across each face, and they began to smile.

James turned from one to the other, smiling too, and in a moment, they broke into great gusts of laughter. The dog barked, and a passing pedestrian glanced nervously up at the window, convinced murder was being done, and in the kitchen, Maggie dropped one of Miss Lacy's best plates, smashing it to smithereens on the stone floor.

It was the first time they had laughed together. Rose, Lacy and James. And, for an instant, Rose's heart beat to the joyful rhythm of shared affection and amusement. Her love for the man was put aside, and they were three friends, who had bestowed upon one another the blessed pleasure of mocking the absurd.

# CHAPTER 25

'A Captain Osborne to see you, sir.'

The portly man at the desk looked up, squinting through the thick murk of cigar smoke which threatened to engulf him. Before him were scattered clutches of paper, notes, ledgers, samples of raw cotton, pens, pencils; the whole coated in a thin film of cigar ash.

'Captain Osborne,' said the portly gentleman, 'Oo the 'ecks 'e when 'e's at 'ome?'

'I don't know, sir. Said he had business to discuss.'

'Business? I don't know any Captain Osborne. What's it all about, Green?'

'He wouldn't say, sir. Said he wanted the top man.'

'Did 'e, by jove? Best send 'im in then.'

The office was large and rather opulent, for the firm of 'Cranshaw and Cranshaw, Cotton Brokers' was thriving, and money was no drawback when it came to comforting the person of Mr George Cranshaw. He was a jovial man, a 'man's man' he liked to say, though he had an eye for a trim ankle and waist, same as the next chap. But a drink and a damned good meal with his business contemporaries was what he enjoyed the best. He loved his work, did Mr George, so called to differentiate between himself and his son, Mr Arthur. And, if it was not for the tiresome presence of his wife in his home in Everton, he would have put up in his club in Bold Street the more conveniently to be at his desk each morning early.

And then there was the discreet villa in Aigburth, where he kept the one distraction he allowed himself from his business, and where he called twice a week. Yes, he liked a bit of feminine company did Mr George, but kept in a separate compartment from the rest of his world, of course. He was a shrewd man, a hard man some would say, but soft where the ladies were concerned, or so he told himself. Witness the luxury of his own home, in which his wife and daughters lolled seven days a week, and the solid comfort of the villa in Aigburth. Still, he didn't begrudge it them, not him. He'd got the brass, and what was it for if not to enjoy, and women were easy to please, bless 'em. Give 'em a bit of a geegaw, and a slap and tickle now and then, and they were as happy as cows in clover.

It was a warm day, and the gentleman who entered his office wore no top coat. His frock coat was a chocolate brown, as was his tall top hat. He wore a striped silk waistcoat the colour of pale sand, which matched perfectly his tapered trousers with dark brown, braided side seams down each leg. He carried a gold-topped cane, and a pair of cream gloves. He was one of the most elegant gentlemen Mr George had ever seen, and he was a gentleman.

Mr George stood up. *Blundered* would be a better word to describe his movement for, like most self-made men – his father had worn clogs only thirty years ago – he was still in awe of those who had been born and bred as gentlemen.

George Cranshaw's father had served his apprenticeship with a cotton spinner in Rochdale, where the damp climate, the abundance of water in the rivers and streams which ran the wheels, was the main source of power in spinning cotton. In 1802 James Watt brought steam power to Lancashire, and said of Manchester 'it is steam mad'. Arthur Cranshaw thought so too, and went to join the madness, taking his son George with him. But son George could see where the real profits lay. Not in spinning or weaving, or the finishing of cloth, but in the buying and selling of it. The market, nevertheless, required someone with experience and knowledge of raw material supplies, and an understanding of the specific technical requirements of the industrial hinterland.

George Cranshaw took these skills, taught him by his father, and migrated to Liverpool. He was representative of the new broker class. He had served his apprenticeship with a fustian manufacturer in Bolton when his father died, and was then employed in a cotton warehouse in Manchester. His experience and special knowledge ensured his importance as a middle man between importers, dealers and spinners in all the main manufacturing areas.

When Mr George began his activities, it had been the practice for the buying broker to make his purchases in the saleroom or warehouse of the importer, but gradually it became customary for the broker to have samples of the raw cotton sent to his own buying rooms to enable him to compare the various qualities and to examine the samples at his leisure.

With the large increase in the production and export of cotton from America, rendered possible by the introduction of the saw-gin machinery in 1793 and the consequent arrival in England of more regularly packed bales, the necessity to examine each bag at the warehouse before making a bid became unnecessary.

Mr George was 'sampling' when the captain entered his office.

'Captain Osborne,' he said hesitantly, unsure whether to shake the fellow's hand, but Captain Osborne held his out in a friendly fashion and Mr George took it, pleased, though he could not have explained why.

They sat, and Captain Osborne crossed one leg over the other, seeming to favour it slightly. He was a good looking man, Mr George conceded, and one the ladies would go for. His figure was rather slender; a bit of meat on his bones would not go amiss, but his shoulders were broad, and he was tall, holding himself erect like a soldier.

That's what he was, a soldier. Mr George felt quite pleased with himself, as though he had solved some ticklish problem, and then wondered what the hell it had to do with anything, and why the chap was here to see him. Still, best be genial, eeh. The gentry was worth keeping in with. Never know where it might lead, and Muriel'd never forgive him if he muffed a chance to mix with what she liked to call 'county'.

'What can I do fer you, Captain Osborne?' he said pleasantly, at the same time shuffling a paper or two, just to let the captain know he was not a man who could afford to waste time.

Captain Osborne flicked an imaginary fleck of dust from the beautiful crease in his trousers, then glanced about him languidly. His face creased into a fastidious look of dismay, and he waved his glove about, as a lady might move her fan. At once, Mr George heaved himself to his feet, and lumbered to the window, like a bear making for food. With a jerk, he opened the window on to Sweeting Street, and immediately the noises of the town drifted pleasantly inwards. Horses' hooves, the sound of iron-rimmed wheels on setts, an organ grinder's sweet but tinny music, and the cheerful whistle of a delivery boy pushing a small handcart along the kerb. The smoke quickly dispersed, and Mr George took his seat, shamefaced as a boy who has made an unpardonable aroma in his trousers.

'Why, thank you, Mr Cranshaw, that is most civil of you. You see . . . my chest . . . has not been the same since Sebastopol, and the skirmish in India did me little good . . .'

Begging forgiveness silently to those who had suffered in the 'skirmish' in India, James Osborne beseeched Mr Cranshaw to take no further trouble; reassured him that he did not require a drink, a more comfortable seat, or the window opened any wider; and said yes, he had been a soldier until he resigned his commission, and how did Mr Cranshaw guess? He supposed it to be Mr Cranshaw's astute eye, trained to observe, and his business mind, which must make quick judgements every day of the week.

A most pleasant ten minutes ensued, and when Captain Osborne casually mentioned his cargo of raw cotton which was going begging, and was ready to be bid for, it happened to be the very thing Mr George was looking for, as he had a buyer from Manchester coming that very afternoon.

''ow much are we talkin' about, Captain? Seventy five bales . . . mm . . . that's about twenty two and a half thousand pounds. Yes, well, I would certainly look at a sample, if yer care to send it over 'ere.'

Mr George was delighted to do business with a gentleman, for it somehow gave the whole affair an added sense of gratification. Not that he would allow this to impair his judgement, that which Captain Osborne had already perceived. Oh no! The cotton would be inspected most thoroughly before a farthing changed hands. Gentleman or not, Mr George trusted no one, especially those he had not dealt with before. It seemed strange that this . . . dandy was here at all, for gentlemen as a rule had representatives to deal with such matters. He wondered if he could bring up the question. Captain Osborne seemed an affable fellow, and done tactfully . . .

'Er, 'ow long since yer came from India, Captain?' Mr George drew on another cigar, and leaned back in his chair.

'A month or two now, Mr Cranshaw, but I have become so devilish bored, I thought I would . . .'

'Quite, quite, but what made yer come into this business?'

James smiled amiably, a picture of elegant ennui. 'I suppose having a family business which deals with such . . .'

'A family business?' Mr George interrupted quite rudely, and sat up in his chair.

'Not . . . Osborne's the shippers? Why, I've done business with your father many times, Captain. Why didn't yer say so, lad? Yon Mr Matthew an' I 'ave . . .'

'But this is nothing to do with my family, Mr Cranshaw. I am branching out on my own, so to speak. I shall be having one or two small cargoes to dispose of in the future. Not all of cotton. Please, I beg you, do not confuse me with my father's business. I and a partner are doing this entirely on our own.'

Mr George tapped the side of his nose and winked.

'Say no more, lad. An' a little bit of, shall we say personal supervision, will give you a start, by gum it will. Though the others won't like it.'

He grinned hugely. 'But we need say nowt about that, need we. Keep yer own business ter yerself, I say.' Brisk now, he began to jot a note or two upon a scrap of paper. He muttered and scribbled, and then, calculations complete, he looked up at James.

'I think you an' me can do business, Captain Osborne. If yer can send me a sample and I like t' quality, I'll buy yer cotton. You understand I take nowt unseen, an' it's money up front. I don't give nor take credit. No offence intended, but I like ter see brass before I part wi' owt, an' when I buy it's the same.'

James stood up and reached for his top hat.

'Mr Cranshaw,' he said, 'It has been a pleasure to do business with you. Now I must be off. I have a luncheon appointment with a lovely lady.'

He smiled broadly, and Mr George warmed to him. By gum, he was a decent sort of a chap, and not averse to a bit of a joke with those who many of his class thought beneath them.

'Off yer go then, lad. Yer can't keep a lady waitin', or she'll tek the 'ump. There's nowt gets their back up quicker than waiting' on a gentleman.'

'You are right, Mr Cranshaw, indeed you are. Oh, and by the way.' James turned as he reached the door, 'I shall bring my partner along to meet you at the first opportunity. I am sure you will get on famously.'

'Do, Captain, and p'raps if yer could spare t'time we might all 'ave a bit o' lunch together. My club is not far away. By 'eck, it's bin a right pleasure ter meet yer, Captain. It's a fair treat ter deal wi' a gentleman. Now off yer go, or yer lady will 'ave tekken up wi' someone else.'

On this laughing note, they parted. Mr George was well satisfied with the morning's work.


James raised his glass, and the champagne in it sparkled in the ray of sunlight which fell through the window of the York Hotel in Williamson Square. Its pale amber lucidity was shot through with a thousand tiny bubbles, which rose interminably to the surface, spraying the glass and James's hand with a fine mist. He smiled, first at Lacy, and then at Rose.

'Ladies,' he said, 'a toast.'

Lacy's eyes were as brilliant as the champagne, and her face was flushed to rose above the pale cream lawn of her dress. The basque bodice was trimmed with palest pink satin ribbon about the neck and at the edges of the pagoda sleeves, and her cream straw bonnet was tied beneath her chin with the same ribbon but of the width of her hand. Her hair was

368

parted in the centre, and drawn to a chignon at the back of her head. She had refused to have it cut and frizzed about her ears according to the current fashion, but the usual vagrant tendrils escaped and wisped rebelliously about her white forehead and neckline.

Rose wore a costume of vibrant raspberry pink surah, unadorned and simple, with a well-fitted bodice and huge skirt. Her bonnet matched her dress, and beneath its brim was fastened a tiny bunch of white silk rosebuds. Her dark hair was as severely fastened back as was Lacy's, but her white skin and slanting green eyes gave her a rich vivid and almost oriental beauty.

The dining room of the hotel was filled with elegant and wealthy people, all equally fashionable and as well dressed as they. But, somehow, it was these three who drew the most interested, admiring and shocked glances. James was splended in his well-cut frock coat, and the slight limp he still had, and which he supported with his cane, gave him an air of vulnerability which set feminine hearts a-flutter. His hair was glossy in the sunshine, and his warm brown eyes glowed with some emotion which seemed to be a mixture of satisfaction, hope, excitement and something else known only to himself, and to one of the young ladies he accompanied.

They had caused quite a stir when they entered the dining room, for they were a striking trio. A sibilant hiss ran through the room as diners were frozen to gasping silence by the sight of Miss Lacy Hemingway, a well-known nay, *notorious* young lady of genteel society gliding gracefully to the best table, accompanied by her own maid, who sat with her, and the most eligible bachelor in town.

None other than Captain James Osborne.

Society watched open-mouthed as James raised his glass.

'A toast to "Hemingway and O'Malley". May they reign long and proudly, and may their humble representative continue to give service as ably as he has done today.'

'Are we really on our way, James, really?' Lacy said wistfully.

'Can you doubt it?' James smiled gently.

369

'But one broker? Will it work, do you think? Will he continue to buy and sell our cotton when he knows who imports it?'

James reached across the table and took her hand. It lay soft and boneless in his, defenceless it seemed to him, and scarce strong enough to wield a brush, let alone rule a shipping empire. He smiled into her eyes.

'Lacy. Is this the brave girl who was to conquer the business world and become the largest ship owner since Mr Cunard? Smile, my dear, for you have just made your first "sale".'

'*You* have made it Jamie, not I.'

He looked tenderly down at her hand resting so trustfully in his, and thought sadly of this morning's work. Yes, he had done it. He had done it for her. Without him, she might have finally persuaded these dogmatic, hardheaded Lancashire businessmen to accept her as a merchant, but what would it have done to her? What would it have cost in bitterness and frustration, as she battled, perhaps for years, to gain admittance to their world? He was a front for her and, once her goods had been bought and accepted for several months by their purchasers; had been acclaimed as worthwhile, and a bargain at her prices, she would reveal herself as the owner of the firm who had sold them. She was banking on the cupidity of these men, who, once they had struck a bargain, and had been served with efficiency and honesty, would be willing to continue their commercial intercourse with her.

Would they turn their backs on her when they knew?

He did not know. He only knew he must help her. Though it did his own cause no good, he must help her to do this thing which was an obsession with her. He wanted nothing else in the world but to take her away, and make her his, and continue to love her to the end of their days, but he was aware that it simply would not do. She would not have it. She could see nothing but her certainty that she was meant to be other than what she called 'some man's plaything' and, until she had proved it, she would only look upon him as a friend. She found him good company. Her laughter proved it, and her welcome each time he called upon her.

Now she was in his debt. Perhaps her obligation to him would do his hopes no good, for those who borrow seldom see the lender as friend, but he must take the chance. Because he loved her.

'Lacy, listen to me. Do not begin to doubt yourself because of this one small task you cannot do for yourself. You have done so much in the past two years, more than many a man. Small firms and shipping lines are going under every week. Even the most sound founder under the cost of running such a diverse organization. But you have kept your head above water by your own judgement. You have made wise investments which have kept a small capital growing. Now, you can go ahead and continue to buy your cargoes, for you have a market. Ship your iron bars, your cotton pieces, your pottery and copper, and bring back all the goods which you know you can sell now.' He held up his hand, silencing her, as she would have interrupted.

'Do not say it again. I know I am selling it at the moment, but under your supervision and instruction. Do you think I would know how to sell a bale of cotton to the Mr Cranshaws of this world if I had not got you to tell me how to go about it? Oh, Lacy, do not sigh because you could not break a pig-headed bigot who has been wedded for years to the belief that women are good for . . .'

He began to laugh, and bent to kiss her fingers, and she touched his cheek, her eyes warm with affection. He nearly broke then, and it took all his self control not to babble of his own conviction that Mr Cranshaw's ideas for women were bloody good ones, and why the hell was she wasting the lovely years of their lives in this nonsense. There was no need for it. None. He was a wealthy man. He could give her all she was used to, and more. He could give her so much love she would float in it, drown in it, and the place for her right at this moment was in his bed, in his arms, and in his heart.

Some emotion must have shown in his face, for she drew back uncertainly, a mist dimming the crystal brilliance of her eyes. From depths he did not know he had, he found the strength to grin boyishly, to turn away in a friendly fashion, and to say to Rose who sat quietly beside him.

371

'What do you think, Rose? You are the other half of this partnership. Do you not think Lacy is foolish to doubt even slightly her own capability? She wants to do it all with help from no man, but compromise is always a good tactic, is it not? I was taught that as a soldier.'

Rose smiled coolly. 'She wants to prove herself, Captain Osborne. Can you take that from her?'

'Please, Rose. How many times must I tell you it's *James*? Captain Osborne has gone now. He is useful in offices such as Mr Cranshaw's, but you must call me James.'

'Very well, James.'

'Tell me that you agree with me, Rose, and prove to this stubborn young woman that it is not a noble thing to refuse a helping hand.'

He knew he was using Rose to distract Lacy from what had been in his face moments ago. Besides, Rose was very pretty, and it was pleasant to flirt a little with a pretty woman. He leaned towards her, touching her glass with his.

'Let us drink together, and ignore this child who wants all the kudos for herself, shall we?'

Lacy was beginning to laugh again, the strange moment gone. James's eyes were a warm, melting brown as he looked into Rose's, and his lips moved to part across his even white teeth. In the past two months his health had improved enormously, and the time he spent with Lacy and Rose, walking Copper on the beaches which lined the River Mersey, had put the colour back into his face. He had put on weight and his leg, through regular exercise, was progressing each day. His engaging, merry charm had returned in the company of the woman he loved, his wit had sharpened on hers.

He still found Rose a prickly individual, hard to know, with a reserve which was unusual in one of her race. He had served with several Irishmen, and their drollery and complete lack of seriousness in the face of hardship had endeared them to him, and he wondered at the often colourless inscrutability Rose affected. He had heard her laugh, seen the transformation in her face when she did, but he was still convinced at times that she did not care for him.

She looked at him serenely now, and he was suddenly taken with the fancy that he would get her to lower her guard. He would make her laugh, melt a little, perhaps indulge in a small flirtation; do something to show she was human. She was looking at him with a coolness that irked him somewhat, for he had never had this effect on a woman before. She appeared so supremely indifferent to him, it was as though he must challenge her to see him, if not as a man, then as a friend.

'Come, Rose, let's you and I go elsewhere, and leave Miss Hemingway to her enormous ego. If she must do everything herself, then let her tackle the bill. We shall amuse ourselves in this fine town and . . .'

'Oh, Jamie. Stop it. You are embarrassing Rose with your foolishness. She does not care to be made fun of, do you acushla?'

Lacy had picked up one or two of Rose's Irish whimsies in their long relationship, and she often interspersed her pure, well-bred English with an Irish nonsense or two, such as now.

'I am quite able to deal with Captain Osborne's . . . foolishness, Lacy,' Rose said equably, 'and do not need you to take up on my behalf.'

Lacy pulled a face, laughing, and drank another half glass of champagne, more than a little exhilarated by the amount of wine she had taken.

'Whoops! Sorry, Rose. Of course you are. Anyone who can tackle Lancer . . .'

'Lacy.' Rose's voice was like the crack of a whip.

There was a deep silence and James looked, mystified, from one lovely face to the other, but neither would look at him. Their glances were locked, and the sparkle had left Lacy's eyes.

Rose turned to him abruptly. 'I think it about time we moved on to our next conquest. Do you not think so, Captain Osborne?'

'Who is Lancer, Lacy?'

She bent her head to peer into her reticule, as though searching for something of vital importance. Her fingers trembled with the clasp, and he was about to lean towards her, filled with a longing to hold them in his own and warm away her sudden alarm, when Rose spoke again.

'He is my stepfather, Captain Osborne. Lacy and I do not . . . greatly . . . care for him.'

Diverted, as Rose had intended, James turned to her. He knew nothing of her family, and was about to ask politely where they lived, and all the usual questions good manners demanded, when she stood up quickly.

'I think perhaps we should leave now. You do have other customers to see, Captain Osborne.' She smiled steadfastly at Lacy. 'Shall we make our way to "Masons", allannah? You did say you wished to buy a parasol, did you not?'

They left quietly, and as James settled the bill, he pondered on the mystery of where the fine, bright sparkle of the day had gone.

Rose stood at her window and watched a procession of fat, snuff-coloured clouds laze along the line of rooftops on the opposite side of the road. The sky was dark, almost navy blue, but the sun, gone half an hour ago, still touched them, shading them to gold, to amber, to brown and finally, as she stared sightlessly, to a deep pewter grey.

Her hand groped blindly at the curtain, which was still drawn back, and she swayed heavily against the window frame as though she would fall. Her eyes glittered in the dark and tears began to run, singly at first, making a thin shining path across each cheek; then as her sorrow overcame her, in a flood; a curtain of wetness which dripped upon the lovely rose fabric of her dress. Great splotches appeared, and she felt her own tears wet her breast. Her breath moaned almost soundlessly in her throat, and she swayed, pulling at the curtain in her hand. Her knees began to give way, and she sank down, resting her arms and head against the padded window seat.

She screamed silently into the cushions, but no one came to inquire why she cried so, and in her dementia she wondered if the padding took the noise, or had she even made it? For an hour she gave way, rocking and weeping in the night. Then gradually, she became quiet.

She got up from the floor and sat upon the tear-soaked seat, leaning her head against the frame of the window. A half-moon sailed across the blue ocean of the sky, casting a silver wash over the chimney pots. Outlined for a moment against the top of a wall, a tom cat stalked an unwary mouse which crept along its base.

Rose sat calmly now, the storm gone, though it had left the havoc of its passing upon her face and spirit. She moved to the table beside her bed and, with a steady hand, lit the lamp which stood upon it. The lemon glow touched the pretty room, gilding the shining surfaces, and tinting the white walls and bedspread to gold. She sat upon the bed, and stared wide-eyed into the centre of the glowing lamp, seeing his eyes and his warm, sensual mouth, and felt herself shake. She put her hand to her eyes, as though to blot out some unendurable sight, and turned, burying her face in the softness of the pillow.

A whisper sighed about the room.

'James, James. Oh, Captain Osborne,' it said.

# CHAPTER 26

The woman was dressed completely in black. Her bonnet was pulled about her head and her heavy-booted feet made a clack-clacking sound on the setts on Naylor Street. A thick shawl was held warmly about her shoulders. She could have been anything from nineteen to ninety, so little of her was visible, but she stepped lightly. She carried a large, unwieldly basket, which appeared to be stuffed to its brim, for it was obviously heavy, dragging at the woman's arm, making her walk with a curious lopsided gait.

She paused when she reached an alleyway on her left and, before turning into it, she looked back, signalling to an enormous man who stood on the corner. He returned her wave, but continued to stand like a small mountain, and as firm, watching as she disappeared from his view.

'She's gone,' he said over his shoulder and another fellow, equally formidable, who sat upon the box of a carriage pulled by four smart horses, passed his hand across his face which was a peculiar shade of green.

'Christ, an' I 'ope she's not long. This stink's enough ter turn ya' over. 'Ow the 'ell do they stand it?'

'Dunno,' said the first man unconcernedly, never taking his eyes from the alley. 'Back up a bit so we can see each other, Jack. I'm just gonner take a stroll up 'ere. See nuthin' un- usual's takin' place, like. Keep yer eye on those bleedin' kids an' all will yer, or they'll 'ave the shoes off the flamin' 'orses.'

'Right, Jonas, but don't be long. Strewth, what the 'ell does she come 'ere for, d'yer think. It's . . .'

But Jonas had gone. It was his job to keep Miss Rose from coming to harm on her monthly visits to her mother, and he was not concerned with smells or thieving kids, or even why she came.

Captain James had sent his carriage and his burliest groom,

and between them, they were to see she was safely delivered, and as equally safely returned, to her home in Upper Duke Street.

Strange really, the way she had gone up in the world. He remembered her years ago when she had come to Silverdale. A scrawny little thing she'd been, with great green eyes. He had been a year or two older working under Mr Arkwright in the stable, and too scared to open his mouth, even to her, for it was his first time away from his home in Garstang. It is a long way from Garstang to Liverpool when you are eleven years old, and know you won't see your mam for a year. No one had bothered much with him. He had a northern dialect you could cut with a knife, and they could make nowt of him, but Rose'd often grin at him, cheeky as you please, when she idled in the yard.

For a while, as she grew from a skinny child to a sudden breathtaking roundness, with a face like the pretty cat who lived in the stable, he had fostered hopes of getting to know her better. But she and Miss Lacy were thick as thieves, and she had no time for the likes of him.

No, Sally was more his sort, and they'd made a good do of it, him and her. Well, they had to, with two kids and another on the way, but he had never got over that feeling he had for Miss Rose. She was worth looking at, by God, and looking after, an' all, and that's just what he intended doing.

'Darlin', is it yerself then. Come away in an' shut the door. 'Tis cold enough ter freeze yer bum. 'Ere, give us a kiss then, an' let's be lookin' at yer. Eeh, Rose, Rose, will yer not listen ter me. I've told yer an' told yer not ter wear the black. It doesn't suit yer, lovely. Faith, yer too young ter be wearin' such a miserable owd colour. When I was yer age I 'ad the loveliest blue, sprigged with forget-me-nots an' a little blue ribbon in me 'air . . .'

Rose smiled, and hugged her Mammy to her, walking with her across the ice-cold floor which had frozen overnight, and towards the cheerful fire blazing in the fireplace. She had to smile, well laugh really, for she well knew that when Bridie was twenty-one she had five children, and there wasn't a farthing to spare to buy a hen's egg, let alone a bit of blue ribbon for her hair. But she said nothing, for Bridie lived on her memories: memories of the lovely days when she and Sean had been young. Somehow, those days had become so inexpressibly dear to her that they were endowed with more treasure than she had actually had.

'I know, Mammy. I know, and I do have some gowns which are a truly beautiful colour, but I feel they would be out of place here. You know I like to slip in and out without a great deal of fuss.'

Bridie looked at Rose with her head on one side, as the voice and speech of gentility, which her daughter had gradually adopted from Lacy, came from the lips of the elegant lady before her. Her eyes became wary, as though she was a child who had thought herself to be holding the hand of a familiar parent, only to find she was clinging to someone she scarcely knew. She smiled uncertainly, then gestured to Sean's chair, as though offering a visitor a seat. But before she had time to step back towards the safety of the group of children, Rose took off her bonnet, threw it on the table, and said in the thickest of Irish brogues:

'Sure, an' I could moider a cup o' tea, Mammy. Me mouth's loik a tinder box fer want of a drink. Make us a cup, darlin', an' we'll be lookin' ter see what I've brought yer fer Christmas.'

Instantly, Bridie was herself again. Faith, an' wasn't it her owd Rosie, all dressed up grand, to be sure, but just the same darlin' child. Beautiful she looked, in her best black dress, put on no doubt in honour of the Mammy, and it was Sunday. Will yer look at 'er, she said to herself. Quite the lady, but still the same Rose underneath.

Reassured, she began to swirl about the room, sweeping piles of what looked like rubbish, but which Rose knew to be the children's clothing, to the floor, lifting the steaming kettle from the hob, and pouring boiling water into the teapot. Instructions bubbled from her mouth to the assembly of silent children, and they moved about listlessly.

There were six of them now, and though at first they stared curiously at the woman who hugged their Mammy, they were used to her monthly visits. After a moment or two, they began to shift the mouldy spread of mattresses, piling them in a corner, and flinging bits and pieces of old rags, blankets, boots, and even a miserable, mewling kitten from God knew where, onto the top of the heap. They were dressed as usual in a ragbag of odds and ends, and Rose wondered resignedly which pawnbroker had the warm clothing she had provided at the start of the winter. She had thought that if she brought clothing, instead of giving Bridie the money to buy it, the children would benefit. But Bridie, with a few pence in her pocket, would be down to the gin shop before Rose had reached the end of Naylor Street. It seemed she could not win, whatever she did. It all ended in the same way: with Bridie reduced to a muddle of hiccuping stupor, escaping for the moment from the squalor in which she lived, and maudlin in her remembrances.

Rose looked about her as she sat in the festering chair. It was exactly as it had been ten years ago when Bridie had lost her Sean. She had regained her whimsical good humour to some extent, but the life she led with Lancer – she usually had the beginnings or the end of a black eye – and her liking for a 'wee drap o' gin', kept her always in a state of disordered penury. Thanks to Rose, she now had no need to go out to work, so her children were reasonably well looked after. Bridie had borne Lancer eight children, the last in 1856. She had named her Mary Kate and, as if having run out of the names by which her first family had been called, she had had no more.

She traipsed about now, her feet in a pair of Lancer's old boots, on her head an old cap he had discarded. Her partiality for doing nothing, and the twenty children she had borne, had put great rolls of fat upon her. It oozed from beneath her chin, and drooped from her arms, but it had a peculiar unhealthy greyness, as though the sun had never touched it, nor even the outside air. She was thirty eight years old.

'There darlin', a lovely cup of tay fer yer. Now will yer 'ave a bit o' somethin' ter eat?'

She looked about like a hostess undecided upon which delicacy to press upon a guest, and Rose shook her head hastily. She could see a pan upon the stove, from which the kitten had just withdrawn its tiny head, and she shuddered delicately, praying her mother would not notice. Half the woman she once had been, Bridie yet had a spark of pride, particularly where her daughter was concerned.

For half an hour Bridie and the children ooh-ed and aah-ed over the huge hamper Rose had brought for Christmas, which was only two days away. The children stuffed rich Christmas cake into their mouths, interchanging it with a leg of turkey, a mince pie or two, and even a spoonful of strawberry jelly.

'Mammy, it's fer Christmas,' Rose remonstrated, but Bridie smiled and sipped her tea, and begged Declan to pass her a 'cakie' to have with her 'tay', and Rose sat back and sighed. What was the use? It was not as if she cared overmuch what they did with the food, or the clothing she gave them. They were nothing to do with her, these carrot-haired children of Lancer McGhee. She brought the stuff for Mammy's sake and for no other reason. Her only concern was for Bridie and, at last, she was going to do what she had dreamed of doing since the day she had first seen Lancer McGhee fasten himself on her mother's white flesh. Her cheeks flushed in anticipation, and she sat up in her chair. Oh, Daddy, can you see me down here in your old chair, the one in which you always sat? She smiled secretly, knowing how Sean's heart would gladden up there in the lovely Heaven, where he surely was.

The toddler, Mary Kate, began to grizzle as her brother snatched a bit of frosted icing from her fingers, and Rose turned irritably. Dear Mother, was she never to have a bit of peace to tell her Mammy the wonderful news she had for her?

'Can't you keep them quiet, Mammy? I've something to tell you.'

Bridie looked up, surprised by the annoyance in Rose's voice, and, perhaps for the first time, realizing that Rose did not care overmuch for her half-brothers and sisters. Why this was so she couldn't imagine, for they were lovely children, and the apple of her eye. Even though each one had been given her as a result of Lancer's animal rutting, without an ounce of warmth or affection to soften their begetting, they were as dear to her as . . . as dear to her as . . . Here her mind, surging to lock out the memories of the children of Sean, became confused. She could not quite remember who it was she compared them to.

'Faith, Rosie, they're only babes. They're enjoyin' the good things yer fetched 'em. Let 'em be. Now, what did yer want ter talk about, alannah?' Her face lit up, and she leaned forward. 'I know, yer gettin' married, that's it, isn't it?'

She clapped her hands in delight, and her mind rushed forward to grandchildren, and her Rose and herself absorbed together in the wonders of motherhood, but Rose frowned and said sharply, a queer glint in her eye,

'Of course not, Mammy. What on earth put that idea into your head?'

'An' what's so strange in a mother wantin' ter see 'er child safely wed, I'd like ter know?' Bridie asked huffily, as though Rose's welfare was her responsibility, and the arranging of her future the dearest wish of her heart. 'Every girl should be havin' a husband, darlin', an' children. Why, I was the mother of five when I was yer . . .'

'Yes, yes, I know, Mammy. You've told me,' Rose said crossly, 'but it's not that. I shan't marry, ever, so you might as well . . .'

'Not marry! Of course yer will, Rosie. 'Tis yer duty as a good Catholic girl ter marry an' 'ave . . .'

'Mammy, will yer shut up and listen to me, please. I have something wonderful to tell you, so stop yer blather, and let me say it.' She turned to the quarrelling children, and banged her hand upon the table.

'Will yer be quiet, the lot of yer. Fer God's sake, take the blasted hamper and go in the corner. You an' all,' she said to the wide-eyed toddler and, used to instant obedience at the command of their father, Teresa and Seamus lifted down the basket, carrying it to the back of the room. Here, they pulled down a palliasse, put the basket in its centre and sat about it, just as though they were basking in the sunshine of a picnic.

'Anyway, where's the other two?' Rose queried. She could not bring herself to call Bridie's two eldest children by her absent brothers' names. The bright-eyed, lively spirited boys who had disappeared into the world of overworked, underfed, exploited children, had not been seen for ten years. For all she knew they were dead, and she still grieved them.

'Oh, they're away to their jobs.'

'Jobs?'

'Aye, Lancer put 'em ter the chimneys a week or two back.' Bridie spoke equably, the repeat performance of what had happened to the first Patrick seeming to give little concern.

For a moment, Rose was sorry she had spoken sharply to the children. Her mother loved them. They, more than Rose, had kept Bridie from going under completely and, for this, if for nothing else, Rose was in their debt. On the other hand, had the children not arrived yearly, her mother might have made something of her life. Or did she need the comfort of motherhood to keep her reason? Had they not been born, might she not indeed have gone mad?

Rose shook her head in confusion, and sighed, then brightened, as she turned again to Bridie.

'Now listen carefully, Mammy, for I want you to understand what I'm saying. Where's the man?'

'Oh, 'e's away ter the purlin', lovely, an' won't be back til late.'

'Good. Now, how soon can you be packed?' Rose's eyes sparkled, and she seemed to hold her breath.

'Packed?'

'Yes, packed, Mammy.' Her joy bubbled over now, and her face was alight with it. She put her hand upon her mother's arm, then leaned forward and hugged her.

'You're comin' with me, Mammy. The carriage is outside waitin' . . .'

'But the basket . . . Christmas . . what . . ?'

'Oh, that was just in case *he* was here. An excuse, for I knew I could say nothing if he was, but now . . . Oh, Mammy, I've waited for this day for ten whole years. Ever since Daddy died, I've wanted ter bring yer from this place ter somewhere clean an' good an' healthy. Somewhere yer could be as yer were when Daddy . . . and now I can.'

'But Rosie, darlin' . . .'

'Don't talk, Mammy. Just get together the things you want to take . . .' Rose looked distastefully about the room, as if studying every poor article, and already consigning each one to the devil. There wasn't a shred or stitch that was worth taking, or that would fit into the lovely place she had prepared.

'. . . in fact, Mammy, let's just go and leave the blessed lot. You won't need them. Everything is ready for yer. Oh, Mammy . . .' She turned rapturously to her mother, her hands together like a child at prayer, her eyes stars in her rosy face.

'It's taken a long time, Mammy, but Lacy and I are doing well now,' she said proudly, 'and I have money. I can afford to keep you in a nice place. Tidy, neat and clean. Oh, Mammy, you'll love it. A cottage on Captain Osborne's place near Tuebrook. There's a little garden, and a yard at the back where you can keep . . . Mammy, Mammy! What is it? What's wrong, Mammy?'

The silence was as thick as the pall of polluted smoke which hung above the rooftops of Bridie's home. It seemed to gather about the two women, as ominous as a pack of rats circling a frightened terrier. It stretched on and on, and Rose felt her mouth dry up with the first stirrings of fear. Her mother was staring like one who has suddenly come upon some unexpected and alarming discovery which puzzles beyond belief. Her eyes were clouded with unease, and an expression of animal wariness settled on her face. She drew back as though into the safety of a lair.

At last Rose found her voice. 'Mammy,' she croaked, then cleared her throat, and put out a hand to her mother.

Bridie drew back a little more, then smiled disarmingly, saying brightly, 'Faith, child, 'twill be dark soon an' yer with all that way ter go back up there. Now come along an' get yer bonnet on, our Rosie, an' wrap up warm fer 'tis a cold day out.'

She turned to the children who sat like small, inscrutable sphinxes upon their mattress. The food was scattered about the place in nauseating heaps, and from a corner, two bright eyes and the twitching whiskers of a brown rat could be seen. Bridie saw it and advanced upon the horrible creature, holding her skirts and flapping them until it vanished into whatever crevice it had come from. 'Yer 'ave ter watch the divils, or they'd 'ave the very food out o' yer mouth,' she fretted.

Rose might not have spoken.

For all the concern Bridie took in her last few sentences, they might have been about the chill of the day, or the price of mutton in St Johns' market. Rose sat, her face slack, watching Bridie bustle about, as she brought Rose's bonnet and her shawl, stroking the fine wool, and exclaiming at its warmth and softness.

She has not understood. She thinks I speak of someone else, or the gin has pickled her brain until she is incapable of comprehending something which is unfamiliar. Rose felt her heart move in compassion for her mother. She does not realize that I am offering her a lovely home in the country, where she will be safe from the attentions of Lancer McGhee, she thought. Where she can be clean and respectable, and can bring up her children . . .

Her thoughts quickened as sudden understanding came to her. Of course, that's it. She thinks I mean to take her away from the children: that she is to come alone, and leave them here to die. She is afraid I am attempting to part her from the only blessing she has. She might have abandoned them years ago, if she had a mind to it. Have gone from here and found employment in a decent house. Perhaps returned to her home in Ireland, but because of them she has suffered Lancer, and the filth with which he has coated her in his evil. She is afraid. Afraid.

Rose began to smile with relief, and she stood up.

'Mammy. Listen ter me, Mammy. Did yer think I meant

384

yer to come alone? I mean yer can take the kids with yer. There are three bedrooms in the cottage, Mammy. Just think o' that. Three bedrooms an' a lovely little parlour, an' a big kitchen with a range, so yer can cook all the things yer want, an' bake as well. An' wait till yer see the garden. Of course there's nothin' growin' at the moment, 'cept a pretty rowan tree with berries as red as a ... Mammy, Mammy. Oh, please, Mammy ...'

Her voice faltered uncertainly, as Bridie's face retained the blank closed look of a person who not only does not hear what is being said, but does not want to hear. Rose babbled on, talking of a cow and hens, and a pig or two, and a bit of a vegetable patch, convinced that if she continued long enough her Mammy would understand. The idea was so incredible, so hard to believe, Bridie was confused, but in a minute she would grasp it. Then they would all be away in the carriage to the cottage where Maggie waited, tending fires and heating water, for they would all need a bath, and then Mammy would sit in the big comfortable armchair which Rose had picked herself, and the fire would warm her, and the cup of tea in her hand would be good and strong, and ...

'Mammy?' Rose's voice trembled like that of a child in the dark. 'Mammy. Please, Mammy. Talk ter me. Tell me yer understand. Don't yer know what I'm saying? I've come to take yer ...'

'No.'

Rose flinched and her face quivered with a fearful pain.

'Mammy, I don't know what yer mean. I'm wantin' yer ter be away wid me ter a lovely 'ome. The Irish lilt real now, as a terrible fear took Rose in its grip. 'Please, Mammy. Don't look like that. Say yer'll come wid me. Say yer will.'

Bridie backed away, and her eyes searched the foetid room, looking for somewhere to hide. She put out her arms to her children and gathered them about her, frantically lifting the youngest into her arms, pressing the small apricot curls to her cheek. Rose held out her own arms beseechingly and tears poured down her bewildered face.

'Mammy, ger yer shawl, Mammy, an' put the children's

boots on. Quick. Oh, quick, before he gets home.' She moved unsteadily towards her mother, But Bridie's voice, shrill and terrified, stopped her.

'No, our Rose, no. Don't make me, please don't make me.'

'Make yer! Make yer! Mammy.' Rose shook her head, horrified.

'I can't leave 'ere acushla. This is me 'ome. I can't leave 'ere.'

"Ome!' Rose's voice was shrill with disgust. 'This is no 'ome, Mammy. I've got a 'ome fer yer. A lovely 'ome where yer can be daicent again. Look at yer, Mammy. Me Daddy wouldn't know yer.'

Bridie's face crumpled, but Rose's pain was too great for her to see.

'I'm givin' yer a chance ter start again. Ter get away from the muck yer wallow in, an' yer say yer can't leave yer 'ome. All these years I've wanted ter fetch yer from it, Mammy. It's all I've thought of each time I've come 'ere an' seen what yer've sunk ter, an' now yer say yer can't leave 'cos it's yer 'ome. Holy Mother, I wouldn't keep pigs 'ere. Them at Silverdale in their sty live better'n yer.' Her voice gasped and choked, as though she could not get the air quickly enough to her lungs to speak the words.

'Daddy'd turn over in 'is grave if 'e saw what yer've become,' Rose said.

Bridie put her head back and howled, and the children began to sob. They had seen so much, these creatures of the slums in which they were forced to live. Bad and evil things. They had experienced cold and hunger, and had watched indifferently each night, as their father grunted upon their mother, but he was a familiar devil. They had turned their heads from Bridie's drunkenness, for it was as natural to them as the lice they scratched. But they were not equal to the sight of their mother howling like an animal.

In all her predicaments Bridie had taught herself to be quiet as the grave in which her love lay, for in silence was quick release from Lancer, a hiding place from his drunken outrage. But now, in her sorrowful anger and fear, she cried out at the fates which had brought her escape too late. She was angry for the first time since Sean had died; angry because she knew there was no deliverance for her; and sorrowful for the child who had tried to help, but who had been too slow about it.

'Rose. Aah, Rose, don't. Don't say such things ter me. Don't hurt me any more, fer don't I know what I am, alannah.'

'Why, Mammy. Why?' Rose was passionate in her desperation. 'What are yer afraid of? Lancer won't be able ter . . .'

'I know, I know. It's just that . . .' Bridie turned away, hugging the child to her, and the rest stared balefully at Rose. 'I can't explain, Rose. So much 'as gone . . .' Her voice became soft, thready, as memories came to knife her. '. . . all the ones I loved, and the good times . . . Everythin's bin taken. 'Cept this. This room I lived in with yer Daddy.' Her frame shook convulsively. Rose took a step towards her, and though Bridie's back was turned, she seemed to know.

'Don't touch me, darlin', please. Just go away ter yer grand life. If only yer knew what joy it brings me, Rosie, ter know that me girl is . . . livin' so foin an' so 'appy.'

Rose felt her insides twist, and she gripped her fists to her side. Oh God, she thought, if only she knew. But Bridie was still speaking, and the smiling face of James Osborne, which had for a moment distracted her, fled away with Bridie's words.

'But yer see, lovely, if I was ter leave 'ere I'd 'ave nothin' left of them days. I sit in the chair,' her voice was soft and reflective, 'an' I talk to 'im an' I'm pretty an' 'e loves me. So sweet, Rosie, so sweet. I can't leave 'im, Rosie. I'd be afraid ter go in case 'e didn't come wi' me. This is where I belong, Rose. Until I go ter join 'im, this is where I belong.'

'No, Mammy. 'E'll come wid yer in yer 'eart. Please Mammy. 'Tis a beautiful place. Yer'd be so 'appy, an' I could come an' see yer every week, an' the children would get fat an' healthy, an' . . .'

'No. Stop it, Rose. I said no.'

Time stopped, and movement, and sound. Even the

children ceased their whimpering, though they still clung to their mother's skirts. Rose stared at Bridie's back, then her eyes slid away to the palliasse, where the rat, his stealthy approach unnoticed, was gorging the remains of the feast. The fire snapped, and a voice from the courtyard screamed to someone to 'give over or I'll knock yer nose off, yer little bugger!'

The kitten stirred, leaping frivolously to its feet, saw the rat and retreated behind the pan of congealed stew, then as if reminded of its own hunger, put its paws upon the rim of the pan and delicately lapped the skim of fat within.

Rose felt her stomach begin to lurch, and the breakfast she had eaten so recently, and in such excitement, began to heave towards her throat.

'Mammy,' she whispered despairingly, 'Please . . .'

'Put yer bonnet on child, and be away. Thanks fer the 'amper an' all.' Bridie did not turn, and her calmness was terrifying, for it signified to Rose the awful finality of her dream.

'Now yer be 'avin' a nice Christmas, darlin', and' we'll see yer in a month's time. Don't fret about me, Rose. 'Tis long past the time fer frettin' about me. Get on wid yer own life. Yer're a good girl, Rose, an' I always ask the Dear Mother to look after yer, 'cos yer deserve the best. No mother could've 'ad better. Now, be off wid yer. Wrap up warm.'

The men on the box of James Osborne's carriage listened aghast to the demented weeping inside, as they careered round the corner from Vauxhall Street, across Dale Street and into St Johns' Lane. Jonas was tempted to get Jack to stop the horses' headlong gallop, and allow him to enter the carriage to comfort the woman within. To Jonas, Rose was still in many ways the whimsical child who had grinned at him so many years ago, and when they had shared their homesickness. But, he reminded himself, as the sound harrowed him, she was neither child nor servant now.

Rose was calm when they arrived at Upper Duke Street. She thanked Jonas politely, as he handed her down from the carriage.

# CHAPTER 27

It was nine months before James introduced his partner to the
men with whom he had been doing business since August of
the previous year, and as Lacy had predicted, though they
were at first belligerent in their outrage at being outwitted by
a woman, swearing they would find another importer from
whom they would buy their sugar, rum, cotton and fruit, they
did not take their custom elsewhere as they threatened. They
were not fools. They were men of commerce, whose profit
very often depended upon the saving of a farthing on a pound
of cotton or fruit. Their livelihood was made up of such
small amounts shaved from the cost of a purchase, and upon
the reliability of deliveries. They needed to have the
reassurance that the goods they bought were quality; that the
merchant with whom they dealt was honest; and that his word
was as good as his bond.

For nine months, with Captain Osborne, they had found all
of these things. Consternation reigned for a month or two, but
as Lacy and Rose moved into the world James had opened up
for them; walking the road which, but for him, they would
never have been able to take; their quiet demeanour; their
knowledge of their own business; their skill with a row of
figures; and the information which they seemed to have at
their finger tips about world market conditions, impressed the
men who had turned them laughingly from their doors for
almost two whole years. Even the daring, and sheer bloody
cheek, with which Miss Hemingway and Miss O'Malley had
outfoxed them, seemed in a strange way to have earned the
two ladies their admiration.

And the two ladies never appeared to forget that they *were*
ladies, and often charmed a grudging disbeliever into thinking
it wasn't so bad after all, doing business with a woman.
Gradually, as the months went by, James moved im-

perceptibly away from 'Hemingway and O'Malley', until Lacy was in complete control at last of her own business. From her office in Strand Street, she overlooked the unloading of her goods for the warehouse in Gorée Piazza – as yet she had not built her own, although she intended to – watching the competent way in which Michael O'Shaughnessy dealt with the men who worked under him, supervising the removal of one cargo to allow in another.

She paid for the space on many vessels now, as the tonnage she shipped increased, and she was at that moment awaiting the arrival in India of a young man she currently employed to act as her agent in the purchase of Indian tea, silk and rice; and was biding Mr Moore's approval of another, whom she proposed sending to Shanghai.

The Burrows brothers and Sheridan Bonfleur had gained her permission to buy and sell produce on their own behalf, as speculators, sending back goods to England in return for shipments which they sold in the markets of the countries in which they worked. She had ensured that no cargo they bought or sold interfered with the profits she made, before saying yes, and she knew from Mr Moore that his nephews, becoming as astute as their uncle, were beginning to build up a steady market; not only for her but also for themselves.

'I shall have to look for new agents, Mr Moore, for they will soon be starting in business on their own,' she joked, as he told her proudly of their endeavours. But he had been quite shocked, as if she had questioned the integrity, yet again, of his family name.

'Never. Oh, never, Miss Hemingway. Let me assure you that they have your best interests at heart. They both employ men now, who act as *their* representatives to negotiate the purchase of the commodities they freight. But you, as their . . . patron, if you like, have first call on their services. They can never forget that you gave them their start.'

Under Mr Moore's watchful eye, she invested wisely in many small shipping lines and bought as many shares as she could get her hands on in the bigger ones.

Then there was the matter of another type of cargo, which

was beginning to catch the imagination of Lacy Hemingway and which, in her opinion and those of other shippers in Liverpool, could only prove to be one of the most lucrative of the century.

Until three years before, most of the Liverpool emigrant trade had been carried by American companies, with bigger and faster ships than those of their British competitors, which sailed on regular schedules. Then, as the import trade of Liverpool grew, and small companies such as Lacy's were founded to deal with it, the supply of British shipping space increased, and surplus capacity sailing west went begging. Something had to be found to fill it, besides Sheffield cutlery, Manchester piece goods, Yorkshire woollens, coal and salt. So what better than the human cargo which was flooding the American continent like a vast tidal wave?

Liverpool was the ideal jumping off point for these human flotsam, who appeared to be obsessed with deserting the Eurpoean communities into which they had been born for the unknown 'New World' which beckoned. They went in their thousands, leaping like lemmings from the lands they loved into an unchartered sea.

From France and Germany, Russia and its surrounding offshoots; from Ireland and Scotland; and across the North Sea from Scandinavia they came, looking for the most economical way to cross the Atlantic. The railway ran like arteries to the heart of Liverpool, offering reduced rates for those who had pre-paid tickets. To travel steerage on a packet ship cost eight guineas. The ship might carry about 640 adults, and fifty or so children in its holds, depending on its size and allowing approximately 1s per passenger per day for food, the profit was obvious.

But that was before the Act of 1855, which regulated the horrendous conditions under which many of the passengers travelled. Requirements for space were increased, and a doctor had to be carried aboard those vessels which carried more than three hundred passengers. There were to be separate water closets for women, and all unmarried men over the age of twelve must be found quarters in the forward part of the ship.

Profits fell from then on. The large returns from the human cargo trade were not as easy to come by. The journey by sailing ship was now not only hazardous, and fraught with difficulties, but also subject to financial loss, as passengers were no longer allowed to be crammed into the hold like bales of cotton.

But the steamship would change all that.

A steamship of her own. A whole fleet of steamships flying the flag of the 'Hemingway and O'Malley' line. A flag of her own.

Lacy turned her chair towards the deep bow windows of her office, and stared across the milling wharf to the clustered masts of the sailing ships. They were like graceful women, swaying and curtseying in the last cotillion at the ball. They had glided for centuries across the dipping waters of the River Mersey, out to the estuary and beyond, their frailness carried by the wind to Ireland.

As they grew bigger and stronger, their courage took them hesitantly, but bravely, to further shores, carrying cargoes which they exchanged for others, more exotic, often priceless. They were beautiful, most of them, as they danced in the fading light on the shining water, lit by the spring sunshine which turned their cream sails to gold.

An American clipper from Shanghai had docked an hour since, and her beauty as she rode the swell at the mouth of the harbour tore the heart from Lacy, and made her blood pound in her veins. Tears had come to her eyes as she watched, for she knew she witnessed a dying race, like the lovely horses which pulled James's carriage, but which were giving way already to the railway, and no doubt, in the future to other mechanical contraptions. The ship was long and lean, with sharp bows and a vast nimbus of sail, and it had quivered as it knifed through the water, its masts, it seemed, at breaking point, as every scrap of canvas almost lifted it from the seas that held it; as if it was trying to fly.

The loveliness of it had stopped her breath in her throat, but she had turned her back, studying determinedly the plans of a steam ship which lay on her desk.

Steam. Not paddle steamers like those of Mr Cunard, but iron-hulled, propeller driven ships. Iron was stronger, lighter, less easily damaged than wood. It could match a paddle steamship in both speed and manoeuvrability, and its success as a carrier of emigrants across the Atlantic was assured. The initial difficulties of propeller driven steamships were overcome now, and with the new tandem compound engine, reducing coal consumption, it could undertake longer sea voyages, even to the China Seas and the trade there.

Lacy swivelled round again in her chair, but this time did not see the beauty of the sailing ships which rode at anchor almost beneath her window. Her eyes were clouded with dreams, not of sails and lovely, racy bows flying through the water, but of a fleet of fast, efficient, black-hulled steamships, flying at their mast the flag of the 'New Hemingway and O'Malley Steamship Line'.

It was in May that Matthew Osborne died of a coughing fit. It flung his already weak heart into a convulsion, and he gave up life as tamely as he had tried to implant it into the womb of his wife.

James Osborne became heir to the Osborne wealth and estate. As he said wryly to Lacy, when they sat at dinner alone the next night, Rose having suddenly become struck down with a headache – a frequent happening these days, and one which worried Lacy – Matthew had been most opportune in the timing of his death.

'Why, Jamie? What do you mean?'

'Well, having completed one term of employment, I find it almost convenient at this moment to begin another.'

'Yes. I can see what you mean. It would have been most remiss of him to leave us whilst you were working for me.'

James laughed.

'You really are the most heartless jade I have met. Does it not concern you that my brother has died?'

She looked up from the peach she was peeling, and paused before she spoke.

'I must be honest, Jamie. I scarce knew Matthew. He was

393

so much older than you or I. He seemed more of my . . . of your papa's generation than yours. How old was he?'

'He was only forty, Lacy. No great age at all.'

'No, I suppose not,' she said, although, at the age of twenty-two, it seemed as old as Methuselah. 'Will you go to live at Highcross?'

Assuming that Matthew would inherit Highcross, the family home, James had bought a charming house, Beechwood Hall, on his return from India. It lay in the vicinity of Tuebrook, and he and Lacy had spent many pleasant hours filling it with lovely pieces of furniture, supervising the clearing of acres of garden, refurbishing and redecorating, and employing servants to run it. It was a pleasant family house, with eight bedrooms, and a vast amount of space in a wing which would be ideal for a nursery, he had thought hopefully. He had lived in it now for three months, forsaking the rooms at his club, but with the death of his brother, he supposed his place was at the home which would one day be his. His father was old, nearly seventy, and the running of the estate was beyond him.

James shrugged his shoulders and leaned back in his chair, one arm across its back. His left hand toyed with some grapes upon his plate. The pale gleam of the lamp fell about his bent head, lighting the deep brown of his hair to chestnut. His eyes were vague, unfocused, and his thick lashes cast a shadow on his cheek. As Lacy looked at him, awaiting his answer, she was struck with the thought of what an exceptionally attractive man he was. She had not noticed it before.

The past three years she had concerned herself with nothing but the starting of her business. Men as men, not business associates, had not featured in her affairs. She did not look upon them as the male sex, attractive or not, only as a means to bring about that which was closest to her heart: the acquisition of ships, wealth and power; and the knowledge that, if she had these things, she would have won, despite what her father and Luke Marlowe had done to her. They had scarred her lovely, trustful spirit, firing it in a furnace of hatred to a blade-like hardness.

Only for one man did she have respect, trust and a strong affection. He sat opposite her, absently picking at a black grape, squeezing it between his fingers. Lacy felt her face form in a soft smile, and a strange tremble moved in her breast. Her eyes were half closed as she studied him, and her hands were still upon the plate which held the half-peeled peach.

Suddenly, as James exerted more pressure on the skin of the grape, it burst, and the juice squirted upwards onto his white ruffled shirt. He jumped, and so did Lacy, and the moment was shattered in rueful laughter.

'Damnation! It's all over me. Sorry, Lacy. I do apologize for my language. No leave it, my dear. Do not concern yourself. The mark will come out when the shirt is washed. I was miles away, considering your question.' He turned and picked up his glass of wine. 'Shall we sit by the fire?'

They moved to the chesterfield, which was set before the fireplace. Copper turned his head to look at them as they sat down, then flopped back on to the comfort of the rug, sighing in the way a dog will when it is content with its place in life, and the company it keeps. He was eleven years old now, and though at times as frivolous as he once was as a puppy, he was now beginning to enjoy the compensations of the elderly, and was inclined to lie in a patch of sunlight or close to the fire, as though his bones needed the warmth.

'You were asking me whether I will move back to Highcross now that Matthew is gone. I suppose I should. Father will be taking me to the office for a while, until I settle into the supervision of the business, but the nine months I have spent with you will have stood me in good stead. Of course, he is retired, but I do not suppose he will mind coming out for a while. Mama can be very trying. She regulates his day like a nanny in charge of a child, and he can scarce go to the . . . to the . . .'

'Bathroom?'

'Yes, bathroom.' He laughed, and shook his head, taking her hand in his. 'Lacy Hemingway, you never cease to amaze me. You say things to me my own sisters would not say to each other. It is a joy to find a woman who is not afraid of uttering a word which is perfectly ordinary, but which seems to fill the minds of most women with the utmost horror. I remember, years ago . . .'

He grinned at her, kissed her fingers affectionately, and returned them to her lap, and Lacy was disconcerted by a small feeling of disappointment as he did so. The touch of his warm, firm hand had been pleasantly comforting, and she had enjoyed it but did not know why. He had touched her before, held her arm and hand, and, in a brotherly fashion, had thrown a careless arm across her shoulders. She had thought nothing of it. She looked at him wonderingly, but he was speaking, his voice trembling with laughter.

'. . . I remember when you and Rose had your sixteenth birthdays, and you slipped away to the beach. Do you recall it?'

She smiled, the memory washing away the strange sensation. The light polished her rounded cheeks to rose, and he caught his breath, but he was practised now in the art of concealing his love.

'Yes, I remember,' she said wistfully, 'we were children then.'

'Aah, but do you remember the talk of ladies' un-mentionables?'

'Unmentionables!' She turned to him and began to laugh. 'James Osborne! How dare you?'

'You were laughing then as well, Lacy. A little girl who had a birthday, and went to share it with another who had not the good fortune you had.'

'Rose, poor Rose.'

'Yes,' he said, unconcerned for poor Rose, 'but do you not remember what you said?'

'Jamie, it is bound to be rude or you would not laugh so.'

'Do you really want me to tell you?'

'Jamie, do not be so annoying.'

'You said to Rose that if she did not stop making you laugh you would . . . you would . . . wet your drawers.'

'And if *you* do not stop making me laugh, James Osborne, I shall wet them now.'

*

396

The sound of their laughter reached the room in which Rose lay, and she put her hands to her ears, and turned to the wall. She stared, dry eyed, at the lemon roses which clustered delicately on a trellis of gold upon the wallpaper, and wondered numbly how much longer she could go on.

She was amazed that neither of them had seen it yet, her deep love for James Osborne, for she was convinced it flowed in a visible beam from her eyes each time she looked at him; that it was there, mellow as honey in her voice, and as sweet, as she spoke his name. It wrapped itself in tentacles of steel about her body, so that she could scarcely move when she was in his presence. She had no control over her own hands, and was certain James and Lacy were surprised at the number of times she dropped something: a cup, a spoon, a pencil, when he was in the room. To her, her love was a tagible entity, part of herself, and as obvious as the fingers on her hand, or the curling swathe of hair which hung down her back. Each time he came to dine she made some excuse – a headache, a toothache, the feeling that she might be catching a chill – sure that Lacy, usually so sensitive and sympathetic to the small ailments which beset a woman, would notice and remark. But she did not.

Rose turned and looked at the square of window, seeing the familiar outline of the chimneys on the roofs of the houses opposite. She was suddenly struck by the thought that perhaps they had taken note of her absences, and were glad. Possibly they thought her tactful. If they were . . . if they were already . . . Dear Blessed Mother, what if they were already deep in love, and thought she knew, and was keeping out of their way so that they might be alone.

James loved Lacy, she knew that. She had seen it begin in him, on that day when she and Lacy had splashed like children in the water pools in the sand. She had seen it flower and grow in the last year. It was in his eyes, in the way he spoke to his love. It showed in the protective way he held her elbow, and shielded her from what he thought might distress her. To Rose, his very stance when Lacy was in the room gave off an air of deep and tender love, but she had thought that

Lacy was unaware of it and, certainly, even if she knew of it, that she did not return his feelings.

It was as convoluted as the chinese puzzles Lacy had had in the nursery at Silverdale, she thought. I love James, and feel convinced that he and Lacy must see it, and if they do not, think them blind. James loves Lacy, and I, believing she does not return his love, wonder why she cannot see it, as it shines about him like a silver cloak.

She sighed and turned on her side. Tears of anguish scoured her cheeks, and she wanted to scream, shout and laugh at the same time. She tossed on the bed, and wept until her eyes were hot and dry and contained no more moisture, then she slept.

'Will you come with me, Lacy?' James asked, as she held out his coat for him. His voice was serious now, all signs of merriment they had shared gone.

'Go with you. Where?'

'To the funeral.'

'James, don't be absurd.' Her face closed, and her eyes became that brittle silvery grey which told him she was displeased.

'Why not? You were . . . *are* a friend of the family. You knew Matthew and his wife, and were a friend of my sisters. I would like you by my side, Lacy, when my brother is laid to rest. Why will you not come?'

'You know perfectly well why not, Jamie.'

'Your quarrel with your father has nothing to do with my family, Lacy. I would like you to be . . .'

'I cannot come, James. I should have thought that perfectly clear. I can go to no place where . . .'

'Can you not say his name, Lacy? Your own father. What can have been said?'

'James, you know the story. You know why my family disowned me.' Her lips twisted bitterly. Her voice broke a little and he moved towards her, yearning to comfort, but she stepped back, in control of herself again.

Yes, James knew the story of her infatuation for a sailor on

398

a ship of her father's line, and of her quarrel with her father because of it. But she had been a child, only seventeen or so, and it had come to nothing. Surely words spoken in heat could be forgotten, and the rift mended. He knew Lacy to be proud now; proud of what she had achieved. But she was also compassionate in her dealings with others. Or had been. She had shown concern for the conditions of the men in his regiment, and the harsh lives they led, and had also been aware of the sufferings of the poor of Liverpool, though how he did not know. But her bitter grudge against her father, whose only crime, it seemed, had been to disagree with her choice of a man who she, in her youthful innocence, thought fit to marry, was almost fanatical. She said they had disowned her, which was, he was sure, an exaggeration.

A word, a move on someone's part could heal the breach. Perhaps a family gathering, sad though it was, would be the answer. She had told him very little of her life since the day she had left home. Only that she and Rose had worked, had found rooms, and that the jewellery she had inherited from her grandmother had started them in business. But she had been vague and the story was disjointed. He had not questioned her too deeply, not yet, for when he spoke of her past she became haughty, saying she did not wish to be reminded. She was looking at him now as though she thought him out of his mind.

'Do not be silly, James,' she said coolly. 'I cannot come to the funeral, and that is an end to the matter. Now go quickly, and we will say no more. I do not wish to quarrel with you after such a lovely evening.'

He left her, the evening which had held such joy, and the promise of something more, was spoiled.

Lacy watched from the first floor window as he climbed into his carriage, and felt a strange restlessness fall over her. His words about her father, and his wish for her to go with him to the chapel at Highcross and then to the funeral, was absurd, and yet, it would be pleasant to see her sisters again; and Thomas and Robert; and all the nieces and nephews who had been born in the last few years, and whom she had never seen. To be amongst people with whom she had grown up. To talk of memories shared. She had always liked Sophie Osborne, and had often wondered at her friendship with her own mama. Sophie was forthright and outspoken, but had a warm heart, and had always treated her with kindness.

They had all been brought up – these people who were part of her past life – with certain beliefs fixed firmly in their minds. She had broken rules, and so was beyond the pale, and she supposed it was useless to blame them. When James had spoken, her heart had weakened and grown soft for some of the sweetness of her childhood. She had loved her home. Silverdale. Its very name spoke of beauty, like the part of the Lake District after which it had been named. Sometimes the longing came upon her to walk up to Woodhouse Close, or to wander across the great, smooth lawn to the spinney which led to the edge of the river. The lovely spacious rooms, and the settled peace of the old house called to her, when the washed sunlight fell from a pale spring sky, or when the bracing winds of autumn drew her along like a child dragging at the hand of a staid adult, as it had on the hill at the back of Silverdale.

Oh, James. You should not have reminded me.

Lacy clicked her fingers, and the dog heaved himself to his feet, and came to her, laying his head beside her skirt. She sat down upon a small chair, and he leaned against her, gently caressing her hand with his rough tongue. He knew she was sad, and his heart strained to tell her how much he loved her. He watched her face, waiting for her to speak and when she said his name his plumey tail moved to the rhythm of his heart.

# CHAPTER 28

'There is a Miss Hemingway to see you, madam.'

Miss Yeoland pricked her thumb, and almost uttered out loud a word she had not used, nor heard, since the days of her childhood, when her father, a farm labourer on the estate of Lord Beckett in Old Swan, had cursed the sow her mother kept in the back yard of their cottage, and which had pinned him regularly in the corner of her sty.

The blood welled from the pinprick and, before she could prevent it, a spot fell upon the fine stitches of the exquisite smocking with which she was embellishing the bodice of a nightgown, which was to be part of the trousseau of Miss Susanna Bradley, daughter of George Bradley, one of the most important men in the Borough of Liverpool. It was this fact which had the needle in her fingers, for Miss Yeoland employed twenty girls to do her sewing, but her smocking was the very best, and Mr George Bradley was very influential.

For a moment her usual calm was shattered, and the thin, black-gowned apprentice who had announced the visitor was beguiled by the sight of the severe features of her employer crumpling, as if she were an infant about to dissolve into tears. It might have been the stain upon the garment intended for the virginal Miss Bradley which was ruined and would now have to be re-made, or was it the name of the visitor which had perturbed Miss Yeoland so? The young apprentice did not know. She had not been in Miss Yeoland's employ two years ago, when the dreadful scene had occurred.

It had been spring, a Monday. Miss Yeoland remembered it well, for Monday was usually a quiet day, but it seemed the mild April afternoon had turned the heads of all the ladies of Liverpool to thoughts of a new bonnet, the planning of the coming summer's wardrobe, or just the purchase of a gay sprig of artificial flowers with which to perk up last year's headgear. The salon was full, both the lower and upper floors packed with ladies, most of whom knew one another, and the polite gossip had reached a crescendo of chattering which had given Miss Yeoland a headache.

It was to soothe her head and her nerves after a tense discussion with Mrs Petch, who was enough to shatter the most resilient temper, on the merits of garnet Giselé velvet or Pekin point for her new evening gown, that Miss Yeoland had slipped away during a ten-minute lull to sip a comforting cup of orange pekoe tea in her private sitting room, and so was not there to see its beginnings. Her deputy, Miss Lake, of impeccable good manners and infinite tact, had taken over from her and witnessed the whole sorry affair.

They had met on the stairs, and what occurred was all over Liverpool by the time the salon closed its doors. Mrs Edward Lucas, mother-in-law to Thomas, and a dear friend of Sarah Hemingway, had come face to face with Sarah's disgraced daughter on the sweeping staircase which led from the lower salon to the upper. Miss Hemingway was on her way down, and those who saw it said she looked her most fetching, and that her face had lit up with pleasure at the sight of Mrs Lucas.

'Why Mrs Lucas,' she said, 'how lovely to see you. You look so well. How is Mr Lucas and Julian? Oh, and Celia? How nice you look. Is it not a lovely day. It makes one think of a new bonnet, does it not? I have just . . .'

Mrs Lucas's Celia, moving up the stairs behind, almost crashed into her mama's broad back as she stopped, momentarily speechless. Mrs Lucas had her foot poised halfway between one step and the next, her hands were occupied with the fullness of her gown, and a nasty accident might have ensued, had Miss Hemingway not put out her hand to steady her mama's friend, saying charmingly,

'I am so sorry to startle you, Mrs Lucas. You almost missed your footing. Is not a crinoline difficult to manoeuvre, particularly when one is going upstairs. Allow me . . .'

Mrs Lucas went from her usual pink-faced calm to a brilliant, outraged scarlet, and then, with the speed of a flagon of red wine being poured away, to a cold, blanched white.

402

'Take your hands off me, miss,' she said in her cool, well-bred voice, '. . . and kindly step aside. My daughter and I wish to get by.'

'Why, Mrs Lucas. I beg your pardon. Do you not remember me? It is Lacy Hemingway. My brother . . .'

'I know who you are, and I have no wish to be associated with you.'

Lacy recoiled, and her face became as white as that of Mrs Lucas. Her eyes, so bright and filled with thoughtless pleasure at this meeting, went blank, then filled with pain. She stepped backwards, her heel hit the rise of the stair behind her and, had not Rose been there with her steady hand, she would have sat down gracelessly.

All about the smart salon ladies had come to a full stop, and conversation had ceased completely. One matron, trying on a bonnet of frothy tulle and crimson roses, was quite blinded as the assistant's nerveless hands tipped it over her eyes, and was mortified to miss even a moment of the scene. A seamstress, her mouth full of pins, kneeling at the feet of the wife of a prominent member of the Borough Council, swallowed one before spitting the others in a frenzy all over the lady's stockinged feet.

It seemed to go on forever, the awful deathly hush, and the four women on the staircase were frozen in a grim tableau. Then Miss Yeoland was there, running down the stairs faster than she had moved since the same sow which had given so much trouble to her father, had chased her across the yard when she was ten years old.

She cast one beseeching look at Lacy, then turned.

'Why, Mrs Lucas. Are you hurt? You have gone quite pale. May I not offer you my private sitting room, and perhaps some tea? What a dreadful occurrence. I really thought you were about to fall. Come, let me help you. Miss Lucas, you look quite faint. Do follow me. Would you like to hold my arm?'

Lacy and Rose might not have existed.

Miss Yeoland's quick wits, self preserving, knew instinctively which of the ladies could do her the most good or harm and, in a moment, she had turned the nasty incident into one in which the notion that Mrs Lucas had stumbled, and nearly fallen, began to formulate in the minds of the onlookers, and had it not been for the contemptuous words uttered by Mrs Lucas, and Lacy's rigid figure upon the staircase, they might have believed they had misunderstood. They whispered to one another, and Lacy's story was around the Misses Yeoland's salon before the elder had Mrs Lucas upon her own chaise longue, with a fresh cup of orange pekoe in her hand.

Lacy stood rooted upon the stairs in humiliation, suffering a sense of disgrace so deep and dreadful she felt her body tremble in shame. Every eye was upon her. She heard whispers, and her own name, and she could not move. She was paralysed, and would be for ever, and those who came to call upon the Misses Yeoland would be compelled to step around her as she clung to the banister. She would be preserved always in the position she had assumed when Miss Yeoland brushed by her with the outraged Mrs Lucas. She felt scorned and lowered in the eyes of all those who stared at her, and she did not think she would ever be able to hold up her head again.

'Lacy.'

It was only a whisper. A hand touched her arm gently and she caught a whiff of the delicate scent Rose used. Rose. Rose was there. Rose was behind her as she always was. Behind her and beside her, and what else mattered? Rose was Lacy Hemingway's friend, and who else counted in this room full of old biddies?

Lacy lifted her head and her eyes glittered. She and Rose had got through far worse than this. She was not about to let a lot of silly women take from her all she had accomplished in the past year, nor let them see that the lashing words and disdainful looks had meant more to her than a momentary nuisance.

She looked around proudly, and the eyes which stared at her dropped hastily. She turned and smiled at Rose, and together they glided down the stairs and across the salon towards the door. It was closed. Lacy turned haughtily, and immediately a young assistant rushed forward to open it, bobbing a respectful and admiring curtsey.

Lacy had cried when she got home, and later, when Miss Yeoland had come in a hackney carriage and begged to be allowed to speak to her, she had at first refused. But Rose, sensible of Miss Yeoland's position, had coaxed her, and she had coolly agreed.

She had never seen the self-possessed Miss Yeoland so genuinely distressed, and had listened, and had been sorry for the woman who, like herself, had a business to run, and could not let sentiment stand in her way.

'You see, Miss Hemingway, though you and your family have been valued customers over a number of years, you are not the only ones. I make gowns and bonnets, indeed, all manner of garments for the good families in Liverpool and thereabouts. My sister and I have worked hard, harder than you can imagine, at building up our connections. We have slaved far into the night to make up orders before we were able to employ the staff we now have. It has been a long, hard struggle, but we succeeded. You, in your position, must surely understand that. I knew, for who cannot hear the gossip which goes about that you and your companion,' she bowed her head in Rose's direction, 'are just beginning to take hold with your business, and you will appreciate the difficulties . . . Miss Hemingway, forgive me, but you see, Mrs Lucas has much influence in this borough. She and your Mama . . .'

She put out a hand to Lacy as Lacy's face, understanding and sympathetic until now, became cold again, and turned from her.

'Please, I beg of you. They are friends, related by marriage, and with what your mama decrees her friends concur. I will be blunt. If you continue to patronize my establishment, you will be my only customer. Mrs Lucas has made it quite clear that she cannot enter my salon if . . .'

Miss Yeoland did not go on. There was no need. Lacy understood. Miss Yeoland had not set eyes upon Miss

Hemingway from that day to this, and now here she was, in the lower salon, asking to see her.

'Oh, Lord, Emm,' she exclaimed to the second Miss Yeoland, who was as dismayed as herself. 'What on earth can the woman want? Surely not to order a gown! I made it plain we could not accommodate her last time.' She thrust the ruined nightgown from her and paced the room.

'I hope to God none of the Hemingways' friends are downstairs. If they should see her here, they will think we are designing for her, and will go elsewhere. Wouldn't you think, after all these years – how many is it? four or five? – they would let the poor woman be. Gawd, the gentry never cease to amaze me, Emm. They really don't. You and I run a business. Successfully, too. But that's different, I suppose. It's sex, you know.'

The second Miss Yeoland gasped, and thought not for the first time their Gladys was too forthright for her own good. It was as well she kept it to herself in the shop.

'Yes, that's what it is. They don't want their menfolk having anything to do with a pretty woman, and the men, well, they're afraid of a woman they think will take away their masculinity. Eeh, Emm, I'm glad I never married.' She tutted irritably. 'Well, I suppose we'd best see her. We can't leave her hanging about downstairs.'

They circled mentally and conversationally about one another for half an hour, these two astute business women; one young, and with her foot on the bottom rung of the ladder; the other elderly, and at the top. The severely plain but smart Miss Yeoland watched the beautiful face of the woman before her, feeling none of the homely woman's envy of a lovely one. She saw not the beauty, but the strength and character that showed in the stubborn jaw, the firm mouth, and the clear, steady gaze of the unusual eyes. They took tea, and spoke of the dreadful weather, and the possibility that spring might be here soon and, at last, Lacy told her why she had called.

She smiled as she spoke, her humour warming her grey eyes, revealing to Miss Yeoland that she was completely recovered from their last meeting and, in fact, now found it rather amusing.

'I have not come to embarrass you by purchasing one of your lovely gowns, Miss Yeoland, though I would dearly love to do so.'

Miss Yeoland smiled also, and bowed her head over her teacup, admitting to herself that she liked this unusual young woman. She looked into the shrewd face, and was quite amazed as she became aware that this was no social call, but one of a more commercial nature.

'Why have you come, Miss Hemingway?'

Lacy did not look away or fiddle with her gloves, as she said directly.

'Have you any money to spare, Miss Yeoland?'

Miss Yeoland did not even blink, though her sister did, and began to squeak like a little mouse surprised by the sudden appearance of the cat.

'I might have, Miss Hemingway. What did you have in mind?'

'I intend to build a steamship, Miss Yeoland, and I am looking for partners who will be willing to put in their money. Shares will be issued, and I thought you might be interested.'

'Are there not gentlemen who . . . ?'

'I am not inviting gentlemen, Miss Yeoland. Only ladies.'

'Only . . . ?

'I want this to be a venture financed and run solely by women.'

Miss Yeoland digested this slowly, her face showing nothing of her thoughts. She might have been considering the merits of the woollens known as Valencia and Vienna, but inside she felt her elation seethe, and she longed to break out in a great cheer. It was not that Miss Yeoland was partial to flinging her hard-earned money about like a man with no arms, as her father used to say, but that here was a woman who had the guts to do something to loosen the hold of men on the world of business. There were not too many about, she thought wryly, and in her youth, had she the capital and training, she might have been one herself. But, oh, how she would champion this one! She had made up her mind in the first moments of comprehension, for she knew she was looking at a fighter, but it did not do to appear to be 'easy pickings'. Let Miss Lacy Hemingway know that Gladys Yeoland would be a partner who knew what she was about. She said,

'It is a big step to take. A risk. I know nothing about shipping, nor the financial successes or failures of your business.'

'You may study my accounts, Miss Yeoland, and Mr Moore at the Royal Union Bank in Castle Street is more than willing to tell you of my financial stability. My business is in a healthy state.'

'Then why do you need money with which to build a steamship? Can you not finance it yourself?'

'Have you any idea how much it costs to build a steamship, Miss Yeoland?'

'No, I have not.'

Lacy told her, and Miss Yeoland, her composure shattered, gasped. But before she had time to remark, Lacy's enthusiasm and her knowledge had her in a state of enthralled silence.

'Have you a notion of how many emigrants are leaving these shores, Miss Yeoland?'

Miss Yeoland murmured again that she had not.

'They can be counted in thousands.'

Miss Yeoland was silent, waiting.

'Next year I estimate that at least twenty thousand will embark from Liverpool alone. Do you know how ideally suited this port is for the trade?'

'Tell me.'

'Everything leads here, Miss Yeoland, from all over the Continent of Europe, and from Scandinavia. Railways start from their very homes and lead right into the Borough of Liverpool. The Irish, for instance, who are going in their thousands, can only sail from Liverpool. The potential is astronomical. They go by sailing and packet ships now, paying six to eight guineas per head, and the journey is unreliable.

408

But with a steamship, travelling time could be cut to ten, or even seven days, and the same back. A fleet of fast ships could earn thirty thousand pounds a year, Miss Yeoland. Ocean-going travel would be cheap. Not only would emigrants fill the ships, but also travellers who wished to cross the Atlantic in comfort, and speedily. And on the return journey, the ships could carry all the merchandise the vast continents of America and Canada has to sell. Raw cotton, of course, and wheat, timber, rubber, sugar.'

She paused, then added quietly.

'It cannot fail, Miss Yeoland.'

The room was quiet. Miss Emily Yeoland sat quietly in the background, upon her chair by the fire, looking as though she expected the hordes of Irish who were to sail to the New World to do so from this very room. Her pale blue eyes, shortsighted from thousands of hours spent sewing in the soft glow of a candle, squinted in the firelight.

She had always, during their long partnership, allowed her more forceful sister to lead the way, and Gladys had never failed her. They had made good, two country bred girls, moved by the kindly auspices of a spinster aunt to be apprenticed for five years to a dressmaker in Liverpool. When they had learned their trade, their combined talents had made them bold, and they had opened their first tiny shop, sewing for twenty hours a day, building up a growing clientele amongst the middle class women who lived in the vicinity. But it was not until a lady in society, noticing the elegance of the wife of her husband's solicitor, had asked her loftily who 'did' her gown, that the Misses Yeoland had moved from the middle class to the 'gentry', and even, on more than one occasion, to the aristocracy.

Miss Emily had done her bit, she thought to herself, working harder than her own farm labourer father in the fields. She did not begrudge it, especially now, as she and her sister approached retirement, and the money they had earned was tucked away ready for the day when they would go to live in a small house in the country, not far from where their father had laboured.

Now, in a moment she could not yet believe, it was all to be risked on the whim of a chit of a girl, who had never done a hand's turn in her life. Emm spoke up for the first time in thirty-five years.

'No, Glad. Not this time.'

Glad turned and stared in amazement at her sister, and so did Lacy, thinking as she did so that it was the first time she had ever heard the second Miss Yeoland speak.

'No! What on earth do you mean, Emm?'

'I mean that I am not risking our savings, *our* savings, Glad, on some fantasy scheme about steamships and the like. You know they won't take on. Everyone says so. Sailing ships will be here when those nasty things are all at the bottom of the ocean. Why, Mrs Petch's husband told her that the most economical way of carrying cargo was in a sailing ship.'

Her sister regarded her with astonishment.

'Whenever did you and Mrs Petch discuss the most economical way of carrying cargo, Emm? Why, she is the most empty headed ninny who ever walked into this shop, and she knows nothing about shipping.'

'Her husband has shares in shipping and . . .'

'But how did you and she come to talk of it?'

'She was telling me of her son's desire to take up marine engineering. It seems he has designed . . .'

'Oh, so *one* of the Petch family has faith in steam.'

'Oh, Glad, please don't do it. Don't risk our savings on . . .'

Miss Yeoland turned to Lacy, who sat, quietly amused, between the two sisters. She could see it was going to be an uphill battle convincing many of the women who were on her list. The elder Miss Yeoland had the far-sighted vision rare in women of the day, but most would be like poor Emm, running small businesses, mostly in the garment trade. Always ladylike, of course, and afraid to venture into the world of men.

'Let us think it over for a few days, Miss Hemingway. If I might, I will call on you at the weekend. Your office is in . . . ?'

'Strand Street.'

'Strand Street. I will give you our decision then.'

Lacy was wrong. In her pride, she had thought herself and perhaps the elder Miss Yeoland to be the only ones who had the courage to risk all they had on what was, after all, almost a new invention. But she was wrong.

With the same dogged determination and flashing enthusiasm she had shown Miss Yeoland, she went from shop to shop, for those were the businesses most of the ladies ran; describing in detail what she was about; how the enterprise would work; the organization of a company; the shares, their prices and how many would be available. Within six weeks, she had encouraged milliners, dressmakers, corsetieres, drapers, lace and flower designers, shirtmakers, and even a country woman who had opened a cheese and butter shop and was doing very nicely, to invest whatever cash they had to spare in the 'New Hemingway and O'Malley Steamship Line'.

An innovation they called it, the steamship which began to grow in the dockyard at Birkenhead. From the keel which was laid on their twenty second birthday, to the last rivet, she and Rose watched it emerge from its chrysalis, and Lacy loved it as passionately as once she had loved the graceful sailing ships.

It was *hers*.

She had done it.

She had started the line about which she had dreamed for most of her life. Through her own endeavour and determination, and sheer bloody-minded audacity, she had done it. From virtually nothing, she had built up a business which no one could take from her now. She knew with every instinct that flourished within her, that she would make a success of it. It was all there waiting for her to grab. She had all the weapons, now she would go out and conquer the world.

On the day of the launching, she watched raptly, like a woman sending a lover into battle, as her ship slid down the slipway towards the water which waited for it. The wind blew from the river and, like that first time, her bonnet slipped from her head, and her lovely, living hair lifted and flew like the flag at the mast of the ship. The flag. Her flag! Miss

411

Yeloand had designed it, and it snapped briskly in the wind, full of its own importance, convinced, it seemed, that it would fly forever. A deep red rose, surrounded by a circlet of silver lace, on a background of black, it flew proudly, defiantly, and Lacy felt her breath catch in her throat.

On her face was an expression of such joy, such blessed rapture, that James, who stood beside her, could not take his eyes from her face. She slipped her hand into his, and his heart constricted in anguish as the thought came to him that he would give half of his life to have that look directed, just once, at him.

'Oh, Jamie,' she breathed, 'Oh, Jamie. Is she not the most beautiful thing you ever saw?'

'Yes. The most beautiful thing I ever saw,' he replied.

But he was not looking at the *Alexandrina Rose*, the steamship which had just been named and launched.

# CHAPTER 29

Lacy Hemingway and Rose O'Malley moved to Beechwood in November 1859, buying it lock, stock and barrel from James Osborne, including his carriage and the four matched greys, and taking over his entire staff.

James had returned to Highcross several weeks after the death of his brother, and had spoken to Lacy and Rose of his intention to put Beechwood up for sale.

'I am afraid I must. Father is old and, though he does his best, he is no longer able to manage the estate. Matthew's widow has returned to her family in Chester, and, with all her children gone, I know Mama is alarmed to be alone. But I shall be sorry to sell Beechwood. I enjoyed the time I lived there, and felt I had put something of myself into it. I had plans for that bit of land to the rear and had intended . . .'

His voice was wistful, his eyes vague and unfocused, as he looked into the secret future he had envisaged for himself and Lacy, and several small shadowy forms, on that bit of land to the rear. He was confused for a moment, when he heard Lacy's voice saying:

'Name your price, James Osborne. If it is the right one, we might do a deal.'

James was dining with Lacy and Rose, as he did at least once a week, and both he and Rose gaped with astonishment.

'You don't mean it,' he stuttered, the turbot he was about to place in his mouth, falling from his fork to his plate.

'Lacy Hemingway, sweet Mother o' God! Whatever next! First 'tis steamships, now a foin house in the country. Bejabers, 'tis mad ya are.'

The brogue was thick on Rose's aghast tongue. She was as overwhelmed as James, and said so at length, but it did no good. It seemed Lacy could stand not another moment in the 'pokey' rooms in Upper Duke Street, which once she had so admired, saying she wanted some space around her, and a place for Copper to run, and would it not be splendid to ride again.

'So, name your price, Jamie, and Rose and I will consider if it is fair or not. We will not be done, you know.'

James laughed, he could not help it. But into his mind came the desolate thought that if Lacy had a home of her own, besides the other impediments which kept her from him, would it not further dash his hopes one day of having her for his wife?

He named a price, ridiculously low, and was rewarded by a cool gleam in the eye of his prospective purchaser.

'This is not a joke, James, but a business deal. You have something to sell, and I wish to buy. Were it anyone else, I would gladly take advantage of you, but I wish to buy, not to steal it from you. Please do me no favours.'

'Lacy, for God's sake. You and Rose are my friends. It would give me the greatest pleasure to sell Beechwood to you, but I beg you, allow me to set my own price.'

'Then there is no more to be said.'

'Damn it, woman, I have yet to meet anyone as stubborn as you.'

'Then James, you must sell your property elsewhere, and I am sure you will have no problem disposing of it at that price . . . and I am *not* stubborn!'

Lacy's eyes flashed now, and Rose looked helplessly from one to the other. Two strong personalities, each determined to have their way, and herself in the middle. For the past ten years or so, she had had the same clashing encounters with Lacy, and knew it was not the way. James had not yet learned. Though he loved Lacy, and wanted her to have all that she wished, surely he must know by now that she would be *given* nothing. She would work for it, earn it by her own endeavours, win it by cunning in the face of competition, or do without.

'Suggest a price to James, Lacy.' She broke into the argument, cool on Lacy's part, heated on James's, with a composure which was slowly becoming a part of her own fiery nature. She had learned it in her long climb upwards from scullery maid and, in the past year, it had helped to conceal the turmoil which her love for James had set boiling in her breast.

They broke off their wrangling and, diverted, as Rose had hoped, Lacy's face took on an expression of guile. She smiled sweetly, and said,

'I shall not make the same mistake as you, James, and offer an enormous sum because you are a friend. I shall suggest what I consider a fair price, and then we . . .'

'But what you consider fair might not be . . .'

'I cannot help that. I will not be made . . .'

'Faith, the pair of ye will be at it 'til the crack o' doom at this rate.' Rose's soothing voice, a mite irritable now, broke in again. 'Why do you not have the blessed house valued, and then come to a decision?'

And so they did, and on the night before the *Alexandrina Rose* was to sail on her maiden voyage to New York, and a week after they had moved in, the two young women – only twenty-two years old, but already owners of a growing fortune in property, a steam ship, an importing/exporting concern, and shares in numerous business ventures – sat together in companionable silence, and sipped a cup of chocolate before retiring to bed.

Lacy broke their peaceful reverie, speaking her thoughts out loud.

'It will be lovely, Rose, to be able to sketch and paint again. I was looking at that bit of spinney at the back of the house today. The waterfall is superb and will make a good subject to paint, and the view is magnificent through the trees to the house. Do you know, it is so long since I had a brush in my hand, I can scarce remember how to hold one.'

Rose looked at her sardonically, and Lacy raised her eyebrows.

'What is it, Rose? Do you think me unable to paint any more?'

'Oh no, I'm sure you can paint as well as you ever could, but when will you find the time to sit still long enough to put

415

brush to paper? You won't do it. You would be afraid that, whilst your back was turned, someone might send a cargo to the wrong destination, or perhaps lay a finger on the hull of the sainted contraption you call a ship.'

'She is a ship, Rose,' Lacy said indignantly. 'Just because she has no sails does not mean she cannot. Sail, I mean. Why, that sainted contraption, as you call it, will fly across the Atlantic quicker than you could ride to Strand Street in a carriage. Do you realize that tomorrow she will take hundreds of emigrants to another world. Just think, I shall be instrumental in the beginning of a new life for all those souls who will travel on the *Alexandrina Rose.*' Her voice was filled with awe, and she gazed into the fire as though it held a thousand secrets, and she would know them all.

'My ship,' she said wonderingly, 'my ship. Do you know, Rose, there were moments in the past when I thought I would never live to hear myself say those two words. *My ship.*' She turned hastily, her empty cup held limply in her hand. 'Oh, it is yours as well, Rose. You have a share in her, and all the other shareholders too, but she is mine really. Is she not, dear Rose?'

She looked uncertainly at Rose, who softened immediately, and bent to kiss her cheek. Though Lacy Hemingway was, as Rose often told her, as 'tough as owd boots' when it came to business, there was a vulnerability about her, born perhaps in that moment when she had lost both the men she loved on the same day, that could not be resisted, no matter how exasperating she was. She had a pig-headed stubbornness, an iron-willed confidence that would not conceive that anyone was right but herself. And yet at times, as now, she became like a child who has had a beloved toy stolen, and is afraid that the new one just bought will go the same way.

'Lacy, you know she is,' Rose reassured her friend. 'She has been yours from the moment when first we walked from the office to the *Annie McGregor* and put your proposition to Paul Ellis. Do you remember?'

'How could I ever forget?'

'That was the day you started, Lacy. The day it all began,

416

and tomorrow is the consequence.' Rose smiled and they were close again, as they had been as children; closer than they had been for a long time, though Lacy had barely been aware of a lack.

'I have just clung to your coat tails,' Rose continued, 'hanging on for dear life lest I be left behind.'

'No. That is not so, Rosie. I could not have done it without you, or Jamie.' Rose's face lost its animation for a moment, but Lacy still stared into the banked fire.

'You may have been behind me, Rose, but you were pushing me, not holding me back by clinging to my coat tails. Every time I turned to look behind to see how far we had come, there you were, encouraging me to go on. Now look at us. In just over three years we have the start of our own shipping line. I wonder what . . .'

Her pensive face became sharp, and she stopped abruptly.

'What do you wonder?'

'Nothing. Well, nothing important.'

'This is Rose here, alannah. Rose O'Malley.'

'Oh, Rose, I was wondering what . . . what Papa makes of it all.'

'He would be proud of you, darlin'.'

'I wonder.'

'Jane tells me . . .'

'What, Rose?'

'She said he asked if you were well.'

The silence was sombre now, as if they spoke of one who had recently died. It stretched out, and Rose thought she had said too much, but Lacy only sighed, and then said softly,

'Men are such fools, Rose. They hold dear values which are not important, and despise the only things worth having. They honour their pride above all else, and are vain of their standing in the community, and yet will throw away carelessly something which is precious and rare.'

'I know.'

'I do not speak of material things, Rosie.'

'I know.'

'Rose.'

'Yes?'

'Do you think I shall ever love again?'

The question came softly, but it struck Rose like a blow from the clenched fist of a prizefighter. She made a faint sound in her throat, and something in it made Lacy turn from her contemplation of the burning logs to look at her.

They were in Lacy's bedroom. It was a beautiful room, full of slender furniture, pretty and delicate, all picked by Lacy herself. James had let her have her head, though at the time he had not known, of course, and neither had she, that one day it would be hers.

'Pretend you are decorating it for a . . . well bred lady of fashion who is to be . . . my guest,' he had said.

'Now then, James Osborne, which well bred lady do you have in mind?'

'Perhaps yourself,' he teased.

'Now that would set the borough of Liverpool upon its ear. Do you not think they have tattled enough about Lacy Hemingway?'

'Well then . . . some imaginary lady who relishes comfort and luxury and all the finer things of life . . .'

'Like . . . ?'

But James would go no further with the delicious teasing, almost a flirtation; at the last moment he became afraid and drew back for he saw nothing in her eyes but affection and trust. With another he would have gone on with the game hoping to lead into the dalliance so sweet between man and woman. With another it would not have mattered should he be spurned but the rest of his life depended upon the way he acted with Lacy Hemingway now, and he treated her for the moment as he would a dear friend.

The room had scarcely any colour. It was white mostly, with a carpet of champagne with a haze of pale peach swirls upon it. The curtains at the window were a froth of white muslin, lined with a rich peach satin, and upon the plain walls were only Lacy's own paintings. Deep velvet chairs in cream stood before the huge, open fireplace, and on each side were shelves, a dozen of them, upon which stood lovely porcelain, crystal, and many, many books.

'What is it, Rose?'

Rose took a deep breath, and for a moment the screaming voice in her head nearly burst out. You do not see, it wanted to say. Are you blind? Are you so besotted with yourself and your toys that you are not aware of the deep and everlasting love, which is there for anyone to see? Maggie knows of it, the very servants in this house. Even Jane, wrapped about as she is in her good works, has asked me if he has spoken to you yet. He comes alive when you enter a room. His voice moves down a tone, rich and deep with tenderness when he speaks to you, and when you leave him, it is as though a candle has been blown out. It stands there waiting to be lit and perhaps another hand can put the taper to it but the flame would not take hold.

'What is it, Rose?' Lacy repeated, her face anxious. 'Have you another headache? Oh, Rose, dear. Why do you not let me call the doctor? You suffer so much with those migraines of yours. I am sure he would give you . . .'

'No. No, really, it is not my head.'

'Then what is it?'

'I was . . . pondering on your question.'

'Aah, yes.' Lacy sighed again and, picking up her brush, began to smooth her hair with long, languorous strokes.

'I was . . . conjecturing, that is all, Rose. It seems so long ago, that . . . passion . . . that desperate longing to be with one person. One is convinced, at the time, that life is not worth having unless one is in the company of the beloved. In between there appears to be nothing. Just emptiness. The day shines only if one has been in the . . . the arms of the man desired above all others. It is an obsession, and one is willing, eager to throw away everything which was once dear to minister to its needs. How strange it all seems when one looks back. Where does it go, Rose, all that emotion, all that love, that desperate yearning?

'I feel nothing now. I can scarcely remember what Luke Marlowe looks like, and yet, at the time, my whole life was hinged upon his comings and goings. Will I ever know that feeling again, do you think? And you, Rose, what of you? Do you never wish to be married, to have children, a home of your own? Do you not wonder how it would be to love a man?' She laughed shortly, not waiting for an answer. 'I can tell you that, Rose, but then you know, do you not. You saw where love led me.'

She shook her head and her hair stirred about her shoulders like a cloth of silver.

'We are twenty-two, Rosie, and considered by the standards of our day to be old maids. Shall we stay so, do you think, or shall we take a lover each?'

She laughed mischievously.

'Society has me an immoral woman now. Unladylike into the bargain, which is worse. So why do I not assume the role they already have me playing? The trouble is, I do not think I could find the time. My day is so taken up with business that by nightfall I am fit only to fall into bed, and alone.'

Rose was laughing now.

'First 'tis painting, now lovers. Sure, an' you'll be talking of a holiday next, and then I will know the mind of you has gone!'

She stood up and began to move across the room towards the door.

'I'm away to my bed. All this chatter of lovers and such makes me weary. Do you suppose that is a sign of spinster-hood?'

'Rose.'

Rose turned to look questioningly at Lacy, her mood calm now, the moment of sadness gone.

'What?' she said.

'That cottage is still empty, you know, by the gates. Do you suppose, if I came with you, I could persuade your mother to come and live in it, or would it be awkward, now that you and I are here?'

Rose began to walk back towards the fire, her smiling face becoming strained. The pain was less acute as time passed, and she had come to accept the realization that Bridie would never leave Naylor Street, but each time she went by the lodge at the gates to Beechwood, she imagined her mother, round and rosy, pottering in the small flower garden which fronted it, and her cheerful Irish voice, calling to her children. She had not mentioned it again. What was the use, she asked herself? Bridie muddled her way from day to day, draggle-tailed and slovenly, sinking deeper and deeper into a gin befuddled state which would never end. Her children ran wild, and were certainly not suitable to be brought to live in Lacy's lovely acres. A year or two ago, whilst they were still biddable, it might have been possible. They would be likely to steal everything that was not nailed down now. While Bridie could still manage to get through the day on only a glass or two instead of a couple of bottles of gin, it might have been feasible.

It was too late now.

'No. It would do no good, Lacy. She's too far gone now.'

'Oh, Rose, I am so sorry. Is there nothing . . . ?'

'No. Even if she would come, what would she do? She is beyond performing a decent day's work. Beyond even keeping herself and her home clean. I thought perhaps, being near to me and away from . . .'

'From Lancer?'

'Mmm . . . she might pull herself together. But it's too late.'

'Oh, Rose. Dear Rose. We have such problems with our parents, do we not, you and I?'


The *Alexandrina Rose*, launched in September, had taken two months to be fitted out, but now she was ready to steam to the New World. Her owners, and those who held shares in her, stood on Clarence Dock to watch the start of her first journey across the Atlantic Ocean. Her destination was New York and her cargo, besides freight, was 500 steerage passengers. Most were Irish.

There were several cabin passengers who had paid £30 each and a dozen or so who travelled second class for the lesser sum of £20, but the rest, all emigrants, had paid eight guineas for each adult.

They expected to sight New York Harbour within seven to ten days.

They formed a tight-knit, respectable little group, the

shareholders. All women, and all looking slightly nonplussed by the seething activity which went on about them, as though they pondered on how they had come to be set down in this alien world. But in their eyes shone a quiet excitement. None of them had set foot on a quayside before, and several drew their skirts about them to avoid the rough persons who jostled them, but their faces wore identical expressions of pride, and they gave the appearance of being certain that they wanted to be nowhere else in the world. They parted their closed ranks to admit two elegant and pretty young women, there was a gradual relaxing of tight faces, and smiles were seen, and even laughter.

'It has come then, Miss Hemingway, the day you have awaited so eagerly?'

'It has come, Miss Yeoland.'

The day was clear and blustery, and the ladies had to hold on to their bonnets, and cling to the skirts of their full gowns, for fear the wind would remove the one or tip the other, revealing the fluted frills of their petticoats.

The quayside was crowded with hundreds of people, many of them sailing on the *Alexandrina Rose*; the rest, it seemed, intent upon seeing them off.

'Shall we move to the rear of the dock and watch from there?' Rose asked anxiously, as several burly Scots staggered by, carrying a huge tin trunk. They had evidently come directly from a public house, for they sang lustily and apologized profusely, in a language completely unrecognizable as English, as they stepped upon her toes.

'Oh, no! It is much too exciting to watch from afar.'

'We could go aboard and sit in Captain Jefferson's cabin until she sails.'

'Oh, Rose, I could not sit still. I want to be amongst the crowds and feel the thrill. Look at all the people who have come to see her steam away.'

Lacy's face looked exactly as it had done nearly twelve years ago, when her father's ship had been launched. Brilliantly sparkling eyes beamed out of a rosy, flushed face. Her lips were parted in an endless smile, and she clutched her reticule to her with the glee of a small child at a treat. She had given up the effort of holding her bonnet, and the wind blew beneath its brim, wisping her hair in strands of curling silver across her face. She brushed impatiently at them with her free hand.

Officers were shouting commands relayed from the captain, who stood in the wheelhouse, and seamen began to juggle with ropes and cables. A dense billow of black smoke shot out of a funnel, then a plume of white steam, quickly shredded by the wind. The deep roar of the ship's siren echoed about the buildings on the quayside, and the noise it made quietened the screaming, shouting mass of humanity, which became recognizable as family groups, individuals and friends parting company.

An elderly woman sobbed brokenheartedly upon the chest of a sad-faced man, constantly looking from her husband's black frock coat to wave jerkily to a young couple upon the deck of the ship. Several children leaned against young parents, unconcerned, it seemed, by the grieving of their grandparents. It was probable they would never see them again.

'Mary, Mary!' a woman screamed, 'Don't forget to write now.' And Mary, leaning on the ship's rail, bowed her head in anguish, and clutched her bag to her, as though it was the only link she had with the world she was leaving.

Everywhere people wept and clung together, inconsolable with the pain of parting. A man sat upon a pile of rope, his face hidden in his cloth cap, and a woman patted his shoulder, saying, as one would to a child, 'There, there now. It won't be long, it won't be long,' though to what she referred was a mystery.

A curious quiet fell upon the crowded dock, as the *Alexandrina Rose* moved imperceptibly, inching away from her mooring. The sliver of mucky water, six inches wide, between the ship and the dockside, became a foot, a yard. Hands reached out to the vessel as if to make contact for one last time with a departing son, daughter or brother, but the gap was too wide.

The noise had stopped now. Those who were left behind stood quietly, as did those on the deck of the ship: both looking, as they well knew, for the last time at one another. A man's voice began to sing, strong and sweet. He was not of the land from which he sailed, and the language he sang in was unknown to most, but the exquisite sadness of the song tore at hearts which were breaking, and tears poured unchecked from a hundred pairs of eyes.

The fine, glad rapture of the day had gone, as Rose and Lacy stood side by side and watched the wrenching sorrow of those who were left. The ship was a hundred yards away now, and the pure voice of the man who sang could hardly be heard, as the cheerful sounds of a quayside returning to normality after the sailing of a ship, took over. Dockers whistled and shouted, and pushed their way, unconcerned, through the silent press of people who watched the steamship. They had seen it all before. But the crowd, with Lacy and Rose amongst them, watched until the ship was gone.

'Come on, acushla, let's get back,' Rose said gently.

'Yes.' Lacy sighed deeply, turning with Rose towards Strand Street.

For the brief moment which it took to turn, take a step, and look into the eyes of the man who stood directly behind her, Lacy was conscious only of a mixture of emotions brought about by the sailing of her new ship. There was compassion for those who had parted, together with pride that, although her ship brought heartache to some, it was the instrument which would give hope and a fresh life to those who sailed in her. There was a gladness and an excitement which contact with the river always gave to her. And in her businesswoman's brain, there was the cool consideration of the profit to be made.

All these feelings vanished, as she turned and saw, with agony, standing on the dock, only a foot away, Charles Hemingway.

'Lacy.'

Charles Hemingway's voice was soft, almost a whisper, and if Rose had not seen his lips move and shape his daughter's name, she would not have known he had spoken.

Lacy swayed, her feet fused to the spot on which she stood. Her face was the colour of skimmed milk, with almost a sheen of blue in it. She could not move.

'She is a fine ship, Lacy. You must be proud of her.' His words could be heard now, as the crowd disappeared and quiet fell, and as if encouraged by the fact that she stood and listened to him, he smiled.

'I stood and watched her go. I knew she was yours, and I came down especially to see her go, Lacy.'

He held out his hand to her, his face pleading for her understanding. She flinched away, staring at it as though it were a cobra about to strike.

'Lacy, please . . . I am so proud . . . you always said you would . . . When you were a child, you said you wanted . . . Lacy.' His voice broke a little and, despite herself, Rose felt her heart go out to him.

'Lacy . . . If you knew how I feel. That a daughter of mine should . . .'

'I am no daughter of yours. You have no daughter called Lacy.'

His face muscles jerked, and he reeled back in horror.

'Come, Rose. We have a busy day ahead of us.'

Taking Rose's arm, Lacy began to walk steadily across the wharf, towards the steps which led up to Strand Street.

# CHAPTER 30

'It is your birthday, and I insist that we celebrate. Ye Gods, woman, do you realize how long it is since you had a party?'

'I refuse to give a party, James. There would be no one present besides you, Rose and I.'

'I am not asking you to give a party. I intend to give a ball for you.'

'A ball! You must be mad, or drunk, James Osborne.'

Lacy shook her head, throwing it back in the extravagant fashion which Nanny Wilson had deplored, and laughed loudly. Her shallow-crowned wide-brimmed leghorn hat fell to the back of her head, held by the ribbons tied beneath her chin. James watched her carefully, his expression unreadable. She moved ahead of him on the grass, turning so that she walked backwards, and her face was as merry and relaxed as a child at a picnic.

'Oh, Jamie, be serious. If you insist we celebrate, we shall, Rose, and you, and I. But really, we are twenty-three, and surely long past the age for . . .'

'I am perfectly serious, Lacy.'

'Oh, Jamie, really you are the most . . . the most . . .' She stopped in front of him, and her voice trailed away uncertainly. The smile slipped from her face, her cheeks quivered, and her eyes were bewildered. The expression in them seemed to say that she was not quite sure whether or not to laugh, but should it all prove to be a joke, she was quite willing to share it.

It was the beginning of June, and the sun shone from a deep blue sky. Far away to the west, a procession of pure white clouds lazed along towards the river, and the Irish sea, like a line of fat lambs in the wake of their mama. It was pleasantly warm, and James had left his coat in the house. His shirt sleeves were rolled up to just beneath his elbow, and he had removed his cravat. His arms and throat were already brown. The wound in his leg was completely healed now, and he had discarded his stick. He looked fit and healthy, and his eyes shone with a curious light which Lacy had never seen before.

They stood facing one another beside a group of young conifers, recently planted. Beyond was a cluster of grey, pitted rocks, from the crevices of which grew alpine plants. Their clean, green, yellow and white leaves and petals almost covered the stone. The grass had been mown right up to the rocks, but tufts grew around their base where the gardener's shears could not reach. Older pine trees and junipers formed a semicircle at the bottom of the grassy slope, which undulated from the house, and a bench had been placed beneath their shade. Further on, a small lake swam in a haze of midges. It was edged with chickweed, comfrey and willowherb, their reflections still in the flat, placid water.

Looking back, the outline of the house could be seen, honey-coloured in the golden sunshine, its stone garlanded with ivy. There were many chimneys, big bay windows and turrets, the roofs of which were tiled in pale green, at each corner. All about the house were the beech trees which gave it its name. It had a look of patient endurance, like a comfortable mother surrounded by her family.

'Jamie.' Panic gleamed in Lacy's eyes.

'Yes, Lacy?' His were sure and steady.

'Do you mean . . . do you mean that you will give a party at Highcross for my and Rose's birthdays?'

'Yes,' he replied quietly.

She flung her head in the air imperiously.

'Then you *are* mad.'

'Why?'

She turned angrily, but her eyes held a strange expression, and he knew suddenly she was afraid. She had thought him to be teasing when he spoke of a celebratory party at Highcross, but now she could see he was not, she was afraid. She would not admit it even to herself, so she became angry, pretending that it was at his own foolish perversity. But James Osborne

427

was getting the measure of Lacy Hemingway after almost two years of her constant companionship. Scarce a day went by when he did not see her, and her character, her emotions, her personality, the way she thought, the manner in which her reasoning moved were becoming as familiar to him as his own. She still had the power to surprise him, but he considered himself an expert now on the ways of her mind. He should do, he told himself, for had he not studied her and her every mood with the passion of a scholar coming to grips with a subject which consumed him. He worked towards one objective. His life for two years had been concerned only with the reaching of it and before that, since he had known her, she had held his interest as no woman ever had.

He looked into the anxious depths of her crystal eyes and thought she had never been more beautiful, and that he had waited long enough. Seven years was apprenticeship enough in the wooing of Lacy Hemingway. He was thirty-three years old, and ready to settle down and begin his own family.

Why the moment, this particular moment, was inexplicably the right one, he was never to know, or even what it was that made him rush to seize it. But some instinct, perhaps an expression which seemed to linger about her eyes now and then; something he was aware of, but reluctant to test for fear of rejection, now made him bold. Bold as he had once been with others. Bold but not cocksure. James Osborne was never that.

He watched her as she flounced up and down the slip of water and smiled again, outwardly this time, for never had he thought to see Lacy actually flounce.

Her gown was of saxony blue, glazed taffeta with a fichu of embroidered tulle of the same colour, and her Italian straw hat was trimmed with ribbons and white silk lily of the valley, clustered beneath its brim. A broad sash whittled her already tiny waist to nothing, emphasizing her small breasts, which had rounded nicely with maturity.

He walked slowly across the grass towards her. Taking her hand, he tucked it beneath his arm. Drawing her with him, he strolled towards the lane which led to the road. It was split

428

about halfway down by what were known locally as 'kissing gates', and beyond the gates was the little lopsided lodge which had once been intended for Bridie O'Malley.

They reached the dry stone wall which edged the lane, and stopped. Lacy bent down and plucked at a white stalk of the 'field mouse's ear' which grew in mad profusion beside it, then turned to gaze across the lane towards the woodland garden on its other side. Rhododendrons and azaleas grew alongside camellias and all manner of flowering shrubs which thrived under the trees. She was struck by the beauty of a sycamore tree. On the side where the sun touched it, the leaves were a bright and vivid green, but in the shade, the green was dark, almost black. A breeze had sprung up, and the foliage rippled like sea water. Light and shade. Pale and dark. The branches, which barely showed, were brown and woody under the dense foliage, and the leaves danced and turned away from the wind.

For an instant, everything was forgotten, and her fingers itched to be about a brush. Her eyes narrowed, and she planned the colours she would mix. She could see the first strokes upon the paper.

James watched her and knew he must speak.

'Highcross will be mine one day, Lacy, you know that.'

'Yes, Jamie.'

She spoke like a child who had been told to stand up smartly and speak out clearly.

'My father takes no part in the running of the estate nor of the business. He is getting old. He likes to sit in his chair in a corner of the walled garden, and watch the flowers grow, he says.' James smiled. 'He is a kindly man, Lacy, led by my mother. He has only a few years left, and is content to leave all the management to me. My Mama is wrapped up in her grandchildren. She has become a little vague since Joanna married. There is only myself at home of all her children. She finds me intolerant of her desire to gossip, but she is fond of me, I think. What I am trying to say, dear Lacy, is that neither of them are ogres. They will not turn away if I wish to bring you to my home.'

'And Rose?' Lacy's voice was abrupt. 'Rose was once a servant, James. Will she be as welcome as you seem to think I will? And, before you say another word, let me tell you I go nowhere Rose does not.'

'Rose is fortunate to have such a loyal friend.' A flicker of pain crossed James's face.

'Rose is *my* friend, Jamie. My one true friend beside you.'

James turned away to hide his face, and Lacy stared at the back of his brown neck, as though daring him to speak against Rose.

'Let me do this for you and Rose, Lacy. Please.'

Lacy sighed, and shook her head. He does not understand, the gesture seemed to say. As he turned to look at her again, James caught the tail end of it, and grinned suddenly.

'Why is it, Lacy Hemingway, you always think you know better than anyone else what is best for you?'

'Because I know myself, and because I know those who once called me friend.'

'But that was so long ago.'

'They will not forget, Jamie. Do you think that polite society will come to a ball where a fallen woman is to be present? You are a fool if you do. No one will come. There will be you and I and Rose, and, if you say so, your mama and papa, but no one else. I am content with what I have, and I would not go back to that stifling way of living, even if I could, but your mama would be humiliated. Would you do that to her?'

'Leave it to me to worry about that, Lacy. Just say you will come.'

'Will you invite the Hemingways?'

'Of course.'

She was quiet. They were both so quiet and still a dozen butterflies, small, blue and exquisitely lovely, drifted about their heads, attracted by the colour of Lacy's dress. One landed upon her shoulder, but she and James continued to stare across the garden, deep in their own thoughts.

'I do not think I could bring myself to greet Mama and Papa, James,' she said in a low voice.

430

'Why not, Lacy?' His voice was warm with compassion, for she spoke in a tone of unutterable sadness.

'It is too late.'

He took her hand and bent his head to look into her face. 'No! Do not say that. They will be overjoyed to be reunited with you. Your quarrel will be mended and . . .'

'It was more than a quarrel. You do not know what was said. You do not know . . . what I did.'

'Lacy. Oh, Lacy.' He was smiling, as though at a child who confesses artlessly to some trivial misdeed. 'I am sure it is nothing which cannot be put right, and if you and your papa never meet, you will never . . .'

'We did meet, James.'

He was still then, and incredulous. Lacy looked up at him, into his steady candid eyes, and was suddenly ashamed. He was so fine, James, so good and fine. She relied upon him for so many things, and whenever she needed him he was always there beside her. Trustworthy, but quiet about it. Not boastful. A man of his word. A gentleman. She shook her head, for she had made him into a milksop, but he was not. He made her laugh sometimes with his droll crudity on many subjects, and he was not averse to an oath or two, but he would never, never understand how it had been with her and Luke Marlowe. James, she knew, liked a pretty woman, and she was sure he was not celibate on that score, but she knew with a fine instinct that he would never seduce a virgin girl of seventeen, as Luke had done. How could she explain, therefore, what had transpired between herself and her father?

'What happened? Where did . . . ?'

'It was the day the *Alexandrina Rose* sailed for the first time. He came to see her. He spoke to me.'

'And you?'

'I turned him away.' She said it sorrowfully, almost vaguely. Her expression was clouded, as though she were a million miles away.

'Why? Why did you do it?' he said urgently.

Her expression hardened, and her eyes chilled to chips of crystal.

'Papa had . . . hurt me. What he did to me was unforgivable. He destroyed our relationship with his actions, but I know now he was . . . influenced by others. He allowed his usual compassion to be clouded by pride, by horror at my own behaviour. I was . . . an ignorant girl, made so by the way in which I had been brought up, and my inexperience led me to . . . But I thought he would understand. I wanted to be honest, but he could not bear it, the truth, and sent me away. I told myself I would never forgive him. That until I died I would never forgive him. And I never will. I never will, Jamie.'

She held the flower between trembling fingers, looking down at it fiercely, her face cold and set in a frost of remembrance. James leaned back against the wall and folded his arms, his face wary, as though at the sudden sound of distant guns. She looked up and saw it, and was filled with remorse, knowing she must tell the truth. That look of unease would turn to disgust, but she must tell him the truth. She could not allow him to continue his plans to give a ball at his home in honour of her birthday, without telling him all that had happened. Her heart ached at the thought of losing his friendship, but she realized that she had it now only under false pretences. There should be trust and truth between friends, as there was with her and Rose. Nothing kept hidden in shame, for fear of losing that friendship.

James was looking out across the green folding curves of the lawn, his face set in lines of dread, and she wondered at the clenched sternness of his mouth, and the blackness in his usually merry eyes. He looked like someone who is about to be told he has some terminal illness. As if a death sentence was about to be imposed upon him. She put her white hand on his warm brown arm, and felt the muscles tense.

'James,' she said softly. He looked down at it, and it was as if he knew already what she was about to tell him, but of course he could not. He could not begin to imagine what she had suffered, she and Rose, nor the act, committed in the name of love, that had caused it.

'Tell me, Lacy. Tell me all of it. Tell me why your father

thought you so disgraced he disowned you, and why you swore never to forgive him.'

She bowed her head and let go of his arm. Her hands hung limply by her sides, and she began to speak.

'I met him in Papa's office. His name was Luke. Luke Marlowe. He was the most handsome man I had ever seen. His eyes were blue ... so blue and bright that, when he smiled at me, I thought I would faint.'

James made a small, tight sound in his throat, and turned away from her. His hands fell to the row of stones on the top of the wall, and he gripped one tightly. His eyes were almost black, and cold as anthracite.

'We met secretly. I was allowed to go to the Royal Institute ... painting, you know,' she said distractedly. 'Rose was with me, of course, and Arkwright, but Luke and I went into the garden at the ...'

Each time she said the man's name, James flinched.

'He wanted to marry me, he said. Papa intended giving him the *Breeze*, his new clipper ship. To be her master. He loved that ship. He loved her so much he wanted her more than anything in the world. I did not know how much.' She laughed harshly, her face contorted, and tears misted her eyes.

'No, I did not know how much. I thought it was only me, you see. I wanted to tell Papa, but he would not let me. No, he said. Wait. Not yet, he said. He was afraid, Jamie. He knew if Papa found out about us he would take the *Breeze* from him, so he held me back, month after month. He wanted to make certain that not only did he have me, he had the *Breeze* as well.'

Her voice died away to nothing. High in the sky, a blackbird filled the silence, calling joyously as it swooped towards a stand of trees. The notes which trilled from it were as sweet and pure as any James had ever heard, and he felt the pain of the moment in every part of his body.

'He must have thought it time to seal our ... our secret betrothal, for one day he took me back to his rooms, and ...'

'Don't. For Christ's sake, don't, Lacy.'

433

He might not have spoken, so deep in the tragedy of the past was his love.

'I was not unwilling, James. No one had ever told me what lovers do, you see. Only Rose, who knows everything, and she was . . . kind. She did not describe the . . . what it would do to me . . . So when he . . . when he . . .'

'Lacy. Sweet Jesus, Lacy. Have you no pity?' James said savagely.

'It was all over in five minutes. I felt nothing extraordinary except the . . . it hurt me . . . He seemed to think it commonplace, and was more concerned with my appearance than with what he had done. I was returned to Rose like a parcel which has been opened, a present at which the recipient had a preliminary peep, then fastens it up again to be enjoyed more fully at a later date.'

James turned slowly towards her, and the expression of anguish on his face began to fade a little. Her simple, toneless monologue; a story of pain and humiliation so great it must be told without emphasis, or she would break, drew him from his own desolation, and he felt pity begin to melt his heart.

'Go on,' he said quietly.

'That night I could bear the deceit no longer, and I told my papa. Not what I had . . . what had been done to me,' she said hastily, 'but that Luke and I loved one another, and wished to marry.'

Tears began to slide like great, fat raindrops across her white cheeks.

'He sent me from the house. He threatened to bring the police to Rose for her part in it, and he said . . . he said . . .' She began to sob quietly.

'. . . He said he had no daughter called Lacy. He said he had no daughter called Lacy, Jamie, and that we were to be gone within fifteen minutes.'

James stared, appalled, and put out a tentative hand to her, his own despair overshadowed by hers.

'We walked to Luke's rooms, but he did not want me either, Jamie. He said I had lost him the *Breeze* and he did not want me any more. I had no one but Rose.'

434

At last James Osborne began to understand the great and unbreakable link which bound Lacy Hemingway and Rose O'Malley together. In all that had happened to her, Lacy had been left with only one steadfast handhold in her life to sustain her. That of Rose O'Malley. Turned away by father and lover, confused and in pain, deceived and left without the support of her family, she had no one to cling to but Rose.

'We stayed with Rose's mammy.'

The bald statement told him nothing. He looked at her, surprised by her expression, and by her use of the word instead of mother. She seemed to have retreated into the past, and spoke like someone who has been given a part to learn, and speaks it, verbatim, without substance or colour or inflection, and yet the tears continued to stream down her face unchecked.

'Rose's mammy lives in Naylor Street. Do you know it, James?' she asked politely. He was about to say he did not, but she went on without waiting for an answer.

'It has only one room. A cellar. The smell at first caused me to vomit quite badly, but I became used to it, but the lice were a nuisance. They would creep into the most private parts of one's body and bite . . .'

'Dear, sweet God. Oh, Lacy. Lacy, my love . . .'

'. . . and when one awoke, it would be to find a rat sitting upon . . .'

'Lacy, please my darling . . .'

'But the worst, I think, was Lancer.'

'Lancer?' His voice was hoarse, trembling with shock.

'. . . for he would pull the clothes from Rose's mammy, and throw her on the mattress, and . . .'

Fiercely, James took her in his arms and held her. Her voice was muffled against his chest and she patiently turned her head as though she must finish her tale of horror, now that she had begun.

'We had been there a month or two when it was discovered I was . . . to have a child.'

'Lacy. Lacy, my lovely girl. Oh, my love.' His arms cradled her, and his hands stroked her hair. He rocked her as sorrow

435

tore at him. All reserve was gone, and she began to cry dementedly.

'Oh, Jamie, they put a needle . . . a needle . . .'

'Ssh. Ssh, there. It is all gone now. You are safe here with me.'

'It hurt so, and I was ill, and Jane came, and . . .'

'Jane?'

'Yes. Rose sent a note to Papa to say I . . . was ill, and she needed help, but he would not come. But Jane did. She brought us food and made me well, but the baby was never born. They killed the baby, Jamie.'

James Osborne's tears of compassionate love fell upon her head, and he held her close to him. She struggled in his arms, as though trying to escape the memories which tore at her, and he soothed her; whispering of his love; stroking her hair, her back, her shoulders; holding her face between his hands, to gently kiss her eyes and cheeks, until she began to quieten.

He thought he had never heard such desolation, nor felt it. Her arms had crept around his back, and she clung to him, and his cheek rested at last upon her tumbled curls. The pins which held her chignon had come loose, and her hair hung in a thick dishevelled mass about her face and shoulders, falling down her back to her waist. His hands gripped it, and his arms folded about her shivering body, and his love, strong and incontestable, was undiminished by the knowledge that his innocent love had been taken first by another. His love had been reinforced, rather, by her pain, and the horrors she had known. He felt a great surge of reverent admiration for what she had achieved, for what she had overcome; and a humility that was strangely unfamiliar.

They stood together at the wall, locked in an embrace which contained not only love and longing, but also a calm peace, found at last after half a decade of striving, of friendship, and the knowledge that the truth lay shining between them, the burden of it more easily borne by two.

She raised her head and looked into his face. He smiled. A smile of such blinding sweetness, understanding and love, she knew then what was in him, and felt a surge of astonishment.

How extraordinary, I did not know before now that I love him. He has been my friend for so long, the idea that he should be anything else has never once occurred to me.

She smiled back, and raised her lips for his first kiss.

# CHAPTER 31

'My mother is ill, Lacy. I must go to her.' Rose stood with her back to the room, and stared out on the overgrown wildness of the sunken paved garden at the rear of the house. It had once been as neat as the stones which lay in straight lines to form an octagon in its centre, every square of soil containing flowers which stood to attention like soldiers. Steps, wide and shallow, led down to it, and to the octagonal pond in the middle, but since the owner before James had lost the wife whose pride and joy it had been, it had become overgrown and luxuriantly untidy; its flowers, shrubs and plants growing in an ecstasy of colour, spilling over onto the paths, half blocking the steps. Lacy said she liked it that way. It was as nature intended it, with a charm and personality of its own, and she quarrelled daily with the gardener, who wanted to tame its wild beauty.

So far she had won.

'But when did you hear, Rose? We have only been outside an hour or so.' She smiled brilliantly at James, and held out her hand to him, and he took it, bringing it to his lips reverently. His eyes glowed. She felt her inside flutter and, if Rose had not been there, would have flung herself into his arms, begging for more of the kisses he had showered upon her in the garden. She could scarcely bring herself back to Rose and her problem.

'I . . . I was down by the drive, and took the note myself. A carter brought it. She is not at all well. You will not mind if I go . . . stay a few days.'

'Oh, Rose, of course not. James will look after me, will you not, Jamie? And keep me from being lonely.'

She turned reluctantly from her new-found love, chiding herself for being so engrossed in her own happiness. It was difficult to concentrate on anything when Jamie looked at her

438

as he did, but she must see to Rose first, help her to get together anything which might be needed. The carriage must be called, and perhaps Mrs Hamilton might be persuaded to fill a hamper . . .

'I'm sorry, Rose, forgive me. At the moment, it is . . . Oh, Rose. I should be sad for you, alannah, but with James and I so recently . . . You do understand, do you not? We are so happy . . . and to come indoors and blurt it out to you, and then find you have bad news. Let me help you to get ready. James will not mind, will you?' She paused and added '. . . my love', then blushed deliciously and James was enchanted with her and they would have started all over again.

Rose said baldly, 'I'll go and pack.'

'Of course. I will come and help.'

'There is no need. Stay with . . . James.'

'No, I insist. Jamie has waited seven years, as he so . . . persuasively told me in the garden, so another hour will not go amiss.'

'May I help you, Rose? Is there anything I can do? Perhaps a doctor?'

'No thank you, James. I will take a hamper, Lacy, but until I see what is needed, that and my clothes will be all I will take.'

She began to walk steadily towards the door, her back straight, her dark head held high. She held her hands clasped before her, and James was suddenly struck by the clamped expression of determination upon her face. She looked as though the drawing room door was a goal of such enormity and distance it would take all her strength to reach it.

Lacy drifted behind her, glowing like a star in a dark sky, her hair still hanging down her back in disarray. Diverted by his love, James grinned, and reflected that she looked like not only a woman in love, which she had vowed to him passionately that she was, but also a woman who had been tumbled in love. She gave the appearance of a lass who has just come from a romp behind a haystack, he thought, and only needs a straw or two in her hair to complete the picture, and by God the moment Rose has gone, we will have the most joyous loving romp; and not behind the haystack, but in the bed I helped Lacy to choose. To hell with waiting for the marriage vows to be exchanged. For seven years I have deferred this day, and I will be damned if I will procrastinate for another hour. I shall marry her before the month is out, anyway. Oh Lord, did I ever think it would be as . . . ? There is no word for it, this feeling, and the joy of being loved by her at last. I can scarce wait to . . .

James Osborne watched his love leave the room, and sat back to enjoy his daydream, contemplating the bliss which was to be his. Lacy turned at the door smiling impishly, and blew him a kiss, and he sighed like a lad of sixteen, and grinned like an idiot, impatiently waiting her return.

As they went up the stairs together, Lacy turned suddenly to Rose, clutching her arm.

'Listen, Rose. Why do you not put Bridie in the carriage, and bring her back to the cottage. I will send Maggie down to supervise the cleaning and airing. She can light fires and make up beds . . .'

'No, I think not, Lacy,' Rose's voice softened, but she did not turn round. 'She will not come. I told you six months ago she would not come.'

'But if she is ill she will have no choice. Just tell Jonas to pick her up, put her in the carriage, and fetch her here.'

'What of the children? I cannot leave them without their mother.'

What a strange way she has when she speaks of them, Lacy mused, just as if they were nothing to her, as I suppose they are not, in a way. But they are her half brothers and sisters, even if she detests the man who is their father.

It did not take long to pack a bag with Rose's oldest gown, a shawl and clean underwear, though Rose snorted to herself as she put her fresh, lavender-smelling drawers in the bag. How long would they remain like that, she agonized.

They saw her off together, James's arm possessively about Lacy's shoulders. As Rose put her foot upon the step into the carriage, Lacy moved away from him and touched her arm, drawing her back.

'Rose,' she said softly. 'Do not stay away too long. I cannot manage without you, you know that. You must not stay at Naylor Street. It is not for you now. This is where you belong. Bring your mammy back here. Will you promise?'

Rose looked into the clear crystal depths, and wondered for a moment how eyes of such a pale, cool brilliance could be so warm and loving.

'I promise,' she said huskily.

Lacy put her arms about her and hugged her, then kissed her soundly on the cheek.

'Give my love to Bridie,' she called as the carriage began to crunch across the gravelled drive.

Rose looked back for a moment, and watched as Lacy ran like a bird into the arms of her love. Before the carriage had reached the 'kissing gate', they had disappeared inside the house, and Rose began to cry brokenheartedly.

The shock of seeing them walk towards her, arms entwined, had sent Rose reeling into a black hole of desolation so deep she felt she would never clamber out. She had no one to hold out a friendly hand. No one to say, 'Grasp this, Rose, and I will steady you. Take my hand and I will pull you from the hole', for the only friend she had in the world had pushed her in to it. Not on purpose, of course. But, nevertheless, it was as though Lacy had stood behind her, and Rose, not looking, had been flung into a pit of despair.

It is not as if you had not expected it, her broken mind said. He has loved Lacy steadfastly since she was sixteen, and it was a certainty that one day his love would awaken hers. Ever since he returned from India, you have watched for the answer in her face; the answer to what flowed in his, and now you have seen it, and they will be together. At this moment, they will be together in Lacy's bed. She knew, for with the perception of her own love, Rose had seen what was in James Osborne's face as she had left the drawing room. He could not wait for her to be out of the house, so that he might get Lacy into that bed. The blinds would be drawn slowly down, and Lacy would glow towards him in the dimness. He would love her slowly, tenderly and delicately, as a woman dreams of

441

being loved. No hasty, furtive fumblings, such as Lacy had described when Luke Marlowe took her; but the deep, sensuous, drowsing love which sharpens and heightens until . . .

Dear Blessed Mother, look down on me and have pity. I feel I am spying on the two people I love most in the world. I cannot tear my mind away from what is happening in that bedroom. Pray for me, Mother, and put into my mind some thought which will divert me from the agony of imagining his flesh on hers. I would sell my immortal soul to be where she is now, and that is a sin, a sin so deep it should not be contemplated. I cannot even bring myself to make the sign of the Cross.

She thought she had screamed, for the carriage slowed, and she was convinced Jonas was about to leap down from the box and enquire whether she was unwell. She had seen him look sharply at her as he closed the door of the carriage.

The sun shone heartlessly through the open window, and a thrush sang its heart out somewhere. They reached the outskirts of Liverpool, and the heat became oppressive. Soon, when they crossed Dale Street, and had been drawn inexorably into the maze of squalor beyond, the smell would begin. She was not accustomed to it now, as once she had been, and she would be sick for days.

Lancer would grin and sneer, and harp on about 'fine ladies an' 'igh-born nancies. Turn yer stumick, does it, madam?' he would say, 'well yer ain't smelled anythin' yet', and he would turn and strain and fart in his pants, and laugh until tears ran down his face, as she averted hers. She would have to live beside him now, until he either died or left home – which was not an impossibility, for he was as unpredictable now as he had always been, sometimes disappearing God knows where for days on end. That would be her future now, for she was aware that, as surely as summer follows spring, she could never again live beneath the same roof as Lacy Hemingway.

Lacy Hemingway, who would soon be Lacy Osborne.

The carriage reached Vauxhall Road, turning right into

Naylor Street. Rose heard Jack calming the horses, and the jingle of the harness as he drew on the reins. Immediately, as always, they were surrounded by a score of undernourished ill-clad children, legs bowed with rickets, eyes enormous in their pinched faces. She saw one of her half brothers amongst them, but for the life of her could not remember whether he was Seamus or Declan. They fell back as Jonas cleared a circle for her, looking intently at her reticule, for sometimes she threw a few coppers to get rid of them. She had been brought up with children such as these, and with the heartlessness of one who has lived with something which has become so familiar as to be commonplace, she ignored their poor deformed bodies, too cemented in her grief to care.

'Thank you, Jonas. If you would just carry the hamper, I will manage the bag.'

'Give it 'ere, Miss Rose. I'll carry 'em.'

She caught his eye, and was surprised by the look of concern in it. But the moment was fleeting, and she fell back into the black pit of despair.

She had been there for a week when Lacy came for her, with James. She had eaten nothing, and the soft, creamy flesh had fallen from her bones like a dish of butter left in the sun. She wore the same clothes she had worn when she left Beechwood. Her eyes stared vacantly at the creeping fungus on the ceiling, and she scratched endlessly; her finger nails raking her skin, leaving thin runnels of blood.

Bridie snoozed tipsily in Sean's chair, her mottled flesh awash with sweat, which ran down her face through the layers of dirt. The children, sitting beside their half sister on the ravaged mattress, stared incuriously at the strangers. The room was like a furnace, for Bridie had closed the windows and door before she flopped in the chair, saying brightly to the inert figure of her daughter, 'Sure, it would keep out the dreadful smell, an' wasn't it just like that Mick Geraghty ter empty 'is bucket on me clean doorstep. Never mind now, darlin', I'll see ter it later, when I've 'ad forty winks.'

For a moment Lacy thought James was going to crash to the floor in a faint, and she remembered that he had never in his life been in a room such as this. But James Osborne had seen the obscenity that had been done at Cawnpore, and the aroma there had not been flowers, and had lived in the stink of the hospital at Scutari before Miss Nightingale took over. He was soon giving orders to Jack and Jonas, moving this and that with his toe, not sure in his distaste what it was that he moved, and not about to look too closely.

Jonas was like a rock. He lifted Rose from the bed, and did not flinch from the appalling smell which came from her. Jack was not made of such stern stuff, and was heard to gasp and mutter an oath as he picked up the youngest child.

It took the three men to get Bridie into the carriage, for she fought them every step of the way, screaming she'd go nowhere without Sean. James was about to go back for Sean, thinking him to be another child, but Lacy just shook her head, afraid if she opened her mouth and swallowed some air, she would fall to her knees and vomit.

They all huddled together in the carriage, with Rose lying across James's knee, and Bridie sagging from side to side, as it took the sharp corners. It went at breakneck speed, for Lacy had instructed it, thinking to shorten the journey, and the awful feeling of claustrophobia which had come upon her, as the smell in the carriage built up again.

The children clung to their mother, drawing comfort from her, as the terror of the journey turned their white faces even whiter, and their eyes into round blobs of fear. As they thundered along West Derby Road towards Tuebrook, Rose seemed suddenly to become aware that she was no longer dying, as she hoped, upon the palliasse in her mother's kitchen. The movement of the carriage, the sun flashing across her closed eyelids, brought her from the senseless state in which she had lain for seven days. Her eyes opened, but for a moment she could see nothing, for the sunlight blurred the occupants of the carriage in its golden rays. James leaned forward anxiously, his eyes warm and solicitous.

'Rose,' he said. 'Rose, we are here. We have come for you . . .'

Rose's face lit up with a look of disbelieving joy. Her eyes shone in the filthy pallor of her face, and her mouth, cracked and broken, opened on his name.

'James. Oh James. My love, my love,' she murmured. Then her eyelids fluttered and closed, and she settled against his chest, his arms about her, like a child who has come home to the blessed comfort of its mother.

James and Lacy looked at one another, their hearts wrenched with pity and with horror. In her delirium, Rose had give away the secret of the love she had carried in her heart for James Osborne for the past seven years.

They had all been bathed, except Rose, who had been sponged down tenderly by Maggie, and put to bed. The children ate everything that was put in front of them, but Bridie grumbled, and asked where the bejabers was the gin. But the doctor gave her a sleeping draught and, for the first time since Sean died, she went to her bed clean.

James said later, as he and Lacy lay together, her head on his shoulder, in their bed in the lovely bedroom at Beechwood, 'If it had not been so deuced sad, I would have had a damn good laugh. I shall never forget Jack's face when Bridie ran naked down the path, screaming to be taken home.' He spoke with awe. 'I do not think I have ever seen such flesh, and all going in different directions at the same time.'

'Oh, don't, Jamie,' Lacy sat up, and put her hand to his mouth. 'Do not make fun.'

'I am not making fun, my darling. Far from it. What I have seen today makes me almost as bitter as the sights I saw in India. What I cannot bear to contemplate is that you lived in such surroundings. That you were . . .'

'Hush. Hush, my love. That is past. My life is now more beautiful than I could ever have imagined it to be. And it is not of me, but of Rose, we should be talking.'

The moon shone through the opened window catching on her shimmering hair, and she tossed it back impatiently; then sat up again, crosslegged and naked, and began to plait it. He watched her, fascinated, enthralled, and lost. The world could go hang, for all he cared.

'Lacy,' he breathed, and his hand reached to the nipple of her breast. It was small, like a pink pearl in the light which shone from the window and, as his fingers touched it, it peaked and hardened. But Lacy was not having it, or so she thought. She slapped his hand away, laughing.

'No, Jamie. First we must . . .'

'Never mind, first we must . . . We must do this first, and this . . .' His mouth covered hers, and Lacy fell into the rapture which had been hers a dozen times in the past week. It was like nothing she had ever known, and she was constantly amazed as she thought back to that first swift time with Luke, wondering if perhaps she had imagined that fumbling moment on the bed. The emotions which flared in her, the sensations of unbelievable delight which James awakened in her, were almost more than she could bear. To compare them to that groping embarrassment on Luke's bed was like putting a candle against the glorious rays of the sun.

'Now can we talk?' she said an hour later. 'You know what has happened to Rose, do you not?'

'Yes,' he said. Serious now.

'She loves you.'

'I think she has some . . . feeling of . . .'

'She loves you, and we have been blind not to see it.'

'We have seen only one another, my darling.'

'That has been during the last week only, Jamie. I mean before that.'

'You did not see my love for you, so why should we see Rose's?'

'Then it is I who am blind.'

'Lacy, you have had so much. You cannot be blamed . . .'

'Very well, Jamie. Let us now talk of what we must do.'

'Very well, Lacy. Let us do that.'

'Jamie, stop it. If you continue to tease I shall . . . I shall sleep elsewhere.'

'Try it.'

'Oh, Jamie. Please,' Lacy gasped, 'this is getting us nowhere.'

'But is so delightful trying, do you not think so?'

446

'James.'

'I am sorry, my love. I am sorry, but can you not see how impossible it is for me to talk of other matters, when you are naked in my arms. I think perhaps we should arise, put on our gowns, and sit by the window and talk. If I do not look at you, but stare earnestly across the garden, I should manage for five minutes.'

It took longer than that, and James was wise in his council. His concern for Rose and her family was genuine, and his sensitivity, perhaps gleaned from the years he had hopelessly loved Lacy, gave him the insight to see the misery Rose would suffer if she was made to share the home he and Lacy would have.

Lacy thought she could not love him more than she already did, but as he spoke, she felt a strong compulsion to weep, and she leaned forward and took his hand, holding it desperately to her. If I should lose this man, I should want to die, she thought simply, and an appalled wave of pity for Rose swept over her. How can she stand it? To live each day, and see him with me, and love him. It cannot be done and yet we are all she has. Her mother is less than useless, drink-sodden and needing care herself.

As the thought passed through her mind she felt a tingle of excitement, and she looked at James, and was amazed to see the glimmer of understanding in his eyes. It was as though she had spoken. She had not, but he had known.

'Bridie,' she breathed, 'and the children.'

'Yes, but will Bridie stay?'

'But, do you not see? She will think she is caring for Rose.'

'Of course, each will think the other needs . . .'

'And they will.'

The children are only five or six. They could be . . . civilized.'

'Oh, Jamie. You speak as though they were savages.'

'No, I only meant that . . . given a decent life . . .'

'I know. I love you very dearly, Jamie.'

'Will it work, do you think?'

'Rose must have a . . . goal, Jamie. A crusade, if you like.

447

Since her father died, and her mother became as she is . . . And then, when I . . .'

'Yes. Yes, I know.' Pain creased James's face.

'I was it, Jamie. She cosseted me. Though I needed her so desperately, she needed my need just as much.' Lacy's eyes were soft and unfocused.

'She always longed to bring her mother from Naylor Street. Ever since Sean died, but Bridie would never come. She was afraid, Rose said, and I suppose she could see no reason to come away, especially with all those children. I wonder where the rest are?' she mused, then shook her head.

'But now, if we tell her how dreadfully Rose needs her, if we can get her away from the gin. So many *ifs*, but it might work. The cottage is far enough away. We could be separate, and yet still together. We could look after her. Jamie, I should like to try.'

Her face was agonized.

'I could not stand to lose her, you see. If I stay with you my darling, and I must, she will go. She cannot be blamed for it. We do not choose where we love, and to see you and I . . . It could not be borne. But,' she added sadly, 'she must never know, James. She must never know that we know.'

'She is strong, Lacy, and brave. To see her mother restored would give her great joy.'

They sat hand in hand, and looked across the moonlit landscape. The ball was forgotten. A dog fox barked in the spinney at the side of the small lake, and Copper lifted his old head. Deciding it was nothing to do with him at his time of life, he thumped himself down again and sighed.

'Shall we be married soon?' James said, almost idly.

'Whenever you like, Jamie.'

'A small affair, do you think?'

'As small as possible.'

'Just you and I, then?'

'And the parson. I think he is necessary on these occasions, my love.'

They sighed, in perfect accord, and as contended as the dog.

448

# CHAPTER 32

Without Rose beside her, Lacy was forced to work harder than she had ever done before, even at the pickle factory. Rose had been in the habit of doing the vast amount of paperwork which accumulated, whilst Lacy organized the shipping of goods. She had clerks working for her and, whilst Lacy visited the cotton brokers who distributed her cotton, Rose had kept mainly to the office in Strand Street.

Now, cargoes from abroad, unloaded and stored in the warehouse under the care of Michael O'Shaughnessy, must be dealt with and sent on their way to the merchants. There was so much work to be done, the absence of Rose forced Lacy to do what she knew she should have done months ago: with her marriage to James pending, she began the job of finding men, or women if they were willing, to help her to run her growing business. It was no longer possible for her to make trips to St Helens, to Manchester, to many parts of Lancashire to do business with those who dealt in the goods she shipped. 'Hemingway and O'Malley' was no longer a business which could be managed by two people, let alone one.

Lacy had been accustomed since Mr Cranshaw had taken over the brokerage of her cotton to travel to Manchester – keeping her eye on the market, she called it – and visiting the Royal Exchange, which was the focus of buying and selling the raw cotton. The main hall was crowded from one end to the other on market days, for this was the most important cotton market in the world. Merchants, expert in appraising the quality of the bales for sale, now bowed most politely to her, for in two years she had become well-known and respected.

The most expensive cotton had the longest fibres, and she stood besides these men assessing its cleanliness, colour and maturity, and they accepted her. Cotton bought on the spot was called 'spot cotton', but there was also a complicated procedure of buying and selling cotton before it arrived in the country, though the 'futures' market, which enabled the ups and downs in the price of cotton to be compensated for. Thousand upon thousand yards of cloth from surrounding towns such as Bolton, Bury, Rochdale, Oldham, Ashton and Stockport were stored in warehouses in Piccadilly and Portland Street, and shown to buyers. The streets were filled with large, heavily laden horse-drawn waggons, piled high with bales of cloth.

Certain streets in the city dealt with certain articles. Shirts were made up in one, underwear in another. Lacy revelled in the nervous excitement, the intensity of the bartering, and the sheer exhilaration with which the busy city infected her; and it was with a great deal of unwillingness that she prepared to give it up. She told herself that she had pledged her life now to James, her beloved Jamie; and that she would, no doubt, be busy with children for several years. Until she could come back to it all, she must have men she could trust to look after it for her.

A book-keeper was employed to take over the work Rose had done, with a young clerk to help him. A permanent agent was given a room next to her own, which would be kept ready for whenever she wanted to be there; and that was whenever she wished, Jamie said. The agent dealt solely with the increasing tide of emigrants who wished to travel on the *Alexandrina Rose*, or failing that, on other steam ships sailing to America. They were now able to cross the Atlantic in relative safety at a reasonable price and, despite all weathers, on schedule. Provision of such a service required a high degree of managerial skill and, already, the keel of a sister ship was being laid over the water at Birkenhead for an owner must maintain technical and economical efficiency in the building of a fleet. More capital was required and, encouraged by the success of their first venture into the world of stocks and shares, the tradeswomen – and men – of Liverpool were clamouring to be allowed to 'get in' and have a second flutter in the 'New Hemingway and O'Malley Steamship Line'.

Competition, not only from lines in Liverpool, but also from Germany and America, was fierce. Fluctuation in the levels of trade, particularly of fruit; and the raising of raw cotton, which was seasonal; and other similar factors, demanded fresh attitudes of mind and a great flexibility in the use of resources. Young brains were needed; belonging to those who could change and bend with the new, exciting times. Those who could not adjust, and there were many, failed.

For the first time in five years Lacy was forced to relinquish, albeit temporarily as she told herself, her complete and obsessive involvement in her work. She still travelled each day to Strand Street, to keep her 'finger on its pulse', as she said beseechingly to James. But she had two people now, three if you counted Bridie, to whom she must give her time and caring.

She and James were married on 30 June 1860. There was no one present in the ancient Chapel of Toxteth, which stood at the foot of Park Lane, besides the parson, and his wife, and her widowed sister, who were arranging flowers for next Sunday's service, and who were delightfully flustered to be called upon to be witnesses.

The parson was reproving, saying he really did not know what would have become of them, had his wife and her sister not been available, and implying in his admonition that they might have been compelled to live in sin. James had been forced to put his hand to his mouth, and had not dared to catch Lacy's eye.

The quiet service, the unhurried and peaceful serenity of the small church; the absence of smirking onlookers; and the presence of the two slightly delirious elderly ladies, one of whom presented Lacy with a half opened white rosebud, gave their wedding day a charm and quiet joy which pleased them both. They felt no lack of family, though Lacy knew a moment's sadness that Rose could not share her happiness. Through all the bad times, she thought, she has been with me

451

taking the load, and now, when gladness comes, she is not here.

They told no one they were married, not even the servants at the house and, though they had been aware, as servants always are, that Captain Osborne spent his nights with their mistress, it was none of their business they told one another. But, even Maggie, that indomitable champion of 'her' young ladies, was mortified each morning to find her young mistress awaiting her breakfast in her bedgown, with Captain James lounging beside her. It was one thing to know of something, she said tearfully to Cook later, but to actually *see* it was another, and wouldn't you think Captain James would be gone wherever he went by the time Maggie took Miss Lacy's tray. But there he was, as bold as brass, right on the bed, with Miss Lacy drifting about in a garment made of cobwebs, and which was like nothing Maggie had ever seen before. Loyal was Maggie, and no one ever dared say a word in her company against Miss Lacy or Miss Rose, should they want to, but even she was shocked by Miss Lacy's behaviour.

Rose must be the first to know, Lacy said. Before anyone. That day, whilst James rode over to Highcross, she walked beyond the garden and down the lane to the cottage which housed Rose and Bridie and, as it turned out, Declan and Mary Kate. As she passed beneath the arch of the 'kissing gate', she thought back to the last three weeks, and was astonished that so much could have happened in so short a time. Their lives: her own, James's, and those of Rose, Bridie and her two children, had been completely turned around over the period.

James had gone nowhere near the cottage. As Lacy said, it would be rubbing salt into an open wound to have him smiling and nodding as though everything was perfectly normal, and Rose would need a long and restful time to recover her equilibrium.

'I can imagine the agony she is going through, James. I love you too, and the thought of you with another woman in your arms is not to be borne. To think of you and all your love which enfolds me being directed at someone else is, well, it is . . .'

She had clutched him to her fiercely, wrapping her long

452

slender arms about him with passionate ferocity, pressing his dark head between her two small breasts.

'Dear God,' she cried, 'she must be in hell.'

Bridie was tackled first. Whilst Rose slept that first day in a drugged sleep, after being spoonfed with 'pobs', as Maggie called the sweetened bread and milk she had eaten obediently, Lacy led the fearful, fretful figure of Rose's mother into the sun-dappled garden at the side of the cottage. It lay just inside the main gates of the small estate, facing the narrow lane which led up to the house. A dry stone wall rioting with campanula enclosed the sides and back, but the front door led straight out onto the grass verge which edged the lane. Foxgloves grew, and dozens of wildflowers: vibrant blue speedwell; pale lilac sea lavender; lady's smock in pink and white; and like a thing demented, upon each wall of the cottage were sweet rose briars so thick they almost covered the white plastered walls, and so beautifully scented the aroma filled the air. The contrast to the horrendous sights and smells of Naylor Street could not have been greater, and yet Bridie glanced about her as though expecting the devil himself to jump from behind the mulberry tree which grew in the corner.

There was a garden seat beneath the tree, and Lacy sat Bridie upon it. The difference in Rose's mother was unbelievable. Scrubbed clean, her hair washed, wearing a snowy white mob cap belonging to Cook, and a decent black dress retrieved from some cupboard in the house, she was unrecognizable as the slattern who had greeted Lacy amiably for the past ten years.

She sat down reluctantly, the drooping flesh of her face wobbling in dismay.

'Where are the children?' Lacy began sweetly.

Startled, for she was ready with a long list of excuses why she must return at once to Naylor Street, Bridie looked around as though she might spy them hanging about somewhere, then smiled unwillingly.

'Sure, an' the last time I saw 'em they was sittin' at the table shovellin' porridge inter their faces as fast as their two 'ands could lift their owd spoons. That there Maggie was after makin' 'em another panful, for 'twas plain as the nose on yer face they'd be inter the next like pups ter their Mammy's milk.' This last remark seemed to remind her of who she was, and that certain responsibilities lay waiting for her at home, and she continued placatingly.

'. . . an' that's what me others will be wantin', beggin' yer pardon, Miss Lacy. They've no one ter see to 'em.'

'And you. You feel better in yourself?'

Surprised, Bridie looked down at her amazing clothes, and she was Sean's Bridie for a moment, her pride in her own appearance seeming to be more than she could comprehend.

'Eeh, Miss Lacy. I've not felt so comfortable fer . . . but yer see . . .' without a pause, she began again, 'there's things ter be done . . .'

'Does not this country air smell good, Bridie? Could you not just eat it?'

Bridie sniffed politely, but it was becoming plain she was not having much more of this blarney. She must be back at Naylor Street by nightfall, or Lancer would be looking for her, and the children to be fed and, besides, there was Sean. His place by the fire must be kept for him, and his . . .

'Rose is not well, Bridie.'

Bridie turned sharply, and the sudden movement made her headache worse. A drop of gin was what she needed. That would cure her a treat. It was the blasted birds that did it, singing fit to burst a lung. It was enough to give anyone a headache. But what was it Miss Lacy had said?

'Rose?' Her voice was anxious.

'She has been ill all week, Bridie. Did you not notice? She lay on the . . . the bed at your . . . house. Did she not complain?'

'Not a word. Honest, Miss Lacy.' Bridie was sharp in her denunciation of the idea that her daughter might be ill, and she not to know of it, and in her own house as well.

'She was tired, I could see that, but she never mentioned bein' poorly.'

454

'The doctor says she must be kept quiet and rest as much as possible.'

'What's wrong with 'er?' Bridie said suspiciously. Her mouth craved a sip of gin and she began to feel irritable.

'It is anaemia the doctor says, and needs constant nursing.' Anaemia seemed as good a name as any to give to what ailed Rose.

'Never 'eard of it. She looked all right ter me last time I saw 'er.'

Bridie was confused now, and frightened. Sean, she said, though her voice could not be heard. Sean.

'Come and see her, Bridie. Come and see Rose.'

Together they climbed the steeply angled stairs of the cottage, stepping into the tiny room under the thatched roof where Rose lay sleeping. Her face in repose was like that of a child. Her hair had been tied into two thick plaits, one over each shoulder across her breast. Her face seemed shrunken, and enormous violet smudges circled her closed eyes. A young girl sat beside her, placidly crocheting some bit of a thing; and the peace in the room, warm and golden, broken only by the gentle sound of the birds in the mulberry tree, could have been the peace of a church.

'Rose. Oh, darlin'.' Bridie fell in a tumble of mother's love to her knees beside the bed. Her voice, though a whisper, reached into the consciousness of her daughter, and Rose slowly opened her eyes.

Her gaze slid about the quiet room, taking in the white walls, the pretty flowered curtains at the window, the bowl of bright marguerites glowing on the polished dresser. Her hand moved lovingly upon the patchwork quilt, caressing its clean smoothness, and as her eyes finally came to rest upon the transformed Bridie, they lit up with delight, and she held up her arms weakly.

'Is it really you?' she said.

'It is, it is that, acushla.'

Bridie held her and rocked her, and the first step had been taken.

She worried about the rest of the children though, saying

they would be roaming the streets like rag-a-muffins with her not there to see to them. So James lied to her, saying he had arranged for a kindly woman to take them in, not telling her that though he had searched the ghastly streets for days, as had Jonas, questioning the neighbours, even the truculent Lancer, they could not be found. Three of them, Seamus, Teresa and Terence, had vanished off the face of the earth. Even the police had been informed, though the local constabulary had been most perturbed when asked to enter the stews of the Scotland Road area to seek for three children who had been missing for a week. They all looked alike, the police constable had remarked, astonished by the request, and by the obvious gentility of the man who asked; there were hundreds of them. Could the gentleman perhaps give him some clue where to begin?

Lacy wondered privately to James whether they had been gone, unnoticed by Bridie in her gin-hazed oblivion, for a long time. He was inclined to agree.

'That Lancer fellow seemed most unconcerned, and quite appallingly vague about how long it was since last he had clapped eyes on them, and was only discomfited by the loss of his wife's services. I gave him a couple of guineas, and I think we will hear no more from him.'

Lacy spent most of the next week supporting Bridie's fluctuating emotions: of motherly concern for Rose; anxiety for her children 'at home'; craving for just a 'sup' of gin; and bewilderment at the cleanliness, the unearthly peace and the kindness of the servants; and fear of the great open spaces around her. Lacy knew it would take months, perhaps longer, to bring content back to Bridie. Just to place her in a snug house where she was clean and had plenty to eat was not enough. Her spirit was damaged, not only her health, and it would take more than this to mend it, but her growing joy in her babies, as she called them, was indescribable.

Declan was five years old, and Mary Kate four, and for the past forty-eight hours, when they were not eating, they had clung with their thin, stick-like arms to their mother, reminding Lacy of the baby monkeys she had seen at the

Zoological Gardens. Eyes like saucers staring in bewilderment from behind Bridie's skirts, and they could not be coaxed to utter a sound. In the tub, though their mouths opened wide in terror, their screams were silent. But they were children and therefore curious, and when nothing worse than soap and water was laid about their persons they became a little bolder, peeping out into the garden, putting a tentative wondering finger to a flower, skittering back indoors at the sight of a passing labourer, or at the sound of Buttercup lowing from the meadow.

Bridie watched them flourish, and saw her elder daughter's face soften and smile when she brought her up a good bit of broth, and the green eyes of Sean were there in Rosie, and she realized that, after all, he had come with her.

It was a month after the incident at Naylor Street, and the whole borough was beginning to rock with the scandal of Lacy Hemingway and James Osborne, when Lacy told Rose of their marriage. She was stronger now, peaceful, and overwhelmed by the joy of her dream for Bridie coming true.

They sat in the warmth of the scented garden, and watched as Bridie shouted directions to Declan and Mary Kate, who were exploring the apple trees in the small orchard. The apples were beginning to ripen, and the smell of them, brought out by the heat of the sun, filled the air of the soft afternoon.

'No. No, alannah. They're not fer pickin' yet. They're still green an' as 'ard as owd boots. Next month we'll have a few an' I'll make us a bit o' jam. See, that's the one fer bakin'. Them's fer eatin'.'

To hear her, one would have thought Bridie to have been a country woman all her life. And yet, that was how she had begun, Lacy reflected. Her roots were in the green land of Ireland, and until she had come as a young woman to the black filth of Liverpool, she had looked out of her window each day on to gentle rolling hills, green and smooth, to trees, and to hedgerows blossoming in a profusion of wild flowers. She really was only back to where she belonged.

The gin craving still had her and, telling her it was their

secret, James gave her one bottle a week. She sipped a small glass appreciatively each night before going away to her bed, and blessed the kind gentleman who had taken up with Miss Lacy, while the flabby white flesh of her began to firm up and grow pink.

Rose's hand rested relaxed upon the arm of the wicker chair which Jonas had brought over from the house. Lacy took a deep breath and, turning, put her hand upon Rose's. It was warm from the sun, beginning to brown a little. Rose looked at her, smiling as Lacy touched her.

'Rose, I have something to tell you,' Lacy said. She put out her other hand, holding Rose's between both her own. Rose's eyes darkened. As though the sun had slipped behind a cloud, her face emptied of all expression. It was the hardest thing Lacy had ever done. The stage lost a player in me, she was to say wryly to James later that night, for she must act the part of the blushing bride with just the right amount of gladness, and yet, at the same time not appear too ecstatic, for it would be as though she gloated over her catch. The man Rose loved.

'We did not wish to give you too much excitement, dear Rose. The doctor was adamant that you had a complete rest, and you know how huffy Doctor Bentley becomes when his orders are not carried out. Oh, Rose. Say you are happy for us, will you not?' She paused and smiled. 'James and I were married a few weeks ago.'

She looked off into the distance pretending not to see the faint returning colour, which had begun to pink Rose's cheeks, recede and drain away. Lacy held her hand lovingly, prattling on about having a small celebration when Rose was well, and the notion of a holiday – she did not mention the words 'wedding journey' – being out of the question.

'The work that piles up is becoming quite out of control, Rose, but I have employed a man or two to help. Your mother needs you at home now, and the two children. Are they not sweet, Rose? To think that Lancer is their father is extraordinary. Perhaps soon you will organize some education for them, and I know Bridie . . .'

Lacy watched as Rose's colour crept back, and the hand

which lay flaccidly between her own became firm, and gripped hers, and still she babbled on as though there was nothing untoward in Rose's lack of response.

'James says . . .' She knew she must mention James's name, or Rose might be suspicious, '. . . that he would be glad if you could look at a paper or two he had brought home. Some account that has him mystified, and you know how inordinately vague he becomes when presented with a row of figures. When you feel up to it, of course, he will bring it over.'

It was said.

Rose knew, and though the strain showed in the stiff set of her shoulders, and the faint trembling of her cheek muscles, she was in control. Lacy watched her as she looked towards her mother and the two squealing children. She saw Rose's face relax a little and a look of relief come into her shadowed eyes. It was as though she had suddenly become aware that her salvation lay before her. She had a family. A family of her own, and one that needed her.

She turned and smiled tremulously, and her eyes were soft with tears. But that did not matter, for everyone cries at the sight of a new bride's happiness.

'Alannah, I wish you every joy, you and James. Go now, I'm tired. Come again tomorrow and . . . tell James if he should need any assistance with his accounts, I shall be only too happy . . .' Her voice broke, and she managed a laugh.

'See now, you have made me cry. Why do women weep when they are happy?' Rose said.

Lacy walked slowly through the late afternoon shadows, back across the lawn to her home and her husband, and wondered at the incredible bravery of Rose O'Malley.

That night, in the privacy of their bedroom, Lacy and James repeated the vows they had made in the chapel at Toxteth, and the heavy golden wedding band, which had lain for nearly a month between her breasts upon a narrow ribbon, was replaced reverently upon Lacy's finger. They kissed and looked at each other, then grinned hugely. James Osborne carried his wife to their bed, and made love to her as though it

459

was their first night together. Later, Lacy Osborne was to observe,

'Do you know, Jamie, that is the sixty fourth time we have made love? You would not care to make it sixty five, would you?'

She smiled in the darkness as her husband slept, already planning the teasing he would get tomorrow.

# CHAPTER 33

They had their first quarrel three weeks later. It was too late for the birthday but they must have the ball, James said, to celebrate their marriage, and to introduce her back into society.

James's meeting with Richard and Sophie Osborne at Highcross had been trying, and though James's father had been willing to hold out a welcoming hand to his son's wife – after all, she was a Hemingway, and it was what he and Charles had always hoped for – Sophie was less agreeable. Richard, becoming delightfully vague as he grew older, could only remember the splendid parties at Silverdale when the pretty child and her sisters had romped restrainedly with his own daughters. He recalled his long-standing friendship with Charles and, somewhere, lost in the memories that were more recent, Lacy's misdemeanour of the past five years had escaped him.

But they had not escaped Sophie. Her mind and memory were vividly sharp. When James rode over to Highcross on the day Lacy told Rose of their marriage, his task was somewhat more difficult.

Sophie was 'at home' that afternoon, and several callers sat about her drawing room preparing to stay for the customary fifteen minutes, which was polite. None were more than vaguely familiar to James, and none stayed longer than five minutes from the second he walked into his mother's drawing room. When Sophie had bidden them a gracious farewell, her impeccable upbringing holding her together for the necessary length of time, she told the footman she was no longer receiving callers, then sat upon the chesterfield and fell into enraged weeping.

'How could you? How could you do this to your Papa and me? I can scarce hold up my head. All this time, and not once

461

have you come to see us, and the whole county whispering. No, not even whispering, for Beatrice Dickson was heard to say *out loud* at Mrs Girvan's in the Upper Arcade, to Edith Taylor, that you are seen leaving that creature's home each morning, and make no attempt to be discreet . . .'

'Mama, may I just . . .'

'Nearly seven weeks, and you have not had the decency to acquaint us with even your presence in this house. Oh yes, James, I know you return to fetch your clothes from time to time. My own servants inform me that you have called. I will not have it, James. Not here, on my own doorstep. I know that young men have their . . . fun, but they have the decency to keep it from the world in which their family moves. And to . . . to associate with that . . . that woman . . .'

James had been ready to apologize to his mother, for he knew he had been remiss, and that his parents must have been distressed, but now his face hardened, and he stood up abruptly. His eyes were cold, and his mama was quite taken aback, for usually James was good natured and tolerant of her meandering admonishments regarding his 'pranks', as she liked to call them. In her mother's heart, perhaps because he had never married, he was still a boy.

He walked away from her, and looked beyond the terrace to the vast rolling parkland which one day would be his, and his sons'. His back was straight, and Sophie recognized the stance, for it was one he had taken as a small boy. Stubborn, Nanny had always said he was, stubborn. But be that as it may, this thing must be stopped, or James must learn discretion. It just would not do.

'Where is Father?' James spoke to the shining window.

'Why . . . I think he is in the garden. He has . . . but what has this to do with him, James? This is between you and me. I do not wish him to be further flustered. You know how he has become. He sometimes cannot remember to change his . . .'

'I would like him to be here, Mama, if you do not mind,' James said politely, still staring from the window.

Sophie sighed and looked slightly alarmed, then said

462

irritably, 'Very well, ring the bell if you must, and send Ashworth to find him.'

Richard Osborne came into the room fifteen minutes later, with the hesitant step of a mole just come from its burrow. James was like him, or as he once had been. Brown eyes, kindly, a trifle confused, hair still thick and curly, but iron grey. Tall, bent now, stoop shouldered, though still slender. He loved his garden, the small area allowed him by the head gardener in which to do as he pleased; planting exotic shrubs from far distant places brought out on his own ships. Most died in the cool, damp climate to which they were unused, but he was never discouraged. He was to be found ambling about and muttering to himself; surveying the ornate and precisely ordered rose garden, the herbaceous borders, the neatly mown lawns; followed at a respectful distance by the suspicious gardener.

'James,' Richard Osborne said warmly. 'My dear boy. This is a pleasure. Have you just come from India?' His eyes misted for a moment, then his face cleared and he added, 'Of course you have not. I am an old fool, but time gets away from me now and again. Do you know, James, the other day . . . when was it, Thursday or Friday? I cannot quite recall . . . but I thought Grace's little one was Grace herself and I said . . .' His face quivered into a half smile, and his eyes twinkled.

'Yes. Yes, Richard, we know that, my dear.' Sophie's impatient but fond expression fell upon her husband, and he stopped suddenly.

'I am sorry, my dear. I am rambling again, am I not?'

He winked at James, and James felt a surge of affection for him.

'It is not that, Richard. It is just that James and I . . . well, we are discussing a certain matter, and though we are well able to dispose of it . . . er . . . without troubling you, James felt it imperative that you be here.'

'That is uncommon civil of him, my dear.'

The brown eyes, blurring and faded with age, looked from Sophie to James, and James was aware that the old man was not quite as vague as he pretended. The amiable obfuscation must have saved him from many of Sophie's tiresome discourses.

'Yes, my dear?' he said gently.

Sophie found it hard to mention the girl's name. For five years the very sound of it had been anathema to dear Sarah and Charles and, as things do, the crimes against society which she had committed had become so great a lady could not repeat them. The manner in which the girl had ingratiated herself into the world of the businessman was bad enough, but to trade – that word when connected with a lady was obscene – yes, *trade* in competition with her own father, was beyond speaking about.

Sophie wet her lips and began.

'We were talking of James's association with . . . Lacy Hemingway.'

Richard looked mystified.

James stiffened, then relaxed again before he spoke.

'She has changed her surname, Mama.'

'I beg your pardon,' Sophie's eyes, which had been staring modestly at her lap as she spoke of this dreadful thing, turned sharply towards her son, and her mouth fell open.

'She has changed her surname.'

'I do not understand, James.'

'She is no longer Lacy Hemingway.'

The awful, awful truth was beginning to sink into Sophie's mind, but she held it resolutely at bay.

'No longer called Hemingway,' she said desperately. 'Then what is she called, pray?' Her elderly face sagged.

James put his hand on her shoulder, looking down at her, and was sorry. She was not to blame. Society made her as she was, and though she had a kindly heart, she knew no better than to revile the girl who had fallen out of step with the rest of them. He knelt before her and held her hands, then, turning to his father who sat upon the opposite chair, he told them of his love, and when he had told them, he spoke the last words proudly.

'Lacy and I were married in June.'

'Why that is marvellous news, my boy. Charles and I have always been of the opinion that . . .'

'Richard!' The shriek of despair lifted Sophie's King Charles spaniel to his feet, and he began to bark, sharply and fearfully, in his alarm. Richard fell back in his chair, and over his old face came such a look of astonishment, James almost laughed. There was a knock at the door and Jefferson, Richard's butler, put a stately head around it, surveyed the scene with interest, then quietly withdrew.

No one noticed. Sophie's wails of blighted hopes and dread continued. What would be the consequence of this alliance upon her own place in the order of things? How was she to accept a 'fallen woman' into her home, even as her own daughter-in-law? Fresh moans, as the pictures crowded into Sophie's mind of Charles and Sarah. Dear Lord, what would they think of her? They would of course, no longer be expected to call, and she and Richard would not be welcome at Silverdale. They would never forgive her for allowing . . .

She cried for an hour. She drank hot chocolate and was soothed by her husband who, at first, not understanding or remembering the fuss about the Hemingway girl, was all smiles and congratulations. He had to be reminded by his distraught wife, but the last bullet to Sophie's maternal pride, her sense of her own status and the rightness of her actions, and her high hopes for her son had yet to be fired.

James pulled the trigger.

'Mama, in order to re-introduce my wife into the society in which she rightly belongs, I intend to give a ball here at Highcross,' he bowed to his father, 'with your permission, sir, of course. But it must be seen that Lacy is once more an accepted and . . . beloved part of a family. Our family. It could be held at Beechwood, but I am not fool enough to believe anyone will come. They would not and, in fact, it is too small for the occasion I have planned.'

Sophie sat like a figure carved from stone, the only movements being those of her tears as they slipped down her cheeks.

'I want this to be the most lavish and spectacular affair anyone has ever seen. The whole family, every one of them, will be here. Lacy will be protected not only by her husband

465

but by her husband's . . . Oh, Mama!' Control gone, James knelt before his parents, and his eyes were a soft warm brown as he spoke with the ardour of his love. He must impress upon these two the depth and width of his adoration of the woman who was the centre of his life. Who *was* his life. Without their backing, their acceptance of his marriage, and their willingness to make Lacy one of their own, it would be hopeless. He and Lacy would still be happy. They needed no one, only each other, but he wanted to see her reinstated. He did not care overmuch and neither did she, but what of their children? His voice was strong, determined.

'She is not a bad woman, Mama, as they say she is. Years ago, as a young girl, she became infatuated with an older man.' He looked into his mother's ravaged face and smiled.

'Do not tell me, Mama, that before you met Papa you did not once have a . . . fondness for some handsome sprig who made eyes at you?' Not for a minute did he consider telling them the complete truth about Lacy. They would not understand.

'James,' his mama cried, 'that may have been so, but I did not leave home over it, my dear boy.' But her hand touched his, and he was encouraged to go on.

'If her father had been wise, the whole thing might have gone its course, petered out. But she was strong willed. You know that, Mama, for Sarah Hemingway is your friend. She went against her Papa.' He spoke quietly now, simply, and the two old people were listening intently.

'She was forced to work to support herself, Mama. She had some jewellery left her by her grandmama. She approached a banker, a man of high repute, and under his guidance invested her money and, again with his help, went into business.'

He was deliberately painting a picture of a poor, deserted victim of some dreadful mistake; alone and defenceless and, as a lady should, turning for protection and help to a gentleman. Though he would never to himself denigrate what Lacy had done, he was fully aware he was taking away from her, though she did not know of it, some of the bright victory she had won. But it was the only way he knew to soften his mother's heart.

'And in all that time, Mama, she had the chaperonage of her maid.'

'That chit.' Sophie's voice was contemptuous. 'She is no older than Lacy. If it were not for her deceitful connivance this . . . this affair might have been avoided. Sarah has not a good word for her. Two young women, or rather, a lady with only a maid, living alone in rooms. It is a disgrace.'

James hesitated, then plunged again. Not lies, he told himself, just a tiny deception to help his beloved on her way.

'They lived for a while with Miss O'Malley's mother.'

The memory of the foetid cellar in which Miss O'Malley's mother had resided was smothered with such force, it was as though he feared he might transmit it in all its horror to the ignorance which was his own mother's mind.

'Miss O'Malley, as you so politely call her, was once a scullery maid in the kitchen at Silverdale,' Sarah remarked scornfully. 'I cannot imagine that the home from which she comes can be one of genteel domesticity. I believe it is in the area of Scotland Road where the Irish congregate.' One might have thought Sophie spoke of Hottentots.

James rose from his knees and paced the room, at every turn stopping to stare sightlessly at the lovely view across the undulating swathe of green towards the river. They were on high ground here, panoramic landscape of the fresh fields of Toxteth Park. It was a chequerboard of colour, varying from palest lemon, to olive. Tiny hamlets, cottages, farms, roosted like flocks of birds in the sunlight, their thatched and slated roofs, smudges of umber on the land. The air was clear and the sunlight turned the waters of the Mersey to silver. He could see the Welsh hills, a pale purple mist shrouding their peaks, and the lofty blue arc of the sky seemed to lie tenderly about the acres he loved so well. It would be his. With or without his parents' blessing, he and Lacy would call this their home one day and rear their own family here. He wanted her to become a part of it; for it to become as dear to her as it was to him. But whilst his mother refused to receive her, she must remain at Beechwood, and he with her. But he wanted his son to be born here, as he had been, and his father before him.

It all lay with his Mama. With her protection, however grudgingly given, the pilloried ghost of Lacy Hemingway would be laid to rest, and Mrs James Osborne would take her place.

Strangely, it was his father who put a blunted, soil-encrusted finger upon the weak spot of the whole structure which James had built, dashing with a few words the carefully balanced bricks of half truths.

'And what of the Hemingways, my dear fellow. Are they to come to the ball you intend to give in your wife's honour?'

It was not said maliciously, but with an air of genuine interest.

The silence which followed was like a humming bird inside James's head. The grandmother clock ticked away the seconds with the indifference it had shown all dramas, whether big or small, for the past hundred years.

Sophie stood up, her dignity and pride, bred in her since childhood, giving her the regal air of Queen Victoria herself. Sarah Hemingway was her dearest friend. Charles, though not so fondly thought of, was a part of her life and of course, as Sarah's husband, must be considered before all else. The words spoken by her own husband brought her back from the vacillations which had beset her, weakening her resolution.

Sophie's heart quailed at the notion of father and daughter having 'words' in the receiving line, and of Sarah storming from Highcross vowing never to return. Oh, what a turmoil, she agonized. Why could not the silly boy have chosen from the dozens of suitable young maidens who were available to him? Besides – her thoughts were jumping madly now – if Sarah and Charles made it evident that they would not come to the ball, neither would anyone else.

Her kind heart ached. She loved this attractive son of hers and longed for him to put a grandson in her arms. But not from Lacy Hemingway. She could not say she actively disliked the girl. It was the stigma which was attached to her which made the whole terrible affair so difficult. Perhaps, later, when the scandal had died away, she might consider having the girl for luncheon. Test the water, so to speak, and if society showed no signs of disapproval, from there a relationship might be developed.

But it was too soon now, and especially for the lavishness of a ball.

'I am sorry, James, but if you insist upon giving this ball, you will be forced to do so without a hostess.'

James's face was rigid, as though he had determined upon a path of self control.

'My wife will be hostess . . .' he began coldly.

'Not in my home, James. Not while I live.' The words were harshly said.

James seemed to sway, and the colour left his face, leaving it a curious murky grey.

Richard Osborne rocked his old frame in an effort to get up the momentum to lever himself from his chair. He took his wife's hand but she drew it away, and began to walk towards the door.

Deeply shocked, James took a step as though to follow. 'Mama, you cannot mean you will . . .'

'I shall not receive your wife, James,' she said over her shoulder, 'not whilst I call Sarah Hemingway friend. She chose her way of . . . living, and you chose her. I cannot alter that, and neither can you. Nor can we change the codes of the society in which we live.'

She turned imperiously at the door, her eyes wide and blurred with tears.

'I am so sorry, my dear. I wish . . . I wish it were different. Perhaps one day when . . .'

She did not finish the sentence. The door was opened by an unseen hand in the mysterious way of a house which has servants lurking in every corner, and Sophie Osborne swept from the room.

Richard coughed, then rubbed his hands together, as though the soil upon them had just come to his attention. He looked at his son sadly. James was still halfway to the door. As it clicked softly to, he turned at last, and looked at his father.

'She . . . she is adamant then?'

'For the moment, dear boy. For the moment.'

He was angry in his disappointment, and Lacy hushed him, as she held him in her arms in the privacy of their bed.

Maggie had gone after the customary fiddling about, which was her idea of putting away Lacy's discarded clothing, smirking smugly over the newly wedded state of her young mistress. Her joy was unbounded, for it had offended her Christian heart to see Miss Lacy so free with Captain Osborne. She had taken to calling her 'Mrs Osborne' at every chance she had, putting it at the end of each sentence, until Lacy told her sharply that 'Miss Lacy' was still acceptable, and made a mental note to employ a proper lady's maid as soon as possible. Maggie was a good-hearted and willing soul, but not used to the work in a lady's boudoir, and inclined to use the same heavy handed manner she had in 'her' kitchen in Upper Duke Street.

James buried his face between Lacy's soft breasts, holding her to him as though she was the most precious thing in the world. His voice was muffled, coming in spasmodic bursts. It was beyond belief, he said, that anyone could be so intransigent . . . so unfair . . . the damned fools could not hold a candle to what she . . . and could you credit . . . and what the blazes did it matter if . . . his father was for it, he could see . . . he liked Lacy but then, so did Mama . . . they would all come, darling . . . but if only his Mama . . .

'Hush my love. Hush, Jamie.' She soothed him with her gentle, loving hands, those which could scratch and claw in the wild abandon of her passion. They stroked his shoulders, and smoothed the back of his neck where his thick hair curled. She lifted his face to hers and fluttered kisses about his cheeks and eyes, and stayed his mouth with her own, but he did not respond. She began to move against him, using her body to detach him from this obsession he had, smiling sensuously into his angry eyes.

'Oh, darling,' he said desperately, 'what are we to do?'

'Do?' she laughed, 'why, just what we are doing now. Can you think of a more pleasant pastime?'

'Be serious, Lacy.'

'I am serious, my darling James.' She reached downwards and ran her hand across the downy flatness of his belly.

He sat up abruptly and she saw that he would not be seduced away from his anger. He wanted this thing with an intensity which surprised her. He cared not a fig for rules, for convention, nor the opinions of those who moved in his world. He had no men friends, and needed none, he said. Those he had loved as brothers had fallen at Delhi and Lucknow and Balaclava. But now, inexplicably, he was consumed with the notion that a ball must be held, and all those who had reviled her must be present.

She lay back on the pillow.

'What is it, my love? Why is this thing so important to you?'

He turned towards her passionately and, drawing her into his arms, cradled her against him, his love so strong she could feel it against her skin as acutely as the soft woollen blanket which lay tumbled on the bed.

'It is you, sweetheart. Do you not see? They must be made to see how fine you are. I am so proud of you. Proud of what you have done. Proud to love you, and have you love me. They must be made to see what you have accomplished, and be made to accept you again. You are an Osborne and, as such, part of . . .'

He got no further. With a cry of rage as shrill as a parakeet's, she tore herself from his arms and from the bed, a slender white stem in the dim light, her hair a swirl of mist as she turned.

'Accept. Accept? Why Jamie, what *do* you mean?' Her voice was mocking, but her face was like a death's head, her eyes and moving mouth black holes in it. 'I cannot quite take your meaning, my love. Please explain.'

'Lacy. For God's sake, woman . . .'

'Am I to believe that you are making this magnificent gesture in order to force the good people of the borough to accept me into their midst again?'

'Lacy, do not be so . . .'

'So *what*, James? So silly? So stupid? So like a woman?'

471

She tossed her head and her hair was a veil of pale frost. She began to stamp around the room, like an animal caged and maddened beyond reason.

'I see it all now. Mama and Papa Osborne will take me under their protective and highly respectable wing, and from there I shall be assessed by the women who have crossed the road to avoid me; who have swept by me as though I were a cowpat in a field, and just as objectionable; who have forced me to shop elsewhere lest I lose my dressmaker valued custom. They are to be invited to relent and forgive, and accept me again. I am to be given a chance to return to the sacred fold. Ha!'

She made a derisively rude gesture, picked up at the pickle factory in Mervyn Street, and James recoiled.

'Well, listen to me, James Osborne, for I have news for you. I do not wish to be accepted. Those . . . sacred cows mean nothing to me, and never will. Never will, do you hear? I have my life exactly as I want it. I have my work and I have you.'

'That is the order of importance, I suspect,' James said coldly, throwing back the covers and rising from the bed. He reached for his gown, his face averted.

'You have your work and you have me,' he repeated. 'You have what you want, you say. But do you give a thought to what I might want?'

'You wanted me. You said so. You have me, but I'll be damned if I will allow you to parade me, shamefaced, before a . . .'

'I had no intention of parading you, as you so quaintly put it, before society. I wished quite simply for my wife to be by my side, in what will one day be our home. If I used the word "accepted" inadvisably, I apologize. Now I shall remove myself to . . .'

Moving as though in great pain, he turned slowly and looked uncertainly in the direction of the bedroom door. His face was anguished, and yet at the same time, his mouth was set in a line of grim defiance. He knew he was right, it said, and he would be damned if he would stand down. But, oh, the agony of the rage which had flared and spread between them.

Lacy was poised for further attack, eyes flashing, every inch of her white flesh quivering, but as she glared at him something in his proudly held head, and his shoulders slumped in desolation, touched the love she had for him. It grew so abundantly, day by day, she had told him tenderly that she would be unable to confine it within her slim self, and would grow fat with it. And now look at her. One small aggravation, and she was at him like a tiger, her love forgotten. In the space of a pulse beat it sprang up. It fought with her anger, winning with a sureness which swept her towards him like a moth to the light.

'Jamie.' Her voice was plaintive, afraid; the virago replaced by a woman loving a man, and hurting at the pain she had inflicted upon him.

'Jamie, don't, please don't, leave me. I cannot bear to see you ... I will go to the damned ball if you say I must, but please, I beg you, do not let me ... be like this.' She could not, for she was Lacy Hemingway, say it prettily, but what did that matter. She was in his arms, and he felt the tears prick his eyes as the love they shared fused them to one.

She had the last word, as she drowsed in his arms in the aftermath of their loving.

'I will go to the ball, if there is to be one, my love, but I am damned if I will enjoy it.'

# CHAPTER 34

The crisp and furious determination with which Rose had tackled everything – from the mud traipsed across the kitchen floor in her first days as a scullery maid at Silverdale, to the battle she had fought for the life of Lacy Hemingway; from cobwebs to broken hearts – had softened now; become gentler with her final acceptance of the marriage of Lacy Hemingway to James Osborne. The impatient and vigorous attack she had once engaged upon her day and all that must be done in it; the firm belief that no one was capable of managing even the smallest task without her efficient superintendance, had weakened, almost failed. It was as though the confidence she had built up, first at Silverdale, and then when she gained admittance into Lacy's business life, had crumbled away. It had been made to do so by her unreturned love for James Osborne. She felt, in her own eyes, a lesser person. A failure.

Not only had the man she loved, loved another; but the life she had lived had been taken from her abruptly. She and Lacy had been like two young trees standing together on open ground, driven this way and that by fierce wind, lashed by storm and, at times, basking briefly in the sunshine of the good days. It had been as though they were held together and upright by one support, driven firmly into the harsh ground, and giving to each other the strength to stand with head held high. Sharing, always sharing.

The bond that had merged them into one spirit would always be there, but the link was stretched now. The cord, like elastic, allowed them to walk away from one another, but without becoming free.

The weeks which followed Lacy's news of the marriage were like an elusive dream for Rose. She was not actively unhappy. Just empty. She felt no pain, nor joy, nor anti-

474

cipation each morning at what the day would bring. She was quiet and introspective, smooth; all sharp edges gone, prickles sanded down. That moment in the garden, and her deliverance from it in the shape of Bridie and the children, had been totally forgotten.

For three months, she moved tranquilly about the cottage and garden, as elegant and attractive as she had always been, her health fully restored. She looked strangely out of place in the quaint, countrified setting, like the lady of the manor visiting a tenant. She cut and arranged flowers, did *petit point*, and read the books which Lacy brought her. When the weather was fine she could be found in the garden, a leghorn hat perched prettily upon the dark shining mass of her hair, the wicker chair in which she sat placed beneath the mulberry tree; or she would drift to a corner of the orchard where the grass grew almost to her knees, and lie upon a rug watching with seeming absorption the movement of a cloud or two.

If the children came she moved. Saying nothing, showing no emotion, she would rise slowly in the way she had now, and saunter away as though they did not exist, finding another secluded spot to contemplate the quiet empty spaces of her mind.

She avoided the house and its surrounding acres, going nowhere that was more than five minutes' walk from the cottage. When Lacy called, which was every day, she smiled, and made small talk, and waited for her to go, and was very polite. With James, who made the pretence of consulting her on a tricky point of book-keeping, she was the same; asking courteously after the state of the market, and showing him to the door with the gracious ease of a well-born lady.

In November, she returned from the calm, stultifying eye of the hurricane in which she had been held and, though the force of the returning pain was almost impossible to bear, she was in control of it, and Rose O'Malley again.

It was Bridie who dragged her back.

Rose had walked that day across the orchard and, for the first time, had climbed the stile which led to what in summer was a narrow leafy lane, edged on each grass verge with a line of elm trees. It meandered in a country fashion in little curves and bends, apparently leading nowhere. Each tree had been stripped by the autumn winds and layer upon layer of browning leaves clung about her boots as she walked. She came to a gate and leaned upon it, looking at the meadow beyond. It was rough with thistles and a myriad small bumps, as though an army of moles had taken it over. She was pleasantly tired after her walk, and went early to her bed that night, falling asleep immediately.

It was the crash which awoke her. It sounded as though some beast had entered the kitchen, and with animal strength had overturned the dresser in which the crockery was stored, and was now savagely trampling the lot beneath its hooves.

There was a crunching noise, like shells being walked upon; a thud; the sound of a door being opened, then crashing back against a wall; and from the open back door directly beneath her window a hoarse, demented voice began to shout.

'Where is it? Where in all that's Holy have yer hidden it, yer divil? I've searched the owle bloody shebang, but there's neither sight nor smell of it. 'Tis 'ere. Oh yes, 'tis here. Fer didn't I see the bottle meself, but yer've 'id it somewhere so's Bridie can't 'ave a sip. Just a sip ter be sure, that's all I'm wantin', captain.'

The voice became wheedling and began to move away from the cottage, as though the speaker was walking – or lurching – towards the gate at the side which led across the field towards Beechwood.

'Aah sur, would yer be denyin' me a bit o' peace now an' then. A foin man like yerself can manage me a nip, ter be sure. Don't be keepin' it all ter yerself now. Yer'd not begrudge . . .'

The voice became fainter, as Bridie drew further away from the house.

Rose lay rooted in her bed and waited, as she had waited for the last three months for someone to deal with the fuss which was knocking on the door of her serenity. Whenever a problem arose, if she ever became aware of it, someone had always been there: Lacy, James, or Peg, the maid who came each day, to brush it out of Rose's path, so that she might step quietly on. But it was late, and Peg was not here. She slept each night up at the house, for there was no room for her at the cottage. It had only three bedrooms: one occupied by Rose; the other by Bridie; and the third by the children.

Rose felt her heart trip, the first time it had moved beyond its customary rhythmic beat since the day she had learned of Lacy and James's marriage. She sat up slowly, then threw back the bedcovers, and went hesitantly to the window. The sky was clear and a touch of frost seemed to light up the garden and beyond, as a million stars reflected on it. A movement in the orchard caught her eye. She was just in time to see Bridie, dressed like a corpse in its winding sheet, heave herself against the gate, with the obvious intention of going through and making her way to the house. She stumbled, falling to her knees and, distinctly on the crisp soundless air, Rose heard her swear, loudly and obscenely.

'Damn the woman,' Rose O'Malley muttered through her teeth and reached furiously for the thick, quilted gown which Lacy had bought her 'just for nothing, dear Rose, but because we love you', and in the urgency of the moment, the sweetness of the words she had not heard then pierced her. But she had no time to consider them.

Pulling her gown about her as she ran, Rose was down the angled staircase, and about to rush on into the kitchen when she saw the carnage. There was broken crockery over every inch of the floor; shattered cups, plates and saucers lay like fallen leaves all about, and in curious piles, as though someone had guiltily tried to tidy them up. She could not go through without cutting her bare feet to tatters, and she had not the time to go back for her slippers.

Swivelling about, she turned to the front door, but a sound on the stairs halted her for a moment. She looked up as she ran. Two little faces peeped worriedly down at her, bright apricot hair all awry. The look of strained apprehension which had been continually theirs three months ago was back again, but Rose had no time to give for reassurance. Her mother would be knocking at the front door of Beechwood before you could spit.

'And you two can get back ter yer beds,' she screeched. 'Go on, off wid yer!'

The two faces disappeared instantly. It was language they understood.

Wrenching open the heavy front door, and leaving it swinging, Rose hurtled across the garden and into the orchard, bare white feet flashing and flinching against the frost-coated grass. She reached the gate which Bridie had left open, and skidded through. She could hear her again now, singing this time, as she weaved her way through the shrubbery of rhododendron bushes. It was the song Rose and Lacy used to sing, as they pronged the fat pickles and smart red gherkins into their jars at the factory of Mr Price and Mr Roberts.

'. . . *I kissed her twice upon the lips,*
*I wished I'd done it thrice . . .*'

She caught her at the edge of the drive, before the house. With a force multiplied by furious and mortified anger, Rose swung her about and, though Bridie was a big woman, Rose almost lifted her from the ground as she pulled her across the lawn.

'Will yer let go me arm! What the divil d'yer think ye're doin'? I was only goin' ter ask the captain fer . . .'

'Be quiet, yer stupid woman. D'yer want ter be wakin' the owle 'ouse?'

'Let go o' me.' Bridie tried unsuccessfully to release herself from Rose's firm grip, becoming truculent, as she was dragged like a resisting sack of melons through the gates and into the orchard. She muttered and groaned, and beseeched Rose to let her be, she was only 'afther a wee drop', but Rose was unrelenting.

'Just walk on, Mammy,' she said through clenched teeth, 'and be quiet, or I'll land yer such a crack yer'll 'ave a mouse as big as the stable cat in the mornin'.'

'Rosie, darlin'. Oh, Rose. I was only . . .'

Dropping the querulous, weeping, fretful Bridie into a

chair, Rose first blew on the dying embers of the fire, throwing on slips of apple wood, then bigger pieces, until a lovely bright warming blaze filled the huge open fireplace. The kettle simmered above it, on the little tripod which swung out over the blaze. They were both shivering with cold, but as soon as the first chill had been thawed, Rose stamped upstairs for her stout walking boots, looking so comic in them with her pretty blue quilted gown, that even the mawkish Bridie smiled.

Rose clattered into the kitchen. It was as though the silence in which she had lived for the past three months was gone, and everything must now be done with as much noise as possible. Savagely, she began to sweep up the debris of the crockery. She could not lift the dresser by herself so, leaving it where it was across the kitchen, she rummaged about until she found two unbroken cups and a jug of milk, and within five minutes she and her mother were sipping tea, knees to the fire, like a pair of gossipy old ladies about to divulge the latest scandal.

Rose waited until Bridie had slurped appreciatively, emptying her cup, before she began. She sat back in her chair and fixed her mother with a look of stern determination, like a parent who intends getting to the bottom of her child's latest prank.

'Now, Mammy, perhaps you will be so kind as to tell me how you came to be drunk?'

There was no sign of 'the Irish' now.

'Drunk? Why, daughter, 'twas not drunk . . .'

'Drunk, I said, Mammy. You were drunk as a fiddler's bitch.'

'Now, Rose, yer musn't speak . . .'

'I shall speak as I see fit. It seems someone has been giving you . . . something, and I intend to find out who it is, and why. I thought you to be cured.'

'Sure, an' how would you know?' Bridie had her dander up now, the notion of being chastized by her own daughter bringing her long-lost Irish temper to the burn. Though her head was clearing, the last vestige of gin-induced courage sparked her tongue.

'Wrapped up in yer dreams, so ya are, takin' no notice of no one. Like a ghostie, carin' fer no one but that laddo up there at the . . .'

'Mammy!' Rose's voice pierced like an animal in torment, and her angry, flashing, green eyes turned almost black.

''Tis true, so don't yer come babblin' ter me over a bit o' drink. I know what it's like ter love a . . .'

'Mammy.' Again, Rose's voice cried her agony. Their roles were suddenly and frighteningly reversed, and it was Bridie who had the upper hand. Almost sober now, though she had drunk the whole of the bottle of gin left her by James that day, instead of merely tasting a drop or two before bedtime as was her custom, Bridie had her wits about her. But she was falling short of the compassion she had felt in the past three months for her daughter.

''Tis 'imself who brings it ter me, yer see. When 'e comes 'ere with 'is bits o' paper 'e slips me a bottle.' Bridie laughed gleefully. 'An' a gentleman 'e is ter do it, an' all.' She became self-pitying. 'I can't stop now, acushla. It's bin ter long.' Her face was sheepish and sly at the same time.

'I 'id it from yer, Rosie, not that yer'd o' noticed. Faith, if I'd drunk it in front o' yer, yer'd not o' noticed. But I kept it an' just 'ad a little sip before me bed. A bottle'd last me a week.' This was said proudly, as though worthy of com-mendation. Then, her sorrow for herself returned, and she added, 'but I was . . . a bit . . . down tonight, lovely.' She sighed deeply and stared into the fire, her eyes melting with sadness and remembered joys.

'I think on 'im a lot up 'ere, Rose. More than ever.' She shook her head wonderingly. 'I didn't want ter come fer I thought the memory of 'imself'd die if I wasn't where . . . where we'd bin together, but all the time I'm out and about in this lovely place, I keep thinkin' ter meself, "Bejabers, wouldn't Sean love this".'

Rose was silent, her own misery forgotten.

'Can yer not just see 'im, darlin', with that dratted pig. 'E'd 'ave loved the very tail of the cratur, curl an' all.' She laughed, and leaned forward to give the fire a proprietary poke.

'An' this cottage an' all.' She looked about her at the shining warm simplicity of the small room. "E'd a bin in 'eaven 'ere.' The incongruity of the remark passed them both by. 'Makin' things, a few shelves, yer know 'ow 'e was fer fiddlin' about. An' the grand garden. We'd o' bin snowed under wi' onions an' taters. Yer Daddy would o' loved it 'ere, Rosie,' she said simply.

Rose leaned towards her mother, reaching for her hand.

'I know, Mammy. I know, but wherever he is, he will know that we are here, and that will make him glad.'

Bridie brightened.

'Yes, ter be sure, an' yer right. Oh, an' darlin'.'

'Yes, Mammy?'

'I'll tell no one, Rosie.'

Rose's face closed abruptly, not yet accomplished enough to guard against the expression of pain which moved over it.

'I mean about the captain.'

'I don't know what yer talkin' about, Mammy.'

Bridie gripped the hand which still held hers, cradling it in both her own. Her eyes were bright and loving now, and steadfast.

'Faith, would I be a mother an' not know when me own child was hurtin'?' 'E's a foin man, an' worthy of any woman's love. I know 'ow yer feel about 'im, Rosie, but no one else does, so that's a blessin'. Only the Holy Mother, an' the two o' us. We'll keep it that way.'

They both sat in silence for half an hour before the fire, both women knowing the other's weakness, and aware that nothing would change either of their yearnings, nor give them what they yearned for.

James and Lacy were at breakfast the next day when Maggie came, red faced with excitement, to say Miss Rose would like to see them if it were convenient. They were not dressed, for it was Sunday, and they had just spent a most satisfying hour upon the soft white rug before the huge bedroom fire, and they still glowed with it. For a dreadful, guilty moment, both James and Lacy felt the urge to clutch their gowns about them and hide, like two lovers caught in an unlawful act, but Rose seemed not to notice.

She was exquisitely dressed in a rich, gleaming Poult de Soie, the colour of saffron. She wore a patelot trimmed with contrasting claret velvet bands, and her bonnet was of the same shade, with a swirl of claret plumes about its brim. Her sleeves were cut wide at the wrist to reveal white lace undersleeves, and she wore gloves. She had dressed her hair carefully and it shone like jet, alive and bouncing. Her eyes were afire, flashing such a look at Maggie, the poor girl cast back into her mind in an endeavour to remember some misdeed which might merit such a glance.

Lacy said afterwards to James that she felt exactly as she had when Nanny came marching into the nursery, causing small heads to rise apprehensively, and straight backs to sit straighter in anticipatory dread.

'Ah,' said Rose, beginning to draw off her gloves, 'I'm glad I caught you together.' As though the idea of husband and wife sharing a moment on a cold Sunday morning was unusual.

'Rose,' breathed Lacy, but James just gaped in a most ungentlemanly manner.

'It's about my mother,' Rose said sternly.

'Your . . . ?'

'Yes. I hope last night did not disturb you.'

James closed his mouth and looked as though he were about to have a seizure. Lacy put a cautionary hand upon his sleeve, for she alone knew that nothing short of a troop of Guardsmen marching through their bedroom would have disturbed what he was about last night.

'Er . . . no, I cannot recall . . .'

'Oh, good. Now, I can assure you that it will not happen again, but to ensure it, might I suggest I have control of all gin supplies, James?'

James choked and coloured, and Lacy stared in astonishment.

'Gin supplies?' she said faintly.

'Might I sit down for a moment?'

Instantly James was on his feet again, for he had risen awkwardly as Rose entered, and then returned to his seat, feeling more composed sitting than standing in his gown.

He brought a chair and drew it to the fire, and offered Rose a cup of coffee. There was a slight hitch in the proceedings whilst a cup and saucer were sent for, and during which time, Rose remarked upon the cold weather, and how delicious had been the frosty air upon her face as she walked up.

Lacy and James were dumbfounded.

'Now,' she said, after she had drunk her coffee, 'I feel I must say that . . . well . . .' She hesitated, as though at a loss for words, but it was not that which held her back, but her honest-to-God-Irish temper that this blasted feller-me-lad had had the effrontery to feed gin to her Mammy, whilst she herself had been . . . unwell.

She exploded.

They sat through it, as shamefaced as two children.

'How yer can sit there in yer foin brocade, smirkin' like some eejit whilst the Mammy is 'alf the time fallin' down drunk, an' yer the culprit is beyond me. Yes, you, I'm talkin' about, James Osborne.' She pointed her finger at him, and James quailed. 'Do yer not know any better, yer great lummox? Sure, she's an owd woman an' the cravin's bin on 'er since me Daddy died, an' I know it comforts 'er, but 'tis not right, 'tis not.' The lilt of the Irish on her tongue became thicker as her agitation grew.

'A bottle. A full bottle each week! God knows what she might o' done if I 'adn't found 'er. Glory be, she'd o' bin up 'ere wid you, beggin' for a wee drop, an' you . . . you all asleep, and the servants 'a talkin'. Holy Mother, James Osborne, I thought yer'd more sense, so I did. Yer should see me kitchen . . !'

Lacy was choked. It was Rose's kitchen now.

'. . . She damn near wrecked the place an' not a cup in the 'ouse unbroken. The little 'uns drinkin' their milk from the jug, so they were. Now I'm sayin' this only the once, so get it straight, James. She's ter 'ave no more gin. If I think she needs a drap I'll buy it fer 'er, not yer.'

Rose's head was held proudly high, her cheeks burned, her eyes were brilliant, and James Osborne could not take his eyes from her. She was magnificent. A memory returned to him,

483

sharp as glass, of the arresting, cat-like face of a young maid. A living, swirling curtain of rich, dark hair, sparkling with seawater like a shower of diamonds; and a full, bursting, poppy-red mouth. She had forced him to look at her then, and away from Lacy Hemingway, and she was doing it now. He was disconcerted, suddenly, by the stirring of warmth beneath the low belt of his gown.

Lacy stood up and took Rose's hand, pulling her from her seat. She put her arms about her, and hugged her; then held her at arms' length. She welcomed back a friend, a beloved friend, who had been absent and had returned.

'Oh, Rose. I am so sorry. This husband of mine has only your welfare, and that of Bridie's, at heart, you know. He gave her the gin, I am sure, in order to lend her comfort. She has been through such a lot, we both know that, but it will not happen again, will it, James?'

She turned to smile at James, and he was looking at Rose, and on his face was the strangest expression. She had seen it somewhere, on some other man's face, but for the life of her she could not remember where, or what it meant. He turned away and his eyes met hers, and into them came his own lovely, warming, familiar look of tenderness and complete love, which was for her alone, and the memory faded.

James grinned and held up his hands.

'My God, Rose, let me be hung, drawn and quartered if I so much as breathe my brandy-soaked breath upon Bridie in the future. I would not dare.'

He became serious.

'Forgive me, will you?' he said sincerely. 'I meant her no harm. I have seen a man, an officer in my regiment . . . He drank more than he should. We tried . . . he wanted us to help him . . . We kept spirits from him, but he ran berserk, Rose. So we gave him a tot each day. He looked forward to it, lived for that moment when he held the glass in his hand. Gradually we weaned him from it, but it took a long time.'

Rose smiled, the Irish hell-cat gone. Her eyes were bright with a purpose which had long been missing. Her expression

484

was one of spirited determination, the lacklustre apathy of the past three months had disappeared, it seemed, overnight.

'Right, well as long as we have that sorted out, I'll be off,' she said briskly. 'I have some things to do today, and then tomorrow, if I might have the carriage, I must go to town and replace the chinaware the Mammy smashed up. Oh, and by the way, Lacy.' Her voice was so casual, she might have been announcing her intention to take a ferry ride across the river. 'I shall be returning to the office on Monday. That lad who has his nose in my ledgers can find himself another job, for he'll not be needed when I get back.'

She smiled, then impishly bobbed a small curtsey at both of them.

'Your servant, sir. Ma'am,' she said, and was gone.

'Well, I'll be damned.'

'So will I.'

'Can you believe it?'

'No, Jamie, I cannot. But whatever it was that brought Rose back to her old self, I thank God for it. I thought never to see again that lovely sparkle, and hear the Irish lilt from her. She had become so horribly ladylike. Oh, how wonderful to hear her temper again, and to see her eyes flash!'

James said no more, as he stared into the fire.

# CHAPTER 35

The months which followed were a period of composing, little by little, day by day, the pattern that was to be their lives together. The ball was never mentioned again, nor the estrangement of Lacy's and James's family, and for the moment, James was prepared to let the situation lie in abeyance. His rapturous delight in his bride was complete, without flaw. Even small, unimportant quarrels added relish to their marriage, and gave to him such joyous fulfilment he was reluctant to pick up the matter of a reconciliation with their respective families.

Each morning at seven, Maggie would bring in their breakfast tray. The fire would be repaired, the small round table at which her master and mistress breakfasted set up before it or, if it was sunny, by the window overlooking the small lake, and Lacy and James would take a light meal. They would often bathe together in the enormous, clawfooted bath, which boasted a drainage pipe, but which must still be filled from the copper jugs of hot water brought up by a succession of nimble-footed, panting housemaids. Then, after dressing, they would take the carriage to the dock area and their respective offices.

Precisely at five, James would call for his wife, drawing her away, often reluctantly, for even now she was unwilling to delegate a part of her work to her competent clerks or Rose, and they would drive home together in the carriage, her hand in his. For some reason, unspoken but fully understood by them all, Rose always took a hackney cab from Strand Street to Beechwood and back, and James and she rarely crossed paths.

She, too, now had to divide her attention between the work she and Lacy shared, and her new-found resolve to 'make something' of her family. She waged constant war on her mammy's frequent falls from grace into the gin-soaked world which brought Bridie release from her sorrows, but they had settled together amiably enough. Providing one did not try too drastically to alter the other, they found their newly restored family closeness as fulfilling as once it had been.

As she grew accustomed to her new way of life, Rose began to derive quiet enjoyment from the training of her small brother and sister. They had inherited none of their father's viciousness. Perhaps any spirit they may have had, had been frightened out of them in the first four years of their lives, for they were shy, flitting behind a chair, or scampering for the safety of their mother's skirts, when Rose spoke to them.

At first they simply ate. Anything and everything that was put before them. Whilst Peg's back was turned, they slithered like two sinuous marmalade cats, their orange hair flaming in the shadows, into the kitchen, and stole any scrap of food they could lay their hands on. Peg, who was sent from the big house every day to help Miss Rose, would screech, and clap her hands to her mouth if a skeletal white hand appeared from beneath the table. There would be such a commotion that the two children, like young animals who have been taught by the harsh lessons of life to take advantage of any food available, and to make themselves as inconspicuous as possible whilst doing so, would freeze into stillness, not even their eyes moving.

Their legs were rickety, and neither medical care nor nourishing food would ever straighten them, but the flesh began to build up on their bones, and their hollowed cheeks filled out and became almost pink. They had freckles, big as farthings, on each snub nose, and their eyelashes and brows were frankly ginger. Their hair, clean now and well brushed – first grumblingly by Bridie and then, as they became used to her, by Rose – was soft and curly like the feathers on the breasts of the hens in the garden. Bridie could not quite recall when they had been born, she said, eyeing them fondly, but she thought them to be four or five years old.

The first time they spoke to anyone – everyone in the household assumed they conversed together when alone –

was on the day that Jonas brought a nanny goat down to the orchard, in order to clear the luxuriant vegetation which had been left untended since that first time of hopeful expectancy of Bridie's arrival at the cottage, years ago. The summer growth had never been cut, and it swayed, teeming with wild flowers, insect and animal life, even this late in the year.

Jonas had been employed by Charles Hemingway since he was eleven years old. When he was nineteen, and the last faint hope he had nurtured for himself and Miss Rose O'Malley had flickered and died, he had married Sally Jenkins, who worked at Silverdale as a dairy maid. A year later Sally gave him his first son, and one each year thereafter. When Captain Osborne had bought Beechwood and cast about for a head groom, Jonas – prodded by the heavily pregnant Sally, who was sick of falling over squabbling toddlers in the two-roomed cottage bestowed upon them by Charles Hemingway – asked diffidently of the captain if he might apply for the job. Mumbling of his experience, of his love of horses and of the ever growing responsibility of his sons, which would keep coming, twirling his cap about in trembling fingers, for he was presumptuous to accost a gentleman in such a way, Jonas had been left speechless and red-faced when the captain said casually that he would do, and the cottage would be ready for them by Friday.

'It has only four rooms, I am afraid . . . er . . . Kingsley, so I hope you and your family find it large enough.'

Large enough! It was Heaven to the harrassed Mrs Kingsley, and she said so endlessly. She stuffed all the babies into one of the rooms and ignoring her enormous stomach, she thanked Jonas so ardently he was quite bewitched. She would do a bit of scrubbing, she said, when this 'un came, to earn a few pence; or work in the laundry, helping out the woman who came once a week; or even, God willing, and if she had the chance, go back to her old trade in the dairy.

When Miss Lacy bought the house from Captain Osborne they remained, of course.

It came to Jonas' ears through Sally, who had it from Maggie, who had it from Miss Lacy, and so on, that the orchard at the back of the cottage was 'getting beyond a joke'. He took it from that remark that the grass needed mowing. The goat was part of a small herd, which were kept for their milk in a little patch of fenced meadow at the back of the spinney, and in no time at all, they had shorn the place to the smoothness of green alabaster.

He had his eldest boy with him that day, a plump and friendly three-year-old who went by the name of Albert, but who was called Bertie by one and all. He had his father's serious face, which broke into an engaging grin on the slightest pretext, endearing him to even the most forbidding individuals.

Bertie held a cord at the goat's neck, leading it as fearlessly as though it were a kitten. At every sudden, skittish move the goat made, Bertie would turn sternly, and in his broad Lancashire accent tell it to 'give over, do, or I'll clout yer', and the nanny would again walk sedately by the side of the child, who came scarcely to her shoulder.

Jonas, Bertie and the goat reached the gate which led to the side garden of the cottage, walked through the almost waist-high grass, towards the back of the orchard, and called out to Bridie, who was turning over the potato plot ready for next year's planting.

'Just bringing' t' goat, Missis, ter get rid o' that there grass. Don't, yer'll not see them trees next year.'

'Right ya are, lad. There's a cup o' tay in the pot when ye're done.'

Importantly Bertie lifted the latch, which he could just reach, led the goat through, then jumped nimbly back, shutting the gate behind him with the air of a man of seventy; wise, experienced, and standing no nonsense from a nanny goat.

'There's a reet feed for 'er there, Dad,' he said sagaciously, then climbed onto the bottom rung of the gate and leaned upon its top, watching with enormous pleasure the way the goat fell immediately upon the grass, as if she had not eaten for months.

They stood for a moment, father and son, then Jonas

turned away, ready for a cup of tea and a chin-wag with old Bridie. She was perplexing to the servants at Beechwood, being the mother of Miss Rose, who until recently they had considered one of their mistresses. Nevertheless, they treated Bridie with casual kindness, like some odd creature that came to the back door, begging, and could not be turned away by those who considered themselves Christian. Not that Bridie begged, but she was inclined to pop up in odd places, and engage a maid or a gardener in what she obviously thought of as one of her old gossips with Mrs Geraghty. She missed that, did Bridie. The long and involved discussions which could be enjoyed with one's own kind.

As Jonas began to walk towards the back kitchen door, which stood open, he remarked to Bertie that they must not forget to tether the goat when they had had their tea, or it would eat its way out of the orchard and be in Aigburth by nightfall.

'Yes, Dad,' said Bertie, trotting behind. A flash of orange against the pyracantha bush, which thrived upon the back wall of the house, caught his eye, and he stopped, intrigued, his inquisitive child's mind sorting through the possibilities of what it could be. There was another! Then both vanished, bobbing down behind a mock orange bush, which quivered gently, then was still.

Jonas had gone into the kitchen and his voice could be heard mingling with that of Bridie's. She laughed. There was a clink of cups, then the door was slammed shut. It was a cold day.

Bertie had his father's patience, so he waited quietly and, sure enough, the two heads, for that was what they were, rose slowly until four bright blue eyes stared into his, looking like two rabbits fixed by the presence of a snake. They were older than Bertie, but they were no bigger.

''Ello,' said Bertie cheerfully, undaunted by their look of terror. He had never known terror in his life, so he did not recognize it as such.

'What yer doin' in there? Playin' 'ide and seek? Me an' our Alfie' – Sally had called all her children for the Royal Family

– 'do that sometimes,' he said confidentially, then went on to more important matters. 'Me and me Dad've just brought 't goat up. D'yer wanna see it? She's a grand goat. A good milker an' all. Yer orchard were that bad, well, me Dad ses grass'd be up t' top o' trees by next year so we fetched t' nanny up. Come on, I'll show yer,' he said magnanimously.

Without waiting to see if his words of knowledge had been received with attention or not, he turned and began to walk back in the direction from which he had just come, confidently expecting them to follow.

They did. Perhaps it was the reference to 'their' orchard, two human beings who had owned nothing in their lives but the rags on their backs, or maybe it was the cheerful acceptance of their presence, but they trooped obediently behind the diminutive boy like two soldiers in the wake of their sergeant.

They were found together half an hour later, three small figures standing on the bottom rung of the gate, heads together, discussing the merits or otherwise of the goat, who had already stripped a square yard of pasturage. Bertie, of course, was the natural leader, answering all questions put to him with an authority which impressed the city-born children to awestruck adoration. Jonas heard the tiny girl say, '. . . an' will yer let us 'elp yer, Bertie?' to which his son replied airily that he would, and would be down first thing to collect them. Their voices rose and fell, and for several moments their shrill, childish laughter warbled about the goat, which looked up irritably.

The moment Declan and Mary Kate saw Jonas, they leaped from the gate and scuttled to the far side of the garden, but Bertie had no time for that.

'Give over,' he shouted cheerfully. 'It's only me Dad. We've got ter tether t' nanny. Come on Dec.' Jonas smiled. Dec, indeed. 'Give us a 'and. You 'old t' gate, Mary Kate.'

Trepidation like a mask upon their faces, the two children did as they were told, obeying the three-year-old Bertie with an alacrity which grew increasingly bolder, and even addressing a remark or two to Jonas.

That night Rose was taken aback, when, as they ate their tea of hot muffins layered with blackberry jam, Declan turned to her and, as though it was the most natural thing in the world, said the first words he had ever spoken to her.

'We 'elped Bertie with 'is goat terday, Rosie.'

Rose grew to love them from that moment, and they her. She let them settle in that winter, before embarking upon her plans for them. She made a home for them, which they began to take for granted, as children should. When she was not with Lacy she took them on hikes, as she called them. Not far, for they were young, and not yet as strong as their beloved friend Bertie. She took them to the back of Beechwood, amongst the trees which gave the house its name, sharing the astonishing joy of crunching the thick spread of yellow and bronze leaves beneath booted feet. Sometimes they went across the winter fields to see the gentle giants who would pull the ploughs in spring.

It snowed after Christmas and, as she opened the kitchen door the next day, the two children stepped back, shaken it seemed by the breathtaking beauty of the new white, shadowed world of their orchard. The grass and the goat had gone now. Every tree stood sharp as ebony against the clear blue sky. Their branches were heavy with a patina of glittering ivory, and through them the sun shone like a brilliant lamp held behind lace, throwing long umber shadows to the cottage door. The trees stood in misted, gilded ripples of crisp, pure snow; untouched, except by a single track, where the dog fox had passed, leaving dainty black imprints on its purity. The shadow at the far side, cast by the gentle slope which led up to the main house, was a deep purple. Ferns, dead and withered, stood frozen in pearl and silver.

The expression on the children's faces made Rose want to cry. Mary Kate's hand crept into hers and Dec, as he was now called, reached out and grasped her skirt. Snow, they said wonderingly, as she told them what it was. They had seen it in Liverpool, they said, and it was not like this. Dirty heaps and mucky layers upon window sills; piddled in and made yellow by wild cats; fouled by wandering dogs, and having not the smallest connection with this world of loveliness.

They were reluctant to walk on it. It was too beautiful. It dazzled them, and shouldn't they fetch Bertie, they said, for he was an avowed expert on everything from his new brother's wind problems, to the habits of the tomcat who ruled the harem of stray tabbies which lurked about the hayloft above the stable. He would know how to tackle it.

Rose coaxed them out in their stout boots, wrapping them cosily in warm clothing: woolly caps, mittens and mufflers, and, watched by Bridie from the snugness of the kitchen, led them along the path, which was only a couple of inches deep in snow, towards the drifts which the wind had brushed up into neat, smooth slopes against the hedge.

The children placed their feet with the care of a heavy man walking on quicksand, convinced they would fall through into some unimaginable region below the familiarity of the garden, but when Dec looked back and saw his own small footprints, and Mary Kate's beside them, his face split into a delighted grin. He began to make patterns, placing his feet this way and that, jumping and landing heavily to make the imprints deeper.

Gaining confidence from her brother, Mary Kate did the same, leaping along the path until it was a crisscross, rutted arrangement of abstract designs. They laughed and squealed like piglets, until Declan lost his balance and fell into a drift. It was no more than eighteen inches deep but, for a moment, panic struck him, as the cold feathery crystals of white closed about him. A handful fell across his face, touching his lips, and he licked it, and as his warm tongue melted it, his expression of dread changed to delight and, as daring as Bertie, he grasped a handful.

Dec sat there, an imp in a muffler big enough for a grown man, his face lit up with that unholy glee which is the sole prerogative of small boys. Shaping up the snow with both hands until it was just right, he lifted his arm, and threw his first snowball.

They were appalled, then heartbroken, when the cold snap

ended and the snow disappeared, but were somewhat comforted by the reappearance of Bertie, who told them not to fret for it would come again one day and, anyway, he had come to fetch them to see the new litter of puppies which their Lou had produced a few days ago. If they liked, he would let them hold one.

'Can we go, our Rosie, can we?' they shrilled, turning, as they did more and more frequently now, to Rose; in a fever of impatience, their sorrow at the loss of the snow-filled world removed by the prospect of another, equally delightful adventure.

Rose's face was soft and smiling as she knelt before them, suddenly filled with an enormous feeling of satisfaction. They came to her expectantly, trusting, and she held out her arms. It was the first time she had done so and, for a moment they hesitated, made unsure as they always were by anything new. Then Mary Kate moved, delicately placed herself within the circle of one arm and, with a sigh, leaned comfortably against Rose's shoulder. The arm closed about her, and Rose kissed her cheek. Declan was slower. Well, Bertie was watching wasn't he? But something in Rose's face drew him and, shuffling awkwardly, he thumped into her arms where he clung for a blissful moment, then was away, his eyes bright and happy.

She went with them, walking behind their running, leaping, hopping, skipping figures for even on this short walk they covered more ground than if they had walked to Tuebrook village.

Lou – christened again for the Royal Family, for one could hardly call a dog Louise, said Jonas – was a small, pretty dog made up of cocker spaniel, a dash of retriever, and some other indeterminable breeds from way back. She had the most beautiful moist brown eyes Rose had ever seen. But her pups, a week old and getting quite lively, had a familiar look which brought a spark of glee to Rose's eyes.

'Why Copper, you randy owd divil, and there was us thinking you were past all that kind of thing,' she murmured delightedly to herself.

# CHAPTER 36

On 16 March 1861, aged seventy five years, the Duchess of Kent, dear mama to Her Majesty Queen Victoria, died. On the same day, as he contentedly surveyed the black patch of soil he intended to plant with onions, which decision he had confided to his wife that morning, Richard Osborne was struck down in a surge of agony, and died before his body hit the ground.

'His heart,' the doctor explained. 'He was a good age, Mrs Osborne, having reached, and surpassed, his allotted span of three score years and ten.'

'Balderdash!' said his weeping wife, 'it was those onions, and I shall never forgive myself as long as I live. Onions! Why, Doctor Bentley, Dawson was perfectly capable of doing such things. But no, Richard would insist upon digging, and other ungentlemanly occupations.'

'But he was content in such an occupation, my dear Mrs Osborne. Would you have had him sitting about . . . ?

'I know, I know,' sobbed Sophie. 'It made him happy, so I suppose I must take some comfort from that.' She became brisk, herself again, for what the good doctor said made sense, and poor Richard had had more years than most. There were arrangements to be made, and of course James must be informed.

He had not called upon her once since the day on which he had informed her and Richard that he had married Lacy Hemingway and, though Richard had consulted with him a time or two down at the office in Water Street, for he had liked to potter about down there occasionally, keeping his eye on his son's progress, she had not seen James since. She bitterly resented the fact, and felt nothing but cold hostility towards the woman who had come between herself and her son.

In the beginning, although she had been shocked and unhappy, her unease had been lightened by the belief that given time, everything would turn out splendidly. She was an optimist and had been fond of Lacy. If society relented, as she was sure it would, for James was well liked, Sophie would have been charmed to have her as a daughter-in-law, for there was no denying her breeding. And if society did not, well then, her son would come and visit her, perhaps dine, and when the children came James could bring them over to Highcross to see their grandmama.

But James had said coldly that he could go nowhere where his wife was not welcome. Sophie had been appalled.

The shock waves which had reverberated through the county when news of the marriage came out had scarcely stopped at its boundaries, rippling northwards into Scotland to the Hemingway cousins, and southwards even as far as Bath, where dear Joanna, Sophie's youngest daughter, had gone to live following her marriage. For months poor Sophie had scarce felt able to go calling, or to receive her friends, for the topic, dissected and discussed ad infinitum, until she felt she would scream or go mad, was the very subject which she did not wish to hear mentioned.

Her friends commiserated with her upon the sadness of losing one's only son to a . . . They did not say the word, for in truth they did not quite know what Lacy had done, save that it was too horrendous to be mentioned to a lady. And, of course, when Sarah called, the atmosphere was frosty, sharp and brittle – like a sliver of ice. Sophie began to feel that the blame for her son's actions was being laid at her feet. The subject was never even hinted at in Sarah's presence, of course, for Sarah would not have her daughter's name spoken in her hearing. One afternoon, she had been seen to stand imperiously and glare at a lady who had confided that she admired the Honiton lace upon another's gown; the very word *lace* sending her gliding from the room like an infuriated swan.

Now, in this time of mourning, just as the scandal had lost its impetus, the whole sorry mess was to be brought to the boil again. James would naturally attend the funeral of his own father, and there was no doubt in Sophie's mind that he would insist upon bringing his wife.

Sophie Osborne's mind went round and round in anguished circles, as she waited for her son to come to her and as she brooded on the problem, she wept, not tears of grief for the loss of her husband, but the tears of a tired child who cannot understand why life is such a puzzle.

James and Lacy were standing, as Richard Osborne had been when he died an hour earlier, in the garden. The subject of the neglected shrunken tangle, which Lacy liked to call her own private jungle, and which Turner the gardener privately termed a 'right bloody mess', had come up again. Lacy was in heated disagreement with Turner's proposal to dig the whole lot up and start again.

James leaned against the waist-high dry stone wall which surrounded a bed of rioting forsythia, the soil the level of the top of the wall. The stones were encrusted with lichens and had the rough texture of age. A mass of spring flowers, yellow iris, crocus and miniature daffodils were caught by the sun, hesitantly warm. James squinted into the sun's rays, watching his wife as she led the frustrated gardener from spot to spot, indicating what she would like here, or there, or over yonder. Nine months they had been married and she drew him to her still. Her beauty stunned him and her crisp humour, her indomitable determination held him in a thrall of adoration. She was part of his flesh and spirit. Her ardour in the sweetness of the night had been an added bonus, he thought, but if she had been submissive and dutiful in their marriage bed, he would still have loved her for her flash and sparkle and bravery, out of it.

And yet there was a sweetness about her, a candour which was so disarmingly endearing he swore she was two souls in one body. Her love and pitying concern for Rose, or for anyone in need, was instant.

Only in business was she ruthless.

He smiled and folded his arms and waited patiently for her as he had done for nearly eight years.

The note was put into his hand by a white-faced and trembling Maggie. The groom from Highcross who had delivered it, had told them what it contained and, as she handed it to lovely Captain James, who had captured her heart, so to speak, from his first glance, she began to cry.

'Ooh, sir,' she sobbed, bobbing a curtsey before turning and running up the steps towards the house.

Lacy turned at James's cry and smiled, believing him to be calling her to his side, bored by the whole thing. He was no gardener and suffered the occupation, or the supervising of it, only for her sake.

'What, my love?' she said, and Turner looked away politely.

'Lacy.' His voice was strange, and for the first time she became aware of the tension in him. Where moments before he had lounged now he was rigid, and his face was strained and pale.

She began to walk towards him, skirting the little octagonal pond, brushing past the bursting growth which spread across the walks.

'Darling?' she said enquiringly, then began to hurry, then run, until she stood before him. 'What is it?' she whispered.

He held out the note, and Lacy read the words which made her mistress of Highcross, and the wife of one of the wealthiest men in Liverpool.

She looked up at him, her eyes soft with love.

'You will come with me.' It was not a question but a statement of fact.

'Of course.'

His face relaxed, and his shoulders, and he held out his arms. She moved into them and he clung to her, and she felt him shudder. She soothed him with her strength and love, and he even managed a wry smile in his sadness and she knew why. For the first time in six years she would stand amongst her own again.

'That is, if they come,' she said out loud, and though he had not spoken, he knew what she meant.

They both wore black as the white-faced butler admitted

them to the large, square hall of the Georgian house in which James and Richard Osborne had both been born.

It was a simple, well-proportioned family house with plain brick walls, pierced with rows of flat, sash windows, over each of which was an arch. On either side of the large glassed front door, wide curving steps led to a balustrade, and a terrace stretched at the level of the first floor across the front of the house. A gravelled drive, edged on both sides by masses of immaculately neat spring flowers, led to walkways around the side of the house. Virginia creeper and wisteria, planted when the house was first built, grew up its walls, almost to the roof. On its left side had been built an octagonal, delicately lovely glasshouse, set in a position to catch most of the day's sun. Trees stood about the house, but far enough back so as not to block out the light; and like a crinoline of green velvet, for the house stood on a slight rise, ran acres of smooth lawn.

Sophie was alone when they were announced, for her other children, four married daughters, had further to come than James. She turned from her sad contemplation of what her future would hold, and held out her arms to James. He held Lacy's hand protectively, but she took it from him gently and, with a nod of her head, she urged him forward to his mother. He would have taken her with him, but Lacy stood quietly by the door. It was not the time to force Sophie Osborne to greet her daughter-in-law. Let her have her moment of comfort with her son.

For a second Sophie's eyes caught hers, and there was a flash of gratitude in them, and then she was held in James's strong arms, and she wept again.

'Oh, James. What am I to do?' she said at last, and he knew she did not refer to the gap in her life which her husband's death had left. He smiled as he knelt at her feet, looking for the strong streak of good-humoured kindliness which he knew her to possess. He kissed her cheek affectionately, then got to his feet. He turned and looked at Lacy, holding out his hand to her, his love clothing her in an armour so strong she was afraid of nothing.

She walked towards them, the graceful folds of her simple

black silk dress swaying elegantly. She had no black bonnet, so she had pulled back her gleaming hair into a fat chignon. Into it she had fixed a comb of jet, and from that fell a veil of black lace. The absence of colour, the severity of her dress and hair, and the filmy lace about her forehead, gave her the appearance of a serenely lovely nun. Sophie watched her and prayed that those who would come to her house – no, this woman's house – this day, and in the days to follow, would accept her. She was a fitting wife for her son.

James waited with his breath caught in his throat, his eyes turning from his wife to his mother, and back again.

Lacy stopped in front of Sophie Osborne where she sat in her chair, as royal as a queen on a throne. Lacy smiled, then dropped into a graceful and respectful curtsey, the folds of her dress billowing about her like the petals on a black silk rose.

'Mrs Osborne,' she said, then rose and waited.

Sophie looked her up and down, then into her eyes, and saw there compassion, a certain wariness, but no regret, and certainly no humility. The silence lengthened and thickened, and James felt his lungs begin to burn with the breath he had held for so long. Then, with a suddenness which made Lacy jump, Sophie threw up her hands, reaching once more for her handkerchief. She patted the seat beside her and said tearfully.

'Oh, for pity's sake. Sit down, Lacy Hemingway. I just cannot abide this foolishness another moment. I don't care a fig for the rest, but I insist upon having my family about me at a time like this. You are family now, so behave as such, and give me a kiss.'

They came to pay their respects to Mrs Sophie Osborne in those days before the funeral, and were thunderstruck to find sitting beside her upon the sofa, Mrs James Osborne. Not Grace, nor Alison, nor Eleanor nor Joanna, who were Sophie's daughters, but little Lacy Hemingway, who smiled imperturbably and received graciously their condolences upon the sudden death of her father-in-law. It was obvious that Sophie Osborne, having taken the decision to accept her

500

son's wife, was determined not only to let those who called her friend know of her will, but also to stuff it resolutely down their throats.

'I know you or one of your sisters should be here to receive with me,' she told Grace, 'but I am intent upon this, so do not try to dissuade me. Now go and sit elsewhere, and take that truculent expression from your face, miss.'

She did not expect Sarah and Charles Hemingway, and in this she was not disappointed, but her reaction to the sight of dear Jane, and Amy and Edward too, was childish delight.

After paying their respects to Sophie, Jane and Amy turned to their sister. Jane, who was a frequent visitor at Beechwood, had soft candles of affectionate pleasure in her eyes. Drawing Lacy to her feet, she embraced her warmly, the presence of others deterring her not one bit.

'The occasion is sad, Lacy,' she murmured, 'but I think I have never had a happier moment than when I came through that door and saw you in your rightful place, beside James's mama.' A tear shone, trembling on her lashes. 'I feel most guilty, for I was fond of James's papa, but it was almost worth . . .' She put her hand to her mouth. 'Oh dear Lord, forgive me, but I am sure He knows what I mean.'

Lacy held her other hand and smiled understandingly, then turned to Amy. Her eldest sister had scarcely changed since that long ago day when she had stood at the altar in St Anne's Church. She was plumper, and her face was as severe, but her eyes wore a gentle expression, as though the experience of motherhood had given her the understanding of loving another.

'Lacy,' she said quietly and leaned forward to put her cheek next to that of her sister, and Lacy knew the gesture meant as much as Jane's more effusive greeting. Amy's husband, Edward, kissed her in brotherly embarrassment and they all took seats near her, prepared to sit for fifteen minutes, as was customary.

No sooner were they seated than Thomas Hemingway was announced with his wife, Emily; then Robert; and following hard on their heels, Margaret, now the wife of John Bradley, who was at her side. They came forward, a hesitant group, in their respectful black, to bend over Sophie's hand and kiss her cheek, but their eyes darted constantly to the upright figure beside the window.

They had known, of course, that she would be there. It was the only topic of conversation in any gathering which did not include Sarah and Charles Hemingway. But here she was, and what were they to do?

James stiffened, his tall figure straightening as he stood behind his mama, ready to move protectively to his wife. But he should have known. After all these years, he should have known.

'Robert,' she murmured, 'Have you no greeting for your sister?'

Robert smiled, and James relaxed as he moved to put his hands upon his sister's shoulders, kissing her cheek warmly.

'How well you look,' he murmured admiringly.

They had no choice, the others, and having made the move, it seemed natural to group themselves about their sister, talking quietly of family matters. They stayed longer than was deemed good manners, but Sophie was beyond caring. They presented a reconciled family picture to every caller, giving the impression that Lacy Osborne was again an acceptable member of their close-knit, well-bred society.

The next day they followed the gleaming hearse, taking Richard Osborne on his last journey across the land he had loved so well, towards Aigburth Road and the church of St Anne. The lane was bordered with a silent strand of estate and farm workers, men and their wives who worked upon Richard's vast lands, and many who had never spoken to the man himself but who had benefited from his generosity.

As the cortège passed by, they fell in behind, and followed to the little church which Lacy had last entered as a demure bridesmaid on the occasion of Amy's marriage to Edward Lucas. The church was so full it was impossible to see anyone except one's immediate neighbour, and it was not until Lacy stood with James and Sophie beside the grave in which the coffin would shortly be lowered, that she came face to face with her mother and father.

James gripped her arm tightly as she swayed a little. He had foreseen what would happen when she met them, and had deliberately placed himself between her and his mother.

Across the open grave, Lacy looked at Sarah Hemingway. She wore a dress of black bombazine, and a bonnet of best silk crape with a long thick veil. Where her face was, only a shimmer of white could be seen beneath the veil, and her black-gloved hands were still at her waist, holding her prayer book. She might have been the blackened stump of a tree, thick and as immovable. Not by a twitch or tremble did she acknowledge the presence of her youngest daughter.

But it was at Charles that Lacy looked.

He wore a coat of black cloth without buttons on the sleeves, and a plain lawn black cravat. His tall black hat was banded with black crape. Every gentleman was dressed exactly the same, and each lady mirrored her neighbour. They might have been poured from the same mould. Even the inferior folk wore their good, black Sunday best. The only splash of colour was in the bright yellow trumpets of the daffodils, which grew in wild splendour about the gravestones and beneath the trees.

As the parson intoned the words which disposed of Richard Osborne, Lacy and Charles looked at one another through her filmy veil.

His eyes were blurred and rheumy like those of an old man, though he was only sixty-one, but they seemed to be trying to say something to her. Across the open grave grey eyes looked into grey, and his were the first to drop. His hand trembled on the arm of his wife, and in his ears, drowning the voice of the parson, his daughter spoke again the last words he had heard her speak.

'You have no daughter named Lacy.'

The sound of earth hitting the lid of the coffin brought them both back to the present and, as she watched the old man who was her father shuffle away, behind her veil Lacy's tears flowed, not for the death of Richard Osborne, but for that of her Papa.

She knew she would never see him again.

# CHAPTER 37

Lancer McGhee was not happy. He stood at one end of the bar, scowling fiercely into the smoke from two dozen long-stemmed pipes, his enormous calloused fist about a pint pot of stout. He leaned his greasy-jacketed back and shoulders against the rough wooden wall, around which a thick line of grime showed where hundreds of others had done the same.

Now and again he crashed the pot to the counter as if the explosion of his thoughts demanded some gesture of violence, although he was not yet full enough to take the final step. He growled from time to time, drawing nervous glances from those about him, and the circle of emptiness in which he stood grew wider.

The sign at the back of the bar read 'The Noted Stout House' and beneath it, '3d a pint'. There was a wide shelf under the sign upon which rested half a dozen barrels, from which the slattern who served drew ale or stout. The woman wore a frilled cap, jaunty and foolishly incongruous with the rest of the grimy tatters she had on.

Men stood about in battered top hats. There were sailors, with arms about one another's shoulders, in the last stages of mawkish drunken comradeship. Two young children loitered in the doorway waiting for whatever might come their way for one never knew when a man far gone in drink might be tricked into parting with a farthing. They wore no shoes, and every so often would take a long pull from a pot, when its owner's back was turned.

Lancer glared about him and his voice rose in a thunderous demand for another pint. The room fell silent for a moment. Lancer was well known in here and it did not do to get in his way when the drink was on him. Though he was not half the man he had been thirteen years ago, he was still a force to be reckoned with, and the woman behind the bar immediately left the customer she was serving, smiling ingratiatingly at Lancer as she placed another pot of stout before him.

Lancer had been irritated by Bridie's disappearance, but not unduly so, and the loss of his children caused him no concern. His first, faint feelings of pride in them, a token of his virility, had evaporated when his vicious temper had broken their spirits. Who could be proud of a son who runs to hide behind his mother's skirts? It had made quite a change, he considered, to bring a bit of young back to his bed. Bridie was old and fat at the end, and lay supine beneath his nightly assault upon her, but the more youthful women who came willingly at the sight of his money, were active and sexually satisfying.

The problem was, they never stayed. In the dim glow of daylight which fought to press through the layer of filth upon the window, the true state of the hell-hole they had entered in the dark of the night was revealed to them, and even they, born and bred in, and accustomed to, the slums, had found it too much for them. Satisfied by his night's rutting, and pacified in the belief that this one would do, Lancer would trot off to work leaving his new 'wife' to see to things, but the moment his vast bulk had thundered away up the alley, the object of his affection would slip away, vowing never to frequent that part of town again.

He became well-known; the prostitutes passed the word about and, should he have offered them a gold clock and five bob a night, nothing would have induced them to take him on.

Now Lancer wanted Bridie back.

As time moved on, her true worth became increasingly apparent to him and, besides, his pickled, slow moving brain said, there was the kids to think of. In what connection he was not certain, for he had not seen any of them from the moment Bridie went to this day. But as the weeks went by and his lust was unfulfilled – he didn't count the woman next door, whom he raped each time her husband was at work, and who was too terrified to complain – his animal urgings began to long for a grain of order in the basic necessities of his life. He was tired of eating food bought from street hawkers, and it was time

505

the bed was changed, and the bloody rats were getting a bit too much even for him. The place needed a bit of a clean, and it would be pleasant to come home to a fire and a woman. Old and fat as Bridie was, she was always available.

He knew where she had gone. Oh yes, he knew where she had gone. That cow next door had told him as she gibbered dementedly in his grasp, but he had not cared overmuch at the time. Tuebrook, she'd said in her terror. That was all she had known, for Bridie, though boastful of the fine house in which her daughter lived, had been vague about its name and specific whereabouts.

Lancer's cunning was that of the fox. When dawn blushed palely in the east and the floating mauve mist which lay a foot deep about the fields on his right began to ebb away, he climbed the railings which surrounded the Zoological Gardens on West Derby Road, burrowed about until he found a sheltered corner, and immediately fell into a black sleep. He did not move that day, except to relieve himself a time or two, falling back instantly into a slumber which was almost death-like.

He woke as the sun slipped beyond the rippling lip of the Irish sea. He was hungry, ravenous, but that was nothing compared to the appetite which lurked in his greasy trousers. He felt full of life, bursting with vitality, like a bull who maddens in a field, separated from a herd of cows by a thick and impenetrable hedge.

He waited until it was completely dark before he moved. Keeping to the grass verge at the side of West Derby Road, he began to walk in the direction of Tuebrook. As he moved beside the blackthorn hedge which bordered the fields, the smell of hawthorn, apple blossom, snowberry and dogwood, brought out by the gentle warmth of the spring sun during the day, filled his nostrils. Stumbling across the ditch which divided the grass verge from the hedgerow, crushing with great clumsy feet the coltsfoot and willowherb, meadowsweet and fool's watercress, which grew in the trickle of water at its bottom, he found a gate, and blundered into an orchard which adjoined the back of a solitary farm. A dog barked frantically,

506

but Lancer was impervious to its warning shout. His stomach rumbled alarmingly as he thrashed about the trees, laden now with blossom. In his ignorance he looked for apples, and when he found none he was disbelieving, muttering fiercely of the stupidity of an orchard without fruit.

He reached Tuebrook about midnight, standing in the centre of the cluster of cottages along the high street which made up the tiny hamlet. He turned left into Tuebrook Lane and stumped along, waiting for some instinct to tell him he had found what he was looking for, but after about a quarter of a mile and utter blackness, he turned and retraced his steps to the village.

This time he took a righthand turn along Green Lane, but nothing filtered into his brain bar the awareness of night sounds, the smells of the countryside and the consciousness of the rutted lane beneath his feet. He was not a countryman but the great black emptiness did not alarm him. There was not a light anywhere, though he passed several small farms and a scattered cottage or two.

He shambled slowly back to the village. It concerned him not in the least that he could not find whatever it was his mind would recognize. He was quite enjoying himself, like a hunter who follows a trail, stalking his quarry, taking pleasure from the pursuit, knowing he was near, but in no hurry for the kill.

This time he went on through the village along West Derby Road. There were several larger houses the further out he got, and though he stood before each one for minutes, studying the black silhouette against the paler black of the sky, even circling one cautiously, he knew they were none of them right.

He was aware instantly when he came to it. There were gates, standing carelessly open, ornate and well kept, obviously leading to a house which was not just that of a wealthy tradesman or merchant. The others he had seen had been homes of the well-to-do, but this, with its air of well maintained prosperity; its fine, carved gate posts; its railings which led away on either side into the blackness of the night; this belonged to gentry.

He breathed deeply, the air entering and filling his lungs in a most satisying way, then strode confidently between the gateposts and along the gravelled drive. Within twenty yards he came to a cottage. Even in the dark he could see the pleasing shape of it, and distinguish the faint, lingering smell of baked bread, the spring freshness of lilac in the garden at its rear, and detect that certain aura which denotes the snug abode of an estate worker whose occupants are all asleep.

His brain was not in any way logical, but animal instinct once again came to his aid. His Bridie, fat, dirty lump that she was, would scarcely live at the big house of the woman who was the friend of Bridie's gel. She would be housed in some discreet hideaway, where she would be less likely to offend the sensibilities of those who had taken her in.

He was confused, for though his sixth sense told him Bridie was near, it did not seem likely they would put her in this conspicuous spot. They must pass here every day, as they moved in and out of the estate, and it seemed strange that they should not take exception to the sight of a gin-swilling filthy old woman, pottering about beneath their very noses. Surely they would stick her at the far reaches of the grounds where no one would see her?

But still, intuitively, he felt the nearness of his victim.

He decided on a bit of reconnaissance. Perhaps he would find something to confirm his belief that within those four walls he would find what he had come for.

Inside the cottage the five-month-old pup lifted her head from where it rested on the pillow between Declan and Mary Kate, and her ears moved, turning in all directions, as she tried to pick up and identify the sound which had awakened her. She got quietly to her feet and, without disturbing the sleeping children, jumped off the bed and moved towards the open door, sniffing, lifting her head apprehensively. Though there was no further sound, she was frightened, sensing some dreadful danger.

Lancer had the back door open. The bolt was not even snapped across it, and he marvelled at the carelessness of country folk who took not even the most elementary of precautions to protect what was theirs.

He was in a kitchen. He had walked for so long in darkness that

508

his eyes were accustomed to it, and he could make out the shape of a big table, and a dresser against the wall. He almost fell, drawing in his breath with a sharp hiss as first one, then two cats rose from before the empty fireplace, shimmied up to him, then abruptly, with the knowingness of animals, drew back into the corner, spitting, huddled together for courage.

Lancer stepped across the kitchen towards the door which led into the parlour. He made not the smallest noise, moving as lightly as the cats themselves, searching for he knew not what, but some positive indication that he was in the right – or wrong – cottage. He had no wish to announce his presence to some irate householder, alerting whoever lived here and the rest of the estate of his existence.

The dog at the head of the stairs began to growl. Her young voice was tentative, for she was stiff with fear, and her snarl became a forlorn whine, as though begging for someone to come and lend a hand. She began to yip. She knew the being who had entered her territory stood at the foot of the stairs now, and she backed away towards the safety of the children's room. Suddenly, it all became too much for her and she began to bark dementedly, her voice resounding about the low-roofed bedroom.

Lancer cursed, and was about to turn tail and run, when a sound from the chair in the corner of the room caught his attention. The chair had its back to him and he had not realized that someone sat in it, but as the mumble, fractious and still half asleep, began, he turned like a boxer on the balls of his feet. A face, white in the darkness, the frilled mob cap on top all askew, peeped round the wing of the chair and Bridie's voice said querulously,

'Will yer stop yer clap, yer daft dog. Faith, a body can't get a minnit's peace wid yer. Now, be quiet or I'll put yer out in the yard.'

She did not see Lancer until his hand came down on her shoulder, and his shape loomed over her like a great bat out of hell. For a second, petrified and paralysed, she allowed him to lift her from the chair where she had dozed off, a tot of gin in her hand. He was muttering in his own way, placating her to silence and conveying at the same time his desire to have her back by his side. If Lancer could be said to have a soft edge, he was showing it now in his endeavour to beguile her quietly from her chair, and back to the home they had shared for nearly thirteen years.

Bridie began to scream, shrilly, but in her terror so weakly, she could not have been heard by anyone who was not within immediate earshot. Lancer, not unduly put out, urged her towards the open doorway whining of a 'bit o' good grub, an' the room wants doin' an', besides, a wife's place is wid 'er 'usband.' His purpose was to get her away from the vicinity of the estate. Once he was away up West Derby Road she could scream her bloody head off. He'd soon take care of that. Hadn't he always. A good slap about her silly, open gob 'd shut 'er up an' if she went on any more 'e'd do it 'ere an' now. But Lancer wanted her on her feet. If he knocked her senseless as he was tempted to do, he would have to carry her, and her weighing a bloody ton. They must've fed 'er a bit o' good grub, he thought, ter make her so hefty. Never mind, he liked a bit o' flesh.

The dog barked with the hysteria of an animal almost beyond the edge of reason.

Rose was in the depth of a luxuriantly sensual dream in which her flesh fused with that of James Osborne. His hands were at her breast, his lips played with hers, and in her sleep she writhed beneath her bed covers as though it were his body which lay on top of hers. He loved her, he wanted her, and she wanted him so desperately she fought for several minutes the sounds which were trying so hard to drag her from him. She would not go! She would *not* leave him, no matter who called her. She clung, in that half waking, half sleeping state which comes before full consciousness, to the delicious sensation the dream had aroused in her, and even when the barking dog, and the voice which was so familiar to her, began to insinuate itself between her and James, she shut it out, fighting to stay with her love.

'Jesus, will yer shut that bloody dog up!' the voice bellowed.

Below, in the pitchy black of mortal terror, the dreaded

voice pierced Bridie's blind unreasoning panic, and she began to scream with all the force that was held in her powerful lungs. The ornaments on the mantelpiece seemed to lift and glide, and the man who held her felt the hairs on the back of his neck prickle.

'Shut yer gob, woman,' he hissed, his anger beginning to surge. He longed to yell at her again, to let out some of the growing rage which was exploding in his easily provoked mind. He had felt the compulsion to whisper, though God alone knew why, for the combined hullabaloo made by Bridie and the dog was enough to waken the dead. Bridie continued to scream, resisting with all her strength the pull of Lancer's vicious grip.

Lancer, who had never panicked in his life, never having had reason to be afraid, panicked now. His rampant temper, held back by the need for quiet and the effort it took to spirit Bridie away before anyone was aware of it, broke through the bonds, never strong, which held it.

'Be quiet, yer daft bitch!' he thundered, and in the pretty bedroom upstairs, Rose the lover parted company with the man in whose arms she dallied, and Rose O'Malley opened her eyes.

Lancer was out of control now with the sudden shift in his temper so well-known in Naylor's Yard and its vicinity. It had strong men blanching and women cowering, and for a moment Rose O'Malley cowered like an infant in her bed, paralysed by the 'bogey man'.

'*Be quiet,*' the voice shouted. 'By God, if yer don't shut that great gawpin' 'ole of yers I'll bloody shut it fer yer. Ye're comin' wid me, d'yer 'ear, back where yer belong. I've 'ad enough o' this so shut yer gob. Shut it, I said.'

He struck Bridie across her face with a hand like a brick, and her nose split with the sickening sound of a rotten tomato hitting a wall. For a moment she was silenced as the blood flowed, filling her open mouth, and he dragged her unresisting figure through the doorway into the kitchen.

The dog continued to bark, then suddenly sensing what was to come, began to howl dolefully. The two children, awake and sitting up in their beds like two china dolls, white and sightless, made no sound. This was how you were when Lancer spoke, and through long practice they fell into the remembered pose.

From the warm safety into which she had instinctively retreated, Rose peeped out, confused, frightened and devastated still by the loss of her dream. The noise was terrible. A man was shouting, a woman had screamed and Copper . . . Copper? No, not Copper. He was up at Beechwood. A dog was howling . . . Dear Mother of God, what was happening? She must get up and . . . Bridie would be asleep in her bed, and if she woke and heard the noise . . . Sweet Mary . . . what . . . ?

Bridie, at the door which led from her new kitchen into her equally splendid garden, and which were part of the home she loved, where she had been happy for the first time since Sean, made a last desperate stand. Putting out both her hands, Bridie gripped the door frame on each side of her, standing like one crucified.

'Rose!' she screeched. 'Rose. Rosie, please . . . don't let 'im take me.'

But Lancer was incensed and mindless. He turned and grabbed her round the neck with fists like sides of ham. The blood which gushed from her nose flowed over his hands, making them slippery, but he had a good grip on her, and he did not let go as she screamed in despair for her child.

As her own name rang in her head, echoing about in an ever growing crescendo of desperation, Rose at last threw off the pall of insensibility which had kept her fast in her hiding place. From somewhere, God knows how, Lancer had come upon them. Leaping from the bed, all fear gone now, thrown off like her dream, she was out of her room and at the top of the narrow staircase which led down to the parlour in seconds. Her frantic mind noted absently the fixed, frozen shapes of her brother and sister as she bolted past their open door, but she was concerned only with what went on downstairs.

'Ye're comin' wi' me,' Lancer's voice roared, and Rose felt

her bladder contract painfully, as though she would lose control, but she was down the stairs, her nightgown flapping about her feet, which scarcely seemed to touch solid ground.

He was there.

In the open doorway to the back garden, he was outlined against the pale night sky, and in his grasp was Bridie. He had her by the neck. He shook her as though to impress upon her the meaning and resolution of what he said. Shook her and shook her and shook her, lifting her bodily from the ground as though she were made of straw. Her hands had released their hold on the door frame, and her arms swung about like those of a stuffed doll, and she looked like a woman performing a lively jig, as her feet danced six inches from the ground.

Rose screamed.

For miles around, every creature which flew or crept in the undergrowth became still. She hurled herself at the man who held her mother, smashing her clenched fists into the rocks of his arms, kicking at his thick legs with her bare, fragile toes. She spat and clawed, and her hatred flashed like a living entity, and the man dropped the lifeless thing he held, for she was a dead weight and too much for even him.

Bridie folded to the ground in a heap of black, her snowy white cap falling last from her head. Rose instantly gave up her attack and froze to awful, knowing stillness, staring blindly, senselessly at the tumble of flesh which lay on the doorstep.

Lancer appeared not to have noticed her, nor her attack upon him. He gazed uncertainly, his hazed mind bewildered by this sudden turn of events. He did not look at Rose, nor she at him. Both of them were fascinated by the thing on the step.

'Gerrup,' Lancer said hesitantly.

Bridie lay inanimate, and he aimed a kick at her side. He'd get 'er up an' bloody quick, fer wid all the row someone'd soon be 'ere ter see what it was all about.

Rose might have been a gnat which had momentarily flown about his face, for all the notice he took of her. He landed another one with his foot, and his boot almost disappeared into Bridie's unresisting flesh, and her head wobbled in an unnatural way.

'Gerrup, yer stupid cow,' he roared, afraid suddenly and not knowing why. Yet, deep down, knowing.

'Bridie,' he said, 'Bridie!' and began to edge away. He turned as though to run, then came back, and stared down at the peculiarly angled position of his wife's head.

He was quiet now, and his heart tripped, and he felt the first stirrings of fear.

'Bridie,' he quavered. 'Fer God's sake, woman, gerrup.'

The dog still howled, and up at the house Copper answered, and so did Lou in her box beside Bertie's bed. Lights were going on in windows, and a door was heard to open. Men's voices rang out across the shrubbery.

'Holy Jesu. Oh, Jesus.' For a moment Lancer McGhee stood like a hunted fox with the hounds fast closing in, turning this way and that, his head moving on his thick neck as he searched for a way of escape.

Then, a voice of authority spoke from somewhere, coming nearer.

'For God's sake, Jack, hold up that bloody light, or we will both be down. Hurry man, hurry.'

Lanterns bobbed between the trees, and circles of light moved across the lawn. With a shuddering cry, Lancer began to stumble towards the gateway through which he had come only fifteen minutes before.

Deep in shock, Rose stood on the cold step, and stared down at her mother's body.

# CHAPTER 38

James and Lacy attended their second funeral in as many months, as they followed the magnificent black hearse carrying Bridie O'Malley towards the city, and the quiet grave at St Xaviour's which she would share at last with her Sean. The cortège was splendid as though in death Rose meant her Mammy to have what she had never attained in life. There were a dozen carriages.

The first held James, Lacy, Rose, Declan and Mary Kate, but the rest were stuffed with servants, and those with whom Bridie had become friendly during the twelve months she had lived on the estate. James had insisted, not knowing how to remove the awful look of dragging pain from Rose's face, that any and everyone who might like to see Bridie off would be provided with the time and the transport to do so. Most of them had genuinely liked the old woman and if they had not, they had cared for her daughter.

Poor Miss Rose.

They would never forget her screams that night. They had topped those made by her own mother as she had struggled with Lancer McGhee and when he was caught lurching through Tuebrook village and brought back by half a dozen stalwarts, gibbering that he hadn't meant to do it, it had taken another half a dozen to hold back the dead woman's demented daughter from him.

Lacy and James had been at Highcross. It was Jonas who had ridden to fetch them. But they arrived at Beechwood Cottage two hours after the event. Groups of servants still stood about, calmer now, but nervous. Lancer was trussed like a fowl ready for the oven. Bridie still lay upon her own doorstep, though someone had covered her with a blanket, but beyond that their minds seemed to be incapable of knowing what the next step should be. Even the constable dithered about like a man asked to deal with a live explosive, for never in his working life had he been at the scene of a murder. Petty theft or a bit of poaching, and the warning off of a gypsy or two were the full extent of his activities in the upholding of the law.

Rose knelt beside her mother, and in her hands was the rosary which her father had made her thirteen years before. Her fingers moved, and the beads clicked, as she sank deeper into the hypnosis brought about by the familiar rite.

When James supervised the lifting of Bridie from the step, Rose began to cry out for him to leave her mammy be, but Lacy was there to hold her, and she turned like a baby, nestling in the curve of Lacy's neck.

The doctor put her to sleep, looking at Lacy as though to say, 'What next, poor woman? What next?' and left.

They had to fetch Bertie to Declan and Mary Kate, and it was not until the strangely expressionless face of their friend appeared before them, and asked in a hushed voice if they would like to come up to his place, that they were persuaded from their shock-induced trance.

'A few days in the company of your lot will bring them round, Jonas,' James had said apologetically, blessing the day he had employed this steadfast fellow. 'It will be a bit of a crush for you, but I fear they need the company of someone cheerful and . . . normal, and who better than Bertie and the other children.'

'Don't you fret, sir. We'll manage,' Jonas had said stoutly. He'd do owt fer Miss Rose would Jonas, as he often said to himself. And fer Captain James. His Sally, with another already on the way, always said what was one more, or even two, with their tribe?

It was the last day of May, mild and sunny, but the way through the town to St Xaviour's was not pleasant. The smell was always worse in the summer, but the warm spring had set it off early this year. As they moved at a respectful pace along Howard Street they passed the borough gaol, and Rose's eyes turned for a fraction of a second, green and brilliant with hatred for the man who lay awaiting trial within its walls.

His children sat, one on either side of her, a hand in each of hers. They were dressed all in black, their pale, freckled faces peeping like those of dormice from beneath bonnet and cap. Their feathery, pale hair was completely hidden. They had recovered somewhat, the irrepressible Bertie bringing them cheerfully back to stand on firm ground beside him, but their bewilderment and apprehension at the present ceremony was plainly written on each young face. At the same time, in their eyes was an expression which said that as long as their Rose was with them they would be all right.

Their Rose had no one now but these two, and she bent her head towards them as the goal passed from her sight. They were her last link with her old world. In their veins ran the blood of Bridie, as it did in hers, and as she rode towards the moment when she would say her last farewell to her mammy, their small hands in hers were the only thing she had to cling to – to keep her from going completely insane.


'What will Rose do now, do you think?'

Lacy looked up in surprise, her mind still preoccupied by a report in *The Times* on the quickening progress of the American Civil War. Her face was creased in an expression of concern. She had known, of course, that there was trouble coming when Fort Sumter was fired upon in April, but that was not what worried Lacy at the moment, as she read the written word before her. It was the awareness that as hostilities got further under way, they would be bound to affect her infant shipping line.

She had two steamships now.

The *Alexandrina Rose* had a sister, the *Sweet Jane* and plans were under way for a third. During the past year, she and Rose had made profits amounting to a little over £15,000, but without the constant supply of raw cotton which flowed across the Atlantic, and the stream of emigrants who packed the ships on the outward jouirney, her cargoes would be reduced to a mere trickle.

Lacy might be able to pick up low-grade cotton from India, Chile and the West Indies, but all the other shippers would be trying to do the same, and there was not enough there, even should the quality be fine enough, to make more than half a dozen ladies' handkerchiefs apiece. She had her Mediterranean trade, but that was only the bread of her business, bringing in just enough to keep alive on. The jam which sweetened it lay in the Southern States of America; and in the thousands upon thousands of Irishmen, and the rest, who looked for a better life in the New World; and who stuffed her steerage space as close as peas in a pod.

James lay on the dishevelled bed, his legs crossed at the ankles, his arms behind his head, as he stared up at the ceiling. He still wore his dressing gown, which had fallen open to reveal his long, slender legs. They were downy with a light brown fluff, like that on the head of a new born babe, until they reached the confluence of his thighs, where his penis lay serenely hidden in the darkness of his pubic hair. The soft mound caught Lacy's attention and she smiled, diverted, the words she was reading and Rose's future temporarily forgotten, as she surveyed the male beauty of her husband's body.

He was thirty four years old, and at the peak of his manhood. There was not an ounce of fat upon him, for though he sat for most of the day in what had been his father's chair in the office in Water Street, in the long summer evenings and at the weekends, he and Lacy rode and walked and swam in the narrow, private strip of water which flowed across the back of Beechwood. It was well-known by the servants that Miss Lacy and Captain Osborne swam in the nude, but they discreetly looked the other way when their employers vanished into the wood behind the house. The servants were becoming so used to the eccentricities of their master and mistress that it no longer seemed unusual, besides, kind ones such as they were hard to come by.

Lacy put down her newspaper and began to saunter across the bedroom, her eyes misting to luminous sensuality as she studied James's half-naked body. She stood beside the bed, and he turned to look at her. He saw where her eyes caressed him, and instantly his penis stirred and grew, and he smiled, and held out his arms. Lacy removed her bed gown, slowly, slowly, holding it to her breasts, revealing first a smooth white shoulder, a tiny sliver of thigh, another shoulder, inch by inch, until her gown fell to her waist, and her small breasts peaked towards him. The garment dropped, and her slim and lovely body swayed languorously an inch from his seeking hands.

'Come here, woman,' he said thickly, his eyes brown and hot.

'Now you,' she said huskily, and he undid the belt which held his gown, drawing his arms from the sleeves. He stared up at her as she stepped up onto the bed, one foot on each side of his body. He grasped her ankles to pull her down, but she said sharply,

'No.'

He released her, mesmerized by her sexuality, and the inventive love play she devised. She stood above him, letting him look into the most secret parts of her body, then sank slowly to her knees, onto the spear which waited to impale her, and he groaned as though it were he who had been pierced.

Afterwards he kissed her, every inch of her slicked body, his adoration of her complete, his hands trembling as he smoothed her damp hair back from her face. Her eyes were half closed, the post-coital euphoria giving her the look of one who is hypnotized.

'You are the most magnificent woman in the world, do you know that?' he murmured tenderly, leaning on his elbows to look down into her face. She smiled and mumbled something, and lifted a languid hand to his cheek, then pulled him down to lie beside her. Lifting her right leg she put it across his body, and snuggled her cheek into the curve of his shoulder. Her right hand lay on his chest which she stroked lovingly.

'What were you saying about Rose, my darling?' she said wickedly.

They walked that day to the wood which lay thickly at the back of the twenty-acre estate. It was not warm enough to swim, so they sat beside the small waterfall which cascaded down the smooth steps of rock into the tumble of the river. It was not as forceful as it was in the winter, for there had been very little rain this spring, but it looked lovely still – like the tiers of a wedding cake, or the skirt of a lady's gown, frothing in a tracery of white lace to the river bed. As the water fell hitting the smooth rock beneath, it created a fine spray, lit by the sun to spun sugar and frozen into a timeless shape. The surrounding foliage, even the shining rocks down which it flew, were a vivid green. The only sound was the symphony of the water, its music a fitting background for the peaceful beauty of the scene.

They held hands as they sat in stillness, and then, as though nothing had happened since James had asked the question, Lacy said,

'She will find her solace in the children.'

As usual, he knew exactly who she meant.

'But will it be enough for her?'

Lacy sighed and shook her head.

'I do not know, my love. She seems obsessed with the business, and works long after I leave, but I feel it is only to fill the gap in her life.'

'It is barely a month since Bridie was killed.'

'Oh, I know it is too soon to expect her to be as she was, but I feel . . .'

'Yes?'

'I feel those children will be her salvation. Have you seen the way in which they cling to her? They have such a need of her, it will be that which will keep her . . .'

'Yes?' James asked again.

'I was going to say *sane*, but that is too vigorous a word. Rose is too strong. She has had so much to contend with and yet, each time, she rises up and seems more invincible, not less. Do you not think that is what happens to people who are asked to carry a heavier burden than most? But she . . . still loves you, you know.'

'Oh, Lacy, I am sure by now she is . . .'

Lacy turned and looked at him almost pityingly.

'It is not a girlish infatuation, James.'

'But surely!' James protested, embarrassed as always, by the mention of Rose's feelings towards him. He would be glad when they moved to Highcross, which would be soon, for then he and Rose would not meet so frequently, and the suppressed empathy which existed guiltily between them would be exorcized. James scarcely admitted it to himself. He loved Lacy passionately, but he was often disturbed by the feeling which the strange green of Rose's eyes and the strong thrust of her breast caused in him.

He cleared his throat and held out his free hand to a rock plant, which thrived in the spray of water which continually drenched it.

'Will she stay in the cottage, do you think, or look for something more . . ?'

Lacy hesitated for a moment, then turned and looked at him, determination in the set of her small jaw, the expression in her eyes almost truculent. He always smiled to himself when she looked like this for it meant she was about to bludgeon him with what she considered a wonderful idea to which she was unsure of his reaction, but about which she would brook no argument.

'I have decided,' she began imperiously, and his mouth twitched.

'I have decided not to sell Beechwood when we move to Highcross,' she said, and looked him straight in the eye.

'Good idea,' he replied equably, 'and then Rose and the children can live there.'

Her mouth fell open, and he roared with laughter.

'You knew,' Lacy gasped, her face pink with indignation. 'Oh you,' she said, and aimed a cuff at his head, and laughed too, then went on,

'You see, she has lived so long now as . . . as we do. The cottage was suitable whilst Bridie was alive and, if she had not died, no doubt Rose would have continued to live there, even when we went to Highcross. Bridie could never have lived happily at Beechwood.'

Tears misted her eyes, and James put his arm about her shoulder.

'She was so goodhearted. Life made her ... what she became, but she was kind, and Rose loved her dearly. But she would not have fitted in at Beechwood.' Lacy gave herself a mental shake and became brisk.

'But Rose will, and the children are young and will learn.'

'I know, my love. Of course she must live there. There is nowhere else.'

'She has an income from her shares in the line, but not enough, I fear, to run Beechwood. And then, if the war in America continues, even those might ...'

He stopped her lips with a kiss.

'Lacy. The least of your worries is money. I am not ... without a guinea or two, you know.'

He grinned engagingly.

Instantly she sat up, her expression cool and stubborn. She lifted her chin, and her eyes looked at him as though he had said something offensively rude.

'What has that to do with it, James?'

James shrugged, bewildered, the smile slipping from his face.

'I mean, my dear wife, that I am well able to care, not only for you, should your business suffer through the exigencies of the American Civil War, but also of Rose, and the children, and Beechwood as well. I am a wealthy man, Lacy. I am not boasting, simply stating a fact. Rose may live at Beechwood. The children will be given a good education. You and I will live at Highcross, and take up the lives which befit our position in society ...'

'You pompous ass!'

James's mouth fell open, and his hand dropped to the stone on which they sat, as Lacy leapt to her feet. Her face was scarlet with outrage and her eyes flashed like the beacon at Rock Perch Lighthouse. She positively quivered from head to foot, and her hand trembled as she pointed an accusing finger at him.

'You patronizing, self-opinionated dolt.'

'Lacy, for God's sake, what the ...'

'Do not Lacy me, James Osborne. You have the gall to sit

522

there and speak to me of looking after poor Rose, as though she were some old retainer who has given good service, and must be suitably rewarded . . .'

'Lacy, will you . . ?' James's voice was becoming dangerously quiet, and he stood up to face her.

'No, I will not. I will not be quiet. I have listened to men telling me what I must or must not do all my life, and I'll be damned if I . . .'

'I am not trying to tell you what to do. I am telling you what I intend to do.'

'Yes, and that includes infiltrating your wayward wife back into the ranks of . . .'

'You are being childish. You seem to be obsessed with the notion of those who were once your friends . . .'

'Yes, *once* my friends maybe, but where were they when I needed them? Only Rose stood by me . . .'

James clenched his teeth. His eyes were brown and flat, like currants in a cake, and his face was white with anger. He wanted to hit her.

'We are not talking about Rose's goodness to you when . . .'

'I am. I cannot ever forget it, not how she worked beside me to build up the business we now have. Half of it belongs to her. Without her I could not have done it. Now she is to be forced to accept charity. I am your wife and must live at Highcross . . .'

'*Must* live at Highcross?' James was appalled.

'Yes, and as it is your home, you will of course maintain it, and I can accept that. I will also accept that if my . . . my business fails I shall be forced to . . . to be supported by you, but, oh James, I shall not be happy doing it. My independence has been the dearest thing in the world to me, as it has to Rose, and to lose it will make us . . . will make us . . .'

Her voice trailed away to nothing, as James turned from her, and began to walk towards the path which led out of the wood. Lacy made a small sound in the back of her throat, and her hand flew to her mouth.

Oh God, what had she done to him? Always she seemed to strike at him, bringing him to his knees with her increasing desire to be herself, her own person, dependent on no one.

523

Not even on him. It took only a word, a gesture unthinkingly made by him, and she brushed him aside as though he offered charity. He was her husband. He loved her. All he wished was her happiness and peace of mind, and again she had thrown it back into his face, like an unwanted gift.

He continued to walk, steadier now, across the soft growth of grass, making no sound, his back straight, his head lifted to stare ahead.

'Jamie.' He did not hear her whisper, nor her footsteps as she ran after him.

'Jamie.' She caught at his arm, but he shrugged her off and walked on towards the sunlight which shone at the edge of the wood.

'Jamie, please stop. Please.' She stepped in front of him, planting her feet apart, but he stepped around her politely, not even brushing her arm with his.

'Damn you, James Osborne,' she screamed. 'You shall stop, you shall.'

Running before him, she turned to face him once more, and as he moved to go around her again, his face stiff with pain, she raised her hand and hit him full in the face. Again and again she hit him, and a bright spot of blood flew from the corner of his mouth, where the diamond in her ring caught it.

'Listen to me, listen to me. You shall listen to me.' Her voice rose in a peal of terror, and at last he recognized what it was that was still buried deep in her. Deep, so deep, it had not been revealed even to Rose. Lacy was desperate to be the master of her own life, and to give to Rose the dignity of being the same. She loved him, he knew it, and was secure in that love, but he must not take from her the belief that she and Rose relied upon no one. Not even him.

His own complacent assurance that he knew this woman who stood before him was laughable. There were depths in her that no one knew, would ever know, and he should be proud that the love and trust she gave him were his alone.

His body sagged, he gave a great cry and wrapped her in his arms, which were strong, but weak with relief. She cried upon his chest, and begged him to forgive her. She had hurt him, she wept, she who loved him more than life itself, and he knew that to be true. More than life itself, but not more than her own emancipation.

It was just before Christmas that the heavy toll of the great bell of St Paul's gave the first intimation that the Prince Consort was suffering from a dangerous illness. A rumour or two had gone about, saying that His Highness was confined to his apartments with a feverish cold, but it was not until 13 December that it was reported that the Prince was not only dangerously ill, he was sinking fast.

The bell tolled again at midnight over a hushed and waiting city and the news of the Prince's death the next day was flashed along every wire throughout the United Kingdom and the Continent of Europe.

Albert, Victoria's 'Beloved angel' had gone. Grief was universal, pervading every household as if each had lost some dear and honoured relative, and the whole country was plunged with their Queen into the deepest mourning. Except for those of inferior station, who could not afford to, everyone wore black. It was considered a public duty, and a mark of respect.

And so it was that Rose's black crape and bombazine called forth no comment as she stood that morning, flowing from head to foot in a veil so thick it was almost impossible to discern her pale face behind it. She wore it though not for Her Majesty's dead husband, but for Bridie O'Malley.

It was three days before Christmas, and though the nation could hardly celebrate as it would have wished, with Prince Albert not yet cold in his grave, there was an air of subdued excitement as Rose's carriage passed from the stable yard towards the drive which led to West Derby Road. The young lad who helped Jonas to hitch the greys to the carriage, thinking himself unobserved, darted behind the tack room, a bunch of mistletoe at his back, and a girlish trill trembled on the air seconds after he had vanished.

Only Jonas accompanied her. It was cold and bright and the dusting of hoar frost turned the drab winter fields and hedgerows to a splendour more often seen in summer, when the wild flowers grew thick. A swirl of seagulls circled the barren fields, their white underbellies, tipped towards the low sun, turned to gold.

They laughed jeeringly and Rose shivered.

The carriage did not touch the town but turned right into Upper Breck Lane and on to Walton Lane. As the vehicle approached Kirkdale gaol a small crowd was already entering the yard, and Jonas turned the horses expertly to pull the conveyance directly in front of the gates. He tied up the reins and leaped nimbly to the ground. Opening the door to the carriage, he helped Rose to alight, looking anxiously into her veiled face and saying beseechingly,

'Let me come with yer, please, Miss Rose. It's not right as yer should go alone. Yer never know what might 'appen. Some o' these folks can be funny at a do like this 'un.'

Rose touched his arm reassuringly.

'No, Jonas. Thank you, but this is a . . . private thing. I must do it alone.'

She stood with the shifting murmuring crowd in the corner of the yard before the gaol. She kept her back to the wall as though its solid granite strength gave her a feeling of security and stared with hypnotic intensity at the great door to the prison, waiting for it to open.

The huge door creaked slowly open and a dread silence fell about the assembly as the figure of a squat, shambling man with dull orange hair and a face the colour of the grey building from which he had come, stepped reluctantly from between the wide doorway, coaxed by several men in uniform. There were others about him, perhaps a clergyman but Rose was not aware of them, only the man in their midst.

He was urged up the steps of the gallows, his feet feeling for each one with the uncertainty of a man ascending unfamiliar stairs in darkness. There was a few minutes of shuffling about and words were spoken, but it might have been a performance in mime for Rose heard nothing.

She lifted her veil and fixed her eyes upon the man above her.

He saw her at last and seemed to surge against the restraint which had been put upon him by those about him and his mouth opened in a black hole of outrage but no sound emerged and if it had Rose would not have heard it.

He was held firmly and at last the noose was placed about his neck with the thick knot just behind his ear. The men who held him moved away and a signal was quickly given and with a sharp snap the platform on which he stood dropped away and with it went Lancer McGhee. As he fell the six feet into oblivion, the rope tightened and instantly fractured the upper bones of his spinal column. The rupture broke his spinal cord and within five seconds he was dead.

Rose was still there when the wooden box carried away the body of the man who had killed not only her mother, but her brothers and sisters, and her own peace of mind as well, watching as the small hand cart was trundled inside the grim walls of the gaol.

She was the last to leave the prison yard and had to be persuaded by the gentle touch of a prison officer, who was surprised to see so elegant a lady at such a gathering. Jonas took her from the man's grasp and put her in the carriage, saying soothingly, as he did to his horses,

'There. There now. There, there.'

Her face was completely devoid of expression as she replaced her veil when the carriage began to move, but the stony blank stare which had deadened her eyes for almost eight months was gone.

# CHAPTER 39

It was after Christmas before James and Lacy moved to Highcross, for they had felt compelled to stay with Rose and the children until after Lancer's hanging.

The cottage had been taken over by Jonas and Sally Kingsley and their five children. Sally had given birth to a daughter, at last, born in the very room which had once been Bridie's, and as the wails of the new girl child floated down to the kitchen, it was as though her sad ghost stumped off in the old boots she had always worn, glad to be gone at last to Sean's Heaven.

Sally enquired diffidently through Jonas if Rose would mind if she called the baby Bridget, and Rose was pleased, another flake of pain peeling away like old paint, from her heart. She and the children had lived at the big house since Bridie's death, Dec and Mary Kate overawed to trembling silence by the enormous rooms, the long quiet hallways, and the majestic presence of Miss Lacy and Captain James. But, with the resilience of children, they soon found a haven of comfort in the warm and cheerful chaos of the kitchen, petted by the servants, who were sorry for the poor motherless mites.

Again, James and Lacy had been forced to subterfuge, in order to cushion Rose's intense pride and horror of charity, implying that if she did not stay in the house they would be forced to sell it.

Sophie Osborne moved to what she grandly called the 'Dower House' on 1 January 1862, though it was, by Highcross standards, really no more than a glorified cottage tucked away beyond the ornamental gardens at the back of the house. It was surrounded by a high, red brick wall and lay in the exact centre of a carefully tended garden completely secluded from the rest of the estate. A small drive wound round the main house, so that her friends might visit in their carriages should they wish, and with a small staff of servants, carefully hand-picked from those who had been with her for years, she settled happily to her declining years, positive in her mind that within the year she would be supervising the upbringing of James's first son.

Highcross, like Silverdale, ran from Aigburth Road down to the River Mersey, though it lay further south. It was very similar to the home of her childhood, and Lacy soon began to feel at ease there. She and James chose a suite of rooms on the corner of the house, facing south and west, and from the windows she could look across the lawn, and the now stripped branches of the little wood which separated the property from the surrounding farmland, towards the river, and across it to the Wirral Peninsula.

Lacy, to Sophie's consternation, had begun to redecorate the rooms to her own taste. The sitting room captured the morning sun and she seemed to imprison it for the rest of the day with the buttercup yellow, the white, cream and gold of the soft furnishings with which she filled it. The master bedroom had been shared by Richard and Sophie for forty years, and about it lay the softness of the gentle love they had known together, but the furniture and decorations were of an era long gone.

Lacy had transformed it from a cluttered, rather oppressive grandeur, into a restful, airy and light sanctuary, in which she and James might share their love-filled nights. The walls glowed in coral watered silk, the draperies were all in white traced with apple green, and the carpet was deep moss, thick and soft. The dressing room which ran off it was papered in the same moss green as the carpet, which ran through from the bedroom, and the woodwork was painted a glossy white. Beyond the dressing room, in what had once been an enormous walk-in linen cupboard, James had installed a bath and water closet.

Lacy had brought several of the servants from Beechwood, but not Maggie.

'Oh, I couldn't leave Miss Rose, not on 'er own like,' Maggie had said, horrified by the very idea of Miss Rose alone, in that big house.

Lacy knew it was inevitable that she would have to make an assault on society, and she fell upon the task with the same determined enthusiasm that had made her the best pickle-sticker in the factory in Mervyn Street.

She and Sophie went carefully through Sophie's list of friends, whittling out those most likely to decline an invitation, until they had short-listed twenty or so whom they both thought might be inclined towards tolerance.

They came to her dinner party, as she knew they would, and the happiness which shone in James's warm brown eyes as his friends bowed over his beautiful wife's hand, or kissed her smooth cheek; and the gratification of Sophie Osborne, as she glided the dignified dinner route on the arm of an elderly widower, was reward enough.

Lacy's air of polite indifference seemed to charm her guests, and made those who had come declare that they had never known such an enjoyable evening. The success of it spread through the borough and, within a week, she and James had more invitations than they knew what to do with.

'But we cannot accept them all,' she said aghast. 'I am to chair the meeting of shareholders on Wednesday and have an appointment with Mr Moore on Thursday, and you know I always see Captain Jefferson whilst *Alexandrina Rose* is in port.'

Diverted by her own words and uninterested in the stack of invitations which James held in his hand she changed the subject to what was the stuff of life to her.

'Tell me, have you heard, James, of the rumour which abounds concerning the increase in dock rates? Has it reached your ears? Really, it should . . .'

'But what about these invitations, Lacy? I cannot just ignore them,' James said as if she had not spoken. 'There is one from the Lucases asking us to join them at the Opera and another from Henry Dickson and his wife to . . .'

Irritated, Lacy grumblingly conceded a little.

'Very well, I will dine with Amy and Ned, if you like, but I cannot . . .'

'But the Dicksons are old friends, and Henry seemed to find you . . .'

'I do not care, Jamie. I am far too busy. I have done as you asked and the dinner party was most enjoyable but until I have . . .'

'Do you mean to say you will accept none of them?'

'I said I would see Amy and Ned.'

'Because Amy is your sister?'

'And what is wrong with that, pray?'

James could see they were becoming perilously close to a repeat of the sharp exchange which had taken place at Beechwood. He had been convinced that once Lacy had tasted the sweet and delightful victory which had been the outcome of the dinner party; when, as had happened, the invitations had begun to appear as a sign that she was 'forgiven', though he would not have couched it to her in such terms; then, she would be so enthralled, that their immediate return to the social scene would be assured.

It was not that James particularly cared for what he called the 'butterfly round', but in his love and pride in her, had wanted it for *her*. He would have been content to continue to live the simple life they had shared for the past eighteen months, with the occasional family gathering, or a small dinner party with congenial friends; but he must, now that his father was dead, continue what he considered to be his duty as the heir to his father's position in society. It was taken for granted that the activities in the community in which Richard Osborne had taken an interest would now pass to James. He had a sense of ongoing responsibility that he felt bound to fulfil. He could not neglect those new obligations: to his tenants; to those who served him; and to those who had called his father friend.

On the occasion of the discussion over invitations, he and Lacy were at breakfast in their spacious sitting room. Their half-eaten meal lay on the snowy cloth of the small table which was placed before the fire and scattered across it were envelopes, some opened, sheets of thick notepaper, and invitation cards.

James watched as the expression of irritable exasperation on his wife's face changed to one of stubborn disagreement. He knew it well and his heart plummeted.

'James, I just have not the time to . . .'

'Nor the inclination, it seems,' he interrupted coldly.

Lacy lifted her chin, and her eyes turned to ice.

'May I ask if you have read the newspapers, James,' she said distantly.

'I can see no connection between our social obligation, and what is written in the newspapers.'

'Can you not,' Lacy's voice was chilling.

'We are bound by duty to accept . . .'

'Do you not feel the least concern about the war which is being fought in America?'

'Oh, for God's sake, Lacy. Does your mind forever run on business? Have you no thought for your duties as my wife?'

Her face went white, then scarlet, and she flung the sliver of toast she nibbled to her plate, and stood up, rocking the table and all its contents. Coffee cups went here and there, and the coffee spilt in ugly brown stains upon the pristine cloth, and the squares of notepaper.

My duties as your wife? And what are those, pray? To sit at home and wait upon your pleasure, and those of your friends? To let my ships founder and my concerns go to the bottom for lack of attention? To live the life of your mother, chitter-chattering over the teacups, gossiping with relish over some petty scandal? To visit the same fools day in, day out and have them visit me? That is not my life, James, and never will be. I think it might be advisable if you were to accept that. I am a businesswoman who happens to be your wife. I have obligations to . . .'

'Do be careful what you say, my dear, for words have a way of coming home to roost, like birds,' said James, perilously close to striking her.

The tension in the room was like the violent stirrings of a storm and Copper, who lay like an elderly pampered friend before the fire, struggled to his feet and slunk away to the door, as though waiting for it to open and allow him to escape.

'And what does that cryptic remark imply?' Lacy whispered menacingly. 'Do I take it you mean to threaten me in some way?'

'I would say the boot was on the other foot?'

'Will you for God's sake say what you mean, James Osborne. You know, or should do by now, that I will not become as your Mama is, or Amy or any of the wives of your friends. I am what I have been for the past seven years. You knew it when we married, and accepted it. I made no pretence then that my business was anything but of the utmost importance to me, and that I would continue to run it despite our marriage. It comes first . . .'

'Before our marriage, you mean,' James said quietly.

'No. No, I did not say that. Let me finish. It comes before . . . before others. It always has. If I must choose between the friendship of these people and my work you know where my choice will lie. Do you not see,' she said desperately, 'that just at the moment, with things in such a turmoil in America, and the decrease in my cargoes, I cannot be expected to socialize . . .'

'It seems you can be expected to do nothing that pleases me.'

'Pleases you,' she shrieked, incensed, but he had turned away, his rage white hot, unable to stay in the room for another moment.

Striding towards the door which led into the dressing room, he wrenched it open, his dressing gown swinging about his bare legs. She did not go after him this time, but stood as the door crashed behind him.

It was the first time neither one of them had backed down.

# CHAPTER 40

The precise nature of the disagreement between North and South in the conflict of the American Civil War was subject to much debate and conjecture by those who were not involved, and many who thought the clash to have been brought about by the question of slavery were not aware that that issue was merely incidental. True the South sought to defend itself against the abolitionists, but this was a simplistic view, for there were many other factors involved.

Eleven Southern States led by South Carolina wished to withdraw from the Union and become a new self-governing nation. The North argued that the South had no constitutional right to do so, and that the Confederate States, as they wished to be called, were rebels.

Some christened it 'the brothers war'.

It began in November 1860 when Abraham Lincoln was elected President of the United States of America, and in December of the same year, South Carolina voted to leave the Union. By February 1861 six more States had followed suit and Jefferson Davis was sworn in as President of the Confederate States of America.

In April, Fort Sumter, which was an island in Union hands off Charleston in South Carolina, was fired upon by Confederate troops, and President Lincoln called for the mobilization of Union forces and proclaimed a blockade of all Southern ports.

The Civil War had begun.

Lacy stared across the road to the quay from the chair in the bow window of her office in Strand Street, *The Times* hanging limply from her hand. A fine drizzle fell across the panes of glass, nearly obscuring the scene before her, a gossamer drift of vapour which shadowed the gently swaying masts of tall ships to a ghostly forest. Though it was mid-morning, the light had barely lifted the dark of night, and street lamps were still lit. Carriages moved in a silent world, the yellow blobs of shifting light illuminating their passage, the outline of greatcoated coachmen barely discernible against the sulphurous yellow and grey of the sky. The setts of the road gleamed, creating reflections of blurred figures as they hurried along, moving in and out of the glow which spilled across the pavement from the window of the spirit merchant who had the ground floor below her own office.

The weather exactly matched her mood.

Lacy thought she had never felt so low in spirit since the days when she was recovering from the horrors of her illness in Naylor's Yard. She sighed deeply, then stood up and moved across the spacious room to stand before the cheerful fire, the wide black belt of her merino skirt swaying gracefully as she walked. The newspaper which she had been reading was still gripped fiercely in her hand, and with a sudden movement she threw it furiously across the room.

'Damn them, damn them, damn them!' she whispered and her shoulders slumped. She rested her forearm upon the mantel above the fireplace and bending her head placed her brow on it.

If only Rose were here.

If she had someone with whom to discuss the desperate situation, which was growing steadily worse, it would help to clear the frustration and despair which seemed to clog her brain, and which made her unable to think. Always in the past, Rose's quiet attention, her readiness to listen whilst Lacy talked out the problem which was troubling her, had seemed to put the words, the thoughts, the ideas into their true perspective; sifting through them until they stood, neat as a row of books on a shelf, and all in their correct order. The answer would then be found. They had been like two horses pulling in the same harness.

But Rose was at home, interviewing governesses for Declan and Mary Kate.

She would talk to James. He would listen, be sympathetic

535

and understanding. All the shipping merchants suffered the same difficulties, himself included, but the big lines and those with a mass of capital to tide them over would survive. They had a large fleet of ships which could travel all over the world to alternative markets; bringing other cargoes from the Balkans, the Far East, Australia; and taking merchandise to them. But she had only her two steamships, plying furiously between the States of America and Liverpool, and they were already travelling no more than half full, sometimes not even that.

Yes, she could discuss it at any time with James but his advice, lovingly given, would not be without a certain unconscious satisfaction. She knew he would never knowingly try to jeopardize what she had, but if it meant she would spend more time at home, he could not help feeling relief that her business was floundering.

Poor Jamie. Torn between his pride in what she had overcome and his longing to have her kiss him goodbye each morning from the tranquillity of their room, and for her to be there to welcome him as he returned in the evening. She smiled sadly, and shook her head as though to clear it of all unnecessary and clouding emotions, and resumed her meditation.

The emigrant trade, which in 1854 had totalled 420,000 each year, had dropped over the past nine months, and the estimated figure for 1861 was only a mere 72,000. She had had her share, but it was not enough.

It was cotton, 'King Cotton', which must be her salvation.

Lacy paced the room, turning at each corner with a little kick of her skirts.

There was an answer.

There had to be an answer.

And she would find it.

She had not come this far to have it all swept away on the wave of the brutal war which was beginning to gather momentum in America. Names like 'Bull Run', 'Manassas', 'Beauregard', 'Johnson' and the 'Shenandoah Valley' had been on everyone's lips, at least those upon whom the war had a direct effect, and now, as the store of cotton which was almost gone could no longer be replaced, other names had crept into the newspapers. Port Royal Sound on the South Carolina coast had been taken by the Union navy in November, and the blockade of that coast was becoming tighter and tighter. Mills in Lancashire were cotton-starved, and already manufacturers were being forced to close down.

Lacy clenched her fists and her lips thinned into a grim line. Going to the door, she opened it and called to the young clerk who sat at his tall desk in the outer office. So swiftly had she appeared, he did not have time to stand respectfully, but fumbled foolishly with his hair as though he was searching for his top hat to raise to her instead.

'Call me a carriage, please, Mr Johnson,' Lacy said peremptorily.

'But your own has . . .'

'A hackney cab will do, Mr Johnson, and at once.'

The young man was so dismayed by the idea of a respectable and elegant lady like Mrs Osborne riding in a public conveyance that, for a moment, it looked as though he might remonstrate with her. But Mr Fisher, head clerk for three years to Mrs Osborne, and used by now to her eccentricities, gave him a look, one which could quell a small rebellion in less than five seconds, and the lad ran out of the room and down the steps to the street to call a cab.

'I must see Miss Millbury who is the last one, then we will talk,' was all Rose said as Lacy swept despairingly into her small, but pretty, sitting room on the first floor at Beechwood.

Lacy whirled about and moved to sit down on the low chair by the fire but as she did so, her crinoline, flattened in front and with a bustle at her back, according to the very latest fashion, tipped alarmingly, and she exclaimed irritably.

'These damn things! Why ever fashion decreed we should wear such monstrosities, I cannot imagine.'

'Why wear the thing then?' Rose said placidly.

'What, and be thought dowdy? How dreadful!'

They both laughed and before Rose knew what she was about, Lacy had slipped off her capacious skirt, and sat down comfortably in only her bodice and white, frilly ankle-length drawers.

'Lacy Hemingway, you will never change. Faith, 'tis good to see you though, for there is no one makes me laugh like you.'

Lacy leaned forward and took Rose's hand, grinning, relaxed, business stress forgotten.

For half an hour they laughed and chatted and drank hot chocolate before the brightly burning fire in the cosy room, and the world outside was forgotten and everyone in it. Including James.

But then a silence fell, and Rose knew Lacy would tell her now the reason why she had come.

'I can speak to no one but you of this, Rose,' Lacy said, 'not even Jamie.'

Rose dropped her gaze and a flush came to her cheek, but Lacy thought she knew the reason, and was not dismayed.

'Go on,' Rose said.

'You and I have always been able to see the other's viewpoint. We seem at times to share the same mind and solutions to what troubles me can often be found in your head.'

'And the reverse, acushla.'

'Yes, I know.' A quick smile of affection.

'What is it then? The war in America?'

'There you see! Even before I speak, you know what is in my mind.'

'I read *The Times* as well, Lacy.'

'You know the problem, then.'

'The blockade.'

'Yes. Port Royal's gone, and Pimlico Sound, and all the major sea ports are stopped up tighter than corked bottles with squadrons from the Union Navy. The emigrants are still going over in small numbers, of course, but to the North, so *Alexandrina Rose* and *Sweet Jane* are coming back without the cotton we so desperately need. Paul Ellis managed to slip out of New Orleans but he was fired upon and narrowly missed being captured. He says Sheridan Bonfleur has gone into the

538

Confederate Army. The cotton trade is of secondary importance to him now that his family is involved in the war and . . .'

'Is Paul in Liverpool?'

Surprised by the interruption, Lacy looked up from her anguished contemplation of the blazing logs in the fireplace.

'Yes,' she answered. 'He is coming into the office tomorrow.'

'Was the *Annie McGregor* damaged?'

'Yes, he says he does not know how he . . .'

'Could he command *Alexandrina Rose*. A steamship? He is used only to sail.'

'Well, I suppose . . .'

'With a fast ship, two fast ships, or even three, when the third is ready, could not he and Captain Jefferson run the blockade? He knows those waters, that coast better than anyone. There is cotton there, you have cargoes cramming the warehouse, which will be snapped up by those in the South. Essential supplies. They must be sore pressed for manufactured goods. They have no industry and the . . .'

'Oh Rose.'

'You could make a fortune.'

'A fortune . . .'

Lacy breathed the words. Eyes shone brilliantly and the flush of success already glowed beneath her skin. She could see it all. As she had known it would, Rose's mind had struck the spark which kindled her own, and the whole perfect plan fell neatly into place. Her brain ticked quietly now, urgency and despair gone, working coolly upon the steps which must be taken to put the whole thing into action.

They took lunch together, still talking, planning, deciding and it was not until the dim light of the afternoon had vanished completely, and the two women looked towards the maid in the doorway who had come, she said, to light the lamps, that they realized that the day was gone.

The next day, Lacy and Paul Ellis were closeted for the better part of five hours together in the office in Strand Street. It still rained, but now the warm excitement in the office generated a feeling so intense it was all Lacy could do to stop herself from grabbing the now tubby figure of Captain Ellis and doing an energetic polka about her littered desk. Captain Jefferson was sent for. When he had been brought up-to-date and was still open-mouthed at the fact that he was to become a blockade-runner, it was Mr Fisher's turn.

Stock lists were gone over, for it was Mr Fisher's job to keep a sharp tally of all the merchandise which was stored in the warehouse at Gorée Piazza. The next few days would be hectic as preparations were put under way to load cargoes of iron, rails, hoops and a dozen manufactured goods which would fetch the highest prices in the Southern States of America, and Lacy worked late into the night, supervising the choice of these cargoes and the loading of them into the holds of the *Alexandrina Rose* and *Sweet Jane*.

'What will become of the *Annie McGregor*, Paul? You cannot mean to abandon her in Liverpool.'

Paul Ellis and Lacy stood in the window of her office on that last night, watching as Michael O'Shaughnessy checked the final crate of Manchester piece goods as it was lowered into the hold of *Alexandrina Rose*. In the darkening rays of the winter sunshine, the outline of the ship's funnels, laced about by spars and rigging, was black against the pale pearl of the sky. Captain Jefferson appeared on the deck of *Sweet Jane*, who was berthed alongside Paul's new ship, and spoke to his first mate, and they both moved to the side of the ship to stare in deep contemplation as the last shovelful of coal was tossed into the bunker.

It was almost dark, though barely five o'clock in the afternoon, and the tempo of the dock was beginning to slow down. Paul Ellis drew on his cigar, his mind darting beyond the evening of pleasure he promised himself in Juniper Street, to the vague sadness he felt at the loss of the ship he had sailed for almost ten years.

'She is not completely lost, Lacy. With some repairs done on her she is still capable of completing another day's work. As a matter of fact I have already had an offer for her. A fellow I know back in Charleston has been looking for a ship to purchase and when he heard of *Annie*'s run in with the Union Ships, he asked if he might take her off my hands.'

'And will you agree?'

'I really have no choice. As you said, I cannot leave her to moulder in dock, and with my new command I have not the time to see to her refitting. Joel Ashton will give me a fair price. He has a hankering to try his hand at blockade-running now that his activities in "blackbirding" are to be curtailed by the war.'

'Blackbirding?' Lacy turned to stare at Paul.

'Mmmm. He has made a nice profit from the Guinea trade over the last six or seven years.'

Lacy looked again at the rapidly darkening scene before her. She was quiet for a moment, as though her thoughts had momentarily distracted her. Then, wistfully, she said:

'I was always sorry I had not a chance to be in on that. There must have been a fair profit to be had from . . .'

Paul turned and laughed.

'Lacy Osborne! Does your mind ever stray far from thought of profit? I have never known a woman like you.'

'Thank you, Paul. You are most kind,' she said, and they both laughed.

'Just contemplate the lovely ship you will have from the profits *you* will make from this venture.'

At the beginning of February 1862 Lacy stood quietly on the quayside, her back to the steps which led up to Strand Street. She had said her farewells to both captains as the heavily laden steam ships were ready to cast off, then had slipped unnoticed down the gangplanks and moved to a secluded position where she might watch her hopes steam away to the mouth of the river. She knew that both men, their crews and her two ships were sailing into danger. The enforcement of the blockade by the Union Navy was strict. The whole of the 3,500 miles of Southern coastline was of course impossible to guard; it would not be necessary. Their aim was to stop the commerce of the major seaports, and a blockading squadron was stationed off each of these.

But Paul Ellis and Captain Jefferson were both experienced

and natural seamen, brave and filled with the expectation of a generous bonus, should they succeed. The stakes were high. Not only would the profit on the goods they took out be enormous, but Lacy would be able to name her own price for the cotton they brought back. Mill owners, those still in business, would be knocking at her door begging to be allowed to purchase it.

Lacy stood until the two ships had become grey blurs against the pale horizon at the mouth of the river, then turned slowly and ascended the steps to Strand Street, crossed it more quickly, and entered her office, throwing off her mantle briskly. There was work to be done. Goods must be purchased to refill her warehouse, empty now of the merchandise which had lain there for weeks. Within a month *Alexandrina Rose* and *Sweet Jane* would be back in Liverpool, and she must have new cargoes waiting for them.

Not for a second did she consider the notion that they might never return.

That night in the flickering light from the fire which glowed in their hearth, Lacy Osborne told her husband of what she had done.

For the past three weeks, since her refusal to accept the score of invitations which had descended upon them after their dinner party, they had barely been on nodding terms. James had made no move to heal the breach in their relationship, and she had been too busy and tired to try. He had enquired politely of her health, as he had sat opposite her each morning, hiding his deepening concern at the sight of the grey circles beneath her eyes, and the strain on her face. She ate hardly enough to keep herself alive, and it took all his determination not to take her in his arms, and hold her fiercely to him, declaring his protective love and despair at what she was doing to herself. She could barely walk sometimes when she came into their room at night, but her expression told him to hold his tongue.

He lay beside her as she slept, her breathing as deep and regular as an exhausted child. Once she fell asleep upon the bed without removing her clothes, and his heart had tripped

542

with his love for her, as he sat beside her in the lamplight, watching over her, drowning in his need to hold her. He had undressed her gently and she had not awoken even as she lay naked in his arms. He had kissed her softly, covering her, before undressing himself and climbing into the bed next to her. For an hour he had watched her sleep. Her eyelids had fluttered, the long cinnamon lashes beating a frantic tattoo upon her cheek as she re-lived some problem in her dream, and her head had tossed fretfully. Only when he took her in his arms did she quieten, sighing against his chest.

He waited with the patience he had learned over the years for her to speak. He knew that whatever crisis had held her in its grip for the past months was temporarily over, she had returned that day to the house early, had dined with him, smiling a little as they spoke of small things. She was relaxed, and softer than she had been for weeks.

He lay now, one hand behind his head, and stared at the ceiling where the merry-go-round of the reflected flames of the fire whirled in gold and orange circles. She lay quietly beside him, her arms resting upon the coverlet which lay across her breasts.

'Jamie,' she murmured at last.

'Yes?'

'May I speak with you now about . . . about our life together?'

'You know that you may.'

'We have not seen eye to eye on so many things, but I hope you know how much I love you.'

'Do you?'

'You know I do, Jamie. Do not dishonour me by pretending otherwise.'

The remark surprised him and, for a moment, discon-certed, he was incapable of replying. Dishonour her? What the hell did she mean by that? He raised himself up on his elbow and looked down into her face.

'Let us talk, Jamie, not argue,' she said, seeing his expres-sion. 'When I speak of dishonour it is meant to tell you that you do me an injustice if you think me capable of being your

543

wife, lying with you in love, if I did not care deeply for you. Do you understand?'

Though the light was dim, James could see the softness in her face, and the honesty of what she said was in her eyes. The truth shone there, and for a second he was tempted to reach for her. Then he drew back. It would solve nothing if they ended the dissension between them by making love.

'Do you understand, Jamie?' Lacy repeated softly.

'Yes, I do, and I will listen.'

'Not just listen, but *talk* to me.'

'I love you too, my darling.'

Lacy held back from reaching for him, just as James had done a moment ago, then began to talk. She told him of what had been happening in the preceding weeks. The words flowed in the warm darkness and he listened, at first appalled, then angry, hurt and horrified that she would send men into certain danger, but equally distressed that she had been unable to come to him. She spoke softly but firmly for nearly an hour, whilst he leaned on his elbow and looked into her face. The only time his eyes flickered away was at the mention of Rose's name and, again, Lacy was certain she knew the reason why. It had embarrassed him to discover that Rose loved him; and Lacy understood.

'Now you know what I have done,' she concluded, 'and why I have been as I have. I had to find the answer without you, my love. I have found it, and whether you agree or not, it is done. More important, you must realize now, that what I do must be my own decision. You must love me as I am, Jamie. That is the lesson you must learn, but I have learned a lesson too. I cannot live with you as we have been for the past weeks. You have to compromise with my needs, but I must do the same with yours. I must share my . . . life with that of being your wife, the hostess in our home, and the mistress of your household. I am prepared to do so because I love you more than any other person in the world.'

There was silence, then she said.

'Now it is your turn to show me what is in your heart, Jamie. Tell me. If it hurts me as I have hurt you, then so be it, but let us have the truth between us, always.'

It was dawn before they slept, tight in each other's arms,

cemented together by the sweat of the passion they had forged in their reunion. Their words to each other had been violent at times, but the truth of their love and need, not just for one another, but for the life they would have together, was as clear and bright as the morning star which pricked the sky above their window as they slept.

# CHAPTER 41

In the same week that *Alexandrina Rose* and *Sweet Jane* slipped across the Atlantic in the direction of South Carolina, the Union Navy captured Roanoke on the coast of North Carolina and, in March, New Bern in Pimlico Sound fell to the North. In April it was the turn of Fort Macon and New Orleans, and the only port left open to the stealthy approach of Lacy's ships was Charleston.

Paul Ellis commanding the *Alexandrina Rose* and followed by the *Sweet Jane*, under the command of Stanley Jefferson, whispered past the Union Fleet in the dead of night, taking Lacy's cargoes and bringing out the raw cotton to the famine-stricken mills of Lancashire. The months went by and, somehow, they contrived to be successful, eluding the guns of the Union Naval vessels. But though they, and others, brought in thousands of bales of raw cotton to the port of Liverpool, by December 1862, half a million cotton workers in Lancashire were unemployed and on Relief.

The distress was appalling. In Preston, Blackburn, Manchester and Stalybridge whole families were close on starving. It was that or the Relief and many men to whom the word 'beggar' was the foulest obscenity, seeing their wives and children in such dire straits, went cap in hand to claim it. These towns, from bustling, noisy places, filled with the clangour of the pole of the knocker-up on the window, and clogs upon cobbles as they clattered to the mill, became populated by wraiths who slipped by with scarce a sound as they searched for sustenance.

Pawnshops thronged with goods, which were worth a penny or two to the man behind the counter, but were treasures to those who pawned them; and warm family homes became cold hovels.

In an effort to draw attention to their plight, Lancashire

operatives marched from Stalybridge to London. Not only did they draw the strength somehow to complete this mammoth walk, but at its end they entertained the interested Londoners with their band music, which they reckoned to be the best in the world, playing their instruments with all the verve of the North-countryman who loves nothing better than the music of a brass band.

Some were found employment under the Public Works Act, clearing ground for buildings or parks. Free coal was distributed to the cotton workers, but the pride of the Lancashire women was shattered by their need to queue for their allowance; and for the Relief tickets, which were exchanged, after more queueing, for bread and flour.

General sympathy for the plight of these people was enormous and tons of clothing were collected from all over the country, and sent via depots to Lancashire. Soup kitchens were formed, and the unemployed queued again for their breakfast.

But the destitution afforded privilege to some fortunates.

Classes were begun in Manchester. Shoemaking and other alternative trades were taught. Reading lessons were well attended, and former mill girls learned needlework at a school organized by the Manchester and Salford District Provident Society.

But the cause of it all, the war in America, ground on. It seemed the tide ran strongly in favour of the South, and the Union forces were pushed back at the second battle of Bull Run, at Freidericksburg, and in May 1863, at Chancellorsville. But at Gettysburg the Confederate Army was defeated, and General Lee retreated for the first time.

It seemed the two vessels of the 'New Hemingway and O'Malley Steamship Line' bore charmed lives, as did many other blockade-running ships. In the beginning, five out of every six ships which were engaged in the same daring practice as Captains Ellis and Jefferson got through the blockade and derisive words were spoken of the failure of the Union Navy to effectively bottle up the Southern ports. Many of the blockade-runners, making a dash for Wilmington or

Charleston through the Federal warships, relied on their small size and speed to escape detection, or to get out of trouble when spotted.

But the average tally of loss was rising fast, and Lacy speeded up the construction of her third steamship, with plans for a fourth on the drawing board. Now, as the war continued into 1864, it was only one in three ships which successfully returned to Liverpool, then one in two, and Lacy felt she lived on the edge of a cliff between each voyage. When they sailed for Charleston, she would stand on the quayside and watch the two ships go up the river and wonder if it would be the last time she would see them. They would be long gone before she turned back to her office and, for hours after her return there, she would rise continually and gaze from her window, as though her willpower could protect and speed them back.

Her smile was clouded, as were her eyes, until the swelling sail of *Alexandrina Rose* or *Sweet Jane* flew round the curve of the Rock Perch Lighthouse.

The three men sitting in the office sipped a glass of sherry, and talked in desultory fashion. Two were Americans, speaking in the flat drawl of the Southern gentleman but the third was English, a North-countryman by the sound of his broad dialect.

A shaft of sunlight fell through the dust-coated window, pointing a finger at the clutter of papers, samples of raw cotton, ledgers, pens and cigars, and placing a glint of gold in the pale amber of the opened bottle of sherry. A window in the opposite wall looked out into a vast shed, a warehouse which was rapidly being emptied of its contents by half a dozen sweating, barefoot negroes. They carried the huge bales of lint cotton, each one weighing almost five hundred pounds, between them, lifing them onto long-handled wheels with apparent ease. A white man supervised their work, walking from the rear of the warehouse as each man trundled his load to the wide doors which stood open to the quayside at the front. The supple, well-muscled young negroes moved easily, gracefully, chanting a rhythmic and monotonous song as they worked. Their bare feet slapped across the stone cobbles of the dock, and they stacked the huge bales they transported onto the tidy mounds which lay beside the ships moored there, before returning for another load.

It was peaceful and warm in the office as the men sipped their sherry. The American placed his feet upon a chair, tipping back the one on which he sat, his glass resting comfortably on his swelling paunch.

'High tide at four, did you say, Anderson?' he asked.

'Just so, Captain Ellis.'

'We'll be away by then, providing the purser has all our requirements from the chandler. If he hasn't that's just too bad. The men will have to make do with short rations. I want to take advantage of Admiral Farragut's absence and be well away by nightfall.'

'Where was he last sighted, Paul?'

The second seaman, the Englishman with the strong Lancashire accent, spoke quietly, almost sleepily, as though the gentle spring warmth had him in thrall, but his eyes were sharp, and there was an air of tension about him.

'I heard there was a flotilla off Savannah a day or two ago, but rumour has it they will go South rather than North.'

Captain John Jefferson put his glass upon the cluttered desk top and got to his feet. Both he and Paul Ellis had been on the quayside in Charleston since dawn, supervising the final loading of the raw cotton so frantically needed in the mills of Lancashire, onto the *Alexandrina Rose* and the *Sweet Jane*. Both ships had been coaled soon after their arrival in port, for their Captains wished to have the filthy job over with, and besides, it was fast developing into a case of first come, first served, as supplies of coal in the war-torn Southern States of America were becoming harder to obtain, and though both ships were rigged with sail and engine, the latter was desperately needed for the speed to get clear of the Union warships which attempted to blockade the Southern ports.

A shout from further down the quayside turned the heads of the three men towards the door which led out on to the dock, and Captain Jefferson took an uneasy step towards it. Tension was so high these days in this busy, blockaded port, the slightest thing had men jumping like frightened women. The work on the loading of the two vessels was halted as seamen, and the dockers who were engaged in hauling the cotton bales aboard, all stopped to stare at the youth who ran like a hare across the dock, his mouth open in a frantic, ear-splitting cry of warning. His flying, leaping figure was the only one with movement, as all activity in the vicinity came to a halt. Hearts thudded in chests and pulses quickened, and the men who were to sail that afternoon on the two vessels turned to look anxiously into one another's faces.

'Come on lads, put yer backs into it,' a voice shouted, and the men resumed the furious urgency of loading which had been interrupted.

The youth almost fell into the office, and for a moment he could not speak, but only point with a trembling hand back towards the way he had come. Captain Jefferson took his arm.

'What is it, lad?'

'Let him get his breath, Captain.'

'What the hell is it? Come on, man, spit it out.' Paul Ellis stood over the youth threateningly, as though the news he brought, obviously bad, was of his causing.

At last the boy had his breath.

'Ships, Mr Anderson. Dozens of them . . . moving towards . . . Charleston . . .'

'Blast and damnation . . .'

'Union ships, sir, and . . .'

But Captain Ellis waited to hear no more.

'Come on, John, look lively man. We can still beat 'em. They'll be relying on us waiting for the tide, but if we go now . . .'

'But what about the rest of the cotton? It's not yet loaded and we shall be sailing without . . .'

'Damn the rest of the cotton. If we sail with what cargo we have we can still get away, but if we wait . . . Send the ship's mate to round up the rest of the crew, there's a good chap, and fetch the purser back from the chandler's. Come on,

John, don't stand there like a damned figurehead. Let's get moving.'

For half an hour a scene of indescribable urgency took place on both the British vessels. Men ran in feverish haste about the decks, scrambling and fretting, replacing hatch covers and generally preparing the decks for sea. A flurry of ropes and cables seemed to be in immediate likelihood of tying themselves in knots, and Captain Ellis was heard to curse loudly and lewdly on the parenthood of several British seamen.

Just as the tide began to reach the full, both ships took on their pilots, loosed the ropes holding them to the jetty and, calm now they were under way, made for the open sea.

By the time the pilots were dropped into the waiting cutters it was early evening. The light was beginning to fade, and Captain Ellis decided to take the opportunity to be rowed across to the *Sweet Jane* to have a last minute discussion with Jefferson on their tactics. It was decided that if Union ships were sighted they would separate and head in different directions, Paul Ellis making off up the coast whilst the *Sweet Jane* made a run directly out to sea.

Both ships got under way again, making their best speed possible. Sea conditions were ideal with nothing more than a long, lazy swell to contend with. For several hours, as the last glimmer of the spring evening drew towards its close the two ships crept stealthily across the soft slopes of the Gulf Stream and the Atlantic Ocean. The sky faded to a silver grey, tinged with a blush of pink at the horizon, and a dusting of stars appeared to the north. Everywhere was quiet but for the soft sound of the engines. The slap of the swell on the hull of the ship was muted and a lone seagull, who had followed them hopefully from land, turned back, heading for home and safety.

It was as the last light of the day gave way finally to night that the lookout, perched high in the sky where the crow's nest swayed above the foremast of *Alexandrina Rose*, yelled to the deck below that ships were in sight, ironclads of the Union Navy, he said, and, his voice shaking with excitement and dread, the enemy ships had sighted the *Alexandrina Rose* and had started to turn towards her.

Paul Ellis did not hesitate.

If he made his turn now, and retreated with all the speed he had, there was a chance the Unionists would not notice *Sweet Jane* who had fallen a mile or two astern. She was not as fast as *Alexandrina Rose* and Captain Jefferson did not know these waters as well as he himself did. Given a small start, which he would gain if he went now, there was a good chance that he could not only get away with his superior speed, but lead the ships of the Union Navy away from the other vessel.

'Full speed ahead,' he bellowed down to the engine room and the exultation in his voice seemed to spread to the men who stood beside him in the deck house, and down below to the men who stoked the boilers. Their faces grinned in anticipation of the chase and their eyes gleamed. Eighteen knots was reached, the ship's maximum speed, and the smoke became as black as the hull of the ship, contrasting with the white wash at her stern and, as Paul Ellis watched, the Union ships turned even more sharply, as they tried to cut off his escape.

'You don't stand a chance,' he roared joyfully, and his men laughed, and urged on their brave ship with sharp movements of their arms and fists, like boxers flexing in the ring.

Captain Jefferson watched her go as she led the naval ships away from him. The plan had worked and in twenty minutes, when it was completely dark, he would slip off unnoticed leaving the *Alexandrina Rose* and her captain to merge into the coastal waters which Paul Ellis knew so well. In eight hours, under the cover of darkness, he himself would be far away from his pursuers. During that time, guided by her captain, *Alexandrina Rose* would shimmy by the enemy and follow *Sweet Jane* home safely to Liverpool.

He almost made it.

Six feet to port or starboard and he would have slid by without even being aware that the unmarked reef was there. The jagged rocks, just feet below the surface, were invisible in the calm weather, no heavy waves broke on them, no clouds of spray were thrown to reveal their presence. Paul Ellis was knocked to the deck, his face quite comically thunderstruck, for it was his boast that he knew every reef and rock on this bit of American coastline. Over the sound of fractured metal and falling masts, he was heard to shout obscenely that he would have the skin flayed from the back of the man in the crow's nest who had let this happen.

The cold grey sea flooded noisily into the holds of the drowning ship and the bales of cotton, loaded only hours ago by the cheerfully singing black men, crashed heavily against the hull, forcing the ship to list grotesquely to port. The graceful masts cracked and were viciously ripped out of the decks to fall slowly, slowly over the side of the ship. The rigging festooned the crew, who scrambled about the deck like fleeing ants, and many were carried screaming into the black sea, caught in the thousands of yards of rope.

On and on the sounds went. Splintering, tearing, crashing, screaming, shouting . . . Paul Ellis thought it would never end, as he lay beneath the wheel of the ship he had commanded for over two years. He had thought he would never love her as he had the sailing ship *Annie McGregor* but now, as he prepared to die with her, he knew that he did. He lay quite peacefully, a seaman from first to last, a man of the sea, dying in her arms and not unhappy to do so.

As the momentum of the ship carried her over the reef to the deep sea beyond, only the cries of the injured remained, and the hiss of escaping steam; then even that was gone as Lacy Osborne's first-born ship died, and sank to her grave.

Many miles astern Captain Jefferson heard her final cry as her boilers exploded, then he turned to the white-faced, silent men about him, and with hardly a tremble in his voice, he quietly gave the order which would take the *Sweet Jane* back to Liverpool.

It was as though Lacy had heard of the death of her own child, and she was inconsolable as James held her in his arms. The news had come to her as she sat in the office of Mr Moore in the Royal Union Bank in Castle Street.

She felt afterwards as though the gods had watched her gloating with the elderly bank manager over the state of her bank balance, and the investments which poured the guineas like a golden shower of rain into her lap, and had laughed and murmured to one another.

'Now is the time to balance the accounts.'

The boy burst into Mr Moore's office without even the most perfunctory knock and Mr Moore turned sharply to admonish the lad. 'Mason,' he said sternly, 'can you not see I am engaged with Mrs Osborne, and have you not the courtesy to knock . . .' but he got no further, for the boy ignored him and stared breathlessly at Lacy, as did the rest of the stunned staff in the outer office, who crowded sympathetically at Mr Moore's doorway.

'What is it? What on earth is going on?' asked Mr Moore.

'Oh, ma'am.' Was all the boy could say, and a dreadful sinking apprehension pricked against Lacy's skin and knocked at her heart as she stood up slowly.

'Mrs Osborne, ma'am,' the boy repeated, and being only a lad of twelve who ran errands from the bank to the dockside, but with a Liverpool man's love of ships, he began to weep.

''Tis the *Alexandrina Rose* ma'am,' he wept. 'The word's just come in. Captain Jefferson's on 'is way.'

The tears the boy shed were repeated a dozen times in the next few weeks by Lacy, as she sat in her office and stared bleakly across the silver grey waters of the River Mersey. The sun shone mockingly on her sorrow, not only for Paul and his men but for the lovely ship which had been her first step to the goal she dreamed of. Lovely. She was hardly that, but like a mother who sees no fault in a beloved child, a first born, Lacy grieved as though the drowned ship had been a flawlessly beautiful clipper, one of the unforgettables she had thrilled to as a child.

Strangely, for always in the past James had been her main support whenever sorrow or adversity came to grip her, her husband was cool and almost indifferent to her pain. Whenever she turned to him for the comfort of a good cry over the loss of her ship he seemed curiously unconcerned, and gave her the most perfunctory of embraces.

For the first time in their relationship she felt he had let her down and, true to herself, she said so.

'You do not seem to care too much about the loss of the *Alexandrina Rose*, James. Does it mean nothing to you to see a ship go to the bottom, nor to see how sad it has made me? I would have imagined, as a shipowner yourself, you would grieve as I do.'

James looked up from the book he was reading and, for a moment, he smiled at the sight of his wife's woebegone face and tear-filled eyes. She held a scrap of lace to her nose and sniffed dolefully, and his heart went out to her. She was genuinely devastated by the sinking of her ship, and seemed unable to recover from its loss. He knew she would, for she was composed of tough fibre, made tougher by the life she had led; but just at this moment she was allowing herself the weakness of regret. He held out his hand to her, and she came to him, ready to be petted back to smiles. But he was not prepared to pet her.

'Sit here beside me, darling, and listen to what I have to say.'

She sat, leaned her head on his shoulder and sighed.

'You say I am uncaring at the sinking of the *Alexandrina Rose* but I am not, Lacy. It so happens I am most concerned, but more at the loss of the men who sailed in her than the ship herself.'

Lacy sat up and stared at him, and her eyes, so soft and clouded with her own misery, became cool and glinting.

'Don't look at me like that,' James went on. 'You have not once mentioned those men. Only the ship and the cargo; and the time it will take to claim the compensation from the underwriters, and how long it will be before you can get your third ship in the water . . .'

'James Osborne. Are you saying that I do not care that my men are drowned?'

'That is how it seems, Lacy. Tell me I am wrong. I pleaded with you years ago not to put your men in more danger than was necessary, but you ignored me and went ahead with this blockade-running. Now, when you are hurt by it, you expect

555

to be comforted as a woman is comforted when she is troubled. You are a business *man* as you have told me often enough, and must expect . . .'

'But I had to do it, James, you know that.' Lacy's voice was high with resentment. 'My business would have gone under if I had not done it. There was little cotton coming in and my goods rotted in the warehouse for want of a buyer. What else was I to do? And I resent the implication that I am not able to conduct myself as a business . . . *man*. Am I to . . .'

'Is your concern only with the making of a profit then, to the exclusion of everything else?'

'Of course not, but my business . . .'

'Aah, your business . . .'

'Do not start on that tack again, James. We have been through this so many times before. Sometimes I take what I know is the only course open to me.'

'Even when it causes men to die?'

'Don't be ridiculous. They were seamen and expected to be put in danger.'

'They were men, and were put to unneccesary risk by your . . .'

'Yes?'

Lacy's face was dangerously still and her voice was coated with ice. James hesitated. To his horror, he had almost spoken the word which was uppermost in his mind. The word was 'greed', and yet he knew it to be not strictly fair. Lacy did not covet the wealth which her transactions brought her, nor even her growing power and the esteem in which she was beginning to be held by her fellow businessmen. It was, he knew, the ingrained compulsion born in her, bred in her unknowingly by her father; the compulsion to compete and win in a man's world and it forced her onwards, always onwards until she could scarce choose between an honest profit in an honestly run concern, and her obsessive desire to beat the whole of the conglomeration of male shippers who competed with her for trade. He had felt strongly against the placing of good English sailors in the middle of a war which was none of their concern, and all for the making of a profit, as he saw it. He had argued with Lacy when she had told him of her intention. There were other markets in which her goods might be disposed of, and other commodities to be purchased in those markets. The profits would not have been so high, nor so quickly accumulated, but Lacy's ships and the men who took them across the oceans of the world would have been put in no more danger than was normally to be found in a mariner's life. Storm and tempest were the sailor's enemy, but they were used to fighting those foes, for they were familiar ones, and had done so for centuries. But to be aware of a danger, as his wife had been, and yet to go head-on to meet it for nothing more than the incentive of a larger profit, was not only foolhardy in the opinion of James Osborne, but wicked.

'You were not impelled to gain merchandise from America nor to send yours there,' he said evenly, though his face was stiff with suppressed anger. He loved her, knew her faults better than anyone, and still loved her; but, By God, the way in which her mind ran sometimes, frightened him.

'There are other countries where a cargo might be had and where you can send yours. I do not see the necessity to put the men on my ships in constant danger. I find I make a profit without . . .'

'But you are well established, James,' Lacy interrupted fiercely. 'Osbornes have been shippers for decades. Your Papa, like mine, inherited a flourishing concern. You can afford to take a smaller profit whilst this damn war in America holds up the cotton. You have business in many countries, whilst I do not. For eight years I have been slowly building up my concern, gaining the support of those who are in with me on this and now, in one harsh blow, I have lost half my fleet. Two ships I had, and now one of them is gone and I must start again. Captain Jefferson is not the man Paul Ellis was. He has not the daring to go where Paul went, or the knowledge of those coastal waters. My third ship, or should I say second now, will not be launched until August and until then I must carry double the cargo on the vessel I have. My profits will be more than halved unless I do so and . . .'

'And that is still your chief concern, is it?'

Lacy had risen from her seat beside him, pacing the room with fierce, angry strides. She turned as she reached the window, kicking the flowing hem of her skirt behind her, raising her arm as though she would strike him. Her lip lifted to reveal her white, even teeth and curled. She moved towards him, impelled by a passion of rage and mounting frustration, her upraised fist clenching.

Suddenly, she stopped, confusion clouded her fine eyes, and a look of utter sadness smoothed the violence from her face, leaving an expression James was to see more and more in the months and years to follow. Indecision waxed there as though two emotions fought inside her for supremacy. The bright spirit of the trusting, honest girl she once had been was slowly being usurped by the invading ruthlessness of the hardheaded woman, who seemed impervious to her own changing character. But at that moment it was as if she had recognized the fallibility of her own creeping resolve; her uncompromising belief that her way was the only way, and he saw her falter. James watched the shift of expression in her eyes as, one after the other, doubt, uncertainty, and sadness softened them. Then, with an unconscious straightening of her shoulders and a resolute lift of her head, they were gone, and she shone with that complete belief in herself that was characteristic of her.

'I am in business to make a profit, James,' she said softly, 'and for no other reason. I have a duty to my shareholders, those who have put their trust in my credibility as a shipping merchant, and I must do what I think is best on their behalf. You must run your venture as you think fit, and I will do you the courtesy of allowing you to do just that without my interference. Please do the same for me.'

In August 1864, her third ship was born and Lacy christened her the *Bridie O'Malley*. She and Rose wept again as the ship ran eagerly to the water, and in May 1865

*Alexandrina the Second* followed. But by then the war between the North and South in America was over for on 9 April, at Appomattox Court House, General Lee had surrendered his army of less than 25,000 men to General Grant. The North had won.

As the year 1865 drew on, and the tension and the striving of the past three years loosened their clutching hold on Lacy Osborne, she found she missed intensely the excitement of combating her wits against the competition of other ship-owners, and the planning and organization of cargoes to fill the holds of her three ships which had obsessed her during the American war began to slip away. She *needed* to keep her flashing brain turning and striving to its ultimate peak. She *needed* the stimulus which had filled her veins and beat at her heart for the duration of the Civil War and without it she was ... well ... bored.

Alfred and Ernest Burrows had enlarged their own and her holdings in the West Indies and the Mediterranean, and Sheridan Bonfleur, minus an arm lost in the siege of Savannah in December 1864, had rebuilt his connection, and cotton was once more coming in an increasingly steady flow into Liverpool.

What else was there for her to achieve, she wondered?

She had proved, not only to Charles Hemingway and those who had shunned her ten years ago, that she could survive their scorn and build herself a new life, but to herself, which was more important, and she had done it with only Rose to help her.

Why then was she so restless? She admitted to herself that the peace following the excitement of the past few years must be the reason, but surely, she could not and should not live for years on the edge of her seat, pitting her wits against rival lines, biting her finger nails over the non-arrival of a ship at the mouth of the river. She could not exist solely to drag the foundations of an enterprise by its very heartstrings from sinking to firm ground. Could she?

Lacy Osborne looked about her at the home she had made with James, at the perfection with which her life suddenly ran. When, after a night of love in her husband's arms he brought up the subject of a child to inherit their combined fortunes, Lacy *did* consider the idea, for was not this indeed a new challenge?

# CHAPTER 42

Not once in the five years she had been married to James had Lacy Osborne concerned herself with the question of why she had not conceived a child. She had been subconsciously aware that James wanted a son, though he did not say so often for the words were too easily linked with those of 'housewife', 'duties', 'hostess', and 'social obligation', which were now never spoken between them. But without speaking and without meaning to do so, James gave away his longing for a child.

When his five sisters came to Highcross, trailing behind them a horde of small boys and girls, James was amongst them. He organized croquet teams, or cricket for the boys, dandling charming small girls upon his knees and watching, unashamedly covetous, the first hesitant steps of Cynthia's latest, a boy of just twelve months old.

Sophie Osborne, getting on in years and seeing her chances slipping away of holding in her arms James's son, was not so reticent.

'You are twenty-six . . . twenty-seven . . . twenty-eight . . .' Her entreaty became more anxious with each year that passed. 'You should have a nursery full by now, my dear. At your age I had seven children, and you have not yet begun. I cannot understand it. Do you not think it might be your attention to business which is somehow diverting the . . . well, the . . . ?'

Not quite certain how to word it, but leaving Lacy in no doubt as to her meaning, Sophie continued to pronounce upon the subject at every meeting in which she found herself alone with her daughter-in-law, and even upon several occasions with James himself, as though somehow he was flagging in his duties as a husband, and must be encouraged to put more effort into it.

She voiced a fear which lay dormant in James's thoughts.

'You do not think her . . . barren?' she whispered, the very idea too horrific to be spoken out loud. Surely not the wives of both her sons, her bewildered heart said, remembering Matthew's timid wife.

'You have been married so long . . .'

'Five years, Mama,' James had murmured at the time. 'There is no hurry.'

The subject was delicate, even for someone as forthright as Sophie Osborne, but the idea that Lacy might be barren was not a new one to James. He thought of the harrowing tale Lacy told him before they married, and dread struck him. But then he mentally shook himself, and put the thought from him. He would not have it. No, Lacy, had conceived once, and there was no reason why she should not do so again.

And so, heedless of the thousands of nights in which they had lain together, and of the seed which James had spilled endlessly into her womb, they embarked joyously upon the task which James called 'transforming my woman into an interesting condition'.

It was a joke, a lovely private joke at the beginning. Wherever they might be, in whatever company they might find themselves; a word in her ear, a look, and the Osbornes would find themselves suddenly obliged to leave the gathering, confessing apologetically to an urgent duty which called them home.

'Never have I embarked upon a more pleasant obligation with such determination,' James remarked cheerfully, his face splitting into a grin of idiotic proportions. The tops of his ears moved up into his thick tumble of hair, and his eyes almost vanished into the folds of his cheeks, 'and I have waited to begin upon it for so long. Time and again I have almost been persuaded that you were ready, my love, but some emergency would keep you fastened to Strand Street or another would lay claim to your attention. But now you are mine. Oh, my darling.' His voice was soft.

'Do you know what this means to me. To have a child?'

The first month when her courses flowed in their usual manner and at their customary time they were disappointed but said, smilingly, that they had obviously not tried hard enough.

'Shall we meet at lunchtime?' Lacy grinned impishly. 'You might call on some pretext and we could lock my office door.'

'You are a devil, woman, do you know that?' James laughed, and swept her into his arms, 'and if you continue to tantalize me with such schemes, I shall be quite prostrate not to have the delights of them when you are pregnant.' His eyes gleamed in a warm, brown delight, 'but then it will necessitate the whole procedure being started upon again for I do not intend to stop at one, you know.'

It was in the New Year of 1866 that Lacy began to know alarm, not because of her failure to conceive, but at the transformation of an impulsive act of loving into something mechanical. Spontaneity had vanished. James and Lacy Osborne had a love for one another that was rare. They had found great joy in their lovemaking, but when the only motive for that bodily love seemed to be getting Lacy with child, it began to fail them.

There came a night when Lacy's deft, practised fingers could not arouse James to his part in the action.

'Come, my love,' she whispered, her mouth slipping wetly across the springy hair which matted his stomach below his navel. 'I cannot do it alone.' Her fingers gently touched his flaccid penis, and she felt the despair move in her husband. He groaned and raised his arm, putting it across his eyes as though to hide a shame. Lacy lay her cheek against his flat stomach and for several minutes they lay quietly, neither speaking.

At last she sat up and, leaning across him, lit the candle which stood on the table beside the bed. She sat cross-legged, her hair hanging in a long, tousled curtain to the bed. James had turned his head away, staring miserably into the flickering candle flame. Lacy took his chin in her hand and turned his face until he looked at her.

'We are trying too hard, my love.' She smiled. 'Did you ever think to hear one of us say that? We, who are as eager to be about one another, as we were five years ago.' She was rewarded by a gleam of humour in James's eye. 'We are putting too much ... importance upon this desire for a child. I am so tense sometimes, in my eagerness, I take no joy from it, and now look what it has done to you.'

She bent and kissed him tenderly upon the lips and felt them move beneath her own. 'You who are like a bull and could service a whole herd of frisky cows ... My darling, I am not laughing at you, but we must keep this thing within perspective. Once, just once in thousands of hours of love, you have been unable to show your love. But you are not alone in that, Jamie. A woman is more able to hide her ... apathy, that is all. I love you dearly, and want to have your child, but for the past six months we have thought of nothing else to the exclusion of our own enjoyment.'

James lifted his hand and cupped her cheek, then ran his fingers lovingly beneath her chin. She could see he had relaxed, the tension brought about by his failure to be a husband to her, dissipating beneath her loving, comforting words. She lay down beside him and adopted the position in which she always fell asleep in his arms, one arm across his chest and one leg across his thighs.

He sighed and stroked her shoulder. 'You are a wise woman, Lacy Osborne, and I know you are right, but it unmans one somewhat when one is unable to ...' He laughed, and Lacy saw the flash of his white teeth in the soft shadows thrown by the candle. She laughed too.

'What, Jamie, when one is unable to ... what?'

'It is a crude masculine expression.'

'Say it to me. I am a crude man's wife.'

'It is the first time I have been unable to get it up. There!'

'Get it up! Oh, Jamie, how lovely.'

'Lovely! You are incorrigible.'

'But it says exactly what it means.'

After the laughter had died down and they lay comfortably in that drowsing state which comes before sleep Lacy said clearly in the candle-lit darkness,

'Do you think you might get it up in Paris, Jamie?'

*

564

Three months later, after one perfect, unflawed week of love-making in Paris, and a year almost to the day when they had begun upon the delectable task of conceiving their first child, and what they were convinced would be a son, Lacy and James Osborne walked, stony-faced, down the three steps from the consulting rooms of a distinguished London doctor. James handed his wife into the carriage which awaited them.

The doctor's words rang in their ears, uncomfortable and embarrassed, for he had found it difficult to speak to a lady and gentleman of what had been, even to the most inexperienced medical eye, a botched back-street abortion.

'You may speak freely, Doctor,' the husband said, 'my wife and I have no secrets.'

'But this is of a delicate . . .'

'My wife . . . had . . . an abortion many years ago. I know of it. Do not be afraid to discuss it.'

The doctor was visibly relieved, for the difficulties of dealing with such a thing were completely beyond his experience. He spoke quietly.

'I am sorry. There is absolutely no question of there being another child.'

James's face drained to a ghastly sallowness, and his hand trembled in Lacy's. She made a small anguished sound, and her eyes became as blank as stones.

'The damage is quite extensive. Might I ask if you have suffered pain when . . . you and your husband . . . ?'

Really, it was most indelicate to speak of such things when both husband and wife were present. It would have been more correct for the husband to be told and in his turn pass on the diagnosis to his wife.

'No.' The word was chipped, agonized.

'The infection you see, beside the damage caused by the . . . by the . . . er . . . instrument . . . I am sorry.'

'You are saying I will never have a child.' Lacy's voice was clipped, staccato, and her lips barely moved. The flesh of her face had fallen in, and huge hollows appeared beneath her eyes and cheekbones. Every scrap of colour had left her, and the vivid hyacinth blue of her gown seemed to seep into her skin, lending it a deathly bluish hue. Her hand gripped James's marking his flesh with great snow-white indentations and he almost winced, so hard was the desperate strength of it.

In a moment, his own agony was put aside, and before the awkward gaze of the doctor, he stood up and pulled the rigid figure of his wife into his arms. Though she made no further sound, he shushed her and petted her, until she relaxed against him.

James Osborne thanked the doctor most courteously, shook his hand, then led the tranced figure of his lovely wife from the consulting room.

# CHAPTER 43

She tried to ease the heartbreak beneath the palliative which had always worked in the past: going each day to Strand Street, throwing herself like one demented into the building of her shipping fleet; driving herself so hard, and others with her, that they were thrown into confusion by the very sound of her sharp voice. Her business grew, and with it her wealth, and the respect with which her opinion was treated. Men who once had laughed behind their hands when she walked the sacred acres of the Royal Exchange in Market Street, Manchester, now bowed politely and sought her advice on the possible state of 'futures'.

All that she had dreamed of, yearned for, years ago had come about, but the sadness she saw in her husband's eyes turned it to nothing. She knew it would pass, this sorrow, but the wound would be slow to heal. James had been so patient and careful of her feelings but never once had he doubted that he would one day have a son to follow him. They were late, by the code of the day, in starting their family, but it had not mattered, for Lacy was achieving what she had most desired, and was happy.

Now it was gone, the sweet vision, and she was astonished by her own deep disappointment and, more to the point, her simple naïvety. How could she have gone on, year after year, and not wondered at her own failure to conceive. As for James, much more experienced than she, why had he not been at least surprised that he had not given her a child?

But, she told herself, it did no good to brood. There were some problems which had no answer and they were best put aside and forgotten.

She was the first to recover from the blow, but it seemed James would never do so. He was as loving, even sometimes as merry as he once had been, but when he thought himself unobserved, particularly when his sister's children swarmed about him, his face became still with a poignant sadness which broke Lacy's heart. At night as he slept and she lay beside him, the guilt would creep into her heart, and she wept for the man who neither in word, deed nor expression had once reproached her for what she had done.

But as the months slipped by, so, apparently, did the grief, and Lacy settled back into the routine of her early married days. She and James rose early and breakfasted together before going in the carriage to their respective offices. Often she would send her husband, grumbling, on home alone, whilst she and Rose sat across from each other by the dying fire in her office, mulling over today's business and the prospect for tomorrow. They were comfortable together, she and Rose, and when Rose voiced a proposal which had been for some time in her own mind, she was not surprised, for had they not always been so?

'We are making too much profit, acushla,' Rose said, almost carelessly, 'and have not the capacity in our ships to take the cargo those profits should be buying. We need more space and there is none to be had. We cannot leave money around doing nothing, Lacy, but must find something in which to put it so that it earns its keep.'

'Mmm, I know.'

'The immigrant trade is swelling.'

'Yes.'

They did not look at one another, but stared, hypnotized by their own converging thoughts, into the heart of the softly sighing fire. Both, though they had been at their desks since nine that morning, were as alert as they had been then.

'Becket and White are . . . struggling.'

'So I heard.'

'They invested heavily, and too late, in three new ships in 1864, meaning I believe, to engage in blockade-running. Now they are in debt and cannot pay off the shipbuilder who is dunning them for the money they owe him.'

There was a pause, as both women contemplated this engaging item of gossip, then simultaneously they looked up and grinned.

'Damned fools.' Lacy began to laugh.

'Quite.' Rose joined in.

A month later, Mr Moore signed the last document on behalf of the 'New Hemingway and O'Malley Steamship Line', and the three new propeller-driven steamships of the 'Beckett and White Line', of appproximately 1,800 tons each, able to steam at ten knots, and to carry over 500 steerage passengers, flew the flag of their new owners at their masts. They were re-named *Lucinda Fraser* – 'for how would we have begun it all, Rose, without Grandmama Lucinda?' – *Girl Sophie* in honour of James's ageing Mama, and *Lacy Rose* for themselves.

Competition to carry immigrants was fierce. Sharp practices were adopted to encourage migrants to travel on a particular line, and the copy in advertisements was quite at variance with reality. In the decade between 1861 and 1870, 2,250,000 immigrants set sail to the now United States of America. Most were Irish. The average time for crossing to New York was nine days and, if a profit was to be made, speed was of the essence. The cost of carrying immigrants was small, but the profit, even at the lower fare of six guineas which prevailed as competition grew, could be anything up to £3,000 per voyage.

'You will soon be bigger than me,' remarked James wryly, as he stood beside her on the day that *Lacy Rose* took to the water for the first time under her new colours. 'Five ships now, and more to come, I'll be bound.'

'Of course,' said his wife confidently.

They were laughing as they walked back, arm in arm, towards the offices of the 'New Hemingway and O'Malley Steamship Line', unaware that at that moment Charles Hemingway lay dying, his youngest daughter's name on his lips.

James and Lacy, and even Sophie attended the funeral. Although Sarah Hemingway swore she would not be at her husband's graveside if Lacy were there, at last even she gave in, and agreed to Thomas's frantic appeal not to cause a further scandal.

They stood about the open grave, the Hemingway family. Thomas, Robert, Amy, Margaret and Jane, surrounding the dignified figure of their mother. It was natural that Lacy should stand with the Osbornes. She was one of them now, and besides, Sophie, who was becoming frailer with age, needed her arm. The hundreds who attended the funeral saw nothing strange in the exclusion of Charles Hemingway's youngest and most beloved daughter from the family group.

Lacy, who had last seen her father at another funeral, that of Richard Osborne six years earlier, felt nothing but sadness as the earth fell upon Charles's coffin. The bitterness was gone, and the sorrow. What had seemed so momentous was no longer of importance. The years of affection which might have sustained Charles in the latter part of his life had been denied him. By his own pride and vanity, and by the influence of the woman who was invisible now beneath her widow's weeds. Lacy knew that if they had once spoken all the past would have been forgotten, and joy in their common love of the sea and ships would have given him great peace. Even his implacable disregard when she had been ill, was forgiven, for she knew now herself what it was to love and suffer, and to be proud.

It was a week later that she crossed the threshold of Silverdale for the first time in twelve years, and was quite astonished by her own lack of concern. She had thought the moment would bring memories flooding back, with disturbing thoughts of her childhood and her Papa, but she found it left her unmoved. It was as though the young girl who had lived and loved here had long since died, and the person who was Lacy Osborne had sprung, fully grown, from the love given her by her husband, and from her knowledge of her own worth.

Lacy Hemingway no longer existed.

There were many people crowded into Sarah Hemingway's drawing room for the reading of the will. The family sat or stood in a close-knit circle immediately about the lawyer, and Lacy could feel the protective hands of James upon her shoulders as he leaned against the back of her chair.

It took a long time to wade through the dozens of bequests, small and large, which Charles had laid out in his meticulous fashion. Chapman, his butler for twenty-five years; Mrs Johnson, still in charge of the housekeeping; even Nanny Wilson, though she was over seventy now and scarce knew what it was all about. All received some benefit.

The house, the estate on which it stood was disposed of. Sarah, her sons and three eldest daughters provided for, and at the last Charles gave Lacy what she had always demanded of him as a child. Recognition. Not as the wife of one man, nor the daughter of another, but as herself.

'. . . and because she has proved that she is capable of not only earning but also maintaining the respect of those with whom she does business, and is eminently able to rule and uphold a commercial concern as well, if not better, than any man, I bequeath all my shares in the "Hemingway shipping line" to my youngest daughter, Alexandrina Victoria Osborne, in the sure and confident belief that she will build and grow, and continue to prosper.'

Lacy and James left the house while the shrill voices of protest and rage from Sarah and Thomas still echoed about the genteel drawing room. Sarah was last heard to say, as they descended the steps to their carriage, that if Sophie Osborne continued to associate with that . . . that . . . apparently no word horrendous enough could here be found . . . she need call no longer at Silverdale.

Lacy stood in the centre of the office in which she had first seen Luke Marlowe's bright blue eyes smile into hers, and her own smile was no less brilliant. She sat down in Charles Hemingway's chair and looked out upon a scene identical to the one she saw each day from her own office. Ships, men whistling and shouting as they went about their work; huge patient Shire horses waiting between the shafts of the waggons they would pull. Barrels and bales and coils of rope, and beyond, the backdrop of the great dockyard and river. It was as familiar as the face she saw in her mirror each day. She loved it all, she always would. It was as deep and strong in her blood as it had been in that of Charles Hemingway, and of her grandpapa Thomas and of the man who had started it all, Robert Hemingway.

She sat back in the chair, and in the dim, hallowed peace of the all-male preserve which had once been Charles Hemingway's own, Lacy his daughter, smiled, her eyes gleaming like slanting silver coins in the palely flushed smoothness of her face. She was dressed all in black, the slender shape of her merging into the gloom of the shadows which gathered around the walls of the room. The overskirt of her gown was caught up and draped at the sides, according to fashion, the crinoline flattened in front across her stomach and built into a bustle at the back. It was made of the finest foulard, richly embroidered in black jet. Her hair was smoothly winged from a centre parting, coiled into a thick plait at the back of her head, and she had discarded her black 'Dolly Varden' hat, throwing it carelessly on to the chair before the fire.

She looked about the large room, studying the cases of books about the sea and shipping; the bureau on which her father kept his sherry, port and whisky for the reviving of callers; the stately Grandfather clock which had ticked and chimed since Robert Hemingway first set it there; large, dimmed pictures of sailing ships and stormy seas, all as old as the office itself, and all of which she had seen a hundred times and more on her visits to her papa.

She had been a young girl the last time. Seventeen and instantly in love with the arresting stranger who bowed over her hand and glowed like a candle, beckoning the innocent moth to its flame. She had flown to the brightness and heat of him and had been dreadfully burned, but it was that moment which had led to this. It had set her on the inexorable path which had brought her to this place, which was now hers.

Alexandrina Victoria Osborne, once Lacy Hemingway, dear pet of the man who had given it all to her, smiled brilliantly, and leaned forward to ring the bell which would summon her brothers, now her employees, to her presence.

# CHAPTER 44

It was midsummer's day and the years had ran backwards to that time when she was sixteen years old, and her friends had come to pay court to the daughter of Charles Hemingway.

There were nearly one hundred people at the celebration to honour Lacy Osborne and Rose O'Malley on the occasion of their thirtieth birthdays. Although several of the older ladies were hesitant about socializing with someone who had once served them they lost most of their doubts when confronted with the calm and elegant manners of Rose O'Malley. After all, she was Lacy Osborne's dearest friend and was apparently used to dining with the Osbornes 'en famille'. She was courteously friendly and enquired most knowledgeably about their children and grandchildren, showing an interest that was genuine with no inclination to toady. Her dress was simple but very fashionable, her speech as polished as their own, and her decorum with the gentlemen beyond reproach.

Thomas, becoming plumper with every disgruntled month, relinquished his plain wife Emily and their six children to the covey of other forsaken wives, and headed with rude speed towards the prettiest unattached lady there. He was thirty-five now, but still retained his predilection for the 'ladies' of Juniper Street, and to Thomas, Rose was still his mama's kitchen maid. A little flirtation, leading perhaps to something more excitingly delectable, would brighten up a decidedly dull family gathering. But Rose sent him packing by calling him 'Mister Thomas' and speaking in a brogue so thick he could not understand a word she said. He was constrained to ask of Robert what he made of this strange attachment between his sister and the Irish 'biddy'.

Robert, gentle, timid, and devoted to his Alice and their children, said he did not understand what Thomas meant. He found her most gracious, he said, and went to sit beside his wife who was beginning to show the gentle curve of early pregnancy beneath her light shawl, taking his small daughter upon his knee.

Amy came with her Ned. She was matronly at thirty-three, but her face was calm and untroubled as she watched Nanny re-tying ribbons and pulling up socks, and her hand rested on the slight mound of her sixth pregnancy. Margaret sat beside her, complacently watching the precocious behaviour of her own undisciplined family, and seemed quite deaf to Sophie's sotto voce remark that in her day such antics would have been rewarded with removal to the nursery.

All of James's sisters were there except Joanna, who lived in Bath, and in their midst was Jane Hemingway, who often said she had no need of marriage for had she not dozens of children in the shape of her nephews and nieces.

Wherever she went Jane seemed to collect children, and now she and James were in a huge circle of them playing 'Ring a ring a roses', as the ladies stepped from between the long windows which led from the drawing room to the terrace. Lacy and Rose were laughing, separated from the others, standing apart as though their shared birthday gave them an intimacy from which the others were excluded. Their heads were close together, the pale fairness of Lacy's smooth and shining chignon contrasting with Rose's slightly tumbled dark curls. Rose looked as though she might have just removed her bonnet; she appeared completely relaxed, and James was disconcerted by the rapid tattoo which beat momentarily in his chest.

He still felt a warmth – more than that if he were honest – for her, but she diligently avoided him in anything but large social gatherings, and he was grateful. Though his love for his wife was the most treasured part of his life, he admitted to himself that Rose O'Malley still had the power to stir him, and more than once wished she would meet some fellow who would whisk her off to Land's End or Scotland.

They were singing, all of them, the children getting out of hand with the informality of it all, 'Happy birthday to you . . .

'. . . Happy birthday, dear Lacy and R.o.o.o.se, happy birthday to you.'

James joined together the two small hands he had been holding and walked towards the two laughing women, lazily smiling in that certain way that he had, a way usually reserved only for his wife. But as the smile drifted from one beautiful face to the other, it was as if he were temporarily hypnotized, for upon both of them was an identical look of love. Love and desire. He had seen that look many hundreds of times upon his wife's face, and on the faces of other women in his past. It said quite plainly that they were available.

But for their colouring, the two vivid faces might have come from the same mould. They were dressed simply, as were all the other ladies of the party, for it was a picnic and the magnificent gowns were reserved for the dinner party which would take place once the children had been removed by their nannies. Lacy's gown was of the palest blonde tarlatan with wide coffee velvet ribbons at her waist, and her white lace parasol was ruffled in the same colour. Rose was in the tender green of spring, a colour which turned her eyes to the hue of woodlands.

In an instant James was beside Lacy. He took her hand and raised it to his lips and his eyes were warm and melting.

'Send them all away and we will celebrate alone. I know just the place,' his eyes wandered wickedly upwards to their bedroom window. '. . . and the birthday gift I have for you looks at its best when laid against skin which is quite, quite bare. I shall remove that pretty thing you are wearing and replace it with something equally lovely, but somewhat more revealing.'

Lacy smiled and glanced about her demurely, rosy at the contraint she was obliged to show. She felt her flesh prickle and her breath quickened.

'You rogue,' she whispered. 'Have you no shame? What will our friends think to see me blushing? You are most unfair to say such things when I can do nothing about it. Behave yourself, and let us join our guests. You shall give me your gift later, and I shall allow you to "dress" me in it with the greatest of pleasure.'

He kissed her hand again and grinned. They turned, a

charming, handsome couple, and walked down the steps of the terrace towards the groups of guests upon the lawn. The loving scene just enacted had gone unremarked by everyone present for James Osborne's devotion to his wife was well-known and no longer a matter of astonishment amongst their friends and relatives.

Lacy turned and held out her hand.

'Rose. Rosie, now come along. It is your birthday too, is it not? We were born on the same day and shall share every moment of this one.'

Lacy remembered that day.

When one grows old all the days of one's youth and child-hood are remembered and cherished, and events which occurred when one was twenty or thirty are as clear as those which happened yesterday. Small details of that day would lie in her memory forever.

Lacy sat with Amy and spoke of their days in the nursery and schoolroom, and Amy laughed as she remembered the escapades which Lacy would have them get up to, and she did not see where Lacy's eyes looked, for she was cloistered in that state which comes to pregnant women as they sit and wait.

Rose leaned her back against a tree, a glass of lemonade in her hand. She sipped from it as she listened to something which James said to Ned Lucas. Her eyes never left his face, except when he gestured with his hands, and then they followed his movement as though she watched the flight of two lovely brown birds. She pointed at something, and James and Ned turned to look. As they did so, Rose stared at James, enchanted, it seemed, by the line of his strong jaw and the curve of his brown throat.

It was as though the day had laid a spell on them and they had not the strength, nor perhaps the desire, to escape it. James turned again, laughing, to look at Rose, and saw the same expression on her face. The smile slipped away, and then Lacy saw what she had never seen before.

James's eyes darkened into that deep, chocolate brown she knew so well. They narrowed and became hazed, and his face

576

softened. His lips parted and he wet them with the tip of his tongue. The gestures were all familiar to her, well known and loved. Like the banging of a kettledrum her heart began to knock frantically against her breast bone and the breath left her.

James! James! James and Rose! Crash! Bang! Bang!

Her heart thundered, and she turned, desperately looking for an escape from the pain, from the pain of seeing James look at Rose as he had looked only at herself for the past seven years. She twisted away from Amy, from the hordes of silly people who seemed somehow to have become as huge as giants, and from the day, the lovely bright day, which was now turned to black midnight. She concentrated madly upon the vivid blue beauty of a cloud of butterflies which hovered above the bush of buddleia, and a corner of her frantic mind acknowledged that it was after all called the 'butterfly bush'.

Amy placed her hand upon her stomach and contemplated the swarm of children with the complacency of one who is sure of her place in the world and is content in it. She was perturbed when Lacy leapt to her feet, but nodded equably when Lacy said, 'I must go and speak to . . . Will you excuse me, Amy? See, Jane is coming to ask of you . . .'

Almost running, the delicate blonde of her dress blurring against the dark trunks of the trees which edged the lawn, Lacy reached the slope of grass which led up to the terrace at the back of the house. She must get away. She must reach the safety of her room, lock herself in. Bar the door and be alone, safe. She could not stand amongst these people another moment, nor see Rose, for if she did she would tear her nails across her smooth white face and rip and . . .

'Lacy. Lacy, darling, where are you going?'

At the entrance to the drawing room, the French windows of which still stood open, Lacy stopped abruptly as the beloved voice reached her almost deaf ears.

'Where on earth are you rushing off to in such a hurry?'

She could hear the scrape of his boots on the stone as he came up the steps, but she did not dare to turn. Her hands gripped the brocade curtain just within the window, and she stared blindly into the room which seemed dark after the brightness of the sunshine.

'Lacy?'

James's voice was questioning, and his hands were warm on her shoulders. He turned her to him gently and looked into her face. She looked up into his eyes and saw there his great and everlasting love for her and, with a cry, she fell into his arms, coming home.

'What is it, sweetheart? Tell me. Who has upset you, my love? My love?'

'Jamie, Jamie, Jamie,' was all she could say, and he moved her away from the window into the seclusion of the room, and held her to him as she sobbed wildly.

'Darling, what is it? Tell me. It is unlike you to weep. You are the most brave . . . Tell me, please. Is it something I have done?'

The moment, that strange and familiar moment which had happened between himself and Rose was forgotten. His love for this woman drove out all other thoughts and emotions, and her distress appalled him. Rose's green eyes, which had so often fascinated him; her pale, cat-like face; the rich, heavy darkness of the hair he had wondered about; that intensely sexual aura she gave off when he came near; and the knowledge, which, man-like he could not ignore, that she loved him, were flung carelessly to the furthest corner of his mind.

This, *this* was the woman who had his heart, and whose smallest pain concerned him more than the whole of Rose's agony. He was not an insensitive man, nor cruel, but his love for Lacy went far beyond that of most men. Although he would, if he were truthful, find it delightful to dally with Rose O'Malley as he had once dallied with all pretty women, it did not lessen his feelings for his wife. Rose attracted him. She was beautiful and had a strong sexual power which he as a warm blooded man, recognized but beyond that she meant nothing to him. She did not even begin to touch his emotions bar that of an affectionate regard and gratitude for the friendship she had always given Lacy.

James held his wife in his arms and kissed her brow, her cheek, the hollow of her neck. He pulled her down onto the sofa and sat her upon his lap, and was about to slip his hand into the front of her dress to cup her small peaked breast, to free her lovely shoulders, when the sound of small footsteps rattled on the terrace steps, and a childish voice piped up,

'Uncle James. We are going to play croquet, Uncle James, and Rupert says he is to start, but you told me I was to . . .'

The child's voice was strung out and breathless, the vexation scarcely to be borne as she clumped up the steps towards the French window, clearly intent upon retrieving Uncle James to be her protector.

Hurriedly, still kissing the tears which were wet on Lacy's cheeks, but restored by the warmth which had replaced the fear in her eyes, James put her back together again and smoothed her hair. He stood up as his young niece stalked determinedly into the room, eyeing her aunt and uncle suspiciously.

'What are you doing?' she asked accusingly. 'You promised to play croquet with us. You should not be here.'

'No, Rosemary, we should not, and I apologize.' He turned to grin engagingly at Lacy. 'Come my dear, let us join our guests.'

He took her hand but, as the child turned away, he said quietly and seriously, 'Later you shall tell me what it was that upset you so.'

That night, when the last guest had gone, and they were secure in the private world of their bedroom, James was so enthralled by the sight of his wife dressed only in a magnificent golden chain on which was set one sparkling diamond, that he forgot the scene in the drawing room – as she had intended.

She moved quite shamelessly, swaying before him, and the diamond rolled between her white breasts, touching each pink nipple as she danced for him, and in the loving which followed they were aware not even of themselves. They were two bodies, two hearts moulded into one.

Afterwards, as he slept beside her, Lacy knew that her fear,

579

her jealousy and her brief hatred of Rose were foolish. She had probably misunderstood. The light had been vivid, the sun in her eyes, but none of that mattered, for there was one thing that was certain in her mind, James Osborne would never love another woman, not even Rose O'Malley.

# CHAPTER 45

Lacy Osborne had never felt more at peace with herself. It was as if that shining instant of mutual appreciation between James and Rose had brought to her the full realization of what her own love for James meant to her, and of how despairing she would be if it were taken from her. She resolved never to allow the incident at the birthday party – or anything like it – to happen again. From that night onwards she made it her business to ensure her husband's glances never strayed a fraction from her side. She made certain that they left the house together each morning and returned to it each evening – together. And if Rose was aware of it, she said nothing, working on alone far into the evening.

James Osborne was bewitched, as she had meant him to be, with the docile submissiveness of his wife. Knowing her as he did, he was quite prepared to see it end as suddenly as it had begun. When was Lacy ever *submissive*, he asked himself? But there was no doubt that the weeks following the garden party were a source of joy to them both.

In those weeks he could not stand against her, as she declared that she was tired of nothing but work, work, work, and could they not have an outing to see them through the lovely summer days until autumn was upon them. She seemed to be intent upon a rest, or so she said, and did he not think a trip on the ferryboat *Queen* to Woodside would be just the thing on such a lovely summer's day. It would be a pleasant jaunt, James admitted, and, coaxed by his wife in a most lighthearted manner through the double wicket gate at the top of the slipway, even managed to enjoy with her the splendid panoramic spectacle which lay before them as they set foot on the deck of the ferryboat.

From Woodside they rode in a hired carriage to Bidston Hall, through countryside which was bursting with the full

581

growth of the fading summer and glorious autumn. They climbed the hill at Bidston and even to the top of the lighthouse, which cut the sky like a spear, looking towards the west and Wales; south to Chester; east across the river to Liverpool; and north to the channel. Lacy was solemn as a child at an important function, insisting upon signing the visitors' book. James gave the unctuous keeper a small gratuity, and together, arm in arm, he and Lacy took the footpath down the hill to Bidston village, where there was an Elizabethan Hall, and a church which bore over its gateway the armorial bearings of the Derby and Stanley families who used once to own the land.

Another day, they travelled along the shoreline to the village of Bootle in the smart curricle James had bought and drove himself, and they walked on the sweeping sands which lay before the fine summer houses of the wealthy millowners of Yorkshire and Lancashire.

James watched Lacy during those peaceful weeks and was gratified to see her expression change from a certain tension to tranquillity, wondering as he did so, how he had failed to notice that she was tense, and why?

But sunshine, the smell and movement of the sea; the high, clear, summer sky, the wild flowers spilling their simple beauty at their feet; the call of the sweet blackbird, and the joy of being alone together worked its magic on them both.

Six weeks later, secure now in the certainty of their continuing love and need for one another, they agreed that Lacy should return to work.

She toured her extended warehouse, bustling now with a score of 'dockies' under the guiding hand of Michael O'Shaughnessy. She discussed with him the advisability of stealing an inch of capacity from the densely crammed quarters of the steerage passengers on *Bridie O'Malley* to accommodate a cargo of iron hoops which a purchaser in Philadelphia had telegraphed – by the 'new' cable laid across the Atlantic in 1865 – that he needed most urgently. They had decided, she and Michael, that for the space of no more than ten days, a dozen Irishmen could be squeezed into an area meant for six.

Other matters came up. The state of the half-rotten consignment of oranges from the Mediterranean, which had inadvertently been overlooked, allowing the fruit to spoil. They agreed that it might still be saleable, and arrangements were made for its disposal, still with a margin of profit of course.

A cargo of tea had just arrived from Shanghai on the fastest ship of the fleet, the *Lacy Rose*, and the exquisite tea chests in which it was packed were being carefully stored ready for sale. Lacy watched with satisfaction the busy scene, sighing with pure animal pleasure at the hustle and bustle which was the very air she breathed. It was the safe ground she walked upon, the comforting assurance that her world was right and secure. Then into that world, with the devastation of a cannonball exploding at her feet, walked the handsome ghost from her past.

The man was tall and bearded and moved with the graceful, rolling ease of a seaman. He was hatless, and his hair, which once had glowed with the autumn shades of chestnut and copper, was bleached to pale gold by the hot suns of the tropics; his skin had the colour and sheen of mahogany. His vivid blue eyes were squinting against the sudden dimness of the warehouse, and he did not immediately see her as he stepped between its wide doors. The sun shone behind him, outlining the breadth of his shoulders; the slimness of his waist and his tapering legs. He hesitated for a moment, allowing his eyes to become used to the gloom, and though his back was to the door, Lacy saw the immediate interest which sprang to them as he became aware of her.

She stood stock still.

She knew who he was.

His name had been Luke Marlowe.

He took a step forward and inclined his head respectfully. His seaman's cap, the kind worn by an officer in Her Majesty's Navy, was held to his chest. He wore a casual frock coat in a soft shade of blue, under which an open-necked frilled shirt gleamed whitely. His tight breeches were buff, tucked into high riding boots, and held to his narrow waist with a broad leather belt. He gave the appearance of a brigand, arresting and vigorous, caring for no one and certainly unconcerned with the niceties of dress. Even his walk and posture as he stopped before her giving the impression of a pirate.

'Ma'am,' he said politely, smiling. She felt her legs tremble in the way they had done thirteen years ago and her heart thud out of rhythm. Her mouth dried up so that she was unable to speak.

'Ma'am,' he said again. 'I beg your pardon if I have startled you. I am looking for Mr O'Shaughnessy, and was told he could be found here.' His voice was deep and soft, just as she remembered.

'I apologize for disturbing you but . . .'

He hesitated, and as he did so, Lacy stepped from the patch of dust-filled shadow in which she stood, and the bright autumn sunshine fell upon her with all the radiance of the Rock Perch Lighthouse.

She wore a simple morning gown of apple green jaconet, very fine and misty. Her crinoline was wide, with a bustle at the back draped above falls of green velvet ribbon. The sleeves were long and tight, the neckline high, and, tipped above her forehead like a pancake, down at the front and up at the back, was a 'Dolly Varden' hat, the straw dyed to the same shade as her dress. Her hair was caught in a mass of curls at the back of her head and twisted in it was a length of green velvet ribbon to match that on her dress. It gleamed in the sun, as did her silver grey eyes, and the pale ivory of her skin was flushed a deep pink on each cheekbone.

There eyes met, pupils widening, and they stood, petrified by time and memory, immobile as marble statuettes. Their eyes clashed, locked, and time drifted on forever in a small vacuum of dust-speckled sunshine. In the space of thirty seconds it was all said, the venom and detestation, the enmity and bitterness, and though the expression on each face was smooth now, polite and careful, grey eyes had hissed their message and been answered by blue.

He was the first to recover. He bowed low, his expressive eyes instantly hidden, but his mouth curled in an amused smile.

'Miss Hemingway,' he said softly, 'this is indeed a pleasure.'

Lacy came at last from her trance. The ignorant, impressionable girl she had been fled away, and she was Lacy Osborne, wife to James, renowned hostess, successful businesswoman, respected member of the Liverpool community. As such, though remembrance knifed her, she was well able to deal with a man such as this. Well able to deal with any man, for was she not one of the most powerful figures in the borough?

With cool disdain her chin lifted, and she smiled politely. In her heart was raging, tormented loathing for the man who had changed her life with his self-centred 'love'; changed it, moulded it, and tossed it aside when it was no longer useful. He had almost killed her. He had certainly killed her child and the hope of any children she might have had, and as he smiled engagingly as only he knew how, it was all she could do not to leap at him with bared nails and teeth, and mark the smooth curve of his brown cheek with long, furrowing, bloody tracks. But all she said was,

'Good morning, Mr Marlowe. It seems we meet again, though I myself would hardly deem it a pleasure.'

'Come now, Miss Hemingway. That is not the way to speak to an old . . . friend. Surely, after all this time we may call each other thus. As I remember you were ever . . . amiable.'

His lips spoke the easy, urbane words, but his eyes said others, and she recognized them. He still condemned her as he had done when, in her innocence, she had dashed the command of her father's ship *Breeze* from him and, though he was as civil as any gentleman with a lady, he could not control the expression in his eyes. They were as cold as the blue seas of the Arctic.

'We were never friends, Mr Marlowe, not then and not now, but it does not signify, for I doubt our paths will cross in the separate societies in which we move.' For a second a speculative gleam touched her glacially silver eyes, as though she wondered how he came to be in Liverpool after all these years.

'If you would be kind enough to step aside now, I will leave,' she continued silkily. 'I have much to do this morning and must be away immediately.'

'You have a busy social calendar then, Miss Hemingway,' he said easily. He smiled. 'I call you Miss Hemingway, though I doubt that is still your name. Some scion of society must surely have claimed you for his own by now. A beautiful woman such as yourself, and one with the wealth and position of your family would not remain long unmarried.'

Lacy smiled just as smoothly.

'I am Mrs James Osborne now, Mr Marlowe. My husband is in . . . business here in Liverpool. Shipping.'

'Aah, indeed. Like would marry like, as I found to my cost, but please, do not let me keep you Mrs . . . er . . . Osborne. I am sure your friends await you . . .'

'I cannot say that they do, Mr Marlowe. I have no concern with the . . . social calendar, as you put it.'

She smiled brightly.

His brow creased in a frown of confusion, and he lifted an eyebrow, then grinned in his easy familiar way.

'Then it must be a . . . relative who brings you down to . . . these quarters. I assume that . . .' he nodded in the direction of the sign above the door of the warehouse, '. . . Hemingway and O'Malley are in some way connected with your family?'

'Indeed they are.'

A slight look of discomfiture crossed Luke Marlowe's face, and he appeared to hesitate, as though he would speak of something which might cause awkwardness, but his brilliant smile erased the look, and he bowed carelessly.

'Then I would be obliged, Mrs Osborne, if you would refrain from using the name of Luke Marlowe. I travel under the *nom de plume* of Joel Ashton, and have done for many years.'

A bell tinkled at the back of Lacy's mind and she heard a voice. It was speaking of ships and . . . and blackbirding . . . a

man from Charleston who . . . It came to her then, the words
Paul Ellis had spoken at the onset of the American Civil War.

'. . . she is not completely lost, Lacy. With some repairs
done on her, she is still capable of completing another day's
work. As a matter of fact, I have already had an offer for her.
A fellow I know back in Charleston . . . Joel Ashton will give
me a fair price for her. He has a hankering to try his hand at
blockade-running now that his activities in "blackbirding" are
to be curtailed . . .'

This was the man who had bought the *Annie McGregor* from
Paul Ellis!

Luke was still speaking.

'. . . I would not like to cross swords with your father again.
He and I did not see eye to eye on . . . certain matters, and I
doubt . . .'

'My father is dead.'

'Aah.' He put on his face a suitable look of condolence,
then lifted his eyebrows questioningly.

'Your brother is then the owner of . . ?'

'No, he is not.'

'Then who am I to do business with here?'

'I really cannot say, Mr . . . er . . . Ashton.' Her heart
pounded with joy at the look of confusion which began to
cloud his fine blue eyes.

'I beg your pardon. I was told to see Mr O'Shaughnessy
with a view to making an appointment with the company's
owner. Mr O'Shaughnessy would tell me if I might obtain a
cargo for my ship.'

For the first time the pose of casual goodwill dropped from
Luke Marlowe's shoulders, and confusion deepened the
frown about his forehead.

'I am to sail for Nova Scotia the day after tomorrow, and I
have space . . .'

'I doubt the firm of "Hemingway and O'Malley" have a
cargo for you, Mr Ashton.'

'Perhaps you will allow me to find that out for myself, Mrs
Osborne. I have business to transact with your brother, and I
would be obliged if you would go about . . . your concerns and

587

let me do the same.' He was becoming angry now, and a strange prick of uncertainty glinted in his eyes.

'Now, if you will excuse me, I must find Mr O'Shaughnessy.'

He bowed with the fluid grace and contemptuous gesture of a man who brooks no argument from anyone, least of all a woman. He flipped his cap to the back of his head and began to stroll casually in the direction of the hubbub of activity at the back of the warehouse, where Michael O'Shaughnessy harangued half a dozen workmen.

Lacy had never known such a moment as this. The delirious feeling of power flowed through her veins like fire, and the knowledge that she could play with this man as a cat plays with a mouse was almost more than she could bear.

'Mr Ashton.' Her voice whipped across his back as he moved away.

He turned impatiently.

'What is it, Mrs Osborne? I'm afraid I have not the time to gossip.'

By God, he would pay for that!

'I must be about my business if I am to be loaded by . . .'

'You will do no business here, Mr Ashton.'

'So you have implied, Mrs Osborne, but your brother is surely the one to decide that.'

'No, he is not. You see, my brother works for *me*, Mr Ashton. For me and Miss O'Malley. You remember Miss O'Malley, do you not? Rose O'Malley?'

Her voice was derisive, but her smile was sunny.

'Rose O'Ma . . .'

He had turned back to her but still, it seemed, did not fully comprehend what she was saying. His masculine scorn of all things female, except in their ability to please him sexually, was so complete, the idea that Lacy might be the 'Hemingway' in 'Hemingway and O'Malley' was utterly preposterous that he gave it only the merest consideration, his mind still grappling with 'Rose'. Rose O'Malley, who it appeared he was supposed to remember.

Lacy watched in grim delight as the facile smile slipped

from his face. His breath eased from between suddenly slack lips, and his eyes darkened until they were a rich, dark blue, like the midnight sky. He put his hand to his brow, then reached to his cap and took it off, and, for a moment, she thought he would scratch his head.

'Rose . . . Rose O'Malley? The one who was your . . . your maid.' His voice peaked most unmanfully and, for a moment, the boy he had once been years ago when he had first come to the 'Bluecoats' school as an orphan, cried through the shadows of time, marking the man's face with dread.

'Do you mean to tell me . . . you and that . . . that you are "Hemingway and O'Malley"?'

'We are.'

'But I am to do business with . . .'

His voice slipped away, but even as it did so, Lacy saw the expression on his face begin to change from confusion and dismay, to the self-seeking and shrewd consideration of what he must do to turn the situation to his own benefit. There was, of course, no question in his mind that he might not be able to do so. In a way, Lacy could admire the speed with which he changed his coat. His brain had assessed, deciphered and hopped adroitly to a new plan of action, in the time it took to blink his thick brown eyelashes.

She could almost hear the working of his mind, that which knew how to bewitch and enchant, as it switched immediately and, with scarce a ripple of expression, into the playing of the role which here was needed. She had seen it before, but had not recognized it then for what it was. But now she did, and her blood raced and tingled. It was here in her grasp, here at last! Though she had not consciously longed for it, nor, for the past many years, even thought of Luke Marlowe, she was suddenly aware that she had never forgiven this man, and here was her vengeance, come by chance in the shape of his disinterred and ever-charming ghost.

'Yes, Mr Ashton,' she said, 'you are to do business with . . . ?'

Her voice rose on the last word.

His eyes crinkled fetchingly, and his generous lips curved

589

in a most attractive smile about his white teeth. His cap was placed gallantly against his chest as he spoke in his most appealing and humorous voice.

'Why, with your charming self, it appears, Mrs Osborne. I will try to make amends for my confusion, and for causing yours, but you see my ship and I are to sail as soon as we have a cargo.' He twinkled most persuasively.

'I had been informed that freight was to be had at . . .' Another charming smile. '. . . at "Hemingway and O'Malley" and, believing I should never be recognized by . . . well, after so many years we are all changed, are we not, Mrs Osborne? Though on you the change is only improved upon. But I do have space to offer . . .' He shrugged expressively and smiled again. 'If we could retire to your . . . office I am sure we could arrange matters in a way beneficial to us both.'

'Why, of course, Mr Ashton, by all means let us retire to my office. I would be fascinated to hear what you have been up to since our . . . last meeting.'

He looked almost shamefaced for a moment, but, believing he had the encounter turned about to his own advantage, he smiled boyishly, shrugged again and curled his lips in a wry and humorous manner. The implication was that much water had gone under the bridge, but now they were two different people.

'I am afraid I have an appointment in five minutes, Mr Ashton . . .'

'Joel.'

'I beg your . . .'

'Please, Lacy. Call me Joel.'

'Very well, Joel. I would like nothing better than to renew our . . . acquaintanceship, but I am afraid I am a very busy woman. I have six ships of my own line you know, and I inherited the major shareholding in my father's company. He had twenty-three . . .' She allowed this to wash over him, and was gratified by the look of envious regret which glanced from Luke Marlowe's bright blue eyes.

'. . . but if you wish to come to my office in Strand Street at two, I shall make it my business to be free for the rest of the afternoon. We can exchange reminiscences and, by then, I shall have thought hard on . . . what I am to do with you.'

Her smile was arch, bright and crystal clear, and Luke Marlowe felt his pulse leap. He congratulated himself on his continuing ability to beguile any woman as he bent over Lacy Osborne's dainty hand. Then, with the sure and certain awareness in his mind that today was to lead to a gleaming future for 'Captain' Joel Ashton, he strode gracefully across the quay with a cheerful, silent whistle upon his lips.

He was unprepared for the two beautiful, smiling women who waited for him in the spacious office in Strand Street from which Lacy ran not only the 'New Hemingway and O'Malley Steamship Line', but also 'Hemingway and O'Malley', and the 'Hemingway Shipping Line' which had once been her papa's.

Supremely confident of his ability to hold his own with anyone, Luke Marlowe smiled his best smile as he bowed over each white hand. Their eyes were clear and unclouded, and their lips smiled and made polite remarks. They listened attentively as he told them proudly of his achievements since last they had met.

He had gone 'blackbirding', he said, when he left Liverpool. First mate, then captain, on an old tub which plied between the coast of West Africa and the Southern States of America, carrying thousands of men, women and children to slavery. By 1863, when the American Civil War had put an end to such endeavour, he had made, as he put it, a tidy sum. He had been able to purchase a ship with his money, and had run the blockade of the Union fleet with a hundred others. He had not, he remarked ruefully, put into Liverpool, thinking it best to avoid the place where . . . He smiled ingratiatingly and shook his head, as though they were all fully aware of why he wished to avoid Liverpool. It seemed he had made a further tidy sum and, after buying a small brigantine from a fellow from Charleston, was now carrying freight in his two ships for whoever would pay him. He was in the process of building up his capital in order to purchase a small shipping concern which he had heard was under difficulty, and which he intended to have.

'Would that be in Liverpool, Mr Ashton?' Rose asked artlessly, but he tapped his nose and smiled.

'Aah . . . that would be telling, Miss O'Malley. It is very small compared to your . . . er . . . concern. Only two steamships built and used for blockade-running during the American Civil War, but like so many shippers who left it too late, the profit to pay for the vessels was never made. They are holding out for . . . a certain sum, but I am optimistic that they will take my offer. Then I shall be in a position to . . . Aaah well, I must not reveal too much of my planned future operation.'

He smiled suavely and crossed the immaculately tailored smoothness of his trousered leg. His white-frilled shirt opened slightly to reveal the deep brown skin of his throat, and the spring of brown hair at its base. He exuded virility, confidence, strength and arrogance, and his manner said plainly that he was prepared to do whatever was needed to get what he wanted. He had worked towards a goal since he was a boy, and once he had almost had it in his grasp. Though he had been thrashed, and his ill-fortune had almost destroyed him, he had clawed his way up and was again poised to break through to gain not only command of his own ship, but also of his own company. Could he help but be overbearing in his self-esteem?

He leaned forward patronizingly.

'And now, if you two ladies would like to tell me what it is you wish me to carry for you . . . That is, if you have a cargo. If you have not, I am sure I will find one elsewhere.'

Lacy offered him a consignment of Manchester goods, to be collected the next day. He was delighted and smug.

'Well, I admit I find this very pleasant. To trade with two, such charming ladies instead of a . . .' The afternoon passed most pleasurably for Luke Marlowe, marred only by Miss O'Malley . . . Rose's . . . regretful refusal to dine with him that evening. She had a prior engagement she said, but perhaps the next time he was in port . . .

Lacy watched, quite fascinated, as Luke Marlowe tripped merrily on towards his doom. His callous disregard for the brief past they had shared, manifested by his eager desire to dine with Rose, was surely the mark of a man without any finer feelings, conscience, or nerves; of a man detached from goodness, pity and even remorse. It was as though she and Luke Marlowe were mere acquaintances who had agreeably been reunited, and the emotions they once shared, the final words he had screamed at her, had never been. He bowed over Rose's hand and, as he turned at the door for one last charming smile, it was all she could do to return it.

When he had gone, they stood in the bow window and watched his jaunty, insolent figure crossing the setts of the road to the berth where his ship lay. He turned as though he knew they would watch him, tipped his cap, then vanished round the corner of the warehouse.

Lacy turned to Rose.

'I could vomit.'

'The divil has nothing on that one.'

'To have the effrontery to ask you to dine!'

'Even to kiss my hand . . . it turned me sick.'

'How could I have imagined myself in love with . . . ? He is so . . . shallow, so . . . *obvious!* Do you suppose there are women taken in by him still, as I was?'

'You were so young, acushla, inexperienced.'

Lacy sighed and sat down at her desk.

'You are certain you are with me on this, Rose?'

'Lacy. Was I not there when . . . ?'

'I know. I should not need to ask. Now, you know the firm he speaks of?'

'I soon will.'

'Pay whatever they ask.'

'Of course, but it will be high, Lacy. When they know who bids for it they . . .'

'It cannot be helped. Now, as you go out will you ask Stevens to fetch Michael O'Shaughnessy? I have a . . . job for him. And ask him to find out where Captain Ashton's ship is berthed. Oh, and I shall need to speak to Mr Moore. He knows all the bankers and . . .'

I could almost feel sorry for the divil.'

'Don't, Rose. Not if you love me. He deserves it.'

'I know, acushla. I know. You were always aware of my . . . aversion to him.'

For a moment, their glances locked in shared sorrow, then, with a brief smile, Rose turned and left the office.

# CHAPTER 46

The man stood beside the gatepost, his back pressed stiffly against its grey, pitted stone and, with the air of a hunted animal, he turned to peer cautiously in the direction of the house. The building could not be seen. It was too far from the road, and was hidden beyond the stand of trees, but he knew it was there. He had reconnoitred the ground so many times he knew every tree, bush and shrub; every path, drive and walkway; every inch of garden and shrubbery. Should he have been asked to find his way from the gateway, where he stood, to the back of the house almost half a mile away, he could have done so at midnight, and with the ease of one born there.

The rain fell relentlessly in a cold, steady stream, its sound was a constant, rhythmic thrumming against the sodden winter ground; down the high stone wall, stretching away to the left and right; across the roof of the gatehouse standing just inside the gates; on to the tree trunks, and into the very fabric of the man's greatcoat.

A pale wavering light from the small, square window of the lodge shimmered through the downpour off to the right, its glow hovering on the remnants of the pruned rose bushes, which graced the verge of James Osborne's driveway. In summer, the heady scent of the lush blooms was the first thing a visitor noticed as he entered the Highcross estate, but now there was only the dank smell of wet vegetation, of rotting leaves, and the faint, salty tang of the river as it drifted on the rain from Garston Sands.

The man stepped carefully away from the gateway, walking with the swaying graceful gait of a man of the sea. His boots disturbed the smooth, wet gravel and the sudden, small noise brought him to an abrupt halt. He remained completely still for several minutes, balanced lightly on the balls of his feet, and not until he was certain that the sound had passed unnoticed did he hasten on, keeping to the grass.

As he left the parkland behind, the ground began to rise gently in a series of wide-lawned slopes. The man skirted ornamental flower beds edged with box as though he were walking in broad daylight, and then he was at the house. He knew its layout exactly, and precisely where he might gain entry, but he made no move to do so. Instead, walking quietly around to the left-hand side, he stood to survey the elegant glasshouse. Then further on he went, through arches and along paved walkways, glancing up at windows and wisteria-covered walls savouring, it seemed, a moment of anticipation before his entrance.

A faint lustre from the dower house lit up the night sky, soft as a candle, but the man did not go near the retreat where Sophie Osborne dozed away her declining years.

As he reached the rear of the big house, moving steadily through the kitchen garden and stable yard, across wet-slicked, slippery cobbles and to the paddock, he paused and stared intently at a row of lighted windows which stretched on either side of the kitchen door. There were more glowing rectangles above, and it was less dark here, where the illumination from the house diffused the night.

After a moment or two he moved on, stepping through an arched porch on to a crazy paved path, which led across the right-hand side of the house and towards the front. Suddenly, his shin caught against something at the side of the path and, with an oath, he knocked over a wheelbarrow, scattering its contents of wet leaves across the path. The clatter as the wheelbarrow tipped noisily on its side made him flinch, and, for a second, as he lost his nerve, he stood poised for flight. Then a dog barked frantically and, above his head, a face appeared at the scullery window, peering into the black night. Mesmerized and still, the man watched the face, knowing he could not be seen, and breathed a sigh of relief when it smiled and laughed, as if an unseen voice had scoffed at the watcher for his nervousness.

The man was at the front of the house again now. On silent

feet, he inched his way up the staircase which curved on either side of the huge front door, stopping, shadowy and motionless, on the terrace which stretched across the front of the house at the level of the first floor. Every window was lit up although most of the rooms were empty. Keeping well away from the rectangles of light which reflected in the wet paving stones of the terrace, the man moved soundlessly along beside the balustrade until he came to the tall French windows of the drawing room.

Then, cat-like, he padded across the terrace, to press himself tight against the wall beside the windows. Moving his head a fraction, he swivelled his penetrating eyes until he looked directly into the room. Hissing with pleasure, in his eyes an ugly inner glow, Luke Marlowe watched the couple who lounged comfortably upon the deep chesterfield which stood before an enormous fire. He also saw a dog stretched out before the flames, its body totally relaxed in blissful ignorance of the intruder's presence – which was some measure of Luke Marlowe's stealth.

James and Lacy Osborne had dined alone that night and, though it was not considered 'correct', they had not dressed for dinner. James was comfortable in a velvet smoking jacket, and Lacy wore a soft, flowing robe, high-necked and full-sleeved in peach panne velvet. As a gesture to her husband, who was only slightly more conventional than she, and partly for the servants, who would have been shocked had she left it unconfined, she had twisted her mass of hair into a gentle knot, tied about with peach velvet ribbon.

Luke heard Lacy Osborne laugh, and his teeth drew back across his lips. His eyes narrowed as he saw her husband lean to kiss her lovingly, and for a moment he watched as the man's hand went to his wife's hair, toying with a loose curl.

It was into this tender domestic moment that he stepped.

The couple on the sofa were engrossed with each other, filled with happiness and a feeling of quiet well-being; their senses lulled by close proximity to one another, the shadowed warmth and comfort of the room, and the feeling of security brought about by the contrasting violence of the storm outside. Even the dog, a puppy merely, was comically amazed as the French windows burst inwards.

Glass scattered, and the salt-laden wind lifted the curtains moving dainty ornaments across polished surfaces. The fire, fanned by the sudden draught, exploded into leaping flame and smoke filled the air. The man who stood so violently in the open doorway, his back to the wind-tossed clouds and black outline of trees, appeared fresh-flung from the depths of hell. His eyes were the eyes of a devil, and in his hand was a pistol, held steady as a rock and pointed directly at Lacy Osborne's head.

Lacy had her back to him. With the sharp reflex of a soldier, and the instinctive reactions of a man who will protect what he treasures most, even with his life, James Osborne moved to place his body between his wife and the man who glared dementedly at her. But they were sitting down, and there was no way he could perform the movement which would put her behind him. He could do nothing but wrap his arms about her head. She struggled and tried to turn, but the voice of the intruder froze her, appalled.

'Don't move. I warn you, don't move, or I will put a bullet in your shoulder. First the left, then the right. After that, perhaps the elbow or the kneecap. I won't kill you, not yet, but should you not do exactly as I say, I will cripple you, both of you, before you can call for help.'

The couple on the sofa became obediently still. The dog whimpered but remained where it was. James spoke but did not move. His hand quivered on Lacy's neck, as if to soothe and reassure her nervous fear.

'What do you want?' he said evenly.

The man laughed and pointed his pistol more definitely in Lacy's direction.

'She knows. Your lovely wife knows. Ask her and then . . .'

As he spoke there was a knock, urgent and loud, at the door which led into the hallway and a man's voice begged Captain Osborne to tell him that everything was all right.

'We heard a crash, sir, and thought . . .'

'Tell him go go away.' Luke's voice was harsh. 'I'll kill her now if you don't . . .'

'It is all right, Winter. A table knocked over, that is all.'

'May I send a maid to clear . . . ?'

'No, no . . . We can manage . . .'

'But sir, allow me to . . .'

Luke Marlowe took a step forward. His face was set in lines of menacing rage, and James heard his own voice go up an octave in desperate fear for his wife. The trigger of the pistol moved a fraction.

'Dammit man! You heard me. We can manage. Now take yourself off and get to your beds, all of you.'

'To our beds, sir?' Winter was clearly bewildered. 'But it is scarce nine o'clock . . .'

'Go to your bed, Winter. And the rest of the servants. That is an order.'

'Yes, sir.'

Winter's voice was slightly affronted, for never in all his years had the captain, or Mr Osborne, now dead and buried, ever spoken so harshly. Muttering to himself, the old butler shuffled uneasily down the long passage which led to the servants' quarters. He'd discuss it with Samuel and William, the footmen, so he would, and he'd half a mind to fetch the grooms. He hadn't liked the sound of Captain James's voice one bit. Go to their beds indeed!

In the drawing room, Luke Marlowe clutched at the last remaining particles of his reason, the shredded thoughts which were all he seemed able to assemble these days, since . . . since . . . she had . . . cut the ground from beneath his feet, her and the other she-cat. Three months ago she'd done it, and in that time he had festered from one hell-hole to another in the stews of Liverpool, torn between stowing away on a ship to the other side of the world, and suicide. For what was left to him now? And what else, but his life, had he left to lose? Nothing mattered. Peace was all he wanted. Sleep and peace in the restful arms of the sea, the one enduring love of his life. To sail across her, or to slip into her watery embrace was all that he had left to him, all that he now desired. But

599

first . . . First *she*, must be made to pay for what she had done. Look at her, shivering in the arms of her husband like some whipped bitch. Tricked up in her satins and velvets like the whore she was. She thought she was so clever, and able to do anything she wanted. But look at her now. She could do nothing but tremble in terror, for she knew what he would do to her. He cared for nothing now but vengeance. She understood that for, in a way, she was like him. Ruthless. Yes, ruthless once, but not any more. Now, now she was far too afraid.

'Well Lacy,' he said conversationally, 'here we are again. Our paths seem destined to cross, do they not? But this will be the last time, my dear. You have done for me with your schemes and money and power, but it will do you no good at the last.'

'Who the hell *are* you?' James interrupted roughly. 'What the devil's going on here?' He looked down at Lacy's face, trying to find an answer written there, but her eyes were lowered and her expression told him nothing. 'Who is this man, Lacy, and how does he know you? Lacy. Answer me, damn you.'

'It appears she is too demoralized, Captain Osborne. Captain. That is correct, is it not? A brave soldier so I have heard, and the lucky fellow who bedded my . . . discarded mistress.'

Luke laughed and, as he did so, Lacy turned swiftly. Her face was white, like alabaster, and so were her lips and her eyes glittered between her tear-sodden lashes. But she was neither fearful nor sorry: she was in the grip of an ice-cold, venomous rage.

James was speechless, frozen in shock.

'You crawling bastard, you,' Lacy hissed. 'Do you think that by coming to my house and waving a pistol you can make me tremble in fear? And my husband? Do you think to terrorize him into submission by mouthing lies and insults, and pointing that . . . Why, I shall stand up now, and so shall he, and if you are half the man that he is, a quarter even, you will kill us both, for we shall neither of us cower to you. But

600

you have not the nerve. You are nothing but a loathsome, creeping, thing. I am glad that I have ruined you. Glad, glad.'

She struggled frantically now to escape James's stiff restraining arms and Luke Marlowe began to move the firearm in a trembling circle, aligning it directly with her maddened face. His own was a bright suffused purple, blotched in great round circles. The cords of his neck stood out quivering and tense, and he moaned bestially.

James Osborne was no longer transfixed. Fear for his wife overcame all other emotions.

'Jesus, Lacy. Be still. For Christ's sake, be still. He will shoot, dammit.'

'Let me go, James, let me go.'

'Stop it, be still,' he thundered, never taking his eyes from the wavering pistol. 'And tell me who the devil this is, or I will kill you myself.'

'It's Luke, can you not see? It's Luke Marlowe.'

'Luke . . . ?'

'The man who . . .'

The sound of his name seemed to calm Luke and he smiled. He was once again in charge of himself and of the situation. Lacy had confused him but now he knew who he was and what he had come to do here.

'Yes, Captain Osborne,' he rejoiced, his eyes gloating horribly.

'I am Luke Marlowe, late lover of your wife. Suitor once, or I had hoped to be, and I almost commanded the loveliest clipper ship of the "Hemingway" line. *Breeze*, that was her name, and she was to be mine. I had them both, the most beautiful ship and the most beautiful woman in Liverpool, Captain. *Breeze* and Lacy Hemingway in the palm of my hand. We were to sail together, *Breeze*, Lacy and myself, but . . .'

Again, Luke seemed about to disintegrate into mumbling turmoil at the agonized memory of that day when his bright and lovely dream had splintered. With an effort, he returned to the present and was calm again. It was the awful calm of utter despair.

'She told her father, you see, Captain, and of course that

was the end of it for me. Twelve years swept away by a foolish girl's desire to be honest.' His lip curled in a sneer. 'Will you look at her now, Captain, and try to believe that once she was honest. It is hard to credit, is it not? Her honesty then caused me to be put on a ship for America, against my wishes, of course. I did have a choice, I must admit. Africa, America, Australia, Charles Hemingway was . . . indifferent to where I fetched up. Providing I did not return to Liverpool, he was careless of my whereabouts. I landed in New York without a guinea to my name.' He laughed bitterly.

James and Lacy were quite still.

'And all for a tumble with a child who had not the wit to keep her tongue still.'

James recoiled, and made a small painful sound in the back of his throat.

Luke shrugged his shoulders and continued dreamily.

'But I did quite well, Captain Osborne. You see, I was a seaman in the true sense of the word. A man of the sea with all the instincts of one who knows and loves her as a man knows and loves a woman. I had no trouble finding work, and with my knowledge and experience, I became invaluable to the mostly drunken and inept men who were engaged in the trade I took up. It helped to be drunk, you see, dulled the sensibilities, as it were. Mine were not involved. You have heard of the term "blackbirding", I am sure. A very lucrative trade. Oh, yes. But you need to know the sea, the ships and the men who sail with you to carry the cargo we carried, and I knew all these things. I was allowed to . . . buy cargo of my own and ship it on the vessels I sailed, and I began to put a bit by for the day when I would . . .' He stopped, and a dreaming, contemplative expression softened his eyes to a gentle, faded blue.

'I would have my own ship one day, I knew I would. For eight years I worked in filth and obscenity. I became inured to it, for it would lead me to . . . one day . . .'

The pistol drifted fractionally to the left but neither James nor Lacy appeared to notice. The utter desolation of the man who held it seemed to have them both in thrall. The silence as he stopped speaking was broken only by the gentle crackle and spit of the logs on the fire, the sighing of the dog, and the steady hissing of the rain beyond the open window. The curtain swayed in the wind and the room grew slowly colder, but the participants in the drama now being played were engrossed, unheeding.

Luke collected himself and continued vaguely.

'I bought my ship in 1863. An old paddle steamer, but I worked on her, loved her, until she would do anything I asked of her. She was good to me, that old ship. I ran cotton, brought back guns and iron, other things . . . I was sorry when . . . she sank, but she had to go. She was too old and could no longer do the work, so it was more profitable to me if . . . she went. The insurance was high but the compensation was more than the worth of the ship and the cargo together.'

He grinned wolfishly and James felt his skin prickle, and the hairs on the back of his neck lifted. 'It was quite easy,' Luke went on. 'The ship was so overloaded she was flush with the water amidships. She sank as soon as we left harbour. I had a small crew, well paid, and we took to the boats.'

He grimaced and his eyes smiled derisively into Lacy's.

'Remember it, my dear. It is a good way to earn a quick dollar if you can get away with it, let me tell you, and one I am sure you would have done yourself, should you have thought of it. The compensation bought me the fine ship I now have.'

Lacy's eyes were like chips of diamonds in her white face, but she did not answer. Her mouth was clamped to a savage line, her jaw jutted and, for a moment, Luke was diverted by the strange phenomenon of her likeness, beautiful woman though she was, to her dead father. There was the forceful determination; the assertive and compelling steeliness in the vivid eyes; the resolution to do whatever *they* were convinced was right, regardless of others; and their own utter belief in that conviction. It was written in the lovely face just as surely as it had been written in the hard and handsome features of Charles Hemingway. But Luke saw something else. Another expression overlaid that customary look of Lacy Osborne's. It

603

was sweet, bright, trustful, honest, loving, and ethereally youthful and Luke Marlowe knew it to be that of Charles' daughter, Lacy Hemingway, as she had been at seventeen.

Lacy Osborne spoke now scornfully.

'Do not concern yourself with my ability to earn a quick dollar, as you put it, Luke Marlowe. I have done it and succeeded beyond your wildest dreams. With nothing more than an emerald necklace and my own wits, I acquired what I now have – with the added disadvantage of being a woman. Do not expect me to feel sorry for you in your . . . adversity, for I have known it myself and most of it was thanks to you. Did you imagine I had what I have, given to me? Did you? When you . . . discarded me, so did my father, and had it not been for Rose . . .'

'Aah, yes. Rose,' he sneered. 'She has always been a staunch support, has she not? Was it herself or you who lured my men to your employment and . . .'

'We do not need to do these things ourselves, Luke, or is it Joel still? We have only to put a word in the right ear, and anything can be achieved.'

James turned his head slowly, taking his fierce gaze from Luke Marlowe and the pistol in his hand. What was being said distracted his plans for disarming the almost insane man. The words Luke now spoke were loud, clear and horrifying.

'. . . and beguiled every shipper in Liverpool to outlaw my ship when I sought cargo. And the company I was to buy. Of a sudden it was no longer for sale. The ships' chandler could no longer supply me with provisions, and dozens of small things prevented me from doing business. My banker unexpectedly found he could not extend my credit and, more, that if I did not pay him what I owed, my ship would be impounded. Now, I cannot trade, for I have no cargo. I cannot steam away to another port, for I have no crew nor provisions. My ship sits and moulders at her berth and . . .'

'Are you saying my wife has done this to you, Mr Marlowe?' James's voice cracked incredulously, whether in pain or disbelief it was difficult to tell.

'Keep out of this Jamie. It has nothing to do with you.' Lacy did not even turn her head to look at him, but continued to stare balefully at Luke.

'Nothing to do with me?'

'No, this is between . . . this man and I. We had a score to settle. It is settled now, and we are even.'

'Oh, no! We are not, Lacy Hemingway.' Luke's face became once more insane with hate and a lust for revenge.

'Years ago, when I began to see a future for myself again, I was willing to forget what had been done to me. You were a child and with a child's mind you thought . . . But now . . . Did you think I would simply fade away from your life after what has been done to me *again*? I have nothing.' It was said simply. 'I have nothing now, nothing to lose but my life, and I care not a whit for that. If I cannot live upon the sea I would sooner die. You are to come with me.'

He lifted the wavering pistol and aimed it coolly at Lacy's head. It was steady again as was the look of determination on his face. Her face was carved from marble, clear-cut, delicate, unlined and as beautiful now that she stared death in the eye as it had always been. Her utter contempt for the man who was to kill her was manifest in her narrowed, translucent eyes, the lift of her arrogant head and the disdain which curled her lip.

Then James spoke and the moment was averted.

'Did you try for a cargo at "Osbornes", Mr Marlowe?' It was said quite calmly, as though they sat in his office and discussed business like three civilized shippers who had commerce together. Luke turned his inflamed, weary eyes from Lacy and spoke indifferently.

'I tried every shipping line in Liverpool, Captain.'

'I gave no order that you were not to be supplied.'

'I was refused.'

'By whom?'

'I do not recall his name. Does it matter? It is too late now.'

'I do not believe so, Mr Marlowe. I imagine I can find men to sail your ship and a cargo for you to carry.'

Luke's body seemed to sway and then in a strange way, as though every muscle had been held rigid but had suddenly been let go, each part of him sagged, little by little. But his pistol remained at the ready, its muzzle still lined up on the shining head of Lacy Osborne.

'It is too late, Captain. I have had enough. This woman, your wife and her helpmeet have brought me down. I have determined she shall . . .'

'Surely, Mr Marlowe, you cannot mean to turn away from what you tell me you most want from life. A ship . . . your ship . . . a cargo to get you on your way again.'

'Stop it, Jamie. He is not worth it. He is nothing but a . . .'

'If you say one more word, Lacy, I shall knock you senseless. It is your vindictive . . . '

'Vindictive is it? Who was it cried with me over what this man had done? A child . . . my child and now yours . . .'

'Stop it I say! It cannot be undone . . . what is done, and I for one do not intend to see you, and possibly myself, killed for the sake of . . .'

'You can both stop arguing for I have no intention of accepting . . .'

It was Lacy's eyes which warned him.

James had seen them come but had not moved his gaze a fraction from Luke's wretched, demented face.

But Lacy, untrained in the ways of a soldier, could not help that tiny flicker of acknowledgement, nor keep her expression under control. Even so, it was too late for Luke Marlowe.

As he turned, a pair of strong arms gripped him about his chest whilst two hands grasped the pistol, pointing it up at the ceiling. In a moment, Samuel and William and two of the grooms disappeared in a heap behind the chesterfield and beneath them lay the weeping, defeated, flaccid form of Luke Marlowe. If her husband had not restrained her it is likely that Lacy Osborne would have joined the pile of servants, adding her blows to those still rained on the already beaten man.

A week later the slightly decaying and rusted hulk of a steamship, under sail until she cleared the river, slipped from her berth at Waterloo Dock. It was December and the sun had not yet risen, but the tide was right, and it would be daylight within an hour.

The ship was low in the water for she had a full cargo. Her crew dodged nimbly about her deck, securing lines and making ready for their voyage across the Atlantic.

Her captain stood beside the pilot who would guide her from her safe harbouring. His face was drawn, the fine sunburn he had sported when he steamed so confidently into Liverpool four months ago turned to a pasty, mustard yellow. But he was smartly dressed, with a high polish on his boots, and a freshly laundered white shirt beneath his soft blue frock coat. A cap was set at an impertinent angle upon his thick mass of hair. His eye was bright and his voice glad as he gave commands to the seamen.

He did not once look back at the great seaport of Liverpool.

# CHAPTER 47

The horse's hooves dashed like great hammers against an anvil, and sparks flew from the rocks over which they galloped. The animal's ebony coat was slippery with sweat and rain, as smooth as if it had been greased and, around his mouth, great drools of spittle fluttered and trailed in the wind. His heart pumped and his flanks heaved, but his loyalty and his strength showed in his willingness to go on, forever if needs be, to the tune of his master's command.

The man on his back was dressed in a sombre riding outfit. Dark grey with a white cravat, and high black riding boots. He wore a great, black, double-collared cape and, clapped down over his dark brown hair, was a tall, black top hat. He wore riding gloves and carried a crop.

The rain fell steadily from a surly sky, pouring down and sweeping across the countryside in great blinding sheets, lifting and shifting, parting occasionally to reveal the rough fields, the hedges over which the stallion jumped effortlessly; deep rutted lanes, dangerous and awash with stretches of muddy water, and the stark and winterish outlines of the trees.

It was nearly mid-April. Sheep huddled beneath hedgerows, bunching tight like fearful matrons as horse and rider thundered by – frequently sailing over their heads – and the rain dripped sullenly from their oily fleeces into the soggy ground.

There were orchards now on the rider's left and right, girdled by blackthorn fences. Ditches edging the lanes overflowed into them and onto the surface of the roadway, and the animal, beginning to flag now, cut flashing swathes of water with his hooves.

A dry stone wall was jumped. The horse's rear hoof caught the top, and he hesitated, almost crashing down. Righting himself, he went on courageously, but the near-accident appeared to bring his rider to a sudden realization of what he was about.

With an anxious murmur, he pulled on the reins, and slowed his horse to a walk.

'Jason, sorry old boy. Whoa. Steady, steady. What a brute I am. Sorry old chap, sorry.'

They walked on, horse and rider, heads bent to avoid the sleeting rain, shoulders hunched in the same tired posture. Water dripped from the brim of the man's hat and ran in a steady trickle onto his hands as they held the reins. The stallion lifted and shook his head, and droplets of moisture from his mane flew about as James cursed silently.

They passed through a village where the noise of the horse's hooves brought faces to windows of snug cottages, setting curtains twitching to see what simpleton was about on a day like this. Rosy light fell across puddles, turning them to polished flame.

The horse seemed to be familiar with the road, for he turned independently and with confidence into a narrow lane. The man, his head sunk between his shoulders appeared not to notice but gazed down at his hands, letting the animal go where it would.

The noise of running water could soon be heard some way off. Not the persistent splash of raindrops, but the thunderous roar of a river in full flood; the sound of a torrent exploding against rocks, and the man lifted his head. He looked about him, bewildered, then emitted a harsh, grunting laugh.

'Well, I'll be damned. How the devil did we get here, lad? I had no intention of fetching up at this place of memories. The last spot on earth . . .'

His voice trailed away. Horse and rider moved on and then, suddenly, there it was. A cascade of water so thick, and yet so fragile it might have been made from lace. The noise was overwhelming but the man was deaf and blind to all but the beauty of his memories, and of his remembered love.

Her white body shimmered, insubstantial as the spray

which gauzed the glade, and her voice rang out, sweet as the lark, earthy as the black soil.

'Jamie. Quickly, quickly, I cannot wait . . . aah . . . ahhh . . . My love, my love . . .'

She was everywhere.

Knee deep in the summer flow of the waterfall, its icy waters gentle but sharp upon her flesh. Quiet, absorbed, before her easel, a smudge of paint upon her cheek. Racing like a boy, a boy in drawers and bodice, with a cascade of hair like water tumbling down her back. In his arms, her back against his chest, serene as a madonna, her quiet voice telling him of her love.

She was here.

The horse had stopped and James Osborne slid down from his back.

'Stand boy,' he said quietly, and though his voice would not have been heard by a man a foot from him, the animal heard and obeyed. James kept his arm about the stallion's neck, and together they watched the racing water. Then, alone, his pain observed by no one, he allowed the angry, bitter hurt to pour from him into the animal's ear.

'She will not forgive me, Jason, nor seems to notice that I even speak. I cannot conceive of a moment in our life together when she has put me before her ships. But now, she is obsessed with them.' He paused. 'I tell you this, when she considers my love before her own for her business I shall know she truly loves me.'

He bent his head and rested his brow against the neck of the animal. His hat fell to the ground, rolling away beneath the animal's belly, but James seemed not to care, and the rain fell heavily upon his dark head. The mist from the thundering waterfall merged with the rain, forming a curtain of water about the two still figures until they were almost invisible. The man's voice was muffled.

'I sometimes curse the day I met her, for I have had no peace since then. She will not let me . . . treasure her. She fights me . . . fights for the right to be distinct from me in a way no husband and wife should be. I have known and been delighted in her spirit from the day we met, but now that very resolution of her will divides us. And I cannot speak of it to her, for I would not quell it if I could. I love her so, you see, and the very trait which seems to separate us is the one I love the most.'

The stallion stood, patient as a docile mare. His namesake, the first Jason had fallen in the Valley of Death, his grey coat awash with his own crimson blood.

'It seems I must take her as she is, my friend, for there is no other way.'

James sighed, and moved near to the froth of water, standing on the edge of the boiling river. The horse followed quietly. The water at the bottom of the fall was a dark, viridescent green, but at its base, as it hit the river, a little light falling between trees touched it to a brilliance which was almost emerald.

James stared, fascinated, his mind struggling to recapture the image which the lovely colour evoked in his memory. Droplets of water formed stars of brilliance in its green depths, and he knew then.

He turned and looked towards the path which led to the house, and felt no surprise when he saw her standing there. It seemed natural. Her eyes had flashed in the light on the water and it was as if he had brought her there with his thoughts.

She walked towards him, the hem of her woollen gown brushing against the undergrowth. She wore a deep red cloak with a hood, but the rain had soaked through the material and it clung about her heavily, the moisture from it dripping like tiny diamonds about the skirt of her dress. The hood framed her face but did not protect it nor her hair above her forehead, and her clear white complexion was glistening with rain.

She appeared to be as little surprised as he. They looked at one another steadily for a long moment, then Rose glanced hastily away. She spoke first.

'You are far from home, James.'

'I was . . . restless, and needed to get out of the house.'

'And I was the same. Mary Kate and Declan were lively, and I felt the walls close in on me. I wanted . . . some air.'

611

They smiled at one another and a tiny spark flared, then dissolved quickly.

'What made you come this way?' she asked.

'Jason brought me. I gave him his head. He thought he was making for home, I suppose.'

They watched the stallion, who tossed his head as though in agreement, and they laughed. But they had begun to avoid one another's glance.

'It will be nice to have the spring, James. It will soon be here, I hope,' she said politely and, equally courteous, James agreed.

The silence was filled with drips and rustles, and the sounds made by the horse, who snorted, impatient now to be warm in his stable.

'You are not settled at your work, as Lacy is this Sunday morning?' Polite still, James broke the awkward silence, a hint of bitterness in his voice.

'No . . . I had . . . I shall leave it until tomorrow.'

'Very sensible. A day's respite is needed now and again.'

'Yes.'

Their eyes, which had avoided one another, began to cling now, sending urgent messages. It was the first time they had ever been completely alone and, like escaping birds which have been caged, the signals flashed from one to the other, darting on the wing from eye to eye. The silent, invisible cord, denied by James even to himself, stretched between them, as it had done for nearly nine years. The nearer they drew to one another, the tighter the tension became. They were conscious of it but it did not seem to matter. There was no one here to see. Always before, there had been Lacy's presence, and the need to keep their eyes expressionless had been acute. And, despite the attraction he felt for Rose, James's eyes had always gone involuntarily from her, drawn to his wife by his deep love.

But he had, without exception, been conscious of Rose and, like a gemstone which glows at the perimeter of one's vision, though she had not been clearly seen, the awareness of her was forever there.

'It is an uncommon bad day for a walk, Rose.'

'Yes.'

They faced each other, less than a yard between them.

James watched as the rain fell onto her dark hair, fascinated by the mass of tiny curls which sprang upon her forehead. Droplets of moisture slipped to the end of each shining tendril to fall upon her eyelids, to hang upon the ends of her lashes. She blinked and, travelling smoothly across her wet cheeks and down the length of her small, straight nose, they gathered like great fat teardrops on her red lips. Her lips parted and the rain ran between, and her pink tongue flicked out in an innocently sensual gesture, to lick away the moisture.

James felt the heat flame in his belly.

He removed his riding gloves and, without appearing to be aware of what he did, he put a finger gently to her face, and brushed a raindrop from the sweet curve of her chin. She did not speak or move, but her eyes darkened almost to black as her pupils dilated.

'You are absolutely soaked, Rose,' he said dreamily, and smoothed the back of his hand against her cheek. 'What the devil made you come out, today of all days? It is a day for staying beside the fireside or in . . .'

The word was almost out. The word which was at that moment uppermost in his mind. More than anything in the world he wanted at that moment to take Rose O'Malley to bed. Had she then made the smallest seductive gesture; had she indicated in that way women know, that she was willing, he might have taken her quickly then in the storm of the winter waterfall. But Rose was inexperienced and senseless in her love. She was not Rose O'Malley, merely a body, a thing of the flesh. All that existed in her world was the hand of this man and his hot, dark eyes upon her, and his low voice. But he was drawing back. His eyes, so warm, were confused, and she could not bear it if he did not . . .

The knowledge came to her then, as it does to every female.

'James.'

Without knowing how she knew, Rose smiled enticingly, and James's eyes were drawn again to her mouth. Her lips stretched against her white teeth and the rain beat down upon her upturned face. She was like a white rose which lifts its petals to receive the blessed moisture which gives it life. Her hood fell back to reveal the living black mass of her hair which she had bundled up carelessly in her eagerness to be away from the house. It lay across the red of her cloak and the rain began to slip down it.

Lost now in the exciting beauty of her – white and black and vivid red – James put his hands at each side of her face and drew her to him. He placed his mouth against hers and tasted the cold rain, and then as her lips opened, her warm tongue, and with a long, shuddering sigh their bodies fused together from breast to knee. His hands twisted in her hair, pulling her face to his, drawing her closer. They were both moaning and the noise of the waterfall seemed to accompany them, thunderous and strong.

With fingers wet and slippery with rain, he undid the cord at the neck of her cloak, and it slipped in a circle of red to her feet, a vivid splash of colour against the winter grass. Her arms clung to him and her mouth to his, as he ripped away the collar of her dress. There were a dozen buttons at the front of the bodice, but they were beyond him and, demented with longing, Rose tore them open before lifting her clawed hands to his wet hair, dragging down his head, obsessed with having his mouth on hers again.

Her shoulders were a startling dewy white, as though they were lit from within, glowing and gleaming against the dark tree turnks. His hands found her breasts: full, ivory, pink nipples erupting. The rain poured across them and his hands warmed them, and his mouth, as he licked the moisture from them like a babe at its mother's breast.

'James, James, James,' she cried over and over again, beyond anything but the need to lie down in the mud with him, and to have him inside her. Her eyes were like those of a wide-eyed kitten, staring into his, soft, luminous and infinitely lovely, and the sounds which came from her throat sounded strangely like those of a purring cat.

James's hands were at the ribbons around her waist. Her gown fell from her like the delicate shell which enfolds a newborn chick. Her bodice and drawers were next, and she emerged, white and cream and tawny rose, and so gloriously beautiful James was as lost to her as though he was bewitched. Helpless to resist temptation, to withstand her shining, slippery body, he cupped her breasts, the nipples hard between his fingers, slipping his hands down to span her waist and the full curve of her hips, until they held her buttocks, straining her to him.

Her arms about his neck were like the tendrils of ivy on the great oak trees which grew in the park about them, and her mouth was as hot as flame upon his as he removed his own clothing. Only when at last they stood flesh to flesh, breast to breast, the heat of their passion making them impervious to the cool air about them, did he speak.

'Rose. Oh, my wonderful, glorious Rose. You are like a . . .'

'Sssh . . .,' she whispered, and drew him down to the wet-slicked grass beneath the shelter of the tree.

From somewhere deep, deep in his inflamed mind a voice cried out sharply, despairingly, and for a brief moment he hesitated. Then her hand found his penis, and he was without sight and hearing. She seemed to know every curve and crease of him, every pore and strand of hair; every inch of his flesh was explored and tasted, and her hands were about him until he was nothing but one exploding mass of feeling with no name, no past, no future. She lay upon him and under him, and the day drew on, but still they fell upon one another, time and again, as if each knew this was the first, and last time.

The rain stopped, and the silence was complete, but for the soft cry of their voices. After those first words when he breathed her name, James did not speak, and nor did Rose. Not words. At last it was over.

James looked down into Rose's face. Her eyes were closed, but her expression was one of peace, of perfect tranquillity, and he relaxed and leaned to kiss her. Her eyes opened and she smiled candidly. There was no shame, no guilt, no false modesty. She lifted her hand and touched his face tenderly. Her fingers traced the firm outline of his mouth. In her eyes was a well of love which was without bottom, and she spoke the words she could not speak before.

'I love you, James Osborne,' she said.

'Rose . . . I . . .'

'No, don't, James, don't.' She smiled serenely. 'I know you don't love me. She, the one you love, waits at home for you.' James moved to sit up, but she held him to her. 'No, James, one more moment, please. It is all I ask. Just this one time, allow me to speak, to say what I have buried deep for many years. It is alive, my love for you, and yet I have been impelled to dig a grave and lay it to rest, and there it must remain until I . . .'

Her eyes slid away from him to the pounding cascade of the waterfall. She began to shiver now, as the blaze of their lovemaking died down, and he pulled his cloak about them.

'I have loved you for fifteen years, James, as long as you have loved her, and I have wanted you since then.'

'But Rose. How can . . . ?' He looked at her in anguish and the full significance of what they had just done was written on his face.

She went on as though he had not spoken.

'That is a long time to watch the man you love, love the woman you hold as dear as a sister. To see in his eyes as they look at her, the love you covet. Yes, covet, James. I have coveted your love and your body. I have imagined how it would be . . . This . . . this . . . and . . .'

She ran her hands across his muscled shoulders and down his long, hard back. They lingered about his narrow waist and hips and taut, flat stomach, and she felt him tremble. His eyes darkened and, instantly, he looked away from her as if the temptation was more than he could bear.

'Rose, Christ, Rose. If you care at all . . . let me go, for I swear I am not strong enough to . . .'

He stared steadfastly at the rough bark of the tree trunk. He was the embodiment of all men who have dined at a forbidden table and are not sorry they ate, but fear they will be found out. James Osborne, a man so in love with his wife he would willingly die for her, was no exception. He longed to

616

explain away the extraordinary circumstances and his own behaviour, to lay the blame elsewhere, but the look in Rose's eyes stopped him.

He shook his head and his strong face lost its penitent cast and became gentle. The shamefaced play of his features died away. His eyes were steady and honest, and he did not avoid her gaze as he spoke.

'Rose, I will not lie to you and deny that I have . . . that you have always attracted me. There is something special, something fine about you, an indescribable, magnetism which draws me to you. Although I love elsewhere . . .' It was as though each was reluctant to mention Lacy's name, here in one another's arms. '. . . you have always held a fascination for me. I have seen the challenge in your eyes, though I am sure you were unaware of it. Men are weak creatures, Rose, when their manhood is involved,' he said bitterly, 'and cannot resist it. But I swear I would never have . . .'

'Never have made love to me if I had given you the time to think? But then, neither of us had time to think, James. This was not premeditated.'

Rose laughed softly and reached for his mouth with her own, and despite himself he responded, sinking his lips into the softness of hers. But his body was armed now, against her; prepared by his clearer mind, and the lusty hour they had just spent. The surfeit of love she had given him had strengthened him, though he took no credit for it.

'God, Rose! What are we to do? How can we face . . . ?' He did not finish the sentence. He did not need to and Rose knew finally that, scarcely begun, it was over.

'Don't worry, James. We shall not have to face one another, nor break our hearts for what we do to Lacy. Even if you were willing, which I know you are not, we could not degrade her, nor each other, with such complications. But there is one thing, James, which you must promise me.'

'Just ask.'

'Guilt sometimes makes a person . . . foolish.'

James looked at her, his eyes steady, then turned away.

'Yes, I know. I will not tell her . . . of this.'

'It would serve no purpose, only annihilate her. You must bear the burden. Do not put it on her.'

'I promise.'

'She . . . loves you so. There is nothing she would not do for you.'

He bent his head. 'Strange as it may seem, after . . . after what has happened between you and I, I am the same about her.'

'I know. But all men are allowed one fall from grace, James. You have had yours. Now you must cherish her as never before.'

The smooth, sliding tears began to flow down Rose's face, tears of such devastating sorrow they seemed to come like a flood, swamping the greenness of her eyes and the whiteness of her flesh. She clamped her lips together, and looked up at the bare branches of the trees, as she tried to bring herself under control.

James watched her sorrowfully, his eyes filled with compassion. He knew there was nothing he could do to take away her pain. Nothing. He gently disengaged himself from her arms, and then sat up.

'We must go now, Rose. I feel we shall . . . not . . . not meet . . .'

'Don't! Please don't, James.'

Her cry rent his heart.

He bent his head and kissed her for the last time.

# CHAPTER 48

Lacy was surprised when Rose failed to make her usual Monday morning appearance in the office. She could not remember a day when Rose had been indisposed, as her note said, since the long ago day when she and James had brought her back from Bridie O'Malley's foetid cellar. Then, she had been out of her mind with fever, lack of food and proper attention, driven so by her awareness that Lacy and James were lovers. She had run to hide from the knowledge and had been stricken down in the disease-ridden place her mother called home. She had never, Lacy knew for a fact, suffered a day's illness since.

Now it appeared she was 'indisposed', whatever that might mean, and was to take the day off, and hoped it would not inconvenience Lacy too much. Lacy snorted impatiently. Inconvenience! Of course it was inconvenient. Every day that Rose did not work beside her was inconvenient, for they were a team which could and did best every other shipping line in Liverpool. And today – when they were to re-launch the two new steamships they had bought – was the most inconvenient of them all.

They had bought the two vessels of approximately 2,900 tons each for a total of £100,000, only a fraction of their original cost and therefore a bargain, but it was still more than they need have fetched – for the firm which Luke Marlowe had been about to purchase had upped the price when it became known that 'Hemingway and O'Malley' were interested. The two ships were to be re-named *Emily Yeoland* and *Gladys Yeoland*, sister ships, in honour of the two ladies who had first had faith in the infant firm of 'Hemingway and O'Malley'. Poor Miss Yeoland the younger, Emily, timid and always in the shadow of Glad, had gone to her maker in the winter of 1866 in an epidemic of influenza which had swept

619

the borough, but the elder Miss Yeoland still commanded her large establishment with an iron-willed grace.

A new vessel was being built in Dumbarton for the 'New Hemingway and O'Malley Steamship Line' and, when she was completed in a few weeks time, would be brought to Liverpool, where she would lie awaiting engines currently being fashioned in Bolton. Lacy and Rose did not follow the shortsighted – some might say loyal – policies of many of their competitors, who gave their business to shipbuilders in Birkenhead and Liverpool; but sent their agents to builders of ships in all parts of the country, to find the most competitive prices for the most efficient job. The new ship, of over 4,000 tons, was to be ready for the opening of the Suez Canal in 1869, and was to sail on a 'Grand Oriental Cruise' via Gibraltar, Malta, Port Said, the new Suez Canal, Singapore, Hong Kong and thence back to San Francisco. It was a project never before conducted by a ship owner in Liverpool, and the great liner would cater to those wealthy enough to afford the opulent luxury with which she was to be fitted out.

Already, *Lacy Rose*, *Girl Sophie* and *Lucinda Fraser* had earned the firm of 'Hemingway and O'Malley', £100,000 each from the freight of tea from China. They were fast and reliable, and the competent agents Lacy had placed in Shanghai and Singapore ran the Eastern end of the two-sided venture with speed, efficiency and an ever-growing experience in what was a large part of her trading. They knew to a nicety which palm to grease, and by how much, in the getting of the choicest cargoes.

Lacy and Rose were not only responsible for their own rapidly expanding concern; they also had to watch closely over Lacy's holdings in Charles Hemingway's line. Almost every day Lacy would confer with Thomas, Robert and the quietly efficient men who now ran the business, those trained by Lacy herself to do what she had not the time to do. Each week she would preside over a meeting to discuss company policy, and each month a board meeting of shareholders was held in her newly appointed boardroom. She now owned the whole building in which once she and Rose had rented a room, and three of the warren of offices had been knocked together into one, and refurbished with dignified good taste. Here she presided as chairman of the board, at the head of the enormous rectangular table, with Rose at its foot. Often, when the heads of her deferential staff were bent over the papers scattered on its polished surface, she and Rose would grin and exchange a sly wink at the thought that they had come a far way over the last decade or so, from Mr Roberts' and Mr Price's pickling factory in Mervyn Street.

Now Rose was to be absent on this important day, and only she, Lacy, and Emily Yeoland would be on the dock to see the two new ships of the line go down to their element. Even James had intimated politely that he could scarce find the time to be at yet another launch of one of his wife's ships, and she had not pressed him, for the crack in their relationship was strained to breaking point since the debacle of Luke Marlowe. Even now, she could hardly bear to dwell on what she considered to be her husband's deliberate faithlessness, and she failed completely to see his point of view when he put it to her.

He had been aghast, he said, by her ruthlessness, and filled with sadness that she could be so cruel and unforgiving.

'Is he not to be allowed to pick up the pieces of the life your father destroyed? Is he to be blamed for his ambition . . . ?' James asked.

'Ambition! Do you mean to tell me you condone what he did to me in the name of ambition. Is the knowledge that his *ambition* has deprived us of a child . . .'

'Stop it, Lacy,' he said wearily. 'We cannot keep digging up that old bone over and over . . .'

'Dear God, James. Is that how you see it? An old bone . . .'

'Of course not. No one could be more . . . agonized than I . . .'

'Then why have you gone against me in my desire to punish him as he once punished me? Can you not stand by me in . . . ?'

'I cannot be the cause of a man's death, Lacy. I have killed men in battle, but never in cold blood.'

'I do not intend to kill him, James.'

'You will do so, if you take his ship and the sea from him.'

'You pious bastard. Have you no feeling . . . ?'

'It does no good to call me names, my dear. I am adamant on this. I will not allow you to stoop to such . . . degradation. I shall give the man a cargo and have him gone forever from our lives.'

His face contorted, he had tried to take her in his arms, but she struck out at him and yelled her fury, and the words he spoke whispered away unheeded to the high ceiling of their bedroom.

'I am as wretched as you, my love,' he tried to say, but she would not listen. 'I can barely stand the pictures which come to my mind of you in that man's arms, nor of the horrors you endured because of him, but I cannot condemn him as you do. I have . . . seen too much, Lacy. Too much suffering . . . at . . . Balaclava, Scutari . . . Cawnpore. I cannot do it to him. Try to understand . . .'

But Lacy had gone, and the servants cowered in the kitchen as the sound of her rage tore through the house.

Since that day they had merely been polite.

Lacy got through the day with her usual speed and efficiency, and the amount of work she accomplished, as she had trained herself to do, was more than many would get through in a week.

Now, at the docks, she smiled and held Miss Yeoland's arm, and felt the thrill she always felt at the small launching ceremony, surprised to see tears on the old lady's face as *Gladys Yeoland* followed her namesake down the slipway. They sipped sherry together in Lacy's comfortable office before Lacy handed her affectionately, for she held Miss Yeoland in high esteem, into her carriage.

At last she was free to take her own carriage to Beechwood.

'Did you think me emigrated to Australia, Rose, did you? Well, you must blame Miss Yeoland, for nothing would suit her but that we reminisce about the day you and I came face to face with that old faggot Mrs Lucas on the stairs of her establishment. Do you remember? She went on and on in the way of the elderly, and I thought she would never go, but here I am, and what in heaven is this about an indisposition?'

Without pausing for breath she went on.

'But I will admit it was rather nice to talk of old times. Do you think it a sign of encroaching middle age, Rosie?'

She turned and smiled, and took Rose's hand affectionately, then frowned, concern showing in her cool grey eyes.

'Why Rosie, you *are* indisposed, are you not? You look as though a sea cruise would not come amiss. You seem to have become positively skinny. What have you been doing? It seems I have only to turn my back for a day or two and you melt away to nothing. Look at you, a shadow of yourself. Are you really unwell, acushla?'

Rose denied it.

'No, no. Of course not. A headache, that is all. 'Tis lovely to see you, darlin', and looking as bonny as the day. Will we sit on the terrace and enjoy the spring sunshine? Who would have imagined after the weather . . . only . . . only yesterday, so wet . . . but today is almost like . . . Now, what will you have? Tea? Or would you prefer something else?'

'No, tea would be lovely.'

Rose instructed the hovering Maggie, who clattered away across the worn flags of the terrace and into the drawing room, banging the door behind her. Rose smiled and shook her head, as they arranged themselves in the white wicker garden chairs, spreading the width of their skirts about them.

'That girl, will she ever learn? So independent and bossy and full of her own importance, and I swear she thinks herself still on her daddy's farm. She stamps about like one of his old plough horses. I have yet to hear her close a door quietly, or sound like anything other than a clog dancer. But still, I wouldn't be without her. She reminds me of myself at the same age. She becomes "vexed" – her word – if I do not eat everything she puts before me. She is fast becoming a tyrant in my life and in the managing of the house. Just because she was with me in Upper Duke Street, she thinks she has the right to order me as she pleases. But she is a caring person. Do you know she even gave me a small Easter gift. A handkerchief she had embroidered herself, and you know how handy she was with a needle. Treated it more like a ploughshare, or whatever implement they use in the fields of Yorkshire. See, I have it somewhere. I will show it to you.'

Rose stood up and moved across the terrace, vanishing for a moment inside the house then re-appeared clutching a large, tapestry workbag in which she kept innumerable small things needed from time to time during the day. She began to rummage in the bag, throwing things this way and that, her voice droning on, and suddenly, with that special understanding which had always existed between them, Lacy knew Rose was nervous.

Rose was not a person to fuss and fiddle with things, nor did she meander on, speaking but saying nothing. She was always, except when her temper was aroused, a calm steadying influence, not only on Lacy but on everyone whose life she touched. Now she was acting as though she was afraid to look Lacy in the face, as though she must be up and about and doing something until the tea arrived, giving herself a task to occupy her hands and eyes.

'By the way that was a wonderful evening at the opera two weeks ago, Lacy. It is so long since you and I used to go together I had quite forgotten how enjoyable it could be and the supper afterwards was delicious. I had a most interesting conversation with Sir Giles Winterton. I meant to send a note to tell you so, but somehow got caught up in this and that, and then I thought to say so personally.'

Lacy watched, quite fascinated by Rose being 'polite'.

'I enjoyed it so much and everyone was most kind. Aah, here it is . . .' She produced the scrap of badly embroidered lawn, its somewhat strange shape blotched with red and blue flowers of unrecognizable breed, and held it up triumphantly for Lacy to see.

'Mmm, very nice, but why should they not be kind?' Lacy, plainly uninterested in Maggie's needlework, was up in arms in an instant at any criticism, hinted or otherwise, of Rose.

'Oh, come now, Lacy. You know why.' Rose looked directly at Lacy for the first time. 'It cannot be a daily event for a Baronet to sit down to supper with a former scullery maid, and one who is Irish at that.'

'Dammit, Rose. Don't bring that up again after all these years.'

''Twas you who took up the gauntlet, not I, Lacy Osborne. I only said they were kind, and so they were. I didn't mean to sound . . . But it was so strange, I suppose, to sit amongst those I had once waited on.'

'But you have done it many times since. That was fourteen years ago and long forgotten.'

'Not by me,' Rose said sharply. 'Still, everyone was most . . . kind.'

'Of course they were, and do be quiet about it, Rose, or I shall quarrel with you. And you did not appear to object to the "kindness" of the dashing Captain Whatsisname. I vow I thought he was about to devour you whole. When he kissed your hand as you left, he looked as though he were eating a peach.'

'I know,' Rose laughed lightly. 'What a fool the man was. Why you call him dashing I cannot imagine. I thought him just the opposite. Begorra, I'd sooner kiss a pig.'

Rose had relaxed now as the laughter spilled out across the peaceful garden, and her face had lost the strained and guarded expression it had worn. When Maggie brought the tea, the two women gossiped for an hour; sending inside for a parasol apiece as the sun became stronger; and dissecting the behaviour, the clothes and the conversation of the guests who had attended the party held for the opening of the opera season in Liverpool's Royal Amphitheatre in Great Charlotte Street. Lacy and James had taken a box two weeks previously and intended to invite a group of enthusiasts such as themselves to each new performance as it was put on. Rose had been included.

They discussed Mr Disraeli's Reform Bill which was being much publicized in the newspapers. His resolutions were, amongst others, that it was desirable that a more direct representation should be given to the labouring classes in the matter of suffrage, and that every parliamentary elector should record his vote by means of a polling paper. It did not much concern Rose and Lacy, for, even they, emancipated beyond any level imagination could have devised, would have smiled at the mere idea that women might one day be included in universal franchise. They did not appear to think it astounding though, that they should discuss these subjects together when most other women were not even aware that such topics even existed.

Rose commented on the Fenian outbreak – Irish home rule being a matter dear to her heart – which had crept across the channel from the County of Kerry, and she talked at length on the injustices being done to her countrymen, for she was still as Irish as the green sod upon which she had been born.

As Lacy listened to her, watching the expressive face, the woodland green of her eyes, the sensation that Rose was chattering in order to avoid speaking of what was really important, crept over her again. It was as though any subject would do, be it lighthearted or serious, providing it kept what Rose really had to say, unspoken.

'What is it, Rose?' Lacy said suddenly, her voice soft with concern.

Rose looked startled, then averted her eyes.

'Nothing, nothing. Why should there be anything wrong?' She was immediately on the defensive.

'I did not ask what was wrong. Is there something wrong?'

Rose stared defiantly, the very glare in her eyes giving her away.

'Sure, there's nothin' wrong, I told yer.'

'Then why are you so touchy?'

'Touchy is it! I'm sure I don't know what yer mean.'

'Rose, Rosie, you are . . . embarrassed. That is not like you. We have always been closer than sisters. No constraint, nor awkwardness. Nothing hidden. Now you are . . . oppressed. Why is that?'

'I'm sure I don't know what ye're blatherin' on about.'

'Let us be honest, Rose.'

'I don't know what yer afther, sure I don't. Will yer stop talkin' in riddles or, faith, I'll think yer mad.'

'You are talking in the brogue, Rose O'Malley, and you know what that means.' Lacy was laughing teasingly, convinced now that she had caught Rose out in some minor discomfiture.

'And why not, tell me that. Sure an' aren't I as Irish as . . .'

'Oh, Rose. Stop it. I know you better than anyone in this world, and it is a sure sign when you get the "blarney" on you that you are either in a temper with someone or you are . . . afraid. Are you . . . has something happened to cause you to be fearful, Rose? Tell me?'

Lacy was serious now.

'Don't be daft, Lacy Osborne. Of what should I be afraid?'

But Rose's eyes were desperate now, with some emotion Lacy could not understand.

'Then what is it? What have you been up to?'

'Up to! Up to! An' what should I be up to sittin' up 'ere like the Queen o' Sheba herself?'

It was as though Rose must keep herself in high dudgeon or her control would be lost. Her Irish temper, whipped up by herself in order to stop her doing the only other thing open to her – weeping like a lost child – was as false as the hair-piece now favoured by the elder Miss Yeoland. In truth, she had nothing at which to be angry; certainly not the woman who sat opposite her, and who was now bearing the brunt of it as calmly as a mother with a fractious child. Clear grey eyes watched her, and Rose knew she had only to put out a hand, and those loving arms would be around her, comforting and safe as they had always been.

Rose made up her mind. It could not continue. Neither she nor James could meet again in this woman's company and expect to appear as two friends and nothing more. If James could practise iron self control and act as though no more than friendship existed between them, she could not. This moment had been decreed years ago, and only circumstances, circumstances of love and loyalty and need, had pushed it along ahead of her, delaying its impact. The pretence must be ended. Before it became a catastrophe, she must leave, and with her going peace would come. To her and to James, and through them, to Lacy.

But before she wrenched herself from these two who were dearer to her than life she must tell Lacy that they must now live apart, and she must tell her why. The truth was all that would do. It was the only explanation Lacy would accept.

Rose steadied herself.

'Rose, what is it? Come on, darlin', this is me here, Lacy. Tell me what has happened to have you in such a pother.'

Rose closed her parasol and laid it upon the stone flags beside her chair. She had her back to the sun and the depth of the shadow hid the expression in her eyes. Her voice was strangely high, almost shrill in her endeavour to be calm.

'Lacy . . . alannah . . . I have something to tell you.'

'Yes, Rose, I know you have.'

'You . . . you know?' Rose stared in astonishment.

'Rosie, you have not been yourself since I arrived.'

'Yes, 'tis true. Me dander was up but it was all . . . all just a trick to be puttin' off the evil moment.'

Lacy leaned forward anxiously, her parasol tipping sideways as she grasped Rose's arm. She dropped the pretty thing irritably, and it rolled away across the terrace, fetching up against the parapet.

'Rose, you are beginning to frighten me.'

'Faith, 'tis nothing to the way I feel.'

'Dammit, Rose . . . will you tell me, or must I shake you?'

'Always impatient but 'tis only to be expected, for weren't you always so. Give me a moment to . . . to pull myself together.' She breathed deeply, her breath sighing out as it left her lungs, and Lacy watched her warily.

Rose looked into Lacy's eyes, and her own were anguished.

'I'm to . . . to go away, darlin'.'

'Away?'

Lacy's face creased in bewilderment.

'Yes, I am going to stay in . . .'

'To stay . . . a holiday? Oh Rose, you are a devil.' Lacy laughed with relief and fanned herself vigorously. 'You alarmed me with your long face and serious voice. I think it is perfectly splendid for you to have a holiday.'

She leaned forward again, putting out her hands to take Rose's, and was surprised to find them as cold and weightless as the first feathers of snow. She began to chafe them absently, her tongue tripping merrily over phrases like '... and where is it to be? ... will you take the children? ... and Maggie? ... Paris? ... oh that would be divine ... and there is Venice ...' and so on, like a rippling brook running itself over stones until it reaches the smoothness of the river and its merry noise is forced to cease.

Lacy's voice slipped away to a whisper, and then to nothing. The sound the silence made was dreadful. It was thick with sorrow and crackling with fear, and it continued as the two women stared at one another, eyes bleak as the river on a winter's day. Lacy's were like smoke, incomprehension and a growing fear changing the clear silvery depths to shivering mist. Her mouth moved to form a question but her face was shadowed with reluctance to hear the answer.

Rose watched with compassion, knowing she was about to club her with a much bigger stick and one which might render her senseless, not only with fear, but with rage.

'It is not to be a holiday, is it Rose?'

'No. Not a holiday.'

'You are ... going away ... to live somewhere?'

'Yes.'

'Rose.'

The word was just a whisper.

'Yes, darlin'?'

'What is it, Rose?'

'It is difficult to explain ...'

'Rose, I do not really care. You can have no reason ... nothing so ... horrendous to make you ... I do not care to be separated from you, Rosie.'

Lacy's voice sounded like that of a child whose mother has just announced that it is to be sent away to school, separated from the only security it has ever known. She was a grown woman, strong and independent. She had proved to herself and to others that she needed no one to help her to force a way through life's obstacles, but in her heart, and Rose knew it for she was the same, was the need to have Rose somewhere about her. And the need was as fierce as ever it had been. Welded together by pain, sorrow, illness and death, it would be as if flesh grown together over the years were to be torn bloodily apart. Even James Osborne did not give to his wife what she needed of Rose, and now it was to be taken from her.

'You know I cannot stand it,' Lacy said.

'You must.'

'No matter what, I will not let you leave me. We are . . . one person, Rose.'

'Stop it.' Rose's voice was harsh, agonized.

'No, no, I will not stop it.'

'I must go . . . *must* . . . I cannot stay . . .'

'Why . . . *why* . . . ?'

Lacy stood up, shrieking the words and the gardener who peacefully planted out the bedding plants for the summer in the walled garden to the side of the house swivelled his head in amazement, and stood up to peer over the warm, rosy stones to see who was creating such a din on Miss Rose's terrace.

As Lacy leapt to her feet, so did Rose and they faced one another eyes flashing, fists clenched. Their loving passion looked like hate.

Beyond caution, beyond the affectionate need to be gentle with this woman who cried her pain, Rose shouted his name at last.

''Tis James, 'tis James . . !' She dropped her chin upon her chest and the tears swept their way across her ashen cheeks. Her hands hung limply to her sides.

'Can yer not see . . . are yer blind, woman?'

Rose's voice was lifeless. It was as though Lacy had taken something precious from her, some secret treasure she had hoarded, and which was now revealed; something which had given her warmth and comfort, and a recognition of her own value, and which was now stripped from her with the sharing.

630

She looked as though she had been shamed, made small; not before others, but before herself. Her face was drenched, blotched with weeping. In her desperation her hair had come down, and for a moment, Lacy was struck with the realization of how like Bridie she was. She looked bedraggled and hopeless, and Lacy's heart swelled with pain, bursting inside until her breast ached.

Poor dear Rose. She had no one but her sister and brother. No man to love her in the night. No one who really cared about her. Only herself. And now she was forced into believing she must leave because of her love for James. She was not aware, how could she be, that Lacy and James had known for years.

Lacy felt the relief driving out the terror and the dreadful knowledge that Rose was prepared to go, away from her love.

'But there is no need, Rosie, no need . . . Do you not see? I know . . . I know about you and Jamie.'

With a great cry, Rose flung herself about, stumbling against the small table on which all the paraphernalia of their afternoon tea was resting attractively. Her breath came gasping in sobs, as though a hand was at her throat. Her lungs laboured to draw in air, and her breast heaved. She reached the balustrade which edged the terrace, half hanging over it as though she would vomit into the flower beds beneath, and the words jerked from her, for she was beyond endurance, and in the nightmare which rushed upon her she was not even aware of what had been meant by Lacy's words.

'Dear Blessed Mother . . . *NO!* . . . *NO!* . . . *NO . .* ! He promised, said he would not tell you . . . would not burden you . . . Just once, only once, that's all . . . I begged him not to . . . Oh, James, James. How could you, how could you . . ?'

Her head jerked and her hands scrabbled on the rough masonry of the brickwork, and blood flowed from a torn finger nail. Her hair lifted and plumed and fell about her face until she resembled one of the inmates of the lunatic asylum behind the high wall in Ashton Street.

As suddenly as they had begun the words stopped. Rose did not quite, as yet, know what the mistake was that she had made, but the terrible silent stillness behind her told her she had just irretrievably blundered into an appalling error.

She turned slowly.

They faced one another and Rose knew that the awful truth stood between them. Lacy was frozen to a slender ice-cold sliver of steel. Her eyes, her hair, even her skin had the look of frosted transparency. Her lips were bloodless and they were drawn back a little, giving her the appearance of a vixen caught by the hounds, snarling in the first moments of self defence. Her voice splintered, like hoar frost beneath heavy boots.

'You . . . You and . . . James, Rose? You and James have . . . some secret which . . . which he pledged not to reveal to me? Some secret which had to do with your . . . loving him? Is that it? Do I have my facts correct? There is something . . . happening between you, which he has promised not to "burden me with", is that not how you put it? Well, he has not, Rose. Oh, dear me. No, he has not. He has told me nothing, for that is the way of men, is it not? But *you* have, Rose. *You* have told me, and now I would like to hear it all.'

Her eyes grew narrow: slits of frosted glass beneath the long curve of her lashes, and some colour crept into her cheeks. She lifted her finger and pointed it at Rose, saying quite sweetly,

'. . . and you are going to tell me.'

Rose straightened, and she flung her head from side to side.

'There is nothing to tell.' Her voice was a mumble of pain and despair and her eyes fled away, refusing to be captured by Lacy's.

'Come, Rose. I expected better from you than that. Nothing to tell? You have just told me there is, for you admitted to me that you begged James not to tell it.'

'Sweet Mary, Mother of God. Let me be, let me be.' The wail of agony slipped across the shaven smoothness of the grass to the gardener, and he felt the skin prickle on the back of his neck. Hastily, he got down from his vantage point and made his way to the comfort of the glasshouses on the far side of the rose garden. It was nothing to do with him after all, he told himself.

'You are forever calling on that God of yours, Rose, to intercede for you, to protect you, and save you from some disaster or other. Well, this time He will not, for if you won't tell me what has been taking place between yourself and my husband, I shall find out from him. Whatever else he might turn out to be, I have not found him to be a liar.'

'Lacy, please . . . Don't . . . 'twas not his fault . . . Dear Mother . . . Please . . . I made him . . .'

'You made him? Made him do what?'

'Stop it, stop it. Let me be, faith, or I'll . . .'

'Are you going to tell me, Rose?'

'I can't, I can't.'

Lacy turned calmly, every movement and gesture regal. Her head was held high, her back straight, and if Nanny Wilson had been alive to see her, she would have been proud, for all the training instilled into young Lacy Hemingway was there to see. But Lacy Osborne's eyes were not the eyes of a child who is forced to submit under a resented yoke, longing to be away to merrier pastimes, but those of a woman drowning in a black pool of despair.

'Then there is no more to be said. Goodbye, Rose.'

'Lacy, wait! . . . Darlin', please wait.' Rose began to move after her. She went hesitatingly at first, as once she had sidled around the kitchen at Silverdale; unsure, frightened, a child.

Lacy stopped, her back poker stiff, smoothed over with tulle.

'Yes?'

'Will you . . . Please don't . . . Lacy . . ?'

The words died away to nothing, and Lacy walked through the French windows into the drawing room.

'Do not bother to see me out,' she said.

# CHAPTER 49

She was gone the next day when James rode over to Beechwood, and with her went Maggie, Mary Kate and Declan. The servants could tell him nothing beyond the fact that the carriage had been brought round to the front door at first light. Jonas had driven it, loaded with boxes and its passengers to the railway station in Liverpool, and had been ordered to return home immediately after he had deposited them on the forecourt. He could not tell the Captain which train Miss Rose had caught.

Questioning the porters and even the respectful Stationmaster had elicited nothing beyond the information that many well-bred young ladies travelled with their maids on the railway train, and it was quite beyond the capability of any of them to remember a certain one.

James Osborne returned to his home and his cold and silent wife, in the certain knowledge that his marriage was finished. He could not see how it could survive after the death-dealing blow which Rose had unwittingly aimed at it. He surveyed bleakly the character of what the remainder of his life would hold. It was not pleasant. In the hissing, tearing, agonizing hurt which enfolded Lacy, she had sworn she would, if he touched her ever again, kill him and Rose, and then herself.

It had been useless to deny what had happened between himself and Rose. The look of guilt which had whitened his own face and, he was certain, that of Rose, told Lacy the truth as surely as if she had caught them in the act of adultery, and he would not belittle her intelligence with a pretence of innocence. He did not even try to justify his weakness, for to do so would have implied that the fault was largely Rose's. In his honesty, he did nothing, said nothing to defend himself, too numbed as yet to consider the surgery and nursing which might mend the terrible wound he had inflicted upon his wife.

Later, she became unnaturally calm. As calm as an iceberg which floats imperturbably upon a sea which no warmth has ever touched and, as she supervised the moving of his clothes, his books, the dozens of small personal possessions which he left comfortably lying about the rooms they shared, into a suite as far away as possible from her own, she avoided him with as much emotion as she would a piece of furniture.

He made no move to stop her. How could they pick up again the lovely threads which had woven into their marriage the love and trust, the delight and laughter, the companionship which had been theirs for almost eight years? They had known and overcome bitter recriminations; desperate, hurtful disagreement over many things. They had shared sorrow, painful and acid, over Lacy's inability to give him a child. But in all this, and through the years of often violent dissent and conflict of opinion, the solid foundation of their absolute love had held the structure of their relationship from tumbling. Even Luke Marlowe's entry into their life, and Lacy's hostility to James's reaction, had not done more than cool their loving warmth momentarily. Each had been fully aware, even as it happened, that given time and tolerance, they would both back down from the confrontation and be as once they had been.

But this was unprecedented, unique, unmatched and hopeless. It had exploded the roots of the life they had built together, and the pieces were too badly damaged to be put together again.

Lacy felt she might wither away and die, like a flower which is left unprotected in the hot sun. That night, as she lay alone in her bed for the first time since her marriage, she held herself tightly, arms locked about her breast, for if she did not keep a firm grip on herself she would run screaming, yes, screaming into the hall-way. She quite simply could not stand the pain.

She must live forever with the knowledge that the man she had loved, to whom she had given the trust which had almost

635

been crushed once before; the man who had bestowed upon her life, stability, reliability, comfort, trust and love, and upon whom she had unconsciously leaned for over ten years, had lain with the only friend she had ever had.

Lain, with. *Lain with*! Oh God, save me from the pain. Rose's flesh mingled with the beloved, familiar inner self that was Jamie. That self, known only, she had thought, to herself. It was not to be borne. Rose. *Rose*. If it had been any other woman she might have forgiven it in time, for men were weak creatures in matters of the flesh, and easily forgot what did not touch their emotions. But how could this be forgotten? For more than twenty years they had been more than friends. It was a betrayal not to be borne.

The problem was insurmountable, for it touched the part of a woman's life which is sacrosant: her man – her treasure, her world. A woman's love for her man and his for her was not to be meddled with. It was her life's blood, unshared with any other; private and revered and unspoilable.

Now Rose had been a part of it, an intruder, had known what Lacy knew, it *was* spoiled, and it was James's doing. How could he imagine that he could . . . lie with, with Rose and not crack the balance, delicate as it had always been, between the three of them?

She did not sleep. Her eyes were dry, bleak as grey rocks in the darkness, and as hard. As she watched James gallop off the next morning to Beechwood – and Rose – her heart was dead, cold as a corpse in a coffin, and just as willing to be buried in the only ground which would bring her a measure of peace.

Work.

She no longer rode with her husband into Liverpool each day, sharing the carriage in companionable silence, or conversation, or even laughing gossip as once they had done. She went alone, leaving the house as early as 6 o'clock in the morning, for she could not sleep. She often returned as late as 10 or 11 o'clock at night, going straight to her room with a tray, and very often did not see James from Sunday until the following weekend.

When he told her dispassionately that Rose had vanished, she was quite surprised by her own indifference, and wondered idly if it were possible to render all feelings to the senseless state of her own and if so was this how the bereaved overcame great sorrow, for she felt nothing now. She had become an automaton. Since that first anguished, agonizing pain-wracked night, she had become nothing, feeling nothing, wanting nothing, giving nothing to those around her, living only for the moment when her brain came alive in her office in Strand Street.

She began to look around her in the weeks which followed for other enterprises in which to invest her time and money. She and Mr Moore, an old gentleman of almost seventy now, but still with the alert brain of a man half that age, kept their eyes and ears open and were well rewarded. Not long after Rose's disappearance it became known to the banker that a salt mine in Cheshire and a salt refinery on the outskirts of Liverpool were available. Their bids were successful, and in May Lacy began to export her own refined salt.

She opened up a new route for many of Charles Hemingway's ships, going against her own brothers' and other shareholders' wishes; sailing round the Horn of South America, a long and difficult passage, to Chile and Peru, taking coal, grain, steel and salt, and bringing back nitrates and hides. The profits were enormous and, as they poured into the dissenting shareholders' pockets, their opposition swiftly died and Lacy's foresight and daring – once called foolhardiness – was praised. From then on, she could do no wrong, and any decision she made was accepted with clapping of hands and cries of delight.

She bid for and won a grant of money from the government for the carriage of the Royal Mail to Alexandria. Many of the tenders put forward were turned down but the *Gladys Yeoland*, the newest ship in her fleet, was also the fastest, with a service speed of twelve knots, which could be increased to sixteen if necessary.

It seemed as those around her lost ships in storms and tempest, foundering some of them before they had done more than half a dozen voyages; breaking in two in monumental seas; sinking in collisions with other ships; running ashore and becoming total wrecks on rocky coastlines. Hers bore a charmed life. She was tempted, as they steamed serenely about the oceans of the world, to save the cost and discard the marine insurance she paid. The premium was high, sometimes as high as ten per cent, the sum which she had advanced during the blockade of the American Civil War. She was tempted to save the money, but a tiny glimmer of superstition, a touching of wood, so to speak, held her back.

At the end of August the first stone was laid in the building of her own warehouse at the back of Prince's Dock. The space she rented in Gorée Piazza these past thirteen years was no longer sufficient for her needs. Michael O'Shaughnessy was given an assistant to help him manage what would be the biggest, most modern warehouse, or shed, in Liverpool; and in the same month Lacy began negotiations for the purchase of a piece of land to the south of the dock area, on which to build a sugar refinery, to deal with the thousands of tons of raw sugar which she imported. She bought tracts of land in Everton, Wavertree, West Derby, Childwall, Gateacre and Waterloo and building began on long rows of terraced houses – hideous in the yellow brick of the Welsh building contractors – across what once had been pleasant fields.

The demand for ships, for docks, new wharves and quays, wet docks, dry docks and all the impedimenta of a bustling, thriving sea port, grew with each passing month. Behind the docks blossomed rows of 'mean streets' to house the dock workers, engulfing pleasant villages such as Bootle and Seaforth in the north, St Michael's Hamlet, Toxteth and Dingle to the south.

Lacy Osborne had money invested in everything that was given birth in that sterile, loveless year of 1868; the year in which she and James walked alone through the bitter, tragic ashes of their marriage.

They had nothing to say to one another, but they maintained a façade. Several times a month they dined with relatives or with friends, and Jane Hemingway was a frequent visitor, her distress at Rose's disappearance real and anguished. She was at a loss to understand Lacy's seemingly casual acceptance that Rose had vanished without a word, and in her anxiety and confusion begged that she might be allowed to search for the woman who held a place in her own heart and, she believed, a special one in Lacy's.

'Why?' Jane asked piteously. 'She was a wealthy woman, was she not, Lacy? How is she to live if she has no money?'

'Her . . . income is paid into her account each month.'

'Then you do know where she is. If she is drawing on her account, can she not be traced?'

'I have no knowledge of what becomes of the money, Jane. I merely leave instructions for it to be put into . . . Ro . . . the account.'

'Lacy, Lacy dear. Please confide in me. Something dreadful has happened between you and Rose, has it not, or you would not take this . . . this uncaring attitude.'

'There is nothing to tell, Jane.'

'Perhaps James could make enquiries. He knows so many people.'

'Perhaps. You must ask him.'

Lacy's voice had begun to crack, her stiff self control spinning away from her on waves of pain. The façade which her work wrapped around her in a protective layer of armour was only present when she entered the sheltered confines of her office. In the months since Rose had left, for sixteen hours a day, she was safe from the despair of it, and when she crept tiredly to her bed at night her exhausted mind and body were felled by immediate sleep. On the occasions when they were not, she would give way to hopelessness and weep for hours on end, tearing her hard-won composure to tatters.

It was at social events such as this – when she was forced to be amongst family and friends and suffer their curious, but well meant interest in the mystery of Rose's disappearance; forced to hear her name and sometimes speak it; forced to sit beside James and recognize the deadness of his love for her – that desolation savaged her battered spirit, and she knew she would weep again that night.

As Jane turned away, almost weeping herself, Lacy's back did not rest against the chair, but was held poker-straight, and her head was set proudly, but inside she was breaking up. Everything was coming apart, ripping into shreds, and when it finally crumbled away she would fold up like a doll whose stuffing has leaked. But until her guests had gone she would hold it all in. Until she could creep thankfully into her bed and feel that warmly welcomed weight fall over and numb her body and spirit she would contain her anguish, and smile and chat as though she and James were as they had always been.

In September James told her that he was going away and did not know how long he would be gone. They did not eat together, ever, except when they were with others, and the servants had become used, as servants do eventually to everything, to their master and mistress taking their meals in separate rooms.

Lacy was before her sitting room fire, built up to comforting proportions, for the autumn day was chilly, when the polite knock came at her door.

'Come in,' she called carelessly, and did not look up as he entered, for she thought it to be her maid. She wore only her peignoir, soft and silken, lace-trimmed and the colour of a pale pink tea rose. Her hair fell casually in a fall of rippling, tangled curls, for she had not yet had it brushed, and her face was relaxed as her hand fondled the ear of the bitch who was now her constant companion, as once Copper had been, going with her even to her office in the carriage.

She turned and looked at him and the softness of her expression, meant for the dog, hardened. Her eyes frosted. She pulled her peignoir about her defensively. She did not speak.

James stood just inside the door, but he did not close it. Even such distant contact as this was anathema to them both, and the intimacy of a closed door implied too much for them to accept.

'I have come to tell you I am going away,' he said lifelessly.

Her heart twisted agonizingly in her breast, and her emotions told her she could not possibly survive the pain of it, but her mind told her coldly that she would.

'Oh?'

'I feel I must search for . . . Rose.'

'Of course. I am only surprised you have not gone sooner.'

He looked bewildered, mistaking her meaning, and should she have looked more carefully instead of glancing with seeming indifference at the dog at her feet, she might have seen the glint of hope in the dull brown of his eyes.

'Why do you say that?' he asked cautiously.

'I only mean one supposes a lover would go instantly to seek out his beloved. It is five months, and you have made no move to . . .'

'Rose is not my beloved.' His shoulders had sagged hopelessly again.

'Come, James. Your actions . . . and regard for Rose give a lie to that remark.'

'Possibly. It happens I do not love Rose, but that is not the issue here. We have . . . discussed at length the day . . . what happened in April, and there can apparently be no forgiveness, nor compassion, not for me, I hasten to add, but for Rose, on your part. I have waited, hoped that Rose would write to you, tell you what . . . how . . . tell you where she is, but she has not, so I must try to find her. It is entirely my fault. I am the reason she has left her home, friends, the work she loved . . . and you. I am responsible, and I cannot rest until I have satisfied myself that she is . . . well . . . secure. There is no other reason, no other motive. Only concern for a friend. *Your* friend, Lacy. We did you a mischief for which there can be no justification, and for which you can forgive neither of us. I would possibly be the same should . . . should you have . . . done what I did, so I cannot blame you.'

He turned quietly to the open door, his composure held tightly to him, his drawn face as blank as a stretch of unmarked snow.

'Where will you go?'

'I thought Ireland.' His back was turned to her and he spoke to the empty hallway. 'I can think of nowhere else she might go. I suppose she could be anywhere. Hopeless really, but I must try.'

'If . . . if you . . . find her . . .'

641

'Yes?' He turned eagerly, as though she were about to give him an affectionate message for Rose.

'. . . will you . . . remain with her?'

He sighed and his shoulders slumped.

'You hear nothing I say, do you Lacy?' he remarked sadly, and closed the door gently behind him.

Whilst James was away the greatest accolade ever granted to a woman was bestowed upon Lacy Osborne when, as the most successful ship owner in the port of Liverpool, she was asked to be the honoured guest of the 'Liverpool and District Businessmen's Association' at their annual banquet and not only was she to sit amongst their august presence, the first woman ever to do so, she was to be allowed to speak to the guests after dinner.

'The 'Liverpool and District Businessmen's Association' had been in existence for over one hundred years, created by the successful merchants of the borough in that curious way peculiar to men when they feel the need to gather and preen and congratulate themselves, and one another, on their own achievement. It was a society which enjoyed the monthly social meetings which took place at the Town Hall, and the sundry functions which the members thought up for their own, all male, enjoyment. It had a serious side, of course, for it was generous in its munificence to the many ladies' charities which abounded in Liverpool. And it was not to be confused with the 'Palatine Club' in Bold Street, which had its roots in the gentlemen's clubs of London's West End. By contrast, members of the Association were sober in their intentions to bring support to those less fortunate than themselves, and felt that they were indeed liberal in their action in allowing Mrs James Osborne the prestige of joining their company, if only for one evening.

She wore a gown made entirely of Persian silk backed by fine velvet, in a rich and shameless geranium red. Her shoulders and arms and the tops of her softly swelling breasts glowed lily white and the diamonds in her hair and about her throat flashed a million stars of light. The costume was almost ostentatious, but her beauty was breathtaking. If James or Rose had been present they would have known instantly what she was about. They would have smiled at her defiance, for the worthy men of Liverpool were spellbound at the sight of so much exquisite flesh on exhibition, and in such a vivid setting. As she moved magnificently about the enormous room, giving her hand and her brilliant smile to the men who once had laughed at her professed intentions, and advised her to run home to her papa, they could not resist her radiance. She was like a flower, a polished, glittering bloom emblazoned in a multitude of dark, shadowed figures. As she took her seat at the place of honour they stood, these men, transported – whether by her splendour or her achievement in attaining the prize they had given her they knew not; nor for that matter did it seem to signify, and they applauded her.

It went on for five minutes and she smiled serenely and bowed, but they would not stop until she raised her hand, then both her hands, and with much shaking of heads in fervent admiration, they agreed to sit and listen to what she had to say.

She made a simple straightforward address. As she continued, it became quite clear to them that Lacy Osborne, far from being overcome by the honour given her, considered it only her due, and was not the least astounded by it all, though she was not simpleton enough to say so outright.

Her smile was sweet as she spoke.

'Gentlemen,' she purred, 'When I was considering my reply to you tonight I was afraid that I would not find the words to adequately express my appreciation of the unique tribute you have bestowed upon me. I realize now that my fears were groundless for, looking at the familiar faces before me, I know I am amongst friends.' She paused and smiled ingenuously. 'I think I might say truthfully that this moment is, quite simply, the pinnacle of my career as a . . . businessman.'

She paused politely for their laughter.

'I have waited for it for a long time.'

The men who listened looked about at one another and

smiled kindly again, for it was true, and must, in all conscience be the height to which any gentleman, let alone a lady, could aspire. They were not as yet aware of the tongue-in-cheek irony of what this woman was saying, this woman who no longer needed their goodwill to survive. Indeed, there were many men here who needed hers, and she knew it, and so did they. But still they smiled in ignorance, believing yet that they were her superior for were they not *men* and was she not merely a *woman*? They drew on their cigars and leaned back in their seats as they waited to be thanked for their goodness and mercy in allowing her to trade with them. Their cigars began to waver in mid-air, however, as she went on:

'. . . but in all that time it never once occurred to me to doubt in my mind that one day I would reach it.'

The gentlemen fidgeted slightly, not quite certain that they cared for Mrs Osborne's pre-conceived, self-assured conviction of her arrival in their midst, considering her attitude and forthright confession of it a trifle out of place in the face of their liberality.

She went on.

'It took many years of bowing and scraping, of bending and bobbing of knees, to get my foot in the door of your masculine establishment, but I was always convinced that one day you would recognize my worth, give me my due, and allow me entrance.'

She smiled brilliantly, looking from face to face, giving each her undivided attention and, hesitating, they smiled back. It seemed she was applauding them for their foresight and good sense.

'You know, gentlemen, we ladies have much to offer outside the role in which you have placed us. In the world of commerce, for instance, although up to now you have not conceded it. Perhaps the traits we are rumoured to possess have held you back in the past. It is said we are devious, and I am sure you believe it to be true; that we cannot make up our minds from one moment to the next; and that if we do so and make an error, we falter and swoon. I believe you consider us to be fragile creatures who delight in flowers and pretty gowns, and the creation only of children and fine embroidery.'

There was a gasp but she ignored it.

'I hope that what I have done will explode that myth, and I also hope very sincerely that . . .' here she grinned again, '. . . you have not opened a Pandora's Box, the contents of which will dismay and alarm you.'

Some of the men laughed a shade uncertainly, others frowned.

'My father, with whom most of you did business often said . . .'

For a moment, a brief second or two, she hesitated and there were those who thought she had lost her nerve. They were not to know of the several ghosts who stood suddenly at her elbow. Two men and a woman, all responsible in their way for this day. They smiled and held her hand, and the woman beseeched her not to 'get yer "dander" up when they treat you like a half-witted child. If yer let 'em see it, sure an' won't they 'ave yer out of the place so quick yer won't know what 'as 'appened. I know 'tis hard, acushla, but listen ter me, will yer? Bite yer tongue.'

That woman, who now stood in wordless sorrow apart, was the one who had kept Lacy Hemingway from telling every man jack of them to go to hell in those years of clawing frustration. She it was who had urged her on, held her back when it was needed; comforted her disappointments, and encouraged her confidence.

The two ghostly men stood protectively, one on either side of her. The elder was grey and sad, but his whiskered face had ever been kind for her, and so it was now, and her forgiveness of what he had done in his love and pride of her winged away to wherever he watched. The younger, aah, the younger – merry and handsome and lively, his love patient and encouraging – where, where now, in this moment of triumph, when they should have stood boldly together, and shared the joy of it, where was he?

Where were they all? Where?

A man coughed, shattering the silence, and Lacy went on

with scarce a pause, and the three ghosts spun away, burned up in the flames of her own victory. She spoke of her father with affectionate remembrance, and the men approved now, for Charles Hemingway had been one of them, and worthy of what his daughter said of him.

'. . . so let me finish by thanking you once more for giving me this . . .' a slight pause and a wicked little smile, '. . . honour, and for the chance to prove to you that women can . . . can do quite well when given the opportunity to try. It was most . . . generous of you to allow it. Thank you gentlemen . . . from us all.'

She bowed her head as though in submission, though her lip curled in a curious fashion, then turned to the Chairman of the 'Liverpool and District Businessmen's Association', who sat beside her, and said,

'And now, Mr Ogden, if you would have my carriage sent for, I will leave you. I have some reports which I must go over before I retire. We businessmen can never afford to relax, is that not so?'

She turned to her audience who appeared stunned, and smiled maliciously and raised her hand, rather in the manner of a queen taking her royal self off after a tedious duty just performed.

'Good evening, gentlemen. Thank you for inviting me to your little . . . get-together.' There was another concerted gasp for Lacy Hemingway had, with a word, reduced their society to the importance of their wives' afternoon tea parties.

'The meal was excellent.'

On a silence as deafening as a salvo from a barrage of guns, Lacy Hemingway, for she would always be called so, glided from the room on the arm of Mr Ogden.

She wept into her pillow again that night and the men who had been rendered almost insensible by her words – for though they did not know how, they were aware that she had mocked them – might have been delighted by her sorrow, saying it was what she deserved, and was it not only to be expected of a woman who was merely that, a woman, and certainly no lady. Although she had thanked them prettily enough, and had said all the correct words to show her appreciation – somehow she had given the impression that she did not really care for the honour they had given her. And after all they had done for her in the past by accepting her into their ranks! It appeared that she had thrown their generosity back in their faces, and in public, too. Tomorrow it would be all over Liverpool that Lacy Hemingway had thumbed her nose, yet again, at society.

On that day of her greatest triumph, and of revenge for the slights she and Rose had suffered together, the grey ashes of it clogged Lacy's mouth. She wept for the two sad ghosts who had haunted her, and who now dwelled God only knew where.

It was nearly eight weeks before James came home, and when they came face to face in the drawing room at Highcross, she not even aware that he had returned, he not even sending word that he had, their greeting was the polite acknowledgement of two barely acquainted strangers.

'Aah,' she said smoothly, 'you are returned from your travels then?'

'It would seem so.'

'And did you find the person you sought?'

The newspaper which he was scanning crashed into a crumpled, angry jumble into his lap as his arms swept downwards, and for a moment she was amazed and strangely frightened by the expression of uncontrollable rage on his face.

'The person I sought! My God, Lacy. Is that the way you speak of the woman who has given her life to your service? I thought you . . . sparing in your granting of affection to others, but to hear you vilify Rose in such a manner makes me . . . want to strike you. Have you no thought for . . .'

'It seems you have, James. Is that not enough? You are ever quick to defend her.'

'Only because she is the one who has been wronged.'

'Indeed. I always supposed it to be the wife in cases such as this.'

'Dear, sweet Jesus. Seven months and your heart has not

softened one bit. You have a stone in that softly rounded breast of yours, Lacy, and stones remain . . . just stones, forever. Will yours?'

'I suppose it will, James. It must, or I could not stand it.'

# CHAPTER 50

It was just after the New Year when the note came.

They had gone through the charade of the season of the year, acting out the parts assigned to them over the Christmas period. They had even sent one another a Christmas card made of satin and lace, very ornate, with a sickeningly sweet verse inside beseeching the recipient to be happy at this special time. Appearances must be kept up, if only for Sophie's sake, and it was expected that cards would be displayed with the hundreds received from family and friends. So, true to tradition, they thanked one another politely, touching cheeks, deceiving no one.

Evergreens were draped about the walls of the hall and in the drawing room, with everlasting flowers entwined. Coloured and gilt paper chains, made by the innumerable nieces and nephews, were laced above picture frames, with mistletoe, holly, laurel and myrtle. Christmas roses and camellias from the winter garden decorated the dinner table and in between each place setting, along its length, was tender green ivy.

There was a Christmas tree, of course. A 'Tree of Love' it was called, brought into fashion by the Queen's 'dear Albert' in 1841; a young fir, cut from the estate and laden with trifling gifts – crochet purses, bon-bons, preserved fruits, alum baskets, charms – and illuminated most charmingly with little wax tapers.

On Christmas Eve the whole family gathered, even the youngest babe in arms, Joanna's last born, to sing 'God rest ye merry gentlemen'. Standing beside one another, Captain Osborne resplendent in his evening attire of black dress coat, white waistcoat and tight black trousers; Mrs Osborne achingly, fragilely lovely in a low-cut, short-sleeved, wide-skirted gown of silver Persian silk, they hid their broken hearts most cleverly with much hearty singing and laughter.

Not once did their eyes meet, for eyes can speak when tongues do not, and neither wished to disclose to the other what was in their heart.

On Christmas Day they drove with the rest of the family in a dozen carriages along the winding drive into Aigburth Road to cram into pews – children, nannies, governesses, unwilling young gentlemen and simpering young ladies. Sophie Osborne on the arm of her son – to listen to the parson's Christmas sermon and to be ignored by Sarah Hemingway who was on the arm of *hers*.

Thirty-eight people sat down at table for the family Christmas dinner. Sophie was allowed the honour of sitting at the head of the table, although it was Mrs James Osborne who should have had the privilege. But she seemed not to mind, nor even care, and put herself amongst the children who did not need sensible conversation.

They ate turkey and goose with chestnut stuffing; and plum pudding which had been stirred by every member of the family, though Sophie had declined this year, saying she was finished with such fiddle-faddle, even if it was in honour of the Three Kings of Orient. They all crunched their teeth, swearing they were broken, on silver charms and threepenny bits, and watched admiringly as the pudding, decorated with holly, blazed brightly.

The day dragged on with the opening of presents. Captain Osborne gave his wife an exquisite solid gold pouncet box encrusted with lapis lazuli, its lid perforated to allow the aroma of the perfume within to escape. She gave him gold cufflinks, and, again, they touched cheeks and smiled, and thanked one another. The rest of the family watched and wondered and were saddened, for once they had been so in love, and Sophie sighed, and longed for the days when Lacy had glowed like the candles on the tree. The flames, azure-tipped with amber and scarlet, burned beautifully, dancing cheerfully. But Lacy Osborne did not.

They played 'blind man's buff' and 'charades', when the younger children became over-excited and the older ones bored. Then, at last, those who lived within travelling distance took themselves off, and those who were guests went thankfully to their bed.

At last Captain and Mrs Osborne were alone.

James now allowed his rich brown eyes to rest upon his wife. His face was grave and sad. His strong body was set off to perfection by his well-fitting clothes, the trousers moulded to his shapely calf. But in his face, before Lacy Osborne turned to him, was vulnerability, uncertainty and a deep hunger. It vanished immediately as her glance touched his sun-darkened face. Of late he had taken to riding every day. No one ever knew where he went, and his wife certainly did not ask, but the outdoor life had returned to him the colour he had once had in India.

For a second their eyes met, then slid hopelessly away.

'I shall go to bed now, James.'

'Of course. I will smoke a cigar.'

'Very well, goodnight.'

'Goodnight, sleep well.'

The nightly ritual over, Lacy gathered up her skirt and ascended the wide sweep of the staircase. She did not turn to look at him as he moved towards the smoking room.

It was nine months since they had been more than coolly polite with one another, and she acknowledged as she moved about the lonely bedroom that she could bear it no longer. Everyone in the house knew, and, she supposed, the rest of society too, for the invisible grapevine which exists amongst servants would spread the news about the borough. But the certainty that she was once again the talk of the town meant nothing to her.

From the time she was seventeen she had provided all of Liverpool with the sensation, scandal and rumour on which those who are themselves above reproach thrive. She had often wondered idly what they would have had to gossip about, if she had not given them the topics which set them on their ears. First her banishment from Silverdale, with some hint of a man involved; her friendship with a girl who once had been a scullery maid, now mysteriously absent; her unladylike behaviour about the businessmen in the town; and, probably worst of all, her business success. The furore following the dinner given by the 'Liverpool Businessmen's Association' in her honour was still a matter for bitter discussion whenever two businessmen met, though they were still politely smiling when in her company. They could not afford to be anything else. Now, it seemed, she could hear them whisper, she had done something which even her besotted husband could not forgive, and she and James lived a smiling lie within their marriage.

Lacy sat down before the gently whispering fire, staring into its coral heart, watching the grey ash drift in a powdery mist to the hearth. She put her elbow on her knee and rested her chin upon her hand. Her eyes were unfocused, glazed with a deep, dredging unhappiness, and her mouth drooped. She sighed and felt a tear form in the lashes on her lower lid, then lifted her hand and dashed it away. She would not cry again. She had sworn to it the last time, and she had meant it. God, she had cried enough to float a clipper ship, and it did no good. The time for crying was past. Even as the determined intention clenched her jaw and firmed her soft lips, her woman's heart let her down and her eyes swam with tears.

'James, James, Jamie.' Silently her heart took up the message. Where are you now? Where have you gone? What is it that has driven us to this? And Rose. Oh Rosie, how can I manage without your strength to hold onto. In one day I lost you both, and for the first time in my life, I am completely alone.

But it was not of your doing, the small and odious voice which came each time to torture her, said softly. It is they who deceived you, the very ones you loved the best. The two you trusted and depended on. But I miss them, she answered silently, love them both still and would forgive . . . How can you forgive and go on living with a man who not only bedded your dearest friend, but hid behind her skirts and would have kept it from you? Her inner turmoil, from which she could find no respite, increased, and her weeping filled the room, as it had done on so many nights.

She got up abruptly and walked jerkily about the room, her

hand to her straining mouth. She jerked her head from side to side, and at each turn her progress dashed back the wide skirt of her gown. She went to the window and drawing aside the curtain flung it open. The bitter chill hit her at once, clawing at the tender flesh of her face, shoulders and the soft curve of her breasts. She breathed deeply, trying to get herself under control, but the cold air scorched her lungs, and she gasped. Closing the window and pulling the curtains to, she fled back to the fire, huddling on her knees before it, the enormous mass of her diaphanous silver skirt dangerously close to the live coals.

She must go. She *must*. There was no plan, no reasoning, just the instinctive reflex for flight from the pain she was in. She had done her best to go on living, for the sake of the Osborne family who had stood by her, for Sophie whom she loved, and in recognition of the life James had given her. He had not asked to her to stay. He had asked for nothing for himself, after that one horrendous finale, in which they had torn one another to bleeding shreds in their agony, and then gone their separate ways. She could not forgive him for what he had done; nor he her, for what she had said. Rose was gone, the property of Beechwood and its attendant acres was occupied by a newly rich merchant and his large energetic family and Lacy wondered if they were ever disturbed by the sad ghosts of the women who had once lived there. Bridie, garrulous, lovable, uncertain in her mind where she belonged, wandering the lanes and across the meadow, searching always for that content she had once known with Sean, and Rose, her daughter. As true and loyal a friend as anyone could wish for but her secret love, her hopeless future clutching at her from the shadow of her past. Did they still linger there, those two sad women, frightening the servants on a dark night or did the dozen noisy children of the wealthy merchant chase them back to the world in which they truly belonged?

Lacy rose from her crouched position in front of the fire and began to undress. She put on her nightgown and let down her hair. She looked like a slim young girl. She slipped beneath the bedcovers, reaching to turn out the lamp. The lambent light of the fire played about the high ceiling and soft coral walls and Lacy Osborne stared intently into the shadows and began to formulate the design for her future.

Their guests had gone, borne away on a tide of cheerful farewells and thanks and good wishes for the New Year, and on the evening which she intended to be her last under the same roof as James Osborne, Lacy Osborne put together the few possessions she was to take with her. James was, she supposed, in the smoking room, or perhaps in his study. With steady hands she closed the lid of her box, smoothed the skirt of her gown, and began the long walk towards the moment which would end her marriage.

Tomorrow, 6 January 1869, she would move from the home she had shared with him ever since his father had died, and he had become master and she mistress, and go to the small house she had rented in West Derby. She would stay there until she had settled her future. Perhaps she would go abroad for a few months. To Italy or France. Relax and sit in the sunshine, and let the solitude ease away the sadness, and when she was healed, she would come back to her roots, and attach herself once more to what was her life.

She needed peace, repose, a breathing space. She smiled, and an Irish voice said, 'Relax, repose. Yer don't know the meaning of the owd words', and the smile, brought about by hope, slipped from her face and pain returned.

She was halfway down the staircase, her hand lingering on the polished wood, when the sound of wheels, the crash of horses' hooves, the cry of a man's voice came faintly to her, through the great sturdy front door which stood at the end of the wide hallway. There were two doors really: the glass one which opened onto the steps and gravelled carriage turn-round, and an inner door made of oak. Both were closed for the January day, which had started cold, blustery and bleak, had worsened into a storm, violent and cracking with thunder. The wind which gusted from the river threatened to tear the slates from the roof, and force in the shuttered windows of the solid house. The sky was purple, black and velvety, like an overripe plum.

Lacy stopped at the bottom stair, surprised, for whoever came to call on them must be mad to do so in this weather. Thunder trumpeted again, the wind howled about the chimney pots, great low clouds whipped across the sky, and snow began to fall in tiny, lashing pellets, stinging the face of the man who hammered on the outer door. He must have discovered in the pitchy black, the bell which hung to the side of the door for it began to ring with frantic insistence, and in a minute the hall seemed filled with men, as Winter trembled across the carpet followed closely behind by Samuel, for it was strange to have a caller at this hour.

James, cigar between his lips, stood in the open doorway of the study.

'What the devil . . .' he said, and for a second the bewildering event drew him and Lacy together in mutual surprise.

'Open the damned door, Winter, before whoever it is breaks it down,' he bellowed, for he had to shout to make himself heard. He moved forward and Lacy stepped down, so they stood side by side in the hallway when the big door was finally opened.

Lacy's dress shifted about her legs and the escaping tendrils of her hair whipped about her face. The flames from the dozens of lights flickered and danced and some went out, but there was still enough illumination to make out the figure of the man who stood there. Burly, white-faced, wrapped about in a great coat and muffler, he almost staggered in on the force of the great wind which struggled with him, and the scrap of paper he held out wordlessly to Winter, fluttered and blew back against his hand.

He found his voice at last.

'For the missis,' he roared and Winter flinched.

''Tis urgent, the woman said, an' I'm ter wait fer an answer.' He made a move to cross the threshold, but Winter, himself again now, put on his most patronizing demeanour, and was about to direct the poor soul to the back door, when

655

Captain James stepped forward and took the note from him. Indecision was written on Winter's face, for it would hardly do to grapple with the fellow within feet of the master, so the coachman was allowed in. To Winter's consternation, he proceeded to warm himself, back and front, by the roaring logs in the fireplace.

Should the note have been placed in Lacy's hand, as was intended, she would have recognized the handwriting, scrawled illegibly as it was, and torn it apart, and the consequences might have been vastly different. But believing the note to concern perhaps a member of her own family, she watched James anxiously as he read it, even placing a hand upon his arm the more immediately to receive firsthand news of what it contained.

She was completely unprepared for James's reaction. His face became ashen and his fingers trembled violently. He put a fluttering hand to his eyes, and then looked up at her, and for the first time in months, addressed his wife without the polite formality to which they had both become used.

'Oh God, Lacy . . . Oh, my dear God.' It was the aching cry of a man in dire need. His eyes were tormented, and despite herself, Lacy took another step towards him, both her hands rising instinctively to help him. In that moment everything that had happened was forgotten, and he was the man she loved. The man she loved more than any other human being, more than Rose, or the ships she had built, and his hurt was hers.

She was about to speak his name, to ask him what the letter contained to bring such pain to him, when he said,

'It is from Rose.'

Instantly, like an actor discarding one role for another, her face changed and the slack-jawed company were treated to the sight and sounds of a woman who had once lived amongst the dregs of humanity, and from where she had learned a choice phrase or two. She used them now, and Winter paled and turned to Samuel, who was equally aghast. James took Lacy by the arm, dragging her like a ill-behaved child towards the study door, and in a moment they had disappeared.

The study door locked behind him, James Osborne turned to the spitting she-cat who darted all over him with the desperate strength of a woman who is consumed with fearful, jealous rage. Her blows fell on him, and her nails tore at his face, and she spat an obscenity at which even he winced. Words of which 'whore' and 'bitch' were the least offensive floated against the ferociously closed door.

'Stop it,' he hissed. 'Confound it, Lacy. Pull yourself together. Stop it, or I shall strike you, and do not think I won't. I swear I have been itching to do it for months now, and if you don't control yourself and sit down, and bloody well listen, I shall be forced to it.'

'Sit down and behave myself? I am expected to submit to being humiliated by the sight of you receiving letters from your paramour. In fact, to hear you boast of it before your own servants, and you . . .'

'Be quiet, you little fool. You arc talking nonscnsc, and you know it.'

'Nonsense!' She was shrieking her pain now, and the schooling she had received in Naylor's Yard, and at the pickling factory, put all the necessary pitch to the tone of her voice.

'You call it nonsense to be dragged from the hallway like a . . .'

'Hell's teeth, woman. What else was I to do? Your foul mouth had Winter about to faint. Was I to allow . . . ?

'Allow? Allow! Your choice of words is disastrous, James Osborne. I shall say and do whatever I please, and you shall not stop me.'

'Will I not? If you do not sit down and listen to what Rose has to say you will get a taste of what I can do, lady.' James's voice was coldly dangerous. His eyes gleamed like the sun reflecting on a brown pool, and around his mouth was a circle of white.

Lacy was beyond caution.

'I do not care to hear what Rose has to say, nor to be locked up in this room a moment longer. It has all been said and is done with. You have had a letter from her, and I dare say it is

657

not the first, presumably to make further arrangements for your . . . assignations. Though why you should wish to share it with me I cannot conceive. No doubt you have been meeting her on your daily rides out . . .'

Lacy's voice rose higher and higher as wretchedness peeled the covering from her nerve ends, leaving them bare, exposed, raw, and her eyes dilated as the pictures which had tortured her for nine months returned.

'Rides out!' James laughed raggedly. 'Rides out! If you are honest and once you were, do you believe me capable of riding out each day to dally away the hours with a woman who was once your dearest friend? I don't even know where Rose is. Why do you think I went to Ireland, trailing about from county to county, speaking to O'Malleys in one village after another. And if I found her, did you imagine I should take her to my bed and . . .'

'You had no qualms about it last . . .'

'Once, only once.'

James's voice rose, and he took a menacing step towards her. Lacy shrank away, for there was a look in his face which said he was driven to the end, and would not hesitate, nor would he be able to stop if he desired to, from hitting her as he had threatened. The silence stretched out as they eyed one another with loathing like two cats caught in an alley.

'How can I believe you?' Lacy said at last, and her body sagged tiredly. She put her hand to the desk behind her, steadying herself, then turned away. She lifted her other hand, and her fingers trembled against her mouth.

'How can I believe you, James? You and she . . . betrayed my . . . my trust and love. I had always known, we both did, of her love for you, but I was honestly not aware that you returned that love.'

'I did not.' His voice was harsh. 'I told you so at the time.'

'Then, why? why? Was I such a disappointment to you that you must find . . . relief . . . elsewhere?'

'No, no, don't twist . . . After all we had known . . . You were aware of my feelings for you. You knew how I loved you . . . do . . . but you chose to pretend otherwise. I . . . once only . . . I was with Rose. Dear God . . .' He ran his hand distractedly through his hair, and the muscles in his face tensed.

'. . . I can scarce believe it happened, or even how. But it did. I was at fault, but I suppose I expected . . . hoped . . . not understanding perhaps, not immediate forgiveness, but a decent consideration of how weak is the flesh. You had . . . once it happened to you . . . though it crucified me to imagine you with . . .'

'But I was not sharing your bed, James. I did not go to another whilst I was sharing your bed.'

James's shoulders slumped and he turned away, defeated.

'No. There is a difference. I can see that.'

They stood tense.

The air was thick with bitter condemnation and the dreadful awareness that the wall standing between them was so strong and high it could never be breached. That they would live divided was a certainty.

Lacy hung her head desolately.

'What is it?'

James was startled for a moment, the reason for this disastrous scene having fled entirely with the onslaught of their combined fury.

'What is in the letter?'

He held it out, crumpled and stained.

'It is from Rose.'

'Yes?'

It was as though James struggled with some emotion too drastic to put into words. On his face, though Lacy did not see it, as she stared at her own slippered foot, were dread and apprehension, deep and palpable; misery and hopelessness. But mixed with these was, strangely, the start of an expression which might only be described as gladness. A look of joy had come to his brown eyes, taking away the muddy look of anger and melancholy, and he put out a hand, the note trembling in his fingers.

'Read it, Lacy.'

'I cannot bring myself to touch it.'

The gladness died a little in James Osborne's face.

'Please, Lacy.'

'Read it to me, if you must.'

'It is really for you. If you read it perhaps . . .'

'Yes?'

'Perhaps the news it brings will be . . . less painful'

'I cannot, James. I can stand no more. It is all I can do to stay and listen to you. I would be grateful if you would allow me to leave.'

Her voice was devoid of expression and her eyes were lifeless.

'Please . . .'

'For God's sake, tell me, or I shall go mad.'

James looked down at the note, his face curiously soft, and his mouth almost curved on a smile. But his eyes were wary, alert with . . . what?

'Rose is to have . . . a child, Lacy,' he said awkwardly. 'This note is to say she is . . . that this morning she began her labour, and that she is . . . alone but for Maggie. She begs you to come to her.'

The silence stretched out forever, and the woman at the window seemed to have lost the use of her limbs, her voice, her senses, for she moved not a muscle.

'Lacy?' James's voice was questioning. 'Did you hear what I said? Will you not read Rose's letter now?'

Still she did not move.

'She loves you Lacy and wishes you . . .'

'Stop, James!' Lacy's voice was high and clear.

'Lacy.' Suddenly the tone of James's voice had changed to the one he had once used in the days when their love was the centre of their lives, the hub of the wheel which turned their days and nights to movement and magic. Soft, tender, loving, so loving it wrapped about her like the warm furs he had bought her, touching her skin with smooth feathers of delight. But she did not turn her head. Instead, she said,

'Put it on the table and leave me alone.'

'Lacy, my love. Forgive me. I did not mean to hurt you. Nor did Rose. Read her letter and you will see.'

'Please go, James,' Lacy's voice was cracking.

James was pleading now.

'Don't turn from her. Don't turn from your friendship. What will she do if you refuse her? What will *you* do if you refuse her? You are her only friend, or were, and she is yours. Lacy, look at me. Say you will not let what I have done . . .'

'Stop it, James.' Lacy's voice was hollow and empty. 'There is nothing to be gained from this. We have said it all so many times. Be still now. Say no more.'

'But Lacy, I must know that you . . .'

'For God's sake, James. I cannot just turn round and embrace Rose as though . . .'

'I love you, Lacy. Always, always. You are my dearest friend, and I have lost you. But don't turn from Rose. You will never forgive yourself . . . later.'

He hesitated, lifting a hand, but she did not see. 'I am . . . Put the burden on my shoulders, but help Rose. Give to her what she gave so unstintingly to you when you were alone.'

She heard the rustle of paper and his voice, stronger now, but soft.

'I will leave you alone. The letter is here.' She heard the door being unlocked, the quiet whisper as James left the room, and then she was alone.

She sank to her knees in an almost leisurely fashion, her hands clinging to the curtains at each side of the window. Her flesh felt as though a million pins were probing it, and her head clanged as if it lay between hammer and rock. She felt her stomach heave, and with a soft cry, rose clumsily to open the window, retching into the frozen winter soil beneath. The angry wind lashed her hair from its pins, and lifted it into a torn cloud of silver about her head. For ten minutes she lay across the window sill, her face like sweating dough, her limbs trembling violently. She closed the window with difficulty and, shaking, swept the crochet cloth from the table on which James's decanters of whisky, port and sherry stood, holding the fragile material to her face as her wretchedness became stronger, and her grief overcame her.

The fire died down, and finally went out, but still she

remained within the room. She sat in James's chair and stared at her own reflection in the black glass of the window. She was so still she might have been dead, but her brain lived and moved. The note was in her hand, hanging from her lifeless fingers, and now and again the flesh of her face twitched, as though at some shaft of indescribable pain. She watched the outline of the trees bend away from the rage of the wind, and heard its howl as it tore at the quivering branches. As it did so a strange sensation, one she had not known for months, touched her, soft as swansdown, and her aching anguish eased a little and onto her face came an expression which, if she had been there, Rose would have recognized.

Lacy had worn it as a child of ten.

She moved stiffly. Her hand lifted the crochet cloth from her lap and dropped it unheedingly to the floor. She almost fell as she stood up. Steadying herself against the wall, she crept around the room until she reached the door. She turned the handle and walked, more strongly now, out into the hallway.

He was there, waiting, sitting on a straight-backed chair against the wall. He stood up immediately, as she moved towards him. His face was drawn, haggard with the look worn by his father just before he died. His eyes watched her, clinging steadfastly to her with the power of his over-whelming, compassionate love. Hers were clear, sure and just as loving.

'Jamie,' she said.

It was enough, and she was in his arms, and they wept their love and need as they clung together. They did not weep for each other, but for Rose.


Rose O'Malley lay neatly in her bed. The bedroom was warmed by a cheerfully crackling fire in the small, blackleaded grate, and its bright flames provided the only light. They slid about the sparsely furnished room, touching the polished mahogany of the dresser, the newel post at the foot of the bed, and the patterned doors of the large wardrobe, reflecting in the mirror which was set between.

Rose turned her head fractionally on the pillow, and her eyes lingered at the painting on the wall above the fireplace, and again the blaze in the hearth turned the outline of the seagulls which flew upon the canvas from white to amber, and the painted chimneys to gold. Her whole attention was centred on the lovely water colour, and she felt herself drawn into the past to stand beside the young girl who played the brush across the sheet of white paper.

'Won't be a moment, Rosie. I must get these gulls on paper whilst the sun touches their feathers to that lovely shade of saffron. Can you see it? Is it not beautiful?'

Lacy was there then, and the tears which had threatened, slid weakly from the corners of Rose's eyes and fell to the pillow beneath her dark hair. The moment was agony, but she held it to her and could not bear to let it go. She wanted her here, not just in imagination, but as she had always been, as *they* had always been, close and trusting since they were children of ten. No one else would do, not even him, though she had loved him. Lacy would hold back the blackness which hovered at the edges of the glowing room. With her lion-hearted courage, undaunted and dashing, she would seize Rose's faltering spirit and infuse it with her own, and the dread and fear and loneliness would be gone, as it had gone all those years ago when her Daddy had died. A young girl's arm had upheld her then and that girl, a woman now, would keep . . . keep . .

Her breath did no more than flutter in her throat, though she was sure she had uttered a deep, wrenching groan. Maggie was there, sad and frightened, and Rose knew she must pull herself together, for Maggie needed reassurance or she would go to pieces, and someone must . . . see to the child, if Lacy did not come.

The light in the room became suddenly brighter as Maggie put a taper to the lamp, turning it up to a steady flame. Then she knelt at the bedside, her face close to Rose's. Rose moved her hand beneath the covers, but somehow could not quite manage to free it to touch Maggie's face. There was a tremble there, though that was all, and again Rose moaned for the end was coming so quickly, and she was not yet ready. There was something to be arranged. She must . . . *must* . . . stay a while longer.

'Maggie.' It was the merest whisper.

'Aye, chuck.'

'The storm . . . is over.'

'Aye. A while since.'

'And . . . they have not yet . . . come?'

'No. Not yet, Miss Rose, but they will. Miss Lacy'd not let you down.'

'How long since you sent . . . ?

Her voice fell away, sighing gently to the ceiling, as her strength was consumed by her need to speak. Her hand moved weakly again, and Maggie saw it and understood, and pulled back the soft blanket, which was as light as swansdown but too heavy for Rose O'Malley to shift. She tried again, as Maggie bent her head.

'What is it, lass?'

'If . . . if I cannot . . .'

'Nay, nay, Miss Rose. Tha's strong, and Miss Lacy'll be over directly to see to things. Don't tha fret none.'

'Yes . . . I know . . . but . . .'

'See, I'm having none of this, Miss Rose. Just you stop your mithering. Now, I'll go and get thee a sip of beef broth, and Peg'll sit beside thee whilst I am gone.'

She rose with fierce determination from her knees, as though this nonsense had gone far enough, and hurried from the bedroom, her great thumping feet for once soft as eiderdown on the stairs.

'Watch her, Peg,' she cautioned the maid, who hovered by the fireside, and headed for the kitchen. She was afraid to leave the unnaturally still whiteness of her mistress, even for the five minutes it would take to warm up the beef tea, but if she could only get a spoonful down her she'd pick up in no time, and with the child to feed an' all she needed summat. Maggie kept hope alive in the only way she knew by doing what she had always done. Making a bit o' summat tasty for 'her young lady' to get inside her.

Peg sat down obediently by the bedside and looked at the hollow-cheeked, ashen, dead-eyed woman who lay upon it. Her eyes were open, but her breath was so light. Peg leaned forward to ensure she would hear it, see it in the slight movement of her breast, and not miss it should it stop. So intent was she on her task and the heavy responsibility placed upon her that the woman's sudden presence made her start.

Instantly she was on her feet, stepping back from the bed respectfully to allow her to approach, and for the first time in nearly a year, Lacy Osborne looked into the face of Rose O'Malley.

Rose lay upon the bed, looking like someone prepared to be placed within her coffin. Gone were her pink cheeks, that sheen of perfect health that had been about her in April. Her eyes had been warm, shining, woodland green, and her hair lustrously glossy. Now, should Lacy have met her on Bold Street she would have passed her by without recognition.

Ignoring Maggie, who had followed her in, and her beseeching whisper to take care, Miss Lacy, for Miss Rose was . . . poorly, she knelt beside the bed, not touching it, and looked and looked at Rose. Maggie fell silent and then, as though sensing a concern as great as her own, moved to the rocking chair by the fireside. She sat in it and began to rock herself, soothed for a moment from the dread of caring for Miss Rose alone. Someone in authority had come and she felt a relief.

Hesitantly, Lacy put out a trembling hand, and touched the thick plait of hair which lay across Rose's shoulder. She stroked it tentatively for, in truth, now she was here and could see Rose's condition, she was overwhelmed by an emotion which had her in a stupor, and she was helpless to know what to do next. Rose's eyes watched her without expression, and for an instant Lacy thought she was already dead, and her own heart ceased to beat, and she could not bear the pain. Her eyes filled with scalding tears, her body shivered, and then she knew, and with a soft, wordless murmur she slid her arm beneath Rose's shoulders and drew her gently into her arms. Rose was light as thistledown, boneless and ethereal, but she seemed to gain sustenance from the arms which held her, and her face turned into the hollow of Lacy's neck.

They clung together.

Lacy knew she would never again know the pain, the shame, the guilt which seized her as she held in her arms the dying spirit of the woman who had loved her, been her comfort and her strength, had done battle for her for most of their lives and now was slipping away to another world, where Lacy could not follow. But she must not go, for Lacy needed her now, would always need her. The truth of it entered her soul and panic clutched her, and she rocked the shrunken figure in her arms in a passion of grieving. Rosie, you cannot go now. I must return to you some of the devotion you have always given to me; return to you what I have kept from you these last months. I have discarded you, abandoned you when you needed me most, and you have come close to death, but death shall not have you. I must be allowed to make atonement for what I have done, and I will. I will.

She looked down into the waxy, white face cradled against her shoulder, and her heart was torn apart as she realized, quite simply, she had come too late. The same loving eyes, sunken and drowsy with approaching death, were there. The same tender smile lifting tiredly the drooping mouth, but there was something else. Something which said, though Rose did not speak, 'don't fool yourself, acushala. This is it, and we both know it. We have always been honest with one another. Do not let us be otherwise now.'

'But I need you. I cannot go on without your strength beside me,' Lacy's eyes answered, and as though Rose understood, as indeed she always had, she smiled faintly, derisively almost, and her head moved a little in denial.

Lacy bent her own head until she and Rose were cheek to cheek, and for several minutes they remained, and she could feel the peace drift into Rose's body.

A touch on her hair, weak as a baby's, roused her, and she lifted her head and looked again into Rose's eyes.

'Lacy,' it was the merest whisper.

'Yes, darlin', what is it?'

'You know . . . about the child.'

Lacy smiled serenely, and saw Rose's eyes clear and her mouth relax.

'Yes, darlin', I know.'

'A boy, Lacy.'

'Oh, darlin', a boy. You have a son.'

Her heart contracted.

'Lacy.'

Rose's face became even whiter and her mouth clenched in pain, and Lacy shushed her, saying she must rest, but Rose would have none of it.

'He is James's boy, Lacy.'

'I know, acushla.'

'. . . and yours now. You must . . .'

'Hush, sweetheart, you must rest a while.'

'No, please . . . the cradle . . .'

Her hand seemed to float, light as air, as it indicated a vague shape in the corner of the room, and for the first time Lacy saw the cradle. A tiny, be-frilled oblong of white, shimmering by the hearth. Maggie had her hand upon it, already proprietorial, as she rocked it gently.

As though she sensed their contemplation of her and the cradle beside her, Maggie came back from her adoration of Miss Rose's baby and stood up. She took a turn or two about the bed, as though to reassure herself that her Miss Rose was not upset, then sank tiredly back into the rocking chair, discreetly out of earshot of the two women. Always on guard, was Maggie, as she turned compassionately towards the two still figures at the bed. Her own eyes were tear-dewed as she watched them. They belonged to her these two, for though she was younger by several years, she had always treated them as a mother might treat two wayward children. Their sorrows as well as their joys were hers.

Lacy looked down into Rose's face and knew what she must do, what Rose would have her do, though how she would find the courage to take in her arms the flesh and blood evidence of what . . . they . . .

Her heart began to bang against her chest wall, then rose in fear to her throat. This was the child of Rose and James and she was afraid to look down into the cradle. She was afraid to look, in case she should hate it; feel revulsion, horror, distaste or jealous rage even. But Lacy Osborne willed herself to look into the face of her husband's son, impelled by some force which she did not recognize. Her head moved stiffly, and her neck seemed to creak as she bent it, and finally she looked down into the sleeping infant's face. As she did so he yawned, and turned his face towards her, and in that tiny movement he was James. James as he settled himself to sleep against her shoulder. In just such a way did he yawn contentedly, after having her undivided attention in the hour of lovemaking. This was how he rested his head. It was James's face lying in the snowy depths of the dainty coverlets, the line of his brow, the way in which the eyes were set in the skull, the tumble of hair, the humorous curve of the lips.

Bending down and, with an expertise she had not known she possessed, picking up the tiny boy, Lacy slowly settled him in the curve of her arm. He turned his face to her breast and plucked from it her heart.

Maggie watched sadly as she walked back across the room towards the bed. Sinking to her knees Lacy placed the child between herself and Rose, and Rose turned her head to look at her son, and then at the woman who was to take her place in his life. He was a beautiful child, dark as a gypsy, or an Irishman, with rosy, rounded cheeks and black, winging brows. He had been washed and his fluff of hair, the exact colour of her own, clustered upon his skull in curling whorls. His fingers plump and pink with health, turned inwards like the petals on a rose, and he yawned again, showing his shining tongue and gums.

Rose's eyes were soft with love for her son.

'He's a fine boy, Lacy,' her voice was thready now.

'Yes . . . a fine boy . . . a fine son.' Lacy could not look away from him.

'You will . . . he will be as if he . . . as if he were your own.'

'I love him now.' Her voice caught and Rose could see it was true and was satisfied.

'James . . . ?'

'We are together again, Rosie.'

'You will not . . . blame him for . . .'

'No, but you must sleep a little. Rest. You are tired. I will leave the boy beside you . . .'

'Yes . . .'

A movement at the door drew Lacy's attention and for a second only she looked up. She was afraid to glance away for longer lest Rose should slip away whilst she did so.

It was James.

His eyes were sunken in his pallid face, ravaged with grief and pain, and Lacy knew he loved Rose with the same everlasting devotion which she herself felt. They had moved through the years together, the three of them, like a tiny battalion which had guarded its warriors against all comers; each protecting the other, supporting, shielding, comforting, defending and, it seemed in that moment, that the child who lay sleeping beside Rose was the progeny of that threefold alliance.

Holding out her hand, but without taking her eyes from Rose, she beckoned to James who came swiftly to kneel on the opposite side of the bed. Rose turned her head wearily, and their eyes met, and they smiled at one another lovingly, but only for an instant. Then Rose turned again to her child and the woman who would be his mother.

'Will we call him Sean, Rosie, will we?'

The woman on the bed lifted her thickly lashed eyelids, and the dazzling brilliance of her green eyes fell for the last time on the face of the woman who had been in her charge for over twenty years. For a moment they looked at one another, and a smile of gratitude tugged at the corner of Rose's mouth. She was beyond speech, beyond any movement in that last moment of her life.

She did the only thing she could. Holding Lacy's glance with her own, Rose O'Malley winked.

# The Egyptian Years
## Elizabeth Harris

The mysterious disappearance of Genevieve Mountsorrel in the Egyptian desert in 1892 was a longstanding family puzzle. Newly married, the young and vivacious Genevieve had sailed for Egypt, happy at the prospect of a new life. No one could explain the tragic turn of events. Only her parasol had been found, hastily discarded in the hot and dusty sand.

A century later, Willa, a distant relative, discovers Genevieve's diary. Drawn immediately into an astonishing story, she learns of Genevieve's secret life and the child she was forced to abandon, the truth about her sinister husband, Leonard, and the extraordinary drama of what really happened to Genevieve Mountsorrel . . .

Acclaim for *The Herb Gatherers*:

'Enormously enjoyable. Elizabeth Harris writes with sensitivity and skill.'
Barbara Erskine

Fontana

# The Juniper Bush
## Audrey Howard

Winner of the 1987
Romantic Novel of the Year Award

The passionate saga of a nineteenth-century Lakeland girl, her search for happiness in a web of conflicting emotions and loyalties.

Lovely Christy Emmerson is the only daughter of an explosives manufacturer and a fine catch for any man. But there is only one man Christy cares about, and when she becomes betrothed to the squire's son, Robin, it seems that all concerned are happy.

But with only a few weeks to go before the wedding tragedy strikes the community, and the Emmerson family. Apparently abandoned by Robin at a time when she needed him most, Christy, heartbroken and confused, falls into a marriage with a local mine owner, the handsome but arrogant Alex Buchanan. As her family grows, Christy becomes increasingly wrapped up in her new life and almost succeeds in forgetting Robin. Then, one day, she meets him again and her whole world is thrown into confusion.

Audrey Howard's other bestselling sagas, *The Skylark's Song*, *The Morning Tide*, *Ambitions* and *Between Friends* are also available in Fontana.

ISBN 0 00 617546 5

Fontana

# Fontana Fiction

Fontana is a leading paperback publisher of fiction. Below are some recent titles.

- ☐ GREEN AND PLEASANT LAND  Teresa Crane  £4.99
- ☐ KING'S OAK  Ann Rivers Siddons  £4.99
- ☐ THE EGYPTIAN YEARS  Elizabeth Harris  £4.50
- ☐ MAGIC HOUR  Susan Isaacs  £4.99
- ☐ THE RELUCTANT QUEEN  Jean Plaidy  £3.99
- ☐ TOMORROW'S MEMORIES  Connie Monk  £3.99
- ☐ WHEN SHE WAS BAD . . . Kate O'Mara  £4.99
- ☐ THE CLONING OF JOANNA MAY  Fay Weldon  £3.99
- ☐ FORBIDDEN GARDEN  Diane Guest  £3.99
- ☐ KING'S CLOSE  Christine Marion Fraser  £4.95
- ☐ MEMORY AND DESIRE  Lisa Appignanesi  £4.99
- ☐ THE ROAD TO ROWANBRAE  Doris Davidson  £4.50
- ☐ SACRIFICE  Harold Carlton  £4.99

You can buy Fontana Paperbacks at your local bookshops or newsagents. Or you can order them from Fontana, Cash Sales Department, Box 29, Douglas, Isle of Man. Please send a cheque, postal or money order (not currency) worth the price plus 24p per book for postage (maximum postage required is £3.00 for orders within the UK).

NAME (Block letters)_____

ADDRESS_____

_____